# The Templar Chronicles

# Book One

## Sam Sabathy

To Sammie,

for believing in me

# TABLE OF CONTENTS

I November 1154 – Ferneham, England ............................................. 1

II Part One 1096 - Normandy, France ............................................. 36

II Part Two 1096 – Paris, France ................................................... 68

II Part Three 1096–1097 - France ................................................. 84

II Part Four 1097 - Italy ............................................................... 107

III Part One 1097 – Constantinople, Byzantium ........................... 122

III Part Two 1097 – Nicaea, Anatolia ........................................... 141

III Part Three 1097-1098 – Antioch .............................................. 159

IV Part One 1099 - Jerusalem ....................................................... 194

IV Part Two 1099–1100 – Lower Levant ........................................ 220

V Part One 1108 - England ........................................................... 229

V Part Two 1113 - France .............................................................. 256

V Part Three 1116 – 1118 England ................................................ 288

V Part Four 1118–1119 - England .................................................. 326

VI Part One 1119 - The Holy Land ................................................ 346

VI Part Two 1119–1128 – Jerusalem ............................................. 365

VII Part One 1128-1129 – The West ............................................. 405

VII Part Two 1129-1135 - Jerusalem ............................................. 435

VII Part Three 1135 - 1136 – Jerusalem ........................................ 452

VIII Part One 1136-1145 - France .................................................. 464

VIII Part Two 1146 – Baalbek ........................................................ 478

VIII Part Three 1146 – Jabal Qasiun ............................................. 490

VIII Part Four 1146-1147 – Baalbek .............................................. 501

VIII Part Five 1148 – Acre ............................................................. 512

VIII Part Six 1148 – Damascus ...................................................... 530

IX Part One 1148 – 1149 - England ................................................. 535

IX Part Two 1149-1152 – Ferneham, England ................................. 553

IX Part Three 1153-1154 - England ................................................. 568

X November 1154 - Ferneham England ........................................... 574

Edward the Confessor 1042 - 1066

William I (The Conqueror) 1066 - 1087

William II (Rufus) 1087 - 1100

Henry I – 1100 - 1135

Stephen – 1135 - 1154

Henry II – 1154 - 1189

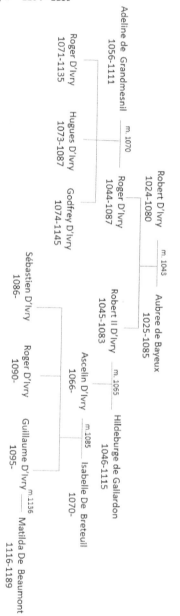

House D'Ivry

Adeline de Grandmesnil 1056-1111

Roger D'Ivry 1071-1135

Hugues D'Ivry 1073-1087

m. 1070

Roger D'Ivry 1044-1087

Godfrey D'Ivry 1074-1145

Robert D'Ivry 1024-1080

m. 1043

Aubree de Bayeux 1025-1085

Robert II D'Ivry 1045-1083

Sébastien D'Ivry 1086-

Roger D'Ivry 1090-

Ascelin D'Ivry 1066-

m. 1065

Hildeburge de Gallardon 1046-1115

m.1085

Isabelle De Breteuil 1070-

Guillaume D'Ivry 1095-

m. 1136

Matilda De Beaumont 1116-1189

William I (The Conqueror) 1066 - 1087

William II (Rufus) 1087 - 1100

Henry I – 1100 - 1135

Stephen – 1135 - 1154

Henry II – 1154 - 1189

# House of Marshal

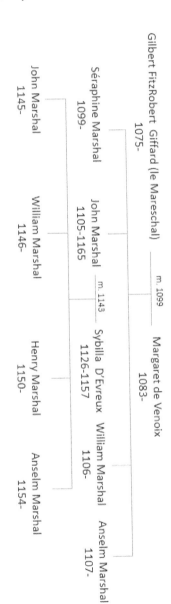

# Robert II Duke of Normandy Familial Relationships

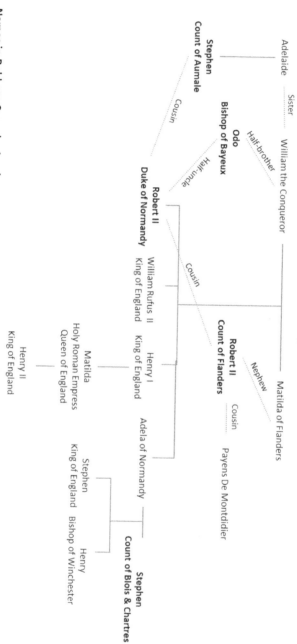

Names in Bold are Crusader Leaders

# Leaders of the First Crusade & Their Men

## Normandy

Robert II
Duke of Normandy

Stephen
Count of Aumale
(cousin to Robert)

## Bouillon

Godfrey De Bouillon
Duke of Lorraine
(brother to Baldwin)

Godfrey de Saint-Omer
(brother to Hugh)

Baldwin de Boulogne
(brother to Godfrey)

Hugh de
Fauquembergues
(brother to Godfrey)

## Flanders

Robert II
Count of Flanders

Payen de Montdidier
(brother to Robert)

## Toulouse

Raymond IV
Count of Toulouse

Pierre
Viscount de Castellon

## Taranto

Bohemond
Prince of Taranto

Tancred d'Hauteville
(nephew to Bohemond)

## Blois

Stephen
Count of Blois & Chartres

Archambaud de Saint-Agnan

## Capet

Hugh
Count de Vermandois
(younger brother to
King Phillippe I of France)

Guy Pagan de Garlande

## Champagne

Hugues de Payns

Geoffroi Bisol

## Byzantium

Alexois Komnenos
Emperor of Byzantium

General Taticius

I am the ninth of the nine. This is my story.

# I

# November 1154 – Ferneham, England

The axe sliced through the air with the precision and grace of a hunting hawk diving for its prey, hitting its mark and cleaving the wood cleanly in half. He sighed contentedly, feeling the ache in his ageing muscles as he leaned down to toss the pieces into the nearby wood pile. How many times had he done just this? Thousands no doubt. In his youth, a chore, but now he welcomed the chance to escape the clatter and clamour of his workers and the townsfolk who made their daily living at the castle and in the nearby town. A chance to think. Or not, if he so chose.

He paused a moment and felt a drip of sweat slip down between his shoulder blades – it had been warm for a late autumn day, was his excuse, refusing to recognize his age. Still a wonder of a man with a body of one half his age, he was unusually tall, with broad shoulders and strong arms, a wide, broad chest, and long legs whose thighs had been strengthened from years of expert horsemanship. His once dark hair now a mass of silvery grey, matching the colour of his eyes, his face not bearded as was the style, but clean-shaven, a habit ingrained from his past. A powerful jaw and mouth were set mostly of late in what appeared to be a passive yet contemplative expression, giving away nothing except the hint of a depth that few could reach now. It had been his way for years.

He knelt and as he reached into the wooden water bucket to scoop a handful to ease his parched throat, he stopped and stared at the water, momentarily stilled by the images of another time when such thirst may not have been quelled so easily. For a brief instant, he was there again, feeling the unending, oppressive heat of the sun, his eyes stung by smoke and tears, and then hearing them. Again. He felt a slight jabbing pain across his entire body.

He drank the water greedily and reached for more, using it to splash his sweat-stained face and then the back of his neck, feeling the necklet as he did so, shaking the thoughts from his mind as he had done many times before. These memories had stayed at bay for years but now they were returning, happening more often, with more intensity. He needed to get on with his work.

Standing to full height, he picked up the axe and froze. The laugh. He swore he heard it. The laugh. It raced through him, electrifying every sinew. He was sure he had heard it. He slowly turned, glancing fervently, searching both near and far of the meadow, studying, listening, hoping to hear it again. His eyes rested upon the impressive grey-white Waverley Abbey, built not so long ago by Cistercian monks, and then carried on to the magnificent ancient yew tree at the northeast corner of the Abbey's grounds. He sighed. A massive colossus of a tree, crafted by the twisting and intertwining of many trunks to form one impenetrable force, branches stretching out further than should have been possible, some bending down and ever-so-barely touching the ground. It too having withstood the test of time and battles, he was in awe of its majesty, and recognized, with a touch of ruefulness, that it would be here long after he was gone just as it had been here for many years before he arrived. And yet, here they were.

A slight breeze rustled through its leaves, and he discovered the source of the laugh as one of the yew's expansive branches bent and yawned with the wind. He smiled, ever so slightly bowed his head reverently, and returned to his task.

Selecting the next log, he placed it on the chopping block and readied his axe. But once again, his movement was stopped. But not by what he saw or what he heard. This time he felt it. And he knew instantly what it was. Vibrations in the ground were warning him of the approach of men on horseback. It was time, he thought. They had come for him as he knew they would.

He lowered his axe and concentrated.

But as the vibrations grew in strength as the approach neared, he realized he was mistaken – this was not men on horseback. This was one. One man on horseback. And arriving at speed. The sound of clamouring hooves on the gravel path that lead to the meadow and the Abbey from the town had reached him and suddenly a figure appeared on the stone bridge across a tributary of the River Wey that ran parallel to the Abbey. The rider was not recognizable at first glance as his dark cloak and hood masked his identity. But something about him was familiar.

The rider slowed as he approached, pulling the breathless horse to a halt a few feet away from the woodpile. The two men stared at each other for a moment.

"Sébastien D'Ivry," the rider stated formally and nodded as he steadied his chestnut-coloured palfrey.

He dismounted and removed his hood, revealing thick, shoulder-length locks of dark brown hair now streaked with grey and a short-trimmed beard to match. Sébastien recognized him instantly.

"Anselm Marshal," Sébastien replied, making no move towards him yet tightening his grip on the axe.

The slight movement was noticed. Anselm smiled.

"No need for that," he said, nodding towards the axe as he removed his gloves. "I come as a friend."

Sébastien stiffened, wary of his visitor.

"It has been a long time Anselm since I have spoken to…" he hesitated slightly, "or even seen anyone in your family," he continued.

"I am aware of that," Anselm responded.

"I said then I wanted to be left in peace, and that has not changed. Your coming here does not bode well with me," Sébastien declared, the warning tones in his voice clear.

"I am not my brother," Anselm countered.

"One can only thank God for that," Sébastien muttered drily.

Anselm nodded slowly. He glanced at the water bucket.

"May I?" he asked. "I have ridden this morning directly from Ludgershall and I have not stopped to rest."

Sébastien stepped away from the bucket, keeping a steady distance between them.

"Help yourself," he said.

Anselm knelt on one knee, drank two handfuls of water, and wiped his mouth and beard with the back of his wrist.

"Why are you here?" Sébastien asked suspiciously.

"I think you know why," Anselm responded, looking up at him before drinking another mouthful.

Sébastien sighed heavily.

"It needs to be told," Anselm said, standing and facing Sébastien.

"It does not need to be told," Sébastien grunted, shaking his head almost imperceptibly.

"Yes, it does," Anselm argued simply.

Sébastien stared at him.

"I have no quarrel with you Anselm," he finally said.

"I know that. That is why I am here and not one of the others," Anselm replied. "They *will* come for you," he added quietly.

Sébastien set his jaw and nodded. This was no doubt true. It was just a matter of time.

He looked up and realized the sun was starting its descent in the west, casting its amber-amethyst glow across the sky, reflected by the swathes of soft clouds floating above them. It had been a good day, he thought.

"You must be tired and hungry," he said finally. "I can put you up for the night if you wish, feed you and your horse, but no more talk of this," he said firmly.

Anselm watched Sébastien as he piled the remaining logs together to await his next visit in the coming days. Sébastien reached for the dark brown tunic he had removed and tossed aside earlier when he had arrived mid-morning, slipped it easily over his head and loose linen undershirt, then fastened a black leather belt around his waist. He picked up the water bucket, emptied it, and began walking towards the stone bridge Anselm had just crossed.

"The beef is good and the wine is plenty," he shouted out over his shoulder, boasting slightly, without turning around to look at his visitor.

Anselm, surprised by this invitation, quickly put his gloves on, grabbed the reins of his horse, and did his best to catch up with his begrudging host whose long legs already had him far ahead.

Sébastien did not take the route Anselm had to reach the meadow but instead headed for another, narrower path back to Ferneham and its castle, a path that, after crossing the small bridge, meandered through a thick wood that led up from the Abbey grounds, and up a gentle slope to the town where they had to cross the main branch of the River Wey. The two men crossed over the first stone bridge and walked in silence, listening instead to the birdsong and the breeze whistling through the leaves, a kaleidoscope of autumn colours reflecting the late afternoon sun. Anselm followed Sébastien, keeping pace with his strides despite the fact he was much shorter. The silence gave them both the chance to reflect on the purpose of Anselm's unexpected visit. Anselm broke the silence.

"I see you no longer wear the mantle," he observed.

Sébastien ignored the comment and pressed on.

"Have you abandoned them completely then?" Anselm continued.

Sébastien stopped in mid-stride, turned, and glared at his companion, shook his head slightly dismissing the comment rather than answering it, and began walking again. Anselm let it be.

Soon enough, the woods began to clear as they approached the edge of the settlement. From its meagre beginning in Anglo-Saxon times, Ferneham had grown so much over the years that it had been included in the Conqueror's Domesday Book as one of the great ministers in the south of England. Situated perfectly between Winchester and London, it provided many a place for rest and re-energizing on long journeys across the lower counties and now was a burgeoning market town with a well-established farming trade. And of course, the glorious Waverley Abbey was close by. It was understandable why the Bishop of Winchester Henry de Blois, grandson of the Conqueror and King Stephen's younger brother, decided to build and expand upon the original manor house which sat at the top of a small hill overlooking the town, slowly transforming it into a dwelling fit for a member of the royal family. Its strategic importance was immeasurable.

The sounds and smells of the town reached them as they made their way through the main gate of the wall that formed a noticeable boundary surrounding and enveloping both the town and the castle. There was a hive of activity, market stall owners starting to pack away their unsold produce and goods before the sunset and the cool autumn evening fell upon them. Children milled about either helping in the stalls or playing in the lanes in between the cottages and various establishments that surrounded the market. Occasionally, the aroma of some roasted meat reached the two men, and both suddenly realized how hungry they were.

As they walked along the edge of the market, townsfolk instantly recognized Sébastien and waved or shouted a cheerful greeting, it was clear he was loved and respected there. Sébastien nodded or waved back, acknowledging and returning the familiarity without breaking his gait. His companion did not fare as well; the townsfolk's demeanour changed upon seeing him and they eyed him with suspicion, protective of their lord even from a distance. Anselm observed it all and avoided making eye contact as best he could.

Once through the market, they followed a winding lane up toward the castle which soon loomed in the distance. Anselm could see even from here the D'Ivry emblem, a shield with three red upward-pointing chevrons on a gold background, signifying wisdom, military strength, constancy, and protection, flying from four flag staffs at the top of the keep.

Originally built in the motte and bailey style with a wooden structure sitting on top of a small hill, Bishop Henry de Blois replaced this with a large stone keep, a third of which was, unusually, buried deep into the motte. But it was Sébastien's changes that truly transformed the site. He had enormous walls constructed from the base of the motte, providing a protective stone shell curtain wall around the keep, with ramparts from which the castle could be defended. He personally designed the curtain wall to have twenty-three sides and five towers, with buttresses for extra support at the base. Crossbar keyhole slots and small Norman arched windows in each of the towers through which arrows could be shot added to the defence of the castle. The gap between the walls and the top of the motte was filled with hardened earth, providing level grounds for structures to be added inside and attached to the walls. Sébastien was extremely satisfied with the result, the castle was an impressive sight to behold. And home for him now.

The gatehouse sat in a southern-facing wall, a small covered wooden gallery protruding above from where sentries could keep watch. To fortify the entry Sébastien installed a heavy, black iron portcullis and a moveable wooden drawbridge, which could be lowered and raised very quickly thanks to a pulley system Sébastien also personally designed. He had put to good use much of the knowledge learned from those he had crossed paths with afar and, for the most part, Sébastien felt very safe.

With the addition of the curtain wall, Sébastien realized he needed a new entrance that would give access not only to the drawbridge above but also to the great hall and chapel which sat below. For this, he came up with an ingenious design. A large, wide stone staircase climbed from ground level up to a landing and then split, to the left and up, leading to the drawbridge and to the right and down, away from it, leading to a covered passageway to the Norman-built chapel, great hall, and kitchens which helped to create a courtyard at the front of the Castle. Everyone living or working at the castle gathered for meals in the great hall and supper was usually a crowded, noisy affair. It would be again tonight.

A well-tended garden could be found on the west side of the castle and two wells providing the water needed to sustain those living and working in the castle were placed on either side of the garden, whilst a third well existed within the keep itself.

A timber guardhouse sat at some distance from the castle's entrance, supplying the sentries not only protection from nature's wrath as they kept careful watch, but also sleeping quarters for them as well. The two sentries on guard nodded as Sébastien and Anselm passed by without making a sound.

As the two men approached the castle, Anselm began to see a number of outbuildings housing everything necessary for the running of the castle: a hay grange, granary, buttery dairy, bakery, larder for storing meats covered in brine, a salt pit, and workers' huts. Some, such as the large stables which housed Sebastian's prized destriers and palfreys, were only a few steps away from the base of the staircase entrance for easy access when horses were needed quickly for departing the castle. Barns for storing the hay carts, a kennel for the hunting dogs, and a dovecote completed the menagerie of structures placed sporadically around the base of the curtain wall. Workers and servants were bustling about as they arrived.

Approaching the stables, Sébastien gave a short whistle and a young stable boy came running. Sébastien turned to Anselm.

"Young Nicholas will take care of your horse, please gather what you need and come with me," he said.

The boy took the reins from Anselm and patted the horse on its dust-covered neck.

"Make sure he's well-fed and watered and brushed down before you turn in tonight," Sébastien said to him.

"Yes sire," replied the boy, grinning at his master.

Anselm unhooked a double leather pouch from the back of the saddle and threw it over his shoulder, resting one pouch each in front and behind him and smiled at the boy. The boy looked at Anselm but did not return the smile.

The men continued on through the open courtyard, towards the staircase. Anselm could not help but admire what he saw, remembering what it looked like the last time he was here, many years ago. Great care and attention had clearly been given here, transforming it from a simple Bishop's house into a rather grand castle.

Whilst not overly immense, its design was unique and efficient and was exactly what Sébastien needed upon his return from the wars. He was honoured to have been gifted it by the Bishop and had been determined to make it suitable for visitors of all stature. And, he had his family to consider. Or what was left of them.

"Impressive, what you have done here," Anselm remarked.

"I just continued what the Bishop started," Sébastien replied, his natural humility preventing him from taking credit.

"No, really. It is remarkable. You should be proud of what you have accomplished," Anselm pressed.

Sébastien winced. Proud, he thought. No.

They reached the foot of the stairs and began the long climb. Reaching the first landing, Sébastien pointed to the right and down.

"Great hall for supper," he said. "And the chapel should you need it."

He turned to the left and continued the climb up to the next landing, passed on the way by a couple of kitchen maids hurrying to the kitchens to help prepare the supper, stopping momentarily to curtsey to their lord then scurrying on, giggling as they went. The drawbridge was down, awaiting his return. He glanced up to the gallery as they approached and spied two more sentries peering over the edge. He returned the nod from the one on the right.

"Well protected," Anselm observed.

"It needs to be, considering…" Sébastien started but did not finish.

They crossed the drawbridge and proceeded through the archway that concealed the portcullis and housed more guardrooms on either side, then made their way into the grounds that surrounded the square-shaped keep. Massive, it easily dwarfed all the other structures built along the perimeter into or next to the curtain wall. The keep's white-washed walls hinted at its number of levels through the many small Norman window slits appearing from top to bottom at each of the four corners which held the interior spiral staircases. Larger Norman arch-shaped windows in the curtain wall towers appeared sporadically in the body of the keep's walls. A steep and narrow stone staircase along the exterior of its western wall provided further protection from potentially hostile visitors as the actual entrance to the keep was at the second level, not ground level, and could be easily defended from above.

Its size was misleading for although four levels could be seen from the outside, two more were buried underneath, providing ample storage for grains, seasoned meats and cheeses that needed to be kept cool, barrels of wine and beer and other foodstuffs, and another well that supplied water for the castle, critically protected in case of attack. Supplies were delivered through heavy trapdoors made from the strongest elm and fortified by cast-iron gates which made entrance impossible when locked.

The ground level contained kitchens and pantries, smaller than those servicing the great hall. Above that was another dining hall that could be used for sleeping quarters for many if necessary. This level held the main entrance to the keep, giving access from a small outer room at the top of the exterior staircase and into the hall. Sébastien used this room primarily to entertain important guests when the occasion called for it.

Above that was a chapel with a small altar on which rested a golden cross, a piscine built into the east wall, a beautifully carved font by the entrance, and wooden benches in between. Behind the altar and off from the chancel was a windowless side room used by a priest from Waverly Abbey or the Bishop if he was visiting, for dressing and private prayer. At the top of the west wall was a private viewing balcony used by the lord of the castle and his family or visiting nobles and royalty. Sébastien had little use for it.

Finally, the top level contained three sleeping quarters, one large, two smaller, each with its own fireplace and privy and with adjoining servant sleeping quarters for retainers and ladies' maids. The two smaller rooms had a connecting door that could be bolted from either side allowing easy access or more security as the case may be. Even though they were sparsely furnished, leaving room for the chests and other accoutrements brought by visitors on their travels, the intricately carved beds, tables, and chairs were of the highest quality having been meticulously crafted by artisans of Bayeux, near Sébastien's familial home in northern France.

The spiral staircases at the keep's four corners ran the entire height of the keep, providing access to each level through a stone arch and wooden door. Inner passageways connected the staircases allowing easy and quick movement between the floors without needing to disturb those in the rooms. Each of the aboveground levels had a fireplace and a privy that emptied into pits below at the rear and side of the keep which was cleaned out each morning and evening. Guards patrolled along the battlements at the top of the keep and the curtain wall towers, keeping watch through the crenels whilst remaining out of sight behind the merlons.

With evening settling in, there was a lesser amount of the usual controlled chaos outside the keep as most of the work to prepare the castle for the night was done and attention was now on the kitchens and great hall below for preparing and delivering supper for many. Sébastien's long-trusted, white-haired retainer and now chamberlain of the castle could be seen walking towards the entrance arch and hurried to meet his master as soon as he saw him.

"Sire," he said, nodding, slightly out of breath.

"We have a guest tonight Osmond, can you please ensure the sleeping quarters in the southwest tower are prepared?" Sébastien asked even though it was more of an order.

"Of course, m'lord," Osmond replied, nodding to Anselm. "Will you be dining in the keep or…?"

"No, no, we will eat in the great hall. Just have another plate and some wine set next to mine at the head table." He turned to Anselm. "Osmond will show you the way to your quarters, make sure the fires have been lit, and bring you fresh water. Make your way back down to the great hall when you are ready."

He did not wait for a reply but turned abruptly and headed towards the keep, reaching it quickly, and bounded up the staircase, taking the stairs two at a time, an easy feat on his long legs. Anselm watched him disappear into the keep.

"If you would follow me?" Osmond said and led Anselm to the southwest tower which formed part of the castle's curtain wall.

* * * * * * * * * *

Sébastien reached the outer antechamber of the keep's dining hall, passed through two doors to enter the hall then made his way to the spiral staircase to his left to continue up to his room, the largest of the three on this floor. He took these stairs two at a time as well, bypassing the entrance to the chapel, until he reached the entrance of his chamber. As with his visits to the meadow near the Abbey, this room had provided a much-needed escape from the necessary and unavoidable drudgery of the day-to-day operations of the castle. It was such a different life from the one he had once led. But more and more now, he was finding that he preferred the sleeping quarters in the southwest tower, those he had just given to his visitor, than up here in the clouds. He wondered if Anselm would realize his gesture.

The only light in the room was the day's nearly faded sunlight coming through one of the arched windows but Sébastien did not really need it, being familiar with the layout of the room. Unlike the two smaller rooms, more attention and care had been taken with this room in its décor as it would be used only by important noblemen or possibly even royalty, travelling from London to Winchester and the southwest of the country. A beautiful large mahogany bed rested against the far wall, canopied and curtained with dark red velvet trimmed in gold. He had had it made by local craftsmen and was terribly pleased with the result. Most of the other pieces of furniture in the room, including two matching oak chests, ornately carved with images of woodland creatures, and a small table and chairs had once belonged to Duke Robert who had gifted them to him and thus was, naturally, of the highest quality.

The single tapestry hanging in the room was older than any other at the castle and beginning to fray at the edges, but even still, one could not escape its majesty. It brought back memories of the Outremer, in particular one stall in the small market in the centre of Acre where the tapestries were all beautifully hand sewn. Sébastien both loved and loathed this room; he returned to it only when necessary.

He found his large leather-covered reading chair facing the empty fireplace and sat down, finally allowing his body to relax and feel the aches from the day's work. He suddenly felt very tired and lapsed into a moment of nothingness, no thoughts racing through his mind, simply listening to the wind easily heard outside the window, especially at this great height in the keep. The stillness and his solitude were suddenly interrupted by Osmond's arrival, who promptly set about lighting a fire and several candles in the room.

"My apologies, sire. We were not expecting a guest, it was assumed you would be in the southwest tower as usual tonight, thus this room is not ready."

"Do not worry yourself, Osmond. Our visitor was not anticipated and I hope his stay is short-lived," Sébastien spoke wearily.

Osmond glanced at his master who could not help but catch sight of the barely noticeable scar along Osmond's hairline on the right side of his face. Sébastien flinched slightly, remembering.

"He is the younger Marshal, is he not?" Osmond asked busying himself with building a small pyre with kindling from a wicker basket nearby.

"I recognized the mark of the House on one of the pouches he was carrying."

Sébastien nodded.

"Yes, he is Anselm, the youngest of the Marshal brothers. A name I had hoped not to hear again," he grimaced.

Osmond raised his eyebrows but said nothing. He was well acquainted with the Marshals, having been at his master's side for over forty years. He busied himself setting the fire and, that accomplished, lit several candles which flooded the room with light.

"Supper will soon be ready, many have already gathered in the great hall," Osmond said, changing the subject.

Sébastien nodded.

"I will be down shortly," he responded.

Osmond slipped out without a word, quietly shutting the door behind him.

Sébastien leaned back in the chair and stretched his legs toward the smouldering and slowly growing flames, crossing them at the ankles. He soon found himself lost in the past, images flooding his mind, leaping from one memory to another in no particular order. Of Antioch, of Jerusalem, of warriors on horseback, hearing the jolting, terrifying sounds of battle, feeling the heat of the fires, seeing the glory of the Temple Mount, the faces of his

Brothers, of Melisende, of Duke Robert, of King Louis and Queen Eleanor, all slipping in and out of his thoughts, then remembering the green fields and thick woods of Bayeux from his youth, and, of course, her. The slight jabbing pain he felt earlier returned.

Sometimes, many times, he wished he had not agreed to go with them, he should have stayed, but at the time he felt he had no choice. And what had he then to live for? He knew now, but then, his grief, his unrelenting grief, drew him away, fully believing he would never return. But his destiny was not to end there, in those lands so far away they seemed as though they and all that happened in them never existed.

Anselm would make a good case, he knew. He needed to decide, tonight, once and for all.

* * * * * * * * *

Anselm was impressed with the room Sébastien had provided. He initially assumed he would be given quarters in one of the north towers which appeared rather isolated, standing apart from the rest of the buildings in the castle. But after entering the southwest tower, climbing the spiral stairs three full turns, and entering the already candle-lit room behind Osmond, he was quite surprised with the grandeur of the room. A sizable four-poster hand-carved, dark oak bed resting against the far wall had a thick feather mattress with linen sheets and pillows overlain by a mass of animal skin coverlets; it was as inviting as it was beautiful. A large stone fireplace already roaring with a well-lit flame and next to it a large wicker basket stocked to the brim with kindling and hewn logs, making the room seem as if it were simply waiting for its next visitor. He felt he had been expected.

Osmond stoked the fire and threw another log from the basket.

"I will send for a page to bring you fresh water presently," Osmond said as he turned towards the door and went on his way without another word.

Anselm watched the door close, dropped the pouches onto the floor next to a small table, removed his gloves and heavy cloak and threw them across the table, then walked up to the fire, leaning against its mantel. He felt its heat at once and welcomed it as the temperature had dropped considerably as the sun set, the last vestiges of which could be seen gently streaming through the arched window as if searching for him before settling for the night.

As his eyes became accustomed to the dim light in the room, he looked up from the fire and noticed a gilded brass disc sitting upright on the mantel. Thick enough to hold the smaller disc inside it, the rim consisted of graduated geometrical marks indicating the degrees of an arc whilst its inner plate was covered with etchings of the celestial bodies of the locality the disc was made for. The smaller disc, held in place with a pin, contained various pointers, each with a curved pointer at its tip, and could be rotated if need be. Anselm was amazed. An Islamic astrolabe, he thought as he studied it. He dared not touch it. He had heard of these but had never been fortunate enough to have beheld one. Anselm nodded slightly. Of course it would make sense that Sébastien would have one.

The unusually warm November day had turned into a chilly evening, he shivered and realized he would welcome and be glad for the skins on the bed later. He wandered over to the western window and took in a glorious view, the setting sun casting its golden glow through the woods and stream nearby and settling on the gardens below. He made a mental note to walk through them in the morning.

He reached for the interior wooden shutters, hooked them closed, and made his way back to the fire. He sat down slowly in the chair and stretched his legs toward the fire, resting his head in the palm of his left hand propped up on the arm of the chair. He stared into the fire and fell deep into thought. So deep he did not hear the page's knock at the door until his third attempt.

"Come!" he called out, startled.

The page boy entered with an ewer, water dish, and linen towel, placing them gently on the table.

"Will there be anything else sir?" he asked.

"No, that will be all," Anselm responded.

He heard the door open and then close behind the page as he left. Once again, Anselm's thoughts turned to what plagued him. How was he going to accomplish what he knew needed to be done?

His thoughts turned to his family and he felt a dull ache when the memory of his mother and father, long dead now, rose and took hold. His mother, the beautiful Margaret de Venoix, born and raised in Caen, had inherited the hereditary title "Le Mareschal" - Marshal of the Stable – from her father. He had ridden with the Conqueror to England in support of his invasion in 1066 and stayed as Le Mareschal and a loyal servant to three English Kings,

William the Conqueror, then William Rufus then Henry. This title passed to her husband upon their marriage. His family had had such an auspicious start, where did it go wrong?

His mind wandered to his three siblings. His older brother William, who had taken holy orders as a young man, had spent almost his entire adult life in service of the church in quaint Cheddar in Somerset, only leaving it for a few years when he agreed to act as Empress Matilda's Chancellor during her brief reign. But he did not stay in the position for long. His falling out with John, who had switched sides in the war with King Stephen and acted as Marshal of the Stable in Matilda's court, created a rift that was never to be mended. A few years after he returned to the church, William had fallen ill, the sweating sickness quickly taking hold and ending his life in a few short days. It had been more than a decade since he had passed but Anselm felt the loss even now. A sweet, gentle lad, William was the kindest of the brothers, clearly the most intelligent of the boys, never raised his voice in anger, strong in his passive way, always the peacemaker. Anselm had visited him a couple of months before he became ill but was unable to return before the plague took him, something he deeply regretted and carried with him every day. He had been the only member of the family to go to Somerset for the burial. John had refused to attend.

Anselm closed his eyes and leaned back in his chair. The warmth of the fire felt very good now. His thoughts turned back to his eldest brother.

Ah, John, Anselm thought, a mixture of conflicted feelings starting to well in him. He was a complex character, his quick intelligence and extreme ambition combined with a strong build and ferocious temper made him a man to be reckoned with. He was notorious for doing what was best for himself under the guise of what was best for the family, even when that resulted in conflict and pain for those closest to him. Cruel and cunning, he was convinced what he did was always right, a stubbornness that sometimes ended in dreadful and devastating consequences. Those whom he loved and trusted were shown an unparalleled generosity of spirit and shared in his worldly goods. But those whom he did not like or, even worse, breached his trust, would often find themselves suffering the impact of his vengeful nature. John never forgot an insult or slight, no matter how small. And having lost his trust, it was never to be regained. Anselm's two brothers could not have been more different.

His relationship with his eldest brother was not without friction. He could not forgive John for not attending their brother's funeral, but John would not discuss it. His behaviour during the wars had been deplorable, accusing their brother William of abandoning the Empress when he had not. And now with the approach of the coronation of her son, soon to be crowned King Henry II following the death of King Stephen a month earlier, it was too late for any reconciliation between the brothers. The rift could have been resolved many times over the years but this was John's way. It was just one in a long list of grudges John held, sometimes rightfully, most times wrongfully, and refused to relinquish. But any change in his character now was unlikely, too much foulness had driven away what little good there was left in him.

Anselm let out a long sigh as his thoughts fell upon the eldest of the siblings, his sister Séraphine. He adored her. All the brothers adored her. He stared into the fire. Of all of them, he missed her the most.

* * * * * * * * *

The great hall was humming with activity by the time Anselm found his way there, retracing his steps out of the southwest tower and down the length of the main staircase as Sébastien had indicated earlier, passing through an outer waiting room before entering the main hall from one of the four entrances. He presumed the two others led to passageways to the kitchens and chapel. He was not sure where the last one led. He found himself in a long rectangular room with two large open fire grates positioned in its centre already ablaze and giving off plenty of heat for the room. Tables layered two deep, surrounded the grates on three sides whilst a single long table being the head table, Anselm deduced, on the fourth side opposite where he stood. There was no dais or platform to set Sébastien and any nobles apart, the only noticeable difference was that chairs sat behind the head table, with one slightly larger than the others, whereas the other tables had benches. Several faded tapestries were hung on the walls separated by cast iron candle holders, each lit candle giving a warm, flickering glow to the room.

The mood in the room was upbeat, many conversations taking place at the same time, with the occasional eruption of riotous laughter momentarily drowning out the rest of the hall. Anselm stepped in and looked around for his host whom he quickly found engaged in deep conversation with someone sitting at one of the benched tables at the far end of the room. One set of doors at the near end opened and the delicious smells and aromas from the kitchen wafted in, followed moments later by servants bringing in trays of various roasted beef and pig, pigeon pies, fried dace, and gudgeon, followed by plates of fennel, leeks, and turnips. Anselm felt his stomach growl.

Sébastien stood, patted the man he was chatting with on the shoulder, and waved to Anselm to join him at the head table. As Anselm made his way through, he could not help but notice a slight dip in the conversation whenever he passed by a table, the diners either outright staring at him or giving him a sideways glance. He tried to ignore it but certainly did not feel welcome. They must know who I am, he thought.

Sébastien was already sitting in his place by the time Anselm reached him and sat in the chair left empty for him to Sébastien's right. Sébastien withdrew his eating knife from his belt, a small, sharp-pointed utensil that speared meats and vegetables so they could be easily moved over to pewter plates and then used to eat with if the food was too hot, and dug into the steaming plates of food in front of them. Anselm followed suit, always travelling with his own eating knife as was custom.

Pewter goblets had already been filled with red wine, imported from France. Anselm reached for his first, taking a mouthful to wash down the food.

"There's ale if you prefer," said Sébastien in between bites.

"Thank you, I am quite content with this wine, it is splendid," Anselm replied. "Loire?" he asked, referring to a region not far from Sébastien's historic family estates in Normandy.

"Côte d'Azur," Sébastien answered.

Anselm was impressed again, his host clearly knew his wines. But then again, why would not he considering where he had been?

Sébastien was ravenous, he had not eaten since morning having spent the day in the meadow chopping wood. He finished his wine in two gulps and signalled for some more as he refilled his plate with more roasted beef. The supper was delicious as usual, he swore he had the best cooks in the kingdom. He turned to his guest and inquired about the meal. But his response was drowned out as the doors to the kitchen opened and more food began to be delivered to the tables greeted by cheers as it arrived, and the chatter increased, so much so it was hard to be heard. Still, Anselm tried, leaning close to Sébastien.

"Your cooks are to be praised," Anselm said again as more platters laden with delicious food were placed before them.

He glanced around the room and at those sitting at the tables, which he assumed were all of the heads of the various offices and their families who lived at and ran the Castle. 'I wish the great hall at Ludgershall had such a buoyant mood,' he thought ruefully, reaching for some warm bread to mop up the juices on his plate.

"Indeed," Sébastien agreed.

He leaned back in his chair and surveyed the room and an almost imperceptible smile appeared. He was content with the state of affairs here. He had, in a few short years, turned Bishop Henry's initial renovations that included this great hall and the chapel into a fortified, secure stronghold, fit for any royal or noble visitor to stop and spend the night.

The two men continued to eat in silence, both preferring for the moment to remain observers of those more animated in the hall. Eventually, the platters were empty and several goblets of wine had been quaffed, satiating their hunger and thirst. Sébastien realized his discussion with Anselm had to be now. He turned to him.

"It is difficult to hold a conversation in here, yes?" he asked rhetorically and continued without letting Anselm respond. "Come with me," he ordered, getting up from his chair and heading towards the kitchen doors.

Anselm followed, the clamour in the great hall diminishing behind them. Making their way down the passageway to the kitchens, Sébastien ducked through the open arched doorway into the kitchen, passing servants still hard at work, and entered an adjoining cool room where various animal carcasses were hung awaiting the butcher. Bypassing those, he headed down a few stairs to the cellar where barrels of wine were stored. At the far end of the cellar a number of lambskin sacks with removable corks and almost bursting to the full of wine were hanging from hooks in the low ceiling, so low that Sébastien just barely fit into the room. He reached for a few of the lambskins and tossed them to Anselm who caught them, almost dropping the first one. Sébastien reached for a few more and then, without a word, retraced his steps up and back out to the passage outside the kitchen. But instead of re-entering the great hall, he opened a small door that led from the passage to the open courtyard. Crossing the courtyard at quite a clip, he led Anselm to the main staircase they had climbed when they first arrived late in the afternoon.

Within moments, they had ascended the stairs, passed over the drawbridge and through the entry arch, traversed the grounds surrounding the keep, and ascended the keep's stairs, Anselm barely keeping pace. Suddenly, they found themselves through the anteroom and inside the keep's dining hall, where a fire, the only source of light in the hall, was already lit in a massive fireplace built into the far wall. Osmond had anticipated Sébastien's needs as usual. A very large oak table and matching chairs created the centrepiece of the room with smaller tables placed sporadically against the walls. Two larger padded chairs sat on either side of the fireplace. Smaller tapestries than those in the great hall hung from the walls here, and when Anselm's eyes adjusted to the fire-lit darkness, he began to have a slightly clearer view of them and other objects that reflected the dancing flames.

Sébastien continued towards the fireplace and dropped the wine-filled lambskins onto the table. He reached up to the mantel and brought two goblets back to the table, opened up one of the lambskins, and poured, filling both goblets to the brim. He looked up at Anselm and paused a moment before he spoke.

"You have come a long way today, Anselm," he said, replacing the cork and taking a drink from one of the goblets. "I think it is time for you to say what you have come to say," he said quietly pointing at the second goblet and pulling one of the larger chairs towards the fireplace.

Anselm mirrored his actions and found himself, goblet in hand, sitting across from the man his brother had come to despise many years ago, needing to find a way to convince him. He hesitated.

"I thank you for supper, and for the room for the night," he began.

Sébastien nodded but said nothing. Anselm leaned forward and looked at his host, the firelight revealing an expressionless face looking back at him. Waiting. Anticipating. Anselm could see how Sébastien got his reputation.

"I am surprised that we dined in the great hall," he said. "I would've thought you would've preferred to keep my presence as quiet as possible."

Sébastien thought on that a moment.

"I have no secrets here. Not anymore. Besides," he took a sip, "I wanted them to see you."

'No secrets?' Anselm thought.

"They seem wary of strangers," Anselm responded.

"Only those they know," Sébastien replied drily. "You have," he paused, "unfortunate associations."

"He and I have not spoken in quite some time," Anselm tried to reassure him.

But Sébastien only smirked. He knew better than to trust at face value, years of watching those around him ambitiously plotting the downfall of others, even those who were loved could be sacrificed if the prize was deemed worthy enough. And John Marshal was the very archetype of unfettered ambition.

"Your brother," Sébastien started, not able to say his name, "is the devil incarnate. He has no honour, he has no loyalty, his ambition knows no bounds."

Anselm found this difficult to argue with.

"He has had his comeuppance, many times over," he said trying to pacify him.

It did not work. Years of hostility and enmity built from John Marshal's outrageous behaviour had not dissipated over time. Anselm steeled himself for the response he knew was coming.

"Comeuppance?!" Sébastien scoffed, laughing sarcastically. "Your brother is a disgrace to his Office and should have been imprisoned for his treachery as soon as the Treaty of Wallingford had been agreed. The D'Ivrys have been consistent in our loyalty to the crown, once we have sworn an oath, we keep that oath, no matter what misfortune might befall us. But not your brother. No, his ambition controls his allegiances, not any sense of loyalty. King Stephen granted him the Office of the Marshal which he was not owed despite it having been in your family for many generations and what did he do with this honour? He turned his back on his King, taking advantage of his loss at Lincoln, no doubt watching from afar as Stephen was captured and led away to be imprisoned in Bristol Castle. He wasted no time swearing for the Empress, did he?" Sébastien demanded.

Anselm could not argue. Everything Sébastien had said was true. But it was also the way in those times, one either capitulated to the forces around you, or one suffered the consequences. John had chosen what he felt was the only option for him, but Anselm knew saying this now would fall on deaf ears. He let Sébastien continue.

"It seems Stephen's suspicions of your brother were well-founded and his siege of Marlborough Castle was well-warranted," Sébastien said pointedly.

Anselm reflected on this. After King Henry had died and Stephen became King, he granted the castles at Ludgershall and Marlborough to John when he awarded him the Office of the Marshal, giving John a strong power base in the region. As expected, King Stephen had counted on his support and John had sworn fealty to him, just as he had to his predecessor. But John took up residence at Marlborough Castle and began to spend less and less time at court, especially once Empress Matilda landed with her army, and his allegiance seemed to switch to her. King Stephen's siege of Marlborough was enough to convince him he was in real danger and when King Stephen was captured at Lincoln during the wars with Matilda, he wasted no time in swearing fealty to the Empress. It hadn't been the first time John Marshal let ambition win over loyalty, nor would it be his last.

Sébastien did not stop there.

"And your brother's enmity of me is unfounded and hypocritical considering his own, ah, matrimonial affairs," he said. "His repudiation of Lady Aline to marry Lady Sybilla served one purpose and one purpose only, to further his cause. He and Salisbury were at each other's throats just months before, for God's sake, but marrying Salisbury's sister certainly solved that!" he said, exasperated.

"You know Gloucester was responsible for that," Anselm argued. "He convinced Salisbury to declare for the Empress and rewarded him with the earldom. And Salisbury only agreed to stop harassing John if John married Sybilla. It was in everyone's best interests to bring peace to the region, you must acknowledge that at least."

"I doubt your brother barely blinked before agreeing to throw over Lady Aline," Sébastien muttered ignoring the comment.

"Lady Aline was well taken care of," Anselm deflected, reminding Sébastien of her remarriage soon after to Gloucester's uncle, Philip de Gai.

"That is not the point," Sébastien got them back on track. "It exemplifies how your brother has no honour, never did, and never will. He could have fled to Anjou to support the Empress. Many did, he did not. He chose to stay to protect lands that he no longer should have had any claim to," he said matter-of-factly.

Sébastien broke the flow of the conversation to retrieve the wineskin from the table, refilled his goblet and, after offering more to Anselm, set it down on the hearth and sank back into his chair.

"I am surprised the King did not reclaim them when he returned to power," he said, sipping a mouthful of wine, letting it settle a moment so he could savour the full flavour of it, then swallowed.

He gave Anselm a dark look.

"That one-eyed traitor got what he deserved at Wherwell," Sébastien declared sombrely, taking another drink.

Anselm winced at the mention of his brother's disfigurement. How it came to be was now an infamous tale. At the siege of Winchester, King Stephen won the town and Matilda had fled, eventually making her way to Marlborough Castle under John's protection. Closely pursued by the King's men led by William D'Ypres, a Flemish mercenary, John realized he needed to make a stand to give Matilda time to reach Marlborough. He found himself in Wherwell, a small village close to the ford at the river Teste and decided he would stand and fight there. A vicious skirmish ensued and John and his men were forced to take refuge in the village's Benedictine nuns' Abbey. D'Ypres allowed the sisters to leave but soon set fire to the building, slaughtering any who tried to escape the flames. Once the fire took hold, D'Ypres and his men departed, returning to Winchester, believing anyone remaining inside would perish. But they were wrong. John and one of his men had stayed inside despite the burning timbers taking hold. As they heard their enemy take leave, they made their way out of the back of the Abbey. Foolishly, John had taken one last look up at the burning ceiling and was struck in his left eye by a drip of molten lead from the roof which had started to melt due to the heat of the fire that was now engulfing the Abbey. A gruesome injury, John somehow reached Marlborough where he recovered, albeit having lost sight in that eye and left with a nasty scar running beneath on his left cheek which had burned from the red-hot liquid metal. Ever since, he had worn a black eye patch, direly needed as, without it, he looked truly monstrous.

'The outward depicting the inward,' Anselm could not help but think.

He had been momentarily silenced by Sébastien's comment and the memory it triggered. John's treachery was only part of his despicable behaviour. His unfounded resentment of Sébastien because of her never ceased, he seemed to thrive on it. And what he had done to his own family did not bear thinking about. He closed his eyes to ward off the images, but he could not prevent the memories springing to life.

As if reading his mind, Sébastien continued.

"If not for his treachery to the crown at Winchester, then certainly for what followed at Newbury," he said, his emotions starting to build within him.

"Newbury was…ill-advised," Anselm conceded.

"Ill-advised?" Sébastien barked sarcastically. "He handed over his own son as collateral!" his voice seething with disgust.

"It was only a delay tactic, one I am sure you would have…" but Sébastien cut him off.

"By God's teeth, not on your life," he said slowly with a clenched jaw, barely containing his anger, giving Anselm a cold stare.

The room fell quiet again. Both men drank. Sébastien leaned forward in his chair, lowering his voice when he spoke next.

"The boy was six years old, Anselm, six! What father does such a thing? Six," he said in a murmur, shaking his head trying to rid it of the thought and memory of the angelic boy.

It reminded him that he had no sons.

"But that was not the end of it," Sébastien continued, his ire rising again. "No. His 'delay tactic' as you call it, failed in achieving its end, did it not? The Empress needed more time to reach Wallingford and so he broke his oath to surrender Newbury, not surprising considering that is what he does." Sébastien took a deep breath. "The King had no choice, Anselm, no choice but to menace young William, your brother would have known that."

"John must have believed the King would never harm young William," Anselm offered weakly, knowing it was not true as he spoke the words.

"By God's bones Anselm!" Sebastian swore his voice raising again. "Your brother was told his six-year-old son would be executed if he did not surrender the castle at Newbury, and still he refused!"

For Sébastien, this act of cruelty was the ultimate betrayal.

"Horrible things are done in times of war," said Anselm wearily.

Sébastien stared at his guest. He could understand Anselm's desire to support his brother, but surely even he had to admit that John had crossed the line into the realm of the barbaric. What was it Anselm said earlier, that the brothers had not spoken in quite some time? The situation with Anselm's young nephew may have been one of many reasons for the falling out. Sébastien knew the past could not be rewritten and realized rehashing it would not achieve anything, at least not with Anselm.

"Enough," he said, bringing the conversation to a close.

The two men sat in silence, each lost momentarily in their pasts. But despite Anselm's display of friendship and willingness to discuss things that surely would only reopen his wounds which would never fully heal, Sebastian felt uneasy about Anselm's presence and the real reason Anselm was here.

"Shall we get to the point of your visit?" he asked warily.

"You must believe I have come here alone," Anselm pressed.

"How do I know the others are not already here, waiting for your signal?" Sébastien countered.

Anselm chuckled.

"You have more security on your lands than King Stephen had in all of England!" he exclaimed.

"Not much good that did him," Sebastian grunted, pointing out the flaw in Anselm's logic. "The Empress managed to get through it, as did her son," he added, referring to Henry, Duke of Normandy, soon to be crowned the next King of England.

But he knew Anselm was right. He knew Anselm was not his brother John, he knew Anselm was as disgusted and ashamed of his brother's actions as he was. He was also certain Anselm felt the pain and loss of her almost as dearly as he did despite the fact she had not been mentioned. He sighed.

"Very well. Say what is it you want to say."

Anselm breathed deeply and began.

"Sébastien, you and I both have suffered great loss. Parts of our souls have died. Most of our lives since have been filled with doubt and suspicion."

Sébastien remained silent, listening.

"I was just a child, numbed by the shock. I do not think I have ever really recovered. It took me years to understand why you left," he continued quietly. "He, of course, never did," he added, clasping his hands and looking down at his boots.

It was a few seconds before he continued.

"We have led very different lives, you and I," he almost whispered, still looking down. "I, well, I have wandered, never really settling, doing whatever I was told, without question, without argument."

Life in the shadow of John Marshal had not been easy. His brother's reputation had tarred them all.

He stood suddenly, guzzling what was left in his goblet. He reached for the lambskin Sébastien had opened earlier and refilled the cup, turned and silently offered more to Sébastien who shook his head no.

He returned to his chair and, looking at Sébastien square on, pointing at him as sat, he spoke.

"But you? You went to the ends of the earth. You forged ahead. What you did, what you found…" he continued but Sébastien cut him off.

"I did not forge ahead. I went because I did not want to live. I expected to die there and wished it many times," Sébastien squirmed slightly, becoming agitated.

"Forgive me, Sébastien, I never meant to suggest…" Anselm trailed off.

He sighed and leaned back into his chair, screwed up his courage and spoke quietly but with meaning.

"We both know what you and the others discovered changes everything."

Sébastien knew he was right. But he was not willing to surrender the argument.

"If you know everything, why do not you tell it?" Sébastien snapped, now tiring of the conversation.

Anselm gently shook his head.

"You know that is impossible. You were there. You saw. You know. I was not. And I only know part of it, Archambaud kept his secrets. So no one would believe me, especially now with the reputation my family currently has."

He waited and watched Sébastien for some recognition that he was speaking the truth. He thought he spied a brief flash in Sébastien's eyes, possibly recognition of Saint-Agnan's name. He pressed his case.

"Others have the right to know," he said. "You owe it to them. You owe it to your family." He paused. And then, quietly, "You owe it to her."

Anselm waited. Sébastien sat still, deep in thought. But the moment was interrupted by a knock at the door. Sébastien stared at Anselm, only responding when a second knock sounded.

"Come!" Sébastien barked.

Osmond appeared with one of the sentries who stayed at the door as Osmond entered the room. Sebastian stood and met him halfway across the floor. Osmond reached Sébastien, nodded to him and leaned in.

"Apologies, sire, you did request to be informed of Lady de Lacy's arrival," he said so quietly only Sébastien could hear. "The river watchers have sent word that they should arrive shortly, by the next candle mark I believe. The guest quarters next to yours above have been prepared. Shall I escort them to you here first?" he asked, shooting a quick glance at Anselm.

With Anselm's unexpected arrival, his granddaughter's visit had completely slipped Sébastien's mind although, to be fair, they were expected much later in the evening. They had travelled by barge from the De Lacy estates in Pontefract and had been traversing the rivers for several days.

"Ah, good," Sébastien said just as quietly, adding, "Yes, have them join us here for some food and drink, they must be in dire need. I assume the child is with them?" he asked.

Avice was his first great-grandchild, having been born almost a year ago to the day. This was to be the first time he would see her.

Osmond nodded.

"Yes sire, and we assume her wet nurse. Lord de Lacy's retainer and pages will assist with the chests. We will show the rest of their household to their quarters in the northwest tower once his Lordship and her Ladyship have been settled in their rooms," he responded.

"Good. Make sure they have all they need, see that the kitchen servants have supper waiting for all of them."

"Thank you sire. I shall inform them that you wish them to join you here," Osmond said, bowed slightly, turned and headed for the door.

He spoke to the sentry waiting at the door who hurried back down the keep's stairs. Osmond turned at the door, nodded again and left, closing the door behind him.

Sébastien returned to Anselm.

"My granddaughter Alix will be shortly arriving with her husband and my first great-grandchild," he said with a touch of pride, it was no small miracle that he was still alive and able to see her.

"They have been travelling for a number of days and no doubt will be in need of food and rest. I had expected their arrival later this evening, but word has been sent that they are closer than predicted, the rivers must have been to their advantage. I have asked that they join us here for some supper. We can continue our conversation after they retire?" he suggested, adding, "I do not suppose it will be long, no doubt they will be tired."

Anselm nodded and drank from his goblet. Interesting how Sébastien referred to his family, he thought. But he kept silent. Sébastien drank what was left of his wine in his goblet and reached for a long piece of kindling which, once alighted, he used to light the candles around the room, revealing a subtle richness in the décor. Anselm stood and looked around, now being able to see the room better. Pieces of silver plate sat atop the fireplace mantel and on some of the smaller tables. Gold candlesticks ran the length of the dining table, not ornate but plainly designed. The tapestries could now be seen in their full glory depicting scenes of chivalry and nature's beauty.

One in particular caught Anselm's eye, of two ladies in a garden, the nuanced raspberry reds and blueberry blues of their gowns and headdresses and the dark moss greens of the woods and vines in the background made the tapestry appear to burst with colour and yet was delicate and understated.

Stunning, Anselm thought, such exquisite craftsmanship. But then, one of the faces of the ladies caught his attention.

Sébastien saw him staring at the tapestry but said nothing when Anselm shot him an inquisitive look.

"You may stay if you wish," he generously offered, ignoring the look.

"Thank you, I would like to," Anselm responded.

He knew this was difficult for Sébastien and in earlier years he would have been asked to leave. But then again, in earlier years, he would not have been invited back to the Castle and perhaps even taken captive and ransomed.

Sébastien headed for the staircase that led to his room above, the same one he had taken earlier in the day.

"I shall return presently. The privy," he pointed to the entrance to another staircase in an opposite corner, "is through there should you need it."

Anselm nodded and then found himself alone. This will be challenging, he thought, suddenly nervous and feeling the need to relieve himself, having drunk a fair amount of wine. He slipped out of the room, closing the door behind him.

* * * * * * * * *

The town had just quieted down, the last of the inns shutting its doors for the night as some of Sébastien's guards, led by Osmond, rode through heading for the main dock just outside the walls of the town to the south. They had brought extra horses, saddled and ready to carry their precious cargo up to the Castle. Hand carts and some of the Castle workers were already waiting there in anticipation of the arrival of Lord and Lady De Lacy. The air had turned quite chilly and all were covered in heavy cloaks, thick leather boots and gloves, the guards with sheathed swords at their sides. Some of the workers carried lit torches and aligned the dock and mooring areas on both of its sides.

It was not long before the lanterns of the barges could be seen gliding their way up the River Wey towards them. There were four in total, all with covered portions which provided some level of comfort and warmth for the ladies in the party as well as for little Avice and her nurse. The De Lacy emblem, a black rampant lion on a gold background, could be seen easily at both the bow and the stern of each barge, clearly indicating the presence of some member or members of the De Lacy family.

Osmond recognized the man at the front of the first river barge, Jordan De Lacy, youngest brother of Henry De Lacy, the current Baron of Pontefract and Lord of Blackburnshire. He was somewhat older than Alix being nine years her senior, the match had been agreed after the death of Jordan's first wife, Catherine, who had died before they were able to have children. He was a handsome man, fair-haired with a ruddy complexion and a shock red beard that made him identifiable from a distance. He had overseen the Pontefract estates for his elder brother when he was away either at court or travelling overseas and had, over the years, gained ownership of a vast amount of lands in the northeast to complement those of his brother. It was a good match, he was on equal footing with Sébastien in rank and he loved Sébastien's granddaughter deeply.

The first barge slowly approached, a handful of rowers carefully guiding it into place parallel to and up against the pier, bow facing the shore. Ropes were thrown when the craft was close enough and the guards grasped them, bringing the barge into position, then quickly tied the ropes to a nearby wooden post, securing it in place. Osmond stepped forward to the boarding platform to assist with the disembarkation. De Lacy had dipped into the covered section and when he returned, he was followed by both his wife, Alix, and Avice's wet nurse holding the child tightly against her chest, well swaddled against the chill of the night.

De Lacy alit first, nodding to Osmond but declining his hand. Osmond greeted him.

"Lord De Lacy, welcome. Lord D'Ivry has been detained, I am here to escort you and the Lady to the Castle where his Lordship has requested you join him in the keep's dining hall."

De Lacy nodded his approval and then reached out a helping hand to his wife. It had been almost two years since Osmond had seen her last, not since the winter wedding in Pontefract, and as she stepped gracefully onto the dock and into the candlelight he gasped slightly. He remembered a bright-eyed pretty girl of fifteen leaving Ferneham for marriage to a man she had barely met and going to a part of the country she knew very little about, and she had blossomed into a truly striking creature, almost identical in looks and demeanour to that of her grandmother. The likeness was rather unnerving. Long wavy golden locks flowed down her back, kept in place by a small gold circlet around her forehead. Her face with its clear complexion and high cheekbones was that of a classic beauty, set off by dark green eyes the brightness of which could be seen even in the darkness of the night sky. Her heavy gowns were completely covered by a dark fur-lined hooded cloak with a high fur collar which protected her delicate features from the cold. Once safely off the barge, she turned her attention to Osmond and beamed a glorious smile.

"Dearest Osmond," she exclaimed reaching out both of her arms to him, grasping his shoulders and leaning in to kiss him on both his cheeks.

"Lady De Lacy," Osmond said warmly, welcoming her display of familiarity, then bowed slightly reflecting his status. But he was touched by her warmth.

He signalled to one of the guards to help the wet nurse disembark safely onto the pier and then turned to Alix with a smile.

"Unfortunately, your grandfather is detained but has asked that you and Lord De Lacy join him in the keep's dining hall upon arriving at the Castle," he informed her. Then added, "He has also requested that the child be brought to the hall as well, he is anxious to see her."

"I am sure he is," Alix agreed, pulling the fur collar of her cloak tighter. "The household…" she began but Osmond interrupted her.

"All will be taken care of m'Lady, we have brought carts for the baggage and chests, my men will bring all to the Castle presently. We have prepared the guest rooms in the keep for yourself and rooms for the household in the northwest tower, hopefully that will be to your satisfaction."

"I am sure it will all be fine in your capable hands," Alix reassured him.

Osmond pointed towards the horses waiting on shore, saddled and ready to carry them through the town and to the Castle.

"I feel I must make you aware, m'Lady, of the reason for your grandfather's detainment," he said as they started to make their way towards the horses, his voice taking a serious tone.

"He has had a visitor today that was not expected. And I am afraid it was not a friend," he continued and Alix shot him a concerned look. Osmond quickly reassured her, "Not to worry, m'Lady, your grandfather is not in any danger."

They reached the grey mare that had been prepared for her. Osmond turned and looked at her.

"It is Anselm Marshal, m'Lady," he said.

Alix raised her eyebrows, her mouth opening in surprise and slight shock.

"Really? What could he possibly want?" she questioned.

De Lacy helped her up onto her mount and she took hold of the reins as she settled into the saddle.

"I am not sure," Osmond responded. "But they have been in the keep since supper." Alix nodded and glanced at her husband who had mounted his horse.

They waited until Avice and her nurse along with two of Alix's maids were all safely installed in one of the horse-drawn carts for the short ride up to the Castle. Osmond then mounted his horse and pulled up beside Alix.

"Let's get on then, shall we?" she said, spurring her mount to a trot with her husband quickly catching up to her and riding at her side.

* * * * * * * * *

Sébastien and Anselm waited anxiously by the fireplace, both men nervous for different reasons. They leapt to their feet upon hearing the noises from the keep's staircase and Sébastien was already moving towards the door when it was flung open and Alix flew in as if floating on air.

"Papa!" she cried as she ran to her grandfather who picked her up in a warm embrace, spinning in a circle as they hugged.

It was easy to do, she was a fraction of his size and light as a feather even with her gowns and heavy cloak.

'Papa' was what she had called Sébastien ever since coming to Ferneham to live with him at the age of nine when her parents had died tragically within a few months of each other. Alix's mother and Sébastien's daughter Margaux, named in honour of her maternal grandmother, had married Godwin FitzGilbert de Clare, a scion in the prominent de Clare family from Suffolk. With their untimely deaths and being the only child, Alix inherited many lands and became a wealthy but young heiress. Sébastien had been determined to protect her as he had not been able to protect Margaux, had her educated to a much higher level than most girls and many boys of the age and vetted her suitors carefully and thoroughly.

Finally letting go of her, Sébastien pulled back slightly but only to get a better look at the girl he had last seen at her nuptials almost two years prior. His reaction was much the same as Osmond's, the girl had transformed into a beautiful young woman, her radiant smile bringing light to the room. A slight pain tugged at his heart as he saw it, the similarities to her grandmother. To her. It was almost unbearable.

His trance was interrupted by De Lacy reaching out his hand to grasp Sébastien's, followed by a warm embrace.

"Welcome Jordan," Sébastien greeted his grandson-in-law warmly. "I see you have kept my granddaughter safe and sound."

"As promised my Lord, as promised," De Lacy responded heartily.

"Your journey went well, I hope?" asked Sébastien. "Were the rivers calm for you?"

"Quite smooth," De Lacy answered. "The Thames was unusually tranquil considering the time of year."

Alix had removed her cloak, revealing a resplendent gown in dark green velvet trimmed with black lace. She went to the doorway where the wet nurse stood holding the child who, miraculously, had slept through the entire ride, only rousing now as they entered the dining hall. She was drowsily awake, looking around at the strange and new surroundings, rubbing her eyes with the back of her hand. She gurgled slightly as her mother took her in her arms.

"Come Avice, come meet your great-grandpapa," she cooed, removing the girl's little travelling cloak and lowering her to the floor, steadying her on her feet. "Let's show Papa what you can do," she encouraged.

With slow, unsteady steps and the help of her mother, Avice made her way towards Sébastien who was now down on one knee, arms outstretched towards the child. His eyes widened in sheer delight as Avice seemed undeterred and determined to reach what to her must have looked like a giant of a man. But she was not afraid of him, something drew her to him, and she finally reached his fingertips, giggling and smiling all the way. Sébastien scooped her up in his arms and raised her over his head, chatting at her, spinning her around, making her laugh. Alix was so pleased, she had not seen her grandfather enthralled like this. For a brief moment, the cloud that always seemed to be hanging over him had disappeared and he seemed…contented.

"She is beautiful," Sébastien exclaimed.

"Just like her mother," De Lacy said proudly and Sébastien nodded.

Anselm gave a little cough, drawing attention to his presence in the room. He stepped away from the fireplace and towards the family. Alix looked at Sébastien who felt obliged to introduce his other guest.

"Anselm, my granddaughter Lady Alix De Lacy and her husband Lord Jordan De Lacy. Alix, Jordan, Anselm Marshal," he said formally, his throat tightening slightly on his visitor's surname, gesturing with his right arm as Avice was now firmly being held in place on his hip by his left.

De Lacy nodded a greeting which was returned by Anselm. Alix, composed, thanks to Osmond's advance warning, stepped forward and extended her hand which Anselm gently took in his, barely kissing the back of it as he bowed. When he straightened, he met her gaze full-on and found himself transfixed. It was like seeing a ghost, he thought. Alix could not help but notice the gaze and, feeling uncomfortable, extracted her hand and moved back beside her husband. Anselm turned his attention to Avice who had started to squirm in her grandfather's arms.

"The child is beautiful," he agreed quietly.

The room went still for a moment, no one knowing quite what to say, what to do. Avice broke the spell as she started to cry, fatigue and hunger taking over. Alix quickly took her from Sébastien's arms.

"You must be tired and hungry," Sébastien said. "Osmond will arrange some supper to be brought."

"Only something light, bowls of broth and perhaps some bread?" Alix suggested, occasionally looking over to Anselm who had returned to staring at her. "We had a good meal at a little inn about halfway between Godalming and here. The nurse will take care of Avice, she is not weaned yet."

She wrapped the girl in her travelling cloak and handed her to the wet nurse.

"If the fires are lit, I think it best that we dine in our quarters?" she asked, sensing a hint of disquiet in the room and not willing to spend any more time in Anselm's presence.

Osmond answered her.

"Yes, m'Lady, the rooms are prepared and waiting for you. I shall have the pages bring the food. There is wine in the room already, but if you prefer warm mead...?" he asked.

"Wine will suffice," Alix responded, looking at her husband who nodded his agreement.

Sébastien walked up to the nurse and kissed the child on the top of her head, patting her gently as he did so, feeling the soft golden locks slip through his fingers. He then stepped away as Osmond gestured to the staircase at the southeast corner of the room which led to the guest quarters two floors above. Alix watched the three of them go and then approached her grandfather for another embrace.

"I leave you to your guest," she said loudly enough for Anselm to hear. As they hugged, she whispered in his ear, "Be on your guard, Papa."

Sébastien took heed of her words but did not react to them.

"I am very glad to have you here my sweet Alix. And you," he added, extending his comment to De Lacy with a grin. "Shall we meet in the morn before tierce?" he asked referring to the third hour after sunrise.

"Oh I think Avice will have us awake with sunrise at prime," Alix smiled.

"No matter. There will be meat and fish and ale waiting here for you whenever you wake," Sebastian replied.

Alix nodded and touched his face gently.

"Sleep well, Papa," she said, looking at him adoringly.

Without a word to Anselm, Alix made her way to the same spiral staircase Osmond and the nurse had just ascended. Anselm bowed slightly as she and De Lacy exited the room, understanding and accepting the slight.

The two men stood silently in the room, now eerily quiet after the flurry of activity that had just engulfed it. Sébastien stared at the heavy wooden door in the stone archway everyone had just used to exit the room. De Lacy had closed it securely behind him.

Sébastien returned to the fireplace and threw a couple of logs on the fire, leaning down to stoke it to life. He propped the fire iron against the stone surround and, placing both hands onto the mantel he leaned in and stared at the flames in quiet contemplation. Anselm watched him. It was like staring at a statue. He knew better than to say anything.

"If I do this, it is for them, to protect them. If I do this, it is told my way, all of it, from the beginning," Sébastien said suddenly, almost inaudibly, not moving a muscle.

"Yes, yes of course," Anselm responded quietly, nodding his agreement.

Sébastien straightened up and faced Anselm.

"Then go fetch your quills before I change my mind."

# II

## Part One

## 1096 - Normandy, France

My memory of how it began is very clear as if it were only a moment ago. I remember the mid-summer heat had cooled somewhat as the day moved into evening and I busied myself with the task of snuffing out the candles used for the evening service in the cathedral. This was usually a laborious chore but vespers this evening had been a special occasion and I was eager to finish the task as there was more for me to do. Robert, the 2nd Duke of Normandy by that name and elder brother of William Rufus the King of England, had arrived in Bayeux earlier in the day for a visit with his uncle, Bishop Odo. Our world had been alight with crusade fervour ever since the rousing call to arms from Pope Urban during his sermon the previous November at the Council of Clermont. And now, after months of planning, armies were gathering and making their final preparations to depart for the Holy Land.

I was still just a lad, having been sent at the age of eight from my family in Ivry-la-Bataille to Bishop Odo's service in Bayeux. My great-grandfather, Hugues D'Ivry, had been Bishop of Bayeux before Odo, and there was a boundless and long-lasting love and respect between our families. Bishop Odo, my grandfather Robert D'Ivry, and my great uncle Roger D'Ivry had all fought alongside the Conqueror at the battle of Hastings and each had been rewarded handsomely for their support with lands in England. But whilst my great uncle Roger had stayed with the Conqueror in England, my grandfather Robert had returned to Normandy and the young wife and newborn son he had left in Ivry-la-Bataille, and to managing the family's estates. His son, Ascelin, became his sole heir and eventually my father. It was he who decided to send me, his oldest son, to continue my education and training in the service of the Bishop in Bayeux, keeping my younger brothers, five-year-old Roger and one-year-old Guillaume, home with him.

And now, almost two years later, I found my youthful self at the very centre of a world filled with anticipation and excitement. My father recognized that serving in the Bishop of Bayeux's household would place me in an extremely advantageous position and he pressed upon me the importance of this when preparing me for the move to Bayeux. Bishop Odo had seemed impressed with this young and lanky D'Ivry lad deposited with him, finding me to be rather mature for my age. I appeared to be both very clever and capable, obeyed his orders and carried out his tasks without question and to near perfection, or so he told me. I think much of the silliness of the other boys annoyed him. But I was quickly elevated to the status of page in his inner circle, which exposed me to the most sensitive and confidential matters at the highest level of the duchy. I listened and learned from my master, soaking up information and locking it away, remembering everything, forgetting nothing.

Today was no exception. Preparations for the Duke's visit had taken the better part of a fortnight, for even though the body of the army accompanying the Duke had already travelled to and was camped outside Paris awaiting his arrival, the Duke and his senior men who had come to visit would need to be fed and housed in quarters during their short stay, horses also fed and watered and stables cleared for them. Just as importantly, food provisions, extra horses and weapons being supplied by Bishop Odo needed to be readied for the long trek to Palestine. Whilst other members of the household busied themselves with what was needed for the Duke and his men, I had been tasked by the Bishop to report on the progress of the preparation of the provisions for the crusade in addition to my usual duties attending his Excellency.

With vespers over, it was time for the Duke and the Bishop to dine in the Bishop's Palace, a sizable cottage-like stone structure within the grounds of the cathedral. I hurried across the cathedral floor, stopping for a moment to glance up at the magnificent tapestry Bishop Odo had commissioned to celebrate the victory of the Conqueror at the battle of Hastings. I remember my eyes falling upon the stitched image of Odo himself in the battle, with words above him in Latin which read "Hic Odo Eps Bacul Tenens Confortat Pueros", "Here Odo the Bishop holding a club strengthens the boys". The tapestry never ceased to marvel, something new could be seen in it each time one looked at it. What amazed me even more was the realization that my master was both a religious man and a warrior, when normally one would have been at odds with the other. But in Bishop Odo they blended seamlessly, earning him the respect, and some fear, of many across Normandy and beyond.

It dawned on me I was late for helping the Bishop dress for supper so I quickly made my way to the heavy wooden doors in the north transept, carrying the extra candles I came here to fetch. They would light the dining hall during what would probably be a very long evening filled with discussions on the final preparations for the departure of the crusading armies. And no doubt some reminiscing, as these two men had known each other a very long time. Twisting and pulling on the massive black iron ring, I opened one of the doors slowly, just enough for me to slip through, and pulled the door closed behind me. The Bishop's Palace was just a minute's walk from the cathedral, but I ran to its rear entrance which was closer to the internal staircase I needed to take up to the Bishop's rooms. After placing the candles in a large chest in the passage next to the dining hall, I climbed the stairs to the upper floor, knocked on the dressing room door and entered when I heard the Bishop call out.

Bishop Odo of Bayeux, now in his sixtieth year, was still a vibrant and engaging man despite his age, highly intelligent, loyal and dedicated to the cause of right. Half-brother to William the Conqueror, he had supported his invasion of England thirty years earlier, not only taking part in the fighting but also funding the ships that carried the Conqueror and his armies to England. He had been well-rewarded with lands and manor houses across England, but mostly in the southeast, close to the Channel. For years, the Conqueror had considered Odo to be his second in command, but that, unfortunately, did not last, nor did it continue with the succession of his son William Rufus to the English crown. Bishop Odo believed the Conqueror's eldest son Robert should have succeeded as King. This had almost become his complete undoing.

I entered the room and saw the Bishop already changing from his official robes from vespers for the less formal supper with the Duke. His beautiful vestment decorated in an explosion of gold and silver threads forming celestial images on dark red velvet had already been removed and was draped across a chair. I knew it needed to be hung up quickly in the wardrobe to protect it but instead, I first knelt before the Bishop, kissing his ring on the hand that was extended towards me.

"Ah, Sébastien, thank goodness you are here," he exclaimed as he returned to fumbling with his cincture, the red and gold silk ropes that encircled the white alb at his waist. "Please help me with this," he implored.

I leapt to my feet and took over undoing the knotted belt. I noticed the Bishop's pure white thinning hair was slightly messed, probably from taking off the mitre which now sat on a nearby table. I spied the crozier, the golden hooked staff used for various liturgical services including vespers, leaning against the wall in a corner of the room.

"How do you wish to dress for supper, your Excellency?" I asked.

Bishop Odo did not hesitate.

"A white alb will suffice for tonight," he responded, adding, "And the purple silk cincture. And my pectoral cross of course," referring to the gold cross on a short chain that when worn rested on his chest against his heart.

It contained a relic of a sliver of the true cross and was given to him by the Conqueror when he was appointed and ordained as Bishop of Bayeux almost forty-seven years earlier. It lay on the table next to the mitre, its gold gleaming when the early evening sunlight streaming through the arch windows fell upon it.

Once he was unencumbered by the heavy outer garments, Bishop Odo stretched his stiff limbs and took a seat at the table. I hung up the vestment and, wrapping it first in purple velvet, placed the mitre in a large wooden chest made specifically for it. Bishop Odo reached for and took hold of the cross, cradling it in his hands as he stared at it. I came to stand beside him, awaiting his next instructions.

"We are in dangerous and exciting times, my Sébastien," the Bishop said without looking up. "What do you understand of it?" he asked me.

I thought for a moment and when I spoke, my response was steady and measured.

"I know we are in a battle with forces who wish to bring harm to those of us in the Christian faith," I answered. "I know we are in a fight to protect the Holy Land and that his Grace, Duke Robert, is here to lead the armies going there."

Bishop Odo nodded. He then looked at me and motioned for me to sit next to him.

"I want to tell you of what has happened, Sébastien, you need to know."

With some trepidation, I sat down next to him as I was bid. Bishop Odo breathed in a deep breath and exhaled a long sigh.

"Sébastien, by now your religious studies should have taught you about the schism in our great church thirty-two years ago, when our brethren in Byzantium split away to form their own orthodox Catholic church, despite Pope Leo's desperate attempts to prevent it, hmm?"

He looked to me for a sign of understanding and I nodded. Bishop Odo continued.

"In recent months, Byzantine Emperor Alexios Komnenos has been having discussions with our Holy Father Pope Urban regarding possibly re-unifying the east and west churches," he continued. My face must have taken on a look of surprise for Bishop Odo dismissed this by adding, "It is suspected that he is more in need of support from the west against the Seljuk Turks than any selfless desire to pledge obedience to the papacy," he clarified.

I sat silently waiting to hear more.

"Emperor Alexios sent ambassadors to attend the Holy Father when he was in northern Italy at the Council of Piacenza in early March last year. They had been instructed to provide a report on the Turkish incursions and ask for mercenaries and weapons to aid the Emperor in his fight against them. The news they brought was dire indeed. The Turks had made their way as far west as Nicaea, to the east of Constantinople, looting and slaughtering on their way. Men, women, children massacred or taken as slaves, many tortured to death, the women defiled before being put to the sword. I will spare you any more ghastly details," he shook his head slightly as if trying to get rid of the images the words created in his mind. "Pope Urban returned to France last July, determined that something needed to be done and made plans to discuss this at the Council of Clermont last November."

He stopped for a moment and looked at me for a reaction. I found I could not meet his glance, so unnerved was I by hearing this. Bishop Odo studied me for a moment and let me take in what he was saying.

"You were there, at Clermont, weren't you?" I asked quietly after regaining my composure. "You heard the Holy Father's speech to the masses?"

"Yes, yes I did," Bishop Odo answered, as he caressed the cross in his hands. "Senior members of the clergy in France were summoned to join him in Clermont to support his call for crusade and I attended as I was bid."

"I have heard stories about his sermon. But you were there, you heard. What was it like?" I asked, now fully transfixed by the Bishop's story.

"Inspirational, more so than anything I have ever seen or heard," Odo said reverently. "I will probably not hear or see anything of the sort again. The Holy Father knew something needed to be done, he knew that for the Holy Land to be saved, the Christian world would need to come together and fight for its very existence. If the Turks continued pressing westward, we would all be doomed."

Bishop Odo let that sink in a moment. And then he continued.

"So, he let it be known that he would be preaching a sermon for the masses on the last day of the council, on a clear field, east of the town. Thousands attended, coming from the far reaches of France, even from other Christian states, Spain, Germany. Stories were spreading about the suffering at the hands of the Seljuks, people wanted guidance, they wanted to know that God was with them and they wanted to hear this from the Holy Father. He left them in no doubt about that, and about what needed to be done. He did not spare them the gruesome details and gave vivid accounts of the miseries of our Christian brethren, of the grotesque injuries and deaths inflicted at the hands of the Turks. The crowds, massive as they were, stood in silent awe and reverence, shocked, alarmed at what they were hearing."

He paused a moment, deep in his memory of it. I waited.

"And yet, as Pope Urban continued his sermon, one could sense a growing shift in mood, from devastation to revulsion. This was not to be endured. The Holy Father invoked the names of our magnificent Frankish warriors that had gone before, Charlemagne, his son Louis the Pious, and other great kings of our past, those who had fought and overcome our enemies. Of those who had established a Christian stronghold in Palestine, building monuments to our faith, including our blessed Holy Sepulchre, which now were being overrun and irreverently polluted by the non-believers."

The Bishop's voice shook as he was overcome by the thought of it. Getting up from the table, he began to slowly pace about the room, taking a moment to compose himself before continuing.

"He beseeched the crowd to cease fighting amongst themselves for petty, earth-bound accolades and wealth, end whatever quarrels they may have with each other, and, joining together, turn that anger towards those who wish to destroy us, come to the aid of Jerusalem which is now held captive by our Lord's enemies."

By this time, the crowds were beginning to rouse, a strong murmuring in agreement with the Holy Father's words could be heard. He then announced those undertaking this charge would be rewarded by having all their sins forgiven and a single voice cried out from the masses, 'Deus Vult!! God wills it!'" he said, his voice rising with the emotion of the moment, his fist rising above his head. "Soon others were shouting this, the masses started chanting, almost to a frenzied roar and Pope Urban had to raise his hand for silence, so he could continue."

The Bishop stopped a moment and took a seat back in the chair next to me.

"He exempted the old and infirm, declared that women were not allowed to go on their own but only with their husbands, and that members of the clergy would be permitted if given permission by their superiors," he said, looking at me.

I returned a questioning look.

"Yes, Sébastien, the Holy Father had granted his permission for me to join the cause before I left Clermont. I have only decided to tell you now as I did not want to worry you. But now I need you to understand why I have decided to join the Duke in this undertaking. When he leaves for Paris, I shall be going with him," he stated firmly.

I was astonished, I did not know what to say, my mind spinning with this news, so I kept quiet and let the Bishop finish his story.

"The Holy Father then declared that whosoever undertakes this pilgrimage and defence of God would do so wearing the sign of the cross. Bishop Dalmace of Compostella brought him some small pieces of cloth that had been sewn into the shape of a cross and Pope Urban blessed them. Adhémar de Monteil, Bishop of Le Puy, was the first to step forward and kneel before the Holy Father, begging for permission to take the cross. Others quickly followed, myself included, and soon all of the cloth crosses were gone."

Bishop Odo got up from the chair and went to a small bejewelled chest sitting on a table in the corner of the room. Gently opening it, he reached inside and removed a piece of folded silver cloth, brought it over to the table and sat down again. He placed the cloth in front of me and motioned for me to unfold it. I looked at it and then back to the Bishop who gave me silent encouragement. I began to open it, lifting each corner slowly, each movement revealing more and more of what was hidden beneath. I stared at the small cross made of linen cloth coloured red, the deep red of the Christ's blood.

"I shall have this sewn on my cloak before I ride with the Duke," the Bishop confirmed. "I have fought many battles throughout my life, Sébastien, but none ever so grave as this. We are fighting for our very souls. I need to make this journey. Do you understand?" he asked.

I nodded, but I was saddened by this news. I had come to love the Bishop, not only as a teacher and mentor but as a grandfather figure as well, my own having died when I was but three. The thought of him going on crusade was devastating and, for an understandably selfish moment, my stoic facade left me and my eyes welled with tears. Bishop Odo saw this and immediately reached out and patted my arm in an effort to comfort me.

"My apologies, your Excellency," I mumbled, wiping away the tears with the back of my free hand. "It is selfish of me to react in this manner. I do understand your need to go. It is an honour to go. I only wish I could join you," I said with heartfelt earnestness.

Bishop Odo had no doubt I was sincere. He studied me for a moment before speaking.

"I am glad to hear of it. I have thought long and hard about this, Sébastien, and I have made a decision. With your father's permission, of course, I want you to accompany me as my personal squire. You will have the same responsibilities as you currently do, except that you will attend to me and to me only," he said seriously, looking intently for any adverse reaction from me.

I was stunned at first, not sure of what I had just heard, but when I understood, my face changed from sadness to opening up to a beaming smile, my heart leapt with joy at the thought of being able to stay with and continue to serve my dear Bishop. And to join so many other honourable men who have all taken the cross was a rare privilege. I quickly tried to hide my enthusiasm and downplay my eagerness.

"I am unworthy of such an honour…" I began to object, but Bishop Odo stopped me.

"Save the protestations of unworthiness, Sébastien. You are more than worthy. You have shown yourself to have the character of a strong, honest lad who will, with the right guidance, grow into a strong, honest man, and one, I am sure, destined to become a great leader in his own right. This will be the opportunity for you to expand your learnings, experience new and different peoples and cultures, and absorb as much as you can of it all," the Bishop said encouraging me.

But then the Bishop's voice became quite solemn and sombre.

"But I want you to understand this: it will not be an easy thing, our mission. We shall be travelling long distances over land, crossing mountains and rivers and seas. Many will die before they reach the Holy Land and those who survive will then face fierce battles with the Turks. And battle is not something to take lightly," he warned.

"But with the Lord with us, we shall defeat them, yes?" I said, trying to show him my enthusiasm.

The Bishop sighed.

"Yes, God willing, we shall be victorious," the Bishop answered.

"Then I will go with you," I said believing I had decided the matter.

Bishop Odo smiled.

"I shall discuss this with the Duke this evening and if he is in agreement, I shall send for your father immediately," he said. "Ivry is about a day's ride from Bayeux, my messenger should arrive late in the afternoon, probably just after sext. With time for your father to prepare, he should be here by the Sabbath," he calculated.

He grunted in the way that he did whenever his mind was set.

"Now, I want you to serve us tonight and listen to Duke Robert. You will learn much from him, yes?"

I nodded fervently, my dark brown hair falling slightly forward. Bishop Odo smiled again, and looked at me intently. I was tall and strong for my age and had a serious, studied demeanour, all giving the impression of being much older than I was. I had excelled in my education and training in the past months, far surpassing the others being schooled with me. Comfortable on horseback, I was good with a sword, skills that were evenly balanced by the reading and writing abilities which my wonderful mother, Isabelle de Breteuil, had had the priests in Ivry-la-Bataille initiate well before my arrival in Bayeux. All would be needed for the arduous journey ahead of them, Bishop Odo no doubt thought.

"You have the grey eyes of the D'Ivrys, I remember those of your great great grandfather Hugues very well," he said, lost for a moment in the past. "You are blessed to be with us, Sébastien, and we are blessed to have you. Listen well tonight," he repeated, pressing the point.

"I will your Excellency," I assured him.

"Good. Right then, you will need to change," he said, gesturing to my clothes. "I suggest the dark green tunic and make sure your leggings are clean, no shabby knees for the Duke."

I nodded in agreement. The Bishop continued.

"I will wash. Come back when you have changed and help me dress."

"Yes, your Excellency," I said, nodding slightly.

I stood and then kneeled briefly before the Bishop and then, without another word, left the room for my own which was down the stairs, immediately below his. There I quickly slipped out of the light brown work tunic and belt I had worn for vespers, splashed some fresh water on my face to clean off the grime of the day, put on fresh grey leggings and the dark green tunic as commanded by the Bishop. I gave my leather slipper-like shoes a bit of a spit polish before putting them back on – I would look my best for the Duke.

Soon I was back in the Bishop's dressing room helping him with his white alb and fetching two purple cinctures from the wardrobe for the Bishop to choose from. Bishop Odo pointed to the one on the right and I helped him on with it. A knock sounded at the door and the Bishop's chamberlain entered.

"Your Excellency," he began with a bow, "you wanted to be alerted to Duke Robert's arrival in the dining hall. He is there now, I have informed him that you will join him presently."

"Good, good," Bishop Odo nodded his approval. "Is there wine on the table and is the supper ready?" he asked.

"Yes, the wine is already in the dining hall, your Excellency. And I believe supper is ready. The kitchen is awaiting word from you for when you wish it to be brought to the table," he responded.

"Good. I shall have Sébastien with me this evening, he shall let the kitchens and the stewards know when supper is needed."

"Very good your Excellency," the chamberlain responded and left the room, closing the door behind him.

The Bishop looked at me.

"Are you ready, my lad?" he asked.

"At your will, your Excellency," I answered and the Bishop led the way to the dining hall down the stairs on the ground floor.

* * * * * * * * *

Robert, Duke of Normandy, first son of William the Conqueror and his wife Matilda of Flanders, stood next to a Norman arched window in the large dining hall looking out the front of the Bishop's Palace to the magnificent cathedral in the southeast of the grounds. Today's July sun setting in the west cast its warm, unearthly glow across the great church. The dining room was already lighted by several candles dancing shadows across a mural-covered wall. A fireplace stood set but unlit, the warmth of the mid-summer day still filling the room.

Better known to his familiars by his nickname, Curthose, given to him by his father when he was a young man and teasing him about the shortness of his legs, he was nearing forty-two years of age and was beginning to feel it. Despite his father's criticisms of his shortcomings, Duke Robert had gained a reputation as a fine military strategist, if a bit slow to stir. When questioned, he would always say he preferred a life of leisure, proven by his slightly protruding belly from years of devouring rich succulent foods and hearty amounts of drink. But once engaged, few could match his courage and quickness of mind. His dark eyes, nearly black hair and matching short horseshoe moustache, each having a sprinkling of grey hairs, gave him a slightly fierce countenance, especially when combined with his fiery temper. He used this to his advantage.

By birthright, he should have been crowned King of England after his father died, but the Conqueror had chosen a younger son, William Rufus, to follow him, leaving Robert as Duke of Normandy. The inevitable conflicts occurred leaving the brothers estranged for years. Only now, with saving the Holy Land as a common goal, did the brothers begin to mend their relationship. That and the fact that to build and pay for his army, Robert had been forced to lease some of his lands in Normandy to William Rufus for ten thousand silver marks, on the condition that he would get the lands back upon his return from Palestine. Whether or not that would happen, time would tell.

I opened the door and preceded Bishop Odo through it, holding it open for him. The Duke turned to see Bishop Odo glide into the room.

"Duke Robert!" Bishop Odo exclaimed, with a beaming smile and extending both of his arms to the Duke for an embrace.

"Your Excellency," the Duke responded bending a knee and, taking the Bishop's left hand, kissed the ring on his third finger.

"Enough, enough of the formality my dear, dear Curthose," Bishop Odo insisted, helping the Duke to his feet, continuing, "We have plenty of time for that in the days ahead."

Robert rose to his feet and embraced his uncle strongly.

"Uncle," he said, "it has been too long since we last met. And now this tragic business brings us together to fight again. It does cheer me to see you."

"You are looking very well," Bishop Odo declared.

"As are you," Robert responded.

Bishop Odo guided him to the two chairs at the corners of the table next to the open fireplace and, as I had already pulled out the chair at the head of the table in anticipation of the Bishop taking it, he sat, making himself comfortable. Robert waited until his uncle had seated himself and then followed suit. I retreated to a nearby corner, awaiting my next instructions from Bishop Odo. He signalled for me to fill the gold wine goblets that sat in the plate settings on the table. Once filled, Bishop Odo took a moment to bless them and raised his goblet in a toast.

"Deus vult" he said in a rather subdued voice, repeating the cry of the masses attending Pope Urban's sermon in Clermont. "God wills it," he repeated, now in his own language rather than Latin.

"Deus vult," Robert responded and raised his goblet to take a drink.

"How long has it been since we saw each other last?" Bishop Odo asked.

Robert thought a moment.

"Not since last Michaelmas, I am sure," he answered, taking another mouthful of wine. "Business within the Duchy has kept me occupied and of course, my dear brother cannot seem to leave well enough alone," he added, a slight irritation entering his tone.

"Have you actually seen William Rufus recently? Or is he just haranguing you from afar?" Bishop Odo was well familiar with the rift between the Duke and his brother the King of England.

"Thankfully I have not, he stretches his grasping fingers into my lands from afar," Robert responded. "If only you and I had been successful in our battle with him for the throne upon the death of my father..."

"You were the rightful heir," Bishop Odo interjected, adding, "and still are."

"Indeed. We were in the right, and with the support of the English barons we should have been victorious. We almost were, with our siege at Pevensey, if not for the wretched weather delaying our troops. Your spiritual leadership was," he hesitated, searching for the best word to describe it, "inspired," he concluded. "But the Lord shone His light on William and we have suffered the ill effects of his kingship for, what, almost nine years now? And you, having to forfeit your English lands, I shall never forgive myself for that," he said quietly.

"It was a casualty of war," said Bishop Odo, trying to relieve the Duke's guilt. "I made my decision to stay with you because it was right, not because of lands in England."

"You lost the Earldom of Kent," Robert reminded him. "And any possibility of becoming Pope," he added.

"That is true," Bishop Odo admitted. "But being banished to Normandy meant I kept my bishopric here in beautiful Bayeux and, now, we find ourselves together once more, taking up arms again against a common foe."

Duke Robert leaned back in his chair.

"Yes, the past is past. It is unfortunate that I have had to pawn some of my lands here in Normandy to Rufus to fund my army, but what is done is done. No matter, I shall get them back, one way or another."

Bishop Odo gauged his nephew's mood and decided to take the opportunity to tease him.

"I don't think you've ever recovered from having that chamber pot emptied over your head by Rufus and Henry when you were all lads," he said, a laughing smile on his face.

The Duke stared at him and for a moment the Bishop thought he had misread his mood, but he quickly broke into a huge grin and laughed heartily at the memory of his brothers' trick.

"It really was not my fault they were so poor at casting dice, but I did not cheat, I won honestly! I should have known something was afoot when the two of them left the room and suddenly appeared in the gallery above me, I could not move quickly enough!"

"I think your reaction may have been somewhat excessive though now perhaps, in retrospect?" Bishop Odo prodded.

"That was not against my brothers, that was against my father. He never disciplined either of them, for anything, which is why they have both become such quarrelsome, difficult men."

"True, but laying siege to your father's castle in Rouen without really having a chance at succeeding…?" Bishop Odo prompted.

Robert waved his hand, as if dismissing the comment.

"That was something I thought he would appreciate, clearly I was wrong."

"You were lucky your mother's relatives in Flanders allowed you refuge there," Bishop Odo said.

"My mother loved me as much as my father did not," Robert responded.

"Be that as it may, was it necessary to harass the Vexin as well?"

"I almost had him there!" Robert exclaimed, laughing. "If I had not recognized his voice, I would have killed him after I unhorsed him!"

"That may have cost you the English crown," Bishop Odo said, quietly chastising him.

The Duke took another mouthful of wine and continued.

"That is quite possibly true. Even our reconciliation thanks to efforts by my mother only lasted until her death."

They both sat silent for a moment, lost in thoughts of early times. I came to know that each had done things that in the light of hindsight may have been deemed deplorable, even bordering on treachery, by their liege lords. But both had paid a dear price for them. Odo losing his Earldom in England and imprisoned for five years until forgiven by the Conqueror on his deathbed nine years earlier, and the Duke at the same time losing the kingdom of England to his younger brother, his father's favourite, after refusing to attend the Conqueror as he lay dying. And yet, all of it, all of the intrigue and scheming and battles, had brought them here, years later, ready to join forces once again. But this time, they were sure, on the side of right.

The Bishop signalled for me to light the rest of the candles in the room as now that the sun had just about set, the room had become dim. Duke Robert broke the silence and returned to the question at hand.

"I've been kept busy these last months with preparations since the sermon in Clermont," he said.

He quaffed again, emptying his goblet in one swallow. The wine was good. Watching him intently, I noticed the Duke was out of drink and moved quickly to refill his goblet. Robert watched me, smiling his appreciation.

"I've no doubt you have been," Bishop Odo said. "How many men are you now?"

The smile dropped from the Duke's face and he became very serious. He glanced over to me as I had returned to my post in the nearby corner.

"All is good, Robert," the Bishop said picking up on his concern. "Sébastien, come here," he beckoned to me.

I stepped up to the table and stood between the two seated men.

"Who does he remind you of?" Bishop Odo asked now that I had moved into the candlelight emanating from the table.

Robert studied my face.

"There is a familiarity that I cannot quite place…" he responded, his voice trailing off.

Bishop Odo chuckled.

"He is a D'Ivry, Robert. Ascelin's eldest, Hugues's great-great grandson," the Bishop said, filling in the blanks.

"By God's teeth, is he really?" exclaimed Robert.

"Yes, he is. He has been with me for almost two years for his studies and training."

"Come here boy, let me look at you," Robert said to me, pulling me closer to the light.

"Ah, yes, yes, I see it now. I remember his great-grandfather Robert and his great-uncle Roger more so than Hugues, obviously because they were in service to my father and around us most of the time when I was a boy," he admitted. "But sweet Jesu, he does look like Robert! The same grey eyes and the jawline are almost identical," he mused, looking closely at me. "So, tell me young Sébastien, how old are you?" he asked.

"I am ten years, your Grace," I said confidently.

Robert was surprised.

"You are tall for your age, lad! How are you getting on with your studies here with the Bishop?"

"Very well, I thank you, your Grace. I am most fortunate to have His Excellency for a teacher," I responded.

Turning to the Bishop, Robert asked the obvious question.

"Is he as gifted as his elders?"

"It is early days yet. But the signs are there, yes," the Bishop admitted.

The Duke clearly knew what the Bishop was thinking.

"Well, we should bring him, we need good squires. He can attend to you and continue his studies and get some training along the way, he will learn from the very best," Robert declared.

"Precisely what I had in mind, precisely," Bishop Odo was pleased that the Duke did not have to be asked. "I will send a messenger this evening to his father to come to Bayeux immediately, he should be here in less than two days. I do not anticipate any issue with obtaining his permission for the lad to join our mission, but if I am wrong, I am sure you will be able to convince him."

"That is settled then," he said and I returned to my post.

The Duke finally answered the Bishop's question.

"I've amassed seven thousand, and with about another three thousand or so Flanders will be bringing with him, we should have close to ten," he said, referring to his cousin Robert, the Count of Flanders, with whom he had spent a great deal of time of late strategizing and planning for this crusade. "About a third of them are mailled and about half are horsed, all are armed. We shall convene with Flanders near Paris where my men are already camped outside the town walls in Saint-Denis. Blois and Aumale," as he called the two Stephens, the Count of Blois and Chartres and his cousin the Count of Aumale, "are already there with the men, overseeing all of them until I arrive."

"Your brother-in-law is prepared for the journey?" Bishop Odo asked, rather incredulously speaking about Blois.

Robert chuckled.

"Yes, well, at the moment, yes. I am sure he will be in constant contact with my sister whilst he is away, he is rather, ah, devoted to her, even after sixteen years of marriage," he said with a mischievous grin. "Although I have been told he has only agreed to go because Adela insisted he take the cross. She certainly is the Conqueror's daughter."

Bishop Odo smiled knowingly, agreeing with the Duke.

"And how does your cousin?" he asked of Aumale, the son of Robert's aunt, Adelaide of Normandy, the Conqueror's sister.

"Very well indeed. He is eager to get on with it," Robert responded, taking another gulp of wine.

"No doubt he is. What other news do you bring then? What do we know of Peter or Walter?" Bishop Odo asked.

Robert drank some more wine, steeling himself, before speaking.

"The news I bring is not good," he stated with a grim tone. "As you know, all of our preparations have been done to be ready to depart on the 15th of August, as the Holy Father decreed."

"Yes, the day of the Feast of the Assumption seemed appropriate for the occasion. It was unfortunate that they decided not to wait..." Bishop Odo started but was suddenly cut off by the Duke.

"Walter, that impetuous cox-combe!" Robert said, his voice suddenly filled with anger.

"He is a Knight, and the Lord of Boissy-sans-Avoir," Bishop Odo reminded him.

"He would not ride as a Knight in my army," he scoffed. "If this were not as grave as it is, I would not pay him any heed. But his early departure leading a group of disorganized and unprepared knights is not only ill-advised but could place our own mission in great peril!"

"Peter the Hermit's army should provide more manpower when they join them," the Bishop tried to soothe his ire.

Robert looked at him sarcastically.

"Peter's army is no army. A gaggle of peasants armed with pitchforks, no horses, no maille, no shields. They have gone on a wing and a prayer. There is no question that Peter is a brilliant preacher, I have seen him, his passion can be greater than the Holy Father's. But he has no patience, no pragmatism, no cunning. And he is no warrior. He leads with his heart and not his head. They both should have waited for our armies to be ready," Robert declared firmly. "Mark my words, they are doomed," he concluded, sure of their fate.

"Have we had any news of their progress?" asked the Bishop, trying to refocus the conversation.

"Were you aware that Walter and his men reached Hungary in early May? And that they then marched on towards Belgrade? It has been reported that the governor refused them entry to the city – he was not prepared for their arrival of course - and they rioted, rampaging and looting across the countryside," Robert shook his head in disgust. "At the village of Semlin, just outside of Belgrade, some of the knights were captured, thankfully they were released but not until their maille was taken from them and hung from the walls. Disgraceful."

The Bishop shook his head in dismay. Robert continued.

"Most recent reports say they finally reached Constantinople, but needed Emperor Alexios to send men to Nish in Serbia to safely escort them. There they await Peter and his men."

Robert drank some more before continuing.

"As for Peter, he and his throng left Cologne about a month after Walter – Walter could not even wait for him to join and strengthen their numbers, his impatience got the better of him!" Robert exclaimed and went quiet for a moment. "Peter's army eventually followed the same route that Walter had taken," he continued, "but we heard nothing until reports came in from Semlin. They saw the maille and shields from Walter's knights strung up on the walls and foolishly decided to attack. We have been told about four thousand of the local people were killed."

Bishop Odo crossed himself and Robert continued.

"But unfortunately it does not end there, they have also attacked and looted Belgrade. And upon reaching Nish, the Germans in Peter's army could not stop themselves from picking fights with the locals and the garrison commander had no choice but to engage them. Peter," he said resignedly, "lost about five thousand men."

Bishop Odo crossed himself again and clasped his hands in prayer.

"Do we know anything more?" he asked quietly.

"No, that was the latest. Whoever has managed to get out of that disaster should be on their way to Constantinople to meet with Walter, assuming his army has not done anything else rash. We will need to wait for more information," Robert answered and then added quietly, "As I said, doomed."

"Hmmm," the Bishop said softly. "We must pray for the Lord to protect them."

Robert looked away and shook his head slightly.

"We must concentrate now on the final preparations for our own journey. To that end, I have met with Flanders, Bouillon, Vermandois and Toulouse in Rouen," he said about his cousin and the leaders of the other French armies Godfrey de Bouillon, Hugh de Vermandois and

Raymond, Count of Toulouse. "We have finalised the routes the armies will take. We realized it was not wise to travel together, the cities along the way will not be able to support a single army of such great size, but instead agreed to take different paths and reunite in Constantinople."

"Very sensible," Bishop Odo said, nodding.

"Flanders will be coming down from Bruges and he and I will meet Blois in Saint-Denis in a few weeks' time. We shall go to Paris to finalise plans for a united departure with Vermandois. Assuming all goes well, we shall journey to Lyon where we will meet with Toulouse. He will have a smaller army and will travel over land from Lyon to Constantinople. Flanders, Blois, Vermandois and I shall go to Genoa first, then Rome, then Bari and, after crossing the Adriatic to Byzantium, reconvene with the others in Constantinople, where Emperor Alexios should be waiting for us with fresh supplies."

"And Bouillon?" the Bishop asked. "He has the largest army, no?"

"Yes. He will also travel overland leaving directly from Lorraine where his army is camped. I believe he first travels to Ratisbona – another reason why Peter should have waited, he and his army could easily have joined with Bouillon there," Robert sighed. "After that, I am not sure, he will be joining us in Paris so we can discuss what he has decided when we meet then. With God's blessing we should all be with the Emperor by All Saints," he said.

Bishop Odo nodded again. It was a good plan, ambitious, but feasible. There would be more to do before leaving for Saint-Denis, the undertaking ahead of them was enormous and strategically complex. But now, it was time to eat. He signalled for me to fetch supper.

\* \* \* \* \* \* \* \* \*

The ride to Bayeux had taken longer than expected and my father and his two men reached the town just after None, the mid-afternoon prayer service, the following day. They pulled the horses up to the back of the Bishop's Palace where Bishop Odo's servants were waiting to attend to them. My father dismounted quickly and handed the reins of his horse to the first boy he saw. Having the D'Ivry height, he walked in long strides to the front of the building, taking off his riding gloves and loosening his cloak on the way. He entered the main doors and tossed his gloves and cloak onto a table just inside the doors and, hearing someone approach, turned and was surprised to see me come through the passageway leading to the dining hall.

"Father," I greeted him, stopping a few feet short of him and bowing slightly and stiffly.

He was taken aback by the sight of me. It had been quite some time, the previous Christmas in fact, since he had last seen me and no doubt he was amazed at the change he saw before him. Not only had I grown substantially – I would eventually surpass my father, himself being over six foot - but it was my countenance that surprised my father the most. I had become very serious. And there was a confidence about me that I believe my father sensed as soon as I walked into the room. His son was becoming a young man. He seemed pleased to see it.

My father smiled, walked up to me and wrapped his arms around me in a warm embrace which I returned breaking into a huge grin. It was good to see him and I welcomed the show of affection, but I was still tense, especially knowing what it was that was going to be asked of him.

"You are looking well my son," he said, holding onto my shoulders. "You've grown."

"Thank you father, I am well."

"How are your studies proceeding here with the Bishop?"

"The Bishop has been very good to me, I am learning a great deal during my time here," I said. "Bishop Odo is a great teacher," I added sincerely.

"Good, good, I am glad to hear of it," my father replied.

I looked beyond him as if to see if anyone was loitering outside. My father knew who it was I was looking for.

"I am afraid your mother was unable to attend, Sébastien. The Bishop's message was urgent and she would not have been able to make the ride quickly enough."

I winced. My father noticed the reaction and tried to assuage the disappointment.

"She bid me to send you her love, and I have brought a few things for you from her, they are being put in my room as we speak."

I had suspected my mother would not make the ride, but I was sorry she had not just the same. I knew that both the Bishop and the Duke were eager to settle the matter of my joining the Duke's army in the service of the Bishop but if my father agreed, it might mean I would not see my mother again for some time. I could only hope that the Duke would take the path through Ivry-la-Bataille on his way to meeting the other leaders in Paris.

"I understand father," I said, trying to keep the sound of disappointment from my voice. "The Bishop and the Duke are in the dining hall, awaiting your arrival," I said, stepping aside and gesturing to the entrance to the passageway.

My father headed for the doorway, patting my shoulder as he passed by. He reached the closed door of the hall, knocked and waited to be told to enter. Opening the door, we found the Duke and Bishop Odo standing by the table which was covered with several pieces of vellum and parchment, some with writing, some which looked to be maps. My father walked up to the Duke and bowed.

"Lupus!" Robert practically bellowed my father's lupine nickname when he saw his old friend and long-time vassal enter the room.

They embraced heartily, clearly happy to see each other.

"That is a name I have not been called in many years, Curthose," my father responded using the Duke's nickname and smiling in friendship.

"Have the years quieted your temper then?" Robert asked jokingly.

"Years of marriage have, no doubt," he responded laughing. "It has been good to have some years of peace after all the battles."

"Isabelle is well?" Robert asked after my mother.

"Yes, very well. She sends her love," responded my father.

He then turned and walked up to Bishop Odo and knelt on one knee before him to kiss his ring.

"Ascelin, come, have some ale, you must be thirsty after your ride," Bishop Odo offered, motioning for him to rise from kneeling.

I quickly stepped up to the task and poured some warm ale into a tankard from a pitcher on the table and handed it to my father. I then turned to both the Duke and then the Bishop, each waving no to my offer as there was plenty left in their own. I returned to my corner.

"We were just reviewing the strategies in place for our armies," explained Robert. "Come, take a look and let me know what you think," he said, gesturing for my father to join him at the table.

I am sure whatever your Grace has been planning over these past months will no doubt lead to great success," he said as he stood next to him, leaning over to take a look.

Whilst the other two men stood pouring over the maps, Bishop Odo chose instead to take a seat at the head of the table watching them discuss the details and drinking his ale in silence.

The Duke reached for the largest vellum with map markings and moved it in front of my father. Within a few moments he had explained how the armies were being organized and the paths to Constantinople each would take. My father asked few questions and had agreed throughout with the plans.

"With good weather, you should reach the Emperor by All Saints, yes?" he asked.

"If God wills it, yes," responded Bishop Odo, breaking his silence.

My father looked at him.

"So, how may I be of assistance?" he asked, glancing between the two men, settling on the Duke. "The last we spoke, you had requested that I stay to assist your younger brother Henry with managing the duchy, has that changed?"

"You may not be aware Ascelin," the Bishop began, taking my father's focus away from the Duke, "I have decided to accompany the Duke on this journey to the Holy Land. I believe our troops will be as much in need of spiritual nourishment as their daily food and drink to sustain them on what will undoubtedly be a long and arduous journey."

This surprised my father. Bishop Odo was renowned as one of the most powerful churchmen in France and quite possibly in the Christian world, yet he was not a young man and his age might become a liability should the journey prove to be too gruelling. But he was in no position to debate this, it was clear the Bishop was resolved.

"Your guidance will be a shining light for the men, especially as they are all aware that you yourself have taken part in great battles of the past," my father said encouragingly.

"The Duke has no wish to discharge you of your responsibilities Ascelin," Bishop Odo continued, "your experience and wise counsel are vital to maintaining the peace in the duchy, especially as young Henry will be doing the bidding of William Rufus whilst the Duke is away and the duchy will be at risk. So, no, we are not asking you to join us."

My father looked at the Duke who had taken a seat at the table whilst the Bishop was speaking. He nodded, confirming he had understood what the Bishop had said, but did not speak. Whilst disappointed that he had not been asked to join them on crusade, my father knew my mother would be gladdened to hear he was going to be staying in Normandy.

"No," Bishop Odo continued, motioning for my father to take a seat at the table with them, "it is not you we wish to take, you are needed far more here. But the armies are formed and are either already at Saint-Denis or on their way there as we speak. And as you are well aware, our knights and fighting men also need the help of others, squires, to help with their maille and weapons, labourers to help with the camps and so on."

My father nodded again and the Bishop continued.

"It is vital that we have as many as we can to support our warriors in this time of need. And I too am in need of assistance in holding services and masses as we make our progress."

My father turned white as the penny dropped and he realized to whom it was that the Bishop was referring.

"You… you wish Sébastien to… to go with you?" he stuttered, rather incredulous. "But he is just a boy!" he added, his mind swirling, forgetting I was in the room.

"He is young, yes," Bishop Odo countered, "but he is strong and has the skills, or at least robust foundations of them, he needs to continue his training. He needs to develop those skills and his knowledge out in the world, not cloistered away in a religious school."

"I agree, your Excellency, the boy needs to gain his experience in the field, but he is not yet eleven years of age!" my father tried to reason with him.

"I was but thirteen when my father returned to England after the great invasion and left me in charge of the entire duchy," the Duke interjected quietly. "Odo was but fourteen when my father made him Bishop of Bayeux," he said, cocking his head in the direction of the Bishop. "We all have had burdens placed upon us in our youth."

Silence descended on the room. The Duke waited a moment to let my father digest what was being not really asked of him, but demanded of him.

"Have you discussed this with the boy?" my father asked softly.

"I have," Bishop Odo responded. "He is willing and eager to take this journey with us."

"Of course he is, he knows nothing of the reality of battle," my father said, a note of exasperation beginning to creep into his voice. "He is a naïve innocent, he will be damaged by this."

"I think you underestimate your son's level of maturity, Ascelin," Bishop Odo responded. "He has grown much over the past two years, and there is already evidence showing that he maturing into a strong young man. And it has become obvious that the D'Ivry spirit is deep within him, the same spirit that has seen some of your elders rewarded with special positions serving the crown. This will give him the opportunity to meet men at the highest levels in France and England and other Christian states. If managed properly, he will become a fine statesman, welcomed into those echelons of society, possibly even serving a King, be that Philippe or William or another."

"Only if he lives through it," my father muttered.

"We will do our best to see that he stays out of the actual fighting," the Duke said, aware of my father's concern for the life of his eldest son.

My father knew there was no option but to give his permission for me to go with them. They would take me anyway, the request was a formality and offered only because of the respect the Duke held my family. My father would lose face with the Duke if he continued to argue and he needed to maintain his trust and confidence in keeping a watch on the Duke's wilful younger brother whilst the Duke was away on crusade. But he also knew my mother would be devastated by this news.

"It is now almost the end of the month, when are you intending on leaving for Paris?" he asked, resigned to my fate.

"The Duke and I depart in a few days. The supplies are almost packed and the horses that we are bringing have been collected from a number of the Duke's vassals. Do we have your permission to take Sébastien with us?" he asked, knowing my father's answer.

The thought of the possibility of his dear Isabelle not seeing her son again probably filled him with dread. The Duke knew what was troubling him.

"Sébastien will no doubt need some of his belongings from the Chateaux in Ivry?" he asked, knowing full well I had everything I needed right here with me in Bayeux. "I suggest that you take him back with you tomorrow so that he may collect what he needs. Ensuring of course that he is ready within four days' time. We will be changing to river barges on the Seine at Mantes-la-Ville and he can join us there."

It was more of an order than a suggestion, but my father was grateful for it nevertheless.

"Thank you, your Grace," he said to the Duke. He was very familiar with the embarkation point at Mantes, he had spent a great deal of time there as King William's Lieutenant when he returned to Normandy after the invasion of England. "I am sure his mother will appreciate being able to see her son before he leaves for Paris," he added.

"Good, it is settled then," the Duke declared. "We shall talk more after vespers," he said, adding, "I have much to tell you about my brother's latest scheming."

\* \* \* \* \* \* \* \* \*

As my father had predicted, my mother had not been pleased to discover her eldest son was being requested by the Bishop to go on crusade. She had made a tearful argument to my father but to no avail. Once accepting the fact that I not only had no choice but, in fact, wanted to go, she gradually acquiesced.

With not much time before having to leave for Mantes-la-Ville to join the Duke and the Bishop, my mother doted on me and controlled almost every aspect of the preparation. She arranged everything I would need to take with me, various tunics, belts, leggings, shoes, and a black hooded cloak all tucked into a small travelling chest. At supper on the night before my departure, she handed me a silver chain with a medal of the Archangel Saint Michael.

"For strength and protection in battle and healing in the aftermath," she had said to me.

As a final loving touch, she had sewn the deep red cloth cross onto the breast of my cloak so that it hung close to my heart.

My father, in the meantime, had been preparing horses for me to take. He chose Pax, his best destrier, a young yet strong piebald not just over two years old. Like his master-to-be, Pax was tall for his age, measuring almost fourteen hands and more growing to come. An even-tempered yet quick animal, he had been my favourite foal before leaving for Bayeux and I had spent a much time with him before my departure and each time I had visited. After seeing my mother and younger brothers upon my return from Bayeux, I had gone to the fenced enclosure by the stable yard to see the horse. Pax recognized me instantly, trotting up to the gate and nuzzling my head. He would be a good companion, I thought.

A saddle had been specifically crafted for the horse with a well-stitched black leather seat and pommel supported by the underlying saddle tree moulded to fit Pax perfectly. Stirrups attached by strong leather straps hung from both sides and a saddle cloth of the D'Ivry heraldic colours, the red chevrons on a gold background, rested between the saddle and the horse, draping down its flanks. Two saddle bags, containing water flasks, an extra pair of gloves and a few sharp knives, sat on either side of the saddle and a tightly rolled blanket was tied to the back of it. Inside the blanket was a sharp short sword encased in a dark leather scabbard that could hook onto any belt.

My father believed the Duke when he said he would do his best to keep me out of the battle, but he wanted me armed anyway. I had shown my father that I was becoming skilled with a blade when we had sparred in the yard during the couple of days of my visit home, and being trained by some of the best knights in France would hopefully make me an expert swordsman over the coming months. The last item to be added was a shield with the D'Ivry emblem painted on the front. This was hooked onto Pax's tack so that it sat over his rear flank.

My father had selected another four horses, two palfreys, another destrier and one packhorse, to be taken to Mantes-la-Ville to join the Duke's team. The packhorse carried my travel chest and other goods including extra clothes and a small set of tools that I would need on the journey.

At noon on the third day when all was ready, I bid my loving mother farewell and, escorted by my father and two of his men, set off for the first leg of the journey to Saint-Denis, reaching Mantes-la-Ville in a few hours, just before vespers. There, the two of us would spend the night before my departure and over dinner my father took the opportunity to advise me on the ways of war.

> "Sébastien," he started, "I need to ask one last time, are you certain you wish to accompany Bishop Odo and Duke Robert on this crusade? War, and it will be a war of many battles, is not for the faint-hearted and you are still of such a young age that I worry this is too much too soon for you."

I thought on it a moment.

> "It is what I wish to do father," I said, my voice unwavering. "It is such an honour to be chosen by the Bishop to attend on him and, if by some chance or other fortune, the opportunity arises for me to serve the Duke as well, then I will have done what I can to champion this worthy cause."

I could not tell from his expression whether he was annoyed or proud of me. But he needed to know I would not be swayed by this. He pushed his pewter plate away from him, not wishing to finish the meal.

> "Then I must make you aware of what you will face, what you will see. The journey will be both glorious and arduous, sometimes both at the same time. You will see nature's unparalleled majesty of the mountains and the seas, you will be celebrated and loved by the people along the

way who will wish you Godspeed. You will eat foods the like of which you have never tasted and drink wines from the regions that produce the best grape. You will begin to feel invincible, that nothing evil will dare challenge you and the thousands who walk with you."

He took some more wine before continuing.

"But all that will change the closer the armies move towards Anatolia and especially into Palestine. Anatolia is a firepit of conflict, the Seljuk Turks trying to wrestle control from the Byzantine Christians. And in Palestine you will meet Muslim armies whose strength and power match our own. There will be those who will pretend to be your friend who are not. There will be times when you will not know whom to trust – in those instances, trust your instincts, that feeling in your stomach," he said, pointing at mine, "that will tell you right from wrong. Are you understanding me Sébastien?"

I thought I did, so I simply nodded, not saying anything.

"Good. You will be introduced to many new customs, different from our own, but learn from them rather than shy away from them. The best way to defeat your enemy is to know them, take every opportunity to do so. You will want to accept everything at face value – do not, instead keep aware and question, as many and much will not be what they seem."

The barkeep interrupted shouting if we needed more wine, my father waved his hand to say no.

"Sébastien, you must be prepared to see some truly horrible things. You must remember that men are capable of despicable acts when emotion is not in check. Desperate men will do unconscionable things and you will witness some atrocities which may try to change you from the honourable young man that you are – always try to resist this, know thyself, trust thyself, and you will see it through. You will grow on this journey, but make it for good. There will be so many who will try to change you for the worse. Become the man we all know you are capable of becoming. Will you promise me you will do everything in your power to do this?"

"Of course father," I said earnestly, even though I was not sure what he meant by some of his words. I only knew I wanted to make him proud.

He leaned back in his chair and sighed. He could say no more.

\* \* \* \* \* \* \* \* \*

The next morning we were informed that the Duke and Bishop Odo had arrived late the prior evening, having ridden the entire day after resting in Évreux the previous night. It was fitting for the Duke to have chosen Évreux to stop for the night, it had been the site of a battle almost two hundred years earlier between the Franks and Rollo Ragnvaldsson, the great Viking warrior who had become the first Duke of Normandy. So it was an honourable and appropriate place for Duke Robert, the Bishop and their men to rest before embarking on a crusade, and a special night service at Notre-Dame d' Évreux cathedral was held honouring their forebears and celebrating the mission they were about to undertake.

But there was no time to waste, the Duke and Bishop had set off on their way again before dawn, soon reaching Mantes-la-Ville late in the evening. After a short sleep and light breakfast, they were now gathered at the banks of the river Seine watching as empty river barges slowly made their way towards the wooden pier. It was a hive of activity of men preparing to load supplies and horses brought by Bishop Odo. William Tancarville, Duke Robert's chamberlain and retainer, was in charge of the operation and clearly had things under control as loading the horses soon was underway, executed with military precision. The horses brought by Bishop Odo would augment those brought by my father, including my own Pax, and would be the first of the horses to be loaded. Next were Bishop Odo's supplies, travel chests and the trunks carrying his vital liturgical accoutrement, including the mitre in its special case, all to be stored on the royal barge.

My father and I had ridden to where the group of men were standing at the river's edge watching the proceedings and dismounted. After formally greeting both the Duke and the Bishop, I joined my father's men and the boatmen, helping them load the D'Ivry horses, whilst my father stayed with the Duke. My chest was added to the rather large pile that was the Bishop's baggage. I would be travelling on the royal barge with the Duke, Bishop Odo and their immediate entourage. I led Pax onto the barge himself, stroked his neck a few times, whispering some calming words, then returned to help with the rest of the loading. I was watched by my father and the Bishop, the Duke was deep in conversation with his chamberlain.

"You should be proud of your eldest, Ascelin," I could hear Bishop Odo say to him. "I have no doubt he will outshine us all."

My father simply nodded. No doubt his heart was filled both with joy and dread at the thought of his son going on crusade. He looked at the Bishop without speaking.

"God will protect him," the Bishop said, recognizing the worried expression on my father's face.

Within the hour, the loading was complete; twelve barges in total with horses, carts, chests and other supplies were ready to travel down the Seine to Saint-Denis. The royal barge was second from the front of the group, clearly identifiable by the Normandy coat of arms, two golden lions passant on a vivid red background, flying from the staff at the bow. All were on board except the Duke. He stood at the end of the pier with my father.

"Take care of the duchy, Lupus," he said, glancing around at the barges in front of him.

"I shall do my best, Curthose" my father responded. And then added quietly, "Please take care of my son."

The Duke gave him a serious glance and nodded. Without another word, he climbed into the barge and gave the signal for them all to push off. My father himself worked the pole for the royal barge and then stood back to watch the departure. His goodbye to me had really been said the evening before; today, in front of the Duke and the Bishop, I had taken a more formal stance, which made my father smile inwardly. But we did manage to catch each other's eyes as the barge moved forward and for a moment, I felt a lump in my throat. I hoped, prayed, this would not be the last time I saw my father.

# II

## Part Two

## 1096 – Paris, France

The barge pulled farther and farther away from the pier and my father slowly disappeared from view. Even though I had been nervous when I first left for Bayeux, this was different. Nervous, yes, but also tinged with excitement, trepidation and joy that I had been selected to attend the Bishop on this mission. I was determined not to let him down.

The trip to Saint-Denis took less than two days despite the fact that we were travelling upstream. It had been easygoing, the sun had shone brightly both days and the breeze at our backs helped speed us along. I had enjoyed being on the barge, helping out with whatever needed to be done. I loved watching the countryside as we passed through and was taken aback by the small crowds who came to the riverbank to watch us go by. The masses knew we were headed for the Holy Land and we were always greeted cheers and shouts of praise and encouragement; I could not help but smile and wave to them.

The Duke had sent a messenger ahead on horseback several days earlier to alert Aumale and Blois that our arrival was imminent. He had hoped to shorten the trip if we did not stop to rest and if the Duke's men took turns at the oars. I offered to take a turn which earned me a considerable amount of respect.

Likewise, Bishop Odo had sent word of our forthcoming arrival to Guillaume de Montfort, his counterpart in Paris. At twenty-three, he was much older than Odo had been when he had become Bishop of Bayeux but still considered a young man for such an exalted position. There was to be a mass celebrating the commencement of the crusade at the Paris church of Sainte-Étienne, and Bishop Odo wanted to give Bishop Guillaume as much time to prepare.

Making our way along the river, taking the Seine's slow, gentle curve to the south, we approached Saint-Denis, recently constructed piers jutting out into the river coming into view. As expected, word had reached Blois the day before and he had organized a welcome party to meet the Duke, sending his personal retainer, Rollant, and some of his guards to greet them and help us disembark. They could be seen gathering the ropes and poles that would be used to help bring in the barges. The Duke's royal barge was the first to reach the river's edge and the men worked feverishly to pull it to the wooden dock. Even before it was secured, the Duke had leapt off making his way to the shore where Rollant and fresh horses awaited him.

"Your Grace," Rollant bowed low as he greeted the Duke. "The Count bids you a warm welcome and wishes he could have been here to greet you himself, but he has been kept occupied with some matters concerning our supplies," he explained.

"Uh-huh," the Duke replied sceptically as he took the reins of the horse brought for him, placed his foot in the stirrup and quickly straddled him. "And Aumale?" he asked after his cousin.

"Count Aumale was called to Reims to collect a contingent of knights wishing to join your Grace's army," Rollant responded as Robert settled in the saddle. "He anticipates returning to Saint-Denis within a few days, but, unfortunately, most likely not in time to accompany you to Paris."

Bishop Odo and I had disembarked after the Duke and mounted other horses prepared for us, not waiting for our own to be offloaded. Rollant waited until all were saddled then mounted his own and then, joined by an additional three guards on horseback, our group made our way at a fair pace on the well-worn road that lead to the town of Saint-Denis, about half an hour's ride from the river. The Duke was familiar with the route having been in Saint-Denis many times, most recently only a couple of weeks earlier to ensure his army was well ensconced in a camp on the east side of the town and a short walk from Abbey. He rode in silence with Rollant at his side. Occasionally, they slowed the horses because of the unevenness of the path. Bishop Odo and I struck up a conversation when the horses walked.

"I am assuming you have not visited Saint-Denis, Sébastien?" Bishop Odo asked.

"No, your Excellency," I answered.

"Then you should count yourself fortunate to have the opportunity. Not many are able to come to the shrine of the martyr. A fitting place from which to launch our crusade, from the very shrine that holds the bones of some of our greatest kings. Clovis, Dagobert, and Charles Martel the first of our great Carolingians and the grandfather of the magnificent Charlemagne, all are here."

"Is the story about the martyr true?" I asked.

Bishop Odo hesitated.

"Was it true that Saint-Denis was a Christian missionary in times of Roman rule and was beheaded on Montmartre for his convictions? Yes. Did he then get up, walk for miles preaching a sermon whilst carrying his head until he came upon this glen where he laid down and died? Well," Bishop Odo smiled, "what do you think?"

I thought a moment.

"I am not one to contradict the miraculous deeds of a deified saint," I replied. "But I think it does not matter if this actually happened. I think it is the lesson to be learned from the story that matters."

Bishop Odo seemed impressed with my response. He told me much later, after many more late-night philosophical discussions, that he had not met a boy of my age who had such depth to thinking and appeared so confident in expressing theoretical views. Most boys of my age, and many a lot older, simply followed blindly what they were told and did as they were instructed. But I had always questioned what I was told, always tried to see beyond mere words, having already done what my father bid me to do. It surprised me to hear that most others did not.

"And what do you think the lesson to be learned here is?" Bishop Odo asked, interested in hearing my views.

But our conversation was cut short by a shout from a red-headed, pale-skinned, rather stout man on horseback coming towards us, followed by two guards also on horseback.

"Brother!" the man shouted again as he got closer.

Bishop Odo leaned over.

"That is Stephen, the Count of Blois and Chartres," he whispered. "He is the Duke's brother-in-law, married to his sister Adela."

I was grateful for the information. The horses were pulled to a stop as the man who was shouting reached us and slowed his horse to a walk up to the Duke's. Rollant backed up his mare to leave space for Blois to come alongside. Blois's guards fell in behind those already in the group.

"Brother," Blois said, slightly out of breath, as he extended his arm towards the Duke.

The Duke extended his and the two grasped each other's forearms in the familiar greeting.

"Blois," Robert responded without a shred of enthusiasm.

Despite the fact that they were brothers-in-law, Robert refused to use the familial connection or even his Christian name when greeting him, choosing instead to keep his distance. He did not have much time for the man, Stephen of Blois was an administrator, not a warrior, and he had serious doubts about his commitment to this crusade.

"Please forgive my lateness, I am saddened not to have been at the pier to greet you," Blois said earnestly.

Robert said nothing.

"How was the Seine? Was she calm for you?" Blois continued as they got the horses moving again.

The Duke did not want small talk.

"How are the men? Have we had any more recruits? Rollant tells me Aumale is on his way to Reims," he demanded bluntly, ignoring the question.

"The men are settled, we are now over seven thousand and have received word that Flanders will be here within a few days with his. I have arranged chambers for yourself and Bishop Odo in the Abbey," Blois said, having assumed they would prefer to stay in the centuries-old royal basilica that had been consecrated in the presence of the great

Charlemagne. "And of course, the royal tents are still in place," he added, finally getting his breathing under control.

"Good," said Robert, thinking his rather inept brother-in-law might have his uses after all.

"Once we have paid our respects in the church, we shall to the camp. And as soon as Flanders has arrived, we will need to set for Paris, we have plans to meet de Vermandois in three days' time. I have given Tancarville instructions to have our horses ready to take us to the city," Robert added.

"Excellent," Blois said. "And what of Bouillon?" he asked of Godfrey, the last of the leaders of French armies going on crusade, the Lord of Bouillon and Duke of Lower Lorraine.

"Godfrey's army is waiting in Lorraine, he is on his way, meeting with us in Paris," Robert responded.

Blois nodded his understanding.

"Your sister sends her love," he said, changing the subject.

"She is well, I hope?" Robert asked.

"She is very well, thank you. I have made her regent of Blois and Chartres in my absence and, of course, is very busy with the children," he answered.

"Ah yes, you have five sons now and, what is it, five daughters?" Robert enquired of his brother-in-law's brood.

"Yes indeed. My youngest, Henry, is barely a few months old, but he is strong and healthy as are two of his older brothers, Theobald and my namesake Stephen," Blois said proudly.

This was good news indeed as not all of Blois's sons were strong and healthy. His eldest, William, seemed to have some learning difficulties and could not be his designated heir and his third son, Odo, was a sickly child and in danger of not living to adulthood. It was a relief that Blois and Adela had two strong sons, now possibly three, as heirs. Duke Robert must have thought a moment on his own childlessness, something he would need to deal with in the not-so-distant future if he were to secure the duchy.

Our group continued in silence for the rest of the journey to Saint-Denis. There was no turning back, the plans the Duke and Flanders had put into place were starting to come together and each of the riders became more acutely aware of the gravity of the mission they were about to embark upon.

* * * * * * * * *

For the first time in weeks, the skies darkened with the threat of rain. The Duke and Flanders led a small group as they rode the two hours it would take to traverse the relatively short distance from Saint-Denis to the right bank of the Seine, where a large wooden bridge, Grand Pont, would provide access to the Ile de Cité, the heart of Paris. From there it was only moments to the Palais de la Cité, the official residence of Frankish Kings since Merovingian times, where we were due to meet Hugh Vermandois, the younger brother of King Philippe, and Godfrey de Bouillon, to coordinate the departure and movements of the various armies going to Palestine.

Unfortunately, as with his view of Blois, Duke Robert did not esteem Vermandois much. He sarcastically referred to him by his nickname "Magnus" meaning "the Great" which could not have been further from the truth as most knew. Despite the fact he was of royal blood, he had a reputation for being weak, his position as Count of Vermandois gained simply because, as he was the younger brother of King Philippe, he was able to marry Adelaide, the rich heiress of Vermandois. His arrogance was unparalleled in the Frankish kingdom and he was routinely admonished by the King for his lack of diplomatic skills. His insistence on leading an army on crusade had been met with some wariness and doubt of his capabilities and competence, especially as he had announced that his reason for joining was that he had been influenced after seeing an eclipse of the moon earlier in the year. But his brother the King was duty-bound to give his support and was ever hopeful that perhaps this would be the making of him.

Even before crossing the Grand Pont, the old walls of the Palais de la Cité could be seen looming on the island. The Palais inside the walls was a substantial building, originally a Gallo-Roman fortress that was rebuilt throughout the succeeding centuries first by the Merovingians, then by the Carolingians, as each monarch used it as the official royal residence. King Philippe's grandfather, Robert the Pious, had taken particular care in adding to its size and splendour to make it truly a palace fit for a king and his queen.

As Paris began to grow and expand and the town grew into a city of renown, it became the French royal family's main power base and needed to be protected and fortified. Robert the Pious had reinforced the walls and built the massive garrisoned gates facing north towards the Grand Pont bridge. Within the Palais itself was the Salle de Roi, the main hall for the King to hold council with his most important nobles, meet with visiting royalty, and carry out other royal functions. It was here that Duke Robert had agreed to meet with Vermandois, and eventually Bouillon when he arrived.

The group accompanying the Duke, the Count of Flanders and the Count of Blois included their three retainers, Bishop Odo, myself and several armed guards from each of the three armies now all camped outside Saint-Denis. Bishop Odo was without a sword but, although I was not wearing one, I still had my short sword packed away in the rolled blanket at the back of my saddle. There was no real concern of any threat, it was a show of strength and power that the three royals wanted to impress upon any who saw them. And dressed in their finest court attire, flowing robes of silver and gold, the horses clad in the colours of their respective royal houses, flags with the various coats of arms on staffs being carried by the retainers, we were an extraordinarily striking and moving sight to behold. No doubt this had been reported to King Philippe by the sentries stationed at the gatehouses atop the two stone round towers at the north entrance, from whose vantage point they could see anyone who approached the Grand Pont at quite a distance.

Once across the bridge, the riders continued along the well-worn capstone paths that lead to the Palais. In the distance to the east, we could see the Basilica of Saint-Étienne, with its baptistery dedicated to John the Baptist on its northern front. With Paris growing at such a fast pace, it soon would be inadequate to meet the needs of the populace. But for now, with a design based on the basilica at Saint-Denis but much larger, its huge nave and four additional aisles separated by colossal pillars, it had become the model for churches all over the kingdom. We would attend services there later in the day and hold a special mass to celebrate the start of their journey to Palestine. But first, we had business to attend to.

I was astonished by the sight of the massive walls surrounding the palace as I approached Grand Pont with the others. I had never seen the like. And my amazement continued as, crossing the bridge, I spied the basilica in the distance to the east. I turned in my saddle and smiled at Bishop Odo who was momentarily in the basilica's thrall. Despite the considerable amount of refurbishment he had done to his own cathedral in Bayeux, the Bishop could not tear his eyes away from its glorious façade until forced to when the group turned towards the main gates between two large circular guard towers in the walls surrounding the Palais.

Having been given the orders to do so, the sentries had pulled the gates open, giving us a wide berth for our entry into the courtyard, making sure to close them behind us. We dismounted, handed the reins to various stable boys who had come out to meet us and walked quickly to the main entrance, up a triangular set of stone stairs to our right. Once through the doors, we turned right and continued down the hall into the Salle de Roi, which was empty save for the King's guards at each of the entrances to the room.

I was stunned by the majesty of the room as my eyes tried to take it all in. High vaulted ceilings, held in place by towering marble columns, had been painted with a myriad of gold stars, crescent moons and fleur-de-lys on a background of dark, royal blue, the ribs painted gold. The walls were covered with luxurious silk appliqués embroidered in vibrant colours depicting biblical and battle scenes, broken only by a number of tall arched windows along the west and east sides of the room. Two thrones, one slightly larger than the other, covered in blue velvet trimmed in gold, sat against the far wall and seemed dwarfed by fireplaces sitting in between the windows. Guards were placed at the arched doorways leading to other sections of the Palais including the King and Queen's private quarters.

Duke Robert, Flanders, Blois and Bishop Odo moved into the centre of the hall whilst the retainers and I hovered near the doorway we had just entered. The Duke moved to one of the arched windows next to one of the fireplaces and looking out from his vantage point, he could see the courtyard our group had just come through and, straight ahead, the royal chapel of Saint Nicholas. His eyes followed the neatly carved arcading along the outside of the church he could easily see from his vantage point. He was probably wondering why Vermandois was not there to greet them.

Suddenly there was a flurry of activity from the passageway that led to the private royal apartments and without warning, King Philippe of France appeared in the arched doorway with several guards and pages following him closely. A very handsome man with dark hair and well-trimmed beard and moustache just barely showing signs of grey, Philippe's appeal to the ladies was understandable and his amorous escapades renowned, such as those that ended in his ex-communication. But he was a well-liked and respected King, having spent much of his reign dealing with troublesome vassals and settling disputes, bringing a period of peace to his realm. One such troublesome vassal had been Duke Robert and Philippe had, many years ago, taken sides against him during his harassment of the Vexin. But that was long ago and now Robert was Duke of Normandy and had sworn fealty to Philippe, putting aside their differences and being comrade-in-arms for several years. Philippe was pleased to welcome him.

Seeing Duke Robert at the windows at the far side of the hall, he started towards him, then stopped when he saw the others in the room. In unison, and from where we were standing, we all bowed, keeping our positions until the King spoke.

"Robert!" King Philippe exclaimed moving towards him again and touching him gently on the shoulders.

Duke Robert straightened and the two men embraced.

"Your majesty," Robert responded solemnly.

"It is good to see you," King Philippe said, clapping him on the back. "Especially under the circumstances in which we find ourselves, hmm?" he added seriously.

The others came closer but still kept a discreet distance; I stayed where I was.

"Indeed, sire. It is now several months since Clermont and we are anxious to be on our way. My army, along with those of Count Robert and Count Stephen," he said, pointing to Flanders and Blois as he named them, "are ready, and waiting for us in Saint-Denis."

The King turned to look at them, both of whom bowed once again.

"It is good to have you both here. Our Christian forces need as many men as we can muster for this battle," he said to them seriously.

They nodded their heads and said nothing. A low growl of thunder rumbled and a humid breeze blew in through the windows. The skies had become quite dark very quickly, the storm that had threatened on their way from Saint-Denis was upon them. The King motioned to his pages to close the outside shutters whilst others scrambled to light the wall candles around the room. It was then that the King took notice of Bishop Odo who, upon making eye contact with the King, stepped forward.

"Your Excellency," King Philippe greeted the Bishop.

"Your Majesty," Bishop Odo responded, giving a slight nod.

"It gladdens my heart to know that you too are making this journey. It could not have been asked of you. I know that with your spiritual guidance and your knowledge of battle tactics, our success is now assured," King Philippe said sincerely, a sereneness to his voice.

Bishop Odo smiled and bowed his head slightly in thanks for the compliment.

"It is my honour, Majesty," he responded.

The King turned back to Robert.

"I believe you are here to meet my brother, Hugh, yes?"

"Yes, sire. We had agreed when we met last in Rouen, to meet here this week. Godfrey de Bouillon will be joining us here, we expect him tomorrow eve," he added.

We had sensed not all was well here when we had not been met by Vermandois upon our arrival and he still had not appeared. Now we were certain something was wrong.

"Hmmm," the King murmured.

"Your Majesty?" Robert prodded.

"I am afraid I have some, erm, disturbing news, Robert," the King began.

He held out his hand to his chamberlain who brought him a piece of parchment, bowed and backed away.

"Upon returning to Paris late yesterday eve from holding council these past few days in Orléans, I was informed that my brother had already departed for Palestine, taking five thousand men with him. Many sons of many nobles have joined him. His servants have informed that he is on his way to meet with the Holy Father and receive a blessing before travelling to Bari. He is then intending to cross the Adriatic."

Robert was dumbstruck, as were we all. This was outrageous. Not only was his decision to depart earlier than agreed and not wait to travel with the others precipitous and rash, it was also hugely insulting to Duke Robert, Flanders, Blois and Bouillon. Vermandois's narcissistic pride had resulted in leading an army of sons of the highest nobility in France, many of whom had not seen significant battle, into what unquestionably would be some of the most brutal and fierce ever fought. Like Peter the Hermit and his peasants' crusade, this was surely doomed to fail.

The King continued.

"I am afraid that is not all," King Philippe said resignedly. "I have here a copy of a message sent from him to Emperor Alexios in Constantinople, giving him advance notice of his arrival," he said, handing the parchment to Robert and giving him a warning look.

Robert had to read it twice, the second time out loud, to convince himself he was reading it correctly:

> *Be advised, O Emperor, that I am the King of kings, highest-ranking of all beneath the sky. My will is that you shall attend me upon my arrival and give me the magnificent welcome that is fitting for a visitor of the noblest birth.*

The Duke was beyond words. The self-important arrogance was shocking. No King would ever have dared to write such a communique to a foreign ruler. Whilst it was true that Emperor Alexios had reached out to the Holy Father to ask for aid in seeing off the Turks, he was a trusted ally and would play a vital role in this crusade, being in a position to provide fresh supplies during the battle and a safe haven once the crusaders had successfully quashed the threat. There was no doubt this missive would be ill-received and Vermandois could quite possibly have jeopardized the entire undertaking by endangering his men and alienating their main ally in the region.

Duke Robert handed the note to Flanders so he could see the words for himself. Bishop Odo was the last to read it; he looked for permission from the King to keep it, folded the parchment and handed it to me; I packed it away in my satchel. We all looked at each other in speechless astonishment.

"I am told this was sent a fortnight ago, which means the messenger is too far gone to recall," King Philippe said. "My brother has acted foolishly, stupidly. I have sent word to Alexios asking for forgiveness for his dreadful behaviour. I am hopeful it will reach him quickly but that will not be until after he has received this," he said looking ruefully at Robert.

Duke Robert felt rage start to rise up within him, and we could all see him do his best to conceal this from the King but was finding it difficult to do so. Preparations had been underway for months and for Vermandois to head off on his own was unconscionable and precarious, as others who had gone ahead had discovered. Bishop Odo noticed the colour rising in the Duke's face and stepped forward, trying to divert his attention.

"Sire," Bishop Odo began, speaking to the Duke, trying to maintain some calm in the room, "it is no doubt the Count de Vermandois's fervent desire to fight the infidel that has spurred his rash decision. I would suggest that with the arrival of Bouillon tomorrow, we be on our way, the Lord and the weather," he said as a crack of thunder reverberated throughout the room, "permitting."

The Duke, his jaw muscles clenching, barely controlling his anger, turned to the Bishop.

"There is no point in Bouillon coming to Paris," he growled. "As soon as the storm eases, I will send a couple of men to intercept him and bring him to Saint-Denis to wait upon us there. We will depart after the service in the morning," he declared decisively.

"By your leave, of course, your Majesty," he added hurriedly to the King.

Everyone knew there was no point in arguing. It was a logical decision, Bouillon could rest a day after his journey from Lorraine.

"Very well," King Philippe agreed.

There was very little else that could be done.

* * * * * * * * * *

We were soaked to the bone by the time we had made our way back to Saint-Denis. Storms arose once again the next day in the middle of the celebratory service led by Bishop Odo and Bishop Guillaume at the basilica, casting an ominous atmosphere over the occasion. The Duke was still in a foul mood from the previous day which did not help matters. We left Paris with the King's blessing but frustrated by his brother's imprudent actions. No doubt Bouillon would be concerned about why he had been asked not to attend the meeting in Paris as Robert had sent no explanation along with the messenger instructing him to go instead to Saint-Denis.

We reached the Duke's massive red and gold tent that had been erected next to the camps, dismounted and hurried inside to get out of the downpour. Bouillon had been alerted to our arrival and, along with his younger brother Baldwin de Boulogne and two of their most trusted knights, brothers Hugh de Fauquembergues and Godfrey de Saint-Omer, entered the tent a few minutes later to find Robert, Flanders, Blois, and Bishop Odo deep in conversation around an oval oak table. I stayed by the entrance to the tent, almost out of sight but attentive and ready to do whatever bidding was required.

"...this blasted rain," Bouillon caught the end of Robert's exclamation through the linen towel he was using to dry his face.

Draping it over his head, Robert looked up and saw Bouillon had arrived with Baldwin. The tall, strong-limbed, burly-chested Duke of Lorraine and his brother could have been twins so much alike were they in size and stature, both with shoulder-length light blond hair and matching beards.

"Bouillon, it gladdens me to see you, even on such a dismal day as this," he said, greeting his old friend.

"Your Grace," Bouillon responded. "I have been eagerly awaiting your return, what news do you bring from Paris?" Then adding as he looked around the room, "Where is Vermandois?"

"Gone," Robert responded sharply.

Bouillon looked confused.

"Gone?" he repeated.

"Yes, gone. He departed Paris with his army of noble sons days before we arrived, without telling anyone. Not even his brother the King!"

Duke Robert's ire evidently had not subsided. He continued as Bouillon glanced at the others who confirmed he was speaking the truth.

"He also foolishly sent word to Emperor Alexios about his impending arrival, in his typically pompous manner. D'Ivry," he said, motioning to me to produce the copy of the letter.

I quickly retrieved the parchment from my satchel and handed it to the Duke who passed it to Bouillon. He gave him a moment to read it through. Bouillon raised his free hand to his forehead and started rubbing it as he took in what Vermandois had done. He handed the letter to his brother Baldwin who handed it to me when he was done reading it.

"He has made his bed, he will have to lie in it," Bouillon said to Robert, realizing there was nothing they could do.

"The King has sent word to Alexios to try to atone for his brother's arrogance," Robert said. "In the meantime, we must ready our troops for departure."

The six men took seats at the table whilst Bouillon's two knights and I continued to stand. Bouillon spoke first, unrolling his vellum maps to show his intended path.

"My army will be ready to leave from Lorraine at the end of the month. We will travel first to Ratisbona, then to Vienna, then through the twin towns of Buda and Pest, crossing the Danube at Belgrade and then to Constantinople. I am hoping to be with the Emperor sometime in late December if all goes well."

"Excellent," said Robert, settling into the discussion and seemingly having forgotten about Vermandois's folly. "Flanders, Blois and I will depart for Lyon on the 15th barring any unforeseen problems. I shall send word to Toulouse when we are on our way so that he and his army can join with us there."

Duke Robert continued, explaining the routes he and Toulouse intended to take to reach Constantinople. The men sat in silence for a moment, digesting the information. Their thoughts were occasionally interrupted by the sound of the rain, now quite heavy, hammering the canopy of the tent.

"This wretched rain has come upon us rather suddenly," Blois complained, almost repeating Robert's earlier words verbatim.

"Hopefully it will let up long enough for us to take to the roads," Flanders responded.

"And if it does not?" Blois asked.

"We will need to delay," said Robert sharply. "I am not having our armies exhausted from being mired in mud even before they have crossed out of France!"

"I am sure the rain will be brief and the roads will hold," Flanders interjected before Blois could respond. "But I am in agreement with Duke Robert if it does not."

Bouillon stirred from being deep in thought. He had found Vermandois's actions disturbing, the last thing they needed was a renegade. And one so disproportionately unskilled in warfare and battle tactics. Like Peter the Hermit and Walter Sans Avoir before him, Vermandois should have waited for the others.

"Baldwin and I should take our leave, we need to get back to Lorraine as soon as possible," Bouillon said suddenly, standing, his brother following suit.

The others stood to say their farewells.

"Deus vult, your Grace," Bouillon said to the Duke.

"Deus vult," Robert responded as they embraced.

Bouillon turned and caught the eye of Bishop Odo as he headed for the tent flap.

"Dominus vobiscum," Bishop Odo said to him.

"And with you," Bouillon responded.

He and Baldwin ducked out of the tent, Bouillon calling for their horses. Their two knights followed closely. Fauquembergues exited the tent first with his brother following closely behind. But just before he stepped out into the rain, Saint-Omer glanced over his shoulder at me, stared a moment and then slipped quietly out of the tent.

# II

## Part Three

## 1096–1097 - France

The rains in and around Paris had continued for well over a month and there was still no sign of it letting up. Those who had shields slept beneath them, trying to keep as much of the top halves of their bodies as dry as possible but even this was futile after a while. The anticipated departure date came and went. The armies were becoming restless and, with no indication from their leaders, the men were becoming frustrated and small scraps were starting to break out over petty quarrels.

With the skies beginning to lighten as the dawning sun, partially hidden behind heavy rain-filled clouds, started to break the horizon to the east, Duke Robert stood at the entrance to his tent, deep in thought, arms folded in front of him, his bearded chin almost down to his chest, giving him a fearsome countenance. Bishop Odo had sent me to request the King to call upon him in the church. I could tell he was deep in thought.

Something had to be done. But with the information just given to him by his scouts, the roads to Lyon from Saint-Denis were still impassable. He needed to be on the move somehow or he would lose momentum and the men's enthusiasm for the cause. They were already sniping at each other and soon they were at risk of losing some of them out of sheer boredom. He pulled the hood of his cloak over his head and set off at a fast pace to the basilica where he knew the Bishop would be preparing for prime, the early morning services. Despite my long legs, I could barely keep his pace.

Opening the main door of the church, Duke Robert entered, removed his hood, knelt and crossed himself; I followed suit. I had informed him that the Bishop was being dressed in the sacristy, off to the side of the altar. He walked up the centre aisle, shaking the raindrops off him as he went, and made his way to the door.

Without knocking, Duke Robert entered the small room and found Bishop Odo adjusting his vestment. I moved into the room and started pouring water from an ewer into a bowl.

"Good morning Curthose," Bishop Odo said, straightening his alb. "Thank you for coming before prime."

"Good morning Bishop Odo," Robert responded. "We need to speak about our delay."

Robert half-stood/half-leaned against a table up against the far wall and crossed his arms on his chest and legs at the ankles.

"This is not good for the men. They are bored and irritable and infighting is starting to break out amongst the various factions. We need them to remain focused, united in purpose. Sitting around the camps waiting for the rain to let up is not good for their morale."

"I agree," replied the Bishop. "What is the latest from the scouts?"

"Rain in every direction except northwest which is the only direction we have no need to go!" Robert answered exasperated. "We have heard that Bouillon has departed Ratisbonne and is on his way to Vienna. I am not sure how many German fighters were added to his vast numbers but he would have only accepted the best. I think he surely has the greatest number of men now. No doubt they are all in great spirits."

"We need to get the men moving," Bishop Odo agreed. "How are the roads west of Paris?" he asked.

"Passable, but not heading in the correct direction. What were you thinking?"

"We have two problems. First is to get the men moving. Second is to revitalise them, get them enthused again about this mission they are undertaking. How better to do that than to march them to Clermont? It would be a detour from our plan to go directly to Lyon but it would, I think, resolve our problems?" Bishop Odo suggested.

Robert gave this some thought. It was a good plan, he would need to discuss this with Blois and Flanders. In the end, they would agree to whatever he decided but it would be good to get their assent voluntarily. He would speak with them after prime.

\* \* \* \* \* \* \* \* \*

The Duke gathered the heads of the armies with their seconds-in-command in his tent within minutes of the early morning service. Robert's own second-in-command his cousin Aumale, Flanders and Payen de Montdidier, the captain of Flanders's army and also his cousin, and Blois and the captain of his army Archambaud de Saint-Agnan, joined the Duke at the table in Robert's tent. I stood my usual post, ready to do whatever was bid of me by either the Bishop or the Duke, hearing everything, saying nothing. The Duke laid out his proposal to move the armies first southwest to Orléans and then south to Clermont.

"Excellent!" Flanders declared avidly, "When do we depart?"

"I suspect it will take some time to pack up the camps. I suggest we go at the start of the coming week," Robert answered. "By my count, we should have eleven thousand men, including knights, squires, and those to work the camps. It will be a slow slog, the rains have not been nearly as bad as here, but we should not expect the roads to be in the best of shape. But with God's will, we should be there the first week of October."

"Hopefully by then we will know more about the whereabouts of Vermandois," Aumale added.

"Indeed. From there we shall make our way to Lyon where we will meet with Toulouse and finally leave France. We should be in Rome by Martinmas," Robert said.

He paused a moment.

"Is it decided then?" he asked, knowing what the answer would be.

Cries of agreement went up from the men.

"Good," he said, standing. "Let us get a move on then, we do not have time to waste. D'Ivry," he said turning to me, "tell Bishop Odo I need to speak with him."

I stepped forward, nodded, and left the tent, my pace turning into a quick run, my heavy leather boots making deep footprints in the mud, as I headed back to the basilica. I found the Bishop in prayer with a few of the priests in one of the transept chapels. But before going to him there, I retrieved his hooded cloak from the sacristy which I knew he would need to protect himself from the downpour outside.

Reaching the chapel, I stood beside one of the columns at the entrance not wishing to disturb the Bishop who was kneeling and facing the small altar and had not seen me arrive. I waited to see if Bishop Odo would rouse himself and just as I was about to clear my throat to make him aware of my presence, the Bishop crossed himself, kissed the pectoral cross hanging from his neck, stood and, without turning around, spoke.

"Yes Sébastien?" he asked.

I was startled for a moment, not sure how the Bishop knew I was there.

"Ah, yes, your Excellency. Duke Robert has requested you attend him in the royal tent as soon as possible," I responded earnestly.

"Has he reached agreement with the others then?"

"I believe he has, your Excellency. But it would be best to hear this from the Duke directly," I answered, not wanting to speak on behalf of Duke Robert.

I held out the cloak to the Bishop.

"Ah Sébastien, your political skills are coming along, I see," Bishop Odo said with a wry smile.

Turning to the others who had concluded their prayers but remained kneeling, he said solemnly, "Prepare" and then, taking the cloak out of my hands, left the chapel and exited the church with me following closely on his heels. Both the Bishop and I sensed there was a discernible shift in the atmosphere of the camp as we made our way through it to the royal tent. Despite the rain, there was a lot of activity, men running through the camp with heightened energy.

By the time we reached the tent, all of the army leaders had dispersed and the Duke was alone with his chamberlain Tancarville who was busy opening various travelling chests and trunks along the interior walls of the tent. Bishop Odo and I stepped into the tent and threw off the hoods of our cloaks.

"Do we have agreement then?" Bishop Odo asked with anticipation.

"We do!" Robert exclaimed.

"Ah, that explains the hive of activity in the camp, there is excitement in the air!" Bishop Odo exclaimed.

"Good. We need to be ready to move out in two days," Robert said. "How many of the brethren will be joining us?"

"Five priests from the basilica here, three more that arrived from Reims with Count Aumale, and ten lay brothers. No doubt many more will join along the way," Bishop Odo responded.

"We depart at dawn to make most of the first day."

Robert turned to me and continued, "Help your master ready himself and the others, make sure you have what you need, it's going to be a long time until you see France again."

* * * * * * * * *

The journey to Clermont was uneventful despite the colossal effort that was needed to move such a large number of men. Crowds lined the streets of the villages and towns we passed through to cheer us on, and our numbers slowly swelled with new crusaders joining the armies. The rain had eased somewhat and we found the roads in a better state than those closer to Paris.

As was his custom, Bishop Odo sent word ahead to the Bishop of Clermont, Gérard de Baffie, who had been appointed by Pope Urban himself at the Council of Clermont the previous year. He wanted to make him aware of the arrival of the armies and instructed him to ready the cathedral for an onslaught of crusaders wishing to visit and take prayer.

Reaching the edge of the town, the military leaders set about creating a temporary camp as their stay at Clermont would be brief, a couple of days at the most. Only the most necessary structures would be erected, most would sleep under the stars next to open fires now that the October evening chill had replaced the humid downpours of the late summer in Saint Dennis. Within a few hours, open meadows had been turned into a well-organized site that supported eleven thousand men who had decided to take the cross and many wives and children who were accompanying their husbands and fathers on crusade. Many wives had decided to join their husbands on crusade instead of staying at home waiting for their return.

Bishop Odo had sent me to the cathedral to fetch Bishop Gérard to the camp. By the time we returned, Duke Robert's tent was up and in place and an aroma of a hot stew being served for the midday meal could be detected well before reaching its entrance. There was raucous laughter coming from the tent as the heads of the armies settled in to eat and drink beer from a barrel that had been brought in from the supply carts. I entered first and held the tent flap open for Bishop Gérard. Bishop Odo greeted him first and then stepped aside so the Duke could welcome him, which he did without getting up from the table or missing a beat in his eating. He motioned to Bishop Gérard to take a seat next to him which he did and Bishop Odo returned to his. Tancarville brought a bowl of stew and placed it in front of Bishop Gérard, who blessed it, and then left it a moment to cool.

> "What news from our nomadic Holy Father?" Robert asked knowing that Bishop Gérard had been travelling with Pope Urban prior to returning to Clermont.

Bishop Gérard smiled wryly at the description as it was, sadly, accurate. When the German Holy Roman Emperor Henry occupied Rome twelve years earlier, he had installed an antipope there, Clement, in the papal see as the elected Pope Urban and his predecessor before him, Gregory, had refused to do the Emperor's bidding whenever it contravened papal law. Clement had no real power as he was simply a puppet for Emperor Henry. But it did mean that Urban had no real base and so he travelled from place to place, across the western Christian world, wherever he was called.

> "He has been in Lucca most recently," Bishop Gérard replied as he dipped bread into his stew, adding, "where he welcomed Hugh de Vermandois and the noble sons in his army with a magnificent pageant fit for a King's brother."

The room fell silent and still, everyone except Bishop Gérard stopping what they were doing. It was impossible not to see Duke Robert's face turning red.

"It was an overwhelming success, quite the spectacle actually," Bishop Gérard continued as he devoured another piece of bread, oblivious to the fact that everyone in the room was now staring at him.

"Truly?" Robert growled.

Only then did the Bishop realize something was amiss, swallowed the remnants of the bread left in his mouth and stared at the Duke.

"Pray, do continue," Robert said slowly, leaning forward rather menacingly.

"Tell us everything."

The Bishop looked around the tent for a set of friendly eyes and found none. He hesitated before answering, trying to gauge why the atmosphere in the room had suddenly changed so drastically.

"Ah yes, well, erm, Vermandois had come, erm, arrived in L-L-L-Lucca in mid-September," Bishop Gérard started, stumbling over his words.

He found he could not meet the Duke's gaze and stared down at his half-emptied bowl of stew as he spoke.

"The Holy Father had been there for a f-f-few weeks by the time he arrived…"

"Oh spit it out man!" Robert barked at him.

Bishop Gérard took a deep breath and steadied himself.

"Count Vermandois and his nobles arrived in mid-September. Pope Urban had received word of their progress and when they were expected in Lucca and he prepared an appropriate welcome for them," he said, trying to tone down the description.

"Appropriate? Did you not say earlier, and I quote, 'a magnificent pageant'?" Robert pressed.

Bishop Gérard knew he was trapped. He nodded.

"Yes, your Grace, I did. The Holy Father felt that he needed to celebrate the arrival of the first crusader army with pomp and circumstance that would leave an indelible impression on everyone who saw it. The musicians…" he continued but Robert cut him off.

"Musicians??" he said loudly in a voice wracked with sarcasm and false wonderment.

He leaned back in his chair and swept the room with a glance to everyone that spoke volumes.

"Did you hear that, Aumale? Vermandois was greeted with musicians!"

Aumale raised his eyebrows and pursed his lips but said nothing.

"Were there feasts? And games? Gifts bestowed? Jewels presented? No doubt the wine flowed as if Saint Vincent of Saragossa poured it himself?! God's teeth!" Robert bellowed.

Bishop Gérard remained silent, not daring to move. But the Duke would not let it rest.

"Anything else? Surely that cannot be everything lauded onto Lord Maaaagnus?"

Bishop Gérard hesitated and then spoke, choosing his words carefully.

"There was one more, ah…bequest made."

Duke Robert leaned forward again.

"Yes?" he asked, his interest dangerously piqued.

"Pope Urban awarded him…the papal banner to be flown at the head of his army when he enters Constantinople," Bishop Gérard practically whispered.

The Duke was astounded. His reddened face drained its colour and turned an ashen white. Bishop Odo, knowing him better than anyone else, recognized the signs of pure fury in him and moved quickly to diffuse it.

"I am sure the Holy Father will be celebrating each of the armies heading to Palestine and this is just the first…" he started.

"The only reason this is the first to be celebrated is because Vermandois abandoned all of the agreements made with us in the summer!" Robert cut him off abruptly.

"There is only one papal banner to be had. He wanted it for himself. Glory-seeking pillock!" Robert swore loudly.

Bishop Gérard crossed himself at the Duke's profanity. Duke Robert caught sight of it and shook his head as he sprang to his feet.

"Save your prayers for Le Magnus, Bishop! He is going to need them!"

He stormed out of the tent, followed closely by everyone else except the two Bishops and me. Bishop Gérard sat in stunned silence. He looked at Bishop Odo open-mouthed, unable to speak, with a pained expression on his face. Bishop Odo felt he was owed an explanation.

"Count de Vermandois was to have met with the Duke, Count Flanders, Count de Blois, Godfrey de Bouillon and myself in Paris in August as it had been agreed that the armies would travel together, en masse, to Palestine. But when we arrived we discovered that he had, in fact, left several days earlier without giving notice to anyone, not even his brother the King. Duke Robert and the others were understandably, ah, upset by this development. Not only were his actions insulting to the others, his army is made up mostly of young men, sons of many French noblemen, with little or no battle experience," Bishop Odo concluded solemnly, "His impetuous behaviour may result in many of them not returning home."

* * * * * * * * * *

Once his temper had cooled, Duke Robert decided to head to the town and visit the steps of Clermont Cathedral himself. No doubt he felt his enthusiasm for the mission ebbing after receiving the news that Pope Urban had glorified Vermandois by awarding him the right to fly the papal banner, a right that should have been his, and he needed something to reignite his fervour for the fight. The fact that Vermandois was the brother of a king was of no consequence; he too, after all, was the brother of a king. And he was a Duke. And ostensibly the leader of armies that, combined, were three times that of Vermandois. That right should have been his, I suspected he would be unable to shake the thought.

It had not taken very long to reach the town and soon we found ourselves approaching the cathedral, the west entrance gradually coming into view. Right after the meeting with the army leaders, Duke Robert had made for his horse which was still saddled from his morning ride and, in one motion, had leapt onto him, grabbed the reins and headed out of the camp with Bishop Odo, Count Aumale, myself and a couple of personal guards close behind him. Bishop Gérard made the wise decision to stay and help where he could at the camp.

Slowing our horses to a walk, we could not help but observe a cloaked figure of a man, kneeling at the bottom of the steps at the entrance of the cathedral, deep in prayer. Our group slowed to a halt, sensing the intimacy of the moment, not wanting to intrude and regretting for a moment the noise made by the horses' hooves on the cobblestones. We remained still and silent until the figure finished praying. Within a few moments, he raised his head, crossed himself and without making even the slightest movement towards the visitors, stood and climbed the steps, disappearing into the cathedral as if he had not even noticed we were there.

Duke Robert was taken with the reverence shown by the stranger who had obviously come to Clermont for the same reasons he had. To see the spot from which a crusade to save the Christian world had been launched was blessed indeed. To experience that place in the moment, breathe the air, drink in the atmosphere and imagine the sights of the Holy Father preaching his sermon to the masses of believers who had travelled far and longed to hear it. He dismounted and did exactly what the stranger had done, each of us following suit in a solemn, silent reverie of respect and contemplation of what was ahead of us.

When he was done with his prayers, the Duke crossed himself and stood, waiting patiently for the others to do the same. He said he wanted to meet the stranger and find out what had brought him to this place on this day. He moved towards the entrance and the others did the same.

Bishop Odo did not move. I asked if there was anything amiss.

"Not at all Sébastien, not at all. I am merely remembering the day I was last here, it fills me with great peace. Go with the others, attend to the Duke, I shall stay here for a moment," he insisted. "And Sébastien," he added, "make sure you visit the crypt. There are two magnificent marble sarcophagi there that you must see, they once contained relics of Saints Vitalis and Agricola. Go on now."

I grudgingly did as I was told and followed the Duke and the others into the cathedral. The stranger was nowhere to be seen. The men walked up the centre aisle to the altar, Duke Robert making a point to look into the chapels off to the sides to see if the stranger was there praying in one of them. But he was nowhere to be seen. Aumale spoke in hushed tones, keeping the reverence of the place.

"Your Grace, I have been giving some thought as to how we could get the armies into the town so they can have the opportunity to visit this place..." he was saying as I drew near.

I realized they would be engaged in conversation for some time and decided to slip away to the north transept where I found the entrance to the crypt. A few narrow stone steps led down to a small wooden door which was ajar and I peered around it to find more steps leading even further down. It was dimly lit with candlelight flickering on the walls and on the stone floor at the base of the stairs.

I slowly made my way down and once reaching the bottom found a flagstone corridor straight ahead of me which gave out further along to two arched openings on either side, to the east under the altar and to the west under the nave. I tread quietly, reverently, as not to disturb the souls of those buried here and, turning left into the archway leading to the portion of the crypt under the altar, was startled to find the stranger in the shadows at the far end, with his arms outstretched, leaning against one of the two white marble sarcophagi Bishop Odo said would be there. His eyes were closed and his head bowed, giving the appearance that he was in deep thought.

I froze. I felt I should turn and go, not despoil the moment for the stranger. But at the same time I was transfixed by the tableau in front of me. And I did not want to disappoint Bishop Odo who had been so insistent that I see the crypt and touch the sarcophagi of the martyrs as the stranger was doing. I hesitated, not sure what to do and then having decided to leave the stranger in peace, turned to go back the way I came. I had barely moved when the stranger spoke.

"Who are you boy?" he asked, without making even the slightest of movements.

I glanced at the stranger.

"Sir, my name is Sébastien D'Ivry," I responded.

"And the men who arrived with you on horseback?" he asked, still not looking up.

"His Grace, Robert, Duke of Normandy, his liegeman Stephen, Count of Aumale and his Excellency Bishop Odo of Bayeux," I responded without hesitating and with just a slight hint of pride.

The stranger had no reaction to the names. He gently caressed the top of the sarcophagus with his left hand, slowly straightened up and walked towards me. As he came out of the darkness and into the light cast by the candles in the corridor, I could now make out the features that had been so carefully hidden behind the hood of his cloak when our group came upon him on the steps of the church. Fair-skinned and with dark, auburn-brown hair that was cut at the nape of his neck, his beard short-trimmed and matching in colour, it was the stranger's eyes that were his most outstanding feature, a vibrant pale blue-green with a gaze that was both penetrating and welcoming at the same time. I felt drawn to the man and yet a little afraid of him as well.

"Duke Robert, hmmm?" he asked not expecting an answer. "I should pay my respects."

"I believe his Grace was wanting to make your acquaintance sir," I said helpfully.

The stranger nodded.

"Why are you down here and not above with the others?" the stranger asked.

"Bishop Odo instructed me to come see the sarcophagi," I answered. "He said they contained the relics of two saints, Vitalis and Agricola, or had contained them."

"The relics are no longer here," the stranger confirmed. "They were re-interred in Santo Stefano in Bologna where the saints were martyred.

But their power to inspire remains," he said glancing back over his shoulder.

I had felt a strange sensation in the crypt when I had reached the bottom step which had only become stronger as I approached the tombs, something I could not quite explain. The stranger stepped aside and let me approach the same sarcophagus and watched as I laid my hands on top of it as he had done. I felt a quivering, and could not tell if that was coming from the sarcophagus or from within myself. But it did not matter, I was unnerved. I felt the stranger's eyes on me and suddenly did not wish to linger. I was glad when the stranger moved to leave the crypt and hurriedly followed him, taking the steps two at a time as he did.

Duke Robert was in mid-sentence when he spied the stranger striding towards him from the entrance to the crypt and across the nave. He stopped speaking which caused both Bishop Odo and Aumale to follow his gaze to the man approaching them. The stranger stopped just short of the group, knelt and bowed his head.

"Your Grace," he said directly to the Duke.

"Sir," Robert started, "your display of reverence earlier served you well, I hope the boy did not intrude on your prayers?" he asked as I reached the group.

"Not at all, your Grace," the stranger said.

"Good, good. Please, rise and tell us who you are and from whence you have come."

The stranger stood and replied with a slight bow.

"I am Hugues de Payns, from the village of the same name near Troyes," the stranger answered, adding, "I am a knight and vassal of his Excellency the Count de Champagne."

Duke Robert was taken aback, the surprise showed on his face.

"You are a liegeman of Hugh de Champagne?" he asked.

"Yes, your Grace," Hugues answered.

"Why are you here on your own? I cannot see that there are others with you, the Count is not here?" Robert asked.

"No, your Grace. His Excellency is not able to join the crusade to Palestine but has permitted some of his vassals to take the cross. I am one such. I have come to Clermont to pay respect to the place of the sermon before joining one of the crusading armies. I have the support of the Count, there are men and arms awaiting me in Lyon."

Duke Robert seemed impressed with the man he reckoned was not older than five and twenty and yet his intense gaze gave him a worldly and wise air. But in that moment, the Duke's mischievousness kicked in as a thought crossed his mind just who this was who stood in front of him and a sly smile appeared on his face. Bishop Odo caught it and shot him a warning glance, but he continued just the same.

"My armies are gathered just outside of Clermont also waiting to pay their respects. I would consider it an honour to have one of the Count de Champagne's liegemen join us," he said solemnly.

Bishop Odo tried to speak but Duke Robert cut him off with a sharp look. I sensed a strange dynamic emerge between the men and did not understand why. But the Bishop kept silent.

"The honour would be mine," Hugues responded, placing his hand on his heart and bowing his head slightly.

"We go to the camp now, are you able to ride with us?" Robert asked.

"Yes, your Grace," Hugues said, adding, "I need to collect my horse and some belongings with my man at the Hôtel le Lion," referring to a small inn down one of the many cobblestone lanes that led away from the cathedral.

Aumale stepped forward and whispered something in the Duke's ear.

"Yes, I agree," Robert said to him. "Aumale, Bishop Odo and I shall head out immediately. Our young man D'Ivry here," he said pointing to me, "will accompany you to the inn to collect your horse and will escort you to the camp. Come join us in the royal tents when you arrive."

"Of course, your Grace," Hugues agreed, bowing slightly.

With that, the guards who had been watching over the horses handed the reins to their respective riders. Duke Robert, Aumale, and Bishop Odo mounted theirs, turned and made their way back the way we had come. Hugues and I watched them leave and then began walking towards the inn, me leading Pax by the reins. Hugues broke the silence.

"D'Ivry?" he asked confirming that he had heard my name correctly.

"Yes m'Lord," I answered.

"Of Ivry-la-Bataille?" Hugues pressed.

"Yes m'Lord," I answered.

"Then you must be Ascelin's kin?"

"He is my father."

"Ah," Hugues responded. "Then Isabelle de Breteuil is your mother?"

"Yes, m'Lord," I said, wondering how this stranger knew of my family.

"I was with my father when he fought alongside your father battling de Breteuil for Ivry Castle," Hugues explained as if reading my mind. "It was very clever of Ascelin to ask for Isabelle's hand in marriage when he succeeded in taking it back."

"You fought with my father?" I asked. "I am sure the Duke will be pleased to hear that, he supported my father in that battle."

"As did my liege Lord," Hugues said. "How long have you served the Duke?"

"Only these past few months. I had been sent to be schooled by Bishop Odo in Bayeux and he and his Grace wanted me to join them, serve them both and train as a knight."

"Have you had any training so far? How well can you wield a sword?"

"Fair enough, m'Lord. I was able to take advantage of the delay caused by the rains at Saint-Denis to work on my skills in between attending the Duke and the Bishop."

Turning a corner, we arrived at the entrance to the inn.

"Well," Hugues started, "your battle form might be something I can help with, I will discuss it with the Duke and Bishop Odo. Wait for me here, I will bring my horse around."

Hugues disappeared into the inn and before too long he returned, mounted on a magnificent destrier, solid black in colour, two bags on each side of the saddle and a blanket underneath with the distinctive blue, white and gold Champagne coat of arms. I could not help but notice an impressive double-handed broadsword, sheathed in a dark brown leather scabbard now attached to a belt around his waist and a strap across his chest and over his shoulder, hanging on his left side, the hilt within easy reach.

Behind him on an almost equally impressive palfrey was a serious-looking young man I guessed to be a few years older than myself, with blond hair and pale skin, I assumed he was the one the knight referred to as his man earlier. His horse's tack also showed the colours of the court of Champagne so there was no mistaking whom he was with.

"D'Ivry," Hugues said, "this is my man, Geoffroi Bisol. Bisol, Sébastien D'Ivry."

Bisol nodded a silent greeting to me, I returned it.

They waited for me to mount my horse as I had not done so earlier out of respect for the knight, and then watched as I led the way, prodding the horses into an easy trot through the streets, then spurring them into a steady canter once we passed through the town's gates. As we traversed the fields and glens on our way to the camp, I eventually rid myself of the eerie disquiet that lingered after I left the crypt. I wanted to ask the knight if he noticed the strange interaction between the Duke and the Bishop earlier at the church but at the speed we were moving there was no opportunity for conversation. Probably best, I thought and made a mental note to ask the Bishop later.

Riding at a fairly quick pace, we made good time and arrived at the camp shortly after the others. I led the two men to the royal tent where I knew the Duke would be meeting with the captains of the armies to discuss the next movements to Lyon. As we were dismounting, Duke Robert and Bishop Odo emerged from the tent engrossed in conversation, so much so they almost walked past without noticing Hugues and Bisol. It was only when Bishop

Odo called out to me to join them did the Duke realize the knight had arrived and turned to welcome him.

"Payns!" he boomed, "glad to have you with us!"

"It is my honour, your Grace," Hugues started but was interrupted by an angry voice behind the Duke.

"What is this?!" the voice bellowed.

Everyone turned to find a red-faced Blois, who had followed the Duke out of the tent, now stopped dead in his tracks, clearly nonplussed and extremely irritated.

"Ah, Blois, come meet one who had decided to join our cause," replied Robert, his voice a little too cheery.

Bishop Odo sighed quietly, which did not escape my notice. Blois stepped towards the Duke, his eyes flashing back and forth from Hugues and Bisol to their horses. Hugues tilted his head in a slight bow as Blois approached.

"My Lord," Hugues said, "I am Hugues de Payns, vassal of..."

"Yes, I know who your lord is, sirrah!" Blois snapped.

He turned to the Duke.

"What is the meaning of this?" he demanded.

"What do you mean?" Robert responded, trying to keep a straight face.

"You know very well what I mean," Blois growled, pointing at the colours of the horses' saddle blankets. "We agreed months ago that since he decided to remain safe in his bed at home none of his men would accompany us!"

"Did we? I do not recall agreeing to that," Robert said almost flippantly.

This had the expected adverse effect on Blois who exploded in anger.

"You most certainly did!" Blois barked.

"I suggest you remember to whom you are speaking and watch your tone," Robert reprimanded him. He continued, his voice rising, "Payns has taken the cross and I do not doubt his sincerity in joining the cause!"

Blois hesitated before speaking again, aware that he needed to temper his emotions.

"I...I cannot abide this," he said slowly, choosing his words carefully.

Duke Robert glared at him, his private joke beginning to wear thin.

"I strongly suggest you do. He has men and arms awaiting him in Lyon and we need all the help we can get. The fact that you and Champagne are at each other's throats all the time over petty grievances cannot take precedence over what we have been called to do!" Robert retorted, loud enough for everyone to hear.

Blois stood rooted to the ground, mouth agape, watching the Duke storm off. Humiliated in front of subordinates, and clearly not a happy man, he turned on his heel and marched in the opposite direction, muttering indecipherably to himself, occasionally looking back over his shoulder at his man, Saint-Agnan, who followed him.

"Why don't you come with me," Bishop Odo said calmly to Hugues, "and I can fill you in on the Duke's plans."

"Of course, your Excellency," Hugues agreed.

"Sébastien can show your man where you will settle for the night, room has been made for the two of you with Flanders," he said pointing to a smaller but still substantial tent further down from the Duke's.

I glanced over and could already see Montdidier, Flanders's army captain, milling about, moving items in and out of the tent.

"Sébastien," Bishop Odo continued, "come to me when you've done your chores, I shall be with the Duke in the camp."

And with that, he guided Hugues in the direction of the Duke.

I tied Pax's reins to the makeshift hitching post outside of the Duke's tent so I could help with the two horses whose reins Bisol was now holding onto. As we reached Flanders's tent, Montdidier appeared, adjusting the belt holding his sword in place. A slender and wiry fair-haired man, Montdidier closely resembled his cousin the Count of Flanders in not only looks but in his gait and stance.

"I've made room for Payns and his man," he said to me, passing by without stopping.

"Thank you sir," I said.

Bisol and I tied the horses' reins to a post to the side of the tent and unloaded the saddlebags, carrying them into the tent. Once the bags were inside, I made a move to go.

"I thank you for your help today," Bisol said, extending his arm in thanks.

"You are welcome," I said taking it and then, after pausing for a moment, continued, "May I ask a question about your master?"

"Of course," Bisol replied as he started to unpack.

"I do not understand the anger Count de Blois has for him," I said. "Has he offended him somehow?"

Bisol smiled knowingly.

"No, he has not offended the Count. In fact, I am fairly certain they have never met before today. However," he said, moving one of the emptied saddlebags onto the floor, "the same cannot be said for Count de Blois and Count de Champagne."

"Duke Robert seemed annoyed by some petty arguments between them?"

"Do you not know who the Count de Champagne is?" Bisol asked.

I shook my head.

"He is the Count de Blois's half-brother, younger by quite a number of years, born of the same father, Théobald de Blois, but by different mothers."

"And there is animosity between them?" I asked.

"Animosity? Hmmmm," Bisol replied. He stopped unpacking and continued, "There are, shall we say, some rumours about the validity of the marriage between Théobald and Count de Blois's mother. The Count de Champagne has been rather, ah, vocal in expressing his doubt and the Count de Blois resents it."

"Understandable," I said. "If he is correct, then the Count de Blois would be...."

"Yes, he would be. This also means the Count de Champagne would be in possession of far more lands and ruling far more territory than he currently is. He pressed his case with King Philippe which is how he came to wed the King's daughter Constance, joining the houses of Blois and Capet. But as the Count de Blois has been married to the Conqueror's sister Adela for many years, there is no challenging his lineage, so the House of Blois's allegiance lies with the English Conqueror and not with the French King. And Blois regularly reminds Champagne of this, which does not help matters between them."

I nodded my understanding. My world seemed to be drowning in warring siblings. I thought fondly of my younger brothers Guillaume and Roger back at home and hoped the same ill will would not befall us.

* * * * * * * * * *

The journey to Lyon took seven days. As we departed Clermont, we passed the field where the Holy Father had spoken his inspirational sermon and many wished to stop to pray at the site. The roads had dried from the summer rains and were well passable, increasing the speed at which we travelled. Once the masses of armed men, some mounted, most on foot had passed the field, we made slow but steady progress, eventually settling on the outskirts of Lyon, a burgeoning town under the control of the Holy Roman Emperor Henry. Our stay here would not be long; the Emperor's support of the anti-pope Clement against Pope Urban caused friction and though he had given permission for the crusaders to cross his lands and to meet with Toulouse, relations between various ruling domains was tense at best due to this conflict within the papal see. And even though the patronage for the crusade was shared across the Christian states, political power games were not set aside for the cause. Duke Robert knew better than to overstay his welcome.

Meeting with Toulouse in the centre of the city was brief and to the point. Pope Urban's papal legate and the spiritual leader for the crusade, Adhémar Bishop of Le Puy, who had been travelling with Toulouse, attended the meeting with him. Duke Robert was not surprised to see Toulouse's wife, who had decided to accompany him on crusade, along with their infant son. A golden-haired, brown-eyed beauty, Elvira of Castile was the illegitimate daughter of King Alfonso of León and Castile, the royal family of Spain famous for its strength and power under Alfonso's rule. It seemed to be a good match for Toulouse and many could not help but admire her and envy him. Many wives of soldiers had decided to take the cross, but not many of those of royalty had. Most, like Blois's wife Adela, had been made regents and stayed to rule in their husbands' absence. But Elvira's spirit and intelligence were obvious to anyone who spent any time with her. I was captivated upon sight and was disheartened to realize the Count and Countess of Toulouse would not be accompanying the Duke on the journey but would be taking a different route. I am sure my appreciation of her was the source of some humour amongst the older men, a boyish infatuation reminding them of their youth.

The various armies were on their way again within a couple of days, Toulouse and his men heading to Turin in the east, Duke Robert, Flanders and Blois and their armies heading south to Genoa. Toulouse had arrived in Lyon ahead of the Duke with the news that Pope Urban was on his way to Bari in southern Italy and would await our arrival there. Upon hearing this, Duke Robert made some changes to his travel plans. He knew if he left the movement of the troops in the competent hands of the captains and rode with only a few men, he could make Genoa in about six days, Rome in twelve, then another six should bring us to Bari in the middle of November if our stops to rest and gather fresh supplies along the way were brief. The armies should arrive a month later. Duke Robert now had to decide who would go with him as part of the advance guard.

It was clear that Bishop Odo would need to be included. Not only was he the spiritual leader of the combined armies, he was also close to the Holy Father and would no doubt desire to meet with him again. As a papal legate, he would be one of Pope Urban's representatives throughout the crusade and would want his blessing and any other instructions and advice the Holy Father wished to give him. The priests who had joined the crusade in Saint-Denis would tend to the armies' spiritual needs in his absence.

In the end, Duke Robert felt it best Bishop Odo, Flanders and Payns, along with their respective attendants, Tancarville, myself and Bisol - who would be attending on both Payns and Flanders - and half a dozen guards would make the expedited journey with him to Bari. This would leave Blois and Aumale in charge of getting the slower-paced armies to the east coast city, one of the launching points to cross the Adriatic.

We packed what was needed for the journey, not wanting to weigh down the horses, bringing only what was necessary. Three pack horses were added to the group, ensuring that both the Duke and the Bishop had the proper regalia and attire with which to meet the Holy Father. This, of course, meant repacking the mitre, vestment and crozier, taking them out of the larger chests where they had been safely tucked away and onto one of the smaller ones that would be carried by the pack horses, wrapped carefully, protected from the elements. The Duke's red and gold colours decorated each of his men's horses and his coat of arms was clearly visible from a distance, fluttering in the wind atop the pole held by his standard bearer, Pagan Peverel. The young man kept the standard pole in place from the leather holder affixed to the side of his horse. The colours of each of the regions represented by the riders – blue, red and gold for Flanders, blue, gold and white for Champagne, red and gold for D'Ivry - could also be recognized either from what we were wearing or from the saddle blankets draped across the horses' backs. Each rider had to ensure he took a thick hooded cloak as a shield against the chill now starting to creep into the autumn nights. We would need them for protection against the November rains in Bari. And of course, each of us had the crusader's red silk cross sewn onto our cloaks so no one would doubt who we were and why we were passing through.

We made an impressive sight as we travelled through the lands, welcomed and cheered by crowds in the cities and towns and, whenever we stopped, fed the best foods, served the best wines, heralded with reverence and sang about in the pubs and drinking inns. The further south we travelled, the larger the crowds became as word of our journey and the purpose for it had made its way ahead of us. We were told later they cheered the armies even more loudly when they made their way past.

And whenever we rested or stopped for the night, Hugues made sure to continue my training as he had done since we left Clermont, pairing me with his man Bisol. I had been using an old, rusty broadsword as my short sword would not do, and, after a number of sessions, Hugues presented me with my first battle double-handed broadsword and scabbard from his own possessions, made with a very fine Damascus blade. It was exquisite, with etchings all down one side of the blade and a Greek cross engraved in red on its pommel. We were worked to the point of exhaustion, late into the evenings, regardless of weather, and when we were finally able to rest, we collapsed, grateful for the sleep that came quickly and deeply. Without realizing it, we were slowly leaving our sheltered childhoods behind and evolving into the highly skilled knights we were destined to be.

But for now, it was imperative that we reached Bari and the castle of Sannicandro just southwest of the city as quickly as possible, as this is where we would find the Holy Father waiting for us.

# II

# Part Four

# 1097 - Italy

We reached the city of Bari just before midnight and decided to stay the night and continue the final few hours to the castle the next day. We had an early start and departed for the castle shortly after morning mass. We soon came within sight of Sannicandro, approaching it from the east, two of its towers and a section of the curtain wall slowly looming before us in the horizon. It was a large and imposing structure and was one of many Bohemond, Prince of Taranto, owned in the lands he ruled across southern Italy. Once a Byzantine fort, the castle had been rebuilt by his Norman baronial father and now Bohemond used it as one of his main residences, with others in Taranto and Brindisi. With four external towers all connected by a curtain wall, it was surrounded by a wide moat that kept it well protected from unwanted visitors. Inside were another four towers connected to each other through structures that comprised the great hall, living quarters, and such like. Next to the largest tower, just inside the main gate, was the baronial palace running along the northern curtain wall, and next to that the small chapel.

As we approached the heavy drawbridge stretching across the moat we could see we were being watched by wary eyes from the tops of the towers. Bohemond had tripled his guards with the arrival of the Holy Father and, even though we were expected, it was clear he was well-prepared as more of his men could be seen patrolling outside of the walls. The drawbridge was down and the large wooden gates open behind the black iron portcullis which was being raised to allow us through. The sentries had recognized the Duke's standard and were opening the castle to us. With Duke Robert leading the way, we passed through the gate and dismounted in front a small stone staircase that led up to the entrance of the large tower. It was there that we were greeted by Bohemond's constable and standard bearer, Robert of Buonalbergo, a young man who also happened to be his distant cousin.

Buonalbergo greeted the Duke and after a short exchange bid him and the rest of us to follow him up the few stairs into the first floor of the tower and through it into the baronial hall, substantial in size and in décor, the walls covered in exquisite tapestries from the east bursting with colour, thick velvet drapes in bright blue and red, the colours of Bohemond's family house d'Hauteville, and the coat of arms, a shield with a red and white chequered bend dexter on a blue background, hanging from the high ceiling at the end of the hall. The Prince of Taranto's lavish taste meant to impress and it had hit the mark as we marvelled at our surroundings.

Bohemond was waiting for us. Tall and slender with skin so white it seemed translucent, light brown hair contrasted by dark eyes and a short but curly beard and moustache covering his face, Bohemond was striking. This was made all the more so by the vibrant cobalt blue robes trimmed in gold that swirled around him as he moved.

"Duke Robert!" Bohemond exclaimed reaching out to his prestigious guest.

Recognizing the more senior rank of his host, Duke Robert bowed reverently and then embraced him as an old friend even though the two had never met. Their reputations had preceded them and their stations commanded respect.

"Your Highness," Robert responded. "I thank you for your offer of hospitality for our meeting with the Holy Father."

"It is good to see you and your men in good stead. The Holy Father is finishing sext prayers in the Church of St John, just outside the north wall, I broke away when I was made aware of your arrival. He should be with us shortly. A meal is being prepared but for now," he snapped his fingers and the doors opened, allowing a few pages to enter carrying gold trays with silver pitchers of wine and goblets filled to the brim which they brought to each of us, "please enjoy some of our best Calabrian," taking a sip from the goblet handed to him.

We were all thankful for the drink, the ride from Bari had been under a bright morning sun above us in a cloudless sky, and the roads dusty for lack of recent rain.

"Who has come with you?" Bohemond asked.

"Bishop Odo of Bayeux," Robert said pointing at the Bishop who bowed, adding, "Robert, Count of Flanders, Hugues de Payns deputizing for the Count of Champagne, and their men. The Counts of Aumale and Blois are following with the armies, we anticipate their arrival in Bari in a couple of weeks, early December at the latest."

Bohemond nodded.

"I am glad to hear of it. Over the past few months, I have had bands of crusaders pass through my territories on their way to Constantinople and beyond. Peter the Hermit and Walter Sans Avoir with their peasant army stayed in Bari before crossing the Adriatic in the heat of the summer. We received word that Emperor Alexios was not terribly pleased with what reached him in Constantinople in October. He was expecting a highly skilled army, horsed and well-armed, but what greeted him was, of course, far from that."

"I am not surprised he was displeased," Robert said wearily.

"Peter's preaching, mesmerising as it might be, could never have compensated for the complete lack of expertise in warfare, the Emperor found the army was utterly undisciplined," Bohemond continued. "Alexios made them camp outside of the city and so they stayed there until he could decide what to do with them. In the end, he felt it best to get them on their way, and so he ferried them across the Bosphorus, took five days to move them all. That was the last we heard of them," Bohemond said, adding, "the Holy Father might have more recent news."

He drank from his goblet.

"Shall we see if sext has ended and alert him of our arrival?" Robert asked. "I could send our man D'Ivry here?" he suggested pointing to me.

"Yes, it should be over shortly if it hasn't already concluded," Bohemond agreed and turned to one of his guards, "Take Master D'Ivry to the church and bring the Holy Father through the passage, we shouldn't expect Pope Urban to take the longer route back," he instructed.

I bowed to the Prince and followed his guard out of the doorway from whence we had come, retracing my steps out of the castle, across the drawbridge to the other side of the moat. We followed the castle's outer wall first turning north and then west and soon saw the spire rising before us. The church itself actually sat just outside the castle's north outer wall but with no direct access, it was a bit of a walk to reach it from inside the castle. I began to wonder what the Prince had meant by bringing the Holy Father through the passage.

The guard obviously knew his way and found a small door which opened into a side aisle of the nave. Sext was still in session but, being familiar with the service, I knew it would be soon over and so we stood rooted where we were. I could see the back of the Holy Father, his vestment glittering in gold, his mitre tipped slightly forward as he murmured his prayers towards the altar. There was a stillness in the air which was both soothing and unnerving and his presence could definitely be felt. I was eager to meet the great holy man whose words had inspired this crusade.

Sure enough, amen was soon said and the churchgoers, having been blessed, slowly trudged their way out, making sure to kneel on the cold stone black and white checkered floor and cross themselves before they went. With an almost imperceptible flick of his hand, the Holy Father bid us to approach. I followed behind the guard who upon reaching the foot of the altar steps knelt and bowed his head; I did the same. The Holy Father blessed us and asked us to stand. Now was my first real opportunity to get a good look at Pope Urban.

Not a physically imposing figure, the Holy Father stood much less than I did at the time and seemed to be almost drowning in the robes and accoutrement of his post but when one met his eyes, that all faded away. His expression was that of a highly intelligent and aware man, coupled with a peaceful countenance that immediately gave reassurance to anyone in his presence. His bushy white beard and moustache and the curls of white hair poking out from under his mitre gave away his age. I came to find out later he was older than Bishop Odo, but not by much. And when he spoke, I was surprised by the strength of his voice, a strong and low timbre revealing a quiet strength; I instantly understood the power he easily commanded.

"Duke Robert has arrived?" he asked.

"Yes, Your Holiness," the guard responded. "This is his man," he said, referring to me, "instructed to escort you to the barons hall. His Highness has suggested we take the passage."

"That would be expeditious," Pope Urban replied. He turned to me and asked, "What is your name son?"

"I am Sébastien D'Ivry," I responded, trying desperately to keep the nerves from my voice.

"Hmmmm, D'Ivry. From D'Ivry-la-Bataille I presume?"

"Yes, Your Holiness."

"I knew a great man by that name, Roger D'Ivry, he served King William of England well and for many years. Fought at his side at Hastings. Is he your kin?" Pope Urban asked.

"He was my great uncle, Your Holiness," I answered.

"Ah. Duke Robert has spoken highly of your family," Pope Urban said graciously. "How come you here?"

"I was studying with and attending to Bishop Odo in Bayeux when the armies for the crusade began to form, both he and the Duke felt I should be allowed to take the cross and serve them," I answered.

The Pope raised his eyebrows and smiled gently.

"If they decided this, you must be worthy of taking the cross," he said. Turning to his own attendant who had been silently awaiting him at the doorway to the dressing room, he said, "Come, let us get me out of these robes and into something more manageable." Then turning back to the guard he added, "Await me at the passage entrance, I will not be long."

The guard and I waited until the Pope had disappeared into the dressing room and then he motioned for me to follow him to a small chapel in the south transept. There, I saw a small alcove on the left where a marble altar stood and on the wall behind it hung a small but vivid triptych of the holy trinity. Standing to the side of the altar, the guard reached behind the third panel, took hold of something, then gave a strong tug. I heard a sort of grinding groan and then, amazingly, the wall opened outward with the small altar still attached to it, giving just enough space for one man to pass through and revealing a hidden passageway further inside. I looked at the guard with an inquisitive and rather shocked glance.

"A rescue tunnel leading to and from the church, built by the Prince's father," he explained and stepping inside, showed me how it worked when coming from the other way.

I had never seen such a mechanism and marvelled at it how simple it was. Stepping inside I could see a black wrought iron gate, also open; this would be closed and locked behind anyone escaping attackers, providing extra protection for those fleeing. The guard lit a torch which he found discarded just inside the passage and then coughed slightly, knocking me out of my trance and urging me to come back out as the Holy Father was approaching. He would, of course, precede us into the passage. I made a note to come study this trick more in depth later if I could find some time.

True to his word, Pope Urban arrived quickly, now dressed in a simple white alb and dark crimson cloak, his white skullcap covering what I could now see was a bald spot, his white curls creating a ring around his head. Each of us in turn ducked and crossed the threshold into the passageway. The guard closed the false wall behind us, securing the latch but left the gate where it was and stepped in front of us to light the way.

We hurried down a few stone steps onto a hardened dirt slope, eventually reaching an even keel, walking the meandering path dimly light by the guard's torch, feeling the air get cooler and cooler with each step. Eventually the ground beneath us started to rise and we found ourselves at another set of steps that seemed to lead to nowhere. A similar black iron gate sat open, but there was no opening obvious to the eye to proceed through. But as my eyes had become accustomed to the shadowy light, I glimpsed the latch moments before the guard reached for it, cleverly hidden in the shadows. Within seconds, we found ourselves emerging from behind a stairway in a hallway I had not been in before and, within minutes, we were back in the baronial hall where we had left the others what felt like only moments before.

Pope Urban greeted Bohemond first and then approached the Duke, both of whom knelt reverently before the Holy Father and kissed the papal ring. He then spied Bishop Odo and, as if seeing a long-lost favourite pet, he outstretched his arms and enveloped his old friend in a long, warm embrace. Bishop Odo returned the warmth, very happy indeed to see his friend safe and seemingly in good health.

As promised, the Prince had ordered the meal prepared for his guests brought to the hall and, after a blessing from the Holy Father, soon we found ourselves devouring a wide variety of delicacies, some familiar, some not.

But all delicious. Duke Robert eventually brought the discussion around to the purpose behind his visit.

"Your Holiness," he began, "Bohemond has informed us of the progress made by those who went before us, Peter and Walter," he said, adding with a controlled half-grimace/half-grin, "and Vermandois. Is there any further news?"

Pope Urban repeated what Bohemond had told us, that Vermandois had been in Bari no more than a fortnight ago and when Bohemond for assistance in crossing the Adriatic, boastfully displaying the papal banner given to him by Pope Urban in Lucca. Vermandois, arrogantly ignoring Bohemond's advice to wait for a particularly fierce storm to pass, pushed ahead and capsized, his entire fleet shipwrecked off the port of Dyrrhachium. He had found himself in the unenviable position of having to be saved by the Governor of the city, nephew to Emperor Alexios, the very man he had sent his insulting letter to announcing his arrival and egotistic expectations. Duke Robert, not wishing ill on anyone taking the cross, nevertheless took particular delight to hear this. He thought that would be enough to humble any man, but doubted it would have any impact on the dullard Vermandois. Nor would the fact he and his men then had to be escorted like children to Constantinople. That is where they were now, being watched by the Emperor's men.

Pope Urban sighed as he placed his goblet onto the table.

"I am sure Vermandois and his men will recover from their, ah, ordeal," he said facetiously.

He was more than aware of the Duke's intense dislike of the King of France's brother and his resentment of Vermandois receiving the papal banner from him. He would have to do something to remedy that. But in the meantime, he needed to pass on some dire news he had received very early in the morning, not having had a chance even to tell Bohemond. The tone of his voice dropped low, there was no escaping the seriousness of what he was saying.

"As you all are aware," he began, Peter the Hermit and Walter Sans Avoir left France many months ago, crossing the Adriatic from Bari in August, and then, having reached Constantinople, decided not to await the massive numbers coming after and instead continued on to Jerusalem. I am told Emperor Alexios tried to persuade them to wait for our armies but to no avail. They set up camp in Civetot, on the Sea of

Marmara, where they were joined by more crusaders, Italians and Germans. Alas, as expected when there is no strong leadership, there are always quarrels and the armies split, the Germans and Italians followed a man called Rainald, and Peter and Walter lost control of their army to a man, erm, Geoffrey Burel."

He paused to take a drink, and reflect a moment on how to tell Duke Robert and the others what happened next. He continued.

"The two armies set out to conquer two different Turkish strongholds. Rainald and his men were defeated when they attacked Xerigordos, outnumbered and surpassed in skill by the Turkish warriors. Most of his men were killed and those not killed, along with the women and children in his camp, were taken as slaves. Burel, with Peter and Walter in tow, had taken the French army and sacked a number of small towns outside of Nicaea, but had not managed to take the city itself. Rumours abound that they committed unspeakable atrocities when doing so, I cannot bring myself to recount them to you. Shameful indeed if the rumours are true."

He sighed deeply, now reaching the conclusion of his account of the peasants' crusade. Duke Robert and the others sat frozen in place, astonished at what they were hearing. The only discernible movement came from Bishop Odo, whose head dropped slightly in a silent prayer.

"But the infidel Turks concocted a devious plan to wreak revenge for the loss of those towns. They sent spies to infiltrate the French camp and spread rumours that Rainald and his men had actually captured Nicaea and that there was plenty of gold and jewels and bounty to be had. Peter recommended to Burel that they wait whilst he and a few others returned to Constantinople for fresh supplies, but Burel refused to listen and led the entire French contingent, twenty thousand, out of the camp at Civetot, leaving behind only the elderly, the sick, women and children."

He hesitated, not really wanting to go on. Whatever had happened was weighing heavily on his heart.

"About three miles outside of the city, they were ambushed by the Turks in a narrow valley, trapped on all sides. It was an unimaginable slaughter. Seventeen thousand men were massacred, Walter amongst them. Burel and three thousand survivors took refuge in an abandoned castle and would have been had by the Turks if reinforcements from Constantinople not arrived quickly and seen them off. They made their way back to Constantinople where they are now."

We were stunned. This had been an unmitigated disaster. Bishop Odo, white as a sheet, crossed himself, others did the same, including me. No one spoke, no one moved, any food and drink that remained went untouched. Whilst most of us believed that the crusade led by the enigmatic preacher and the reckless knight had been well-intentioned, no one really believed they would get very far and would more than likely turn back, and await the more highly skilled warriors to arrive and join their ranks. This needless loss of life was shocking and never thought possible. But, I suppose, looking back we had to admit that if they persisted with this foolish business, this unfortunate fate was really what had been waiting for them all along.

* * * * * * * * * *

The effect the Pope's words had on the leaders of the armies was mixed. Initially disheartened, Flanders quickly became incensed and wanted to push on to Constantinople as soon as possible, as did Hugues. They were eager to engage the Turks and avenge the deaths of their crusader brothers. The Duke and Bishop Odo were more cautious and decided to wait for the arrival of Aumale and Blois with the armies to reach agreement on what to do next. Duke Robert was particularly hesitant, he had received word from Normandy that as soon as he was out of reach, his brother the King of England, had broken his vow to keep the duchy for his return and was now trying to consolidate his hold on it, bringing it permanently under his rule. Duke Robert needed to decide if he should return.

After spending a few days of Bohemond's gracious hospitality and luxurious accommodations at Sannicandro and having received the Pope's blessing, we decamped to Brindisi, the port town a few days' ride to the coast, large enough to handle the large numbers of crusaders now in our armies, many more having joined as they marched past the many towns and cities along the route.

Shortly after our arrival in Brindisi, we were alerted to Bouillon's progress. Most of his journey had been over land, fording a river now and then, he had made good time, passing through Vienna and the towns of Buda and Pest at speed. He had crossed the River Danube at Belgrade in mid-September reaching Sofia a few weeks later. The report had said if all went well, they expected be in Constantinople by the end of December. This news made

Flanders and Hugues all the more determined not to wait and to make the journey as soon as their men arrived.

I had noticed that Bishop Odo had not quite been himself since first meeting with the Holy Father. He had taken to his bed early that evening and his spirit seemed broken somewhat by the news Pope Urban had shared with us. He became withdrawn, more contemplative than usual, he seemed to tire easily. The November nights were turning colder and he remarked more than once how he was feeling the chill in his bones. I tried not to ask intrusive questions about his well-being, each time I did, they were dismissed with a gentle wave of his hand. The Duke expressed his concern for his old friend, there was nothing I could tell him to ease his worry.

The armies reached Brindisi in early December, about a week ahead of schedule. Duke Robert was overjoyed to see Aumale and even had a warm embrace for Blois. The two Stephens had managed to successfully bring an army of twenty thousand over long distances and through some rough terrain, keeping order and discipline within the ranks, not an easy task.

Once all the leaders had arrived - except Toulouse who, like Bouillon, would be making his way to Constantinople following a different overland route and so would not be joining us in Brindisi - discussions were held on what the best course going forward would be. The weather had taken a turn for the worse, and some were in favour of sitting out the winter and then proceeding, others wanted to get underway immediately, pausing in Constantinople if necessary. After many hours long into the night debating the options, there was no meeting of the minds. Flanders and Hugues were determined to board the ships provided by Bohemond and sail for Dyrrhachium immediately, Duke Robert and Blois wanting to wait out the winter. Bishop Odo was, of course, part of the Duke's army and would go where he was bid.

And so, the decisions made and the armies divided, Flanders taking his Flemish fighters and Hugues taking his men from Champagne onto the ships waiting for them to cross the Adriatic. I was saddened somewhat to know that Hugues was going ahead as we had built a great friendship and I greatly valued not only his mentoring of my battle skills, but also his companionship. It felt as if we were kinfolk, and when I stood on the docks watching the ships pull away I was reminded of similar feelings experienced as I waved good-bye to my father as he stood on the shore of the Seine at Mantes-la-Ville watching the barges disappear in the distance. I was grateful to Hugues as he had decided to have his man, Bisol, stay with the Duke's army so we could continue our training together over the months to come. He had warned us that he wanted to see significant improvement in our swordplay when we saw each other next. He had praised my aptitude with the blade to Bishop Odo who passed this remark to me for encouragement. I vowed not to disappoint him.

After deciding to stay the course rather than return to Normandy – reckoning coming back a crusading hero would be the best way to regain the lands his brother was trying to keep from him - the Duke initially resolved to stay with his army in Brindisi, there were plenty of supplies and work for the men to keep them occupied through the winter months. And he had another reason for wanting to remain in Brindisi: he had become beguiled by Sybilla, the daughter of Geoffrey of Brindisi, Count of Conservano. Not only was she an intelligent, dark-haired beauty, Sybilla was a wealthy heiress in her own right, being a near cousin of the great Prince Bohemond himself. It was a love match enriched by the advantages it would bring to both families and negotiations began for their marriage. And so, the Duke wanted his courting of the lady to continue for as long as it could.

As Christmas approached and the weather worsened with gales blowing down from the north and across the Adriatic, the worrying condition of Bishop Odo's physical health led Bohemond to make the suggestion that he and the Duke spend the winter at his Castle of Scilla in Calabria, almost the most southernly point in Italy. It was not far from Sybilla whom Duke Robert could visit often and Bohemond insisted it would do wonders for the Bishop's fragile state. Blissful to those who visited, he said many found it difficult to leave once they experienced its calming splendour, an idyll where the breezes from the three seas – Ionian to the east, Tyrrhenian to the west and Mediterranean to the south - swirled warm gentle caresses that soothed the body and the soul. And of course, home to his delicious grape, flourishing in the temperate climate, transformed after harvest into the delicious drink Bohemond favoured and shared with his special guests.

When broached with the suggestion, Bishop Odo at first declined, wanting to stay with the men in the camps outside Brindisi. He was, after all, their spiritual leader and felt responsible for the souls of the men who would face sacrificing them in the coming months. But he knew in his heart that he needed to rest, to recuperate, become stronger physically and mentally for the challenges he would face in the future. And so, with some gentle urging from both the Duke and myself, he slowly acquiesced to the idea and we found ourselves packing after Christmas for the relatively short journey to Calabria.

Blois, of course, jumped at the chance to spend the winter in the warmth by the sea. Aumale and Blois's man, Saint-Agnan, agreed to stay in Brindisi and oversee the armies until the time came when we were ready to sail for the east. Bishop Odo and myself, Duke Robert and his man Tancarville, Blois and his man Rollant, Bisol and about twenty of the Duke's guards were to spend the winter at the Castle of Scilla. Bohemond sent word ahead that his royal apartments were to be at the Duke's disposal and that his men were to be well treated. And when he returned to Sannicandro, he sent his personal physician to do whatever he could to help the Bishop.

We arrived in early January, on the day before the Feast of the Epiphany. The castle sat upon a cliff top overlooking the Strait of Messina to the west and the splendid beaches below. Despite its high elevation, the castle was surprisingly easy to reach as the path to it meandered on a gentle slope until it reached the entrance. Or the only entrance it seemed as the key to this castle's defences was the sheer drop from the castle walls to the beaches on one side or into the Strait on another. On the west side was an octagonal tower whose roof could be used as a viewing platform watching anyone who approached. Or taking in the stunning sunsets.

The Duke was kind to his old companion and gave him the Prince's royal apartment over his protestations, and took a smaller but just as lavishly decorated room for himself. Each of the apartments contained curtained feather beds covered in brightly embroidered throws of Byzantine mosaics and furs for the chilly nights. At the foot of each bed was another, smaller single bed for the retainers to sleep in, near their masters, ready to do their bidding at a moment's notice.

Bohemond's men kept his promise and we enjoyed his sumptuous hospitality during our stay. The Duke and Blois kept in touch with their men in Brindisi, sending either myself or Bisol with messages on a fairly regular basis. We received word that Bouillon, Toulouse, and Flanders had finally been reunited and were now camped outside Constantinople, awaiting our arrival, which was delayed by the Adriatic's wintry seas. Hugues had decided he and his men would join with Bouillon which was sensible as that made the armies more evenly balanced in numbers.

For myself and Bisol, our days, when not performing messenger services, were spent mostly training on the sandy beaches and rocky cliff base beneath the castle. Or being taught the skills needed to be the perfect squire, how to quickly shoe and unshoe a horse, how to fix its tack when broken, how to mend the padded chausses worn on our legs and the quilted bodices that would be worn on our bodies under the hauberk, the heavy shirt of maille used for protection. We were taken to a village blacksmith to watch how the maille was created in the blasting hot ovens that made the strongest steel glow a fiery orange and allow itself to be bent and hammered to perfection. We were taught how to sharpen knives until they sliced through tough-skinned fruit as if passing through air. I continued my studies and discovered Bisol had not learned the basics of reading and writing, so I took it upon myself to teach him.

Days turned into weeks and with the help of the Prince's physician, Bishop Odo seemed to improve both physically and in spirit, although because of his ill health, performing the various masses had become rather lax, reduced to just evening prayers. The Duke in particular seemed to be enjoying himself here, no doubt on account of the soothing weather and his newfound lovely lady. He would disappear for a few days at a time during these weeks, saying he matters to attend to in Brindisi but no doubt stopping on the way to and fro and enjoying the hospitality and companionship offered in Conservano instead. We began to worry that, when the time came for us to leave, he would not.

We spent the evenings by the fire, discussing the news from the men, the Pope or from one of the seemingly unending stream of letters from Blois's wife Adele, with the latest from France. The Bishop would regale us with stories of the battles of the conquest, telling of the ferocity of the Anglo-Saxon warriors and the particular reverence held for their leader, King Harold II, who died heroically on Senlac Hill. He was the enemy and needed to be captured or killed, but that did not mean he did not deserve their respect.

Bishop Odo also told us stories of the time he spent in England as the Earl of Kent and of the vast amount of land he once owned there, spread across many counties. And of the glorious abbeys and churches he had seen on his travels across the Christian world. He was eager to see the Shrine of the Holy Wisdom of God in Constantinople, known by the Byzantines as Hagia Sophia. And he spoke fondly of the Byzantine basilica at Palermo, just across the Strait of Messina, on the island of Sicily. It would be a shame, he said, to have come all this way and not pay a respectful visit. We agreed to find the time when he felt strong enough.

I do not recall precisely what the weather was like that particular morning, whether it was sunny or grey, raining or bright. The evening before, the Bishop had taken supper in bed and, not wishing him to dine alone, I brought a small table to use for my supper and sat with him, refilling his goblet before he asked for it. It was a talent I had grasped quickly and was honing every day, the art of anticipation. Knowing what someone wants or needs even before they know it themselves. We talked well into the night, maybe too long? He took hold of my hand a few times, and told me he thought of me as the grandson he never had, would never have. I remember he asked if I knew the meaning of my name, "Sébastien." I had to admit I did not.

"It is of Greek origin," Bishop Odo said smiling, "it means 'Venerable,' 'Revered'," he paused a moment, studying my face. "You will come to earn it."

I was not so sure. I was on my path to becoming a man and had already experienced the sin of lust with my innocent fantasies of the lovely Countess of Toulouse. And some of the pretty servant girls in the castle had flirted with me, or at least that is what I thought they were doing. I blushed when I thought about them. But I thanked the Bishop for his kind words.

In the morning, I brought him his usual morning watery ale, a bowl of fruit and some bread, a basin of warm water and a fresh towel. He thanked me and waved me to leave him.

"Go, go, my Sébastien, leave me to my breakfast. I know how much you enjoy your swordplay with Bisol, you are both becoming extremely talented you know, I sometimes see you from the top of the tower. Very good, both of you. Hugues will be pleased. I think I shall write some letters from the comfort of my bed this morning. Come, let me bless you before you go."

It was not much later that I found myself on the beach standing next to Bisol, sword in hand, sweat dripping down the back of my tunic, a moment frozen in time, numbed, not sure I had heard what Tancarville telling me. I raced back up to the castle, taking steps two, three at a time as quickly as my gangly legs could carry me, almost falling into the Prince's apartment, catching the smooth stone frame of the door to steady myself.

Inside, I could see Duke Robert and Bohemond's physician on the near side of the bed and a priest on the far side leaning over the Bishop who was laying supine on it, blankets in disarray, parchments strewn across the bed and on the floor, an inkwell tipped over in its tray. I remember my eyes filling with tears as I began to comprehend and yet not: Bishop Odo was dead.

Slowly I walked into the room, barely breathing, studying his face as I approached. It was pale, yes, but it had been for so long as he struggled to regain his health. The Duke stood aside and allowed me to lean over to see for myself. Was there a slight smile on his face? Was I imagining that? I reached for his hand which was still warm to touch but I could feel what I could only imagine was the chill of death creeping into it. I knelt by the bed to say a prayer, I felt movement behind me, I thought the others had joined me but did not turn back to look. Fighting back the tears, I murmured,

*"Sanctos, subvenire! Veni ei obviam Angeli Domini! Accipite sisterent eum et animam suam Deo Altissimo. Det ueniam Christus, qui vocavit vos: ut te ipsum; paradisum deducant te Angeli sinum Abrahæ. Requiem aeternam dona ei, Domine, ut et luceat lux vestra eum in saecula. Amen."*

And then ran through the prayer again silently, in my own language,

'Saints of God, come to his aid! Come to meet him, Angels of the Lord! Receive his soul and present him to God the Most High. May Christ, who called you, take you to Himself; may Angels lead you to Abraham's side. Give him eternal rest, O Lord, and may your light shine on him forever. Amen.'

Resting back on my heels, my head still dropped as if in prayer, I only had one thought: 'My God, who would save our souls now?'

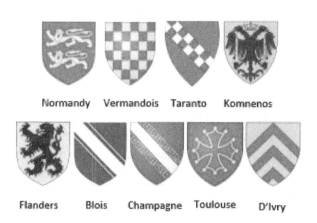

| Normandy | Vermandois | Taranto | Komnenos |
|---|---|---|---|

| Flanders | Blois | Champagne | Toulouse | D'Ivry |
|---|---|---|---|---|

# III

## Part One

## 1097 – Constantinople, Byzantium

The shock of Bishop Odo's death reverberated around the camp, shaking the men to their very core. It was not something any of us had considered possible and if it were not for the funeral procession held in Palermo and interment of his body at its basilica, both witnessed by my own eyes, I would not have believed it. Duke Robert had been gracious and generous, paying for all of the expenses the burial incurred, including the splendid tomb the prelate was laid in. I was told later by Bohemond's physician that the Bishop had been found on the stone floor, having gotten out of bed and then fallen. He and the Duke had come upon him, lifted him up and placed him on the bed, pushing the books and papers out of the way, knocking over the inkpot doing so. The physician reckoned the Bishop must have felt faint whilst he was writing his letters, and had tried to get help. There were no signs of injury or wounds on him, so he concluded it was either a fever of the brain or that his heart had given out.

Duke Robert made it clear, almost immediately afterward, that I was not to despair, that he would find a place for me in his retinue. And whilst the Prince's castle had been an oasis for us waiting out the wintry, gale-lashed seas, it lost its allure and Duke Robert decided to pack up and return to Brindisi. I carefully wrapped the Bishop's things, handling the vestment and mitre with particular care. The crozier had not been freed from the swathes of deep blue velvet cloth it had been wrapped in when we departed Sannicandro Castle and so I simply left it in the chest it had travelled in. I added his pectoral cross which I bundled in red velvet, and then covered all of his possessions with his cloak with the red silk cross sewn onto its breast, folded neatly on top, protecting its cargo awaiting its new owner. I shuddered on the thought, I could not begin to imagine who would take his place.

It was a slow and sombre ride for everyone, even stopping at Conversano to visit with the Duke's betrothed Lady Sybilla did not lighten the mood and soon we were back at Brindisi in the camps with the men. The Adriatic seas were still too rough to cross but this gave the Duke, Aumale and Blois time to revive their respective armies and prepare them for the crossing to Dyrrhachiumn and the trek beyond. Pope Urban and others sent messages conveying their shock and sorrow over Bishop Odo's death, the Duke allowed me to read all of them, each slightly reopening an emotional wound that was taking its time to heal. We were to meet with Adhémar de Monteil, Bishop of Le Puy, the Holy Father's choice for the spiritual leader of the crusade, who was still travelling with Toulouse since they set out from Lyon. But there was time for that later, now we had to make plans for our voyage across the sea.

Bohemond did not meet us in the port city. His nephew, Tancred d'Hauteville, a successful warrior in his own right, had decided to join his uncle to captain his army and the two men had taken advantage of a break in the bad weather a few weeks earlier, just before Bishop Odo's death, to sail forth from Brindisi. By our estimates, they would arrive in Constantinople sometime in April, just short of a month ahead of our own expected arrival.

We had known for a while that Bouillon had reached Constantinople just after Christmas, meeting up with Flanders who had arrived there ahead of him by only a few days, settling their armies just outside the city walls. They were joined by the remnants of Peter the Hermit is army, those that had survived the massacre at Nicaea. Some of them had become religious fanatics, marching barefoot and without weapons, and eating only the roots of plants, believing that God would lead them to victory. They were nicknamed Tafurs, Arabic for poverty-stricken, and they were brutal. Bouillon and Flanders did not mind what they did as long as they proved themselves to be good warriors and so left them alone.

And, of course, Vermandois had been in the city for quite a while and spent his time waiting for the others, hoping that with their arrival and ours he could return to Emperor Alexios's good graces after the debacle his journey had become. But despite a great showing of gifts and warm words of welcome, Alexios had not been completely trusting of the King of France's brother, and had kept Vermandois a virtual prisoner in a nearby monastery. Not that Vermandois realized.

Toulouse and his army were also expected in April, so we needed to get there at haste lest we miss the opportunity to join with the others and galvanise the troops into a united force. Duke Robert decided that as soon as the waters were less choppy, we would set off. That came sooner than we expected, and by early March and with Pope Urban's blessing, the ships were loaded with the men, their families, horses, arms, and carts loaded to overflowing with food and supplies for the long journey to Constantinople once we disembarked at Dyrrhachium.

The seas were reasonably calm for our voyage, the large single-mast cogs carving their way through the waves effortlessly and with little resistance. Only a few times did the waters become choppy and seasickness took hold with the expected result for some of the travellers, but my stomach held firm which was surprising as this was the first time I had been on a ship of this size. The royal galley was magnificent, the regal colours of Taranto flying high above us announcing to the world that we were on our way. I spent most of my time as close to the bow as I could, holding fast to the edge, gazing out to sea, the salty mists stinging my face and drenching my surcoat, but I did not mind. I breathed in the crisp cold air deeply and resolutely – I thought about my teacher the Bishop and silently swore to him I would do him proud. He would never have the chance to see Palestine, to visit the holy sites in the grand city of Jerusalem, to pray at the tomb in the Holy Sepulchre. I pledged I would do these things for him.

We landed at Dyrrhachium in the mid-afternoon of the second day and took the rest of the day unloading and setting up a temporary camp for the night. Bisol and I helped Duke Robert settle first, then helped others where we could. We would not be staying long; once the Duke sent his scouts ahead, we would soon follow.

Duke Robert had been rather reserved since we left the Castle of Scilla, understandably so. Bishop Odo's death had shocked him, probably more deeply than any of us. No doubt we shared the same belief that he was invincible, his death could not be conceived of, that he would always be here, with us, guiding us, teaching us. But now there was a void that may never be filled and this is what I am sure Duke Robert was struggling with. I missed my mentor and sorely felt his absence. We were fortunate to have other matters to occupy ourselves during the days that followed, contemplations of our own mortality were left to the stillness of the nights, staring into the ebbing flames of the fire pits we slept next to.

It was an arduous journey through the Macedonian mountains, facing occasional attacks by renegade imperial soldiers and local bandits thinking they were able to harass and rob; they were mistaken. Even so, the roads to Constantinople were surprisingly well-worn from the flow of trade that was ever-increasing between the Byzantine and the western worlds. Spirits were high amongst the men and the families that accompanied them and only increased the closer we got to the city and the spectacular scene that greeted us as the city walls came into view was unlike anything I, or many of us, could ever have imagined.

The city stretched further than one could see and was protected by a massive, seemingly impregnable, double set of stone walls seventy metres apart connecting four hundred towers and fifty-five gates stretching from the Sea of Marmara to the Golden Horn, manned by hundreds of imperial guards and each tower flying the Komnenos colours of black and gold. Bordered on three sides by water, the Sea of Marmara to the south, the Golden Horn to the north and the Bosporus Strait to the east, Constantinople was the centre of the world, where the cultures from east and west both coalesced and clashed in a vibrant intensity one could not escape. Not that one wanted to, Constantinople seduced men with a disquieting ease, once she touched you, it was difficult to leave her.

At the heart of the city, close to the Hagia Sophia and within sight of the Bosphorus, was the Great Palace which had been home to centuries of imperial rulers and their families. But the years had not been good to it and eventually a new palace needed to be built. The northern slopes of the Sixth Hill on the coast of the Golden Horn was the chosen site for the Palace of Blachernae. Like his most recent predecessors, Emperor Alexios had selected this Palace as his official residence and it was to here that we headed en masse, expecting to see the colours of the other armies who had reached there before us already having set up camp outside the north wall.

We were on our last leg of this part of the journey with just one more day's ride to reach the city ahead of us. Duke Robert had decided to camp for the night so that the preparations could be made to make an appropriately glorious entrance through the Blachernae Gate, with the noble members of the armies dressed in their finest leaving an indelible impression on those watching them approach. We had just finished supper sitting around an open fire when a scout who had been sent ahead to ensure the path was clear arrived back in camp with some unsettling news.

"Sire," the scout said, bowing as he greeted the Duke.

"What news?" Robert asked as he rose to stoke the fire.

"The roads are clear, sire, there should be no issue with reaching the city. We have posted guards along the way to ensure it. There is, ah..." he hesitated.

"Yes? What is it?" Robert barked.

"We gained sight of the army from Toulouse, sire, well encamped outside the north walls. But we were unable to see any evidence of the other armies. We travelled parallel to the walls for quite a distance, but whilst it was clear from the condition of the ground that a large mass of men had been there, they are no longer. Prince Bohemond, the Duke of Lorraine, the Count of Flanders, the Count of Vermandois, none are to be found."

Duke Robert stood still for a moment, then turned to Blois.

"There must be some mundane explanation for this or we would have heard something sooner, Toulouse will tell us when we arrive in the city tomorrow. No doubt our dear brother-in-arms le Magnus has done something to upset the Emperor," he surmised, referring to Vermandois.

"No doubt," Blois agreed.

We all slept under the stars that night, not bothering to set up any tents or structures. It was an easy and early start for all of us and we were mounted and ready to go before sunrise. As the scout had reported, the ride was clear and uneventful and we made good time. Duke Robert did not want to ride too far ahead, he wanted to make his arrival as spectacular and impressive as he could by having his army close behind. When we reached the top of the last hill before the Blachernae Gate, we confirmed the reports were correct and could only see the red and gold, twelve-pointed cross standard of Toulouse waving in the cool spring breeze, interspersed throughout the masses of men camped outside of the gate.

There was no sign of the others. Duke Robert pulled his horse to a halt to survey the sight. We could see the double walls we had been told about stretching from the sea to the north to beyond our sight to the south, the alternating stripes of red and white a meandering river of stone inviting and cautioning visitors as they approached. We spotted Toulouse's tents but could not see Count Raymond himself but we knew the sound and noise of the arrival of the Duke's armies would make him appear.

And so, our long, slow progress was about to reach its first end at the grand city whose Emperor had called for our aid so many months earlier. Our horses picked their way carefully down the rocky hill towards the gate and soon the ground trembled with the movement of thousands of footsteps and hooves and the wheels of supply carts, all pressing forward in a wave of unity towards the same destination. Duke Robert, Aumale and Blois were resplendent in their finest riding attire, with the senior men of their respective armies wearing their lords' colours with large standards being flown from poles either attached to their saddles or carried by hand supported by leather holders on their belts. As I was now officially a part of the Duke's court, I was allowed to have the Normandy golden lions on red flown from Pax but I also made sure the D'Ivry red and gold chevrons saddle blanket was clearly visible too.

It was clear from our vantage point where space had been used outside the city walls by the departed armies and now would be used for ours. Aumale and Saint-Agnan, the captains of the two armies, took instruction from Duke Robert, split away from our lead group and steered the armies in that direction to the south, leaving the Duke, Blois, myself and Bisol and a dozen guards to continue towards where Toulouse was camped along the northern portion of the wall.

As Duke Robert predicted, Toulouse emerged from his tent and spied us at a distance. We could see him giving instructions to one of his men, Viscount de Castillon, who then gave orders to others nearby, causing a flurry of activity around them both. We could also see the sentries coming to post on the battlements of the massive walls to watch our approach. The Emperor would have been notified as soon as we appeared on the horizon and it was expected some message would be waiting for the Duke once we reached Toulouse's camp. And of course I could not help but wonder if the Countess would be with him, I had not forgotten her.

We made our way through the swathes of crusaders in Toulouse's army, the closest immediately stopped what they were doing and stood silently, nodding the respect that was due the Duke. This caused a ripple effect amongst the rest of the army and soon we found ourselves in a sea of quiet humanity, the only movement from thousands bowing their heads or kneeling as the Duke and our group passed by. I felt honoured to be amongst them but I was not without a little twinge of sadness that my mentor was not with us to witness the sight.

Toulouse stood at attention at the entrance to his tent and watched as we dismounted and handed the reins of our horses to his squires who led them away for feeding and brushing down. Once Duke Robert was on the ground, he approached and bowed greeting him.

"Your Grace," he said.

"Raymond!" Robert exclaimed, opening his arms for a friendly embrace. "It does one good to see you well!"

"Thank you, I am well indeed. As are you, I assume?"

"Yes, yes, the roads and the weather were both favourable for us," he responded, taking off his riding gloves. "And even though we had to see off a small number of brigands who we met along the way, they were easily despatched."

"Thank the Lord. I have wine and food waiting for you inside," Toulouse said, motioning towards his tent.

"Excellent, my stomach has been growling for several hours," Robert said smiling. And then, becoming sombre, he added, "I assume you have been informed about the death of our dear Bishop Odo?"

Toulouse nodded.

"Yes. Tragic, not only as a personal loss for you, but also a great loss for our mission. He and his inspirational sermons will be greatly missed."

Duke Robert sighed.

"Indeed. But we must press on, it would have been what he wanted," he said and ducked through the tent's open flaps.

We each followed in turn with the guards remaining outside, Toulouse instructing his squires to make sure they were all fed. Bisol and I took our usual positions near the entrance to the tent but Duke Robert motioned for us to join them at the Count's table. This was startling; even though we had dined with the Duke and the other nobles at hastily built fire pits along the journey and made to feel as equals, we were not. Bisol and I hesitantly took a seat at the far end of the table, keeping a respectful distance from the nobles, gladdened to eat but also ready to do anything that was asked at a moment's notice.

"So, Raymond, where is your lovely Countess?" Robert inquired, and my ears pricked up.

Toulouse smiled.

"Ah, the Countess is lodging with the Emperor. He graciously offered apartments in the Palace, we thought it best that she stay there whilst awaiting your arrival. I shall send for her...."

"No need," Robert interjected. "I am sure we shall have the pleasure of her company when we arrive at the Emperor's court which I am assuming will be shortly? Did he leave any word for me?"

"Yes he did, your Grace. His imperial Majesty has sent his warmest greetings and welcome to you and the nobles accompanying you on this great quest. And he bids you attend upon him as soon as you are able, he is eager to discuss the strategies for the battles ahead," he said, delivering the Emperor's message.

"Good, we shall enter the city tomorrow, could you please send word tonight?"

"Of course, your Grace."

"Excellent. Now, Raymond, where are the others? Crossing the crest of the hill we could see none of the other armies, none of the warriors or any of the colours of the nobles."

Toulouse grimaced and Duke Robert leaned back in his chair, bracing himself for bad news.

"Much has happened but you must first know that the others are safe," Toulouse began.

"I am relieved to hear it especially considering what has happened to the previous armies who passed this way," Robert responded.

"I am sure you are aware of the troubles Vermandois encountered on the crossing the Adriatic? Well, shortly after he and his capsized army had been rescued and escorted here by the imperial troops, Bouillon arrived with his large numbers and the Emperor became concerned about how to provide supplies for such a massive amount of people knowing that more were on their way and due to arrive at any time."

"I am not sure I understand why he was concerned," Robert said. "His support of troops and provision of supplied were part of the agreement he made with the Holy Father when he asked for help fighting the Seljuks, he knew what he needed to provide."

"Indeed. But he seems to have had other issues to deal with. The Emperor has been insisting that the nobles leading armies into his lands swear an oath of fealty to him and to agree to return to him any lands that were his and taken by the Turks. And that is where he found some difficulty.

"Vermandois acceded immediately, he had no choice considering the position in which he found himself, indebted to the Emperor for saving him and his army. It only took being asked once for him to swear the oath. And Bouillon," Toulouse started but Robert interrupted.

"What about Godfrey?" Duke Robert demanded, suddenly concerned about one of this crusade's most important leaders.

"Bouillon refused to swear because his feudal lord is Emperor Henry who is currently at odds with Alexios. So he stalled, refusing to discuss it and saying he was waiting for the other leaders to arrive. But then the Emperor began to withhold food and other supplies, and Bouillon had no choice but to acquiesce. It has, unfortunately, created a rather hostile and distrusting relationship between them. I am not convinced Bouillon has any intention of keeping the oath but time will tell. The Count of Flanders took the oath without incident, I am assuming that is because you instructed him to do so if it was asked of him?"

Robert nodded, taking a long drink from his tankard.

"Yes, that was agreed in Saint-Denis. I am surprised by Bouillon, but then again I can understand why he would not want to upset Henry. He is funding Bouillon's army after all. Henry will not be pleased to hear Alexios is playing games like this."

"Indeed. Once the Emperor was made aware that Bohemond was soon to arrive and my own army soon after, he decided that Bouillon, Vermandois and Flanders needed to be moved on. He convinced them by offering his ships to cross the Bosphorus as well as more supplies and funds than originally agreed. Bouillon and the others thought it best to go, and so they went, now settled in Civetot awaiting our arrival."

"Probably the correct decision although I would have expected him to wait for Bohemond at least," Robert said. "What of him?"

Toulouse sat back in his chair.

"It is unfortunate that they did not wait, Bohemond arrived with his three thousand men and Tancred's two thousand very shortly thereafter. The relationship between Bohemond and the Emperor is strained at best, has been since Bohemond and his father's army waged war against the Emperor a decade ago. Alexios naturally insisted on receiving homage from Bohemond to prove his loyalty which Bohemond did freely, although I suspect he really has no intention to keep it. Especially when Alexios refused to make him his chief commander in Asia. This allegiance may not hold but, for now, it is in place."

Toulouse gave some thought and then chuckled.

"Well, at least it is with Bohemond even if it is not with Tancred," he said taking a mouthful of ale.

"What do you mean?" asked Robert.

"He refused to swear. Claimed he never trusted the Byzantines, slipped away at night to avoid taking the oath. He may be difficult, but I have to admire his moral character, he remained steadfast by what he felt he could or rather could not do even if that meant adding to the wariness betwixt his uncle and the Emperor."

"Let us hope that does not come back to haunt him," Robert said. "And you? "

"I arrived the day after Bohemond and Tancred sailed," Toulouse continued. "I am assuming they will be with the other armies by now. I have met with the Emperor and, as expected, he demanded the oath from me. But this," he sighed, "I could not do."

Duke Robert looked startled and started to speak but Toulouse stopped him, raising his hands in a pacifying manner, calming him.

"Have no worries, your Grace, I reached an agreement with the Emperor that suits us both. I swore an oath of friendship rather than allegiance, and promised to return any Byzantine lands we conquered back to him. He was satisfied with this, or at least that is what he has said to me."

"Keeping Alexios in our good favour is key to our success for our progress through Anatolia," Robert said. "I shall give homage to him tomorrow as will Blois," he added, pointing his thumb at his brother-in-law who had remained silent throughout the conversation, too busy with his stew. Robert stared at him for a moment then turned back to Raymond. "And Bishop Le Puy? Is he here with you?"

"Yes, he arrived last week, he had become ill in Thessalonica, so we continued on without him, I left some of my guard to escort him when he was well. We did not encounter many problems en route, save one involving him. His Excellency had the habit of wandering away from the main body of the marching army, I noticed this early on and instructed my man Castellon to keep watch. Unfortunately, he lost sight of the Bishop on one occasion and Le Puy was set upon by a group of mercenaries before Castellon could reach him. He was beaten and they took what belongings he had, he was only saved when Castellon finally got to him. It frightened him somewhat, but I believe it has cured his habit of wandering too far from the crowd."

"He will need to take on the responsibilities from Bishop Odo, do you think he is up to the task?" Robert asked.

"The Holy Father believed in him, I have no doubt when the moment arrives, he will rise to the occasion," Toulouse responded.

Duke Robert was not convinced but he had more important matters to deal with than a shaken cleric who was foolish enough to stray from the only source of protection near him.

"You will accompany us to the Palace tomorrow?" Robert asked.

"Of course, your Grace. We are united as we ever have been, and the Emperor needs to be shown that."

* * * * * * * * * *

The messenger sent by Duke Robert the previous evening had returned with a warm welcome from the Emperor, a few chests of gold and an invitation to come to the Palace mid-morning the next day, when they could conduct the formalities required between members of royal houses before sharing the mid-day meal. So we rose early the next morning, taking mass before dawn, led by Bishop Le Puy who seemed to have been cured of both his fright and illness as there was no sign of either in his speech and manner.

Afterwards, Bisol and I helped Duke Robert and Blois into their most formal attire, the Duke in his robes of crimson and gold and Blois in silver and blue. Duke Robert thought it best to wear a thin, gold ringlet crown signifying his royal status without overshadowing the Emperor. Toulouse had chosen not to wear his colours which were similar to those of the Duke but instead wore robes of white trimmed in red and gold. All had decided not to wear their maille as that would have been seen as provocative and a display of distrust and there was no desire to insult the Emperor.

Duke Robert had ordered a few dozen of his guards to attend him on his entrance to the city and Aumale arrived leading them on horseback in full military ceremonial splendour. Toulouse and Blois also decided to bring men and had them dressed in colours matching their respective masters. Bishop Le Puy and Bisol, Saint-Agnan, Castellon and myself attending our lords rounded out the leading group in the procession, with the Duke Robert's standard bearer, Pagan de Peverel, at the Duke's side.

At the appointed hour, with a cool breeze coming from the north off the waters of the Golden Horn and the morning sun rising through a cloudless sky, we mounted our horses, me on trusty Pax, and headed out of the camp and along the outer wall to the south, towards Karagümrük Gate. There were a number of gates in wall between where we were camped and the one we were to use to enter the palace grounds, but the Karagümrük Gate was the ceremonial entrance used by Emperors past and present. Duke Robert, whilst intending to pay homage to the Emperor, also wanted to make sure his royal status was recognized. And he also wanted those watching from the towers and the battlements to see him approach, impressed and awed by his formality and ceremony. As would be the crowds that would rush to come see the spectacle once we passed through into city and made our way to the Palace.

As we marched our processional next to the outer wall, our presence was announced by horns blasted from the battlements. We could hear what sounded like crowds gathering on the other side, come to see the western visitors, their curiosity outweighing any sense of threat. We reached the Karagümrük Gate, and saw it had two doors, both unlocked and open, entreating us to come through. We were told later that they were always opened at sunrise as was the custom for all of the entrances to the city. And they would be shut and locked again at sunset. We passed through the arch in the first wall and then through that in the second wall, slowing the horses to a steady walk. Crowds were forming and lining the path to the Palace, wanting to have a good look at the strangers and yet keeping a respectful distance and allowing our group to get through unhindered. We were not the first crusaders from the West to arrive in the city, but seeing the brother of the King of England was a rare sight.

The Palace itself was built to impress and made its mark despite being positioned relatively close to the defensive walls. We had effectively walked back upon ourselves by the time we reached the Palace, and realized we ended up closer to where we had camped than to the Karagümrük Gate where we had entered the city. But this mattered not, we enjoyed our progress through the streets and seeing the people of Constantinople and being so well received by them.

I thought about the others who had preceded us along this path to meet with the Emperor and swear their oaths to him. I wondered if they had been so welcomed as we were now. We had been told that the Emperor disliked ceremonies and rituals and preferred to spend his time hunting; the smaller gates in the walls nearer the Palace allowed him to escape to the forests west of the city and slip back in undetected. It was no wonder that he found himself annoyed by Vermandois who lived and breathed extravagant ceremony and had sent him on his way; it would be interesting to see how he would respond to Duke Robert who shared his views and to Blois who did not.

The path took us to the side of the Palace and then around to its front which faced the waters of the Golden Horn and the imperial port. The red and white striped pattern of the walls continued in the palace's design, only more ornate and intricate in its decoration of the arches and balustrades of the balconies above. There were five large, tall, open arches along this face which led to an open courtyard and the main entrance to the Palace itself. Immense vertical banners with the house of Komnenos black, double-headed eagle clutching silver swords on a background of gold were hanging on either side of the arches. Imperial guards stood at attention and did not move as we approached.

Duke Robert brought his steed to a halt just outside the triple arches and dismounted, handing the reins of his horse to one of his guards who had moved in place beside him. Another of his guards assisted Bishop Le Puy and one each of Toulouse's and Blois's guards did the same for their masters, allowing them to dismount and join the Duke. Glancing around, he pointed first to Aumale and then to me, indicating we should join him and guards moved into place to take control of our horses. Bisol, Saint-Agnan, Castellon stayed where there were, saddled and at attention.

Without a word, the six of us passed through the centre archway into the inner courtyard which was beautifully tiled with a black and white checkerboard floor stretching the length of the building. At the opposite side of the courtyard to where we entered were stone steps, lined with more imperial guards, leading to three more arched entrances. It was through the centre arch that our host and ally, the Byzantine Emperor Alexios Komnenos, appeared without announcement or fanfare but with his retainers in tow, one man in particular slightly ahead of the others.

Not a tall man, the Emperor's strength, much like the Duke's, was in his sturdy build, well-proportioned and muscular, being made all the more impressive with his choice of a gold studded black tunic and matching robes which swirled about him as he strode through the arches and down the steps. His face had a ruddy complexion, muchly hidden behind a thick, woolly black beard and moustache, and emanated a warm, luminescent glow when he smiled. He wore the traditional headdress of the Byzantine Emperors, a gold, enamel and jewel-encrusted diadem that dangled two sets of gold chained pendoulia with precious stones from the gold headband just above his temples.

Upon the appearance of the Emperor, Duke Robert immediately knelt on one knee and we all followed suit with the exception of Le Puy who bowed his head, signifying the respect that was due to the Emperor from a Bishop. Alexios approached the kneeling Duke and touched him gently on the shoulder.

"You are most welcome," he said cordially, adding "Please let me embrace you as a brother."

Duke Robert stood and the two men hugged, clasping each other firmly, each showing their strength.

"I have with me the Counts of Blois and Aumale, and of course you are aware of the Holy Father's representative and our crusade's spiritual leader, Bishop Adhémar of Le Puy," he said pointing to each in turn.

"You are all welcome," Alexios said enthusiastically. "Come, let us drink and celebrate your arrival, we have many things to discuss," he added and turned back from whence he came.

We followed as we were bid. The interior of the Palace was grandly constructed, with marble columns and vaulted arches leading to other open areas and rooms which lead to more open areas and rooms, and giving access to the floors above. It was, rather oddly, sparsely furnished but I surmised that may have been due to obvious renovations being done to extend and fortify the building that I had seen being done to the exterior of the Palace and continued inside.

Alexios led us into a massive, multi-storied hall that could easily hold a hundred or more, its walls decorated with alternating ornate tapestries and more es banners. Its most stunning feature was its vaulted brick ceiling covered in mesmerising mosaic tiles depicting past Komnenos Emperors and Christ and his saints. The artistry of the place was enthralling, the skill needed to create such an architectural masterpiece jaw-dropping. It was all I could do to not stare and gape and try not to look impressed which I could not help but be.

At the far end of the hall was a set of three steps that ran the length of the end of the room, leading to a landing where two large wooden thrones covered in gold velvet, one slightly smaller and less opulent than its mate, stood awaiting their owners. Behind the thrones I could see two entrances at both corners with doors open, inviting us in. Alexios stopped when he reached the top stair and turned.

"I believe we have some formalities to attend to before we start our discussions?" he said without really asking. "I think this would be the appropriate time, Taticius?" he said, again without really asking, to the man who was shadowing him.

"Indeed, your Highness," Taticius responded.

I studied the man for a moment. I recognized his name from listening to Duke Robert and the others tell battle stories of the past around the fire pits in the evenings on our journey here. He was a hard-looking man, military through and through, from many years doing battle in honour of his Emperor, his broad shoulders carrying the weight of the Byzantine wars with the Seljuk Turks. He was the Emperor's right-hand man just as the Count of Aumale was the Duke Robert's.

We gathered in a semi-circle around the Duke and Blois as the Emperor took his seat on the larger throne. Duke Robert took his sword from his scabbard, climbed the three steps and knelt on one knee directly in front of the Emperor, leaning slightly on the sword which was now pointing down touching the flagstones, arms outstretched, both hands grasping the pommel on the hilt. The room went eerily quiet as we all fell silent, waiting for Duke Robert to speak.

"I, Robert, Duke of Normandy, promise upon my faith," Robert began in a strong, confident voice that never hesitated or failed, "that I shall, for as so ever long this crusade shall last, be faithful to his Imperial Majesty, Emperor Alexios Komnenos of Byzantium. I pledge to return to him Byzantine lands lost to the infidel. I vow to never cause him harm and will observe my homage to him completely against all persons who oppose him in good faith and without deceit," he concluded solemnly.

The Emperor leaned forward and wrapped his hands on the outside of Duke Robert's.

"I, Emperor Alexios of Byzantium, accept your most reverent homage paid here today in front of these witnesses and welcome you as a vassal of the Byzantine empire. I vow to support Normandy's endeavours in the battles with the Seljuk Turks and enemies of the empire."

Duke Robert bowed his head and then after a moment, stood, bowed again and then backed his way down the steps and re-joined our group. The Emperor leaned back in his throne, contented that he had received the oath of allegiance from one of the most powerful men in Christendom. We all watched Blois repeat the vow Duke Robert had just given almost verbatim and then was received by the Emperor as a vassal of Byzantium. Even though it was over all rather quickly, the brief ceremony was a vital cog in the wheel of support that we crusaders needed to pursue our goal of defeating the enemy armies we were to face on our way to Jerusalem. We could only hope that the vows given on both sides would hold. It would take some time, but those hopes unfortunately would be dashed.

Before sitting down to the mid-day meal, Alexios wanted to show us his pride and joy, the fragments of the cross and the nails used for the crucifixion, found by Emperor Constantine's mother Helena and sent back to him in Constantinople and which were now in Alexios's possession. This, of course, was what we had all hoped for, to come close to and possibly touch an actual relic from our Saviour's crucifixion.

Alexios guided us through a maze of corridors deeper and deeper into the Palace and then into a series of rooms that led off each other, each manned by his personal guards. Upon reaching what seemed to be the last room, we entered to see an empty room but with what looked like another wooden door on the opposite side, with wide iron braces running back and forth across it, and heavy chains with locks attached on either side. Alexios waited until the doors we came through were closed and then snapped his fingers. One of his men who had entered the room with us unlocked the locks and slid the thick chains through their rings, resting them gently onto the floor. He then took hold of the right side of the door and pushed it along the wall, revealing a recessed area protected by black iron bars that were buried deep into the stone floor and ceiling. Alexios then reached for a lit torch and brought it close so we could all see what was sitting on a stone platform, carved out of the rock.

On a bed of blue velvet sat Constantine's helmet, the very one he had constructed using a few fragments of the cross and one of the nails used in the crucifixion. He had this done for he believed something that had touched the Saviour would give one special powers. Beside that was a bridle that had been made using another nail and in between these two was the third nail and a few more fragments of the Cross. We had seen coins with his image wearing this helmet with the chi-rho symbol as its crest and yet now we were seeing it, sitting in front of us.

The room had gone completely still, no one wanted to breathe for fear of disturbing the peace that had descended upon us. Slowly, one by one, we all crossed ourselves and fell to our knees in prayer. We were in awe, blessed to be in the presence of such great things. Alexios waited patiently for all of us to take in the sight and step up to get as close a look as we could and when we had all had done so, he had his man push the door back in place, re-hang the chains and re-lock the locks, giving the keys to Alexios who pocketed them. The door to the room was then opened and we silently made our way back through the maze of hallways, Alexios leading the way, thankfully as none of us would have been able to remember the way. It was an experience burned into my memory.

The Emperor then treated us to a magnificent meal in his dining hall where there was a lot of talk about those who had come before and what was going to happen next. Alexios confirmed that Flanders, Bouillon and Bohemond had taken the oath, no mention of Bohemond's nephew Tancred's evasion of it was made, probably because the Emperor thought it made him look weak. He thought highly of Bouillon and his brother Baldwin and had confidence in their abilities to lead their armies into battle. He was not so impressed with Vermandois, he thought him arrogant and without honour, and was happy to see the back of him.

Duke Robert and the Emperor fell into deep conversation about capturing Jerusalem, the Emperor considered it to be part of Byzantium and insisted that it be returned to his rule once the crusaders had taken it back under their control. That, of course, would be up for debate if and when that happened. But the real focus was on Nicaea and how to win it back from the Seljuk Turks. Taticius was going to join the fight, leading a Byzantine force of about two thousand men. Having already fought the Seljuk Turks, he would be able to provide a wealth of information on their tactics and fighting methods, and the men would help swell the numbers of the crusader armies. He would represent the Emperor on the field and he was enthusiastically welcomed by the others.

The next few hours were spent studying various maps, determining the best courses to take, imagining as many what-if situations that we could so that fall-back options could be factored in, and sharing as much information known about the tactics of the enemy we were going to be facing. The Emperor had promised gold, silver and other treasure, horses, pack mules, foodstuffs and wine to support the armies when he sent his ambassadors to the Holy Father and he spoke of this promise in detail assuring us that those supplies were at his fingertips and waiting for his instructions. All seemed to be going very well and as planned. Duke Robert and the others seemed pleased with the discussions with the Emperor and his men.

It was as these conversations were waning when the doors to the hall opened and the Countess of Toulouse appeared with two ladies by her side and we all scrambled to stand as she approached. Just as I remembered her, beautiful and radiant. Her dark red velvet gown, with a fitted bodice and long sleeves which widened at the elbows, lined in white silk, flowed around her. A white wimple was wrapped around her head and neck, falling gracefully across her shoulders, completely covering the golden tresses I knew were there from seeing her in Lyon. From her hips hung a silver chain girdle which came together and continued down the front of her skirt almost touching the floor. I felt a flush of excitement, a slight heat rising in my cheeks. Thankfully, this time no one noticed.

"My lady," Toulouse greeted her, reaching out and taking her hand, gently kissing the back of it.

"My lord," the Countess responded and curtsied slightly as did her ladies, nodding to the others in the room. Turning to the Emperor, she continued with another curtsey, "Please forgive the intrusion your Majesty."

"No forgiveness needed when greeted with such beauty," Alexios replied beaming, clearly taken with her.

"I believe our discussions here are done, your Majesty?" Robert asked.

"Indeed," Alexios responded. "I assume you wish to return to your camps to begin preparations for your departure?"

"Yes sire," said Robert, adding, "If our horses could be sent for, we shall depart now before the gates are closed for the night."

"Is this where we are to bid you adieu?" Alexios said to the Countess. "It has been a pleasure having you grace our court."

She blushed and glanced down.

"Thank you, sire. It has been a joy to stay within the walls of the palace but I too must prepare for the departure, and so I return to the camps with my lord," she said, looking at Toulouse with a smile.

"And so it shall be. I have no doubt our paths will cross again," the Emperor responded.

# III

# Part Two

# 1097 – Nicaea, Anatolia

By the time all the armies had come together in early June, we reckoned we would number almost sixty thousand mostly consisting of fighting men but also including women, children, and clergy. It had been agreed during discussions with the Emperor that, with the armies as large as they were, staggering the movement of the troops would be best and so Toulouse and Taticius and their men set off two weeks ahead of Duke Robert's and Blois's armies. We moved to the coast and camped on the beaches of the Golden Horn awaiting the return of the imperial ships to port so we could make our departure as quickly as possible. We crossed the Bosphorus without incident and were shortly on our way over land to join up with the others.

Duke Robert decided to by-pass Civetot and instead go directly to Nicaea as he had been alerted that the other crusader armies had already departed Civetot and marched to the city. Toulouse and Taticius had arrived ahead of us and had joined the other leaders only to find them already entrenched around the city on three sides, the fourth bordered by Lake Ascania which the Turks controlled. The walls of the city were massive, protected by two hundred towers and battlements manned by many. We found Bohemond encamped outside the north gate, Toulouse with Bishop Adhémar outside the eastern gate, and Flanders, Bouillon and his brother Baldwin outside the southern gate. They were grateful not only for our armies to support their numbers but also for the food and supplies we brought as theirs were dangerously low.

We were told once we arrived that attacks on the crusader armies had been occurring with increasing frequency, more so with the hurried return of Arslan, the Sultan of the city, who had rather arrogantly decided that the crusading armies posed no threat – he had, after all defeated Peter the Hermit is pitiful band of warriors - and had left weeks earlier for a conflict in the east leaving his family and his treasure in the city. He had seen off imperial forces before this and apparently believed the new Western armies would do no better. Besides, he had been aware of the crusader presence in Civetot for quite some time and had stockpiled supplies in preparation for a lengthy siege. But the news that reached him was worrisome enough to cause him to return, only to find his capital surrounded by thousands of enemy soldiers setting up camp. He launched a surprise attack on Toulouse who was caught unprepared and if it had not been for Bouillon coming to his rescue, Toulouse surely would have been defeated. Once Bohemond arrived, the crusading armies were organized into a real fighting force and, using the knowledge of Muslim and Byzantine fighting tactics Bohemond had learned when fighting Emperor Alexios those many years ago, the tide turned and the Turks soon fled the field.

Scores of men were lost on each side. After the battle, the crusader dead were buried nearby whilst the bodies of the Turk fighters were moved far away from our camps, upwind so the stench of the rotting bodies did not reach us. But no burial was given, a huge insult to the Seljuks. The Sultan took what was left of his army and escaped to the hills. But we would see him again.

Since then, the armies had been besieging the town for weeks before we arrived, without much success. The lake provided the enemy a way of getting food and other supplies into the town unhampered by any of the crusading forces. Duke Robert knew he had to somehow get ships into the lake to block this supply route and he entreated the Emperor to send some of his fleet as quickly as he could. This would entail sailing to the coast near Civetot and then transporting the ships overland, which would use a large number of powerful but slow-moving oxen and take a considerable amount of time. The Emperor had been keeping himself abreast of all that was happening at Nicaea, albeit from a safe distance, and agreed to send a number of ships as well as his army of mounted archers and light cavalry, ready to engage in battle once they arrived.

The leaders knew they needed a different plan of attack from the lengthy siege, the method of warfare they usually employed and had been so successful with in the past. With regularly receiving fresh supplies via the lake, they knew the city could hold out much longer and that despite their attacks, the tall walls stood steadfast. We needed to find a way in. We gathered in Duke Robert's tent which had been erected next to Bohemond's at the north gate.

"I think I have found it!" Toulouse exclaimed unfurling a crude map of the city, its walls and gates, and pointed to what looked like a tower near the east gate.

"Here," he said and all leaned in. "Gonatas Tower, looks to have taken damage over the years, it clearly leans to the south. Its strength has been compromised, making it the weakest point in the walls. If we could get close enough to excavate the stones at the base, we could topple it," he finished and stood straight, his hands firmly on his hips, staring down at the map.

The others considered it a moment. Bouillon offered his opinion.

"I think it is a good plan," he said, rubbing the beard on his chin. "But how do we get at it? Our men will be felled by enemy arrows before they can reach it."

"I have thought of that," Toulouse said and produced another parchment with what looked like a hastily drawn sketch of a circular siege engine, about eight feet tall and with some sort of covering. "Thick leather instead of a wooden cover to keep the weight manageable and to protect the sappers underneath as they're digging," he said answering the question we were all thinking. "It should protect them from anything being thrown or shot from above. Wheels and push levers underneath to move it in any direction needed. We build it out of range of the Turks's arrows, they will see it from their vantage point but will not be able to do anything to stop it. That should frighten them somewhat."

Duke Robert straightened up and spoke.

"Excellent, let us get it done. Toulouse, take control of this, use whomever and whatever you require."

Suddenly, loud shrieks and cries could be heard coming from outside the tent and one of the sentries rushed in.

"Apologies, your Grace," he said out of breath and looking from man to man. "One of your men, Ralph de Montpinçon, was cut down as he tried to scale the walls. We are unable to retrieve his body, our men cannot reach him because of the arrow shot."

"Show me," Robert responded and followed the sentry out of the tent, the rest of us following closely.

Ralph de Montpinçon was a long-serving, trusted warrior in the Duke's army, brave, steadfast, and obedient and his single-minded attack was quite out of character. We reached the boundary edge safe from the Turks' projectiles and could see his body crumpled at the base of the wall and other soldiers attempting to reach it, only to be driven back. Eventually they all retreated and the enemies' arrows stopped their assault. For a moment we felt we were in a standoff with an invisible foe. Two men then appeared at the top of the wall, hoisting over a strange-looking device with some sort of large metal claws attached to a chain. The men began slowly lowering it until it reached our poor man's body. The claws were dragged back and forth until it caught hold of his clothing and, finally having secured the body, slowly drew it back up and over the top of the wall.

We all stood in shock, watching this horrible scene unravel before us, powerless to do anything about it. But worse was to come. Just as we were beginning to think the spectacle was over, loud shouts came from the top of the wall and Montpinçon, now naked and with a rope around his neck, was dropped down, swaying to and fro like a sickening pendulum. The message the Turks were sending was clear, a warning of what would befall us if we continued to try to take the city.

Duke Robert was incensed.

"Get out of my way," he shouted, rushing through the crowds of men watching this horror in front of them.

But Aumale caught and restrained him.

"Your Grace," he said, holding the Duke by the arm and trying to gain eye contact with him. "He is gone, there is nothing we can do for him."

But Duke Robert struggled to be free of his grasp and turned to Aumale in a fury.

"Despicable," he shouted, his anger unfettered and raw. "We cannot let this go unanswered!"

Aumale did his best to make Duke Robert see reason and shook him.

"Your Grace!" he said again trying to get the Duke's attention, "Your Grace!" and then, quietly so only Duke Robert and those standing closest to him could hear, "Robert, you must let it go. For now. I swear by God's blood, Montpinçon will be avenged, but now you must regain control," he said, almost hissing.

Duke Robert stopped trying to wriggle free and stared at his man. He knew he was right, there was nothing anyone could do for Montpinçon.

"He was one of my best men," Duke Robert answered, his voice filled with incredulity and anguish, "he's been with me since Rouen twenty years ago."

"As long as there is life left in our fight, the Turks will be punished for this," Aumale assured him.

Duke Robert nodded. Retribution would have to wait. He stepped back from Aumale.

"Have our best archer cut him down and retrieve his body under the cover of dark," he said, speaking his words gravely.

Aumale bowed and moved quickly to carry out the orders.

Duke Robert stood a moment, watching the macabre scene. He was determined there would be consequences for this unholy act. This he would remember.

\* \* \* \* \* \* \* \* \* \*

The work on the large circular siege engine began immediately after the incident with Montpinçon, using the natural materials readily available from the nearby woods. As designed by Toulouse, the sappers pushing the war machine would be protected by a thick, hardened leather covering that would deflect arrows from above as well as anything else that could be flung down upon them from rocks and boulders to hot sand.

It took a small group of men a few days to build it, and as soon as it was determined to be war-worthy, it was rolled from behind the hill where it was constructed and pulled it to within full view of the Turkish defenders gawking from the top of the walls, trying to determine what it was they were looking at. A handful of Toulouse's men were selected for the task and positioned themselves inside the machine, ready to advance it to the Gonatas Tower without worrying about being attacked, injured, or worse.

Duke Robert, Toulouse, Aumale, Blois, Bohemond, and Tancred stood atop a rocky outcrop overlooking the camps below. I was in attendance on the Duke as usual and stood next to him fixated, fascinated by the movements below. From this position we could observe the progress of the newly built siege machine and the leaders could shout or signal orders to their men below. It was early afternoon and the winds had picked up which Toulouse reckoned would help once the fires were lit. The time of the day for the attack was chosen specifically as it was hoped that if successful the tower's collapse would happen in the darkness of night, it would heighten the sense of panic that would ensue.

The sappers started off slowly, picking up pace once the large wheels of the engine grabbed hold of the ground beneath it. As soon as they reached within range of the Turkish archers they knew the strength of the cover would be tested and sure enough they could hear arrows and stones bouncing off the leather, landing harmlessly beside them. They reached the leaning tower without loss of a single man and soon were hacking away with their iron tools, loosening the stones at the tower's base, and digging down underneath the tower's walls. The stones were replaced with large pieces of firewood and piles of kindling were added through several trips back and forth to retrieve more. The leaders hoped this would lead to the tower's collapse when the kindling was set ablaze and further weakened the foundation.

Duke Robert stared intently at the action, taking it all in, standing as still as a statue, his arms crossed in front of his chest, his dark eyes missing nothing. As soon as he saw the siege engine starting to reverse its steps after packing the last of the firewood, he knew the sappers' work was done and gave an almost imperceptible nod which was the signal to Toulouse to ready the fire. Toulouse shouted the orders to some men below and we could see flames take hold in the torches the men were gripping, readying themselves to take the place of the diggers as the siege engine approached. The exchange of men was made and they started off again towards the tower, reaching it quickly and setting fire to the piles of wood then returning to where they started, just out of the enemies' arrow range. All of this was observed by the guards atop of the walls and cries soon went out warning of what was about to happen. We stood watching as the Turks's attempts to stop our men failed. The blaze took hold and as expected panic spread and we could hear the shouts getting louder and more frantic.

Duke Robert, satisfied with what he was seeing, turned to the other leaders.

"That blaze will burn for a while, set some guard to keep eye on it through the night. Hopefully, it will do what it needs to and we will be in Nicaea by sext," he said and then left them, returning to his tent.

The fire burned for hours, sending smoke and sparks up into the dark, cloudy night sky like shimmering ghostly spirits flickering momentarily alive and then dying out. The captains took turns to keep watch whilst the others rested as the fire continued into the early hours of the morning. Every once in a while a cracking sound could be heard but none of the crashing sounds of a massive tower coming down we were hoping for. Eventually the flames burned out, and we were left with having to wait til dawn to see what damage had been done. And what greeted us was both shocking and impressive.

Gonatas Tower had indeed suffered damage but not as we had expected. The fire had taken hold and further weakened an already weak base, causing the tower to collapse, but back onto itself, not outwards. If it had, the tower would have come down completely. Remarkably, the damage was negligible and, even worse, had been repaired by the Turks by the following morning. They had used the cover of darkness to their advantage to reinforce parts of the tower to make it withstand any further assault. We had overestimated both the strength of the fire which caused it to burn too quickly thus causing the damage to occur earlier in the night, and underestimated the tenacity of the enemy who wasted no time in getting the tower even stronger than when we had left it the day before. It was devastating and awe-inspiring to see, at least to me it was.

Unfortunately, Duke Robert did not see it the same way and was furious to see our efforts had failed. I watched him storm over to Aumale who seemed transfixed by the sight before him only to have his amazement roughly broken by the Duke snapping at him. Hushed words were followed by Aumale nodding and hurrying away to do some bidding for the Duke. I could tell by the look on his face that this was not going to be good.

I saw Flanders in the distance making his way up the hill towards where Duke Robert and I were standing and was gladdened to see Hugues de Payns behind him. After a short discussion, I saw the Duke gesture towards his tent and pointed to me to join them and I hurried over. Flanders ignored me as he and Duke Robert continued speaking as they walked but Hugues clearly remembered me from our encounter months earlier in Clermont and nodded a greeting.

"Ah, young D'Ivry," he said, clasping me by the shoulder, "I see you have arrived unscathed since Clermont!"

"Indeed I have, m'lord," I responded, adding, "although…"

"I was disheartened to hear of Bishop Odo's death," he interrupted, reading my mind. "He will be missed."

I remained silent, glancing at the muddy ground under my feet.

"Bisol tells me you have become quite the swordsman from your training these past months, yes?" he asked, carefully changing the subject.

"I am working hard on it," I replied, not wanting to appear arrogant and full of myself even though I had felt there was a vast improvement in my fighting skills.

"You can never stop expanding your knowledge," Hugues said. "There is always more to learn, in many things not just your blade."

I wanted to ask what he meant but we had reached the entrance to the Duke's tent and our conversation stopped as we entered. Duke Robert's retainer Tancarville had prepared a meal of biscuits and salted meats and had already poured warm ale in a number of pewter goblets. Duke Robert motioned for all of us to sit and partake. He and Flanders continued their discussion as they sat down at the table.

"It is what they deserve!" Robert barked at Flanders, who gave an almost imperceptible shrug. "What news on the imperial fleet?" Robert asked, taking a swig of his ale.

"They are expected shortly, we believe within the next two days," Flanders responded, breaking off a piece of biscuit and then skewering some salted meat.

"Good, I cannot see another way to conquer this damnable city without taking control of the lake ports and starving them out!" Robert declared.

We finished the rest of the meal in silence.

Within an hour we knew what Duke Robert had commanded Aumale to do. One of the mangonels which had been used earlier in the battles to try to batter the city's walls without much success was rolled into place facing the portion of the wall next to the Gonatas Tower. And behind it came a horse-drawn cart, filled to the brim with something, but with what we could not see as it was covered with a leather tarp. Aumale had alerted Robert that they were ready and we made our way out to where the mangonel was positioned.

Men were tightening the torsion spring made of thick ropes and cranking the cupped arm back into place, making it so tight the entire catapult creaked as if in pain. It was then that I saw what the intended payload was as the tarp was pulled back. Stacked, one on top of another, were heads of Seljuk Turks that had been killed in the battles over the past weeks. Duke Robert had ordered them detached from their bodies and brought here to be used in grisly retaliation against the Turks for what they had done to Montpinçon, for the failure at the Gonatas Tower, and for the relative impotence the crusading armies had had so far in trying to defeat the enemy and drive them out of Nicaea. It was with horror that I saw two or three at a time lifted by their long hair and tossed into the large cup of the mangonel and then, when this was full, launched, with precise accuracy, over the walls and into the streets of the city. It was expected that this would instil immense fear, the dreadful realization that their fighters' bodies not been buried as was the Muslim custom but instead their heads were being used to spread terror and fear and possibly disease throughout the city streets. This sent the Turks into a frenzied panic and terror, exactly what Duke Robert intended.

Over the weeks we had been here and engaged the Turks, I had seen many battles but from a distance, helped with the bloody wounds of our warriors, witnessed many shocking things but had never reacted in either horror or fear. I had been focused, did what needed to be done. But try as I could, I was not able to control the effect this gruesome scene had on my body, dry heaves started slowly but then came more frequently and I had to rush away from the presence of the Duke so he would not see me vomiting up the meal we all had just sat down to. Bent over, my body lurching as it rid itself of the rest of my stomach contents until it had turned clear bile, I knelt on the ground, spitting out what was left. I felt someone touch my shoulder and I looked up to see Hugues standing there holding an uncorked animal skin flask. I was instantly ashamed, mortified that I reacted in such a weak and uncontrolled manner.

"Here," Hugues said, offering me the flask, "clean your face and wash out your mouth."

I did what I was told, grateful to get rid of the foul taste. I wiped the flask down ensuring it was clean and handed it back as I got up. I looked at Hugues beseechingly.

"Why…?" I asked not being able to finish the question, my mind seeing all those bloodied faces and then imagining all the headless bodies they once belonged to.

Hugues thought a moment.

"You are repulsed by this, yes?" Hugues asked.

I stared at him, my silence answering his question. Hugues sighed quietly before he spoke.

"Battles are rarely won by physical combat alone, young D'Ivry. The might of an army is made of many parts. Weaponry skill, physical brawn, strategic thinking, knowing one's enemy. Psychological combat is just as important and effective, sometimes more so than brute force. One must never show an enemy any weakness. The Turks will now be in no doubt as to what we are capable of, barbaric though it might be," he responded seriously.

Even though I understood what he was trying to teach me I still found it abhorrent. But I also realized that I needed to come to terms with it if I were to continue in Duke Robert's retinue, he would not allow another display such as this and I would lose his trust. I squared my shoulders and set my jaw and gave Hugues a look that said so be it. It was a harsh lesson, but one I needed to learn.

\* \* \* \* \* \* \* \* \*

Duke Robert's strategy did have its intended effect and panic spread across the city. This increased when the Emperor's fleet was spotted on the horizon in Lake Ascania a couple of days later, bringing relief not only in the form of badly needed supplies for the crusader armies but also the knowledge that the imperial ships would create a blockade and prevent the Turks from getting supplies from their own ships which were no match for the Emperor's powerful cogs.

Within this fleet, another of the Emperor's generals, Boutoumites, had brought a Byzantine force which would be responsible to attack the ports on the lake when the Duke and the other leaders were ready to launch a coordinated attack on the city. Twenty thousand imperial troops arrived on foot at the same time and brought news and instructions from the Emperor to Taticius. It did not take long to organise the assault; the crusading armies were energized and ready to fight, many, including myself, found it difficult to sleep on the eve of what hopefully would be the final battle.

It was now the middle of June with cool mornings turning to warm days, a curious mist and low clouds hung across the fields and camps, so thick we could barely make out the walls of the city and the massive towers standing defiantly in our way. Looking back, I realize that this should have been a warning to us, that we were, in fact, not seeing things as clearly as we should have, but with vows and oaths and promises made between allies, we had no reason to doubt that anything was amiss.

The attack was planned for dawn, with the sun behind us in the east helping our cause by temporarily blinding the Turkish guards and fighters to our advance. Taticius informed us that the fleet would be ready to attack the ports and then his foot soldiers would attack the city from the east as well, so the Turks would find themselves bombarded from all sides. What we were not aware of was the Emperor had different plans for this day.

After getting into full mailled armour, settling into position and waiting for Duke Robert's signal, all the armies started to march en masse towards the walls, letting loose volleys of arrows and darts and missiles in a coordinated attack, with thunderous roars and shouting coming from the thousands of men approaching the city on three sides. No one noticed at the time that none of Taticius's arrows or projectiles actually reached the walls but fell harmlessly in front, not causing any damage whatsoever.

After about an hour of this attack with most of the mist now dissipating, a strange sight greeted us as we began to see more clearly: the imperial standard was now flying atop the tower of the main gate on the eastern wall. And no Turkish soldiers could be seen along the battlements. What was this? Why had the imperial standard been hoisted? Had the fighters coming from the boats been successful in taking over the city? And if so, how were they able to accomplish that so quickly?

Duke Robert gave the signal for an immediate halt and as it made its way around to the other leaders we could see more imperial standards being raised to fly from the tops of all the towers along the walls. We were astounded. What on earth was going on? Instead of being enmeshed in a vicious battle to determine, once and for all, the rightful owner of the city, we found ourselves stopped in our tracks, squirming in our saddles, confused and bemused of the sight that befell us. Duke Robert ordered a quick retreat and for the other commanders to come to him immediately, including Taticius. Once gathered in his tent, the Duke turned on Taticius demanding answers.

"Just what is that?" he barked, pointing towards the city walls. "Why are the Emperor's standards hoisted? By god's teeth I will have answers!!"

But Taticius seemed to be at just as much of a loss as we were, although no one was really sure of that knowing the penchant the Emperor had of not keeping his promises.

"I am sorry, your Grace, I do not know. My men had started their advance just as yours had…" but he was interrupted by the arrival of a messenger dressed in imperial colours stepping through the open flaps of the tent.

"WHAT?!" roared the Duke at the poor boy who remained silent and, trembling, handed Aumale a small, sealed parchment, bowed and stepped back to await further orders, hoping to escape the Duke's wrath. Aumale passed it to the Duke without reading it.

Duke Robert ripped open the folded parchment and quickly scanned the contents.

"Sard!" he said in a hoarse whisper, handing the note to Aumale before turning to the others to continue.

"The Emperor's forces entered the city from the ports during the night! The Seljuk Turks have agreed to surrender the city to the Emperor. Our men," his voice darkened, "are not to pillage or loot any treasures and only are allowed into the city ten at a time."

"But that is our due, that is our right!" Blois exclaimed.

"Do you not think I know that?!" Duke Robert retorted.

"The Emperor has cheated us!" declared Bohemond. "Tancred was right to distrust the Byzantines, I should never have believed that their ways had changed since the wars with my father. Alexios was never going to allow us to declare victory here and take our spoils!"

"You knew nothing of this?" Duke Robert snapped at Taticius.

But the imperial General remained silent. Duke Robert understood the meaning of the silence and also understood Taticius's loyalty to his master. Furious with him as he was, he could not fault the man's allegiance.

"Boutoumites also writes the Emperor is nearby in Pelecanus, about an hour's ride from here," interjected Aumale. "And has instructed we should join him there if we are aggrieved."

Duke Robert thought a moment on this.

"'If we are aggrieved'," Duke Robert sneered. "Aumale, Bohemond, Flanders and I will go," he said, pointing at the others as he said their names, pointing at me last but not saying my name. "We will find out just what games the Emperor has been playing with us."

"Would it not be wise, your Grace, to have a contingent of guards following?" Aumale suggested.

Duke Robert agreed and instructed him to select fifty men to accompany us but at a pace behind. It did not take long to remount the horses and be on our way and in short order we had traversed the distance to the small enclave where the Emperor had set up camp. Bohemond had requested his nephew Tancred accompany him whilst Flanders had requested Hugues and the Duke agreed to both. Blois and Vermandois, of course, offered to stay behind and keep control of the camps where the men were, understandably, getting irritated about not being allowed to enter the conquered city. Duke Robert agreed to this too, probably silently relieved, he had not wanted to be laden with his weak brother-in-law or, worse yet, the insipid French prince, in this undertaking.

When we arrived we found a well-established camp, they had clearly been here for some time, keeping their distance from the fighting but close enough to keep watch on everything taking place at Nicaea. Duke Robert did not waste any time and did not wait to be announced, he dismounted and stormed into the Emperor's tents followed closely by the rest of us. It was an enormous tent, probably the largest I had ever seen, with many curtained areas and guards posted everywhere. I was amazed that we reached the Emperor's area unimpeded – it was clear we were expected.

Duke Robert got right to the point and demanded answers without bowing or addressing the Emperor as he was due being of higher rank. Duke Robert clearly no longer felt they were allies.

"Robert, Robert, Robert," Emperor Alexios tried to calm the Duke down, coming towards him with open arms as if to embrace him. Duke Robert stepped back to avoid it.

"We know what you have done," he growled. "We now demand to know why."

The Emperor took a seat at a massive table and gestured for the Duke and the others to join him. Duke Robert moved towards the table but did not sit;

the others remained where they were. Emperor Alexios clasped his hands almost as if in prayer.

"Your Grace," he drawled, "surely you must have realized that your crusading armies would not have been able to take the city."

"I believed no such thing! We were making inroads, our attacks were taking their toll…"

"But were they really?" Emperor Alexios interrupted. "Your attempt to fell Gonatas Tower was a dismal failure and the mangonels did not have the power to cause any significant damage to the walls."

"That is why we requested your fleet to cut off the supplies to the Turks from the ports," Duke Robert continued angrily, then stopped for a moment. "But you…you knew we would have to do that. You had this planned from the start, did not you? You had no intention of sharing any of the riches and spoils from the sack of this city, did you?"

The Emperor studied the Duke and knew he needed to placate him. But the tone he took was stern, almost chastising.

"The goal here was to rid the city of Nicaea of the Seljuk Turks and return it to me, that was the vow you made when you swore your allegiance to me," he said looking at each of the leaders directly in the eye. "For my part, I agreed to provide supplies which I have done and which I intend to continue to do. But I simply cannot have tens of thousands of your soldiers running rampant pillaging and looting, stripping my city of its precious treasures. Surely you must see that?" he concluded, giving the impression he was completely unaware of his duplicity.

Duke Robert shook his head.

"If you think I, or any of the leaders of these crusading armies would ever trust in your word again…" Duke Robert started.

Emperor Alexios raised his hand to stop the Duke from continuing and leaned towards him.

"You and I both know that Nicaea is not your main concern. It is a minor impediment on the road to Jerusalem which is your real objective. Whereas for me," he shrugged, "Jerusalem is, ah... strategically unimportant. All I want is Nicaea and Antioch back under my control. I shall keep my vow to you and the other leaders to provide the supplies you need. And you and the other leaders shall be well compensated for your work here," he finished.

Clapping his hands, several men appeared carrying many heavy chests which they opened as soon as they were set down, revealing a vast treasure of gold and silver coins.

Duke Robert glanced at the chests and grimaced. Taking this offering would mean having to acquiesce to the man who had just betrayed them, but without his support it was doubtful the crusaders would be able to defeat the Turks at Antioch and move into Palestine. And the Emperor was right: Jerusalem was our goal. Seemingly deep in thought, Duke Robert moved back to where a couple of his men were standing. As usual, Aumale was the voice of reason.

"We must stand down, your Grace," he whispered to Duke Robert. "Without the Emperor's support in Antioch we will fail. And Jerusalem will be lost to us," he added.

Duke Robert stared darkly at the Emperor as he took in Aumale's words. He realized Aumale was right.

"We...shall...accept your offer," he said begrudgingly as he walked back to the Emperor.

Alexios nodded.

"Good, good," he said. "There is, however, just one condition."

The room filled with dread. What new game was this? Duke Robert met the Emperor's gaze but said nothing. Alexios smiled but it was not friendly. It was vindictive.

"I am sure you all recall when we met last, you pledged yourselves to me, paid homage as I am due? Ah, and yet," he said getting up and walking slowly towards Bohemond, softly tapping the table as he went, "not…everyone. Is this not so, Prince Bohemond?"

Bohemond stared at the Emperor.

"I do not know what you mean," he said emphatically. "I swore the oath."

"Yes, yes you did," the Emperor responded. "But your nephew, the captain of your armies, did not," he said flatly, looking past Bohemond, over his shoulder to where Tancred was standing nearby.

The room was still. The Emperor turned his back on Bohemond and Tancred and returned to his chair, sat, entwined his fingers, and rested his hands on his belly.

"I demand that any senior member of rank in the Christian armies that has not as yet pledged their vow to me do so before anyone departs for Antioch," he stated flatly. "We can start with him," he added, pointing directly at Tancred.

We all looked at Tancred to see what he would do. We knew he despised the Byzantines, had been cheated by them in the past and this betrayal by the Emperor of the crusading armies only solidified his belief they were never to be trusted. He stepped forward and spoke without hesitation.

"If you give me this tent full of coin and as much as you have given to the Duke and the Counts, then I too will take the oath," he sneered insolently.

We were all shocked at Tancred's petulance. One of the imperial guards offended by such disrespect of the Emperor, came at him and pushed him away with contempt. Tancred pushed back, leaving the two of them standing apart, like two snorting, angry bulls, each waiting for the other to make another strike. The Emperor quickly rose and moved to stand in between them. Bohemond reached the two men at the same time and grabbed hold of his nephew, shoving him back.

"Tancred!" he barked, "It is not for you to behave in such an impudent way to the Emperor!" shaking him to get his attention. "You must take the oath," he hissed.

By this time, Tancred was surrounded by all of the leaders, Bohemond, the Duke, Flanders, and Aumale. He looked from one man to another and found no friendly eyes. He knew he had overstepped the mark and needed to make amends; the success of their mission depended on it. He turned to the Emperor.

"I will…take the oath, your…Majesty," he said resignedly, lowering his gaze, knowing he had no choice.

And for the moment, tensions were eased.

\* \* \* \* \* \* \* \* \* \*

With the gold and silver loaded and the supply carts restocked with the various foodstuffs, wine and beer needed to support the crusaders, the slow trek to Antioch began near the end of June. To save face and to give the impression that the Western and Byzantine armies were still working in concert and united in purpose, a story was circulated that said the events at Nicaea had been intended and that it was the quick-witted strategies planned and agreed to by all the leaders that won the city. The truth was buried and we continued on our way with the support from the Emperor seemingly intact. Only those at the highest levels knew any better.

News of our success in recapturing Nicaea made its way back to Rome and France. The Holy Father was delighted and convinced that it was just the first of many victories that we would celebrate as God was with us. Blois continued his copious letters to his wife Adele, telling her, 'Nicaea was conquered after one month, we will reach Jerusalem in 5 weeks' – he would be wrong about this as he was about most other things. But then we did not know otherwise, did not know what was ahead of us in the lands of Anatolia leading us to Antioch and then into the lands of Palestine.

A battle at Dorylaeum met us first. Although it meant the loss of about a fifth of Bohemond's men, it was the making of Bouillon as he masterfully broke through the lines of Seljuk Turks that Sultan Arslan had waiting for us. And of Bishop Le Puy, who outmanoeuvred the Turks with an attack from the rear. Once again, Sultan Arslan fled the battlefield before being taken prisoner. And the Christian world rejoiced again at our triumph.

I continued my training as we moved through Anatolia, being mentored by the greatest warriors in the Christian world. Hugues took a particular interest in my handling of the blade and other weapons, holding swordplay sessions with myself and Bisol, and bringing in highly skilled fighters, Bouillon's man Godfrey Saint-Omer, Blois's man Archambaud Saint-Agnan and

Flanders's man Payen de Montdidier, to challenge us whenever the armies had stopped to rest for a few days.

Bishop Le Puy took me under his wing for my spiritual guidance but, caring though he was, he was not Bishop Odo; I still missed my old master every day. And as the battles raged, big or small, Duke Robert kept his promise to my father to keep me away from the bloodshed, although my work with the wounded continued.

But nothing would prepare me for Antioch. What happened there, insignificant though it seemed at the time, would be the catalyst for the direction of my life for many years to come.

# III

# Part Three

# 1097-1098 – Antioch

The journey through Anatolia was arduous. Although Sultan Arslan had escaped the rout at Dorylaeum, he laid waste to the lands from there to Palestine, blighting the crops and destroying most of what we would normally forage for food. Supplies continued to dwindle, which forced looting and pillaging of the villages on route. Many of the crusaders died including the wife of Baldwin of Boulogne, Bouillon's brother, in early October of that year, prompting him to leave the crusade to find his fortune in helping the Armenians fight the Seljuk Turks in Edessa. His loss was felt keenly by Bouillon as the brothers had fought at each other's side since their youth. It also meant breaking apart the two brother warriors that served them as Hugh de Fauquembergues decided to go with Baldwin and Godfrey Saint-Omer stayed with the crusade and Bouillon.

Antioch was the gateway to the Holy Land. Our armies finally reached the city in late October 1097 and we realized immediately how daunting a task it would be when we faced the enormous walls and four hundred towers stretching for miles encircling the city. It was so vast, we did not think we would have enough warriors to completely surround it so we concentrated groups by leader at the five main gates that served the city. Virtually unreachable from the north due to the Orontes River that bordered it and impenetrable from the east and south because the city walls sat atop a mountain range, it made for a formidable fortress. From a distance, one could see the citadel on Mount Silpius as it soared above the other buildings in the city. A beautiful, shining example of exquisite architecture and mingling cultures living, for the most part, in harmony, Antioch harboured secrets only known to a few. We were to discover some during our time there.

Strangely enough, there were more Christians than Muslims in the city, a mixture of Armenians, Greeks and Syrians. But it was governed by the Seljuk Turks who had become paranoid about potential treachery and betrayal and so had recently expelled many of the Christian leaders and jailed the Christian Patriarch of the city. And so our advance was seen as more of an effort to help rid our fellow Christians of a tyrannical ruler and replace him and his officers with Christian leaders and officers. And many there would be willing to take their place.

Discussions were held amongst the leaders of our armies how to take the city. It was clear that a physical assault would not succeed even though Toulouse put forward a good argument for it. In the end though, everyone agreed to take a more cautious approach and launch a siege.

Cautious though this may have been, it was not a strategy with quick results and days turned into weeks and weeks into months and no progress being made. Our numbers had reduced from the battles and skirmishes since leaving Constantinople and the sixty thousand from all the Western armies were now less than forty thousand which simply was not enough to man the entirety of the walls. Where there were unmanned gaps, and supplies from the nearby river made their way past us and into the city.

And so, whilst the city seemed not be affected at all by our siege, our numbers were falling, many dying from the cold or starvation and those that remained became more and more demoralised through the harsh winter. Blois's letters to his wife Adele revealed some terrible truths of the situation. Archambaud told me he had written in one letter:

> *'We have lived through great suffering and evils beyond counting. Many people have exhausted their finances, and others were saved from starvation only by the kindness of God. The cold is excessive and there are terrible deluges of rain.'*

For once, he was not exaggerating.

The leaders began sending out small groups of men to forage for food along the fertile lands next to the nearby river. It was in early January 1098, on the day of the feast of the Epiphany, when I joined Hugues, Flanders, Bisol and a few others on such a mission setting out in the early afternoon under the cover of dark, cloudy skies that threatened yet another downpour. We decided not to use our horses but to go on foot and wrapped ourselves in heavy winter cloaks with hoods and short swords at our sides, bringing leather pouches to hold whatever we might find. I had taken particular care of Pax over the difficult months, always making sure he was fed and warm and safe amongst the horses of the senior men. Sometimes even feeding him before myself, or even instead of myself. I checked on him before we left.

It was not long before we were out of sight of the city and picking our way through forests at the base of the mountains on paths that to the river. The winter rains had turned them to ribbons of thick mud that we sank into up to our calves, making the going very slow and difficult. We changed tack and moved off the paths, spreading out into the forests which meant we could cover more ground more quickly but also left us more vulnerable to any unexpected attack by bandits or the garrison soldiers who made regular patrols of the areas outside the city walls.

We did not see the Turkish troops until it almost too late. They appeared seemingly out of nowhere and came for us, letting out terrifying shrieks as they did. Hugues had spotted them just before their attack and, turning to me, he shouted.

"D'Ivry! Go! We will find you!" and then drew his sword, readying himself for the inevitable combat.

I turned and ran into the forest, knowing that if I headed to the paths, I would be caught. In the distance I could hear the shouts of enemies smashing into each other, the clash of swords as weapons came together in a fury of fighting, and the agonised cries of those losing the battle. But still I fled, not because I was afraid, although I was, but because it had been drilled into me during training: when ambushed or set upon unexpectedly, one man must escape in order to report back and warn the others. I knew this was my duty and yet that did not prevent me from stopping several times and considering going back. But I knew either we would win the day or lose it with the strength of the men there and so I carried on.

I had just realized that I had been climbing rather than being on level ground when I felt the first drop of rain. I knew the dark clouds were going to let loose a torrent and that I needed to find cover and continue my trek back to the camps once the storm had eased. Looking ahead of me, I spied a break in the trees in what looked like a small rocky alcove that would provide the shelter I needed. By the time I reached it, I was soaked. I stepped under the stone overhang and saw that the alcove was a bit deeper than one could tell from below it. My eyes adjusted to the dimness of the light and could see that the ceiling of the alcove sloped downward as it reached further back – the alcove was actually a cave. With my height now almost six foot, I would not be able to stand up straight deeper in, I would need to crawl if I wanted to explore further than halfway in. But for the moment, I just wanted to rest and stood at the mouth of the cave staring out at the rain now pounding down. I thought about my fellow soldiers out there and worried about their fate.

I heard the snap of a twig and knew instantly someone was behind me. I slowly moved my hand and gripped the hilt of my short sword as Hugues had taught me and in one single move withdrew it and spun around, ready and prepared to fight whoever, whatever, was in that cave with me. But what I saw stopped me short and I blinked, trying to take in the sight. Before me was a slender youth, much shorter than myself, wearing Turkish warrior garb and shaking like a leaf. It appeared the poor lad was terrified, understandably so, my size was intimidating and my clothing told him I was the enemy. But something told me he was no threat. I could see no weapon on him and as if reading my thoughts, he removed his cloak of furs and laid it on the cave floor, then turned slowly around with his arms stretched out, as if to say to me, 'I have nothing which will hurt you.' Whether this was unwise or not, something told me he was not going to attack me. I lowered my sword but kept a good grip on the hilt in case my instincts proved wrong.

I stiffened slightly when he reached for a sack resting at his feet. Looking at me all the time with one hand raised, he slowly pulled it open and reached in, bringing out something bound in soft leather. As he unwrapped it, I could see it was bread, a few pieces of Turkish pita. I stared at it. He broke off a bit and ate it and then offered some to me. I could only guess at the fear he was experiencing to be face to face with his enemy, and yet here he was offering me bread. He must have seen how much I was in need of food. Even though I was wearing layers of winter clothes and a heavy cloak, my gaunt face must have given my hunger away. He placed it on the sack and stepped back, giving me wide berth to retrieve it without being in danger of an attack.

I watched him warily and then stepped forward. Without taking my eyes off him or my hand off the grip of my sword, I reached for the pita and ate it, first slowly then greedily as my hunger kicked in. And for a flash of a moment, my eyes left his and went to the sack where there was obviously more. But still he did not move. If he were shielding a weapon, he could have pounced when I was distracted but he did not. When I finished the piece, he gestured towards the sack as if to say 'there's more' but I stood and backed away. And then he spoke.

"You…West?" he asked speaking haltingly but in my language.

I was stunned. How could he know these words? Granted, over the past months Toulouse had taught us a few words in both Turkish and Arabic so naturally I should have expected my foe to know some of mine but still this took me aback. I simply nodded. We stared at each other. He gestured to the sack again. I shook my head not even though my stomach was telling me otherwise. He pointed to himself.

"Zengi," he said and then pointed at himself a second time. "Zengi," he repeated.

I pointed to myself.

"D'Ivry," I said.

"De-verr-ee," he responded stumbling over the pronunciation.

I tried to hold back a smile.

"D'Ivry," I repeated.

He repeated my name perfectly this time, nodding and grinning. He motioned towards his feet and I could see a small pile of branches, stepping on one of them had given him away. He gestured again, this time using both his hands first with his fists clenched then expanding his fingers all at the same time.

"Fire?" he asked, repeating the gesture.

I nodded. He slowly kneeled beside the twigs and reached into a pocket in his vest; I clenched the hilt again, still not completely trusting him. But all he took out was a flint and within seconds he had managed to start a small fire. I noticed a pile of larger branches further along in the cave; he must have collected them before the downpour started. He sat cross-legged with his back to one of the cave walls, and leaned to blow lightly on the flames. He motioned me to sit across from him on the other side of the fire. I knew instantly why he did this; with both of our backs against the cave walls, we both had the same view of the cave's entrance and a clear view of each other. I took a seat.

For the next couple of hours we sat, wary of one other, each taking turns adding to the fire. And sharing what was left of his food, I became comfortable enough to accept it from his hand. We tried to speak with one another, but we knew too few words of each other's language. We could not explain who we were to each other nor explain how both of us had come to meet in this cave in the woods outside of Antioch. Eventually the night arrived and then the rains let up. Although it was still frightfully cold outside the cave, we were warm inside and from our vantage point we could see the stars starting to peep out from the dissipating clouds.

I am not sure if we both heard the sound of men approaching at the same time but we were on our feet quickly. It was only then that I was absolutely sure he had no weapon for he would have reached for it then as we knew not who it was that advanced towards us. It was only when I heard Hugues calling out my name was I certain who it was. We had been victorious, I surmised, else he would not be so careless to draw attention to himself. I stepped to the mouth of the cave and called back to him. A few moments later I could see first him and then Flanders making their way up through the forest heading towards me. In my excitement of seeing them I had forgotten about my companion and glanced over my shoulder. He was not there. But he had not come past me, I would have noticed; he must be hiding in the darkness at the back of the cave, he was small enough to fit.

"D'Ivry!" Hugues exclaimed reaching me first, adding, "I am glad to have found you alive and well."

"I take it you and the others were victorious? Did we lose any men?" I asked eager to hear the news.

"Not one soul," Hugues replied, leaning into the cave. "You seem to have found a safe place to wait it out, well done," he said looking about.

Flanders arrived and nodded a greeting and also peered into the cave.

"We must go," he said sternly. "Put out that fire and gather your things," pointing to the sack on the cave floor.

I knew my new friend was still inside and probably terrified of these two men who had just beaten the Turkish soldiers in the skirmish we were both hiding from. I had a choice. Reveal Zengi to Hugues and Flanders or let him be. It was an easy decision to make. He had given a starving lad some food. He had not run off when he had the chance to alert someone to my presence. We did not fight. We had tried to communicate. I decided to let him be.

"Yes, my lord," I said and picked up the sack and stamped out the dying flames, but leaving some embers burning, enough so a fresh fire could be started if needed.

The others started to make their way back down towards more level ground. I stood at the mouth of the cave watching them, then glanced behind me straining to see as far back into the cave as I could. But I saw nothing and heard nothing. I gently dropped the sack back down onto the ground, nodded to the darkness taking over the cave, turned and followed the others. Zengi never made a sound.

* * * * * * * * * *

The siege dragged on with little sign of any real gain. Each minor success was met with another failure and Antioch held firm, not suffering the ill effects we had expected them to. It was now early spring and the terrible conditions we endured during winter had passed aided by the arrival of fresh supplies and materials sent from England for building siege engines. We almost lost all of it when the ships were attacked by some of the Turkish garrison, but the combined strength of the armies of Bouillon, Bohemond and Toulouse fought them off, the Turks losing over a thousand men in the melee.

Our men started to occupy themselves with building several siege engines. I was fascinated by the designs and the rather simplistic mechanisms that made them work and I offered my help anywhere I could, anywhere I was able to learn. Others built a fort outside the Bridge Gate which Toulouse took possession of and Tancred oversaw the restoration of a ruined monastery outside St George's Gate and took possession of that when it was complete.

Whilst this bolstered the morale of the troops and kept them busy, the leaders were becoming increasingly frustrated. And worse yet, we had heard rumours of that another powerful Muslim army led by a famous fighter named Kerbogha was headed to Antioch; we knew we had to breach the walls and take the city before his arrival. The siege was not working - other options to accomplish this needed to be found and quickly.

It was now late May, the days were starting to give a hint of the heat that was to come during the summer months and yet cooled off enough in the evenings for fires to be lit for warmth. We heard that Bouillon's brother Baldwin had engaged and beaten Kerbogha's army in Edessa which was the reason for the delay in his armies reaching Antioch. But he had regrouped and was now on his way to us.

Bohemond was already in Duke Robert's tents just before dawn when I arrived for duty. The two of them were in the middle of a discussion, Bohemond pacing back and forth.

"Imbecile!" Bohemond exclaimed. "Who does he think he is?!"

I found an unlit corner of the tent to stand and await any instructions from the Duke, curious as to what had gotten Bohemond so riled. Duke Robert held up his hands trying to calm the Prince. It did not work.

"You make him Commander-in-Chief of the siege and this is how he repays you?!"

I froze. Duke Robert had given the responsibility of leading the siege to Blois, much to the consternation and over the objections of the others. What had he done now?

"He has lost the faith in the cause, Bohemond. It is his decision to go," Robert responded, oddly playing the pacifier.

"Then he goes alone!" Bohemond retorted.

"You know that cannot be," Robert responded, his voice beginning to rise. "Not only is he married to the daughter of a King, he is the Count of Blois and Chartres. He has every right to take what is left of his contingent if he so chooses."

"And just how many is that going to be?" Bohemond demanded.

"About a thousand men," Robert said, shaking his head.

Bohemond's mouth dropped open and for a moment he could not speak. He just stared at the floor for a while before speaking.

"We are already down a third of the men that we came with," he pointed out. "And with Kerbogha on his way, we cannot afford to lose a single man!"

"I am aware of that," Robert responded, motioning to me to bring some morning beer for the two of them which I did quickly and returned to my post. "Mark my words, he will get his comeuppance for this," he said darkly.

The two men thought quietly on that a moment. Indeed, the Christian world in the West would not look kindly on anyone breaking their pledge of taking the cross and abandoning the mission. We could only wonder what his strong-willed wife would think of her husband being such a coward.

Duke Robert changed the subject.

"Has there been any progress on that matter we discussed when we last met?"

"Have the other leaders agreed to my request?" Bohemond replied.

Duke Robert snorted. Some request. A demand more like. If his plan worked, Bohemond expected to be made Prince of Antioch. Toulouse was furious, demanding that Antioch, like Nicaea, be returned to Emperor

Alexios as promised when we were all in Constantinople. But Bohemond no longer had any intention of honouring any oath or pledge, especially after the Emperor's treachery at Nicaea. Duke Robert, Flanders, Bouillon, Vermandois and even Tancred had recognized just how desperate the situation was and had acquiesced to Bohemond's demands.

"Yes, they have. Now, what news on your plan?"

"Excellent, I am sure they will all see it is for the best and what I deserve," Bohemond responded and finally took a seat at the Duke's table. "I believe we have good news. I have found a man who can help find a way in. The commander of the gates at the St George Tower, an Armenian Muslim named Firuz, has made it known that he is willing. He informed a couple of my men that he has had his honour insulted, accused of hoarding food and fined a small fortune and made an example of in public, despite his protestations. He is more than happy to join our cause and have revenge on those who have wronged him."

"Good, good," said Duke Robert. "Get word to him that we will work with him on finalising the plans for a breech through that gate. I think Blois's leaving may actually help us in this. Tell Firuz to get word back to his Turkish governor the crusaders have been frightened by the rumours of Kerbogha's imminent arrival and that we are leaving. They will have already seen Blois and his men leaving, so we will make it seem as though the rest of us are following him, but then we will circle back and enter through the gate as soon as it has been opened for us," Duke Robert spoke as the strategy came together in his head.

It was a good plan. Blois insisted on leaving with his men even knowing this new plan was almost in place, convinced that Kerbogha's looming arrival spelled doom for the mission. We were not sad to see him go; the other leaders expressed a sigh of relief when they saw him saddle his mount and head off towards Constantinople where he would eventually take ships back to the safety of France. Duke Robert did not appear to bid him farewell. He had had enough of his weak brother-in-law and was only sorry to see the much-needed men go with him. I was going to miss his captain, Archambaud Saint-Agnan; he had taught me much about how to defend against an enemy who had weapons when I did not.

The details of the plot were settled for the night at the beginning of June just a few days after Blois's departure. We were ready to go. Duke Robert needed as many men as he could for this battle; I knew it was time for me to join the fighting. He sat me down to tell me what part I was going to play in this.

"D'Ivry, I made a promise to your father to keep you from combat as best I could. I am still going to try to honour that promise. But there may come a time when you will need to wield your sword; I have watched you, you are ready. But be aware, battle is not the same as training, you must keep your guard at all times, never let it down. I am going to place you in the auxiliary guard with Toulouse. Once we are through St George's gate and have opened Bridge Gate, you will follow him and secure the cistern in the east of the city – we control the water, we control the city. Do you understand this?"

I nodded.

"Good," he said. "I have arranged for Bishop Odo's helm to be given to you, seek out Tancarville for your maille. Dress yourself and report to Toulouse once the sun has set."

I did as I was instructed. My father had provided me with maille but I had outgrown it over the past months and Duke Robert had obviously noticed this. I found Tancarville in one of the Duke's secondary tents, he was waiting for me with some pieces of mailled armour. With his help, I slipped the bodice over my linen undershirt, placing my arms in its metal-ringed sleeves. It was heavy. Tancarville then placed a linen cap on my head then added the maille coif which made it all even heavier, I could feel it pressing down onto the top of my shoulders. He removed a conical helm from one of Bishop Odo's chests and placed it onto my head, pressing it down as far as it could go and straightened it so the nasal guard sat directly in front of my nose. He stood back to examine me. I apparently met with his approval.

"Can you see properly?" he asked.

I looked from my left to my right and back again and nodded.

"Show me your attack and defence manoeuvres," he instructed, tossing a broadsword to me.

I stepped back and went through the basic moves that I had been taught over the months, moving around the tent when doing so to show him I was agile. When I stopped, he reached out his hand asking for the sword back.

"You are ready," Tancarville said matter-of-factly.

I removed the helm and thanked him.

"Stay safe Sébastien," he said. "Do Bishop Odo proud."

I placed the helm into a sack made of coarse cloth and slipped my cloak around my shoulders, pulled up its hood and tied it so no one from afar could tell I was in maille, and returned to the tent I had been sharing with Bisol and others to retrieve the broadsword Hugues had gifted me those many months ago. Once inside, I added a plain brown surcoat to cover the maille and attached a belt around my waist to which the scabbard was attached and sheathed the sword. Bisol entered just as I was tugging on the padded gloves that would protect my hands from attack but would still allow me a tight grip on the sword.

"Sébastien!" he exclaimed seeing me in full battle gear. "Impressive. Where has the Duke put you?"

"In the auxiliary guard with Count Toulouse," I answered. "You?"

"I will be with Hugues and Count Flanders in the vanguard behind the Duke and Prince Bohemond," he said.

I understood why. Despite his relatively youthful age, Bisol was already a seasoned warrior and Hugues would want him by his side. It meant he would be in the thick of things before I even crossed the threshold of Bridge Gate. I stood up, picked up the sack that held my new helm and made a move to leave.

"God be with you Sébastien," he said seriously.

"Deus Vult," I responded and disappeared into the crowds.

\* \* \* \* \* \* \* \* \* \*

In the late afternoon on the day of the attack, Duke Robert engineered the movement of the men who were to give the impression there was a mass departure of crusaders who were abandoning the fight. He even went so far as to have Peverel fly his standard slightly higher than usual so that anyone watching from afar could easily make out the Normandy flag and colours. To all concerned, it gave the intended impression of an exodus of the Western armies.

Our forces crept silently back to the deserted camps under the cover of darkness, many mailled and armed, all eager to finally have the chance to meet the enemy after months of delay. As planned, we took our positions and readied ourselves for the signal. It came shortly after midnight.

The Armenian had kept his word and had let down a rope on the west side of the guard tower next to St George's gate where Bohemond and a hundred of his soldiers were waiting. Taking the lead, Bohemond climbed the rope and, upon nearing the top, felt one of his hands being grasped from above. Momentarily concerned that he had been found out, he was relieved when a familiar voice spoke to him.

"Long life to this hand," Firuz whispered to him and helped him over the edge.

Several of Bohemond's men soon joined him up above and split into two groups, one headed for the Turks garrisoned near Bridge Gate where I was stationed, the others followed Bohemond into the tower at St George's Gate. The next thing we knew, the massive locking beam at Bridge Gate was being lifted, the doors suddenly pulled open by some of Bohemond's men. This was met with a torrent of cries as the crusaders in Toulouse's vanguard in front of us rushed through, pouring into the city, quickly joined by Bohemond's men and then Bouillon's once the Gate of the Duke was broken open, followed by Bishop Le Puy's men through the Dog Gate and finally Taticius and his men through the St Paul Gate. The crusaders were swarming all over the city attacking indiscriminately, taking down Turkish soldiers wherever they found them. Unfortunately, that is not all they did.

Toulouse's rear guard followed on the heels of his vanguard and I found myself in the rush of a crowd of fellow-soldiers, making our way through the narrow streets, across the city and the up towards the cistern as were our instructions. '*Control the water, control the city*,' I heard Duke Robert's words ringing in my ears.

We reached it with relative ease; the vanguard had cut down anyone standing in our way, bodies were strewn everywhere one looked. There were several circular stone structures with arches built over them, ropes wrapped around the arches and hanging down into holes beneath. These were the openings to the cistern that sat below us and we were standing on its ceiling, supported by massive stone undercroft-like supports. We surrounded them and stood guard.

We could hear the shouts of our soldiers and the screams of those being attacked. We could only pray that the Christians in the city were being spared, this was, after all, their city. The cloudy skies that had given us cover for our invasion were now clearing, casting grey moonlight across the buildings which threw shadows onto the streets. That is when I noticed a movement down below and slightly to the north of us – it looked like a number of people quickly and quietly making their way towards the citadel.

I am sure it would just be our men making their way through the streets but thought I should report it anyway. I looked for Toulouse, he was not in sight. But one of his men, a commander called Rainard was nearby. I moved quickly beside him.

"Sir," I whispered, "there is movement, I believe quite a number are heading for the citadel."

"Turks?" he whispered back.

"I am not sure, I could not see clearly enough," I answered.

"Come with me," he said and gestured for another man whose name I did not know to join us.

With our weapons drawn, we quickly crept along the streets to the citadel, being careful to stay in the shadows. We followed Rainard and obeyed his signals and soon we were approaching the entrance of a massive stone building, many stories high. This was the great citadel of Antioch, the home of the governors and headquarters for any visiting dignitaries. It could hold several hundred and even had its own access to the cistern below and large food stores and so could easily defend itself from an attack.

Rainard led us past the enormous wooden doors of the main entrance, not wanting to use them as we would be easily seen once inside. Instead, we circled around the exterior, looking for another way in; we soon found one, a small doorway, probably one of many used by servants or workers to enter or exit unnoticed. Rainard pushed on it, it was locked from the inside. We continued creeping along the outer wall, testing each door we came to. We finally had success with the fourth door we tried, opened it and stepped silently inside. The passageway was lit by torches well enough for us to see our way through. Rainard stopped short of entering one of the main halls and knelt on one knee, peering into the room. We knelt beside him. We could see and hear no one. Which was disconcerting.

We moved into the hall and, using the support columns to conceal our presence, crossed the mosaic floor to the other side and down another passageway until we came to a set of curved stairs leading to the upper floors. Rainard motioned for us to follow him climb the stairs.

We had not heard a sound until they were upon us. Two Turkish soldiers came at us with scimitars raised, murderous intent in their eyes. Rainard's man and I turned to take on the first Turk as the second went after Rainard himself. They were strong and highly skilled and forced us up the stairs despite the advantage we should have had being physically above them. Slowly we backed up the stairs and into a circular room, an offshoot from the staircase. I never saw the thrust that took Rainard, I only knew his Turk was now battling the two of us, focusing on the Rainard's man whilst the first Turk took me on alone.

He was swifter than I, his curved sword seemed lighter and easier to wield than my broadsword. But I appeared to have more strength and managed to knock him down a few times but each time he scrambled back to his feet. At one point I caught a blow that sent my helm sailing across the room and knocked me down on one knee, dropping my sword beside me. I felt the warm trickle of blood coming down my left temple and tried to ignore it. That was when I saw the body of the Rainard's man on the floor beside me, still and lifeless, and I knew I was now battling both of the Turks.

They slowly crept around me, trying to decide what would be the best way to attack. They were faster, but I had the longer reach and stronger sword. Finally, they came at me.

"DUR!" I heard someone shout in Turkish.

Both men immediately broke off what they were doing and stepped back from me. I could not see who had stopped my imminent death at the hands of the two Turkish soldiers. I glanced at the floor and noticed blood dripping from my head wound. When I looked up again, I saw who it was.

Zengi walked slowly towards me. The Turks stepped back again and bowed. I was astonished. I could not begin to understand what was going on, how Zengi came to be here and why he had the power to halt what inevitably would have been my execution. He looked different, seemed older and taller than when we had met earlier.

"Ayağa kalk," he said to me and lifted both hands, directing me to stand.

I did, slowly. The Turks shuffled nervously.

"Bu yeterli!!" Zengi barked at them with a side glance.

They froze. Zengi looked at me.

"De-verr-eee," he said grinning.

I did not correct him this time. I just nodded. He reached down and picked up my helm and sword. He handed me my sword first.

"Kılıcını kılıfla," he said pointing to the sword and then to its scabbard still hanging from my belt.

I sheathed it immediately. He then handed me my helm. I took it and tucked it under my arm.

"Arkadaş?" he asked. When I did not respond, he said after thinking about it a moment, "Friend?"

I was astounded.

"Evet," I answered, saying 'yes' in his language.

"Tanrı ister," he said, then translating, "Allah wills it."

"Deus Vult," I responded, then translating, "God wills it."

He turned to the two Turks and said something to them that seemed to be orders. When he was done, they nodded to him and bowed. He looked at me.

"You...go," he said in my language, pointing to the Turks.

I looked over to them, wary and unsure. Zengi saw my distrust.

"Bu iyi," he said with a reassuring tone. "It is...good."

For some inexplicable reason, I believed him. I bowed slightly.

"You keep safe, De-verr-ee" he said.

He sounded like he meant it.

I hesitated, not really knowing what to do or say. We both stared at each other silently for a moment, and then Zengi moved to the side so I could walk past him. I put on my helm and followed the two Turks, across the room and towards the passageway with the stairs. Before I exited, I turned back to have another look at Zengi. He was gone like a ghost in the night. Just as he had disappeared in the cave.

We descended the stairs quickly and quietly, obviously no one wanted to draw attention to my existence. The Turkish soldiers were close but made no move to block me or prevent me from leaving. I suddenly recognized the main entrance to the citadel which Rainard, his man and I had passed by earlier when trying to find a way in. The immense wooden doors which had been bolted from the inside contained a smaller door built within it; it was this that one of the Turks opened and stood back not looking at me. I slipped through and heard it shut and locked firmly behind me. I was free. As I raced back to the cistern, I realized I had been allowed to live because of a kindness I had shown a young stranger. It made an indelible mark.

When I reached the cistern, I searched for Toulouse to report what had happened in the citadel. He was with some men warming themselves around a makeshift fire and keeping a close guard on the cistern openings. He saw me approach and was concerned when he saw the blood on my face.

"D'Ivry!" he exclaimed, "What has happened? Why are you bloody?"

"My lord, once we had secured the cistern, I thought I saw some Turks moving towards the citadel and informed Sir Rainard. He decided to investigate and ordered another of your men to accompany him. I showed them where I thought the Turks had gone. Once we were at the citadel, we found an unlocked door and started to search but were set upon once we were inside," I explained, out of breath from running and trying to get the details out as quickly as possible.

Toulouse motioned for one of his men to attend him. He gave him some instructions which I could not hear and then turned back to me.

"Where is Rainard?" he asked.

I looked down at the ground.

"He was cut down, sir, as was the man he brought with him," I answered.

Toulouse grimaced.

"That is unfortunate," Toulouse said dismally. "Still, I am glad to see you were able to escape."

I decided not to correct his assumption.

"You should have that head wound looked to," he said, turned and walked away from me.

\* \* \* \* \* \* \* \* \*

It took two days of routing the city to take full control of it and even then we had not taken the citadel. Toulouse had given orders for it to be surrounded but it was locked and bolted shut and the Turks remaining inside had no intention of surrendering. So instead, he ordered troops to guard it, so although we could not get in, they could not leave.

In the chaos that ensued with armies from both sides clashing throughout the city, many Christians were slaughtered alongside the Turks that had chosen to stay and resist the siege over the months. The viciousness of the fanatical Tafurs took a toll on the inhabitants; they did not seem to care if those they were attacking were Christian or Muslim. To them, all the city dwellers were the enemy, and that included women and children as well. Their brutality, seen before at Nicaea, was surpassed by their actions here at Antioch. It was discussed by the leaders that they should be reigned back once some calm had been restored, but they had bigger issues to deal with now and they needed them. Kerbogha was still advancing towards us and we had to be ready to meet him.

We did not have to wait long. One day after we captured Antioch, the first of Kerbogha's scouting parties were spied approaching the city from the northwest and we knew he was close, too close for us to replenish the city before he arrived. We would have to make do with what was left which, we soon discovered, was not much. But we were secure in the knowledge that Emperor Alexios was soon to arrive with reinforcements and supplies.

We watched from the towers at St Paul's Gate as Kerbogha's army marched west past the city, just out of range of our archers, as we had been when we had approached the city. I stood next to Duke Robert, amazed at how quickly our fortunes had turned. Three days earlier we were on the verge of starving, Blois had deserted the mission with his men, and our fate was to be determined by the trustworthiness of one who was betraying his own. But we had overcome all and were in possession of the city; it was only time before the citadel fell to us as well. And now, we were facing yet another powerful Muslim army. We the besiegers were about to become the besieged.

"Kerbogha's army looks strong does it not my Grace?" I asked the Duke.

"Yes, but looks can deceive. I have battled smaller armies much more powerful than they seemed on sight. Strength does not necessarily come from numbers. Large armies who are not trained and who do not possess the skills necessary for battle can be a hindrance rather than a blessing."

Bohemond appeared at the Duke's side to watch the troops' arrival.

"Have you seen the great man yet?" he asked.

Duke Robert shook his head and the two men scanned the marchers for Kerbogha himself. Just as we were about to return to the quarters Duke Robert had taken for himself inside the Iron Gate, a great cry was heard from the masses of Muslim warriors and we all peered out to see what was causing it. And then we saw him.

"There, your Grace," Bohemond exclaimed, pointing to a small group of men on horseback.

Gloriously bedecked in silver and gold robes, Kerbogha sat astride a magnificent black steed, surrounded by others similarly dressed and what looked like his personal guard, armed and ready to protect him at all costs. But it was not Kerbogha that caught my eye; it was the person who rode at his side. I was not sure at first, blinked several times to make sure I was seeing correctly, but there was no mistake. The young Seljuk Turk I had encountered in the cave and then again in the citadel was riding next to the Turkish leader. I could not believe my eyes.

"May I ask a question, your Grace?" I asked the Duke.

He nodded, not taking his eyes away from the spectacle.

"Who is riding next to Kerbogha?" I asked.

Duke Robert looked but shook his head. Bohemond, having heard my question, leaned over to see who I was looking at.

"The lad riding to his left?" he asked me.

I nodded.

"That is Imad al-Din Zengi, Kerbogha's adopted son. His father had been Governor of Aleppo but was executed for treason many years ago. Zengi has been raised by Kerbogha ever since and is now his heir apparent," he answered and then turned to me. "Why do you ask?"

I started to reply but the Duke interrupted.

"They will try to storm the city as we did," he said to no one in particular. "They will fail as we did and then they will siege like we did. We need to find out where the Emperor is with the supplies and reinforcements, we will not last long without them."

"Indeed," Bohemond replied, switching his attention from me and back to the Duke.

There were preparations that needed to be done, strategies that needed to be planned. We never spoke about Zengi again and I was quietly grateful for that, I would not have known how to explain my curiosity.

It did not take long for the Turkish army to set up their camps surrounding the city, taking the very positions we had just vacated a few days earlier. As the Duke surmised, the city was stormed but having done this ourselves, we knew how to defend against it. And so, after a few days of failing to breach the gates, Kerbogha and his army settled in for what everyone believed would be a lengthy siege.

Days passed with supplies starting to get low and no sign of the Emperor, the morale of the crusaders started to decline once again. We had already reached what we thought was our lowest ebb before we took over the city with many starving and abandoning their vows, now more were leaving the city under the cover of darkness using ropes thrown over the walls. Our circumstances, though recently improved, were worsening and quite quickly. It was when things had become rather dire when Duke Robert was made aware of curious goings-on with a humble soldier in Toulouse's army who was claiming he was having visions in which different saints appeared.

His name was Peter Bartholomew and he had declared to anyone who would listen that Saint Andrew had appeared and told him that a relic of the Holy Lance, the iron tip of the spear that had pierced Christ on the cross, was in Antioch, buried beneath the church of St Peter. Bishop Adhémar learned of it first and had spoken with Toulouse about whether or not to bring it to Duke Robert's attention. Toulouse was not wholly believing of Bartholomew's stories but he also did not think investigating them would do any great harm. And at this point, anything that could boost the spirits of the troops was going to be a good thing.

"Do you believe these visions are real? Or is the man mad?" Robert asked getting to the point quickly.

"I believe he believes what he is seeing and hearing," Toulouse responded.

Bishop Adhémar sniffed loudly; Duke Robert turned to him.

"I take it you do not believe him?"

"No, I do not," Bishop Adhémar responded. "We have had many claiming they have had visions and yet none has been proved true. Starvation can drive a man insane, your Grace. It is probably nothing more than this. He is also saying he is losing his sight because Saint Andrew is unhappy that he has not searched for the relic. This I doubt very much."

"What harm would it do, your Grace, if we gathered a few men and took a look under the tiles in the church? If he is wrong, we will contain the damage, but if he is correct…" Toulouse started to suggest.

Duke Robert waved an impatient hand at them.

"Fine, take a couple of men, and D'Ivry here," he said looking at me, "I want you to be my eyes."

"Of course, your Grace," I said.

Toulouse and I left the Duke just as Bohemond arrived at the Duke's quarters. Two of Toulouse's men joined us as we walked to the church where we found Bartholomew sitting on the low stone platform in front of the entrance with a few others who were holding tools of varying shapes and sizes.

The church of St Peter in Antioch was really one of a kind, carved out of the side of Mount Starius on the north-east corner of the city, with room for only a simple altar and a flagstone floor surrounding it. It was said that St Peter himself preached the word of the Lord from this very church and so it was believed to be the oldest church in Christendom. I had walked through its doors a couple of days after we won the city and was amazed at the height of the ceilings as it was almost as high as it was wide. A single altar sat on the opposite side of the entrance, surrounded by colourful mosaics on the walls and the floors.

A rumoured tunnel did exist, it was to the left of the altar and I had followed it along as it led out to the mountainside where guards had been posted, ensuring no one still in the city who wanted out could escape this way.

When we arrived at the church, Bartholomew stood to greet us as did those who were with him.

"My lord," Bartholomew said reverently and bowed to Toulouse.

He motioned to us to enter the church, he and the group of men with him following us in. The interior of the church was cool and dark, lit only by the sunlight streaming through three star- shaped openings above the entrance.

"Tell us again what your visions have said to you," said Toulouse.

"Of course, my lord," Bartholomew said. Turning to me he continued, "St Andrew has appeared to me four times, each time telling me that a piece of the Holy Lance, was here. He revealed to me that it had been buried under the tiles here when St Peter himself preached the word of God here. I was to tell the Crusader leaders and then search for it, giving it to the Count of Toulouse when I found it. But I hesitated and each subsequent visit he has been becoming increasingly angry with me for not doing his bidding."

"Not everyone is convinced of the legitimacy of your claims, Bartholomew. However, Duke Robert has given his permission for a search to be done. D'Ivry and my men here shall bear witness."

Bartholomew's eyes lit up with excitement. Bowing again, he turned to his fellow soldiers and immediately set about taking up the flagstone floor so a search could be done beneath it. Toulouse took his leave, telling one of his men to keep watch and if anyone required his presence, he could be found at the citadel.

I wandered about the church again whilst Bartholomew and his men began loosening the stones and moving them outside so they would be out of the way of the digging. With two of Toulouse's men keeping watch, I wandered over to an opening in the wall that led to the tunnel and stopped at its mouth and stared at it. I remember being told that it was obviously an escape route used by Christians whenever the city was attacked. 'Perhaps not just Christians,' I thought.

Once the stones of the floor had been removed, Bartholomew and his men started digging as we kept watch. Hour after hour and nothing was found. Toulouse appeared and left. Bishop Adhémar arrived and was not surprised to hear that nothing had been found. Tried though we did to contain what was happening from the crowds, more and more people began visiting the church to see for themselves and to offer assistance. But still, no sign of the lance. The first day drew to a close and it was decided to start again the next day as the light was now not strong enough to see clearly. I decided to head back to the Duke's quarters and as I came out of the church's entrance and into the street next to it, I spotted Bartholomew engaged in a conversation with Bohemond. I surmised Bohemond was getting a direct update rather than depending on hearsay from Toulouse. It was important to him after all, if we were successful in seeing off the Turks, he was to be awarded Antioch and made its Prince. I thought nothing more of it.

The excavations continued into a second day. Duke Robert and the other leaders were becoming impatient and starting to doubt the authenticity of Bartholomew's visions even as other more senior members of the armies began to join in. There was an excitement building, a tremor of energy that permeated the entire city. People started to believe that the Lance was real, was here and was a divine sign that we were to be victorious in this crusade. The leaders were torn about this; if the Lance shard was found, this energy could easily be turned into a fervour and used in our battles with the Turks. However, if the shard was not found, the morale of the troops would sink into hopelessness and despair from which the crusade would not recover.

When I arrived on the second day to witness the work, I was surprised to see Bartholomew wearing heavier leggings, which was odd because, despite the cool air in the church, the digging would be strenuous and anyone participating soon found themselves needing to strip off some clothes to ease the heat and sweat. But not Bartholomew.

It was mid-day when the diggers stopped to rest a moment and take water. They seemed downhearted and frustrated by not having found anything even closely resembling a piece of the Lance. Bohemond had arrived to observe the work and stood to the side, arms crossed, his face expressionless.

I was standing beside the altar, looking down at the huge pit that was in place of the floor, seeing nothing but more of the same of dirt and stone which had been carried away in buckets after being loosened with the sharp tools used by the diggers. Then, without any warning, Bartholomew jumped into the pit, fell to his knees and started digging frantically with his bare hands, making grunting noises and murmuring to himself as he did so. He suddenly let out a cry and brought up out of the dirt what looked like a piece of iron, about the length of a spearhead and pointed like one.

> "It is here!" Bartholomew exclaimed as tears began to run down his cheeks. "Our Lord God Almighty has saved us!"

He clamoured out of the pit, gripping the piece of iron tightly, as if not wanting to risk dropping it. Everyone else in the church ran to him, shouting, surrounding him trying to get a look at the sign from God that had just miraculously been found, no doubt only due to the persistent faith of the true believers. The only person who did not make his way to Bartholomew was Bohemond. He simply turned and left the church without a word. I stared at the large gaping cavity of earth at my feet and wondered at the convenience of the relic's discovery by Bartholomew at this particular moment when only he was in the pit. I was reminded of the conversation Bishop Odo and I had when we were on our way to Saint-Denis. 'I think it does not matter if this *actually* happened. I think it is the lesson to be learned from the story that matters' I had said. And I remembered his advice never to accept at face value anything that left an uneasy feeling in my gut. I had that feeling now.

Despite the fact that some of the leaders did not believe this was a true relic of the Lance, they did recognise the impact believing it was had on the crusaders. The excitement caused by the knowledge that God had sent a sign and that we were destined to be victorious spread like wildfire throughout the city. Bartholomew was being hailed as a hero and a spiritual leader and when he announced that Saint Andrew had visited him again and instructed the crusaders to fast for five days, they followed him without question. When the fasting was over, the crusaders made it known that they were now prepared to do battle. But the leaders had one last strategy to try before organizing an onslaught.

Bohemond's spies had been reporting to him that Kerbogha's armies were not united under him and were fractious and fighting amongst themselves. So the leaders, thinking that because of this Kerbogha would be open to negotiations rather than fight, decided a parley should be held to discuss terms for ending the stand-off. It would be imprudent to send any of the leaders, if talks went badly, a leader could be held hostage or worse. It was when different options were being discussed that an unexpected volunteer came forward.

Peter the Hermit had been relatively quiet over the past months, doing what he could to keep motivation high amongst the troops but also dealing with his own shame and humiliation at the failure of leading the peasants' crusade to a disastrous fiasco. He felt he could redeem himself by offering to take the parley on behalf of the Christian leaders; it was an idea not immediately rejected by the leaders when discussing it late one evening in Duke Robert's quarters.

"I think it is a good idea," Flanders was saying when I arrived.

I was late getting back from tending the horses, and checking on my own Pax of course, who seemed content and surprisingly well-fed. I never asked but was secretly pleased that Pax had been included in the group of horses that belonged to the leaders and were singled out for special treatment. Especially as many had been sacrificed to feed the starving during our siege of the city. As I stepped into the room, Duke Robert shot a disapproving look at me. I bowed and took up my position in a corner to his right.

"But why would a high-ranking warrior like Kerbogha even consider meeting with someone as low-ranking as the Hermit?" asked Vermandois, clearly oblivious to the impact Peter and the peasants' crusade had made in Anatolia.

"It has nothing to do with rank," Robert retorted, annoyed that he had to include the French King's brother in these discussions.

"He has quite a reputation amongst the infidel," explained Bouillon. "Leading an army of the poor armed with basically nothing but farm implements and their faith impressed the Turks and anyone who heard the stories about them. The fact that they were defeated is almost irrelevant." He turned back to the Duke and continued, "I agree with Aumale, your Grace. I think Peter would be appropriate, Kerbogha will not be insulted."

Duke Robert thought on this a moment.

"I think the Hermit is a good choice and I agree with you Bouillon, Kerbogha should not be insulted. We need to send a small guard with him and an interpreter that we can trust. And a chest of coin to show our respect should be well-received."

Everyone nodded in agreement.

"Go fetch him. We much to discuss," Robert ordered.

Flanders bowed and motioned to his man Montdidier to do as Duke Robert ordered. I knew that this would be my one and only opportunity to speak up and so I approached the Duke, making it clear that I wanted to say something.

"Yes D'Ivry?" Robert asked.

I coughed a small cough, took a deep breath and spoke as seriously as I could.

"Your Grace, someone will be needed to present the chest of coin to Kerbogha, I would like to be that man. May I have this honour?" I asked, standing at attention and not looking him in the eye.

The conversation around the room came to a halt. Toulouse spoke up.

"Not content just having your head split open?" he asked trying not to smile.

Duke Robert moved very close to me, looking up at my face as if trying to gauge the reason behind the request. Even though I was now several inches taller than him, his gaze was still intimidating. But I held firm. Toulouse broke the silence.

"I believe he has earned it, your Grace," he said. "This is parley, he should not be in any great harm."

Duke Robert pursed his lips, probably remembering the promise he had made to my father.

"Very well," he said. "You will be representing all of the noble leaders here, and the Muslims are familiar with parley, so you should be safe. But there are risks, do you understand? If this goes awry, we may not be able to come for you."

"I understand, your Grace," I answered and said nothing more.

"So be it," he said. He turned to Tancarville and said, "Get him suited with the finest you can find." And then turned back to me, "You will go unarmed – do you understand?"

I nodded.

"Thank you, your Grace," I said earnestly.

A date was set for parley with Kerbogha. Duke Robert spent much time with both Peter the Hermit and myself instructing us on what to say and how to behave. A small wooden chest edged with bronze was found in one of the abandoned houses in the city and brought to the Duke who filled it with gold and silver coin donated from the leaders' private cache. Four of the Duke's personal guards were chosen to accompany us to the meeting place and both Bouillon and Flanders offered their men, Saint-Omer and Montdidier, to make a complement of six. All were armed but told to leave their swords sheathed. And they were instructed not to leave our sides.

Kerbogha's men had erected a tent for the meeting between his army camps and the Gate of the Duke. We would have to exit the Gate and then cross the Bridge of Boats to reach it. Peter, as the main emissary, would lead the party, insisted on going on foot. I would follow behind on Pax with the others mounted on their horses behind us. It created a perfect picture and exactly what Duke Robert wanted to convey – our piety supported by our strength.

We were to set out mid-morning as the sun climbed into the sky to the east, appearing above the mountains behind us. Summer had taken hold and the nights' coolness had given way to warm mornings. The seven of us on horseback had gone to the stables to prepare the horses and as I saddled Pax I began to sweat; I was not sure if that was the sun's effect or my nerves. I was about to step into the stirrup when Peter appeared at my side.

"My lord?" he said quietly.

"I am not a lord," I responded gently. "Please call me D'Ivry, or Sébastien if you prefer."

"Very well, Sébastien it is," he replied. "I believe you were a student of Bishop Odo?" he asked. I nodded silently and he continued, "I knew him, not well, but we met a few times over the years. The last was at the Council of Clermont where Pope Urban gave his wondrous sermon. He was a godly and righteous man, and I believe also quite good with in battle?"

I smiled, reminded of the image of him stitched into the tapestry hanging in his cathedral, or what had been his cathedral, back in Bayeux. The memory of it made me wince with melancholy, Peter must have seen a change in me.

"I apologise if saying so has brought any discomfort to you," he said kindly.

"It is no matter. Bishop Odo was very important to me, he will remain with me in spirit no matter where I go," I replied.

"Indeed, I am sure he will guide us through our task today. I would like to offer a blessing to you if you would like?"

I agreed and suggested that the others join us which they did. When it was done, we mounted the horses and walked them out to the Duke's Gate with Peter leading the way on foot. Duke Robert, Flanders, Bouillon, Hugues and Bisol amongst others were waiting, Bouillon holding the chest I was to take to Kerbogha. I saw Flanders engage in a short conversation with Saint-Omer and Montdidier as Duke Robert approached Peter.

"Remember, we offer only the terms we discussed, we accept none from him. You must remind him of the disadvantages of his position and the consequences should he refuse," Robert instructed.

He pointed to our interpreter Matik, a thin older man, bearded and dressed formally in Christian attire but bearing no weapon. He had taken part in the preparations for the parley with Peter and knew well what needed to be done. He came forward and joined Peter, intending to walk alongside him rather than ride.

He motioned to Bouillon to come forward to give me the chest. Without a word I took it from him and tied it to the pommel of my saddle so that I kept my hands free to work the reigns. Duke Robert then turned to me.

"D'Ivry, stay the course, let Peter speak, do not react to anything that is said or done by the Turk, behave as though it is all as to be expected, hm?"

"Yes, your Grace," I answered looking down at him from my height atop Pax.

It was time to go.

* * * * * * * * * *

Our small band, led by Peter the Hermit and Matik and followed first by myself and then the others on horseback, waited for the barriers of the Duke's Gate to be lifted and for the huge gates to be opened. The view that greeted us was curious: in the distance were the different camps of Turkish soldiers separated under their own banners but well in front was a set of plain tents, nothing remarkable, nothing denoting it as expecting any special event. Only the handful of armed guards patrolling outside hinted at who the people inside could be. The statement Kerbogha was making was clear: he did not consider the crusading armies to be his equal. My gut told me this was not going to go well.

Once outside the walls of the city, we crossed the Bridge of Boats that spanned the Orontes River and started to cross the relatively short distance to the Turkish tents on the plains of Antioch. I looked over my shoulder after we came off the bridge and saw the battlements filled with crusaders and others craning to get a view. I could not see the Duke or the others but knew they were watching. I was determined to do him proud and I could not help but wish Bishop Odo were here to witness this. I took a deep breath and urged Pax to keep the pace with a gentle tap of my boots to his sides. He whinnied and shook his head, bristling a bit against the tap.

"Alright, Pax," I whispered gently, "you know what to do."

It took about half an hour to cross the empty fields between the city walls and the tents. As we approached, the guards came to attention outside the tents but with swords remaining sheathed. This, at least, was a good sign. We came to a stop about twenty feet from the entrance and waited for some sign of welcome. Those of us on horseback remained mounted, Peter and Matik stood still in front of us. The only sound came from the walls of the tents fluttering in the gentle breeze coming from the west. The flaps of the main tent were pulled open and a small, elderly man dressed in rich Turkish clothes emerged and walked up to Peter. He looked at all of us for a moment and then began speaking to us. We waited to hear the translation.

"Kerbogha, Atabeg of Mosul, welcomes you," Matik said, "and entreats you to join him," he added, pointing to the tent.

Peter bowed slightly to the Turk and gave his reply for Matik to translate.

"We are honoured," he said.

Once that was done, we dismounted and I unlashed the chest from the saddle. Three of our men including Saint-Omer and Montdidier stayed with the horses and the rest of us followed the elderly Turk as he walked slowly back to the main tent, ducked and entered it.

What greeted us was astonishing. Although the exterior of the tents was drab at best, inside had been decorated with rich, vibrant colours, silk curtains of gold and cobalt blue. It was difficult not to be impressed. We entered an anteroom first where two more guards were posted, still with swords sheathed. Heavy curtains separated this anteroom from the main meeting area; these were pulled back for the Turkish interpreter and we followed him in.

The first person I saw was Kerbogha himself, the former soldier and now proud Governor of Mosul, one of the most powerful of the Muslim cities. He was sitting on an ornate chair on top of a small riser and, although dressed for the occasion, he had a distant, almost bored, look on his face, as if he were tolerating this parley rather than truly wishing to participate in it. He was stroking his pointed beard with his left hand, his elbow resting on the chair's arm and looking at no one in particular. His eyes sparked a moment when he spied the chest I was carrying, always eager to have gold and silver laid at his feet.

As we approached, there was a movement of the curtains behind Kerbogha. Zengi appeared and joined his adoptive father on his left. He looked different again, his black hair now hung loose, straight and long, falling well past his shoulders. We locked eyes in a moment of recognition, but gave nothing away.

We waited until everyone was in place and then Peter the Hermit spoke after bowing.

> "Bohemond, Prince of Taranto and Robert, Duke of Normandy, send greetings to Atabeg Kerbogha of Mosul. They offer prayers for your health and those closest to you and extend their appreciation for your willingness for this parley."

Peter waited for Matik to finish his translation before continuing. Kerbogha nodded his understanding.

> "In good faith, the Prince and the Duke bring you this offering of gold and silver as a demonstration of their good will," he said, gesturing towards me and the chest I was holding.

As instructed by Duke Robert, I stepped one pace forward and stopped. To my surprise, Zengi moved towards me, opened the lid revealing a mound of exquisite gold and silver coin. He looked up at me, tilted his head ever-so-slightly as if to say, 'that will do nicely,' and motioned to one of the guards to take it from me, show it to Kerbogha and then take it away. Zengi returned to his leader where he was handed two small folds of cloth made from fine Turkish silk, each a kaleidoscope of deep-hued colours interspersed with silver and gold threads. Kerbogha pointed at them and then pointed at me. Zengi walked back to me.

> "For...your Prince and...Duke," he said haltingly in my language, holding them out for me to open.

I unfolded each, one at a time and revealed the largest rubies I had ever seen. But remembering the advice from Duke Robert - *behave as though it is all as to be expected* – and kept my face as impassive as I could.

I nodded my thanks, wrapped them in the silks and tucked them into my belt, making sure they were secure. Zengi returned to his post. It was then Kerbogha's turn to speak.

"'Madha turid?" he said directly to Peter.

"His Excellency wishes to know what is requested of him?" Matik translated.

"Our leaders are aware of the difficulties faced by both our armies during this siege and they assume there is a shared desire not to waste bloodshed if agreement can be reached? If so, I have been instructed to offer the terms of trial by single combat by ten or twenty commanders of each army, a fight to the death to determine the outcome of this siege. The victor's army shall be given the city of Antioch; the army which fails shall be allowed to leave unmolested," Peter replied solemnly.

Matik relayed Peter's words and we watched with heightened anticipation for some sign of comprehension and a willingness to consider the terms. But my first impression of Kerbogha had been correct, he really had no interest in discussing them at all. Instead, he laughed, a harsh, mocking laugh.

"Lays ladaya makhawif," he said to Peter with a sneer. "Mawaqifi aman, hdha aleard la yaghrini. 'Ana 'arfid!"

His tone told us what his response was before Matik did.

"His Excellency is not concerned about his position here," he translated, adding quietly, "and he has no interest in this offer. He," Matik coughed slightly, "declines."

This took us all by surprise but no one showed it. We had expected him to come with his own offers and for negotiation to take place, but this outright rejection was unforeseen. I exchanged a look with Zengi who looked powerless to do anything about his adopted father's decision and remained expressionless, looking straight ahead at no one in particular. Peter did his best to follow the Duke's instructions by reminding the Turk about the disadvantages of that position but he was having none of it. With a curt wave of his hand, the parley was over and we were escorted out of the tent.

With very little ceremony, we made our way to the city, going back the way we came. Peter relayed everything to Duke Robert and Bohemond; naturally, both were angered by Kerbogha's response. But it was what Saint-Omer and Montdidier reported that startled me. It seemed they had alternative reasons for attending the parley.

"What did you observe?" Flanders asked of his man.

"It is clear that they are not a cohesive fighting unit," Montdidier replied.

"Why?" Flanders asked.

"We are, undoubtedly, outnumbered by many. But they are dispersed across the plain, and do not give any sign of being united, at least not physically," he responded.

"Of course this could be a ploy," interjected Saint-Omer. "But we have received information from the spies that the Generals of the other factions are more interested in protecting their own lands rather than fighting us, this distance is more than likely intended rather than feigned. We could use this to our advantage."

Everyone fell silent for a moment to ponder the implications of this and Kerbogha's response to our offer. A clever strategy would need to be connived to use this against them. We recognized now that we had no choice but to go to battle.

Once again, it was Bohemond who conceived the plan for attack. Knowing that Kerbogha's army was made up of separate factions from Persia, Palestine, Damascus and others gave Bohemond the edge he thought we needed to break the Turks and send them running. He devised to split our armies into four divisions: Duke Robert and Flanders would take the northern French, Bouillon would take the German troops, Bishop Adhémar the southern French and Bohemond the Italians. Toulouse had fallen ill whilst we were at parley and so it was decided he should remain in the city guarding the citadel with about two hundred men.

Each division would march out from the Bridge Gate but in groups, not as an army as a whole. Vermandois would go ahead of the divisions, taking a regiment of the best arches from all the armies, letting off volley after volley of arrows at the Turks on the other side of the Bridge of Boats with the intention of breaking the Turkish line. He would be followed by Duke Robert and Flanders, then Bouillon, and then Adhémar with Bohemond bringing up the rear. We knew it was a good plan and it had to work or we would die fighting. The leaders decided the battle should be waged the next morning at dawn.

The five days of fasting Bartholomew had ordered before the parley were now over with the expected result of increasing the fever for battle amongst the hungry crusaders. Adhémar also ordered that the fighting men should shave and trim their hair so they could not be mistaken for their enemy. And on the evening of the battle, Bohemond sent messengers throughout the city with rallying cries to encourage the troops. We were down to only about twenty thousand crusaders and with only a few hundred horses left meaning the majority would be fighting on foot, but still there was an air of excitement and belief in our victory. And despite his doubts of the veracity of the discovery of the Holy Lance, Adhémar was willing, as our spiritual leader, to carry it before him as he led his troops.

After prime prayers at dawn the next morning, the armies prepared to carry out the Bohemond's plans. I was mailled and helmed and given a deep red surcoat by Toulouse to wear over top. And I lucky enough to have been allowed to be on horseback on Pax aside Duke Robert on his steed. This was the first time I was to be in the midst of the fighting, every abled body was needed for this battle. Vermandois and his archers stood ready at the gate with Duke Robert and Flanders and their men awaiting our turn to cross the bridge.

At the appointed time, the barriers were lifted and the gates flung open and with great shouts and cries of attack, Vermandois and his archers stampeded the bridge letting out their arrows into the masses of Turkish soldiers on the west side of the river. I happened to look back at the citadel and caught sight of a black flag being raised, those inside giving warning to the enemy that the attack had begun. But this was in vain. Taken completely by surprise, the Turks were seen scrambling, trying to organise a coordinated attack. Vermandois's men did what they needed to do and pushed the Turks back. One of the Turkish factions camped to the north sprang to life and came charging towards the archers, but by the time they reached them, Duke Robert, Flanders and our men, myself included, had already stormed across the bridge and met them head on, reinforced by the others. Those, led by Adhémar, Bouillon and Bohemond, came across the Bridge and spread out in a semi-circle, assailing anyone of the enemy they could see.

We found out later that the Turkish Generals had begged Kerbogha to have his entire army meet ours as we came across the bridge in groups but for reasons we will never truly understand, he dallied and delayed before engaging the bulk of his army. Whatever his thinking, he was too late in sending the rest of his troops and when he finally did, instead of meeting us, they stormed into the retreating vanguard of his own army who had fled from our attack. Once word had spread of the retreat, it did not take long for the Generals to abandon him and flee.

My own interaction with the enemy was short-lived and fleeting. As we rushed across the Bridge of Boats, I saw Hugues to my right, on his black destrier, sword in hand. He shot a look at me and then jerked his horse's reigns to the right as we both stepped off the wood planks of the ramp of the bridge. I followed him and within seconds we were in the middle of the conflict, soon surrounded by Turks on foot. But Flanders's other men were on our heels and quickly engaged them. One Turkish soldier came for me and I veered Pax out of the way of the swipe of his scimitar and met it with my own broadsword coming down hard from above. The power of my blow stunned him and he was down in an instant. But before I could finish him, Hugues, who had just dispatched his own opponent, leapt from his horse and did the deed with his sword, killing the Turk instantly. I had never seen an enemy die in combat so close before; the look in the man's eyes was both surprised and haunted; he had not expected to die this day.

It was over in less than an hour. We pushed forward, beyond the meeting place of the parley and found the camps deserted. No sign of Kerbogha and none of Zengi. But in the distance, we could see smoke starting to appear, first in individual wisps, curling towards the sky and then in ever-growing clouds, so thick they blotted out the landscape behind them. Kerbogha had ordered the ground to be razed as he made his escape to prevent us from pursuing him any further. It was the sign that we had been victorious.

Our troops, knowing they had won the day, began scavenging for food and valuables, anything they could carry or bring with them back to the city. I could see Duke Robert, Flanders, Bouillon and Bohemond gathering at the bridge's entrance we had rode through moments before. I went to see the body of the man I had helped to kill. Hugues was nearby and joined me.

"It was a good fight young Sébastien," he said to me as I stared at the man.

He bent down, took a small knife from his belt, cut a small sack from the man's belt, and tossed it to me.

"I believe this is yours," he said as I caught it.

Opening it, I could see a few gold and silver coins. I did not know what to say. Hugues guessed that I was troubled. He got up, walked over to me and put his hand on my shoulder.

"This is the spoils of war, D'Ivry. You must face that and accept it. Or not go on," he said and then made his way towards the bridge.

He was right of course. But as I stared at the money in my hands, I had to wonder what had happened to Zengi – was he one of these bodies spread across the fields or had he escaped? Although he was the enemy, a part of me secretly wanted him to have survived the onslaught. But there were too many dead to know his fate for certain and I had to be comforted by the thought that he might have gotten away.

* * * * * * * * * *

Kerbogha's haste in fleeing meant he had had no time to pack up the camps and we quickly found hordes of supplies, food, sheep, oxen, wines and a myriad of other goods we desperately needed. All were brought back to the city and shared amongst the crusaders. In the city, word had reached Toulouse of our victory as well as reaching the Muslims who held the citadel and a quick surrender was negotiated – strangely, they insisted on surrendering to Bohemond and not to Toulouse. Whether this was out of respect for his military prowess or that they now considered him the leader of Antioch and had agreed to this before the battle, we were never sure. But it did support Bohemond's earlier demands that he be given the city as a reward which he had raised again and again each time the leaders met. Some made the argument that the city belonged to Emperor Alexios but Bohemond reminded them that the Emperor had abandoned our mission, betrayed us at Nicaea and had not provided the support he had promised and so their oaths to him were no longer valid and they were free to do what they wanted.

Toulouse and Bohemond continued to bicker over ownership of the city. Bohemond increased the number of his standards being flown and both refused to give way to the other over using the citadel as a residence. The squabbling amongst the leaders was becoming more than an annoyance, and many of the men threatened to head to Jerusalem without them. Finally Bishop Adhémar decided to hold a council late in July to decide matters and make plans for the journey to Jerusalem.

The first matter decided was everyone's agreement not to march towards the Holy Land in the middle of summer. The heat would be unbearable and the armies needed to regain their strength before we could go anywhere. Next, Vermandois was chosen to go to Constantinople to obtain the promised support from the Emperor. He left but never returned deciding, once the Emperor refused any further support, to return to France and not fulfil his vow just as Blois had not.

Before the council could be held, Bishop Adhémar suddenly took ill and died, leaving the spiritual leadership of the crusade in chaos along with deciding who should be awarded Antioch. Duke Robert made no claim on the city and left it to Toulouse and Bohemond to work out. It was not until November that Toulouse finally relented after it was agreed that he would be the leader of the crusading armies going to Jerusalem. Bohemond was satisfied, he had his city. He was now known as Bohemond, the Prince of Antioch and ruled lands as far as he could see from the top of the citadel.

And so, with those quarrels resolved and the burial of Bishop Adhémar in the Church of St Peter, we settled in to spend Christmas in the city with fresh supplies arriving unimpeded along the river. But only one thought was on our minds.

Jerusalem.

# IV

# Part One

# 1099 - Jerusalem

The animosity between Toulouse and Bohemond continued despite Toulouse's concessions, and only worsened when Bohemond evicted some of Toulouse's men who had stayed behind to keep an eye on Bohemond in Antioch. Toulouse was determined to have his revenge and thought he had found a way in Marrat, a rich settlement south of Antioch. He and Flanders had departed Antioch the previous November and besieged the city in December only to have Bohemond follow and take possession of Marrat's towers, creating yet another stand-off between the two men again.

This ill will was starting to take its toll on the other leaders and on the armies who were frustrated not seeing any plans to march on Jerusalem. Eventually Bohemond pulled his men from the towers in Marrat but that did not seem to have any impact on solving the growing and mutual hostility. And so another council was called early in January 1099 in nearby Rugia during which Toulouse offered to pay the leaders for their support. To Duke Robert and Bouillon he offered ten thousand gold coins, Flanders six thousand and Tancred five thousand but only Duke Robert and Tancred accepted the offer, Bouillon and Flanders did not, choosing instead to return to Antioch with Bohemond. It was not really surprising to see Tancred's acceptance of Toulouse's offer, we knew he had longed to break free from his uncle's grip for quite some time, this gave him that opportunity. Unfortunately, this meant the armies would split, diminishing the numbers and therefore the strength overall. Fighting the enemy had suddenly become more difficult.

And whilst the leaders were squabbling over such matters, the situation at Marrat was becoming much, much worse. Already suffering hunger again after having thoroughly pillaged the town for all its food and supplies, Toulouse's soldiers were becoming desperate. We found out just how much when he received a report from one of his men he had left behind to keep the city secure. He arrived at Duke Robert's quarters ashen faced.

"Your Grace..." Toulouse started and then stopped, not sure how to proceed.

Duke Robert had just started to write some communiques when Toulouse arrived. He saw the look on his face and motioned for me to fetch him a goblet of wine.

"You have heard from Balazun, I presume?" he asked.

Toulouse could only nod mutely and downed all of the wine in one gulp. I refilled the goblet and handed it back to him. It took a moment for him to collect himself and pulled up a chair when Duke Robert pointed to one. He looked ill.

"I cannot, I cannot begin to tell you of the events these past weeks in Marrat whilst we have been here," he stated flatly, staring at the table. "It is horrid, unimaginable, un-Holy," he mumbled.

"Take a breath Raymond," Duke Robert said gently, using Toulouse's Christian name, "and tell me what has happened."

Toulouse breathed in deeply and exhaled slowly.

"Conditions at Marrat have deteriorated rapidly since my departure to come here for council," he said sombrely, his fingertips lightly touching the table, choosing his words carefully. "Supplies were already running low, especially after some of the senior troops stripped the houses bare of all their goods."

He took another deep breath. Duke Robert waited patiently and said nothing.

"Balazun reports that they have not received any word of a replenishment of food and supplies, so some of the men have taken the most wretched decision to...to...use some of the Muslim dead for sustenance," he said, almost whispering the last few words.

Duke Robert and I both froze, hardly believing what we had just heard. Both of our mouths dropped open in shock, Duke Robert's eyes grew wide and he leaned closer to Toulouse as if he had not heard correctly. Toulouse pressed the palms of his hands against his temples as if trying to rid his mind of the images.

"They, they pulled the dead bodies from the river and cut them..." Toulouse stopped, unable to continue.

My father told me before I left Normandy to be prepared to witness scenes of unspeakable cruelty, brutality, whenever we were at war. 'Desperate men will do unconscionable things' he warned me. But never could I ever believe such an atrocity as this. Toulouse's troops must have seen death coming to have been convinced this was their only way to survive. I honestly could not say I would not have done the same thing if I found myself in the same position.

"You must return immediately Raymond," Duke Robert said quietly but firmly. "This cannot go on."

Toulouse nodded his agreement.

"I leave this evening," he replied gravely.

He told us later that upon his return, his men had started to pull down the walls of the city in a fury at their predicament, believing their leader appeared to rather spend his time bickering over Antioch than being there, getting supplies and preparing to march to Jerusalem. Toulouse had to resolve this and quickly or he would lose complete control of his army. Using a considerable amount of his personal fortune, he secured the much-needed food and was able to placate his men with promises that they would soon be on their way to Palestine. He also knew his time in Marrat was over, he needed to regroup, take control of the mission and finally become the leader he claimed he was.

* * * * * * * * *

Once the Marrat situation had been calmed, Duke Robert's army, including myself, joined Toulouse for the journey to Jerusalem. But even with Duke Robert, our numbers totalled less than five thousand fighters, nowhere near enough to wage any major battles along the route. We desperately needed the armies of the other leaders and sent word to both Flanders and Bouillon to join us as soon as possible but these requests seemed to be ignored. We could not wait any longer so, after hearing nothing from the others, we decided to be on our way, departing Marrat for Palestine taking a route along the shoreline of the Mediterranean. This gave us access to the critical food and supplies that were being sent from Western allies who supported our mission.

By mid-February we found ourselves at Arqa, a settlement near the grand city of Tripoli. For reasons he did not explain to the Duke, Toulouse had decided to besiege it and instructed his men to set up camp around it, forcing Duke Robert to do the same as he could not continue on to Jerusalem without him. We discovered later that it was Toulouse's belief that if Arqa fell, Tripoli would soon follow, and that was the real reason behind his adamance to take Arqa. What Toulouse did not know was that this was an especially resilient stronghold, fortified over the years by Pagans, Turks, Arabs, it would take a massive force to conquer it. But Toulouse was adamant it could be done, probably more out of pride and the desire to rid himself of the reputation he now had due to the atrocities at Marrat. But we also had hoped to see the armies of Flanders and Bouillon fairly soon, for surely they were on their way now that we had proven we were marching towards Jerusalem.

Word of what happened at Marrat had spread quickly throughout the area and it had a rather surprising effect on the neighbouring towns and villages – our reputation was cemented for being brutal and fearless. Emirs and other dignitaries from around Tripoli and Arqa arrived or sent emissaries offering gold, supplies, horses, clothing, whatever they could to convince us to leave their towns in peace. This made Duke Robert and Toulouse and even Tancred very rich and, with supplies and food being supplemented by Greek and Venetian ships meeting us at the coast, our armies quickly regained their strength. But, irritatingly, Toulouse was determined to see Arqa fall and kept besieging the town despite making little to no progress. Duke Robert knew needed to start planning the campaign for Jerusalem as we had a new foe to deal with there – the Egyptian Fatimids who had ousted the Turks from the Holy City – and urged Toulouse to end his siege so we could press on.

Toulouse refused, convinced victory was near, so strategizing our attack on Jerusalem would have to wait until we had dealt with Arqa as Toulouse was determined to have it. But weeks passed without breaching the walls and very soon, the Turks and Arabs of the nearby settlements began to wonder why they were paying so much to protect their own towns when it was clear that we could not take Arqa. That is when rumours reached us of another very large enemy army being formed, this time from Baghdad, that would soon set off to challenge us. Toulouse and Duke Robert realized we simply did not have the manpower to meet this new force and sent many, increasingly panicked, pleas for help to Flanders and Bouillon who finally agreed to leave Bohemond in Antioch and re-join the crusade.

Their two armies had been with us for some time when some strange things began happening in the camps involving Peter Bartholomew. When Bishop Adhémar passed away, our armies were suddenly left without a spiritual leader and Bartholomew, with his cult of followers, had slipped into the role, despite there being a great deal of scepticism about him and the finding of the Holy Lance in Antioch. But it was a gap that needed filling and as long as he kept his place, the leaders decided he would do and left him to his own devices.

Unfortunately, he was incapable of handling the power that came with this position and his preaching became more and more erratic. He made claims of having visitations of saints telling him to purge the armies of the sinful and that only he would be able to tell the sinful from the righteous. This, of course, was dismissed quickly by Duke Robert and Toulouse as nonsense. But Bartholomew persisted, claiming that Bishop Adhémar had come to him in a vision where the Bishop admitted he had been wrong to doubt Bartholomew and begged his forgiveness. This was one claim too far, the breaking point for many, and arguments and brawls broke out between Bartholomew's believers and non-believers. But he was adamant that his visions, including that of the Bishop, were real and that he was prepared to prove himself by trial by ordeal.

All along, Duke Robert had paid no heed to Bartholomew, believing him to be a bit of a charlatan. He never believed he had found an actual relic, having seen what was the real Holy Lance in Constantinople. He had decided to remain quiet – until now. He ordered the priest to attend him and the other leaders one evening, a few days before Good Friday. They were discussing his claims before Bartholomew arrived.

"Surely he cannot expect us to believe his visions of Bishop Adhémar?" Robert asked incredulous.

"Or his presumption of being the sole judge of sin within the camps?" Tancred said vehemently.

Toulouse looked uncomfortable. He had, after all, been a supporter of Bartholomew and had claimed aloud that he was a believer of the authenticity of the Holy Lance. But now, he was outnumbered and was slowly having to admit, with much chagrin, that he may have been wrong.

Bartholomew was announced and shown into the Duke's tents and immediately gave a low bow to the senior men there. Duke Robert did not waste any time.

"Priest, we have been informed of some preaching that you have been doing of late in the camps, saying Bishop Adhémar has visited you?" Robert said.

"Yes, your Grace, the Bishop appeared before me in the early hours of the morning a few days ago. He was enveloped in a heavenly glow and emanated peace and tranquillity. But he was also aggrieved, he seemed desperate to speak to me. He admitted he had been wrong about doubting the find of the Holy Lance and begged my forgiveness," Bartholomew stated with sincerity.

Tancred snorted.

"You must realize how difficult it is for anyone to take you seriously about this? How very self-serving this 'vision' is? It is an obvious ploy to silence those who question the veracity of the Lance!" he snapped at the priest.

"But the Holy Lance led us to victory at Antioch," Bartholomew insisted answering Tancred. "Without it, we would not have been certain of God's will and would not have won the day."

"It was Prince Bohemond's brilliant strategizing that led us to victory at Antioch," Tancred argued, adding, "And without *it*, we would not have won the day."

Duke Robert put a stop to the argument quickly.

"Bartholomew, you must realize that there are many that do not believe the lance you found is the true Lance, for many have seen another in Constantinople, including myself. And many of us here. And now, with this so-called appearance of Bishop Adhémar, well, for many this is too much. The discord being created between your followers and the others is starting to be detrimental to our cause. Something needs to be done, and done soon, the disorder must be quelled."

Bartholomew was becoming agitated. Not being believed was clearly having an effect on him.

"Of course, your Grace, I understand. But I must insist to you that my visions are real, that the Holy Lance I discovered in Antioch is real, upon my life, I have been true and faithful!" he said fervently, crossing himself.

A silence overtook the room. Bartholomew took a deep breath.

"I am prepared, your Grace, my lords, to verify the legitimacy of my visions and of the Holy Lance. I beg of you!" he pleaded. "Put me through a trial by ordeal so I can prove myself!"

The others in the room all glanced at each other. This would decide the issue, one way or another. Slowly, they all nodded to Duke Robert.

"So be it," he agreed.

"I ask for four days of fasting so I can prepare myself," Bartholomew said. "I accept any ordeal of your choice. I am determined, my faith and honour will see me through any trial I must suffer."

And so it was settled. Duke Robert and the others decided Bartholomew should be put through an ordeal by fire. Three days later, after sunset on Good Friday, two large pyres were built, four feet high and thirteen feet long and only about two feet apart. Bartholomew was to walk in between them when they were fully aflame. If he emerged unscathed, we would all know that he had God's protection and the lance he had found was indeed the true Lance. And of course we all knew what it meant if he did not.

The dead olive branches that had been used to create the pyres took hold of the flames quickly, spitting sparks up into the night-time sky. Crowds of crusaders, men and women, including the members of Bartholomew's Cult of the Lance, arrived early, jockeying for position so they could witness the event. I stood at the far end of the pyres next to Hugues and Bisol, both of whom had arrived with Flanders. I was glad to see them.

"Be careful Geoffroi, Sébastien," Hugues warned, "we know not how this mob will react when, if, Bartholomew comes through."

Both of us adjusted our stance to stand more firmly, our senses slightly more alert than they had just been. I could see Duke Robert in deep conversation with Toulouse, Bouillon and Flanders – they all knew the future of this crusade depended on the outcome of this trial.

Bartholomew arrived barefoot, dressed in a simple tunic, and carrying the Lance before him. The crowd hushed to a near silence, all we could really hear was the snapping of the twigs as they were consumed by the flames. He stepped forward towards the entrance of the pyre tunnel now in full flame, raised the Lance above him and, looking around at the faces surrounding him, addressed the masses.

"Here I present to you the one true Holy Lance, discovered beneath the stone floors by the altar of the Church of Saint Peter, the Church of Saint Peter where the venerable Apostle Peter himself preached the word of the Lord! I kissed its point as it protruded from the ground and felt the power of God surge within me! On my faith, on my honour, with the protection of the Lord I shall survive this ordeal!"

And with that, he stepped into the raging inferno, moving quickly through it and out the other side towards us. He emerged, appearing unmarked by the fire, crying out 'God help us!.' The crowd closest to him went wild, his followers shouting and crying in a frenzy, running to him in an attempt to touch him and get a piece of his tunic. Instinctively, Hugues, Bisol and I leapt forward trying to protect him, knowing he would likely be torn apart if we did not reach him in time. Duke Robert and Toulouse had obviously considered this beforehand and within moments we were surrounded by Toulouse's guards, pushing the crowd back and allowing us to carry Bartholomew to a tent where the Duke's physicians were waiting in case they were needed.

We laid him on a cot where he was quickly covered by blankets as he had started shivering. The physicians immediately got to work examining him to see what injuries he had incurred. We could see scrapes and cuts on his legs which probably happened when he was set upon by his followers trying to get a piece of his tunic, or of his own body, for a relic. We also noticed he was not moving his legs and wondered aloud why this was. But most disturbing of all were the red blotches now starting to appear all over his body. It was clear to us that poor Bartholomew had not come through the ordeal unscathed. Quite the opposite. One of the physicians spoke to Hugues.

"His back is broken which is why he cannot move. I believe this was caused when he was trampled by the crowd. There are cuts and bruises but those are of no great matter and probably also happened when the crowd came upon him. He is, however, badly burnt, the swellings over his body will soon blister and may become infected. We will apply ointments with herbs and rose oil to temper the injuries and to soothe his pain."

"Very well," Hugues said, and then turned to us. "I am going to report to Duke Robert and the others, the two of you stay and assist where you can."

The physicians put us to work immediately, fetching fresh water and soaking pieces of flax in a concoction of oils and liquids with herbs and other bits unknown to us. With each application, Bartholomew screamed in pain, and we could see the blistering, now visible all over his body, turning black as infection set in.

It took twelve agonizing days for Bartholomew to die. His followers sat vigil outside the tents, begging for information on his condition but Bisol and I kept silent. It was not our place to say anything, and we went on with the business of trying to relieve his pain in the few days he had left.

The effect of his death was immediate. His group of followers, in shock and disbelief, dispersed, the members demoralised and distraught that everything they believed had not been true. They returned to the armies they had come with and never spoke of it again – the Cult of the Lance was no more.

Toulouse's reputation was now in tatters. He had supported Bartholomew and his discovery of the lance, but now his leadership of the crusade was in question, many doubted his abilities if he could be so easily swayed by such a charlatan. To make matters worse, he received word that Emperor Alexios was on his way, having ordered Toulouse to stay at Arqa and await him. But many now no longer believed in the Emperor, he had betrayed too many times, and we wanted to be on our way. In-fighting raged again amongst the leaders, Tancred, who had supported Toulouse since they left Antioch, now switched his allegiance to Bouillon and even Toulouse's own men threatened to go on their own. Toulouse realized his time as leader of this crusade was done; he would have to share the responsibility, and of course the power, with the others. And once we arrived at Jerusalem, a new leader would have to take us the last few miles to our final destination and battle with the Saracens.

* * * * * * * * *

We were on our way by early May, following a route close to the sea so we could keep receiving supplies sent to us from the West. We expected attacks along the way but with the exception of a few bandits foraging for food, we were left alone by the Fatimid Muslims who controlled Palestine. The battles we had faced over the past few years had taken a toll on the numbers of fighting men, we were down to about twelve hundred mounted knights and twelve thousand foot- soldiers, a fraction of what we had started out with. Our path took us past the port cities of Tyre, Acre and then Caesarea where we camped for a few days on the beaches and celebrated Pentecost. Finally, at the end of May we turned inland at Arsuf and marched towards Ramleh which we planned on taking but found it abandoned, the inhabitants having fled a few days earlier leaving all of their goods, livestock and much else behind. It was a strategically important town for us, half-way between the seaport of Jaffa and Jerusalem. It was here that the plans for liberating the Holy City were finalised.

Over the weeks of travel between Arqa and Ramleh, it became more and more obvious that one of the other leaders would have to step up and take control. Duke Robert made no movement to take over, he wanted to leave that to someone else. That someone was Bouillon. He had gradually become a favourite amongst the troops, and his unwavering focus on rescuing Jerusalem inspired them to keep the faith and their vows. And so, upon arriving at Ramleh, Bouillon took control.

Our appearance there did not go unnoticed. We met many fleeing Christians who had been expelled from the city by Caliph Iftikhar al-Dawla who had issued eviction edicts when he was apprised of our imminent arrival. They warned us that the wells around the city had been poisoned and that al-Dawla had brought in extra provisions to withstand a lengthy siege. And just as in Antioch, we found ourselves under pressure to act quickly, for the Caliph had also put out a call to the Muslim world for assistance in defending the city and rumours abounded that a Muslim Fatimid army was on its way from Egypt.

We expected all of this, having become familiar with these tactics each time we had engaged the Muslim armies during the battles so far. But now, we were just days away from our first assault on the Holy City, and morale was strong despite the intense heat and shortage of food and water. Our purpose was to be realized and very soon and we needed to be prepared for whatever might befall us.

We were strategizing at council discussing how we should attack the city and what fallback positions might be needed, with Bouillon leading the discussions.

"The north walls are most vulnerable, the northeast more so than the rest," he stated, acknowledging he had confirmed this information with more than one of the Christians who had just fled the city.

"Attacking from the south will be difficult with a large contingent, but we should be able to position a smaller force between Mount Sion and the south walls and attack through the gate there. And another force on the west wall, whilst we position most of the armies at the northeast corner, possibly others further along," he theorised. "We will need to confirm this is possible once we have been able to assess the strength and validity of the information we have received."

His suggestions made sense, the others all agreed.

"There is a small settlement here," Duke Robert pointed on the map, "called Nabi Samuil, a where Byzantine monastery has been built next to the tomb of the Prophet Samuel. I suggest we set up our base camp there until we are ready to move on the city? But we will need another, preferably to the south."

"Bethlehem is well-positioned for that," Tancred offered, tapping on the map. "We will need to secure it though, it is currently garrisoned by Saracen troops."

Bouillon did not hesitate.

"Then you shall liberate it," he said to Tancred. "Take Baldwin de Bourcq with you and about fifty men to secure it."

Tancred nodded.

"We will need siege engines," Flanders stated, returning to the problem of the attack on the great city itself. "We can get some of the timber from local forests, but I am concerned there will not be enough, nor will it be hardy enough to withstand the onslaught from the Saracen's mangonels."

"Supply ships are en route but we have no idea when they will reach us, or if they will, so we will have to make do with what we can find here," responded Bouillon. "Set the men to task of hewing what they can. We also need to secure a source of water, set some men to that as well. We proceed to Nabil Samuil in two days."

The army moved to Nabil Samuil the same day that Tancred and de Bourcq left for Bethlehem. Duke Robert and Bouillon and a small group of men, including myself and Bisol, rode ahead and reached the small monastic community before the main army, leaving Flanders and Aumale to oversee the movement of the bulk of the men. The tomb of the Prophet was at the top of a large hill, just south of the settlement and we continued riding until we reached its summit. It was there that we saw a vision unlike any other we had seen thus far.

Jerusalem.

We could see the Holy City in the distance, less than a day's march from where we stood. We all dismounted and dropped to our knees in thankful prayer for being delivered safely to this place, *Deus Vult*, it was clearly God's doing. And throughout the next few days setting up camp, we could hear the cries of joy coming from the top of the hill as crusader after crusader, soldier and civilian walked to the crest and saw the blessed place with their own eyes. The hill was quickly dubbed Mount Joy for the sheer exhilaration one could not help but feel upon seeing the city.

I felt mesmerised by the sight, there had been many times when I had lost all belief that we were going to reach it, and I spent several nights sleeping under the stars on the hilltop so the city would be the first thing I saw upon waking. I was there late one evening after I had finished my chores and most had turned in for the night, having found a relatively soft patch of ground to sit on and leaning against a large boulder to watch the flickering lights of the city when I heard soft footsteps approaching me from behind. My muscles stiffened and my eyes searched for anything nearby that I could use to defend myself, my sword lying next to me but in its scabbard. In my mind went through the fluid steps of taking hold of it, unsheathing it and turning to face my adversary and calculating the time that would take if such actions were necessary. The footsteps continued until I saw, in the corner of my eye, a wiry older man reaching the crest of the hill and standing still a few feet away from me, staring into the distance, his hands held behind his back, transfixed as I had been the first time I saw the sight. I coughed slightly as I was not sure he knew I was there and he flinched with surprise, stepping back and tripping over a small satchel he had just placed on the ground next to his feet.

I could see he was not armed, dressed in well-worn dark linen tunic and trousers and simple sandals, he looked more like a poor peasant rather than any warrior. I leapt up and offered my hand to help him up which he accepted with a great look of surprise on his face. I wanted to know that he was not hurt and asked him so in my own language. To my surprise, he answered, speaking it almost fluently.

"Yes, yes, I am fine, I am unhurt," he answered, brushing the dirt from his backside. "I did not see you there, please, please forgive me."

"There is nothing to forgive," I responded. "You are not from our armies, who are you? What brings you here?"

"My name is Theós, I am a simple leather worker, sir," he answered, dipping his head slightly.

Then seeing Pax's saddle blanket which I had brought to rest my head on for sleeping, he must have suddenly thought I must be someone of some significance as he bowed.

"Why are you here?" I asked again.

"I am just one of the many you must have seen coming from the city these last few days, Caliph al-Dawla has forced the evacuation of Christians upon hearing that soldiers from the West had arrived," he answered humbly.

"Are you Christian?" I asked wary, thinking he looked more Arab.

"Yes, a Coptic Christian, sir," he responded. "My family comes from Egypt, but we settled in Jerusalem many years ago when I was a mere child."

I was ashamed suddenly of the assumptions I had made of the man.

"Where are your others?" I asked wanting to change the subject quickly. "Are they here as well?"

He shook his head slowly, pursing his lips.

"No, sir. I have no family. My mother and father died a few years ago and my wife before them giving birth to my only son who also died. I am alone here," he said.

My heart went out to the man and I felt ashamed once again, feeling responsible for making him relive what must have been painful memories. He seemed to have noticed my awkward unease as he turned back to the view of the city, changing the subject.

"Beautiful, is she not?" he asked.

I was surprised when he used the feminine to describe the Holy City, but then I thought how appropriate that was.

"Yes, she is indeed."

"It is a shame what the Saracens have done to her," he said sadly.

"We have heard stories, but how bad is it really?"

"Very. Most of the Christian churches have been desecrated, some damaged almost beyond repair. And the blasphemous graffiti is everywhere, more appears as soon as we clear that from the night before. We are harassed daily, businesses are being lost, and our lives now are threatened if any dare to stay beyond the date set by the Caliph's edict. If I was being honest with myself I would have to admit that we knew it was coming, it was always difficult, Christians, Muslims, Jews, Pagans, all living in such close proximity of each other, all claiming the holy sites for their own, it was bound to break at some point."

"But surely the Muslims have brought this onto themselves?" I insisted. "Defiling Christian holy ground out of spite," passing along what I had been told by the bishops from the West.

"Yes, of course. But they could accuse us of the same thing, and do. And the Jewish people would accuse both the Christians and the Muslims of violating their holy sites."

'Their holy sites?' I thought to myself. I had a little knowledge of these other religions but any discourse with the clerics about them had always started and ended with an almost fever-pitch evangelizing of their inherent evil. I never fathomed that there could be other beliefs that might have some validity. This roused my natural instincts to examine more deeply what others simply took at face value. I had a sudden urge to know more. I took a seat back down on the hard ground, leaning again against the boulder again stretching my long legs out in front of me, and asked him to explain what he meant.

"Well, to answer you we need to go back in time, much further than when Our Lord walked these streets," he started, sitting down beside me and drawing his knees up to his chest and wrapping his arms around them. "You are aware of the original temple here, Solomon's Temple?"

I nodded.

"It was built by King David's son to honour the site where Abraham bound Isaac, on the mount once called Moriah. This was also the site, according to Jewish tradition, where God created the first man from dust, and it holds the Foundation Stone, the rock from which the rest of the world was created. Solomon's Temple had an inner sanctuary that enclosed this site, their Holy of Holies, in which rabbis were able to communicate directly with God. The Jews consider this to be the most holy of all places on earth."

I was listening with rapt attention. I was fascinated.

"For early Christians, Solomon's Temple was venerated as a site where many events of Christ's life unfolded. Herod had the Temple renamed after himself during his reign, but unfortunately it was eventually destroyed by the Romans who turned the Holy of Holies into a temple for their own Gods. It stayed under Roman rule until the great Emperor Constantine sanctioned Christianity as a true religion at the council of Nicaea."

I knew well the story of Constantine and his conversion from paganism on his deathbed, and that of his mother Helena, the finder of the fragments of the true cross near the place of crucifixion. These were cornerstones of our religion.

"And so began a large influx of Christian immigrants," he continued, "mostly Byzantine, and that is when many churches and holy sites marking the path of Christ from the prison to Calvary were built, including the magnificent Church of the Holy Sepulchre. This site is the most holy for Christians, but of course I am now telling you what you already know."

"Yes, I am well acquainted with the holy sites in Jerusalem, Bishop Odo taught me well. But I am still at a bit of a loss to understand the Muslim claim?"

"The Muslims do not refer to the site as the Temple Mount. Instead, they call it Haram al-Sharif, Noble Sanctuary. And sometimes it is called Al-Aqsa. According to Muslim tradition, the site has great importance in the teachings of their Prophet Muhammad. After the city fell to the Arabs, he decreed the site to be the third most important Islamic site, after Mecca and Medina. This was the place from which Muhammad ascended to heaven, from the very rock the Jews claim is their Foundation Rock. And, like their predecessors, the Muslims renovated this holy spot but now for the honour of Islam, and called it the Dome of the Rock."

He rested a moment before continuing.

"And ever since, the city has exchanged hands between various Muslim factions, each claiming be to be true followers of their Prophet. And each having differing views whether or not to allow Jews and Christians to live in the city or even if they were allowed to enter it. Some were more moderate, and there were times when all lived together peacefully. But it never lasted, and punishments abounded. The Christians created a settlement to the west of the Holy Sepulchre and, for the most part, they were able to keep a careful distance, and were left alone as long as they did not interfere with the rulers of the city. Unfortunately, some of the Muslim factions were not so generous and any non-Muslim could find themselves displaced, ousted from a city they called home for generations. It is one such that rules Jerusalem today, the Fatimids, who no longer wish non-Muslims in the city. And this brings us to where we are today," he said, sighing heavily.

I suddenly felt ashamed again, this time of my shocking lack of knowledge of this land we were now fighting for. There was so much more to the conflicts than I had been taught and this unsettled me and wanted to discuss it more, but I realized Theós was now lost in thought and so I let it lie.

Finally, he spoke what was on his mind.

"I know not what I shall do, nor do any of us really," he said, dejected by the thought of his reality.

He looked back at the city, his heartbreak clear in is melancholy expression. I felt I needed to help this man.

"You say you are a leather worker?" I asked, changing the subject.

"Yes, my father was my teacher, my family have worked with fabric for generations, leather is our specialty," he responded, looking at me with what I thought was some pride.

I looked closer at the leather cap he was wearing, in the dim moonlight I could just make out exquisite patterns woven in and out, around and atop of it.

"Did you make that?" I asked, pointing.

He smiled.

"Yes sir," he answered, quickly removing it and holding it closer so I could examine it. "As you can see, it is a superior leather."

I took it from him and examined it. The stitching was flawless and I said so.

"Thank you sir. I have always believed the key to making a beautiful leather piece comes from the quality of its stitching," and placed it back onto his head.

I thought a moment.

"You seem like an honest fellow," I said.

"I strive to live up to my name, sir," he responded, telling me what his name meant in his native language.

"I may have a job for you…" I started.

"Oh sir, I do thank you for being so kind, but alas, I am no soldier," he said, anticipating my offer.

"No, no, I was not thinking about your warrior skills. Our armies are always in need of your type of craftsmanship, many of our belts and straps are in need of repair and I know Duke Robert is always complaining about the state of his boots," I said explaining myself.

"You…you are acquainted with the Duke of Normandy? We have heard his reputation, he is a great man and an even greater warrior," Theós said in awe.

"Yes, he is my master, I have attended on him for most of our campaign, before that I attended on Bishop Odo of Bayeux until he died. So, what about it? Do you wish to join us or carry on your way?" I said getting to the point.

He looked dumbstruck. I prodded him again.

"Theós?"

"Apologies sir, I am a bit astonished by your generosity. I…I would be honoured, sir, to be at your service," he said, genuinely grateful.

"You may think otherwise soon, there is a great deal of work to be done. Is that all you have with you?" I asked, pointing at his satchel.

"Yes, it only has what tools I could grab before I was hustled out of my shop and home. And I am no stranger to hard work I assure you," he said.

"I believe you. We will stay here tonight and I can get you some fresh clothes back at camp tomorrow. I suggest you get some sleep, we will be up well before dawn."

He thanked me again and again only stopping once he saw me sit back onto the ground and re-roll the blanket making it ready for me to rest my head upon it. He took that as his cue to settle in for the night and not another word was said for the rest of the night. My offer to him was not as altruistic as one might think. I desperately wanted to learn more about the history of this place and I knew in my heart he was the one who could educate me. So I looked forward to the times when we could talk more about these things. I did not realize then just how important my new friend would become to me.

* * * * * * * * * *

The camp was swirling with an eager anticipation and it was this excitement that spurred the leaders into launching a surprise attack a week later. We brought our mangonels and best archers but without any siege engines we quickly realized we did not have the firepower to be successful and a retreat back to Nabil Samuil was ordered. The leaders were becoming concerned about where and how they would be able to secure the materials needed to build these engines, for not being able to do so would bring our mission to an end very quickly. And then, it was as if our prayers had been answered, not once but twice.

Tancred's mission to liberate Bethlehem was easier than had been expected as the Saracen garrison had abandoned their posts upon hearing a Christian army was on its way. He even managed to hoist his own banner atop the Church of the Nativity and proclaim the town for himself. But without much more to do, he and de Bourcq returned to us, leaving a small number of troops to protect those living there. On their way to our camp, they happened upon a set of caves, just south of Nabi Samuil, and discovered to their amazement a horde of timber and building materials, simply abandoned as if waiting for them. As they were being retrieved, we received word that six Genovese ships had come into port at Jaffa, with even more timber, nails, ropes, everything we would need. Flanders and Aumale organized the transport of it all to us and the Genovese even offered to sacrifice two of their ships to provide more wood. Now we needed to decide what type of siege engines we should build.

We learned after the failure of the first assault on the city that a simple attack with mangonels and our archers would not be effective. Jerusalem was one of the strongest fortified cities known to the West. We would not be able to knock the walls down and they were too thick to undermine from below, instead we needed to breach them by going over top. And so, our fighters were given their task: build two immense siege towers that would surpass the height of the walls and could be rolled into place, allowing many men to climb up from within to cross over once a bridge was set. Our men did this in three weeks in Nabi Samuil, the hill of Mount Joy hiding them from sight.

Along with the siege towers, a massive battering ram with an iron cap was also built, as were ladders to scale the walls and wattle screens made of the lightweight wood cut from the timbers and woven with thin branches from the trees we felled. Theós's skills had come to be invaluable during these days, showing others how to best use leather straps in constructing the siege towers and making many desperately needed repairs to our protective clothing and horses' tack. Duke Robert was most pleased when a newly crafted pair of boots appeared outside his tent and was very impressed I had seen how Theós's talents could best be put to use.

To have accomplished creating all of these siege weapons in such a short period of time, under the impossible conditions of oppressive heat, little food and water, was nothing short of miraculous. And to keep the Muslims distracted from thinking any such construction was underway, the leaders organized a march around the city by the majority of the armies, leaving the builders behind to continue their work. Barefoot but in mailled armour and carrying weapons and shields, we walked along the outside of the walls starting from the northwest, around the to the south and ending up in the Mount of Olives, some of us resting in the Garden of Gethsemane, where Peter the Hermit preached sermons all afternoon and into the evening. Obviously this was observed by the Saracens, we must have been quite the sight to those who stood along the battlements at the top of the walls and stared as we walked past, not attacking, but singing hymns.

From what we observed from our march, we quickly confirmed our combined armies were not large enough to surround the city. So the leaders took Bouillon's plan to heart and designed an ingenious attack that still focussed on the weak areas on the north walls but giving the impression attack would come from many sides. There were six gates in total that allowed entry into the city, all heavily manned and reinforced, with armed Saracen soldiers pacing the battlements on either side. Bouillon had already determined not to have all the men placed at one location, and everyone agreed that, like Antioch, the armies would be divided and situated at different gates.

Bouillon and Duke Robert each would command one of the siege towers at the northeast corner of the city, outside Herod's Gate. Flanders would take a smaller contingent to the centre of the north wall and attack at St Stephen's

Gate. Toulouse initially opted to man David's Gate near the citadel on the west wall but on the day when he was joined by Tancred, he moved to the south wall, harassing the enemy as much as he could with the battering ram at Mount Sion's Gate. He knew at some point, if the breach on the north wall was successful, our fighters would eventually arrive to unlock that gate and let his army enter if the ram had not done the trick before then. And it was agreed that only the commanders would have access to their horses, in order to move quickly in between gates if need be. The twelve hundred calvary would leave their horses, including my Pax, with the non-fighting crusaders, for us to retrieve after the battle or in case of retreat if one was called. This battle, for the most part, was going to be on foot.

On the 13th of July, the siege towers were ready to be moved to the city on their gigantic wooden wheels. Everyone, soldier or not, was involved either being part of the teams that moved the towers or packing up the camp at Nabi Samuil as we were not to return. We were either going to be victorious or die trying. We knew what was at stake; if we were defeated, one would hope to die a good death for if one survived it would be a life of slavery, probably taken away into the far reaches of enemy territory, never to see home again.

I was with Duke Robert's party, responsible for providing shield cover for some of the men who were pushing once we were within reaching distance of the Saracen arrows. I glanced around and could see Saint-Omer, Hugues and Bisol with Bouillon's party, we made eye contact, knowing what the other was thinking. All of us were dressed for war in our hauberk maille which rested on top of a thick quilted undergarment. Our heads were protected by great helms, weapons hung from our belts, a sword or mace or flail. Those pushing the towers, including myself, had their shields tied to their backs. This was heavy and awkward but it was nevertheless essential protection for what we were about to engage in. The rapidly increasing temperatures which we were still not used to would make this conflict particularly harsh.

We started out at night when the air had cooled somewhat compared to the mid-day sun, but we were drenched from the searing heat by early morning, filthy from the clouds of dust kicked up by the towers' wheels and the men struggling to push these timber beasts forward to their destination. Once we were within reach of the defenders' missiles, the attacks upon us began, arrow shot, rocks and small boulders thrown, the enemy's own mangonels taking aim and doing their best to knock us back. But still we pushed on. The men started to become frightened, doubting and unsure of the success of this mission. If it had not been for the inspirational words of Duke Robert and Bouillon, many would have abandoned their posts. But still, we pushed on.

It took us two days to move the great towers into position outside Herod's Gate. The Saracens had not been able to halt the progression of these monstrous machines, they must have seemed grotesque and terrifying and unstoppable to those watching them slowly approach. At the same time, the enemy was pummelled at three more of their gates, diverting many of the defenders, thus diminishing the numbers we were going to face.

Finally, in the early hours of the 15th of July, Bouillon's tower was within reach of the gate, so close that its bridge could now be lowered. Our archers let off volley after volley of arrows, trying to protect those working the tower and lowering the bridge from inside. The defenders fought fiercely, throwing everything they had at us, pouring boiling water down upon our men setting up the ladders in place along the wall, shrieking in pain when it hit them. They launched what I found out later were Islamic grenades, almond-shaped clay pots containing some sort of fuel and a small hole for a cloth fuse that was lit before it was hurled. Normally these would have had the desired effect of exploding upon impact, instantly setting alight whatever wooden structure it hit. But the enemy did not realize that whilst the cores of the tower engines were made of the stronger, aged wood brought by the Genovese ships, the outer layers were made from the newly cut timber of nearby forests and would not catch fire as easily. More often than not, these fireballs blew themselves out, rendering them harmless.

It was mid-day when the bridge was lowered and made contact with the northeast wall to the east of Herod's Gate, and a great shout went up from those working the tower as they began to race across the bridge. I recognized the men who breached the gate first, two brothers from Flanders who were part of Bouillon's army, Lethold and Englebert de Tournai. They were followed by scores of others, now pouring into the city, the Saracen defenders in disarray, panicked, running away from us, further into the city, allowing more of our soldiers to use the ladders to scale the walls without being assaulted. I lost sight of Hugues, Bisol and Saint-Omer, having quickly followed Bouillon over the wall. I reached under my maille, kissed my St Michael's medal and wished them Godspeed.

We brought the Duke's tower into position soon after and once its bridge had made contact with the wall to the left of Herod's Gate, the Duke Robert's men soon followed Bouillon's across the wall, racing onto battlements to the left or disappearing down the steps and into the city. I stood, waiting my turn to cross the bridge, sword in hand, ready to do battle with whomever I came upon. Stepping from the shade of the tower out into the bright sunlight, I was blinded momentarily but pressed on, only really gaining my full sight back when my foot touched the stone of the wall. I had made it to the interior of the city.

I was carried by the force of some of the Duke's men along the battlement to my left, towards the Gate of St Jehoshaphat, all the while watching the events happening below. I caught sight of Hugues in the midst of a battle with a couple of enemy soldiers but I could not see Bisol or Saint-Omer amongst the crowd. I raced down a set of steps to come to his aid, despatching one of the Saracens immediately with a single thrust of my sword and then turning to help Hugues rid himself of his. Once we had defeated the enemy in the vicinity, Hugues turned to me and nodded his thanks, too breathless to speak.

Bisol suddenly appeared from around a corner, returning to find his master after having become separated from him in the mêlée. As soon as he saw us, he knew instantly what had taken place and grinned at me. We took a moment to catch our breath, and then moved deeper into the city. We knew the Temple Mount was near and that most of the enemy would gather there hoping to find refuge in one of their most holy of places. We found ourselves in a maze of narrow streets, more like alleyways, a marketplace with goods for sale suspended from overhanging roofs and on the ground in front of a myriad of ornately decorated and painted wooden doors and iron gates. We knew not who may be hidden behind these doors, friend or foe.

The further we progressed, the more bodies we came across, it seemed many of our fellow soldiers had preceded us through these alleys, slashing everything they met, human or animal. Blood was everywhere, splattered on the walls and on the stone slabs of the alley floors, so much so pools were beginning to form in the grooves of the well-worn flagstones. The attacks had been brutal, many corpses missing body parts, decapitated, or hacked apart so badly we could not tell if they were Muslim, Pagan, or Jew.

We hurried to the Temple Mount and climbed the steps, seeing its gold dome rise up before us. Its stunning shining beauty contrasted sharply with what was happening beneath it, for lowering our gaze slightly we were met with a scene of utter chaos and bedlam. What we were witnessing was whole-scale slaughter. Several thousand of the city's inhabitants had retreated to the Mount and were now either dead on the ground or running amok in panicked fear. Men, women, children, all being cut down before us as they tried desperately to reach the Dome of the Rock, mistakenly thinking it would give them refuge from the wild-eyed crusaders who simply pulled them out and slew them with no thought.

Our armies' soldiers and enemy alike were stepping through pools of blood, some slipping and falling and becoming covered in it. In some places it splashed as men on foot and on horseback stomped their way across as if passing through a running creek. The horror of it was unimaginable and I recalled my father's words at our last dinner together at the inn at Mantes-la-Ville before I took the cross and joined Duke Robert and Bishop Odo on this mission: '*men are capable of despicable acts when emotion is not in check.*' I realized I was a long way away from days of peace and comfort in the idyllic villages of Normandy. The heat, the screams, would be etched permanently in my mind's eye, I was certain I would never forget.

Snapping out of our momentary paralysed state, we hurried across the raised platform and down a set of steps leading to the Al-Aqsa mosque. I could see several terrified people huddled in the stables to the east of the mosque but it gave no protection to them and soon their lifeless bodies were strewn across the floor. Another group had gathered nears the mosque's arched entrance, standing under Tancred's banner which had been hastily strung up on the front wall. We watched in horror as each was cut down, one at a time, the banner falling to the ground, soaking up the newly spilled blood. The cries of those being attacked and dying was horrific, many in agony calling out 'Franji!!,' the name the local Arabs used for us, yet another image I was sure I would never forget.

Tancred appeared from behind a column on the west side, storming across the Mount towards us, obviously some of Bouillon's men had made it to David's Gate and let him and his men in. He was enraged, screaming at us that he had given his banner to a group of people who had surrendered to him on the Mount, telling them it would protect them, only to see them slaughtered before his very eyes by out-of-control, frenzied soldiers. The roar of the fighting crowd almost drowned out his words and we were helpless to stop the actions of what was now an unruly mob of hysteria-infected warriors. From our armies.

Flanders shouted at us from the steps we had just descended and gestured for us to join him. We hastily left the macabre scene, leaping down the Temple Mount's steps, weaving our way through the rabbit-warren streets, stepping over bodies and body parts and trying not to slip on the blood-soaked flagstones. We reached David's Gate where Tancred had left Toulouse at the city's citadel and found he had not yet secured it. Inside was a large group of defenders who had escaped to it, barricading themselves and continuing to fight throughout the night and into the morning of the second day. But during one of the skirmishes, we discovered the Caliph himself had fled his palace to take refuge in the part of the citadel known as the Tower of David, so now the situation switched from being one of attack to being one of negotiation. As soon as al-Dawla realized the city was lost, he offered to trade the surrender of the citadel and the gift of a trove of treasure, hidden throughout the city, for his freedom. This was part of the accepted rules of engagement since he was of high status and so he was soon escorted out of the Tower of David and through David's Gate with his bodyguard on his honour to go to Ascalon and not return. We watched from the top of the Tower until he disappeared into the horizon of the late afternoon sun. He did not return. But we would meet him again.

The slaughter throughout in the city continued into the second night and fires that had been set across the city, including in a large synagogue, lit up the night-time sky like a blacksmith's forge stretching for miles. More and more inhabitants of the city were killed, many found hiding in the attics of the stone buildings in the marketplace, hoping to escape our swords. Some of the non-fighters in our armies took part, being overcome with the ecstasy of the victory that surely was theirs to celebrate and they looted whatever they found, cutting jewellery off the dead bodies sometimes mutilating them where they lay.

As the morning of the third day turned into the heat of the mid-day sun, the stench from the dead was becoming unbearable and something had to be done now that the fighting had dissipated. So a number of Saracen prisoners were ordered to rid the city of the bodies by piling them outside the various gates in pyramid pyres, lighting them on fire, filling the air with heavy smoke and reeking of burnt flesh. This would take days, there were just so many of them. Others were instructed to rid the city of the blood and remove the stains which were everywhere. Duke Robert later estimated the city's dead to be near forty thousand. Of our twelve thousand foot-soldiers, we lost nearly three thousand and they needed burying as quickly as possible. Bouillon ordered all the crusader bodies collected, shrouded and kept in cool places so graves could be dug for them in the Gehenna Valley just south of the Sion Gate.

* * * * * * * * * *

It was not until the sun was starting to reach its zenith on the third day that I was finally able to enter the Holy Sepulchre, the holiest Christian place on earth and one of many sites which had been desecrated by the infidels. I approached the entrance from the east and found Bisol standing there, staring transfixed. I stood beside him silently for a moment and then, I touched his elbow, breaking his reverie, and we climbed the few stone steps and entered, pushing hard on one of the wooden doors. We found ourselves in the Martyrium Basilica, not expecting the size of the huge columns that soared up to the ceiling far about our heads, the enormity of the church deceptive from outside. Despite the vandalism and attempts to despoil it, we could see its original design coming through and the majesty it projected throughout. We walked slowly, up the centre aisle towards the apse, kneeling and saying a prayer once we reached it.

Spying a door to the right of the altar, Bisol and I and soon found ourselves out in the triportico, an open courtyard covered on three sides, partially in shadow from the massive rotunda across from us. We started in that direction but stopped when I looked to my left and saw it. Calvary. The rock of Golgotha. I pulled on Bisol's arm to stop him from walking any farther away. Frozen for a moment, we took in that we were standing at the very place where Our Saviour had been crucified. It was almost inconceivable to accept that this was our reality.

A small set of steps led up to the rock which rose many feet from the ground. Bisol and I looked at each other, do we dare? Slowly, and with great respect for the place, we ascended the few stairs and stood inches away from the place of the crucifixion. We knelt and touched it gently, reverently, and said a silent prayer.

After a few minutes, we descended the steps and crossed the courtyard to the Anastasis, the large rotunda that held the tomb of Christ. Upon entering, we instantly felt the coolness of the place refreshing our sweat-stained skin, the temperature having dropped considerably from the extreme heat outside. Dim inside due to its shape, torches and lamps had been lighted and blazed throughout, revealing, when our eyes adjusted, more of the same type of damage and heretical graffiti that we saw in the courtyard and the basilica. It was cavernous in size, column after column bearing the weight of the great rounded roof, soaring to the clouds above. It was glorious. And in the middle was the once ornate small structure built to honour and protect the Saviour's tomb, now stripped of its rich silver and gold engravings and adornments, with pieces of the structure having been hacked away, pocketed no doubt by common thieves. And yet, despite many attempts over the years by non-believers to destroy it and any semblance of our faith, it stood, ready for our worship again.

Other crusaders were there but no one was speaking. Most were standing still, taking it all in. We gradually walked around the rotunda, absorbing the breath-taking sight, overwhelmed and yet humbled at the same. When we were ready, we descended the few steps to the tomb itself, a plain enclosure carved out of the rock, with a platform bed at the far end, also carved from the rock. Modest and unpretentious. Perfect for the carpenter's son. We were there only a few moments and then came out so others could make their visit.

Walking back through the courtyard and then into the basilica, we noticed a long set of stone steps, I counted twenty-two, leading down on the south side from the apse. We followed them only to come upon another long set of stone steps of the same number, leading to the small crypt where fragments of the true cross had been found by Constantine's mother Helena, the very same we had been allowed to see by Alexois in Constantinople. The air down here was even cooler, almost cold, and we shivered slightly. The desecration had not stopped above ground but had continued down here as well, we were very saddened to see.

Taking the steps quickly back up to the ground floor, we stepped out into the fading sunset and made our way to the Al-Aqsa mosque on the Temple Mount. We knew that Bouillon was intending on using it for his residence during his stay in Jerusalem and that a council had been planned for that afternoon, so I needed to return to the Duke as soon as possible. There was much work to be done.

# IV

# Part Two

# 1099–1100 – Lower Levant

It took just under a week before the first council could be held in the Al-Aqsa mosque on the Temple Mount for much time was needed for the Mount to be cleared of the dead and the pools of their blood. The stains still remained despite the efforts of many Muslim prisoners, men, women and children, on their knees scrubbing as if their lives depended on it. Bisol and I walked past them quickly, avoiding eye contact, and reached the Al-Aqsa's main entrance, a centre arch slightly larger than its six sisters, three on either side. Each was exquisitely carved, the centre arch more so than the others. The doors were open and so we walked in without hesitating, knowing we would be recognized and not stopped.

Inside we continued to be amazed by the sheer elegance of the Muslim décor. No interior walls existed but instead huge, thick rectangular stone columns supporting the high ceilings, cloaked with Islamic banners, silk curtains and long flowing drapes of deep rich colours. The flagstone floor was highly polished and covered in exquisite woollen carpets in a medley of bright colours and mystical swirling designs in gold and silver threads. Aumale and Flanders were in the process of overseeing the pulling down of the curtains and hoisting our banners the various armies in their place. At the far end of this massive, open expanse I could see Duke Robert and Flanders and his man Montdidier watching as a large table and a number of chairs were set up for them and other members of the council. Duke Robert was speaking with his retainer Tancarville and I joined them, listening to him receive instructions about setting up the Duke's new rooms in what had been Herod's Palace, just south of the citadel. Toulouse and Tancred then appeared, followed a few minutes later by Bouillon and Hugues.

Everyone, including myself, had changed into clean clothes, doing what we could to remove the reek of death that had hung about us for the past few days. Bisol joined Hugues, they spoke quietly for a moment and then Hugues took a seat at the table after Bouillon invited him to after the others had. Wine from vast vats found under some of the market stores was poured and plates of succulent fresh fruit and olives was placed on the tables. But before we ate, Bouillon rose to say a prayer of thanks to God for our victory, just as those he had ordered held in the Holy Sepulchre immediately after the battle had ended. Now, decisions were needed on the way forward, who was going to stay and who would leave and, most importantly, who would rule.

The initial view was that Duke Robert should take on the mantle of ruler of Jerusalem, as he was the most senior ranked of all the leaders still with the crusade, being Duke of the largest duchy in France. Bohemond as Prince would have been considered but he had stayed in Antioch, preferring to rule his principality there. But Duke Robert refused, saying he needed to return and reclaim Normandy from his brother King William Rufus, now that he had enough riches to pay back the loan and then some. He was content to stay awhile to gather more treasure wherever it could be found, but he would not stay for long.

Then Toulouse was offered the crown but he refused, saying he was not comfortable being King where our Saviour had suffered so. He also expressed a desire to return to Tripoli and resurrect the siege there that he had abandoned months ago.

Finally, after much discussion, Bouillon offered to govern but, like Toulouse, refused to be called King, not wanting to wear a crown of gold in the place where our Saviour wore a crown of thorns. Instead, he took the title Princeps, a little-known title used by Roman Emperors meaning simply 'first one.' Such was his pious humility, ever-present and so consistent in the man we had come to know and admire.

Tancred voiced his desire to stay in the Holy Land but needed a position that was worthy of his status being a member of the royal family of Taranto. Bouillon suggested the title of Prince of Galilee and granted him many settlements and the lands surrounding them next to the sea. Tancred was extremely pleased as this would mean he and his uncle Bohemond would then be of the same rank, both Princes, and willingly and readily accepted it.

Discussions then moved to dividing the properties and treasure amongst the leaders, although many of the properties at least had already been claimed. Bouillon said he would keep the mosque as his residence and invited Hugues and Bisol to lodge there as his liegemen. He was extremely disdainful of the Islamic décor, it was clearly not to his liking and planned to set about renovating the entire mosque, removing anything related to Islam, including stripping the walls of all their decorations, burning the prayer rugs, building new internal walls to create more rooms and even walling up the prayer niches with bricks and stones. And he intended to add more gardens for his relaxation. There was a great discontent with the name of the building and its designation as a mosque, both being totally unsuitable for a Christian ruler. Some ideas were bandied about, and eventually the leaders settled on the Temple of Solomon and the stables attached to the east were renamed Solomon's Stables. Everyone seem satisfied with the choice.

Duke Robert confirmed his desire to keep Herod's palace for his own during his stay and Toulouse claimed the Tower of David and the citadel for himself. Tancred was satisfied with this as long as he was allowed a sizeable tower in the northwest of the city which he eventually named after himself. Flanders agreed to take treasure only, his intention all along was to take the cross to save the holy city from her enemies, he intended to return home.

The next order of business was to discuss the missive that was to be sent to Pope Urban, telling him of our victories in Palestine. It was agreed that Bouillon would write it and send it off immediately for news of our capture of the holy city must be shared, spread across the Christian world, people needed to know that this great land was back in the hands of the true and faithful. And that God had shone his munificence and grace upon us and found us worthy. This was done and sent the next day, we estimated it should take a couple of weeks to reach him. But alas, the Holy Father, he who had preached to the masses in Clermont and impelled thousands to take the cross and make this trek to save the Holy Land from its enemies, our spiritual champion for this quest, died on the 29th of July, six days after the letter was sent. He was never to know that his hopes and desires of reclaiming Jerusalem had been realized.

And finally, the leaders needed to decide how they would go about transforming this Muslim Jerusalem into a Christian city. Renovating could not just be kept to the holy sites and royal houses, all signs of Islam needed to be removed. It was agreed that every crescent moon in the city would be replaced with crosses and if that were not possible, they would be torn down and destroyed, and any Muslim images, mosaics, writings or symbols would be covered or painted over with frescoes of Christian saints and events.

The Dome of the Rock was also to be turned into a Christian church, to be used by the ruling family and high-ranking members of Jerusalem's ruling class and anything within it that suggested a link to Islam was to be removed, although the brilliant blue mosaic tiles on its exterior and its gold dome were to be left intact. The rock under the dome was to be turned into an altar for Christian mass and prayers. I thought about Theós's words when I heard about the plans for the rock itself and wondered what the Muslim and Jewish gods would think about this.

And of course, the most important site, the Holy Sepulchre, was to undergo a major restoration. The rotunda was to receive a new blue dome, the structure around the tomb repaired and its gold and silver decorations replaced. All graffiti was to be removed at once and any damage to the walls were to be repaired throughout. The crypt below was also to be repaired and made suitable for prayers and finally the entire site was to be enclosed so that the basilica, triportico and the anastasis would be a single structure. It would be made a shining beacon of God's perfection, unrivalled in the Christian world.

These were ambitious plans indeed, but we knew that once word got back to the Christian states, many of the rich would take pilgrimage and dedicate funds to the rebuilding of the city. It would be believed that our victory had been ordained by God despite the great odds against it, and now the masses would want to partake in it. Bouillon ordered the work started immediately.

* * * * * * * * * *

Pleased though we were with our success, we knew the battles were not over. Alerted prior to the existence of an Egyptian Fatimid army that was on its way to reclaim the city, we knew we had no time to rest and must prepare to fight once again. At the beginning of August, we heard from al-Dawla, the Caliph who was released from captivity in the Tower of David after he paid his way to freedom. He sent emissaries who were received by Bouillon and the others in the newly renamed and soon to be redecorated Temple of Solomon. They demanded our immediate surrender which of course was refused and they returned to the Caliph having been unsuccessful in convincing us to leave.

Bouillon's scouts told us that the Caliph's army was camped just outside the city of Ascalon, a day's ride to the south-west from Jerusalem, and so it was decided to depart as soon as possible to launch a surprise attack on them. Duke Robert and Toulouse initially chose not to join Bouillon. Flanders and Tancred choose instead to wait word from their own scouts before making any decisions on joining the march. But our men and Toulouse's did attend the mass led by Peter the Hermit in the Holy Sepulchre to bless the battle the day before the others departed. But there was really no reason to delay, their scouts relayed the same information the next day about where the Fatimids were and the magnitude of the threat, and so the rest of the leaders quickly rallied their troops and we were soon on the move.

In mid-August, we arrived in the valley of al-Majdal, southwest of the city, and came upon a field full of livestock – sheep, oxen, goats, camels – grazing alone. We found out later that this had been a tactic by the Caliph, hoping we would be distracted by the easy pickings and would spend our time rounding up the animals to take back to Jerusalem. But the tactic failed.

Instead, Bouillon devised a plan that would take the enemy by surprise and give us the advantage. Even with the full complement of all the crusader armies, some nine thousand foot-soldiers and twelve hundred calvary, we were outnumbered, probably by five times as many and so the element of surprise was essential. The armies were divided into nine divisions, Duke Robert and Tancred leading the centre whilst Toulouse commanded inland with his back to Jerusalem and Bouillon with his back to the sea.

At dawn of the next morning, we embarked on our attack, finding a sleeping Fatimid army, wholly unprepared for our arrival. Once roused and organized, they fought bravely but their soldiers were badly trained and ill-equipped to handle our superior fighting force. There was only one moment when the threat of defeat seemed possible when the Fatimid vanguard broke through our line but Bouillon rushed in and despatched any enemy warriors found amongst us.

The enemy began their retreat, seeing their cause was lost, but this seemed to anger our soldiers who went after them as they fled. Some managed to escape to the sea where a Fatimid fleet was waiting for them, others tried hiding in trees but were shot down by our arrows. Even more tried to retreat to the city but were crushed against the walls, the garrison refusing to open the gates for fear of letting us in. We had won the day, made even more absolute when we discovered that the Caliph had escaped on one of the ships and returned to Egypt. Bouillon estimated the enemy had lost almost thirteen thousand men during the course of one day.

Negotiations began the next day with the garrison who were still entrenched in the towers at the gates. They agreed to surrender after watching the city being looted by the crusaders who had broken down the gates and raced about, taking whatever they wanted, killing anyone who stood in their way. But they would only agree to surrender to Toulouse, whose reputation had reached them and for whom they had a great deal of respect. Bouillon of course, could not abide this and we left Ascalon without agreeing to terms, deciding instead to return to Jerusalem to decide the matter.

But simply moving the discussion to the Temple of Solomon did not resolve it. Instead, the bickering that had caused so many problems earlier in the campaign, with Bohemond at Antioch and at Marrat and then again after the siege at Arqa, raised its ugly head, and once again Toulouse found himself in the middle of it. Duke Robert and Flanders supported Bouillon, whilst Tancred took Toulouse's side in the argument. The first attempt to recapture Jerusalem by Muslim armies had failed because we had been united as a fighting force just as we had at Nicaea, Dorylaeum, and Antioch. And yet we still could not find a way to avoid these arguments and disagreements over the spoils. In the end, no resolution was made and Ascalon remained in Fatimid hands, although it was no longer deemed a threat.

* * * * * * * * *

Duke Robert and Flanders were dining together a few weeks later in his quarters at Herod's Palace, with Aumale and Montdidier also at the table. They were discussing the Ascalon matter which still had not been resolved with defeated tones.

"This quarrelling will be the end of us," Duke Robert declared, annoyed.

"I agree," Flanders said. "Toulouse was a great warrior, I can see how the infidels would respect him, his reputation obviously precedes him. But he cannot expect to take control of portions of the Levant after declining to rule it. Bouillon has accepted that responsibility, it is his honour and right to take Ascalon under his rule."

They all nodded in agreement.

"So what now?" Aumale asked. "The threat from Ascalon has been dealt with, Bethlehem, Ramleh and Jaffa now secured and under our control. What do we do now?"

Everyone was quiet, thinking about this. Finally, Duke Robert broke the silence.

"We have done what we came here to do. I have my wedding to the Lady Sybilla to attend to. And taking my duchy back from William Rufus."

He paused a moment and then spoke again.

"I think it is time to go home."

It was a simple statement and true. We all knew he was right. And so with that, our time in the Holy Land was going to come to an end. It would take time to organise the ships needed to take those who wanted to return to their homes as there was no desire to go on foot. By our calculations, our departure would leave Bouillon with only about two thousand foot-soldiers and three hundred calvary, so when word was sent to procure the ships, along with it went a request for fresh soldiers to come to Bouillon's aid.

Our departure was set for late November, Duke Robert wanted to be back in Bari before Christmas. There was one last thing I knew I needed to do before we left and so, with Duke Robert's permission I sought out my new friend to say good-bye. I found him in the camps still in place outside Herod's Gate where many of the expelled citizens we had seen leaving a few weeks earlier were now waiting for permission to return to their homes. He was still hard at work, sitting at a work stool, head bent down, focusing intently on the boot he was repairing. I entered the tent and greeted him.

"Theós, how goes it? I see the Duke has kept you busy?" I said, clapping my hand on his shoulder.

He looked up and smiled.

"It is an honour to do the Duke's bidding, I am happy my work has been put to good use," he said humbly.

I pointed towards an animal skin of wine, asking silently if I could have some. He nodded.

"I have some news," I said, taking a swig and sitting down across from him. "Our ship to return to Normandy has arrived in Jaffa. We are to leave within the next week once Duke Robert has concluded his business here."

Theós's face fell, his expression a mix of sadness and concern.

"You are truly leaving? Does the Duke not wish to stay in Jerusalem? I had hoped he would."

"I do not believe it was ever his intention to stay for long," I answered, leaning across to a nearby table and plucking a couple of olives from a small clay bowl. "He needs to return to take back the duchy from his brother, the King of England. And I must return with him."

"I am saddened to hear of this," Theós said, setting down his leather-working tools. "I have much respect for his Grace, and for you of course. You saved me from a life I cannot even begin to fathom. I shall always be indebted to you for that, I am not sure how I can ever repay you."

"I need you to come with me to the city, so put away your work, the Count of Toulouse can last another day wearing the boots he has on," I said jumping to my feet.

Theós quickly packed everything away and within minutes we had entered Herod's Gate and were meandering our way through the winding alleys which had now been cleared of anything giving the impression a brutal battle had ever raged. Heading to the west side of the city, I could feel Theós becoming agitated beside me, nervous his first time back in the city he had called home for so many years before being forced out of it by those who despised his presence. We passed St Stephen's Gate and followed the alleys almost to the Tower of David but stopped short before emerging into the wide, open expanse in front of it. Theós knew exactly where we were but had no idea why we were there. I pointed to a small black iron door, ornately carved with Coptic writing and symbols engraved all over it.

"This was your shop, yes?" I asked.

Theós looked at me, incredulous and with tears springing to his eyes. He gazed at the door.

"Yes, yes it was sir," he said, his voice barely above a whisper.

"It is yours again. You will need new locks as the others were destroyed by Saracens breaking in, and I am afraid it is quite empty. But I have had it cleaned and of course you may bring what you have been working with in the tents, stools, tables and suchlike. Oh, and here," I said reaching into my belt and unhooking a small leather bag of coins and tossing it to him, "this is from Duke Robert."

He caught it and looked at it as if disbelieving his eyes. He looked at me, his mouth dropped open, unable to speak.

"He thought you would need some help purchasing the goods you will need to start again," I said, explaining the coins.

I opened the door and we walked inside. It was small but the shelves where his goods had once been displayed were still in place and there was ample room for his worktable and tools. At the back, steps led to another floor, I peered up but made no movement to ascend.

"My personal rooms," he explained.

I looked around one last time.

"Well, I must be off, I have a lot of preparation to do before we depart and I am expected back at the Temple soon. Please accept this as our gratitude for your services these past weeks."

"I am at a loss for words, sir," he said. "How can I ever repay such a kindness?"

"Please take care of our men," I said. "They will need your skills and talents, there is much work to be done to bring the city back to her former glory. That is all I ask."

I also wanted to thank him for the many conversations we had in the nights leading up the battle, and enlightening me. But I decided I had said enough.

"I most certainly shall," he assured me.

"Live in peace my friend," I said to him and we embraced.

"Peace be with you," he said, returning my embrace.

I left him there then, once again in his shop, glad that I could help him return to the place he had lived since time of his first memories. And now, I was about to do the same.

It was time for me to go home.

# V

# Part One

# 1108 - England

The heavy wooden door slammed shut, the clanging of the bolt being slid into place and the keys turning the lock reverberating around the small, damp cell. Before me stood Godfrey D'Ivry, a tall, well-groomed man dressed in the finest clothes belonging to a man of his status. He crossed his arms and silently glowered at me as he waited to hear the steps of the guard recede down the passage.

"Get up!" he barked at me.

I scrambled to my feet. Although dressed in rags, I stood proud and defiant, knowing the castigating I was about to endure. Over the years I had grown into a formidable and probably intimidating man, now standing well over six foot and strong as an ox. But at this moment, I felt like the ten-year-old I was before the crusade, about to be chastised. He looked me up and down.

"You should count yourself fortunate," he said matter-of-factly. "If it were not for the good standing in which the King held my father, you would be spending the rest of your life in this dung-heap!"

"I am most grateful to you, cousin," I said to him sincerely.

"You should be, obtaining your freedom has cost me dearly!" he snapped.

He began to pace.

"I have spent the last two years warranting for you and assuring King Henry that you are not a threat to his crown. He would have been content to leave you here indefinitely. For the life of me I cannot understand why you sided with that rogue against his Majesty…"

"I did so because I truly believed Duke Robert was the rightful King of England," I answered, probably too impertinently.

"Enough!" he shouted, his glower deepening. "You shall never speak of it again. That *peasant* will never see Normandy again. He shall never rule there again nor here in England!"

I fell silent. I knew it was no good to argue. Duke Robert had taken his chances and lost and now he languished in another cell at the opposite end of the hall to my own here in Devizes Castle in the southwest of England. His misfortunes began shortly after his marriage to Lady Sybilla with the death of King William Rufus both of which took place after our departure from Jerusalem. Duke Robert's decision to invade England upon our return to Normandy to wrest the crown away from his other younger brother, Henry, who had been crowned before we had barely set sail from Bari, led to years of battles on both sides of the Channel. He should have known King Henry would never forgive such egregious acts of treason and, despite an early treaty agreed between the brothers, within a few years we were at war with him again, this time in Tinchebrai, a small town south of Bayeux. The King had easily taken Bayeux, burning most of it as he pushed through on his way to us. My heart ached upon hearing it, remembering its beauty from my childhood and time spent at the cathedral with Bishop Odo. But I had stood by the Duke and was captured at his side during the final battle. And now I was about to be freed from prison because of the loyalty and service my uncle had shown the English crown years ago as butler to Henry's father, William the Conqueror. My fate had turned because of a man I had never met and who had been dead for many years.

"You cannot be seen in public looking like this," he said, sighing angrily. "I need to return to Winchester for council. My men will arrive in a few days with what you will need, food, clothes, a horse. Go with them, they will take you to the grange at Shirburn where you shall await my return."

He turned to leave, pounding on the cell door for the guard.

"I have written to your father and mother," he said in a softer tone. "They were gladdened to know you are being released and have written letters to you which I have kept for you. You will also find your brother Guillaume in Shirburn, he has been with me for a few years now, helping with the properties and the stables. You should be safe there. Make yourself useful. And for God's sake, Sébastien, do not do anything foolish! I will not be able to save you a second time."

With that the door to the cell swung open and he ducked out without saying another word to me. He was right of course. But I also knew there was something I needed to do before I left this dreadful place and that was to see the Duke. It would probably be the last time I ever would.

As the coolness of the early winter afternoon turned to a chilly evening, I could hear the footsteps approaching my cell bringing me the gruel they served for food. Looking through the small opening in the door I was relieved to see that it was the usual guard on duty. I stepped back to the far side of the cell, my way of telling him I was no threat to try to escape. I had done this every morning and every night when the food was brought or whenever the door was opened. He deftly unlocked and opened the door and let himself in. This time he greeted me differently, he obviously knew I had been granted my freedom.

"Master D'Ivry," he said with a drawl common to the southwest counties.

"Gilo," I responded.

I knew instantly the food was different too as it actually smelled good and filled the cell with the aroma of hot stew. He placed the bowl and spoon on a small table in the corner along with a pewter goblet.

"Good wine for you this evening," he said pointing to it.

I thanked him and asked him if he knew I was to leave soon.

"Aye, I have been told to expect his Lord D'Ivry's men the next day or so. I am to prepare yourself to leave this place then."

I nodded as I took a seat at the table and dug hungrily into the stew.

"I have to say Master D'Ivry, a royal pardon is a rare thing," Gilo said, watching me.

"Indeed," I answered. "Henry is King of England, I must accept the circumstances as they are."

Gilo thought for a moment.

"There are many who are sympathetic to your position," Gilo said hesitantly.

This was treason talk. I needed to stop it before it went any further. I put the spoon down, took a mouthful of wine and thought carefully about how to respond.

"No doubt there are, Gilo. But I believe the Duke's cause is lost. Even his army captain the Count of Aumale, his cousin, deserted him in the end," I said calmly.

"I am sure you are right, Master D'Ivry," Gilo said, accepting that I was not going to take the bait.

"There is something you could help me with though," I said, leaning back on the small chair.

Gilo cocked his head inquisitively. I took a deep breath.

"I would like to see the Duke before I leave. He has been a constant in my life since I left Bayeux as a boy and was at his side throughout the crusade to the Holy Land. I owe it to him to speak with him, face to face. Can this be arranged?"

Gilo did not hesitate.

"Leave this with me, Master D'Ivry. I shall try to fix it for some time during the night tonight," he replied and with that left me alone to finish my meal.

And alone with my thoughts.

\* \* \* \* \* \* \* \* \*

I could tell looking through the iron-grilled window near the top of my cell that the night was pitch black, clouds having rolled in earlier in the evening blocking out the stars and the moon. The only illumination came from the slender tapers I had been allowed throughout my time here. I barely heard the keys turning in the lock this time and had just turned my head in the direction of the door when suddenly Gilo came through, one hand gripping a lit torch, the other with a finger to his mouth instructing silence.

I followed him out of the cell and down the murky passageway, our shadows dancing on the dirty stone walls as we made our way through. I had been mistaken thinking the Duke was on the same floor in the dungeon tower I was; he was actually two stories above. We quickly ascended the stairs and reached the door of his cell undetected. Gilo handed me his torch to hold whilst he found the key. He slid the latch that added more security to the door just like mine, turned the key in the lock and yanked the door lever.

"There is no one else imprisoned on this floor of the tower," he whispered unnecessarily. "I shall wait at the bottom of these stairs, come find me when you are done, there is no other way out."

He took the torch back from me and scurried away. I took a deep breath; I had not seen Duke Robert since our humiliating loss at Tinchebrai over two years ago. Those taken prisoner had been gaoled in a number of places across England, primarily to prevent the chance of any conspiracies to take hold. I pushed the door open.

The sight that met my eyes was shocking and distressing. The Duke Robert I remembered had been a strong, sturdy soldier, had led masses of troops across thousands of miles of harsh terrain to free the Holy Land of the tyranny of the Saracens and the Turks. A brilliant strategist, few could match his cunning and his ploys of outwitting foes had become legendary. And yet, I also knew the gentle side of him, his love and admiration for Bishop Odo and how affected he had been by his unexpected death. His joy upon seeing his new-born son. And of course there was the absolute adoration for his Lady Sybilla and his heart-wrenching grief at her death giving birth to their second son who died a few days after she did. I did not believe he would recover from these tragedies. But eventually he did or at least he seemed to, and threw himself into a determined and steadfast fight against his brother. Which had brought him, us, to where we were now.

But the man sitting hunched over at a small desk, furiously writing on some pieces of parchment did not resemble the man I remembered. Usually impeccably dressed, Duke Robert's clothes had worn thin, threadbare in places, barely able to keep out the cold seeping in through the walls. His round paunch from years of good food and wine was gone, his body slender bordering on reedy and his hair and beard were wildly out of control and had not been attended to in many months. The tips of his fingers were stained with black ink from writing so many notes and letters that probably went nowhere, no doubt by the King's orders. I felt a lump in my throat, pitying the man who had fallen from such high status into this dark hellish place.

I stepped further into the room and he looked up, startled, squinting at me in the flickering light from a lantern next to him. And then his eyes widened in sudden recognition and he leapt up, overturning his chair, rushing to me, his arms outstretched as if seeing an old, long-lost friend. Which, of course, he was.

"Sébastien!" he exclaimed as he embraced me. "I am glad to lay eyes upon you lad! Sweet Jesu, have you grown even more?" he asked looking up at me.

It was true. I now truly towered over Duke Robert but I had not noticed until he mentioned it. The Duke had always been a powerful force despite his short stature and no man would ever have reason to question his strength of presence.

"Come, sit, have some ale," he insisted, pouring some into a couple of tankards.

He obviously knew he was going to have a visitor tonight. I suspected Gilo had provided some extra beer.

"When do you go?" he asked, clearly already aware of what I had come to tell him.

I took hold of one of the tankards and raised it to him.

"I am not exactly sure. My cousin Godfrey is sending men to fetch me in a couple of days to take me to one of his properties, Shirburn in Oxfordshire. My brother Guillaume is already there, has been for a couple of years now."

"Ah, Guillaume. How old must he be now? Fourteen? Fifteen?"

I was amazed he even remembered I had a brother, never mind his age.

"I believe he has just reached seventeen," I responded.

"Seventeen?" he said in disbelief.

"Yes, your Grace," I replied.

Duke Robert glanced at me sharply.

"I can no longer be addressed in that manner, Sébastien," he said rather mournfully. "I have lost Normandy, and all of the lands over which I held dominion. This," he gestured around himself, "is my life now. So for your safety more than mine, please just call me Robert."

I did not know how to answer this. After all we had been through, all he had been through, to be brought low like this was undeserving of such a man. But I had to admit I did not doubt that he would have done the same to the King if the tables had turned and he had won the war.

"But," he added, "I am not sure I would trade the life I have had. What adventures we had, eh? What places we have been, what things we have done."

"I have you to thank for that," I said.

"And dear Odo," he replied. "We must not forget our good Bishop."

We both drank silently to his memory.

"The winter spent in Calabria was most remarkable," I said, breaking the silence. "Learning my sword on the beaches with Bisol during the day and then listening to the stories the Bishop and yourself told during the evenings, it was the best of times. And of course…" I trailed off.

Duke Robert knew where I was heading.

"Oh yes, my lovely Sybilla. I was enchanted the moment I laid eyes upon her. She was standing next to her father in the great hall in the castle at Conversano, my heart was hers in that instant."

He smiled gently, lost for a moment in the memory of her.

"Your wedding was spectacular," I said, urging the good memories.

Duke Robert laughed.

"It was, was not it? I did not think I had eaten or drunk so much ever in my life! And had the belly to prove it! Sadly," he added patting his flat stomach, "that too has gone."

Duke Robert thought a moment and something made him chuckle aloud.

"Of course that was nothing compared to that Easter when we were back in Rouen and I did not make it to mass. I remember spending the evening before with some, ah, rather unsavoury folk, woke to find my clothes, money, everything gone, including my memory of most of the night!" he laughed. "That was lucky for those who robbed me. Of course," he added rather soberly, "my sweet Sybilla was dead by then."

"She was truly beautiful, in so many ways," I said. "It did not take her long to settle in with her ladies at Falaise after our return."

"My homestead was in dire need of a woman's touch. Her beauty and grace were surpassed only by her keen intellect," Robert murmured. "She was a better administrator than I ever could have been!"

"And she gave you your son."

"Yes, my wonderful dear William Clito. I miss him tremendously," Robert said beaming.

But his smile did not last and his expression darkened.

"I fear for his safety Sébastien. I know Henry and I agreed as part of my surrender that he should be raised by the Count of Arques, but I do not trust Henry. He knows my William is in line for the throne after his own William who is but a year younger. I worry he sees my son as a threat."

"I am sure he does. It was no accident that he gave his son the Saxon version of Clito as part of his name."

"Yes, he chose Ætheling for his son's name on purpose. Both words meaning blood prince, he was sending me a message. There may be some, ah, question as to the rightful heir when the time comes," Robert grumbled. "He is determined to make it clear that it is his son who shall succeed to the throne, not mine. But time will tell just whose head the crown finally falls upon when this sorry saga is all said and done."

We were silent again, me remembering the charming smiles and giggles of Robert's little boy who was no more than four when we had to leave him, Robert lost for a moment in his own bittersweet memories.

"My concern for him is quite genuine," Robert said. "I need you to promise to do me one thing after you leave this place if you feel you are able without placing yourself in any danger. Not immediately, not so soon as to draw attention to yourself, but try to get word to Arques of my concern and have him put plans in place to secret the boy away should Henry make any move that gives the impression my boy is becoming too much of a menace. Can you do this for me?"

"Of course your Gra…erm, Robert. Of course. Consider it done and put your mind at ease. Your son will be kept safe and sound."

"Good, thank you. There is actually one more request I need to make of you," he said quietly.

"Whatever it is, it shall also be done," I said sincerely.

"After my lady's passing, I did not spend much time at Falaise as you know, I could not bear to be there without her, nor indeed sleep in our marital bed, or eat at our table. So I had those and many other things moved to Chinon. Fulk, the Count of Anjou at the time, agreed to safe keep it for me until I was ready to reclaim it. But by then, our battle with Henry had taken me north and from there, well, to where we are today. His son is now Count of Anjou, he is also named Fulk, the fifth of that name I believe. I want you to have my belongings, Sébastien, I have no use of them now."

I was astonished. I knew the pieces he had mentioned very well, I had eaten at that very table many times, and I remember the day the enormous intricately carved, dark oak bed had been delivered to Falaise for the Duke and his Duchess. This was a true honour indeed.

"But would your son not be in need of these pieces himself?" I asked, slightly incredulously.

"William Clito is but a babe and needs to grow into his own without the stain of his association with me. I have left a considerable fortune in the hands of those I trust for his care during his youth and use when he is older. He has no need of these items," he explained.

"Then I shall be honoured to have them," I said.

"Good. I have written a letter here for you to take when the time comes," he said, reaching for the parchments he had been writing on scattered all over the table.

Rifling through them, he found the one he needed, folded it, sealed it and handed it to me. I tucked it away in the belt of my tunic. Duke Robert sighed a sigh of great relief.

"Thank you, Sébastien, thank you. My days of battle and conquering enemies are at an end, but perhaps in time my son will be able to fight and reclaim our rights or, at the very least, our family's honour."

I knew I could not stay much longer but dreaded leaving the Duke's presence. I knew it was highly unlikely I would ever see him again. We sipped our ale.

"What shall you do in Oxfordshire?" Robert asked quietly.

"I am not sure," I replied. "The grange in Shirburn needs administering as do a number of other properties my cousin Godfrey has across the south of England. I may settle down to managing some of them for him, I might even take a wife," I said grinning.

That made the Duke smile.

"I remember your first love, Sébastien," he teased.

"Oh?" I asked surprised. "Have had I one then?"

Duke Robert chortled.

"Do not play coy with me! I believe the lovely Countess of Toulouse caught your eye, did she not? Elvira of Castile with her long blond hair and bright eyes?" he grinned mischievously.

I felt my face flush at the thought of her and was glad the light in the cell was dim enough to cover my embarrassment.

"Sweet Jesu!" I exclaimed. "How could you have known that?"

"How could I not have known? Or any of the men for that matter? Your face turned as red as Bohemond's wine whenever she was near!"

"I was but a young'un at the time, how can I be blamed for that?" I said laughing with the Duke at the memory.

"She was a true beauty," Robert confessed. "Raymond was a lucky man."

"Yes…and no," I said. "He never repaired the damage between himself and Bohemond and Tancred. That bad blood continued for years, I truly believe it cost him his life in the end."

"Yes, I believe you are right. I was saddened to receive word he had died just before he was about to attack Tripoli. I think he believed Tripoli was his destiny."

He leaned back in his chair.

"All of the leaders had won some prize in the Holy Land. Bohemond had Antioch, Tancred Bethlehem and Galilee, Bouillon and his brother Baldwin Jerusalem. I have no doubt that Flanders would have succeeded in capturing a Palestinian city had he wanted to but you know he insisted on returning with us. But Toulouse had not found his place, Tripoli would have been that for him."

Again we fell silent for a moment, thinking of the great Count and, of course, his beautiful wife.

"I guess some things are meant to be and some are not," Robert continued. "Even Blois tried to redeem himself in his wife' eyes after his cowardly return from Antioch. I heard from Adela, many times, complaining of her humiliation that her husband had not fulfilled his vow and instead had crept back to France in shame. She expected too much from him I think. She wanted a husband like our father, but he was a rare man among men, few like him. She was destined to be disappointed."

"Still, she must have been proud that he returned to Ramleh for the battle there years later? And it must have been a shock for her to hear of his death there?" I asked.

"Proud? Of him? No, no I do not think so. That battle at Ramleh was an unmitigated disaster. Baldwin completely underestimated the enemies' numbers, it was a miracle he escaped. Blois and the others were not so fortunate. It would have been Blois's worst nightmare come alive," Robert answered.

"Bouillon would not have made such a mistake," I said, thinking of the leader who had accepted the title of Princeps of Jerusalem after refusing to be called King of the city. His brother Baldwin had no such misgivings and gladly took on the moniker after Bouillon died.

"I was shocked to hear of Bouillon's death," Robert admitted. "It certainly cast a shadow on our wedding celebrations. He was the heart of our crusade. Bohemond and Toulouse may have been its best leaders, each in their own time. But Bouillon was steadfast, the most pious and the most dedicated to the cause, bar none. I have always suspected that his illness at Caesarea was contrived."

This startled me.

"You think Bouillon was poisoned?" I asked.

Duke Robert shrugged.

"He was the most fit of all of us by far, I never heard of a time when he was ill in almost four years. And then, suddenly, a year after we have captured Jerusalem and he has been ruling as the chosen Princeps, he dies? And of an illness no one can define? There are many of our foe who would have rejoiced in his death. Baldwin was the logical choice to succeed him of course, Bouillon had insisted on formalizing that his succession should be with a blood relative. Baldwin had done well in Edessa after he left us. And seems to be doing well in the Holy Land," Robert said, taking a drink from his tankard, then refilling it after offering to refill mine.

"Bouillon's man Saint-Omer was one of those who taught me fighting techniques, he was an exceptional warrior. His were the quickest hands with a sword and shield I have ever seen."

"You have become quite the warrior yourself, I saw you stand your ground at Tinchebrai. You are remarkably lissom for a man of your size," Robert said, his compliments pleasing me.

"I have Saint-Omer to thank for that. His best advice was 'never keep still' and he did everything he could to make sure I did not when I was training. It was exhausting! But worthwhile in the end."

"Who taught you your horsemanship? Combat from the seat of one's horse is a difficult skill to learn but you mastered it well," Robert asked.

"That was Montdidier, Flanders's man. He was impressive to watch in the stirrups. His enemies were truly at a disadvantage, his reach and balance on his horse was remarkable. And then there was Hugues de Payns. He gave me my first full broadsword, one of his own. I still had it with me at Tinchebrai. He could wield any weapon, sword, mace, flail, shoot arrows, anything really, either sitting deep in the saddle or standing tall in it. God only knows where that sword is now," I said ruefully.

"Probably one of the most honourable men I've had the fortune meet, far more honourable than me," Robert said with a moment of self-awareness. "I know Bouillon thought highly of him as well, he was glad to have Hugues join his army during the capture of Jerusalem. Did he return to France after Bouillon's death?"

"Yes, the Count of Champagne demanded his return, I believe he reached France even before we did," I said.

I missed these men. Each had played a distinctive part in my adolescence and had a direct impact in developing my character, making me the man I had become. They had seen something in me that I was much too young to have seen myself and they had had faith in me. I could only hope that I would be able to live up to all their expectations.

We continued talking well into the small hours of the morning, reminding each other of stories long forgotten over the last decade and replacing the tapers when they ran low. But at the back of our minds was the fact that, barring some strange twist in fortune, this would be our final meeting and I was sorry for it. I am sure he was too.

It was time. Duke Robert knew it, knew I was reluctant to make the motions and saved me the embarrassment by speaking first. He slapped his thighs and stood.

"Well, Sébastien, I think it best for you to go. It does my heart good to know you are being allowed to go free," he said, trying to ease the suddenly heavy atmosphere.

I rose to my feet.

"You must not waste this chance," he advised warmly, clasping me by my upper arms. "I have watched you over the years become a strong and loyal man, honourable to the core. You have the power and now the chance to make a name for yourself. Go do it."

I found myself unable to speak. He embraced me like a father embraces a son and then without another word, pulled open the cell door, called for Gilo and stepped aside to let me pass. I reached the door and was about to duck to go through it but stopped short, turned and met the Duke's eyes. I nodded knowingly and stepped through, hearing the door being shut behind me. I had a fleeting thought of trying to help him escape but I knew there was only one way out of the tower and with guards posted everywhere and with the castle unknown to us, we would not get far. Gilo arrived and turned the key in the lock and slid the locking bar in place. I watched him do this, resigned to the Duke's fate.

We made our way back down the tower stairs, retracing our steps through the passageways and to my cell. Exhausted, I laid down on the narrow cot which Gilo had brought for me to sleep on after hearing about my pardon so I would no longer have to sleep on the straw on the cold, hard floor. And for the first time since Bishop Odo's death, I felt tears well up in me.

* * * * * * * * * *

The ride from Devizes Castle in Wiltshire to Shirburn in Oxfordshire was going to take less than a day. Godfrey had ended his business in Winchester early and decided to join my escort, having us stop at Marlborough on the way as he had some things to discuss with the King's Marshal. As he had promised, Godfrey's men had arrived with a fresh set of clothes and a horse but no sword – I had to prove my trustworthiness before I would be allowed that. I found myself early in my twenty-second year starting a new life in a new country surrounded by strangers. Godfrey I had never met and the last time I had seen Guillaume had been at my departure from Ivry-de-Bataille for the crusade when he was but a mere babe, less than a year old.

I had not looked back to the prison tower when our horses carried us through the arched entrance. There was no need; Duke Robert could not be watching and I needed to make a break with our past as best I could. So I kept my head down, concentrating on the roads until Devizes was well behind me.

The route took us through undulating rural fields, now empty of their harvested crops, awaiting the frost of the winter. The chill of the dawn had lasted through the morning even with the bright sunshine that broke through the clouds, and the horses' breath as well as our own steamed into the cold air. As we neared the town of Marlborough, my cousin signalled for me to join him at the front of the riders. I spurred my horse on to move up next to him, his men pulled in behind us.

"I have some matters to discuss with Gilbert Giffard, King Henry's Marshal, it should not take long. He is staying at Marlborough Castle overseeing some repairs, so we will be meeting there. He had invited me to stay and hunt in the King's forest nearby, but I have declined. You may explore a bit of it if you wish, but do not wander too far. A couple of my men will accompany you of course."

"Thank you Godfrey," I said genuinely, grateful for the chance to wander a bit even if it was still being watched.

"Gilbert has requested permission from the King to change his family name to Marshal out of respect for the position he holds at court. I believe it will be granted but there is a lot of work re-writing the writs and deeds for the various properties he holds in England, I have offered my assistance. His wife Margaret de Venoix actually inherited the office; she now busies herself with household matters administering those properties. She is a beauty, but also highly capable. You should look to finding yourself such a wife," Godfrey said and then tapped his horse into a trot, his way of telling me our short conversation was done.

A wife? This was not something I had given any thought to, other than jesting with the Duke. My attraction to the fairer sex was undeniable and I had had my infatuations during the years in Palestine but war and battle does not lead one to think much about these things. Most of the men I was closest to were not married, probably reckoning that they would find themselves having marriages arranged based on the successes they had on crusade. Duke Robert had waited until quite late in life to find a mate, I just naturally thought I would do the same. But perhaps Godfrey was right. The days of crusade were long gone and I had a new life ahead of me.

We arrived at Marlborough at mid-morn, having had to cross the River Kennet after passing St George's Church as we approached the town. The castle sat atop the summit of a motte, very high, almost sixty feet, above the town, the views proving to be extraordinary. Access to the castle was by a path that wound its way around the motte several times before ending at an arched entrance with stairs tunnelled through the hill and up to the castle itself.

Not all the men came with us, only Godfrey, myself and two others made the climb around to the peak of the motte. We took our time walking the horses up the constant incline until we reached the entrance and dismounted. One of Godfrey's guards stayed with the horses and then three of us ascended the stairs and emerged at the crest of the motte, I was instantly impressed by the sight that befell me. The keep had been built of solid English oak and was three levels high, with battlements along its roof. The entire keep was surrounded by small gardens and a low stone wall that one could look out from and take in the natural beauty of the forests and parklands extending for miles on three sides, the town of Marlborough taking up the view on the east.

We were waiting for one of Gilbert's men to come greet us when we heard a commotion coming from around one corner of the keep, an adult male voice yelling words we could not understand followed by a youngster's peals of laughter. We all turned towards the noise when suddenly a pony appeared in full gallop being ridden by a small figure wrapped in furs. I only knew it was female when the fur-lined hood hiding the rider's face suddenly fell back onto her shoulders and her golden hair, which had come loose from its ribbons, flew behind her. She did not seem to be in any danger, indeed the peals of laughter continued as she pushed the horse to go faster around the various paths in the gardens in front of the keep. The owner of the male voice appeared soon after on foot, clearly distressed that the rider continued to disobey his orders to stop.

The pony and rider turned the corner of the garden closest to the boundary wall and headed straight for us. It was only then that we heard a male voice, strong and demanding, bellowing from the open door behind us.

"SÉRAPHINE!" the man shouted to her, with a tone that was unequivocal in its meaning. "Séraphine! Stop this instant!"

The girl, distracted by the man's shouting, pulled too hard on the reigns and lost control of the pony which reared up and threw her to the ground before racing off and coming to a stop in another garden. Instinctively I rushed over to her, worried she had been hurt in the fall. She lay on her side facing away from me, her clothes askew, her long hair haphazardly laying across her head and shoulders. As I approached I thought I could hear whimpering and I knelt beside her, gently removing the blond strands from her face. But it was not whimpering I had heard, it was laughter. She rolled onto her back, tears running down the sides of her cheeks as she lay on the ground, her hands holding her stomach.

"Are you hurt, Miss?" I asked, genuinely concerned.

She gasped for air, trying to regain some semblance of control. I helped her to sit up and then to her feet and it was not until she was standing and straightening and dusting off her clothes did she finally look up at me and I saw her eyes. Deep, dark, hazel green with a strength and power too old to belong in one so young. Startled, I actually took a step back.

"Thank you for your kindness, my lord," she said to me with a sweet smile. "I am not hurt."

The others had now reached us and the man who had shouted stepped up to her.

"Séraphine, are you hurt?" he asked looking at her for injuries.

"No, Papa, I am not," she responded.

Her father sighed heavily. His tone changed from caring to reprimanding.

"You have been told before not to do this, why do you persist? Your behaviour is not ladylike. Yet again, I am disappointed in you," he said sternly.

Séraphine lowered her gaze. But I sensed she was not sorry for what she had done. In fact, I suspected she revelled in it.

"I am sorry, Papa," she said. "But…"

He held a hand up to her to stop her from speaking further.

"Enough. Go to your Mama," he instructed and stepped out of her way so she could go.

She curtsied to her father and hurried away before he changed his mind and reprimanded her even further. I watched as her quick steps turned into a bit of a run, she gathering her skirts so as not to trip on them as she scampered up the steps at the entrance.

"Please forgive my daughter gentlemen, she is young and high-spirited and I am afraid loves her pony too much," he said apologetically.

"I thought she rode rather well," I offered.

Godfrey waved his hand as if to say it is of no matter and instead changed the subject.

"Gilbert, it is good to see you. I have brought my cousin, Sébastien D'Ivry, we are on our way to Shirburn," he said pointing to me.

Gilbert shot a look at me but did not extend his arm.

"His Majesty has been generous releasing you, pray you remember that," he said coldly, clearly not agreeing with King Henry's decision. Then turning to Godfrey he continued, "Come inside, I have the papers ready for you."

We followed Gilbert into the castle and into a great receiving room to the right of the entrance hall. The walls were adorned with decorated shields of various members of the royal family going back to the Conqueror. I noticed a new mounting board had been added but was empty of its shield. Gilbert saw me looking at it.

"For Normandy, now that it belongs to his Majesty," he said pointedly.

I got his meaning and, feeling his wariness, excused myself, letting the two of them get on with their discussions. I retraced my steps back outside and decided to forgo the forest and instead walk alone through the gardens and see the views from the perimeter walls. To the west of the castle was the River Kennet, flowing past the Church and meandering south and heading east into the distance towards the River Thames. I knew at some point I would go to the great city of London but not soon. For the time being, I was to be kept out of sight of the King and his family so as not to raise the memory of his brother. I stood for what seemed like a long time gazing out into the distance thinking about my circumstances and where I was headed. I needed to do something with my life, I needed to make a name for myself, get out from under the shadow of the Duke.

I followed the path along the low wall watching the scenery change as I moved around the castle. The marshy land leading to the river rose on the far banks, revealing endless miles of tall green trees. I assumed this must be the forest Godfrey had mentioned to me earlier, no doubt there would be a great stock of deer there for the King to hunt if so. And painful punishment for anyone caught killing any without his permission.

I continued along and started to see the built-up areas of the town to the east of the castle. Looking closer, I could see a bustling marketplace, with many people going about their daily business unaware of the dire circumstances others found themselves in. I envied them, their sense of purpose. I needed to find mine.

I had been deep in thought and knew not for how long when I heard a woman's strong voice call out to me.

"You are Sir Godfrey's cousin, yes?"

I turned to see a beautiful woman wrapped in a fur-lined hooded cloak standing on the path of the garden nearest to me, and behind her a nurse tending to two very young children. I bowed my head slightly in respect.

"Yes, I am Sébastien D'Ivry, son of Ascelin D'Ivry and Isabelle de Breteuil. Godfrey is my father's cousin," I replied.

"You assisted my daughter Séraphine when she fell from her horse?" she asked.

"I asked if she had hurt herself, she had not, Lady Margaret" I answered, letting her know I knew who she was.

"I thank you for that," she said. "My daughter is full of life at her age, sometimes too much so for her own good."

"She will make a fine rider," I said trying to be supportive.

"Not much use in a wife," she said ruefully but with a smile.

Suddenly, there were screams coming from the other two children as they fought over a toy the nurse had brought with her.

"My boys seem to have inherited the same energy as their sister," she said with a hint of pride.

"They must be quite a handful," I said.

"They are well taken care of by the nurses, them and the babe," she said.

"You have four children my Lady?" I asked.

"Yes, Anselm is but a year now, John is three, William just two" she answered, pointing to the boys when mentioning the last two.

Over her shoulder I could see the older of the boys slap the toy out of the hands of the younger and then march over to us.

"Mama!" he demanded as he walked, his little arms swinging at his sides, quite a ferocious look on his small face. And then again as he reached his mother, "Mama!"

Lady Margaret turned and looked down at him. He had hold of her cloak in a tight fist and was pulling as hard as he could.

"No, John, not now, Mama is occupied," she said rather coldly.

He glanced up at me and scowled. She called out to the nurse to come fetch him.

"Marie, please take John and William back to the nursery, they are tired," she said, excusing the behaviour as tiredness.

"Yes Madame," the nurse responded, curtsied, and obeyed, picking up the smaller boy and taking John by the hand.

He stared angrily at me all the way back to the castle.

"John is demanding, even at this tender age," Lady Margaret conceded. "He will need to temper his nature if he is to succeed his father."

"He is but a child, I am sure he will grow out of it," I proffered.

"His one soft spot is his sister. He simply adores her. Her behaviour earlier has kept her to her room for the rest of the day, so she cannot play with them. He is probably annoyed by this. But he must learn he cannot expect everything just because he has demanded it," she said. Then added laughing, "He is not the King!"

No, his is not the King, I thought. It would be interesting to see what kind of a man he would grow into.

"You must be cold," she said. "Let us go inside, I can have some mead brought and you can warm yourself by the fire in the great hall."

I was glad of the offer as I was starting to feel the chill through my cloak. Once inside, I removed it and my gloves and placed them on the back of a chair close to the hearth. I was leaning over towards the firepit, rubbing my hands, feeling the tingling of them coming back to life. The mead when it was brought was good, and warmed my innards quickly, it tasted delicious. This Giffard family, soon to be known as Marshal, knew how to live well.

Godfrey and Gilbert were soon done their business and we took our leave not wanting to outstay our welcome. And we preferred to get to Shirburn before dark if we could. Gilbert bid Godfrey good-bye but said nothing to me. We headed back to the entrance, Godfrey and his guard descended the stair tunnel ahead of me. Before following them, I turned to look at the castle one last time and thought I spied the figure of the girl Séraphine at one of the windows in the west tower. But it was fleeting, I might have been mistaken.

\* \* \* \* \* \* \* \* \* \*

We reached Shirburn with about an hour's sunlight still available to us, we had made good time from Marlborough. Godfrey had considered diverting to another D'Ivry estate in Bucklebury but decided against it, he wanted me settled at Shirburn as quickly as possible. The route took us through the North Wessex Downs, with its rolling hills and forests through which ancient paths had been pressed from years of those travelling from village to village, going to markets and plying their trade. It reminded me of the lands around Ivry-la-Bataille and Bayeux, lush, rich soils and trees whose vibrant colours lit up the landscape like a painting. I felt a pang of longing for my old home and seeing my mother and father. I would have to be satisfied with being reunited with my brother Guillaume. Even though I doubted I would recognise him, nor he me.

The light had just started to fade when we walked the horses through the entrance arch to the grange having passed a set of stone farm buildings I assumed were part of the estate. Once through the arch, I could see the main house, with a rounded tower at the front, one of the four corners of the building and the only tower. The entrance was here but we did not stop, continuing instead around the building to the back to the stables. There we were met by a couple of lads who helped us dismount and took the horses to be brushed down and fed before being locked in the stalls for the night. I took the saddle bag with my meagre belongings and followed Godfrey in.

The dwelling was not large by royal standards and not what I had spent the years living in during my journeys from Normandy to Palestine and back. But of course that was by the grace of Duke Robert and I was fortunate to have been able to experience the luxuriousness he demanded for himself. But it was still sizable and could house a large family if need be. For now, it was more than enough for Godfrey, Guillaume and myself, especially as none of us had a wife.

I walked into the small greeting hall through the front entrance where both Godfrey and I took off our cloaks and gloves. Glancing around, I saw the ceiling was quite high and was made of dark wood crossbeams forming a grid pattern from which a large wheel with candles hung with twelve large tapers all lit, providing enough light to illuminate the room. I was gazing up at it and had not noticed Guillaume coming into the room. Godfrey alerted me to his presence.

"Ah, good, Guillaume, your brother is here as you can see."

I turned and saw myself, only seven years younger. Guillaume was the spitting image of me at that age and seeing him made me break into a huge grin. He grinned back at me and, trying to be formal, extended his arm to me. I pushed it aside and grabbed him in a strong embrace, happy to see a member of my immediate family finally, after all these years, after all that I had been through. After a moment's hesitation, he returned my embrace.

"Come now, enough of that! Lupel, show your brother to his room and then do your rounds, Sébastien, go with him, you can start becoming familiar with the grounds. I expect our supper will be ready when you are done," Godfrey instructed and then left the two of us alone.

I stood back and looked at Guillaume. He was a strong lad, no doubt the years working at the grange had made him so.

"The last time we met you were but a babe," I said smiling at him.

He picked up my bag and started to ascend the large wooden staircase behind him.

"Mama and Papa spoke of you often, I heard much of the crusade and about where you were, what you were doing, the victories in the Holy Land. They have written you letters, they are in your room."

"Why did Godfrey refer to you as Lupel?" I asked, wondering at the strange moniker.

"It is short for Lupellus. Our father gave me the nickname, I can only assume he thought it appropriate to call me "little wolf" since he had been known as Lupus when he was younger."

"Does it fit?" I asked teasing him.

"You will have to determine that yourself," he answered cheekily.

We reached the top of the stairs and carried on down the hallway towards the rear of the house, passing a few doors on the right along the way. A few windows on the left of the hall revealed the existence of an internal courtyard, bordered on all fours sides by the house. When we got to the last door on the right before the passage turned to the left, he opened it and stepped aside so I could enter. It was not a large room, but large enough for my needs. The fireplace would hold a good fire and there was a sizable bed suitable for a man of my frame and a table and chairs sitting in a nook by the windows looking out over the grange grounds to the north. Not for me were the warm rays of the eastern morning or the glows of the western setting sun but I could not complain. It was just what I needed for the time being.

"There are letters," Guillaume said pointing to a couple of sealed parchments sitting on the table as he placed my bag on the bed.

"I will get to them later," I said looking at them.

"They are overjoyed for your release," he said, giving away part of the letters' contents.

"I am glad to hear it," I said, adding, "I am not so sure our cousin Godfrey is."

"Godfrey is not one for showing emotions, he just gets on with it. But he did risk our family's reputation and position at court with his pursuit of your freedom."

It was clear Guillaume was well informed of many things concerning me.

"I hope to gain his trust, as quickly as I can," I assured him. "And yours, of course."

"You already have mine, brother," Guillaume said sincerely. "I would like to hear stories about your time on crusade if you would be willing to share them with me?" he asked.

I smiled.

"I would be happy to. But for now, I guess we should get to the chores? I do not wish to annoy Godfrey on my first night of freedom."

I passed the next hour walking about the grounds with Guillaume, checking in on the livestock and seeing the grain and hay barns now full with their harvested crops. We watched the farmhands from the top of a small hill getting the sheep in their enclosures for the night and then checked that the horses from today were now in the stables and had been brushed down and fed and those in the grazing fields had been blanketed. It was when we were observing the horses in the fields that I got a tremendous surprise.

Standing not too far away from the gate leading into the field was a pair of horses, one older than the other, that looked almost like mirror images of each other, piebald black and white destriers, each taking a turn at munching on the shrubs coming through the fence. I could have sworn one of them was Pax, but how could that be? The last I saw of him was at the castle in Tinchebrai on the day of our surrender to King Henry. I walked towards the two, getting a better look at them the closer I got.

"Pax?" I whispered.

The older horse cocked his head towards me and slowly came over. To my astonishment, it was my dear old friend. I reached out and stroked his nose and neck, feeling him nuzzling the side of my head. But how could this be? I looked quizzically at Guillaume.

"I thought this might please you," he said, smiling. "Father agreed a settlement with the King after the battle for many of the Duke's horses and their tack. He knew we would need them for the properties cousin Godfrey owns here in England and sent quite a few, they have been dispersed to different holdings. Pax happened to be among them and came here. He is still a good workhorse in many ways but his real value is in his stud. One of his many colts," he continued tipping his head at the other horse, "is Lux, he arrived a couple of years ago. All indications are he is taking after his father!"

I was amazed. Pax had been but two years old when we set off on crusade and after my capture in Normandy I was certain I would never lay eyes upon him again. But here he was, at fourteen and still hale and healthy. My heart filled with pure joy at seeing him and knowing that he had been safe and sound these past couple of years.

"His many colts?" I asked, still a bit incredulous.

"He has done well at stud, very well. Several of his colts and fillies are at different stables, we will see them when we travel to the properties. Lux is the only one here," Guillaume said, reaching out to stroke the young fella.

"We can take them both out on a hack tomorrow if you are willing," I said, wishing it were morning already.

"We will need to have a saddle made for you to ride Lux, but you can ride Pax, your saddle and tack is hanging in the stable, waiting for you," he said as we walked away.

All throughout the chores, Guillaume told me more about himself, telling me about his childhood at Ivry-la-Bataille growing up with our brother Roger who was still in Normandy with our parents, working on administering the castle and other D'Ivry lands with our father. It was good to hear his stories, they made me feel reconnected somewhat to a family I had not seen in years. But I also knew of the division within the family who were forced to take sides when the two royal brothers decided to wage war against each other. The family in Normandy continued to support Duke Robert as had I; those in England had supported King Henry. And even though the Duke was now imprisoned in a place from which he was unlikely to escape, the memory of the battles and the outcome were still fresh and raw in people's memories. It would take a long time to rid myself of my association with him.

We ate in the dining hall with Godfrey's servants bringing us steaming hot stew and delectable wines brought from France to satisfy our hunger and fill our bellies. It was a gratifying change from the gruel I had been fed the past two years and I devoured a couple of bowlfuls and an entire loaf of bread. Godfrey was explaining the holdings that were now back in our family's possession, most of which were scattered all over the rich fertile lands of Oxfordshire and Gloucestershire. I was eager to see them and to offer my assistance wherever he saw fit.

"You seem to be in good stead with Giffard," I commented.

"You will need start referring to him as Marshal soon and, yes, I have tried to maintain the good relationship set with him by my father. They were both very close to the crown with first William and then William Rufus, they needed to work together to ensure the efficiency of the court." He then switched tack, asking "What were you and Lady Margaret discussing when we came into the great hall?"

"It was much of nothing. She came out to the gardens earlier to thank me for helping with her daughter earlier. Two of the boys were with her, little John seems to be a bit of a handful. Giff...er...Marshal is lucky to have three sons to follow him."

"He would have had more had the two that followed the girl thrived. Unfortunately, they did not. There was a worry that Gilbert would not have any more sons after the death of the second babe. But, God blessed them with three more."

"Ah, that explains the gap in age between the girl and her brothers," I said, finishing my goblet of wine.

"She is a bit of a wild one, I fear her parents indulged her because of the loss of the two babes. They will need to reign her in if they wish to find a good match, she will be reaching marriable age soon," he said as if he was talking about an uncontrollable filly nearing breeding age.

I knew Godfrey wanted to speak together after supper but the meal had filled me and the day's activities had been draining and I felt fatigue setting in. So I made my excuses and apologies and went to my room. A fire had been set, probably whilst we ate, and fresh bedclothes had been laid out on the bed for me. A basin of water and a clean towel were on a small side table against the far wall and two large candles on the main table had been lit. Beside them was an empty tankard and a full animal skin, I presumed would contain warm ale. I stripped completely and despite the fire, felt the chill in the air hit my entire body as I leaned over the basin and splashed cold water onto my face. The cold did not bother me; I had become used to it in my damp cell at Devizes Castle. I knew had lost weight during the two years spent in captivity and some muscle loss as well, I would need to spend some time rebuilding my physical strength.

But I did not linger on these thoughts, I grabbed the nightshirt and moved to the fire to warm myself. I pulled the shirt over my head and adjusted it over my body, it reached my knees which was surprising; someone must have been warned about my height, now just under six and a half feet. I sat in the chair on the side of the table that was closest to the fire and reached for the small packet of letters that had been waiting for me. I looked at the handwriting on the outside of the first one and recognized a female hand. This was from my mother. I broke the seal and opened it.

*My dearest Sébastien, greetings*

*I cannot express the overwhelming joy felt upon hearing the news of King Henry's mercy towards you in the matter concerning the former Duke of Normandy. Your father and I have been tormented with thoughts of your treatment at the hands of your captors and gaolers and were praying to our merciful God for your release. And our prayers have been answered, glory be to God.*

*Whilst I know of the depths to which your love and loyalty to those who kept you safe from harm and brought triumph in the Holy Land, it is time, my darling, to forgo the past.*

*Your father's cousin Godfrey has been generous in his offering to take you into his home, as he did your brother Guillaume at such a tender age, even younger than whence you went from us to Bishop Odo in Bayeux. Be gracious in this, I know you are so in your heart to those who show such kindness and generosity.*

*I hold you dear in my heart,*

*Your loving Mother*

*Isabelle de Breteuil D'Ivry*

I reached inside the opening at the neck of my nightshirt for the chain and medallion of St Michael which, by some miracle, had stayed with me since the moment she gave it to me the day I left her. It felt good to touch, the raised edges of the saint's image worn over the years but still discernible even against my rough fingertips. I made a silent vow to do as she wished, not only for herself, but for myself as well.

Next I read my father's letter. It did not contain the warmth of my mother's, nor did I expect it to.

*My son Sébastien, greetings from your father*

*I am aware that your mother shall be writing to you and I share with her the elation we have in our hearts at the news of your release. The King has been most kind in his forgiveness of your trespasses against the crown. You must not forget this generosity, it has saved the family from ruin and kept my cousin Godfrey in his Majesty's good graces. The former Duke is lost, you must detach yourself from him and forge a new path. I know this will be difficult, but it is imperative.*

*Your reputation as a strong warrior and expert swordsman has reached far and wide. Use that for good, make a name for yourself that distances yourself from your unfortunate recent associations.*

*I am as always,*
*Your father*
*Ascelin D'Ivry*

I folded the two letters back into their original shape. I noticed a small chest at the foot of the bed, opened it to find it empty, placed the letters inside and closed it. I suddenly felt exhausted as the day finally took its toll, and fell upon the bed, barely covering myself with the many fur coverlets spread across it. Within moments, darkness enveloped me, a deep sleep which no thought or dream dared to penetrate, I was oblivious to the world I knew now and had ever known.

# V

# Part Two

# 1113 - France

My life in Oxfordshire was relatively uneventful for the next couple of years. Helping Godfrey maintain the estates took up a lot of my time and I spent my leisure time training Guillaume how to fight astride his horse and on foot, passing on all the knowledge I had gained from the expert swordsmen who had trained me. This gave me ample opportunity to regain my strength and before long I had put on weight in pure muscle, strong arms and back from doing chores and thigh muscles from hours spent on Lux. It had not taken long to prove to Godfrey that I could be trusted and was soon awarded with a new sword and other weapons I would need in case trouble brewed. The properties flourished making Godfrey a rich man and of course Guillaume and I benefitted from this although the wealth could not be called our own.

As Duke Robert had suspected, King Henry did make a move to gain custody of his son William Clito by attempting to kidnap him but the plot failed as the Count of Arques had given orders for the boy to be hidden whenever he was not in residence and luckily for the lad, the attempt was made during such a time. I arranged for him to be secreted away to Flanders once the threat was gone. And as the Duke wished, I eventually was able to have his possessions shipped to England where they stayed in storage, awaiting their turn to become useful again. Once that task was done so was my association with Duke Robert and I closed myself off to him. I had no choice.

But I realized I missed the life I had come used to over the years spent on crusade with the Duke, Bouillon, Flanders and the others and, for me, at the ripe age of twenty-four, I was itching to be on another adventure again. This desire was made even more so upon hearing of the death of Flanders, a year after my release from captivity. He had sided with the new King of France, Louis VI, against a revolt by a number of the French barons, including Blois's son Théobald. And it was during the battle at Meaux just outside of Paris that Flanders's horse stumbled, throwing him to the ground where he was trampled to death by the hordes of horses taking part in the fight. A woefully unfitting end to one of the crusade's best leaders, I was truly saddened to hear of it.

As for my own personal life, because of my previous associations I was not a worthy candidate for marriage to a rich heiress and so I had put aside any ideas of making a good match for the time being. Not that my private desires were not taken care of, there was the odd flirtation with girls in the villages, but nothing of a serious sort. I needed to complete the repair and restoration of my reputation before I could seriously contend for any significant hand in marriage.

It was just after the new year of 1113 during a visit from my other younger brother Roger that this opportunity arose and I knew my life was going to take another change in direction. Over supper he had told us of the fortunes that some were making at tourneys that were taking place across France and that interest in them was gathering pace throughout the neighbouring settlements such as Flanders and Hainaut. These types of contests had existed for years and we had used them as training exercises for our men when on route to the Holy Land. But they had been part of preparing for battle with the goal eventually being, of course, to kill your opponent. But now these exercises had turned into games and the champions were making themselves not only materially rich but renown across the Christian world for their skill. Whilst I was not bothered about the fame, I did see how this could be my way of restoring my image in the eyes of the barons and the crown itself.

Guillaume and I had taken Roger out to our practice grounds at our property at North Leigh, just north of Oxford, to show him our skills and to ask him to judge if they were worthy enough to compete against those he had seen. Roger was impressed with my swordplay and the control I had of Lux, but less so with Guillaume. Which suited Godfrey, he did not want both of us travelling to the continent and leaving him without anyone to help with the estates. He spoke with the King and obtained permission for me to travel with Roger back to Ivry-la-Bataille to see my parents and then to Valenciennes to take my chances at a tournament being held there in the summer, hosted by the Count of Hainaut. It was to be my first opportunity to use what I had learned over the years and I hoped I could prove my honour and valour. Or, if I proved unworthy, I would be back at Shirburn facing my future there.

I took Lux and a couple of other horses with me and one of the stable boys named Pascal to be my squire and keep the horses shod and fed and to run errands when needed. Godfrey gave me small sacks of gold and silver to pay my way for which I was extremely grateful. And I was allowed to use the D'Ivry colours and standard of red chevrons on gold, the same I had used during the crusade which was gracious of the King to allow. I presumed that as long as there was nothing to indicate Duke Robert, the King would be content for me to carry our family's colours. It was a subtle way of reminding me to whom I owed loyalty now.

We crossed the Channel in mid-March, reaching Ivry-la-Bataille a few weeks before Easter. My mother's delight in seeing me was unbridled, much to the displeasure of my father who preferred restraint over unfettered emotion. But even he could not help breaking out in a grin when we embraced for the first time in many years. I was given my old room which had not changed much over the years bar a new, larger bed, I would have fallen out of the one I left when I was eight. The castle grounds had changed during my absence, many more farm buildings had been erected and cottages added closer to the edge of the crop fields, probably for the workers to stay in during harvest. But the inside of the keep had not changed much and I found it easy to make my way around as the memories of it came back quickly.

At supper on the first night and into the hours of the night we talked about many things, filling in the details which simply could not have been provided in the many letters sent from various ports and cities. My father knew Duke Robert well and lamented his current incarceration but knew one must accept the consequences of one's actions, and so we did not dwell on him very long. It was when I mentioned Hugues De Payns, Count de Champagne's vassal, that my father suddenly sat up as if he had just remembered something important.

"Stay here, Sébastien," he said getting up from the table. "I have something for you," and disappeared through an arched door and down a passageway.

I looked quizzically at Roger, he simply shrugged. My father soon returned, carrying in both hands a long, oblong wooden box, with two latches on one of the long sides keeping it shut. I pushed my goblet out of the way as he placed it on the table before me and returned to his seat.

"What is this?" I asked.

"Open and see," he responded.

And so I did. Whatever was inside had been carefully wrapped in blue velvet and tied with a couple of ribbons which I undid easily and then unravelled the object. I was stunned. It was the broadsword that Hugues had given to me during training when we were on our way to Bari, I recognized the red Greek cross on the pommel and the etchings, now faded and scratched from years of use, along both sides of the blade. It was still a fine sword, only slightly worse for the wear. I looked at my father, my eyes asking the question.

"He appeared one morning quite some time ago, I have forgotten how many years now, on his own, a lone rider out of the mist. He identified himself, said he had come from the court at Champagne, and said he had a possession of yours that he would like to return to you but knew not if he would ever be able to see you in person again. He accepted some warm ale for himself and water for his horse and then he was gone. That was it, the entire encounter lasted less than an hour," my father explained.

I could not even fathom a guess as to how Hugues had come to be in possession of it and was quite taken aback that he had journeyed from Champagne to my father's lands to try to return it to me. I removed the last of the velvet and stood, taking hold of the grip with my right hand, raising the sword out of its box, and then gripping it with both hands. It felt good, familiar, I recognized its weight and balance, it was like meeting an old friend and feeling as though we had never been apart.

Roger came over to my side of the table and pushed aside the velvet in the box, revealing the scabbard that had been sitting underneath.

"Seems you have friends in high places," he said quietly.

'Indeed I do,' I thought but did not say aloud. I placed both the sword and its scabbard back into the box, hooking the clasps, and sat back down. My father and brother stared at me, waiting for an explanation. I felt they were owed one.

"We came upon Hugues on the steps of Clermont Cathedral on our way out of France. Bishop Odo had suggested a pilgrimage to the site of the sermon by Pope Urban would inspire the troops and it did. Hugues had been given men and coin by the Count of Champagne who had decided not to join the mission. He became one of the masters of my training, I learned much from him. He gifted me this sword," I tapped the top of the box, "once he felt my skills were worthy of it. It came from his private stock. It had not left my hand until the end of the battle at Tinchebrai. I never thought I would see it again."

Everyone sat in silence, impressed and yet not knowing what to say. I am sure they were wondering what else I could tell them about my travels and experiences in the Holy Land. But I said nothing more about it or about him. I had no idea where Hugues was now, if he was still alive and if he was, what adventure he might be engaged in. I was determined to find out though. His gifting to me of this sword for a second time would not go unacknowledged.

* * * * * * * * *

At the beginning of the summer, the spring rains had ceased and the ground returned to solid from the muddy mire that had existed only a few weeks before. The call went out for the tourney at Valenciennes, on fields of the Count of Hainaut. All of those who wished to attend had two weeks in which to get to the settlement and establish a campsite in the field set aside for the competitors. It was to be a two-day affair, with participants from the north and south of France making up the two teams who would compete against each other. The main event, the mêlée à cheval, fighting on horseback, to occur on the second day, after the mêlée à pied, fighting on foot, taking place on the first day. And joust combats were going to start the tournament the evening before. I had a lot to organize and very little time to do it.

I sent word of my intention to compete and received instructions from Hainaut on where to go to join the other fighters from the north. My father kindly added to my funds and provided a new helm and set of maille, and two surcoats and shields with the D'Ivry crest. I had purchased items needed to set up camp and extra tools for Pascal to do his job keeping the horses in good shape over the few days we would be there. Most importantly was obtaining a set of lances to use in the jousts. I spent considerable time selecting the best and strongest ash, having many made and perfected, seeking out any imperfections from the hilt to the blunted and rounded coronal steel tip.

It did not take long to load everything onto the pack horse and cart coming with us and soon it was time to go. I am sure I made an impressive sight in the D'Ivry colours sitting astride Lux, my cherished broadsword in its scabbard at my side. I was ready for the challenge.

By the time Pascal and I reached Valenciennes, many others had already reached the camp field and set up their tents, claiming their spot on the grounds for the next few days. I spied an empty place near a large tree with long, wide-spread branches high enough not to interfere with the tent I had brought. I motioned to Pascal and pointed to the area, he nodded and we walked our horses in that direction. It did not take too long to get everything set up, erecting the tent and planting the D'Ivry shield at its entrance so it was easily seen. After having some bread and cheese and ale which we brought with us, I decided to leave Pascal to some chores and take a look at the others who had arrived before us.

Walking amongst the tents of the other competitors, I recognized many of the shields of men from places who had sent crusaders with us to the Holy Land, the emblems of Picardie, Bourgogne, Orléans, Reims, amongst others. When I saw men from Lorraine, I stopped for a moment and thought of Bouillon and of his man Saint-Omer who served him throughout his time in Jerusalem and who had helped me develop my fighting skills. I wondered where he was today. The last I had heard of him, he had settled in Jerusalem and became one of King Baldwin's men after Bouillon had died.

I was reaching the edge of the camps having counted about fifty tents when I spied a shield that looked very familiar to me, blue and white edged in gold, the colours of Blois. A couple of squires were milling about entering and exiting the main tent passing by two others sitting on low stools and chatting outside the tent, men whose countenances were very familiar to me. But it was not until one of them made a gesture with his left hand that I my memory was jarred; these must be Blois's sons, the two he spoke most about during our travels. He had shared so much about them from the letters from his wife Adele that we all felt we knew them without ever having met them. The more I watched them, the more I was certain. I approached.

"Blois?" I asked, pointing to the shield.

"Yes," said the one that seemed the taller of the two. "And you?"

"D'Ivry. Are you of the family of Stephen, Count of Blois & Chartres?"

"Yes, he was our father," responded the shorter one sounding a little wary. "I have heard of D'Ivry, whence come you?"

"Ivry-la-Bataille is my place of birth where some of my family still dwell. Others are now in England, with many properties in Oxfordshire and other counties, it is from there that I have come. I knew your father. I attended Bishop Odo and then the former Duke of Normandy during the crusade to Palestine."

They both stared at me for a moment, appraising me. The shorter one stood and stretched out his arm as a welcome.

"I am Henry of Blois, brother to Théobald, Count of Blois. This," he said turning to the other," is my older brother, Stephen."

I shook arms with Henry and nodded to Stephen who was now openly glaring at me.

"I have come for the tourney," I said, explaining the obvious, then followed with, "this is my first."

"We have attended three others before this. The fields here have hardened well, it is good that the weather has been dry the past couple of weeks. The others were not so lucky, we were up to our knees in muck for the mêlées," said Henry.

"I am surprised to see you here D'Ivry," Stephen said scornfully. "I am surprised King Henry allowed you out of his sight considering your actions at Tinchebrai. Everyone at the English court are well aware of your support of Curthose against his Majesty."

I winced slightly at his disparaging use of Duke Robert's nickname.

"The King of England is wise," Henry said to his brother, with a slightly chastising tone. "He must have seen no threat in allowing this man the opportunity to amend his reputation."

Stephen sniggered.

"Best of luck to you then. I have to admit, I am glad you are fighting for the North," Stephen chortled, looking me up and down. "I would not want to be on the receiving end of your mace. But how good are you on horse?"

"I believe I can hold my own," I said modestly, adding, "I was fortunate enough to have had good teachers."

"Well, just stay by my side during the mêlées," Stephen said arrogantly as he got up and started to enter his tent. "I will take care of you."

I watched him in silence, not surprised at his attitude. It appeared he had inherited some of his father's more unseemly qualities. But I did not dwell on that for very long as moments later a rider in Hainaut colours arrived, dismounted next to what looked like was a wooden pillar and proceeded to tack a piece of parchment to it.

"Ah, the rules have arrived," started Henry, "let us go see what they have in store for us."

We wandered over to the post to see what we were going to be up to over the next few days if we did not succumb to injury or worse. I looked across the open fields, trying to see those I would be fighting against.

"Where are the competitors from the South?" I asked.

"They have been placed on another settlement about half a mile away, on the other side of this open field being used for the mêlées. We will be able to see the herald waving the standard from here, he will be atop that hill with the judges," Henry answered pointing. "The contest on horseback needs much more space than the contest on foot. We will hear them coming before we see them."

"As will they us," I said rather cheekily.

We reached the message post slightly ahead of some others who had also seen the messenger arrive. Leaning in, we read:

# Tournai de Valenciennes

## Joust

1. Combatants are allowed to charge with lances three times, only 3 lances allowed per match
2. If there is no winner after 3 runs, combatants are allowed to charge two times more with other weapons such as maces or flails
3. If still no winner, the match will be fought on ground with weapons such as maces and swords, lances are not to be used
4. If there is no decisive winner, judges shall vote, giving points for skill and accuracy and making deductions for foul strokes

## Mêlée à Cheval

1. Combatants shall approach the battle field from their own settlements and only enter once the herald has called for the mêlée to commence
2. Up to three lances may be used
3. Combatants must remain horsed throughout
4. Once unhorsed, a combatant is considered defeated and must retire immediately
5. Any possessions left on the field by combatants may be taken by victors' squires who shall not be harassed nor harmed

## Mêlée à Pied

1. Combatants shall enter one-third of the battlefield from their own settlements and charge only once the mêlée has commenced
2. Combatants may use any weapon(s) of choice except lances
3. Dropped weapons may not be retrieved
4. Disarmed combatants are considered defeated and must retire immediately
5. Any possessions left on the field by combatants may be taken by victors' squires who shall not be harassed nor harmed

Baldwin of Hainaut

It seemed simple enough. Not only did I need to unseat my opponents during the joust and the horse mêlée and disarm them during the mêlée on foot, I needed to get Pascal to take from them as much as he could carry, as I fight on. And not be unhorsed or disarmed myself at any time. I shot a look at Henry.

"This is fairly standard," he said answering my unasked question. "Of course there are the revelries tomorrow night in Valenciennes after the jousts, you might want to be mindful of your intake of wine. Many tournament novices have fallen foul of over-indulging and then either not making it to the mêlées the next day or failing miserably and losing all their weapons and horses and having to pay enormous ransoms to get them back."

"Advice I shall endeavour to follow," I said. "Where are the jousting lists?" I asked looking around and seeing only open field.

"They are set up just outside the city limits," Henry said as we walked back to his tents. "Ride with us tomorrow, we will take you there," he offered.

I thanked him and after agreeing a time to meet in the morning, I found my way back to my tents. I could not help but notice that I was being stared at as I wandered through the settlement, probably being sized up as a newcomer, possibly a threat to the prizes given for special achievement during the tourney. I decided to keep my head down as best I could and spent the afternoon and evening checking every piece of maille and every weapon was in good shape. After a hot evening meal, I settled in for the night, trying to get as much sleep as I could. Not that that was particularly easy; the atmosphere in our settlement was electric, an edginess mixed with excitement about the events to unfold over the next few days. But soon the sounds of camp diminished and a peaceful quiet descended. I drifted off into a deep, dreamless sleep.

* * * * * * * * *

Daybreak had just begun to crest on the horizon when I stepped through the tent flaps into the misty morning air. I stretched, loosening the muscles in my long limbs and took the tankard of warm ale from Pascal, downing its contents in one mouthful. I could feel its heat making its way down into my innards, it tasted good. Others in our settlement had already stirred and were working with their horses or gathering their weapons. I walked over to where Lux and the other horses had spent the night behind my tent and found that Pascal had already been busy suiting up the horse with the caparison brought for the occasion, the cloth covering made of the D'Ivry emblem and colours, falling across his back and hanging down on his sides and the matching mask with openings for his eyes and ears. My mother had offered to have a new saddle made for the occasion but from my years at battle I knew this was not needed; a new one would be too stiff and inflexible for the riding movements needed in this tourney whilst a well-worn seat would be of greater benefit and form a better, more snug fit between myself and my horse. So even though Lux shone with bright red and gold colours and shining reins and spurs, it was a simple, dull brown saddle for us. He looked good. I smiled at him as I stroked his nose, whispering encouraging words to him.

After attending to my personal needs, I returned to my tent to dress. I pulled a padded undercoat over top of my undershirt and then stepped into the padding leggings. Pascal then helped with the rest, tying the clasps on the arms, legs and then the breastplate.

The final touch was my treasured sword which I slid into its scabbard once I had wrapped the leather belt around my waist and tied it in front.

Pascal had tacked one of the other horses with us and attached the cart which was to carry my helm, gauntlets and extra shield which also had the D'Ivry crest of deep red chevrons on its front, lances and other weapons to the lists where the jousting competition would be held. He also had packed my hauberk, a shirt of maille with maille sleeves reaching my wrists and long enough to cover my thighs. He affixed the standard pole to my horse's gear and hoisted the D'Ivry flag where it gently flapped in the breeze. When it was time, we rode together to the Blois tents where I found only Henry saddled and ready to go with his squire also on horseback next to him. I looked around for his brother.

"Stephen has already made his way to the outskirts of the city where the lists are, he wanted to take a look at the grounds," he explained.

Without another word, our group headed out of the settlement and towards Valenciennes. We joined others on the road and soon the path was a river of men on horseback, almost one hundred strong, all clad in jousting mailled armour, colourful flags with family emblems held aloft all fluttering in the same direction, the wind having picked up slightly along the way. We were joined by competitors from the South and for a little while at least, we were unified, a group of warriors going to battle. There was much laughter and frivolity, sportsmanship before the fight when all kindness and friendship would be abandoned until victors were declared. Roger had told me that even though these were mock mêlées, men had died in these tournaments. So even with the good cheer, there was an undercurrent of solemnity that ran amongst the men.

"What happens once we arrive at the lists?" I asked Henry.

"The two sides will separate, all the fighters from the North to one side, those from the South to the other. Once the Count and his court have taken their places in the viewing platforms, there shall be a review of all of the fighters parading on horseback, one after another, alternating one from the North and one from the South until all fighters have presented," he explained. "All fighters will then put on their helms and choose their starting lances, and then wait, ready to be called. The herald calls out the names of the first two combatants who come to a standstill at either end of the yard. The charge begins at the sound of the herald's horn. This continues until all combatants have participated and victors have been decided."

"And the prizes?"

"There are many, those from the Count of course for the tournament champions. But the nobles place bets as they decide on favourites and you may be rewarded with gold from their winnings. Anything you capture from the field is yours to keep or ransom back to the one you defeated. The squires are also allowed to collect your winnings in the mêlées, so keep Pascal close."

I nodded. I felt an excitement begin to rise within me, somewhat akin to what I felt as we prepared for battle on crusade.

The pavilions and temporary stands built for the spectators came into view, the black chevron-on-gold flags of Hainaut being flown from every post and rooftop possible. We found ourselves being split into two groups and we continued on in the direction determined by whom we were representing. A bivouac had been set up at some distance from the jousting yard and we were instructed to claim an area for our men, horses and carts. Henry spied Stephen ahead of us making his way to an area for themselves and I was able to secure a space next to them and we settled in to wait for the event to begin.

I was patting Lux down and making sure he had water when we heard the first trumpet of the herald's horn, calling us to parade. There was an order in which fighters were to ride, the most noble going first, followed by lesser nobles with tournament novices bringing up the rear. This is where I found myself, both Henry and Stephen having taken their place at the front of the riders for the North. The wooden stands were now filled with crowds of spectators, excited for the tournament to begin and to get a glimpse of our host, Count Baldwin of Hainaut and his wife, Countess Yolande. They arrived with much fanfare, the horns announcing their presence as they made their way up the stairs and to the seating area secured just for them. Once seated, the herald came to stand next to them to announce the opening of the games.

"Upon this day," he boomed, "by the grace and munificence of his lord, Count Baldwin of Hainaut and his lady, Countess Yolande of Guelders, the opening of these games is now declared! Combatants, prepare to present!"

He then reached for his horn and with three blasts, the parade began, starting with a rider from the South whose colours and emblem I recognized as those of Aquitaine. An impressive rider, his shields in bright reds and golds with the single gold lion hanging on the horse's sides, astride a magnificent black steed, he was an intimidating sight. I was wondering who the fighter was when one of my fellow North riders confirmed it for me.

"Ah the indomitable Duke himself," he said, leaning in so he could be heard over the din that was starting to take hold. "There was doubt he would compete, being under threat of excommunication at the moment."

"Perhaps his love of the contest drove him here," I suggested.

"More like his love of money," he said with a chuckle.

I watched as each of the riders took their turn urging their mounts forward when it came their time so that they were in a full cantor by the time they entered the yard in front of the pavilion, each just as resplendent as the last. Shouts and cheers greeted the riders as they rode past, with favourites being called to by name. The riders themselves were shouting different battle cries throughout their part of the parade, each one in Latin, words or phrases from their mottos. 'Victoria!,' 'Honnoris!,' 'Veritas!,' and others, all cried out with passion and vigour, showing the pride and pure joy each was feeling at the moment. Most were swaying, waving their standards back and forth above them. This was difficult to do; standard poles were not light and to control a horse with one hand and wave one's flag with the other is a real test of skill. But as the parade continued, I realized I had no such battle cry. All of my soldiering had been under the banner of the Duke of Normandy which now, of course, belonged to King Henry and so I had no right to use it. I thought hard and quickly about what I should proclaim and was still struggling to think of something when it was my turn to parade.

I spurred Lux into motion and he pushed forward at speed, in full cantor by the time we cleared the entrance gate. I felt the blood rush through my body, the excitement of the moment taking over me and as I reached the royal pavilion I grabbed the standard out of its saddle grip in one hand and unsheathed my sword with the other, stood upright in my stirrups so that I was only controlling Lux with my thighs and, raising both the sword and the standard, I shouted,

*"BEAUSÉANT! BEAUSÉANT! BEAUSÉANT!"*

The crowd roared its approval, and I caught the eye of the Count as I passed by where he and his lady sat. I had made an impression which was what I needed to do. I just did not know if it had been a good one.

I turned Lux around once I exited the yard at the opposite gate and directed him to return to our side where I joined Henry and Stephen and dismounted, handing the reigns to Pascal.

"That was clever of you," Stephen said to me although I was not sure it was a compliment. "A French battle cry in the midst of Latin ones will certainly stand out."

"I did not know it was customary to do this during the parade, and I did not think using anything from my days with the former Duke would serve me well," I replied feeling annoyed that I needed to explain my choice.

Stephen scoffed and walked away. Henry beamed at me.

"Beauséant," he said, repeating my battle cry. "I have not heard that in a long time. Apt, considering where we are. I hope that all of us can 'be glorious' D'Ivry."

"Si Deus Vult," I said smiling, "If God wills."

Our conversation was interrupted by some commotion near our gate entrance to the yard. Henry being much shorter than I asked if I could see what was happening. I scanned the heads in the crowd and noticed men starting to step aside as if they were making way for someone. I was right, I soon saw the Count of Hainaut and his Countess slowly working their way through the mass of men, stopping occasionally to speak to one or another whilst receiving respectful nods or bows from those he approached and passed.

"It is the Count and his Countess, and their entourage," I said.

Henry did not have time to comment as they came within earshot of us. In an instant, Stephen stepped in between us and bowed lowly to the Count.

"Your Excellency," he said solemnly.

The Count stopped short and looked at Stephen.

"How does your brother?" the Count asked of their older brother Théobald, who had been Count of Blois since their father's death many years ago.

"He is well and sends his greetings," Stephen said, continuing his gravitas. "My overlord, Henry, King of England, also sends his greetings and wishes you every success for a triumphant tourney."

"I thank his Majesty and wish him good health," the Count responded.

And then slightly side-stepping Stephen, he continued his progress over to where I was standing. I bowed, but not as low as Stephen.

"You wear the colours and carry the standard of D'Ivry, do you not?" he asked me.

"I do, your Excellency. I am Sébastien, son of Ascelin D'Ivry and Isabel de Breteuil."

"I know this name," the Count said, reaching into his memory. "You took the cross and attended on Robert Curthose during the crusade, did you not?"

"I did, your Excellency. I came to know your father, Count Robert. He was an honourable and worthy warrior, steadfast in his purpose to recapture Jerusalem. I was also fortunate to have spent time with his cousin, Payen de Montdidier, I trained with him, I learned much from him on the art of battle on horseback."

The Count broke into a large smile at the mention of his father and cousin.

"My cousin Montdidier's horsemanship was better than my father's, you had the best teacher. I believe we saw some of that skill in the parade? Hopefully, it will serve you well today and in the mêlées to come."

"I thank you, your Excellency, I will endeavour to be worthy of Montdidier's mentoring."

The Count tipped his head and turned to go. Stephen coughed slightly and stepped up.

"May I remind your Excellency, that this man took arms against King Henry and sided with the former Duke in the battle…."

"That is not of our concern," the Count cut him off sharply, shooting him an irritated side-glance.

Stephen bowed and stepped back. The Count looked over his shoulder at me.

"I will place my wagers on you, D'Ivry. Do not let me down," he said and then he walked away, quickly enveloped by the crowd.

The joust began as soon as the Count and Countess had resumed their seats. The first combatants were announced: Orléans for the North and Anjou for the South. The two men, now in full mailled armour and helmed, their brightly coloured emblemed shields now hooked on one arm, lances tucked under the other and resting across their horses' saddles, walked their mounts to their designated starting places and awaited the blast of the herald's horn. The first sound would instruct the jousters to raise lances, the second would signal the commence. The horses, aware that something unusual was afoot, were restless with excitement and the two riders had some difficulty in containing them behind their lines.

Henry and I found a spot on the far side of the lists to watch from, close enough to quickly return to our horses when we were called, but also giving an excellent vantage point from which to see all the action. The first horn sounded; the combatants raised their lances. And seconds later, the second horn sounded and off they went, galloping at full speed at each other. The thundering hooves were almost drowned out by the shouts and cries from the spectators, all clamouring to see. The two fighters and their horses pounded down the yard towards each other, heads down, lances raised and within seconds there was a huge explosion of sound as the two men came together, lances smashing into shields, each breaking into many parts, the two riders thrown backwards on their saddles, not falling but staying mounted, trying to control their horses as they threw down what was left of their shattered weapons. They headed to the end of the yard, circling back to their starting points where their squires awaited them, ready to hand them their second lances. Anjou seemed to still be struggling with regaining control of his reigns and re-set one of his boots in the stirrups which meant he really was not set and ready for the second run. And so Orléans, taking advantage of this, easily saw him off, unhorsing him on the second run. The crowd roared its approval as Orléans took a victory lap in front of the pavilion. The first of many was done, the joust was firmly underway.

Stephen and Henry both won their bouts but with some difficulty, unhorsing their men only upon the third strikes. Most of the battles took more than one run and some had to move to ground battle after the third lances were used. Some were injured, a few broken bones when men fell from their horses which meant they would not be able to compete in the mêlées. But then my turn came, the herald announcing my name and that of my competitor.

"From the North, Sébastien D'Ivry!" he called out. "From the South, Guiscard de Lyon!"

I gripped the shield in one hand, waiting for Pascal to hand me my helm. I easily straddled Lux who was comfortable with the weight of the mailled armour and Pascal held up the helm which I put on and then took hold of my first lance which I held upright balanced on my thigh. I am certain I made a formidable sight as few men had my height or my physical strength. Now I would be tested on my mental strength. I urged Lux forward and passed Henry on the way to the entrance gate.

"Deus te custodiat," he said looking up at me. "God protect you."

Pascal followed behind me carrying the two extra lances and my sword. I had decided I had no need for any other weapons. This sword had served me well, if I needed it I knew my old friend would not let me down if the joust turned to hand-to-hand combat if both of us were unhorsed. We reached the entry gate and Pascal laid the lances against the fence within easy reach so he would be ready to hand one to me if need be. But he wore the sword and kept it close to him so it would not be lost.

I drew myself to full height sitting in the saddle, adjusted my helm and took a deep breath. My opponent reached his entry gate at the same time I did. The Lyon colours of red and silver stood out as his horse, skittish and nervous, began moving from side to side. Unlike his horse, Lux had come to a complete standstill, facing into the yard, as if staring at his own opponent. I watched my competitor raise his shield and saw my target: the Lyon silver lion rampant, up on its back legs, his front legs raised with claws out, on a solid red background. That would be where I would need to strike him if he were well-horsed. And if he were not, a good strike anywhere would knock him off. The first horn sounded. We raised our lances.

I am sure the roar of the crowds had not abated and had probably even increased as we readied ourselves. But I did not hear any of it. My focus was fixed on the task ahead, just as it had been each time I was readying to do real battle. But I only had one enemy to deal with here. I could feel the heat of Lux on the back of my legs and I whispered to him.

"Alright Lux, you know what to do."

The second horn sounded and I spurred Lux into a gallop from his full stop and within seconds we were racing ahead at full speed. Lux's powerful legs drove us forward in a straight line, I barely controlled him at all, he knew exactly what he needed to do. My opponent rushed at me from the other side, lance raised, ready to strike when the opportunity and timing called for it. I knew that this would be my first chance to impress those watching and, of course, prove myself worthy of the Count's support. I leaned forward slightly in my seat, tightening all the sinews in my body, readying myself for the hit and aiming the tip of the lance, seeing it hit its mark in my mind's eye over and over again.

When the collision came, the dead silence in my head was suddenly replaced by a massive explosion of sound, of the iron tips hitting metal of the shield, of wood breaking and splintering, of crowd shouts and cheers, all now reverberating in my ears. And yet, at the same time, all motion seemed to lose pace, in a sort of slow sinister dance as our weapons clashed with a ferocity that would have killed had the lances' tips not been blunted. But whilst my lance hit its mark and pushed my opponent, his did not. I knew if I could swipe my shield at the moment the tip of his lance made contact, the effect of two objects colliding whilst moving in the same direction would result in deflection. This was a dangerous risk to take, for if it were not timed just right, it would leave me vulnerable to serious injury if not worse. I took my chances anyway.

But I was not hurt. My strategy had worked, the power of his strike on me dissipated and had no effect whilst mine on him was devastating. The force of my blow was such that he was driven backwards off his horse, flying with arms and legs outstretched before him, seeming to hover in mid-air before landing hard on the soft sand beneath him. His helm flew off his head and rolled aimlessly to the edge of the yard, his broken lance falling harmlessly to the side and his horse coming to a halt by the gate I had entered. I slowed Lux down to a walk, turned him around and headed back to check on the condition of my opponent, who was face up on the ground, motionless. I could see Pascal racing into the yard, picking up whatever he could find that had fallen off the Lyonnaise fighter. His squire came running into the yard and knelt beside his master who was alive but winded. He gradually held up his hand to show he was not seriously injured and eventually he was able to stand with the help of his man. I breathed a sigh of relief, I had not wanted to injure my opponent. The crowd, which had gone relatively quiet as the fighter was being attended to, erupted again with more shouts and cries, I could even hear a few calling out my name. I rode past the pavilion and shouted my war cry again when I reached the Count. He nodded his appreciation to me. And with that, I exited the field.

I was immediately surrounded by the other fighters from the North, all wanting to congratulate me for being the first to knock a man off his horse with the first lance in the competition. Henry was the first to reach me of the two Blois brothers and heartily clapped me on my back once I had dismounted.

> "Well done, Sébastien, excellent play!" he exclaimed. "Where did you learn to do that?"

I wanted to remain modest and unassuming, but even I had to admit my plan had worked to perfection.

> "I picked up a few tactics on crusade. It is a ground battle technique, but seems to have worked well here," I said trying not to grin and thanking Saint-Omer quietly in my head for his invaluable teachings.

I wandered over to Pascal who was excited to show me what he had collected from the fallen fighter. Not only had he gathered his studded helm, his shield and a ceremonial dagger which had slipped out of his boots when he landed, Pascal had taken possession of his horse and all its tack. He seemed quite pleased with himself.

> "I am sure Lyon will pay a pretty price to get these back," he said, grinning from ear to ear.

> "No doubt," I agreed.

The rest of the joust competitions soon finished as my duel had been near the end of the list. The North had won the day, having unhorsed more of the combatants from the South than they had of us, so there was a reason for celebration back in our settlement that evening. But I remembered the warning Henry had given me earlier and decided to turn in after joining the others for a splendid feast and downing a goodly amount of wine but not so much that I felt ill-affected. Lyon's squire had arrived during the festivities to negotiate the return of his master's belongings and horse. After taking advice from Henry, we agreed a price, a tidy princely sum for a few moments' work. He returned later and the exchange was made. I doubted I would see Lyon again in the mêlées over the next couple of days.

The next morning sun greeted us warmly, it looked to be a good day for a mock battle on horseback. The Count had a priest conduct mass for each of the two groups, many appreciated this knowing that it was the mêlées where lives would be risked in these tournaments, even though the fighters were not actually trying to kill each other. Once done, we all dressed again in our fighting garb, armour, helm, shield at the ready. We would start with a single lance and were allowed two more to use throughout the mêlée on horseback, so Pascal wore my sword once again.

At mid-morning, we were instructed to form a line bordering our side of the battlefield, grounds that stretched as far as one could see. Our opponents looked like little brightly coloured specks shimmering in the distance, lining the border of the battle field opposite to our own. All of the squires had been positioned along the centre of the third side of the battlefield so they could reach us quickly to retrieve the goods of fallen fighters. Judges sat at raised daises atop a small hill along the fourth border of the field, from which they would watch for exceptional skill or egregious fouls which would be included when assessing the mêlée at the end of the day.

Henry and Stephen pulled their steeds up on either side of mine and stared at the so-called enemy.

"I guess we shall see soon just how good your horsemanship skills are, eh D'Ivry?" Stephen said smirking.

I did not bother to respond, choosing instead to stare ahead, studying the ground and making out what I could about the other fighters going by the colours I could make out. Then the herald raised his horn and blew his first blast. We raised our lances.

"Beauséant," Henry said leaning over to me.

"And you," I said back to him.

As soon as the second horn sounded, we were off, en masse, pushing our horses to breakneck speed as quickly as we could, sizing up our opponents as they started to come into focus. I recognized a few of the fighters directly across from me being from Limoges, Bordeaux and Angoulême. I knew that of the three, Angoulême would be a better win, recognizing the shield as the red and gold checkerboard of its Count and so the rewards should be richer.

So I focussed on him but kept an eye on the others approaching in case they decided to try to take me as their prey.

Angoulême seemed to take my hit well but as he passed me I realized he was actually sliding to the side, his saddle strap had snapped and he was no longer in control of his horse. Within a few moments he was down, falling and rolling, curling up into as much of a ball as he could to avoid the hooves of the other horses. I did not need to call out to Pascal, he was already racing across the field towards the fallen man, taking hold of his horse and shield, and leading the steed off the field in the space provided when the two teams separated and prepared to turn their horses around and take another run at others still horsed. Those who had been unhorsed were limping off the field as they were no longer in play.

I swung Lux around and scanned the field, finding the Limoges fighter in my sights. My first lance had not broken upon contact with Angoulême and so I adjusted my hold on it and charged at Limoges, easily knocking him off his horse with one thrust. I quickly turned Lux on the spot and found Bordeaux on his way towards me. This blow shattered my lance and I dropped it instantly, glancing over my shoulder to see Bordeaux crawling on the ground. I was keeping Pascal busy today.

I directed Lux over to where Pascal had placed my two extra lances and snatched one without breaking speed and headed back onto the field looking for my next conquest. I could see Henry being attacked by a man from Montpellier and I came to his assistance, together he was no match for us. Slowly the number of fighters began to shrink as defeated men dashed off the field so they would not incur any penalties for lingering. Both sides fought well and it was only when the remnants of the South saw they were outnumbered did they give up the game. We would not find out the official winner until the end of the tournament however as points could be taken away for any foul play or broken rules. We would have to be content with our winnings from the field which would be kept until after the next day's mêlée. The horses would not be needed for it anyway and the defeated fighters would have to make do with backup shields which might not be as high a calibre as those they lost.

That evening, more of those from the North started to come talk with me, and I began to make fast friends with some of them over a few tankards of good ale. But we all knew the biggest challenge lay ahead of us and the settlement grew quiet earlier than the night before as men turned in to get their rest. Henry and I were the last ones still sitting around the firepit closest to us.

"Will Stephen return to Mortain after the tournament?" I asked, knowing that he had been granted the county from Henry last year.

"No, I do not believe so. Stephen's place at the moment is with King Henry, he will return to England. He was sent there at the behest of my mother after the revolt of the barons three years ago. It was always her wish, for him to live at Henry's court."

"Your mother Adela is a formidable woman," I said frankly. "I never met her but we knew of her correspondence with your father during the crusade. She definitely had the strength of the Conqueror in her."

"She still is and still does," Henry said with a knowing grin.

"What do you do after the tournament?"

"I? I shall return to my studies at Cluny. I am for the church Sébastien, per my mother's wishes," Henry said. "So this shall be my last tournament."

I thought I heard a slight wistfulness in his answer. I did not know whether to be envious of such family connections and power or glad I was a free man. Or as free as one could be after fighting against the King of England.

"And you?" he asked me.

"I shall return to my homestead in La Bataille and train until I hear of the next tournament."

"Well, if you continue as you are, you will not need to wait to hear anything, they will come to you. A successful tournament brings riches to those who host them and a warrior with your skills would be a huge draw to guests and visitors willing to pay for room and board to see him."

He got up and stretched, I could hear the bones in his neck crack.

"I have already been eliminated from winning the grand prize, and I do not believe Stephen has a chance. But you still have one. There a few in the South that will challenge you. But I have faith in you, I am sure the Count is happy he has backed you in this fight. Just keep doing what you are doing."

He clapped me on my back and disappeared into the rows of tents. 'Keep doing what I am doing' I thought. That would be easier said than done.

Clouds had rolled in during the night and we all woke to the sounds of heavy raindrops bouncing off the tents' canvas. This would not bode well for the mêlée today. The field had been badly torn up by the horses the day before and now it was turning into a muddy quagmire. The rain eased off for a while as we ate our morning meal and so Henry, Stephen and I decided to inspect the field so we could know what to expect. It appeared several others had the same thought and many were already at the fences, peering in.

"This will make it much more difficult to fight," Stephen said patronizingly and with a slight whine.

He was sounding more and more like his father with every word.

"Lucky for us, it will be more difficult for our opponents too," I said and turned away.

The rain started up again on our way back to the camps but not as harsh as earlier. We knew that the mêlée would take place regardless of the weather, it would now be a contest by those who knew what techniques worked best. I reached my tent and found Pascal inside lining up my weapons.

"Which do you want with you?" he asked.

"Only my sword Pascal. I cannot be weighted down with anything else in this rain and in that mud," I answered.

This mêlée started much as did the one on horseback, except all of the competitors had already entered the field, reaching about a third of the way in at borders set by flags placed on the fences on each side of the field. Canopies had been provided for both the spectators and the judges to protect them from the rains, nothing was going to keep them away from enjoying this spectacle.

Having chosen my spot after carefully sussing out the drier section of the field, I stood at attention alongside the rest of the North fighters, my hand on the hilt of my sword, ready to unsheathe it upon the herald's first horn. Weapons were different this time and were to be used in an effort to knock an opponent down until he submitted and declared defeat by crying out, 'J'abandonne!.' But we were only allowed to use the flat side of our swords, and maces and flails had to be rounded and blunted so as not to cause any lethal blows. Any direct hit using a sharpened edge would be a foul and would disqualify a fighter. I had to remember this as I contended with others coming at me and the rain and mud.

The clouds now decided to fully unleash a true downpour, the likes of which I had not seen in years. In an instant, under-clothing was soaked, adding to the weight of us, and we could see pools starting to form in the water-clogged muck. But we remained still as statues, unaffected by the droplets trickling down our backs. The herald's first blast of the horn sounded. Almost in unison, we brought our weapons to the fore, raised and poised, standing ready for the charge. Then upon hearing the second blast we were off, charging with weapons raised, scanning the horizon of opponents who were racing towards us with the same intent as we had.

It was not long before we knew who was going to stand a chance as novice fighters sank ankle-deep into the sticky mud and were finding it difficult to progress. This made them vulnerable to attack and we already started to hear the shouts of 'J'abandonne!' coming from both teams. Once again, my training with some of the best soldiers to take the cross, this time Saint-Omer, gave me the edge. One exchange echoed in my head during a difficult session that took place in the fertile fields of Anatolia which had turned boggy after rain that had not stopped for a couple of weeks.

*"Over there," he had said, pointing to a particularly bad patch.*

*I thought he was joking.*

*"I cannot possibly fight in that," I objected, "I will not be able to move in it."*

*"Then you will die in it," he responded nonchalantly. "Your enemy will not heed your complaints."*

*I took a tentative step in and immediately sank. With each slow step, my boots went down further and further until they were both fully submerged and making gurgling sounds. Saint-Omer just stared at me then, after a moment, told me to come back out but of course I was stuck.*

*"If you cannot move, impale your sword into the muck, it will find solid earth. Then reach into the mud and find the tip of your boot with your free hand, pull back on it, this will create space for air and the hold the mud has on your boot will be relaxed. Use the sword to help with your balance and push yourself out," he instructed.*

*I did what he said and soon I was standing next to him. Without a word, he stepped into the same spot I had just struggled in, but instead of sinking, he moved, quickly, from side to side, back and forth, ending up back next to me on drier ground. I did not really understand how he had not been sucked down into the mud.*

*"Remember what I said about never staying still? That applies here, even more so. And one other trick – move on the balls of your feet, do not put your heels down. The less contact there is with the bottom of your boots the better. Do not allow the mud take hold. Now, try it again."*

We practiced this again and again, first only moving then including sword strokes and using other weapons and then adding my shield until I perfected the technique. From a distance I must have looked like I was dancing across a sea of mud.

This memory flashed through my mind in an instant and I reached my first opponent ahead of anyone else reaching theirs. My opponent fought valiantly but he was no match for me, and I had him down and unarmed within seconds. I glanced around me and made eye contact with Pascal who was already on his way to collect my opponent's weapons. I also chose my next target and headed for him. Fifteen minutes into the mock battle and I already had four 'kills' to my name.

With all the mud being splattered about, it should have been difficult to make out which fighter was which but the rains did a good job of clearing the shields so it was fairly easy to tell who was friend and who was foe. I saw Stephen being beaten down to the ground on the far side of the field, perhaps he should have stayed at my side. He was too far away to help, so I concentrated on finishing the job at hand.

The battle lasted for a few hours as the teams were fairly well-matched but eventually we were down to the last few fighters from each side. That is when I met my match. I had seen the Aquitaine colours on the first day as the Duke led out the South for the parade but had not encountered him or anyone from the region at all in the mêlée on horseback. I was resting after my sixth encounter which had taken place almost directly in front of the spectator pavilions where I had found some solid ground on which to stand by the fence. I was surveying the field when he emerged from the skirmish, heading for me with one goal in mind. I took a deep breath and started towards him, meeting him half-way, shield raised and sword in attack position.

He took his first shot at me using his black German mace whose spikes had been shorn off leaving a rounded stump, effectively turning the mace into a balled club. He hit me on my shield which I had raised slightly above my left shoulder, having seen the move coming from afar. A strong opponent, he was nonetheless not an overly clever fighter and many of his strikes were unimaginative and predictable. But I was to be taught a lesson about complacency.

I was on the attack, thrashing him again and again with the flat face of my blade, taking advantage of every drop of his shield and making contact with his arms and shoulders in an effort to drive him down. But during my flurry of blows on his shield, I took my eye off his mace momentarily and with one strong movement he swung his mace upward, catching my shield on its bottom point and driving it up towards my head, knocking off my helm in the process. There was no rule about combatants surrendering once a helm had been lost, most did simply to avoid any serious injury. It would be foolish, if not mad, not to. But I had been in this position before and, angry with myself at becoming so over-confident, I redoubled my efforts, pounding away at the fighter until he finally fell, defenceless, into the mud, dropping his shield and mace and crying out "J'ABANDONNE! J'ABANDONNE!!"

I stood over him, sword in both hands now as I had dropped my shield, arms raised above my head, breathing hard, sweat and rain running down my unprotected face, fighting the almost irresistible urge to finish him off completely. It was the herald's horn declaring the end of the mêlée that took me out of my stupor. Pascal quickly reached my side, taking the sword gingerly out of my hands as I stood staring at my downed opponent, face down in the mud. Suddenly, I heard what sounded like him laughing as he rolled over and pushed himself up to standing.

"By God's teeth!" he roared as he removed his helm, "you have a mighty sword sir!"

William, the Duke of Aquitaine, stood before me, reaching out to clasp my arm in congratulations.

"Fairly and bravely fought," he said followed by another hearty laugh.

"Thank you, your Grace," was all I could muster, being rather dumbfounded to realize whom I had just defeated in hand-to-hand combat.

I watched him walk away towards the South side of the field where his comrades were waiting for him. I looked around me and discovered there were only a few fighters left on the field and they were all from the North. Suddenly I felt very tired, drained of all my energy. I walked beside Pascal over to the North side of the field and were surrounded by my comrades, all shouting my name. Whilst I was glad for their praises, all I really wanted was some warm ale and to rest. As if reading my mind, Henry appeared, tankard in hand, helping get me through the crowd of men back to my tent. Pushing through the flaps, I laid down on the cloth-covered pile of straw I was using for my bed and within minutes I was asleep.

I only slept for a couple of hours. Pascal kept busy packing away all the spoils he had picked up across the field. And he had cleaned my sword, scabbard and belt so they shone, presentable for the finale of the tournament where the worthy fighters would receive their rewards and riches. He had also cleverly packed a second set of boots as the others were now mud-soaked and unwearable. He knew I needed to look good.

I stood and stretched the soreness out of my muscles and stepped out into a late-afternoon sun which had appeared shortly before I woke. I could see all the other North fighters milling about their tents, watching them make deals for the ransom of goods taken from South opponents or having their own goods being returned to them. It felt rather surreal, had I not participated in the tourney myself, I would have thought I had dreamt the past few days. Pascal tapped me on my arm.

"Sire," he said, leading me to where our pack cart had been sitting. "Those you defeated have paid very well for the return of their goods, given more than we had expected. The Duke of Aquitaine was especially generous. I had to purchase another cart in order to carry it all!"

He yanked a canvas cover off of the second cart to reveal chests of gold and silver coin. I was impressed, I had not expected so much. I was happy to have placed my trust in Pascal to deal with this, I had not really wanted to take part in haggling. I thanked him.

"We need to start closing the tent, we set off first thing in the morning," I added.

The tournament denouement involved a lavish banquet at the jousting yard provided by the Count and Countess where fighters from both the North and South could meet and mingle, making new friends against whom one would undoubtedly be fighting at the next tourney and the next. The yard had also turned into a sea of mud so stalks of straw and hay had been strewn across it on which were placed rows and rows of tables and benches. The evening sun was casting a warm glow and by the time I arrived, a veritable feast had been spread from one end to the other. I saw Henry waving at me from the table closest to the centre directly in front of the pavilion, pointing to space on his bench where I could sit next to him facing the dais. As I walked through the tables, men would shout a greeting or a toast to my successes, some stopped me to introduce themselves and shake arms. I knew I had done well, but I was not expecting such adulation and was somewhat embarrassed by it by the time I sat down. Someone handed me a goblet of wine and patted me on my back. The herald stepped up to the end of the royal platform and spoke to the crowd before him.

"Count Hainaut and Countess Yolande!" he announced, bellowing their arrival.

A flourish of horns sounded and they appeared on the steps to the left of the dais and everyone immediately sprang to their feet. The horns continued playing until they took their seats. The Count made eye contact with me and nodded. The herald continued.

"The Count and Countess wish to express their congratulations to all of the competitors of the Tournai de Valenciennes. The spirit and sportsmanship displayed during these past days have been of the finest quality and they salute each of you for your strength and honour without which this tournament could not have been the great success it has been!"

A great cry went up from the men, all raising their goblets and tankards in a show of respect and admiration for their host's kind words. It was now the Count's turn to speak.

"It is now my great honour to present the awards for the winning teams of each of the three competitions and for individual expertise in skill and performance," he started as pages began to arrive in the field carrying what looked to be the prizes, sacs of gold and silver coin.

"The champion team of the joust.... the North!" he declared. "The champion team of the mêlée à cheval...the South! And finally, the champion team of the mêlée à pied...the North!"

These declarations were met with boisterous cheers and shouts from the men, each knowing that being part of a winning team meant some reward would be coming their way. The pages quickly distributed the prizes, I was happy to part of the team that had won the most. But the Count was not finished.

"And now, the prizes for the best fighter from each side," the Count continued pointing to two chests next to him.

The crowd went silent. Although rumours had flown after the two mêlées as to who had done what and where special merit may fall, it was only just rumour. Many things happened all over the battlefield and the fighters would not have been able to witness all of them. We would have to rely on the judges and the Count himself to determine who would really be the worth recipients of these special honours.

"For outstanding skill and fair play, from the South…William, Duke of Aquitaine!" the Count announced, being met with more cheers and chanting from the men as he stood, bowed to the Count and waved to crowds.

"And for outstanding skill and fair play, from the North…Sébastien D'Ivry!"

It did me good to hear the cries and chants with which my name was met. The loudest came from Henry but that might have been only because he sat closest to me. I followed the Duke's cue, stood, bowed and waved. I lifted my goblet filled with wine and raised it towards the Duke who reciprocated. The Count instructed more pages to deliver these chests to us where we sat. I thought that was the end of it but the Count had one more announcement to make.

"I now have the honour of announcing the man of the tournament, the single competitor who excelled best at all three competitions, whose strength and power was unparalleled and whose sense of honour and rectitude was evidenced by an utter lack of foul play," he said and the crowd went quiet. "The judges and I have discussed what each of us have witnessed throughout these past days, our determination was unequivocal and unambiguous. For superior skill at the joust, unmatched dexterity on horse and exceptional swordsmanship, the Champion of the Tournai de Valenciennes…Sébastien D'Ivry!"

Everyone around me were on their feet, applauding and shouting my name. I stood and gave a slight wave and nodded to the Count and resumed my seat. I actually did not think I had done anything particularly spectacular but privately I was pleased, nonetheless.

"Let the festivities begin!" shouted the herald, and more food, ale and wine was delivered to the tables in copious amounts.

Many of the competitors came by to congratulate me, pat me on the back and tell me they were impressed with my skills, some asking where I had learned them. I told them about having taken the cross and having the great luck of being around some of the best warriors in Christendom on our way to and in Palestine. I neglected to mention Duke Robert and hoped they were not aware I had supported him.

As the festivities moved into evening torches were brought to the yard to light up the area. The Count and Countess had departed shortly after the meal had started, preferring instead to dine in their private quarters. I was engaged in a deep conversation at the table with the competitor from Limoges I had defeated when I felt the presence of someone standing patiently behind me. At a break in the discussion, I turned my head and looked to see who it was. A tallish man who looked to be about my age, dressed in the clothing of a retainer, I did not recognise him.

"Many apologies for the interruption, Master D'Ivry," he said sincerely. "I've been sent by the Count to pay you a portion of his winnings from bets he placed upon you during the tournament as he promised."

He reached inside his cloak, removed a large sack of coin and handed it me.

"I thank the Count," I said, slightly amazed at the amount.

"He also wished to relay to you that your reward for being the tournament champion shall be delivered to you in the morn prior to your departure, if you could be so kind as to tell me what time that would be."

"Are you his personal retainer?" I asked.

He smiled.

"I am one of many who serve the Count," he answered. "My name is Osmond."

"Well, Osmond, please relay my thanks and gratitude to the Count, for being allowed to compete in his tournament."

"I shall," Osmond responded but did not move from the spot.

"Is there something else I can help you with?" I asked.

He hesitated. The competitor from Limoges got up and left us, I gestured for Osmond to take a seat.

"I…I have a request to make, Master D'Ivry," he responded slowly. "Whilst I am honoured to be part of the court of Hainaut and the Count has treated me very well indeed, I feel I may be better suited to work outside the court."

"Many a good man has believed that Osmond," I said gesturing about me. "What is your request?"

"I was fortunate enough to be in the stands watching your performance these past days. I have no doubt you have a great future in the tourneys, they are becoming more and more popular and there are many riches to be made. I have been told that you have but one squire with you and one with your future should have your own retainer. Would you be willing to bring me on to serve you in this capacity?"

This I was not expecting.

"Would the Count not be upset with you if you were to leave his employ?" I asked.

"The Count has many who are already available to do his bidding and many more who would relish a chance at becoming part of his court," Osmond reasoned. "I have no doubt he would be glad to know I was going with you, especially after how much your efforts have brought him in winnings."

I thought about this for a moment. If I were to go down this path of tournament glory, I would need a good man to help with my affairs and manage my house whenever or wherever that might be. Osmond had gained the experience I would need, and he seemed honest enough.

"I have my own horse and tack," he started again in earnest but I waved him silent.

"I think you might be just what I need. But," I cautioned him, "I am not who I appear to be. There are…elements…to my story which are not agreeable to many," I glanced over to where Stephen was sitting. "You may come to regret your decision."

"I am aware," Osmond simply and waited for me to speak.

"Fine," I agreed. "But you must have the Count's leave. We depart at dawn, if you are with us, I will assume the Count has given it. If not, I will assume he has not."

"Thank you, Master D'Ivry," he said, looking pleased.

The Count had been most generous in giving me a share of his winnings, not only were there gold and silver coin, but he had added a small chest of exquisite jewels and six glorious pure black steeds to my reward. He also provided four of his own guard to ensure my safe passage through the County of Vermandois, but that was not really necessary. And he allowed Osmond to leave court and join me on my travels.

And so, it was three who set off in the morning from the fields outside Valenciennes, with full bellies and carts laden with a not inconsiderable fortune. I knew this was the path I must take if I ever wanted to reinvent myself. And although I did not know it, I had just been joined by the one who would see me through the rest of my years.

# V

# Part Three
# 1116 – 1118 England

The next two years were spent traipsing across the western states of Europe, from one tournament to another, travelling as far east as Augsburg, as far south as Marseille and near the shores of La Rochelle. The competitions were challenging, especially those in the Germanic lands, their fighters were very strong and their weapons were weightier. Their downfall was their lack of speed and agility, for one could easily evade the swings of their heavy maces. I did not win Champion of all of the tourneys, but I fought well and earned much for those who backed me. And of course, gaining a significant fortune in the process. My reputation as a tournament master began to precede me and with each competition I made new friends and allies. It was a great accomplishment and for the first time in a long time, life felt good.

But then, in the early summer of 1116, came news from Ivry-La-Bataille. My father had been injured in a fall from his horse when returning from conducting some business in Paris and my brother Roger felt it best that I return. Osmond and my small band of men had been relaxing in the early summer sun on the beaches near Bordeaux after having just finished a tourney there. We packed up camp that very day and rode as quickly as we could push the horses and arrived a week later.

It was early evening when I finally dismounted at the familiar entrance to the castle, leapt up the stone stairs, passed by the open doors and entered the main hall calling out for anyone who might hear me. My mother came to the top of the stairs and seeing it was me hurried down and embraced me fiercely.

"Oh Sébastien my son, thank you, thank you for returning," she said, touching both sides of my face with trembling hands.

"I came as soon as I could Mama," I said. "How is he?"

"He still has not woken since the accident," she said.

"May I see him?"

"Yes, yes of course, come with me."

I followed her up the steps and to the room where my father had been placed when he was brought home. He was laying on the bed, tucked in under a cloth sheet of linen and light furs, seemingly asleep. It was difficult to believe he was not about to sit up and greet me. The only hint of something awry was the bandage encircling the crown of his head. A nurse was at his side, washing something in a small basin. I looked questioningly at my mother.

"His horse startled when crossing the Eure and he fell, hitting his head on the stone wall of the bridge," she said, trying to give me answers. "He was brought here right away and was looked at by our physicians, he has been like this ever since. We just need to give him time, he will either recover or," her voice cracked, "he will not."

She was trying to be brave, but I knew she was devastated to see her once virile husband now laying helpless before her. I heard movement behind me and turned to see my brother Roger in the doorway. I went to him and we embraced.

"Come brother, let us get you something to eat, you have ridden far in such a short amount of time, you must be famished," Roger said.

My mother nodded to me to go with him as she took a seat by the bed. The two of us returned to the dining hall where a meal had been prepared and left for us.

"How serious is this?" I asked him.

"Very," Roger responded. "The physicians are not sure he will survive. The accident was worse than Mama knows, the horse actually trod on him after he fell, he has injuries to his body as well as those to his head."

I sighed deeply. This was dreadful news. Only the year before did we lose our grandmother, having made it to the ripe old age of sixty-eight, dying in her sleep, a few weeks before her birthday. But that had been almost expected, this had not. We sat at the table for a while, not really discussing anything of importance, almost waiting for something to happen. We heard a commotion at the main entrance and our brother Guillaume appeared, having made his way from Shirburn probably about the same time I had left Bordeaux. We filled him in on what we knew and got him some food and ale. And then sat in virtual silence well into the small hours of the morning, eventually heading to bed but only because fatigue was setting in.

My father lingered as each of his sons sat watch at his side, taking turns and giving updates if there was any change, but there really was not much to say. Our mother's worry gradually turned to a saddened acceptance that her husband of thirty-one years was not going to return to her. Each of us tried to find something to do, chores, tasks, anything to keep busy when we were not with him. On the second afternoon, Guillaume and I decided to repair a fence in the far paddock and walked there to get some fresh air and exercise. Guillaume brought up the topic neither of us had wanted to discuss.

"I suppose Roger will be taking over father's role as Lord D'Ivry and be in charge of administering our properties?"

"Undoubtedly," I answered.

"But you are the eldest son...?" he asked trailing off.

"Roger has been father's deputy for more years than I can count, Guillaume," I said, tugging hard at the broken panel of wood. "I would not know where to begin. Besides, his life is here, my life is not. In fact, I will need to return to England soon, I should have returned already, I am surprised Godfrey has not demanded it of me."

"Why would he do that?"

"Because his agreement with the King only allowed me to come across the Channel temporarily, Henry expects me back."

"Ah. Well, with your new-found wealth and reputation for being one of the finest fighters in the West, I am sure you will be welcomed warmly back into the fold. I know Godfrey has been rather proud of your accomplishments in such short a time."

That pleased me. I owed Godfrey much for his belief in me and his support in obtaining my release and I had made a promise to him to do him proud and to remove the stain he and others believed I had brought to our family's reputation by my support of Duke Robert.

"I can only do my best, Guillaume. The real decision here is yours, what do you wish to do? Stay here with Roger or come back to England with me?"

Guillaume did not hesitate.

"England is my home now, Sébastien," he said firmly. "Godfrey has me overseeing many properties now, almost too many. In fact, if you are returning, we should discuss how we could share these responsibilities, if you are willing?"

I finally broke off the offending slat with one last tug and tossed it onto the ground.

"That sounds good, Guillaume, very good actually," I agreed.

Our father passed two days later, almost to the day his mother has passed the year before. Our mother performed the usual funeral preparation of washing his body in holy water to purify his soul. My brothers and I then wrapped him in a shroud of white linen and placed it in a wooden casket in which it would be transported to the Abbey of Our Lady of Bec, where my grandfather had been interred thirty-three years earlier. But before then, our entire family, long-time friends and acquaintances of my father, either through business or through battle, would sit vigil for three days, singing hymns and saying farewell. The priest from the local chapel held mass for us over his body and blessed us as we set off on our journey to lay our father to rest next to his own.

The Abbot was waiting for us as we arrived, having prepared the abbey for the funeral services and masses to be performed. No expense was spared, hundreds of candles lined the walls and aisles and an exquisite dark gold velvet funeral pall with the D'Ivry chevron emblem emblazoned on its centre had been quickly but carefully crafted to cover the wooden box until it was lowered into the stone sarcophagus in the crypt of the Abbey. We gave it to the Abbot to be hung in the Abbey afterwards, along with a sizable donation from both the family and many friends to ensure masses would continue to be said in my father's honour.

I passed the days that followed in a bit of a fog, many tasks to do and ensuring my mother was taken care of, Osmond proving himself to be invaluable in helping her. But I knew, as did she, that I would soon need to leave. And I knew that my nomadic lifestyle roaming from tourney to tourney would need to end. I had accumulated greater wealth than I thought I could and would have stayed in France had I no oath to the King of England or to my cousin. But I did, and needed to go. So at mid-summer, I collected my belongings, including the riches and treasures I had amassed, horses and weapons and pieces of great mailled armour, packing them securely to ensure their safe passage across the channel. I offered positions to the pages and squires who had been with me the last few years to come work for me and most accepted, including Pascal. And of course Osmond who had already declared to stay at my side.

My mother stayed stoic during my departure, she was, after all, a Breteuil, made of stern stuff. I knew deep down she was saddened to see me go, but I also knew Roger would take good care of her. And with relations with Normandy more peaceful since King Henry had been its overlord since taking it from Duke Robert almost a decade ago, we hoped that travelling between the two regions would be without incident.

The Channel was good to us and we made the crossing easily and quickly, landing at Dover then making our way over land until we reached the Thames. We saw the grounds of Shirburn in the distance as we came along the edge of the Chiltern Hills after sailing barges up the river and disembarking at Wallingford, riding the rest of the way. Godfrey put on a magnificent feast to welcome us home but commiserated with us first on the death of our father, being reminded of the passing of his own mother five years earlier. It was also clear the Guillaume had been right, Godfrey was quite pleased with what I had achieved in the last few years and he spoke with me as an equal. And true to his word, Guillaume set about sharing with me the duties to maintain and make improvements to the properties such as enclosing the hunting grounds at Beckley Park which had been owned by Godfrey's father and our great-uncle Roger D'Ivry and passed to Godfrey after his death. Our next goal there would be to build a hunting lodge that would be fit for royalty to visit and keeping the park well-stocked. We started on it immediately, and were very impressed with the results, so much so we decided to spend our Christmas there.

Occasionally Godfrey and I would visit Oxford on business, usually attending the livestock markets or meeting with other landowners to discuss various issues affecting us. Sometimes I would go on my own and stay the night in the town. On one such trip on a particularly chilly September day, after leaving Oxford and heading to Newenham Manor to visit its Baron to discuss a purchase of some of his sheep, I decided to follow the Thames so I could see more of the countryside. I knew at some point I would need to turn to the east and chose to do so after I crossed a small brook, continuing along until I came upon a handful of stone cottages, a pretty, unassuming little settlement. A priest appeared walking along the path towards me, I recognized the alb underneath his cloak.

"Forgive me, priest," I called out to him as we got closer. "Can you tell me the name of this place and who is the landowner?"

"Of course, sire," he responded cheerfully. "This is Sandford on Thames, the land is owned by the Abbey of Abingdon. There is a small rural church nearby, the Church of Saint Andrew, I am going there now if you wish to join me. I have warm mead you are welcome to if you wish."

"Thank you muchly for your kind offer, I should be most grateful to step in from the chill," I responded and dismounted so we could walk the remainder of the way together.

The church was not very far away and we arrived there in just a few minutes. It was a charming little chapel made of limestone rubble and through the orchard that surrounded it I could see an arched doorway on the north side as we approached and a much larger one on south side when we turned its corner. Leaving my palfrey tied to a post outside, I stepped inside when the priest opened the arched wooden iron-pegged door there. What I saw delighted me, a nave only large enough to hold a small congregation, probably no more than thirty at the most. A beautiful white marble baptismal font stood at the back of the nave and looking to the right I could see a stone arched frame through which one would walk to reach the chancel where a tall, narrow arched window in the east wall was letting in the morning light. Two more smaller versions of that window sat in the north and south side walls of the chancel, providing more illumination throughout the day.

'So quaint,' I thought to myself, thinking how very different this was from the magnificent, ornately decorated cathedrals and sepulchres I had visited on crusade. 'But God can be found here,' I thought.

The priest handed me a goblet of warm mead as he had promised and I thanked him.

"What else can you tell me about this place?" I asked, sipping the hot liquid carefully.

"There is not much to tell really. We are a simple village, hardly a village, I do not believe there is even ten cottages. The Abbot also built the water mill on the Thames, you would pass it if you continued south next to the river."

"It is a beautiful bit of land, the views along the river are exquisite," I said.

"May I ask from whence you come today sire?" he asked.

"I had business in Oxford yesterday and now am on my way to Newenham before I return to Shirburn," I answered.

"Do you live in Shirburn?"

"I do, in the manor there. I am Sébastien D'Ivry, my cousin is Godfrey of the same name."

The priest practically jumped hearing my name.

"Oh! Do forgive me, my lord, I did not realize…" he started but I waved him off.

"It is of no consequence. I assume you have been ordained?"

"Yes my lord, have been so these past two years. I am Father Renart, the youngest son of Thomas de Sandford."

"Was it your father then for whom the village is named?"

"No, his eldest brother Ralphe, he provided the funds for the building of Saint Andrews. Both are long gone now," he said, crossing himself.

I followed suit and then made a movement to go.

"Thank you muchly for the mead and the conversation, Father Renart."

"You are most welcome, Master D'Ivry. Please come visit our little place again."

I did, many times, diverting my journey to pass through the lands and to see the water mill operating there. With each visit, I was more and more convinced that I wanted to build my own manor here, on the banks of the river, overlooking the Thames. I mentioned it to Godfrey one evening.

"Really? Sandford on Thames?" he asked, rather surprised. "Would not you prefer the excitement of the city rather than a sedate pastoral life?

I chuckled.

"I think I have seen enough large cities to last a lifetime," I said.

"Well, if you are serious, I might be able help. My mother, bless her, was a patron of Abingdon Abbey, made many donations over the years, land, money, even in the months before she died and in her will. I do not doubt we can ask a favour and obtain a parcel of land for you to build on."

I was pleased to hear it. And after a few discussions with Abbot Faritius, I found myself the proud owner of a tract of land north of the village, on either side of the little brook, stretching from the Thames to the northwest of the church. I obtained the services of the same family of builders who had just completed our hunting lodge at Beckley and very soon the construction of a large manor, stables, barn and gardens was underway. I kept close watch on the work, selecting the materials myself, working out design problems whenever they arose and even picking up a block plane every once in a while. I enjoyed the manual labour, the sweat felt good and it was satisfying to know my own hands had helped create this place. Especially after so many years of destruction. With any luck, the finishing touches would be done by early spring.

On rare occasions, the King and his court would come to stay at the castle in Oxford. This castle was a point of pride in our family. Our great-uncle Roger had not only been a wealthy landowner but a very close friend of Robert D'Oyly, the castle's builder and a favourite of the King William the Conqueror at whose side he fought during the invasion. The two of them together built the great St George's tower inside the castle bailey the year after the main keep was completed. The Conqueror, who was King at the time, was very pleased with the result and rewarded them with land across the south of England. So to be able to attend on the King here was a great honour, and we were grateful when we received an invitation to council there in early December.

We arrived early, crossed the bridge over the moat on the northwest side of the castle, left our horses at the stables and crossed the bailey to the mount. As we walked, I glanced at George's Tower to the east in the castle wall and marvelled at its structure. We took the stairs up to the arched entry, passed the guards and made our way to the great hall. There, other barons and landowners of the region were standing around in small groups chatting and Godfrey caught the attention of Gilbert Marshal, whose surname had been officially changed from Giffard, and beckoned to him. He came over to us, followed by a gangly, angry looking lad.

"Godfrey!" he exclaimed reaching out to shake arms. "I am glad you are here, I am hoping for your support with the King today."

"I have no issue with you taking residence in Ludgershall. It is strategically important to the King and really should be occupied by one of the King's men. With the work you have done at Marlborough, I would think the King would be more than appreciative of your request," Godfrey responded. "You remember my cousin, Sébastien?"

"Yes," Gilbert said, extending his arm in welcome. "We hear you have achieved great things these past years in France. The King was especially intrigued to hear of your successes at the tourneys. I am sure you will be eager now to make your stamp here in England?"

This was a much more warm and friendly reception than the last time we met when his distain of me was palatable.

"Godfrey, I am sure you will remember my son, John," he continued, not waiting for my response, gesturing for the sullen lad to join us. "I do not believe you have ever met?" he said turning to me.

The boy stood beside his father and nodded to Godfrey and then to me.

"Not exactly met," I said with a wry smile. "The last time I saw you, you were but three years, and tugging on your Mama's skirts in the gardens at Marlborough. You were angry for being taken inside by your nurse."

The others laughed at the image but it did not endear me to the boy at all.

"I do not recall you at all," he sneered disrespectfully, but we all ignored him as the King's page called us to order.

We moved in order of status into the meeting hall.

"I do not believe you made a friend there," Godfrey whispered to me.

He had no idea how right he would be.

* * * * * * * * * *

The council with the King ended without incident and although he did look directly at me for a moment, he did not speak to me. I would have to be satisfied that he did not order me from the room. Gilbert was particularly pleased as the King had acquiesced to his request to take residence at Ludgershall although he stopped short of actually giving the castle to him. Gilbert hoped that gift would come to him later, or perhaps later to one of his sons. He was determined that they would follow him in service to the crown, continuing the role he and his predecessors had possession of for a few generations now.

We descended the stairs of the castle down into the bailey and had almost reached the stables when the sound of slow-clopping hooves on the wooden bridge crossing the moat and through the barbican gate reached us. Four riders appeared, two men I did not recognise on destriers at the front and back of the group and in between rode Lady Margaret and another rider who was vaguely familiar, both on palfreys. They rode towards us and, stopping just short, were greeted by Gilbert. A stable boy appeared and took hold of the palfreys.

"My lady," Gilbert said, helping his wife down from her horse, kissing the back of her hand.

The other rider remained horsed.

"My lord," she responded. "Godfrey, it is good to make your acquaintance again," she said to my cousin who nodded to her.

"It is a delight to see you again my lady," he said gallantly. "What brings you to Oxford?"

"We," she said motioning to the other rider, "are in need of silks for new dresses for the festive season, not something for a man to be bothered with." She laughed lightly. "But one of our horses has lost a shoe and being nearby I thought the King's stable might be able to assist in repairing it."

She then turned to me.

"You look familiar, do I know you?"

"This is my cousin, Sébastien D'Ivry, recently returned from France," Godfrey said.

"Oh yes, I remember you now. We met in the gardens at Marlborough, you had just helped my daughter after a fall from her horse," she said.

"You have a remarkable memory, my lady," I said, impressed.

Upon hearing my voice, the still-horsed rider threw off her hood and stared at me and then broke into a smile, and I suddenly realized why I had that strange feeling of recognition earlier. This was the same beautiful face I had glimpsed looking up at me when I bent over her to see if she was injured all those years ago. But this face was no longer merely a child but that of a striking young woman, flawless skin and full blood-red lips. And those eyes.

"Master D'Ivry," she said, breaking what I thought surely must have been an eon of time but was really only seconds, "it seems we are destined to meet whenever I have an issue with my horse."

She reached out for her father to help her dismount. She curtsied slightly first to him, then to Godfrey and then to me, beaming. I was smitten.

"I am, as always, ever gladdened to be at your service Miss Séraphine," I answered, trying to remain as relaxed and diplomatic as possible when my heart was beating faster than it ever had.

But the enchanting moment was not to last as John quickly stepped in between us and began speaking to his sister, purposely cutting off any further discussion. I stepped back and moved over to her horse and looked at the shoeless hoof. I took the reins from the stable boy and slowly turned the horse around and guided him to the stable, leaving the others to continue conversing without me. For some reason I felt the need to do this myself, but it was an easy fix and within a few moments I had tidied the hoof and attached a new shining shoe. I tossed a coin to the stable master and led the mare back out to the group who still stood where I had left them. Godfrey saw me coming and, noticing the new shoe, looked incredulously at me.

"There you are, Miss Séraphine, all good," I said, handing the reins to her.

She blushed, or at least I thought she did.

"My most humble thanks, Master D'Ivry," she said, our fingers briefly touching as she took the straps from me.

"Think nothing of it," I responded.

Godfrey mumbled something about time getting on and so we all bid each other adieu with invitations to visit each other over the upcoming holidays. I was going to make sure I did just that. As we navigated the cobblestoned streets from the castle down to Folly Bridge, the horses in a gentle walk, Godfrey could not help but tease me a little.

"Cat got yer tongue?" he asked.

"I am sure I do not know to what you are referring," I said, feeling the colour rising to my cheeks, glad of the chill in the November afternoon that I could blame it on.

"She has turned out to be quite the beauty, yes?" he prodded.

"Yes, quite," I admitted, trying not to give anything away in my voice.

"You should set her out of your mind Sébastien," Godfrey warned. "Your newly earned riches aside, Gilbert will undoubtedly want a better marriage for her than a nephew of the King's former butler!"

I said nothing. I did not want to reveal anything to Godfrey, especially not of my heart. But although I tried to shake the thought, I knew I had met my mate. I now needed to find ways of being able to see her, but something told me this was not going to be as difficult as one might expect.

* * * * * * * * * *

That Christmas was spent at Beckley Park, my mother and brother Roger having made the crossing to stay with us during the weeks before, during and after. Godfrey invited the Marshals to spend the holidays with us at our newly completed lodge as the rooms at Ludgershall would not be ready for them, and we enjoyed hunting deer and hawking when the weather permitted. Séraphine and I were able to spend some time together, despite John's concerted efforts to keep us apart, speaking by ourselves in corners of rooms whilst others, including William and Anselm at ten and nine years of age now growing into fine little men much happier than their brother, busied themselves with food or games. And whilst her physical beauty would be enough to awaken any man, I soon discovered she was very quick of mind, routinely defeating me at draughts and with strategies that left me defenceless when we played chess.

With her father's permission and Guillaume offering to come along, we went riding the rolling hills of the county, through forests and across streams, wherever our horses would lead us. Often she would break ahead of me, being the excellent rider I had predicted she would become, pushing her mount to a full gallop, a speed no gentle lady had any reason to reach. And throughout, the joy that emanated from her filled the air with glorious sounds and filled my heart to bursting.

One day near the end of her family's visit, we rode to Woodstock where King Henry had built a luxurious hunting lodge in the middle of acres of fine parkland, one far grander than our own which paled in comparison. There, having managed to lose Guillaume on the way, standing on a large stone bridge that spanned the River Glyme, looking over a little island in the small lake that formed there, we shared our first kiss, a gentle touch of lips that gradually built into an impassioned embrace. I took off my glove from my left hand and slowly stroked her rosy cheek, placing my palm fully against it when I realized how chilled it was. She placed her hand on top of mine and looked tenderly into my eyes. The cold January air disappeared, her warmth filled me.

I suspected I had fallen in love with her that day when we were next to the stables at Oxford Castle, but by the time the feast of the Epiphany came I was certain and I was dreading her departure. I was convinced both Gilbert and Lady Margaret were aware we had made an attachment, her brother John certainly was. Each time we returned from a ride he would be waiting, standing outside the entrance to the lodge, arms crossed, the usual scowl on his face. I asked Séraphine once what it was that made him so.

"Oh John, do not mind him," she replied. "He is over-protective of his sister, even though I am almost six years his senior. I looked after him when he was a young child and Mama and Papa were travelling with the King, just as I do now for William and Anselm. And now that I am of a marriageable age, he feels threatened, and behaves like a petulant child at times."

"He will need to temper his emotions if he is to follow in your father's footsteps as Marechal to the King or he will not gain many friends at court, or elsewhere," I said earnestly, being honest with her.

She sighed resignedly.

"I know my dear Sébastien, it is not something that has gone unnoticed. But I cannot intervene, my views are of no matter in our house," she said.

"That would not be the case in our house," I said half-teasing, half-seriously.

She just smiled her sweet smile, leaving me in her thrall. It was a characteristic I came to adore.

Before the Marshal family departed, I was able to have some time alone with both Gilbert and Lady Margaret to formally request their permission to pay court to their daughter. I had mentioned I was going to do this to Godfrey who warned me against it, not believing that it would be well received by her parents. He was right.

"Absolutely not!" Gilbert said emphatically upon hearing my request. "Sébastien, Séraphine is our only daughter and we are determined to make a good marriage for her, perhaps even a royal match. Not with Henry's legitimate heir of course, William Ætheling is already betrothed to Matilda of Anjou, and we would not be worthy of such a match. But King Henry has been prolific in his ability to produce sons even though all but one are illegitimate, so a match with one of those sons might be suitable. Robert, the Earl of Gloucester is out of contention, also already betrothed, but perhaps the next, Richard of Lincoln? There are all sorts of possibilities, and we will have success and soon! I am afraid you would not be suitable, despite your newly acquired wealth."

I realized such a match would solidify the Marshal family's royal connection and bring them many riches in grants of land, property and coin. I felt the air go out of the room hearing their refusal. But I was determined.

When saying our farewells, Lady Margaret dallied inside a moment, seeming to struggle with her gloves. I stood beside her, patiently waiting and staring out the front entrance at the carriage I had just watched Séraphine step into being helped by Godfrey. Lady Margaret could not help but notice my line of vision.

"Master D'Ivry?" she said but I had not heard her, lost in my thoughts. "Sébastien?" she tried again.

"Yes, my lady?" I responded, turning my attention to her.

"Séraphine tells me you are an excellent rider. And you are obviously very good with the maintenance and care of horses. My younger sons would greatly benefit from your skills in battle riding, would you be willing to teach them?" she asked quietly, not meeting my glance.

It took only a moment for me to understand what she was actually saying. I was certain they had others to train the lads, so there was another reason for her request.

"Yes, yes of course, my lady, I would be delighted," I answered, trying not to sound too keen.

"Good. It is settled then," she said, suddenly satisfied with the status of her gloves. "I shall inform my lord to tell the stable to expect you shall we say once a week?"

And without waiting for my response, she went out the door and into the awaiting carriage. She had given me hope.

Even though Gilbert was not happy with this arrangement, he saw me as no threat, he felt he had made their position on their daughter's marriage clear. And he knew it would be shrewd of him to keep good relations with my family, especially now that I was back in the good graces of the King. But try as they might, the options for matches for Séraphine only came and went. Richard of Lincoln remained in France and was rumoured to become betrothed at any moment. Another bastard son, Henry Fitzroy, remained in Wales and another, Fulk, had already taken holy orders. Any others were too young to be considered for marriage, but this secretly pleased us. The more time we spent together, the more we fell in love. Me with her spirit, her headstrongness, her strength, and she, well, she called me her champion. We knew we must marry. But without the approval of Gilbert and Lady Margaret, we would have to do this in secret, and the repercussions would be severe.

Our one saving grace was that Séraphine was not a member of the court like her father. Nor was I, which meant we did not need the King's approval to marry. Nor did she need her father's permission being of age to agree to wed on her own, but his consent would have been a blessing and make this a joyous occasion rather than something that caused displeasure and angry consequences. In the end, we had no choice, this would have to be done in stealth and with as few people in the know as possible. But not in isolation, we needed a witness. I knew who to ask.

As my manor started to take its final shape, I began taking Osmond with me since he, being my retainer, would be the keeper of this house, and he needed to know every detail of it. I valued his input, he had seen some of the greatest houses in Christendom when travelling with me during the tournaments and his memory and advice were both very much needed. It did not take long for me to confide to him my desires to wed Séraphine, something of which he was already keenly aware, having listened to me endlessly discuss my days with her probably ad nauseum. It did not take him but a moment to agree to assist in any way he could.

The next challenges to face were, first, to decide where this should or could take place without raising alarm to members of either family and, second, to decide whom could I trust to bless our union as well as the marriage bed. The former was fairly easy, my new manor was within walking distance of the Church of St Andrews and it would be easy to hold a wedding there in the dead of night without raising suspicion. For the latter, I sought out Abbot Faritius at the Abbey in Abingdon. I visited him there a few days before Easter and walked with him in the Abbey's gardens, the multitude of flowers just beginning to bud. I got right to the point.

"You must realize what it is you ask of me," Abbot Faritius said in his heavily Italian accent. "It is true that le Mareschal is not of royal blood, but he is a trusted servant of the King, you risk his displeasure, you risk that of the King."

"My cousin tells me that you are a favourite of his Majesty?" I asked already knowing the answer.

"Yes, yes, of course. He wanted me as successor to the Archbishop of Canterbury just a couple of years ago and was angered when the bishops refused to allow it, they were not happy with my being *Italiano*. Good enough for our dear Holy Father Paschal as the Papa of the Christian world," he said wryly, crossing himself, "but not for England."

"Did your work as a physician also not have some bearing in that?" I asked.

"Of course! These bishops do not like their own to heal human bodies, just human souls! *Stupido*! They do not know that one feeds the other!" he said passionately. But then, raising his hands in a defeated gesture, he continued, "Ah, it was not to be. But, I was content to come to Abingdon, it has been good here. Your aunt, Lady Adeline," he said pointing at me, "was a great lady indeed, *bella donna*. Her grants of parcels of land has brought substantial wealth to the Abbey, we have been able to do good work here because of her generosity."

We stopped and sat on a stone bench overlooking a small pond. He reached into a pocket and pulled out a few grains and tossed them in and we watched as some small brightly coloured fish arrived in an instant, fighting each other for the precious food only to be displaced by a latecomer who bypassed the others and grabbed most of the food. And then disappeared once he had had his fill, leaving the others searching for any traces that might be left.

"Ah, you see, the dark grey one, he comes alone, from the depths of the pond, every time he does this, he lets the others fight and always wins the prize."

We sat in silence for a moment.

"I will do this for you, Sébastien," he said quietly. "And I will speak to the King on your behalf should the need arise."

I nodded my thanks.

"It is planned for the fifth day of April, at the hour before midnight," I said. "St. Andrews in Sandford on Thames will be at my disposal, I will ensure Father Renart is not present to protect him from any retribution from the Marshals. Are you prepared for the anger that will no doubt come from Gilbert?"

"I expect it. But he has no valid argument, if you assure me the lass is willing, you are able to wed without his permission."

"I can assure you Abbot, she has expressed her love to me, others have remarked on it, it is no secret, our joining should not come as a surprise."

"No, not surprise. But shock. And wrath. You ask me if I am prepared...but are you?" he asked, concerned.

"For the love of this woman, I am prepared for anything," I said, unwaveringly.

"Good, you will need to be. Now come, let me bless you before you go."

Easter that year was particularly warm and the sun shone on the south of England every day from Good Friday to Easter Sunday and for a week beyond that. Séraphine and her two youngest brothers had been invited to join us at the manor in Shirburn for a few days after Easter for hawking and archery lessons, so there was no expectation of her return to Ludgershall on the night we had planned for our wedding. Despite my new manor at Sandford on Thames being only a couple of hours ride away, Osmond packed what we needed to stay a few days in Shirburn.

Now I needed to get Father Renart safely out of the way. A few days before Easter I presented a new mass chalice to him knowing that he would not be able to have it consecrated in time for the Easter service, and I generously offered to pay his way to have it done by the Bishop of Lincoln, telling him Abbot Faritius had suggested it. And so, he departed for the east of England immediately after Easter to spend a few days there, a relief to us knowing he would be out of harm's way and not held to blame for what was to come.

The day of our secret nuptials was like any other. Séraphine, William and Anselm and I rode in the morning, enjoying the fresh, warm air after the cold days of the winter, and stopping for a drink at an inn in the little town of Dorchester. Séraphine and I tried to behave as we always did, hoping there was nothing to give away our mounting excitement of the night to come. After returning to Shirburn, Séraphine spent some hours in the gardens working on her embroidery whilst Guillaume and I worked with the brothers on their sword skills. When the chill of the early evening began to creep in as the sun began to set, we moved indoors and settled by the fire, the boys taking up their reading whilst Séraphine and I played chess. It had always been difficult to concentrate on the game whenever we played, but tonight was especially so. I felt the nerves inwardly and hoped they were not visible. She, on the other hand, was as calm as a sleeping lamb.

After everyone had retired for the night, I found myself pacing in my room, watching the candle clock burn down the time, seemingly much slower than usual. But of course this was just my own anticipation skewing my sense of being in the moment. Finally, the appointed hour arrived for me to go to the church I crept down the stairs and out of the house as quietly as I could. Osmond met me at the stables having saddled Lux for me. We spoke as I checked the straps.

> "You are set to bring Miss Séraphine to the church as we discussed?" I asked nervously.

> "Of course, my lord. All is ready, our horses are saddled, and Pascal took her bags to your manor in Sandford earlier this evening, he awaits you there. All he knows is that you are returning to Sandford late tonight," Osmond reassured me.

This eased my worries somewhat.

> "Good. I shall see you and my dearest at the church at the hour prior to midnight. Thank you Osmond."

> "Ride safely my lord," he said, and I was off.

It took Lux and me only an hour to reach my manor where Pascal was waiting. He took control of Lux and I raced inside to my rooms and quickly changed into my wedding attire, replacing my rough riding breeches with those made of the finest off-white linen with a matching tunic which fell to my thighs and a pair of hose that tied onto the britches at my knees. I wrapped a thick, plain black leather belt around my waist which when hooked together came to rest across my hips. Overtop of this I wore a tight-fitting, deep red velvet cotehardie covering the tunic, fastened down the front with several gold buttons, the D'Ivry emblem emblazoned three times on each side. Another more ornate and bejewelled belt I tied around my waist, and to that I attached a slender but sharp dagger in a leather sheathe on my left side. New soft leather boots had been purchased for this night and I wrapped them around my legs, tucking in my breeches. Finally I was ready,

I grabbed my cloak and gloves and walked at a quickened pace on my own to the church.

I entered from the north side door and found it deserted, with the moonlight coming through the windows bringing the only light to illuminate the church. Opening the south side door, I peeked out, and was met by the stillness of the night, no sound, no movement from the sleeping village. I shut the door and walked up to the altar and back again before going about the nave, lighting a few candles there and then in the chancel where the final blessing would be given at the altar.

Abbot Faritius arrived first, dressed in his simple black Benedictine habit sinched at the waist with a white rope, a black scapular covering his shoulders and a dark cloak with its hood pulled up over his head to keep him warm on his long ride. He wore no jewellery and nothing ostentatious that would draw attention to himself travelling incognito from Abingdon. I let him in and closed the door behind him, only then did he feel comfortable enough to remove his hood.

"Good evening Sébastien," he said, unbuttoning his cloak.

I took it from him and laid it across the font.

"Is all prepared?" he asked.

"Yes, my man Osmond is escorting my lady, they should be here at any moment."

The thought of this had been filling me with a nervous energy but now a serene calm took hold of me. It was as if everything I had been through since leaving Bayeux those many years ago had led me to this point and my life was finally about to have real meaning.

She arrived moments later, I heard the sounds of the horses whinnying as they were tied to the posts. I opened the door and stepped out and saw her standing in the moonlight. She removed her riding cloak and handed it to Osmond and walked towards me, everything about her shimmered. Her dark green velvet dress was fitted to the waist, the bodice buttoned tight revealing her feminine curves, the skirts flowing to the floor. A gold girdle hung on her hips, coming together at the front and hanging down almost to the edge of her dress. She wore her hair loose, thick golden tresses flowed across her shoulders and down her back with strands falling across her breasts. A simple ringlet of gold encircled the top of her head, she wore no other jewellery. She did not need to.

She reached out and took both of my hands in hers coming to stand on the stone threshold of the door. Abbot Faritius joined us from inside the church and, with Osmond standing to the side, we said our vows as was the custom.

"I take you, Séraphine of the family Marshal, to be my wife," I said solemnly, squeezing her hands gently.

"I take you, Sébastien of the family D'Ivry, to be my husband," she said just as solemnly, returning the squeeze.

Abbot Faritius stepped forward and placed a hand on ours and crossed himself. We then followed him into the church, Osmond coming in after us, making sure the heavy door was closed and locked. Séraphine and I walked, hand-in-hand behind the Abbot, through the stone arch separating the nave from the chancel then stood in front of the altar and waited for the Abbot to position himself behind it. Opening his bible to reveal a gold band with a brilliant ruby stone, he offered it to me. I took it and slipped it first on her thumb, first finger, second finger and then finally onto the third finger of Séraphine's left hand. Then, reaching again to cover our hands again with his own, the Abbot spoke.

*"Beloved, let us love one another,*
*because love is of God;*
*everyone who loves is begotten by God and knows God.*
*Whoever is without love does not know God, for God is love.*
*In this way the love of God was revealed to us:*
*God sent his only begotten Son into the world*
*so that we might have life through him.*
*In this is love:*
*not that we have loved God, but that he loved us*
*and sent his Son as penitence for our sins.*
*Beloved, if God so loved us,*
*we also must love one another.*
*No one has ever seen God.*
*Yet, if we love one another, God remains in us,*
*and his love is brought to perfection in us.*
*The word of the Lord.*
*Amen."*

He crossed us as we crossed ourselves and responded with our own Amens. I raised Séraphine's hand to my lips and kissed it gently, meeting her gaze. It was done. We were now man and wife.

We left the church after quickly gathering our things and blowing out the candles. I rode on Osmond's horse with Séraphine in front of me, my arms around her waist felt good and welcomed. Reaching the manor house just before midnight, we were met by Pascal who was waiting for us. He said nothing and had no expression upon seeing not only Séraphine but the Abbot as well. He was a clever lad, I am sure he easily figured out what had taken place that night. But discretion was one of his many best traits. We handed him our cloaks, which he took away, and then entered the great hall which had a fire burning in the massive fireplace. Pascal took the Abbot's bags to a room we had prepared for him, and then returned with some wine for us, placing the tray of goblets on the table and leaving, shutting the door behind him.

The wine tasted good, we needed nothing else to celebrate with. Our wedding feast was going to have to wait until we could tell our families what we had done and there was a good chance there would not be one. We would find out the next day when Séraphine and I returned to Shirburn to escort the brothers back to Ludgershall.

But for tonight, there was only one ritual left for the wedding rituals to be completed and that was the Abbot's blessing of our marriage bed. Séraphine and I retired to separate dressing rooms to prepare and Abbot Faritius was shown to our bedroom by Osmond who carried the holy water for him and then took his leave. I arrived shortly after, now dressed only in my linen breeches and tunic. The room was warm and the many candles which must have been lit by Osmond, brought an almost unearthly glow. The four-poster bed was magnificent and exquisitely carved – it should have been considering it had belonged to Duke Robert. I had it and the other furniture he had given to me brought to the manor when it was ready to be furnished. Despite his short stature, Duke Robert had enjoyed a luxurious lifestyle, with a bed big enough to fit me and then some.

There was movement at the door and Séraphine appeared, her night-time smock hanging loose from her shoulders, down to the floor where I noticed she was barefoot. Overtop of this was a deep blue robe, the colour of purity, edged in gold, cut at the sides so the buttoned fitted sleeves of the smock could be seen. She stood, absentmindedly playing with the new ring on her finger, looking at me expectantly.

Abbot Faritius wasted no time. Having prepared a goblet of holy water whilst waiting for us, he now sprinkled some across the bedspreads and the pillows. And then he gave his blessing.

"Dearest brethren, let us call upon God, who has deigned to pour out the gift of his blessing to multiply the offspring of the human race, that he may himself guard his servants, Sébastien and Séraphine, whom he has chosen for union in marriage; and that he may give them peace, oneness of mind and manners, and the ties of mutual love. May they, by his favour, have the children they desire and may these children, being his gift, also be endowed with his blessing, so that these his servants, Sébastien and Séraphine, might serve him in all things in humility of heart. Through Christ our Lord, Amen," and crossed the bed, then us, and then himself.

And with that, he departed, leaving us alone.

I fell asleep with Séraphine in my arms that night. Séraphine. My wife. She and I, wrapped around each other, our bodies warm under the bedcoverings, were enveloped in world of bliss. For tonight at least.

\* \* \* \* \* \* \* \* \* \*

Needless to say, the peace and quiet of the morning did not last long. I had sent Pascal fetch Godfrey and Guillaume with an urgent message to come to Sandford as soon as possible and they arrived just as Séraphine, myself and the Abbot were finishing our morning meal. Godfrey came through the front entrance and into the great hall, removing his riding gloves and cloak, stopping dead in his tracks when he saw Séraphine sitting at the table.

"Good morn…" his voice trailed off.

Looking from Séraphine, to me and then to the Abbot, he quickly twigged as to what was going on. Guillaume came in from behind and stood, mouth slightly open, staring at Séraphine.

"By God's teeth Sébastien, what have you done?" Godfrey asked astonished. Turning to Séraphine, he said, "I think it is best you collect your things, Miss Séraphine."

"Please address her as Mistress D'Ivry, Godfrey," I said, reaching across the corner of the table and resting my hand on hers. "She is, after all, my wife. And she will be going nowhere."

Godfrey stood still, unable to speak. Guillaume picked where he left off.

"How, how was this done?" he asked and then, turning to Séraphine said, "I saw your maid on the landing this morning, she said nothing of your disappearance."

"I left a note telling her I would be taking a very early ride and that I would be back for tierce. As it is not yet that hour, she would have no cause to raise an alarm," Séraphine answered him, her voice steady and calm.

Abbot Faritius stood and with arms outstretched moved towards Godfrey.

"Come, Godfrey, sit, have some ale. Guillaume, you as well. This is a joyous occasion, we have two blessed creatures in love and now married in the eyes of the Lord. No man can undo what has been done here."

Godfrey ignored him.

"Marshal is going to be furious when he is told! He is a member of the King's inner court! You have just been accepted back into the King's good graces…"

"And there he will stay, Godfrey," Abbot Faritius said. "The King will not object to this marriage, it was not within his gift and therefore he cannot condemn it. And if there is any challenge to it from others, I shall speak with the King myself on the matter."

This did not seem to pacify Godfrey.

"And what about Gilbert? This will tear apart the friendship between our two families, I am sure of it!"

"ENOUGH!" I roared as I stood, having had enough of Godfrey's protestations. Then, seeing the shock on his face as I had never raised my voice to him before, I softened my tone and said, "I love her, Godfrey. And she me. It is done. Instead of being apoplectic I would hope you would be happy for me, for us."

Godfrey sighed heavily and sat down, not willing to accept reason. I waited a moment, then retook my seat.

"Our family has spent years carefully cultivating these relationships, Sébastien, do you not understand? What we could lose? What you could lose? I love you my cousin, but you very well may have brought total ruin upon this family."

"Then expel me from the family," I said. "I and I alone shall bear the brunt of the Marshal family wrath, you shall remain blameless. Because you are. You knew nothing of this, you could not have stopped it. I will not give her up, Godfrey."

We had come to a quiet standoff. He then turned to Séraphine.

"Do you have what you need, Mistress D'Ivry?" he asked sincerely.

"I need my maid to be sent to me. I have everything else here with my husband," she answered and smiled her sweet smile.

Godfrey knew he was beaten.

"I shall send for your maid," he responded. And to me he said, "I will go with you when we escort the Marshal lads back to Ludgershall, we need to go today. Telling Gilbert and Lady Margaret cannot be delayed."

I agreed, although it pained me to have to spend time away from my lady so soon. But Godfrey was right, leaving it any longer than necessary would only make it worse. We would need to travel back to Shirburn first, pick up the lads and then depart, and with changing horses at Newbury we should be at Ludgershall by the early evening. I informed Osmond was aware of our plans and instructed him to make sure Séraphine's maid Sophie arrived later that day. And with a kiss on the cheek of my beloved, I was off.

* * * * * * * * *

The tower of Ludgershall castle loomed in the distance as we approached from the north. Not large but strategically important, the castle was on route to London from the southwest and was also on the well-worn trading route between Winchester and Marlborough, so it was usually bustling with visitors stopping in during their travels or attending markets. King Henry had been known to stay there when on a hunting progress, so the accommodations had to be to the satisfaction of both himself and the queen should she decide to accompany him.

There was a wooden bridge that crossed the ditch encircling the castle and its buildings and we made our way over it and into the open area where we found a number of traders milling about, many of them at the blacksmiths waiting for their horses to be reshod. Pages having recognized the Marshal emblem on the brothers' horses' tack arrived quickly and took the reins from us after we dismounted.

Climbing the stairs of the tower I was suddenly filled with a sense of gloom, knowing what was about to befall me. The boys ran ahead of us into the large entry hall and through to the great hall and we followed, finding Lady Margaret at the table speaking with a couple of her maids. She looked up and smiled a greeting, dismissing them as she did so. The boys ran to her and she embraced them both, happy to see them.

"Lady Margaret," Godfrey said, stepping forward and nodding.

"Godfrey, it is good to see you again. And you Sébastien. I hope the past few days have been pleasant and the boys have not been too difficult?"

"We have enjoyed their company, Anselm is becoming particularly good with the hawk," my cousin responded.

Anslem grinned, glad for the compliment. Lady Margaret beamed and sent the boys to their rooms to change for vespers. Godfrey spoke.

"Is Gilbert in residence?"

"He is not, unfortunately," she replied. "He has business in Pembrokeshire, he rode the same time the boys and Séraphine went to Shirburn after Easter."

At that moment, the door at the far end of the great hall opened and her eldest son John appeared, his face darkening upon seeing me. This was not going to go well.

"Mama," he said, bending down and kissing her on the cheek. "I see my brothers have returned. Where is Séraphine? I did not see her horse in the yard."

They both turned to look at Godfrey, who gave a little cough and moved slightly to the side so I could step forward. I needed to be the one to tell them. I took a deep breath and steadied my stance, looking directly at Lady Margaret.

"Séraphine is at my manor in Sandford on Thames, Lady Margaret," I said.

"Why has she decided to stay and why there and not Shirburn? And why has she not returned here?" she asked.

"My Lady," I hesitated slightly before continuing, "Sandford is now her home. Séraphine is Mistress D'Ivry. We were married last night by Abbot Faritius."

I readied myself for the anger that was sure to come. Both Lady Margaret and John stared at me, dumbfounded, not believing what they just heard. John was the first to react.

"She is *what*?" he sneered at me. "*You were what?*"

I repeated my last sentence, which only served to intensify his rising anger.

"*Did you know of this?*" he spat out at Godfrey.

Godfrey merely shook his head and then looked beseechingly at Lady Margaret. She seemed to be still digesting this news. John meanwhile had turned white with rage and reached for his sword. I did not reach for mine but Godfrey put his hand on his and with this motion, Lady Margaret snapped out of her daze and touched her son's arm, silently telling him to sheathe his weapon. There would be no blood spilled here and John certainly would not have survived any physical battle with us, or even with me on my own being taller, stronger and much better with a weapon than he.

"Is it a match of mutual love?" she asked me quietly.

"Indeed it is," I answered her sincerely.

She nodded.

"*Mama!!*" John shouted at her. "*This cannot be allowed!*"

"John," she started soothingly, "Séraphine's age allows her to make this decision on her own, she needs not our permission." Then turning to me she added, "But it would have been best to have had our blessing."

"Yes, my Lady and I am sorry for that. But when I was denied my request to court her, I, we, worried that an effort would be made to keep us apart and prevent us from being together. I am truly sorry for the deception, but please believe it was only with the best intentions, for I do love your daughter."

"*Love Séraphine??*" John burst out. "*You have the pedigree of a wild dog! You do not deserve to walk at her side, or breathe the same air!*"

"John!" his mother said sharply, having had enough of her son's anger.

He started to pace back and forth next to her as she tried to ease his anger. Just like when he was three. I feared this behaviour would never change.

"Please know that your daughter will want for nothing," I said, trying to quell any concerns she might have.

"I have no doubt of that dear Sébastien," she said. "I must write to her father, he will no doubt wish to return immediately to discuss this situation further. You said the Abbot of Abingdon performed the blessing?"

"Yes my Lady, he did," I answered.

"Abbot Faritius is in good standing with the King, he desired him for Archbishopric see at Canterbury, are you aware of this?"

"Yes, my Lady," Godfrey interjected, "the Abbot has strong connections with the D'Ivry family as well, one of his benefactors was my mother, Adeline de Grandmesnil."

"Adeline de Grandmesnil? I remember her well, a very pious lady. And of course her husband Roger as Butler to the Conqueror was obviously favourited by him. The crown has once again shown favour to your family, so who are we to contradict the King?" she reasoned.

She knew her history well. Both Godfrey and I remained silent, awaiting her next comment. But as usual, her hot-tempered son erupted again.

"*Mama, this is contemptible! The King will be furious once father informs him of this betrayal, he will order it undone!*" he barked.

"Silence!" she said sharply again but this time stronger. "We shall have no more of this! Leave us."

John glared at her but knew better than to refuse her demand. Bowing to her, he made his way past us, Godfrey gripping the hilt of his sword until the boy was out of sight. But he managed a hate-filled whisper when he passed me by.

"This will not be forgiven, D'Ivry. This I shall not forget."

The room was silent for a moment. Breaking it, Lady Margaret spoke with a measured tone.

"As you can see, my son is passionately protective of his sister and he is still young although he should know when to hold his tongue. Sébastien, I am not against this union. I have known for some time your feelings for my daughter and that she reciprocated them. Never in words, always in deed. A mother knows. If the Abbot had not felt this was a good match, I am sure he would not have gone through with it and indeed would have tried to stop it. My husband will undoubtedly be angered by this, but leave that with me."

I bowed to her graciousness.

"There will need to be discussed the matter of dowry…" she started but I cut her off.

"There is no need, my Lady. I have substantial wealth and I shall ensure that Sandford is left to her in the event of my death."

"I shall leave that to you and his Lordship to discuss upon his return," she said and stood, her way of saying our conversation had come to an end.

"Please tell my daughter that I love her and shall visit her soon. In the meantime, I shall have her clothes and other belongings packed and sent to her to help her feel more at home in her new house."

"I shall do just that, my Lady," I assured her.

With no more to say, we took our leave and went on our way. Godfrey wanted to take our night's rest in Newbury but I did not, preferring to push on to get back to Sandford and to my bride as quickly as possible. And so we parted ways at Great Bedwyn. Séraphine was asleep by the time I reached the manor in the early hours of the morning, and I slipped quietly into bed next to her without waking her. The next days were going to be difficult for her, and I did not want to disrupt her peaceful sleep.

* * * * * * * * *

As expected, Gilbert was not as magnanimous as his charitable wife. He received the news badly and rushed back to Ludgershall as soon as he could, leaving his business in Pembrokeshire unfinished. Despite his wife's entreaties to see the good in our marriage, his anger clouded his sense, and his eldest son's fury only added to his lack of rationale. King Henry was approached with a complaint and, as Abbot Faritius suspected, he declined to become involved. Lady Margaret was kind enough, and clever enough, to send Séraphine her dresses and possessions before Gilbert returned home. Unlike her belief that a discussion about a dowry should take place, Gilbert had no intention to initiate this, believing that his daughter had acted without his approval and therefore was owed nothing as was I. With the exception of a rare letter from her mother, Séraphine did not hear from any member of her family for quite some time. She was cut off and we soon learned we were banned from Ludgershall.

Séraphine was disturbed by the behaviour of her father and brother but remained steadfast in her love and loyalty to me and settled easily into her new role as mistress of the manor at Sandford on Thames. She quickly turned the house from a cold set of stone walls into a real home, warmth abounded in every room, and especially any she was in. More servants were brought in to help with running the household and her retinue of maids increased to three in anticipation of our expectation a family would be forthcoming. We hoped that when that happened, when we were blessed with a child, that perhaps the icy relationship with the Marshals would thaw.

I continued to concentrate on administering the properties and looked to gather more along the Thames where I could. I also recognized that the watermill that existed on my property by the river could easily be converted into a grain and corn mill, thus increasing the revenues being made from the land I had obtained from the Abingdon Abbey. And the other D'Ivry properties continued to flourish under Guillaume's careful expertise and as the weeks turned into months, the shock of our clandestine wedding faded into the background and Séraphine was accepted into our family as if she had always been a D'Ivry. Godfrey, attending meetings with the King on his own either in Oxford or in London, reported to us that Gilbert was icily respectful but went out of his way to avoid interacting with him on anything other than official matters. His son John, however, always managed to be unpleasant to Godfrey, even being chastised by the King on one occasion and ordered to give his apologies.

That summer we travelled to Ivry-la-Bataille so my mother and brother Roger could meet my wife. Séraphine and my mother took to each other immediately, and both were quite saddened when it was time to leave. But before returning to England, we toured about Normandy, paying our respects at my father's grave in Évreux and even spent few days in Paris where our marriage was celebrated by many friends I had made during my years of touring. We did not go to Falaise, the last stronghold of Duke Robert, I did not want any suggestion of reliving the old days to reach anyone in England.

We returned to Oxfordshire in late October and celebrated our first Christmas together at Sandford followed by a lively new year. I never spent more than two consecutive nights away from Séraphine, at first concerned that some attempt at abducting her and taking her back to Ludgershall might be made. But as the weeks passed, that seemed less likely so keeping close was now just because it was what I wanted to do. And as the cold winter began to shift into spring and we passed the first anniversary of our wedding, we could at long last began to feel as though we could relax and perhaps, after all this time, we could start mending the ill-will between our two families.

This wish only increased when Séraphine shared with me her joyous news after we returned to the manor after the mid-summer's eve celebrations and blessings. She was with child, our prayers to start a family had been answered. We waited before sending a message to her mother to make sure it was true, but once we did, she arranged to come visit us within days of hearing the news. She brought the two younger boys, William and Anselm, with her, they missed their sister and wanted to see her again after such a long separation. Gilbert was in Pembrokeshire again but Lady Margaret assured us he was pleased to hear our good news. John, of course, said nothing, sent no word of congratulations and did not attend with his mother. His resentment of me and of my taking his sister from him remained fresh and raw as the day he learned of our marriage.

Séraphine's condition progressed well and before too long the mid-wife informed us that we had been blessed with twins. Throughout the next months I watched as my love's belly grew with the life we had created inside, our excitement growing each day, and each time we felt one of the babes kick. The summer had been particularly hot and I did my best to make sure she was always comfortable and did not work to excess, but my wife's fortitude was beyond compare and she insisted on taking care of the household right up to her confinement a couple of weeks before Christmas.

It was about a week into her lying-in that Séraphine's maid Sophie fell ill. We did not think much of it, her fatigue was thought to be due to the extra work given to her because of her mistress's condition. But when a cough and a slight fever emerged, we thought it wise to remove her from Sandford and keep her at Shirburn until she was better and could return to service. We sent our own physician to take care of her and hoped she would regain her health quickly.

Christmas that year was going to be different from the last with the approaching births and Séraphine being unable to join any of the celebrations and having meals in her room. But I spent as much time as I could with her, including sleeping at the foot of her bed when she allowed it. I went to services at the church without her and received the blessing from

Father Renart who had blessed the birthing bed before her confinement. Abbot Faritius assured us that he would arrive as soon as he heard the labour pains had started and would be there to bless the twins' arrival. We had secured not one but two mid-wives, one for each of the babes. All was in order and it looked as if we were going to start the new year with two new additions to our family. I was over the moon with joyous anticipation and each passing day heightened that feeling more and more.

But on the morning after Christmas Day, I awoke to find my cherished love in some distress. She was sweating profusely and her forehead was burning hot. I immediately called for the mid-wives to attend upon her, I did not know if this was normal for labour and was naturally quite concerned. I also sent a message for Abbot Faritius to come to us immediately.

I paced back and forth outside the bedroom waiting for someone to come speak to me about what was happening. About an hour after the mid-wives arrived, one of them appeared, closing the bedroom door behind her so I could not see in. She was wiping her hands on a towel and had a grim look on her face.

"Master D'Ivry," she started, "Mistress D'Ivry is awake and is in labour, her pains started a short while ago."

This news should have filled me with joy but something told me not all was well.

"What else?" I asked.

She hesitated, as if looking for the words.

"Mistress D'Ivry is quite ill. She has taken with fever and…"

"Tell me."

"A small cough has started, with some blood spit up," she said barely able to look at me.

I froze. The mid-wife's tone was frightening.

"May I see her?" I asked, my voice trembling.

"It would be best if you did not, we need to have her concentrate on the birth of the twins," she answered. "But as soon as that is done, you may see her."

I understood.

"I must return to her," she said. "I will bring any news as soon as I have it." And then she stopped, having had a thought and said, "It might be wise to have your physician attend?"

With that she opened the door to go in and I got a glimpse of my lady, writhing on the bed. My heart stopped and as the door closed I dropped to the floor in anguish. 'How could this be?' I thought, bewildered as to the turn of events. I immediately sent word for our physician to return from Shirburn. And I began to pray.

Hours dragged on without any news. Godfrey and Guillaume arrived later that morning and the Abbott that afternoon and we all sat in the great hall, waiting and waiting. Osmond took care of all of us, making sure we had whatever we needed. The mid-wives came to us occasionally, only to tell us nothing had changed. I sat still, not wanting to move or breathe for fear of causing any further ill-winds. Then a thought occurred to me.

"Godfrey, how does Sophie? The maid we sent to you a week ago?"

He shook his head and shrugged to say he did not know. It was Guillaume who answered.

"She is well Sébastien, so much so I thought she would be able to return to your service after the birth. Why do you ask?"

"If I recall, she came down with a cough and fever, did she not?"

"Yes, that is right."

"How did the cough progress? Was there blood? How soon did it clear? How soon did the fever clear?" I asked, getting animated.

"I believe there was some blood for the first few days but that stopped before the fever abated which it eventually did," he answered seeing where I was going with this.

I breathed in deeply.

"Then perhaps, it is not as dire as we may think," I said hopefully but knowing in my gut that I was trying to convince myself that things were not as serious as they were.

The others nodded but said nothing. What could they say? The situation was horrific. We sat around the table, food and drink ordered by Osmond barely touched. The melancholy in the room was broken by the arrival of Lady Margaret who had agreed to join us after Christmas to help her daughter through the birth. She was unaware of the events that had happened this morning and as soon as we told her rushed, panicked, to Séraphine's side.

Shortly after we heard Séraphine's first cries of birth. Unable to sit still upon hearing them, I raced back up the stairs to the anteroom just outside our bedroom, Guillaume and the Abbot on my heels. I was now frantic with worry, sick for being able to help and feeling completely out of control. Her cries continued, seemingly endlessly, her suffering increasing by the minute. I was beside myself, wracked with worry when her cries suddenly stopped, only to be followed by those of a new-born. I straightened up and met Guillaume's eyes and hesitant smile and I began to hope. Within a few moments, the cries of a second new-born were heard and our hearts began to lose their heavy burden and lighten within us. But still, we dared not move or say anything. The door opened and Lady Margaret appeared. She came to me.

"My dearest Sébastien, you have two beautiful daughters," she said, smiling.

But her smile was not one of pure joy. Something was not right.

"And Séraphine?" I asked haltingly.

Her expression turned sombre.

"She has lost a lot of blood and her fever has not broken," she said gravely. "We now just have to wait and pray," she said, looking at the Abbot who crossed himself.

"May I see her?" I asked.

"Give the mid-wives a moment to prepare her and the babes, then you may see them all," she answered and returned to the bedroom.

Godfrey approached me first.

"You are a father," he said gently, taking hold of my arm, trying to bring good cheer into the room.

"Indeed," I responded but my mind was on my wife.

Guillaume came to me and patted my shoulder, but said nothing. What could he say?

One of the mid-wives opened the door and peered out, beckoning me to come in. Though they had done their best to tidy the room, it was clear a massive struggle had taken place here over the past hours. Bedclothes and bedding had been tossed into the corners of the room, I could see blood on some of them. Basins filled with bloody water waited to be emptied though I did not know if that was from my lady or the new-borns. I glanced over to where they lay, wrapped in swaddling, being attend to by the mid-wives. I looked over their shoulders so I could get a better look at them. They were beautiful. My daughters. I felt a surge of pride. But then I turned to go to my lady.

I felt my stomach drop when I saw Séraphine lying in the middle of our over-sized bed, covered by a clean sheet, looking small and frail, her face white bordering on grey, with the sheen of a fever glistening on her forehead. I approached her slowly, not wanting to wake her if she slept, and gently sat on the bed next to her. She opened her eyes and looked at me, offering a weak smile.

"We have daughters, Sébastien," she whispered to me.

I took hold of her hand. It was surprisingly cold.

"Yes, we do," I said, trying to smile an encouragingly smile at her.

"What shall we name them?" she asked.

"We do not need to bother about that now, we have time for that," I replied.

"I was thinking Isabel for your mother and Margaux for mine," she said as if not really hearing what I said.

"That is wonderful, my love," I said. "But now you must rest, you must heal your body."

"Yes husband," she whispered and fell asleep.

One of the mid-wives came over to the other side of the bed and reached over to tuck the sheet around Séraphine. I took that as my cue to leave her in peace. Coming back into the anteroom I found Lady Margaret deep in conversation with the Abbot. They stopped upon seeing me.

"She was awake, we spoke a little," I said. "And the babes are beautiful. She wants to name them Isabel and Margaux."

Lady Margaret embraced me.

"I have sent for our family physicians to come assist," she said. "The mid-wives will stay, but she needs different care now."

I agreed and thanked her. I was about to tell her that our physician was on his way when I noticed Osmond hovering at the door of the anteroom.

"My lord?" he asked.

"Yes?"

"The physician from Shirburn has arrived."

"Show him in," I said and Osmond stepped aside.

He came into the room at pace, bowed to me and entered the bedroom without saying a word. We all looked at one another and no one spoke. We waited to hear the results of his exam with anticipation. It did not take him long. We all looked up when we heard the door open.

"Lady Marshal, Master D'Ivry," he said nodding to each of us in turn. "The mid-wives have informed me of the events of the last several hours. Mistress D'Ivry has a high fever which has taken hold, and a bloody cough that seems to have worsened since its first appearance this morning if the mid-wives' observations are correct and I have no reason to doubt them. My concern is that this coupled with a tremendous loss of blood during the births has placed the Mistress in a very precarious position indeed. I have ordered cooling cloths to cover her body to try to reduce the fever and have administered a poppy pastille, drunk down with hyssop water and distilled wine for the bloody cough. She must receive one every four hours. I will stay and keep watch for any sign of change for the next hours, as that will tell us if she will persevere."

This was the first time I truly understood the possibility that my lady might die. I was rendered dumb, so Lady Margaret stepped forward.

"Thank you," she said. "I have sent for my own physicians from Ludgershall, they should arrive sometime in the night to assist you in any way they might."

"That is much appreciated Lady Margaret," he replied apparently relieved to hear he would not have to shoulder this burden on his own.

"If you will excuse me…" he said and returned to the bedroom.

The Abbot lead us in a prayer, standing there, in the anteroom, all feeling hopelessly inadequate. This was an enemy none of us had ever faced. This fever did not have the usual form of taking arms against its foe, its insidious presence instead lurking sight unseen, not showing its face to us, not giving any of us an opportunity to meet it head-on and beat it down using our traditional weapons of strength and power. My poor Séraphine was on her own in this battle, and all we could do was sit and pray that she, and she alone, had the strength and power to defeat it.

* * * * * * * * * *

The candle had burned down to midnight when I woke with a jolt. I had fallen asleep in a large chair Osmond had brought to the anteroom for me earlier. I got up and stretched. 'At least I have not been awakened with ill news,' I thought. Osmond had quietly provided a water basin for me nearby and I splashed cold water onto my face, through my dark hair and around my neck trying to feel as refreshed as I could. I had a long day ahead of me, I needed to be alert. I reached under the neck of my shirt and found the St Michael medal there, raised and kissed it, then returned it to its hiding place.

I walked down the hall to the room we had converted to the nursery and quietly opened the door, not wanting to disturb either the babes or the wet nurses sleeping there. I approached the cribs and looked down at my girls for the first time on my own. They were so tiny. Both had those dark hazel eyes of their mother. I could see one was slightly smaller than the other, probably typical for when two are born together, I reckoned. I thought of our mothers, Isabel and Margaret. My mother Isabel, although a strong woman in her own right, was of smaller stature than Lady Margaret, and so I silently decided then and there which was to be named which. They gurgled and wiggled in their swaddling but did not wake. I smiled, and for a brief moment had forgotten the turmoil just outside the door.

One of the nurses began to stir and so I left the babes in her care, stepping out into the hall and closing the door quietly behind me. There I bumped into Osmond who had come looking for me.

"The mid-wives need to speak with you sire," he said.

I returned to the bedroom and stepped in. It had been lit with many candles, bright enough to make out everything in the room but soft enough to allow sleep to take over.

"She has been asking for you," one of the mid-wives said.

I went to Séraphine's side and knelt down beside the bed, taking her hand in mine. Warmth had returned to it which I took to be a good sign.

"Come lay with me," she whispered and so I climbed onto the bed slowly, stretching out along her body, on top of the covers so as not to disturb the cooling cloths still applied to her skin.

"I have loved you from the moment I looked up from the ground of the gardens at Marlborough and gazed into those grey eyes," she murmured. "You were my champion, then, always."

My eyes filled with tears.

"And I you, my dear sweet Séraphine," I said, trying desperately not to sob the words, needing to be strong for her.

"I shall not leave you, dear husband," she said, trying to soothe me. "We shall always be together."

"Of course, my lady," I said, trying my best to soothe her.

"Then come, wrap your big arms about me and keep me safe," she said looking up at me with such love.

I leaned down and kissed her gently and then did precisely what she asked. And just like on our first night together and many others since, I fell asleep with Séraphine in my arms, hoping against hope it would not be our last.

It happened a few hours later. I was wakened by Séraphine's convulsions and yelled for the physician to attend. She was soaking wet, drenched in sweat and coughing up blood. I was pushed aside by one of the mid-wives as they came to her aid, the physician hurriedly touching her forehead, neck, wrists and ankles. Some sort of bit was placed in her mouth, no doubt to keep her from swallowing her tongue. Guillaume, Godfrey and Abbot Faritius appeared at the doorway, having heard my frantic calls for help. Lady Margaret then arrived and ordered them out of the room, they retreated to the anteroom. She moved to the head of the bed and tried to hold Séraphine's head still, to no avail. She looked up at me imploringly, almost begging me to save her daughter. There was nothing I could do. I was at an utter loss.

Then suddenly, she stopped moving. Her body just seemed to relax back into the bed. One of the mid-wives removed the bit and the tension in her jaw lessened as her mother laid her head down onto the pillows. She then gave out a great sigh and went still.

My beautiful, beloved Séraphine was gone.

# V

# Part Four

# 1118–1119 - England

It was all rather unreal, trying to comprehend the complete absence of another was not just difficult, it was nigh impossible. And yet, this was now the position I found myself in.

The moments immediately following Séraphine's death were a blur. Lady Margaret's screaming did not reach my ears, all I could see was her tortured face. My own movements seemed to be slow and robotic to me but in fact I rushed the bed and gathered my love up in my arms and held her tight, her lifeless arms not returning the embrace. The sound of my own anguished cries resounded in my head and then lit up the room as the rest of the horrific spectacle came crashing in, the mid-wives kneeling on the floor sobbing, the physician stepping back from the bed, the towel in his hands covered in blood, Guillaume, Godfrey and Osmond bursting through the door, then coming to a standstill, frozen with dread.

Abbot Faritius moved quickly to Lady Margaret, lifting her off of the head of the bed, practically carrying her out of the room, one hand covering a side of her face so she could not see the awful sight as they walked. Osmond beckoned the physician to the basin in the corner of the room so he could wash the blood from his hands and clothes. Godfrey and Guillaume just stood silently, watching me rock Séraphine back and forth, tears pouring down my face. Godfrey tried at one point to get me to release her but I pushed him away, never wanting to let her go, silently begging her to come back to me. But of course, she could not.

After what seemed to be an eternity, it was finally Osmond who was able to convince me with gentle words that I needed to let her go. I laid her down onto the pillows, feeling her golden tresses run through my fingers, then pulling the bedcovers over her body. I touched her face and stroked her cheek, and kissed her one last time. Osmond wrapped an arm around my chest, drawing me slowly away from her. Abbot Faritius returned to the room and started performing the death rites, asking for God's forgiveness of her sins and for the saints to take care of her soul, and finally blessing her. He turned to me.

"My dear, dear Sébastien," he said, placing his hands on the sides of my shoulders.

I just stared blankly at him.

"My Séraphine is gone," I said weakly, tears welling again in my eyes.

"Yes she is, Sébastien," he said sadly. "Come, we need to let the physician do what he needs."

Guillaume and Godfrey who had not left now stepped aside and let the Abbot guide me out of the room, following us down the stairs. Osmond had earlier prepared some warm mead for us and some meats and bread as dawn was approaching, but I touched none of it. I sat silently, listening to the others, quietly discussing the necessary things that needed to be discussed. Lady Margaret had been brought back to her room and given a thimble of dwale to help her sleep. One of Séraphine's maids was staying with her. A message needed to be sent to Gilbert. Decisions needed to be made about the funeral, where it should be held, where she should be buried, who should do the service. I suddenly had had enough of the chatter.

"MY SÉRAPHINE IS DEAD!" I roared, slamming my fist onto the table. "And all you prattle on as if it is just another day's business!!"

Everyone stopped talking. Abbot Faritius took a seat next to me and leaned in.

"You are right, of course, Sébastien. All of this can wait and I will take care of the message to Gilbert. I know this seems incomprehensible to you right now. You need to sleep, you have been up for almost two days. We can discuss things after you have rested."

I knew the Abbot was trying his best in this dreadful situation, but none of that mattered. I simply did not know if I could go on without her, how I could go on without her. The pain was unimaginable, like a hot blade cutting me to the core from my heart to my loins. Again and again and again. I felt I could not breathe.

"I need some fresh air," I said and left them there, looking hopelessly at one another.

Not really thinking where I was going, I walked past the gardens, the gardens where my lady had spent so much time cultivating her beautiful flowers, and headed for the river. Within moments I was at the Thames, next to the watermill and collapsed on the bank there. And the tears came, swiftly and hard, my sobs wrenching my body til every muscle in my body ached. It only stopped when I had exhausted myself and I sat staring at the rushing waters, numb and despondent for god knows how long.

I knew I had to return to the macabre scene and by the time I did, the Marshal physicians had arrived and were helping our own take care of my lady. I could not bear to watch them and, wanting to avoid the others for a while, walked the halls of the house until I finally found Osmond in the kitchens. It was as if he could read my mind.

> "I have prepared another room for you, my lord," he said, knowing full well that I could not return to our marital bedroom. "I think the Abbot is correct, you need to rest."

> "I know, Osmond, thank you for thinking of this for me. I do not wish to speak to anyone right now, please tell the others I have retired for a while and fetch me when Lady Margaret awakes."

With that I climbed the back steps and found my way to the room I knew Osmond had prepared for me. In it was a single bed, just barely big enough to fit my frame, and a table with a basin and jug of water. A set of clean clothes had been draped across the chair for me. I sat down on the edge of the bed, suddenly extremely fatigued. I fell back onto the bed and stared at the ceiling. I begged sleep to come as the images of the night began to swirl, disturbing me and bringing tears again and I was grateful for the privacy this room provided. Eventually sleep arrived and, thankfully, without any dreams.

I awoke on my own a few hours later and for a split second I could not remember why I was in this room and that all was well with the world. And then it came rushing back and the pain of her loss hit me once again. 'This is my life now,' I thought to myself. 'I will never feel anything but this ache again.'

I knew I had to get up and join the others, there were things that needed to be done, and only by me. I splashed myself with water and dressed in the fresh clothes Osmond had left out for me. I stepped out into the hall into a hive of activity, much more active than I would have expected after such a night. One of the nursemaids ran past me on the main stairs without even looking up and I realized something was very wrong. Osmond met me at the base of the stairs.

> "What is it Osmond?" I asked. "What has happened?"

"One of the babes has taken a turn, my lord," he said directly. "The physicians from Ludgershall are with her now."

I walked into the great hall where I found the Abbot and Guillaume by the windows. I did not even need to ask.

"About an hour ago one of the nursemaids asked for a physician to come see one of the babes," he said, basically repeating what Osmond knew. "They have been with her ever since, we have heard nothing."

"And Lady Margaret?" I asked.

"She has not been roused Sébastien, the physicians felt it best to let her sleep," answered Abbot Faritius.

This was almost too much to bear. First Séraphine and now, only hours later, one of our daughters was in danger, I grabbed the back of a nearby chair with both hands, fighting the urge to pick it up and throw it across the room. Instead, I tried to compose myself by staring at the floor. Once again, utter helplessness set in. One of my daughters was in peril and despite my considerable physical strength, there was yet again nothing I could do. She was in God's hands now.

It was not long before our physician from Shirburn appeared in the doorway, he face ashen, his expression sorrowful.

"Master D'Ivry," he said clearing his throat. "I am afraid the little one has not survived."

I just stood there, numb.

"What was the manner of her passing?" the Abbot asked.

"She simply was not able to thrive, Father. It is not uncommon for one in a set of twins to be underdeveloped, which has happened in this case," he said gravely. "It was the smaller of the two who has passed."

"Isabel," I whispered.

"Pardon my lord?" the physician asked, leaning closer to me.

"Isabel, the babe's name was Isabel," I said closing my eyes as if to ward off the pain.

The physician nodded sadly.

"What of the other child?" Abbot Faritius asked.

"We moved her to another room as soon as we were called to attend. So far, she has shown none of the same issues as the other…erm.. as Isabel. She…?" he looked at me inquiringly.

"Margaux," I answered softly.

"Margaux appears to be healthy but the mid-wives shall keep a close watch and of course her wet-nurse shall be with her," he answered.

I was silent.

"Thank you," Guillaume said, stepping forward, taking the physicians arm and walking him out of the room.

I could hear them speaking in low tones but could not make out the words. But I did not care to know. My world had turned upside down in a matter of a few hours, I had lost my wife and a child, I did not know whether to sit or stand. I probably should have been more concerned with the state of Margaux's health, but reason had abandoned me. I simply stared out the window.

But my dulled state was broken by the cries of Lady Margaret who had wakened and, meeting Guillaume and the physician at the foot of the stairs, was given the tragic news. I went to her and embraced her, feeling her pain through her shuddering body. I tried to offer comforting words, but stumbled lamely, realizing there were no words. The Abbot joined us, took hold of Lady Margaret's hands and prayed with her as I stood by watching them. He then made his request.

"Lady Margaret, I know the pain you must be feeling at the loss of your daughter and granddaughter. There is no greater than the loss of a child, for no child should precede a parent into the kingdom of heaven. Please ease yourself with the knowledge that both will be received by our heavenly Father, sinless and full of grace."

Lady Margaret's sobs had subsided and she looked at Abbot Faritius with teary eyes.

"Lady Margaret, I must ask for your help now. In preparation for burial, your daughter must be shrouded, but of course before that…" he started but Lady Margaret interrupted him.

"She needs the ritual bath?" she asked knowing the answer.

The Abbot was silent but his silence was her answer. She raised her head high and straightened herself.

"I shall take this task on myself," she said stoically. "Have one of her maids attend upon me, this shall be done. What of the babe?"

"The young one does not need to be bathed as she passed in the state of innocence. One of the mid-wives will prepare her," he answered.

Lady Margaret turned to me.

"I will let you know when this has been done and when she will be ready for vigil. I wish my lord Gilbert to be here…" she said but I cut her off.

"I believe Lord Gilbert has been sent for?" I said to the Abbot who nodded.

"He is expected by vespers," he confirmed.

"Please let me know when he arrives," she said quietly, adding, "I will go to Séraphine now."

We watched her climb the stairs slowly, dreading her task. It was done quickly with help from one of the maids. Someone, I do not know who, had realized we would need a coffin and later that afternoon I watched sombrely as a plain wooden box was carried up to our bedroom. When it was time, I was called to come up to see her.

Walking into the room, I could see the bed had been stripped down to its frame, everything else on it had been removed. And in the centre of the frame sat the wooden box in which my lady laid, wrapped in a white shroud, only her beautiful face visible. I leaned over her, holding onto the sides of the box and gazed at her. Looking down her body I saw that one of the nursemaids brought Isabel in, wrapped completely in a little white shroud, a miniature version of that which covered her mother, and laid her cradled in one of Séraphine's arms. I touched the babe's swathed head gently and then did the same to Séraphine.

Slowly the others began to appear at the doorway, waiting respectfully until I stepped aside so they could pay their respects. I took a seat in the corner, watching this morbid scene play out. As the afternoon darkened into early evening, candles were lit around the room giving it a haunting glow, the flames not moving at all as if they knew there was no life in this room. Osmond entered and came over to me.

"My lord, Gilbert Marshal has arrived, he is quite beside himself. And the eldest son, John, is here as well," and shot me a look that I understood well.

"Leave this with me," I said, getting up and moving to Lady Margaret where I whispered her husband's arrival.

The two of us descended the stairs, she quickly and ahead of me as I hung back a little, wanting to give them a few moments alone in their grief. She went to Gilbert who embraced her intensely, holding her as she wept. John was pacing back and forth by the door like a caged animal ready to spring as soon as it was able. We locked eyes and he came for me when I reached the last step.

"SON OF A WHORE!!" he roared, storming towards me with sword raised.

I was defenceless, rarely wearing weapons in my own home but I had no reason to fear as Gilbert reached out and caught him by his cloak before he could reach me, knocking the sword out of his hand. Osmond very quickly scooped it up before the lad could get at it. Gilbert shook his son.

"John! JOHN!" he yelled, "Calm yourself this instant!"

Lady Margaret took hold of his face in her hands in an effort to quiet him. Angry tears ran down his red-hot face as he blubbered almost incomprehensibly.

"He, he, it was him, she is dead, if he, if he had not taken her, she, she…" he cried out.

"Sébastien is not the cause of your sister's demise, John. She caught a fever and a deadly cough from which her body could not recover. Especially after the trauma of birthing two babes," she tried to explain as he stared hatefully at me. "John! It was not his fault, he is not to blame!"

But John was obviously having none of it. Although his sputtering venom at me ceased, it was clear he believed there was a devil in this room and it was me. He hugged his mother tightly, but stared deadly at me. Gilbert embraced me and then the three of them climbed the stairs to the bed chamber to see her.

St. Andrews in Sandford was prepared for the funeral after some discussion with Gilbert who was insistent that his daughter and granddaughter be buried within the family plot in Cheddar in Somerset. But I was not going to allow that, this was Séraphine and Isabel's home, this is where they were going to stay. The younger brothers were brought to attend and King Henry sent one of his retainers as a show of respect for both of our families. The service I am told was very good, I do not remember it. I was walking around in a sort of cloudy haze, weaving in and out of the nightmare of reality and then disappearing into my thoughts and memories of her. Although I found comfort there, it did not last long and the pain of losing her returned.

The day after the burials, with Isabel having been buried with her mother and an engraved gravestone hammered into place, the Marshals decided they needed to return to Ludgershall. I walked with Lady Margaret in the gardens of the manor, saying our goodbyes out of earshot of everyone else.

"I know you loved her deeply, Sébastien," she said sincerely to me, taking my arm as we walked.

"From the moment I laid eyes upon her my lady," I admitted honestly.

"You will find life difficult in the near future, but the anguish you feel will pass. Or at least lessen. And when it does, you must move on. Séraphine would want that. And of course, you have little Margaux to take care of now," she said.

But I felt nothing, even the mention of my new-born daughter did not lift the weight from my heart. I did not blame the child, I just could not bring myself to show much concern of her at the moment. Besides, she was well taken care of, the wet-nurse was well trained and one of the mid-wives agreed to stay on longer than usual to ensure Margaux was thriving. I said nothing.

"As for John, I know he feels a great deal of anger towards you, blames you for this. Do not take this to heart," she said.

And then she coughed. It was just a little cough, dry and insignificant. But we both looked at one another for a moment, each thinking the same thing. I began to ask about it but she waved me away with her hand, saying it was nothing.

"I am fatigued only," she said, adding, "and the spring dust affect me," feigning a little smile.

"As you say, my lady," I said but the nagging worry was not assuaged.

Godfrey had come from Shirburn to bid them adieu as had Guillaume. Abbot Faritius had not returned to Abingdon at all during this time and was at my side to see them off. Whilst John was assisting his mother into the travel cart she had arrived in with her maid, Gilbert came to me to say good-bye. During the many months his daughter and I had been married, he had kept his distance although he never objected to his wife's correspondence with us. Now, I could see he was truly heart-broken by his only daughter's death, and he probably rued the time wasted not sharing events and celebrations as families should. I outstretched my arm to him in a conciliatory gesture but he passed it by and grabbed me in a tight embrace for only a moment or two, then quickly releasing me and turning to mount his horse.

Godfrey spoke quietly with him for a few moments, probably wishing him and his family a safe journey back to Ludgershall. I happened to catch John's eye as he paced his horse, anxious to be on his way. There was no expression of farewell, no wishing of good tidings. Instead, he touched the grip of his sword hidden under his riding cloak, an unveiled threat that he was not done with me yet. I ignored him. We watched the small group of horses and the travel cart make their way along the dry road leaving the manor until it was nearly out of sight.

Guillaume and Godfrey and the Abbot stayed the night but then returned to their own homes the next day, leaving me effectively on my own for the first time in days. The silence in the manor was hauntingly uncomfortable and broken only by the cries of Margaux when she was brought out of the nursery and had become fatigues. I did not pay her much attention, her presence ripped open a new wound and deepened the ones already there.

It was the week after the new year that Godfrey brought the dreadful news. Lady Margaret had taken ill upon her return to Ludgershall, the cough had turned bloody, just as Séraphine's had, and we could only hope that she was strong enough to fight the illness as the maid Sophie had before Christmas. But it was not to be. Within the space of less than a month, Gilbert had lost his daughter, a granddaughter and his wife, and John had lost his sister, a niece and his mother. With the one person who kept John in check now gone, his hatred of me would now go unabated. I cared not, for nothing mattered now.

* * * * * * * * * *

The next few weeks were spent in a never-ending cycle of oscillating emotions, feeling much and then feeling nothing at all. I walked through my daily tasks in a fog, everything done by rote. I took long walks by the river and tried to fill my days with tasks that would not remind me of her but it seemed just about everything did. Both Godfrey and Guillaume visited regularly to try to lift my melancholy spirit but nothing seemed to help me. I had stopped going to the church services, always finding one excuse or another despite pleadings from both Father Renart and the Abbot to return. The truth was I was doubting the existence of God now, for how could He impart such cruelty on two innocents? And I questioned what I had done to deserve such a punishment as this. I had fallen into a despair I did not think I would survive.

The snow had held off for the most part that winter, but now it was in full force. A blizzard unlike any we had seen attacked the southeast of England at the end of January, forcing us to take shelter where we were and rely on our large food stores for sustenance. I ordered fires to be built and maintained day and night in each of the rooms and ensured Margaux was carefully watched over even though I still was unable to hold her. On the third day of being confined to the manor, one of my workers burst through the main doors searching for me.

"What is it?" I demanded.

"Beggin' yer pardon, m'lord, but there are problems at the watermill," the old man said, shivering badly.

I motioned to him to follow me into the great hall and stand next to the fire to get warm.

"Thank ye, m'lord," he said grateful to warm his hands through his threadbare gloves. "The Thames has frozen over," he continued. "There seems to be motion underneath, but the top layers are frozen thick as planks, if the ice is not broken the watermill may be damaged."

I sighed. This is not what I needed right now. I decided to go myself to see how dire it was and told the man to stay where was and sent for some warm ale to help calm his shivers and a thick pair of gloves to replace his worn ones. I put on my thick boots and a heavy winter cloak, grabbed my gloves and, shouting out to Osmond where I was off to, bolted out the door towards the river, stopping off first at one of the barns to grab a pointed spade and an axe.

It only took a few minutes to walk the short distance to the mill and, sure enough, the old man was right, the river had frozen right up against the wooden pillars in the river itself and, more worryingly, against the wooden wheel which was straining against the pull of the river and the constraint of the ice. I knew I had to free the wheel quickly or it would splinter and fixing that would be dearer than repairing the pillars.

Stepping inside with the tools I had brought with me, I chose the axe and found the spot where I wanted to start. I began hacking away, being careful to stay a good distance from the wheel so as not to strike it inadvertently. It was painstaking work, but slowly I managed to clear the ice completely away from the wheel and it began rotating on its own, freezing cold water pouring from the troughs as it turned. Not wanting to stay out in the cold for longer than necessary, I turned my attention to the ice by the pillars. This would be trickier, having to break the ice and not fall through it at the same time. The Thames here was deceptive – the surface water appeared fairly calm, but there was a nasty undertow caused by the unnatural presence of the pillars splitting the water flow in different directions, including back upstream, all sight unseen from above.

I stepped gingerly onto the ice, testing to see that it could carry my weight. It could. I brought both the axe and the spade with me thinking I could use them if the ice cracked and I found myself in the river. Making sure I was balanced, I began hacking away at the ice with the axe, slowly removing it in sections, relieving the pressure on the pillars under the mill.

When I was done, I picked up the tools and climbed onto the river's embankment, stood up straight and stretched, exhaling strongly and seeing my breath turning to steam. I looked around and realized this was the very spot I had come to on the day of my beloved's untimely death. I stood for a moment, hearing the soothing sounds of the running waters, watching as they rushed past me. I bundled my cloak around me and stood on the snow-covered ground leaning on the axe and let my mind wander back in time, hearing her laugh as we walked along the water's edge in warmer times, her imagined smile warming my heart again and yet tearing it too.

"D'Ivry!" a voice called out to me from the edge of the nearby forest.

I tightened my grip on the axe, for although the voice sounded familiar I could not quite place it. I pretended not to have heard.

"D'Ivry!!" the voice called out again, a little louder.

Suddenly, the deepest part of my memory tripped and I knew who it was, although I could not reason how it could be, even when I turned around and saw him. Hugues de Payns, my old friend, mentor, fellow crusader, was grinning at me through the heavy snowfall.

Once I got past the shock of seeing him, I climbed the bank and we embraced like long-lost brothers, then quickly returned to the manor to get out of the cold, settling in by the fire with some of my best wine. I was both surprised and gladdened to see him, I had given up any hope of ever seeing any of those I had travelled with to the Holy Land, most had either died, stayed in Palestine or returned to their homes far away from England. So it was with both joy and curiosity that I welcomed him into my home, joy to be able to speak with him again after all these years and curiosity to know why he had come.

"So, how long has it been?" Hugues asked, taking a long drink from his goblet, running his hand through his dark auburn hair which I could see was now speckled with grey.

"Well, let us see. The Duke, ah, former Duke I should say, and I departed Jerusalem that August, going to Bari for his wedding to Lady Sybilla the next spring. So it is almost nineteen years then?" I answered with slight amazement of the passage of time.

"Ah yes, the Duke, or former Duke as you say. I was disheartened to hear of his battles with King Henry after William Rufus's death, you were with him all along?" Hugues surmised.

"Yes, I was at his side for all of it. Including the loss of Lady Sybilla," I said going quiet.

"I was distressed to hear of her death, so very sad at such a young age," he said. "As was the loss of your lady, Sébastien, I was greatly aggrieved to hear of it," he said sincerely.

We sat silently, staring at the flames in the fireplace. Finally, I spoke.

"It is not something I believe I will ever recover from," I said, my voice is just above a whisper. "I will never comprehend why this happened, never."

"Our benevolent God acts in ways we will never understand..." he started but I cut him off.

"God?" I chortled. "God? Is there a God? A benevolent God? What God gives the world such a beauty only to snatch it away, leaving us poor souls behind to suffer their loss? I am not sure such a God exists Hugues," I said, sinking further into my chair.

We sat silently again, letting the air settle between us.

"I too suffered a similar loss," he said quietly.

I was not aware of this. I let him continue.

"I had wanted to stay in Jerusalem but, as you know, Count de Champagne expected me once the city had been secured in Christian hands. I waited as long as I could but returned to France in a few years after your departure, and so thrilled my lord with stories of the great land that he insisted on going on pilgrimage there, taking me as his guide. So I am afraid I was in Jerusalem during all your troubles with King Henry. It was on my second return that I met her, Elisabeth de Chappes, she was one of Countess Isabella's ladies. My lord, the Count, and his lady gave their permission for us to marry and so we did, I think about the same time you were being released from Devizes Castle?"

Hugues obviously knew a lot more about my intervening years than I did about his.

"She bore me four children, Sébastien, Gibuin, Thibaud, Herbert, and Isabelle. The first three were relatively easy births, but things took a turn when Isabelle was born in 1113, and my darling Elisabeth was gone a few days later," he said, looking down into his goblet.

Even though this had happened over five years ago, I could feel his grief even now. It did not escape my notice that two of the most important people from my youth had suffered as I had.

"And the babes?" I asked.

"All healthy and well, and blossoming in Champagne, living with my brother and his family. After Elisabeth's passing, the Count came to me and asked if I would be willing to take some of his men to Jerusalem, and in my state of mind I was more than willing, I simply could not bear to stay in Champagne. And this time I stayed, offering my services to King Baldwin."

I knew exactly how he felt. What I would give to escape this torment that was plaguing me.

"I came back to France only this past summer, having business with the Count and with a new abbey he is supporting, well, relatively new, it is only just over three years old. The Count has given a sizable grant of lands near Langres to a monk who had joined the reformed Benedictines at the abbey in Cîteaux so he could found a Cistercian abbey there. Bernard is the monk's name, or the Abbot's name, I should say, he was blessed as Abbot shortly after the Abbey was made ready. He named it Clairvaux. I was asked to oversee some additions to the charter. I like this Abbot, he seems devoted to the Count as he is to him. But I am not so enamoured of this order, their rules are rather severe, some of the monks fall ill easily. So I was asked to speak with Bernard about easing some of the restrictions which I did."

"I hope you made the Abbot see reason," I said, adding tersely, "dead monks are no use to anyone."

"Indeed," he agreed and then changed the subject. "During my travels, the Count kept me abreast of events in the county and across France. Apparently you have become quite the tournament champion over the past few years, yes?" he said, grinning a bit.

"I suppose so," I said, shrugging. "It seems the training I received from you, Saint-Omer and the others proved valuable off the real battlefield as well as on it. I managed to make somewhat of a fortune, and would have stayed in France if I did not owe King Henry my return to England."

"With your height and strength you were no doubt a formidable force at the tourneys. I would not want to come up against you!" he said, chuckling at the thought of it.

"It helped to have my old sword at my side," I said, giving him a side-glance. "Thank you for bringing it to my father, you made quite the impression on him."

"It was the least I could do for you," he said making it seem as though it was nothing.

"What of the others?" I asked. "What news of them?"

"Geoffroi Bisol is still with me, Godfrey Saint-Omer, if you remember, was with Bouillon after Bouillon's brother Baldwin departed for Edessa. He stayed on in Jerusalem after Bouillon died and Baldwin accepted the title of King. Payen de Montdidier returned with Flanders, Flanders has departed this earth of course, as has Toulouse."

I thought of training on the beaches with Bisol and had to smile. It was good to know he was still with Hugues. And that made me think of Bohemond and Tancred, and so I asked about them, letting him know I knew of Bohemond's captivity upon arriving in Bari.

"Tancred acted as regent until Bohemond's release three years after his capture but continued as such when Bohemond came back to the West in search of new recruits to build an army. Tancred had to give up his rule of Galilee to do so, but he seemed not to mind, both were principalities after all. But not only did Bohemond gain an army in the West, he gained a wife!"

He laughed.

"King Phillip's eldest daughter Constance who, as chance might have it, had been married first to my Count de Champagne. Their marriage was annulled on the basis of consanguinity, but I think really it was because their union delivered no viable children. Which was odd, since once Bohemond and Constance were married and returned to Bari, they had a son. I suppose not all unions are fated to be successful in producing heirs," he said, taking another mouthful of wine before continuing.

"Bohemond became foolish. Instead of returning to Antioch, he decided to have his revenge against Emperor Alexois, forgetting I suppose that the Emperor now knew all his tactics. They never really engaged in a full-scale war but instead both sides endured many smaller battles, each taking its toll on the armies, but Bohemond suffered the worst of the two. Eventually, he had to surrender and as part of that, he agreed to give Antioch back to Alexois upon his death. He died soon after, sometime in 1111, a shell of the man he once was. A shameful end really."

He took a deep breath. That was dire news to hear, the great Bohemond, master of so much domain, reduced to a lordship over a territory a fraction of what he once ruled. I felt saddened to hear it.

"I do not suppose Tancred was very happy to hear of his uncle's capitulation?" I asked, knowing the answer.

"No indeed he was not. Not only did he refuse to obey the agreement when Bohemond died, he pushed his forces into farther territory, even taking Krak de Chevaliers under his control. But he was only regent, acting in the name of Bohemond's son who was, I think, no more than three at the time of his father's death?"

I smiled remembering the time Tancred stood up against the Emperor.

"He was always one to forge his own way, was not he? He seemed pleased when Bouillon made him Prince of Galilee soon after becoming the Princeps of Jerusalem? Even if he had to give it up when Baldwin became King," I offered.

"Yes, but there was always something about the Taranto men, never satisfied, always scheming to capture more. But, then again, I suppose it is not generous to speak of the dead," Hugues said, leaning forward and helping himself to some more wine.

I looked at him questioningly.

"Ah, I thought you knew. Tancred died several years ago, in 1112 I think, from a fever he could not shake. Bohemond's son, Bohemond II, is now Prince of Taranto and Prince of Antioch. And Saint-Omer's brother, Hugh de Fauquembergues who replaced Tancred as Prince of Galilee, remains so," he explained.

'So many gone,' I thought. Bouillon, Flanders, Bohemond, Tancred, Toulouse, all dead. And Robert in prison. Such is the passage of time. Hugues must have caught what I was thinking, as he leaned over and slapped my shoulder.

"But we are still here, are we not?" he said, trying to be jovial.

'Yes, but not really,' I thought.

"I am assuming you heard about Aumale?" I asked.

"Yes, my Count informed me about the discontentment of the Norman nobles about King Henry's management of the duchy after Duke Robert was captured. It was only time before his son William Clito reached his majority and incited them to rebel last summer. I believe Aumale supported William Clito, if I am not mistaken," Hugues answered, telling me what he knew.

"Yes, an interesting choice, considering he fought against the Duke at Tinchebrai," I said irritably.

Hugues smiled at me.

"Forever the constant man, are not you Sébastien?" he asked rhetorically.

"Loyalty means all to me," I responded.

"Do you remember Archambaud de Saint-Agnan?" Hugues changed the subject. "He was Blois's man, returned with him when Blois abandoned the crusade at Antioch?"

I remembered him vaguely.

"After Blois's death, Lady Adela requested he join her son Théobald's inner circle, Théobald only being twelve at the time of his father's death. She felt he would benefit from Saint-Agnan's experience and so he was part of her court for quite some time, retiring only a few years ago," Hugues explained.

"I met Théobald's brothers Henry and Stephen, at my first tourney in Valenciennes which was Henry's last, he told me he was returning to his studies and I believe eventually took orders in Cluny," I said, refilling my goblet.

"Ah, yes, Stephen. We met once at council in Blois, unpleasant individual. He seems to resent his lack of position, his older brother having been given Blois and Chartres," Hugues said frankly.

I chortled.

"He had no time for me at that tourney and snubbed me at others, I think in part there was envy of my success overshadowing his own achievements. But that is the world of competition. Each time he spoke, I saw more and more of his father in him," I said, sarcastically.

Osmond knocked at the door and let us know that some food had been prepared and was waiting to be brought to us. I waved the servants in and soon Hugues and I were devouring plates of roasted meats and winter vegetables and baskets of bread. It was the first substantial meal I had had in weeks.

"So," I said, after a few mouthfuls, "what brings you here, Hugues? It is all well and good that you are visiting an old friend, but not for one minute do I believe you have just been missing my handsome face."

He put his spoon down and leaned back in his chair, chuckling and then, thinking for a moment, became serious, looking around to ensure the doors were shut.

"The situation in Jerusalem is precarious," he said. "I presume you were aware of King Baldwin's death last spring?"

I nodded, the news had reached us just after Easter.

"He had bequeathed the Kingdom of Jerusalem to his brother Eustace but also declared it should be offered to his cousin Baldwin de Bourcq should Eustace refuse to come to Jerusalem. Eustace did accept but de Bourcq had reached Jerusalem quickly and so was elected in his place. It was a practical and sensible choice, Eustace was too old to take this on. So we now have another Baldwin, Baldwin II as the King of Jerusalem. He is a good King but does not have the strength or power that either of his cousins had and we fear we may be losing our grip on the city. There have been incursions in Ascalon which he managed to fend off without having any pitched battles, but the Muslim forces are gathering again," he said, finally stopping to take a breath and more wine.

"That is unfortunate, but with Christian leaders in most of the larger cities, surely there is not a real threat?" I asked.

"There is always a threat," Hugues said seriously but not condescendingly. "What we need to do is increase the presence of Western strength, offering security to those within the city and those on pilgrimage to it, whilst convincing those who might be considering an attack to think otherwise."

"What did you have in mind?" my interest aroused.

"I have already gathered a few men, some of those we have been speaking about, who are willing to return to the Holy Land and offer our services to the new King Baldwin, as sort of, ah, protectors if you will. There are no royal persons involved, most of us are minor nobles, or not noble at all, so as not to draw attention to us. But our connections are considerable."

"And you believe the King would be amenable?"

"Very much so. Anything that can enhance the reputation of the powerful hold he has of the city would be beneficial to him."

I pursed my lips and thought for a moment. This was an intriguing proposition. But I still did not know what part I could play in this.

"May I ask who the others are?"

Hugues took a moment as if considering if I could be trusted.

"At the moment, Saint-Agnan, Montdidier, and Bisol are waiting for me in Calais, Saint-Omer is in Jerusalem. And when I was meeting with Abbot Bernard, he introduced me to a young man, André de Montbard, who was quite eager to go to the Holy Land and the Abbot asked if I could take him with me. He is a vassal of my Count and is also the Abbot's uncle, so I thought it wise to include him. Then we have…"

"Wait a moment. Montbard is the uncle of Abbot Bernard? I thought you said he was a young man?"

Hugues puckered his brow, his way of telling me this was rather complex.

"Yes, he is the much younger half-brother of Alèthe de Montbard, the Abbot's mother, born many years later from the union of their father's second marriage. So even though the Abbot is," Hugues went silent a moment to count, "about ten years his senior, Montbard is his uncle. Such is the way of second marriages with younger wives," he said shrugging.

'Indeed,' I thought.

"And we also have two Cistercian priests from Clairvaux Abbey who have offered to attend on our group, cook, clean, perform secretarial tasks and such like. Rossal, a distant cousin to Abbot Bernard and a founding member of the Abbey, and Gondamer who was visiting Clairvaux from his abbey in Portugal when I was there, he also offered his service. They too are waiting with the others at Calais," he said, finishing and sitting back into his chair again, taking a large drink from his goblet.

I refilled it for him.

"And why have you come to tell me of this, Hugues? What part am I to play in it?" I asked, finally bringing us to the point of his visit.

"I want to you to join us," he said without hesitating, looking me square in the eye.

This shocked me. I thought he might be here to ask for financial support, I never thought he would ask this.

"Whatever for Hugues?" I asked. "My powerful associations are minimal, probably even less now with Séraphine's death. And my life is here, I have responsibilities…" I argued, but he interrupted me.

"Is it? Do you have a life here now that she has gone? You have a child, yes, but she is an infant and will have no need of you for years to come. Your wealth will keep her in comfort and protected. Your properties have managers who are perfectly capable of running them in your absence, you choose to become involved as deeply as you do. Did you really need to go out tonight in this bloody blizzard to clear the ice from the mill? I think not," he said rather boldly. Then adding in a softer tone, "Have not you lost your way Sébastien?"

At first I was offended by his impudence. But deep down I knew he was right. From the moment I knew she was gone, I had felt dead inside, convinced I was now condemned to this bleak world, a waking death. She had breathed life into it, she had brought excitement and exhilaration and love, and without her I was nothing. And I could never be anything again. At least not here. Not like this. I needed my life to have meaning again. And maybe, just maybe, I could rid myself of the intense, pain-inducing guilt of her death, and that of my little Isabel, both weighing heavily and unrelentingly on my heart.

I looked at Hugues and nodded.

And with that, I was on my way back to the Holy Land.

# VI

# Part One

# 1119 - The Holy Land

It had not taken long to get my affairs in order and within ten days Hugues and I found ourselves in Dover, eager to get the journey started. The others Hugues had gathered were waiting for us in Calais and Saint-Omer had travelled from Jerusalem to join us, wanting to take the opportunity to visit his home, a day's ride southeast of the port. Crossing the Channel was uneventful despite the winter winds blowing a near gale, we navigated the choppy waters with relative ease. Hugues had obtained passage for us aboard a supply galley headed to Palestine that would be making a few ports of call along the way, but we had two nights to spend in the city before our departure. It would be good to be reacquainted with my old friends and meet the new men making this journey.

I had instructed Osmond to stay in England to watch over the estate for the time being. Once we were settled in Jerusalem and I was ready, I would send for him. I had packed minimally knowing I could obtain what I needed when I arrived, many of my garments ill-suited for the hot climate there. But I brought my maille and helm, and hanging from my belt was my favourite sword, which I had had no use of for quite some time. I thought I might need some or all of it there. And I made sure to bring a couple of winter cloaks for although the summers in Palestine would be almost unbearably hot, the winter days could bring a chill to the air and the winter nights would be downright cold. Like the others, I was allowed to bring only two horses, so I dressed Lux and Fidem, one of Lux's colts, in their finest tack, checked that their shoes were in good condition and covered their backs with D'Ivry saddle blankets I had made and taken with me to the tournaments those many years ago, the original that had come with me to the Holy Land long worn through.

Saint-Omer met us at the port and helped unload the horses and travel chests. It was good to see him again after all these years.

"Sweet Jesu!" he exclaimed upon seeing me. "You have turned out to be a bit of a mountain of a man, have you not D'Ivry!"

His short golden-coloured beard partially hid the well-tanned face that broke out into a huge smile upon seeing me. He had aged well, the Mediterranean air had been good to him.

"It does my eyes good to see you again Saint-Omer!" I said, taking hold of his arm in our traditional greeting. "I was sorry to hear about Fauquembergues's death."

"My brother has been missed. He was a strong leader, there is no doubt about that, well deserving to take the role of Prince of Galilee when Tancred relinquished it. But he met his match in Damascus. We were lucky to have been able to retrieve his body for burial in Nazareth," Saint-Omer said. "I was saddened to hear of the Duke's misfortunes, that was about the same time, yes?"

"Yes. We fought well at Tinchebrai, but Henry was too strong for us. That was many years ago, much water has passed under the bridge since," I said.

"Indeed, I hear you've become a champion of the tournaments!" he said grinning. "Perhaps when we have some time you can show me what made you so good at it."

"I think you know much of the credit goes to you old friend. Those lessons in the muck proved to be quite invaluable."

He laughed and hoisted a bag over his shoulder.

"Come, we have a meal waiting for us at the Hôtel au Quai where we shall spend the next two nights. Our ship leaves at dawn on the third day hence."

Saint-Omer had secured a large room at the rear of the Hôtel for a private dinner. I could hear the chatter and banter as I ducked in through a doorway and walked down the hall, reminding myself I needed to remember the low ceilings of these Norman public houses. Hugues opened the creaking door and entered first followed by Saint-Omer and then myself. The warmth of the room welcomed us, caused by the blazing fire in the huge inglenook fireplace along the far wall and the collective bodies of several men who had been there for a while. Hugues's appearance quieted the room, mine silenced it.

"Our ninth," Hugues said as his way of introducing me.

"D'Ivry!" said Montdidier, getting up from the table, "it is good to see you again. How many years has it been?"

He came forward and embraced me like an old friend. One by one they came up to welcome me, saying how glad they were to see me, remarking on my unusual height and saying some words of commiseration about the Duke. Hugues then introduced me to André de Montbard, the youngest of our group, uncle to Abbot Bernard of Clairvaux. The two monks Rossal and Gondamer who were going to be travelling with us were not in the room as both were attending vespers at a church a short walk from the port. And then, in the midst of all of these voices came a loud cough from the corner of the room and there stood my dear old friend, the one I had spent most of my time with on crusade, from our first meeting at the Hôtel le Lion in Clermont to our farewell on the beach at Jaffa almost three years later. The Palestine sun had had some effect on Bisol's pale skin freckling it and his blond hair seemed blonder. It truly did my heart good to see him.

We settled in for a hearty meal and tankards filled to the brim with strong ale and pewter goblets of red wine from Saint-Omer's family vineyards. We drank to the health of those who we had known and lost - Bouillon, Boulogne, Bohemond, Toulouse amongst others. And then began the reminiscing, memories of times gone by, the good and the bad. And we talked about what had kept us busy during these intervening years although I did not contribute much during those conversations, I could not bear hearing the sympathy in their voices for my losses and I was not one to boast about the tourneys. So engrossed were we no one seemed to notice the return of our two monks, who slipped through the door and joined the table. Or at least, no one seemed to be concerned about their arrival, quiet though they were, they seemed to fit in with the group effortlessly.

Once the table had been cleared of the remnants of the meal we were able to finally discuss the reason for our group coming together. Hugues stood and started, the room falling silent, everyone staring at him with rapt attention. It was obvious he was seen as our leader.

"I am pleased we have been able to finally gather, and with the addition of Sébastien D'Ivry we are now whole. The situation in the Holy Land is alarming and at its worst since our armies defeated the Saracens twenty years ago this coming summer.

"As you are all well aware, after the victory four crusader states were established in the Holy Land, the County of Tripoli, Principality of Antioch, the County of Edessa and the Kingdom of Jerusalem, each with a Christian leader who had made his mark during the crusade. My own lord, Godfrey de Bouillon, having refused the title of King of Jerusalem, set about undoing the damage caused by the infidels and rebuilding the holy city in the image of our Lord.

"As you know, he was taken from us too soon and his brother Baldwin was called upon by the High Council to come down from Edessa to assume governing Jerusalem. He did of course, and he did take the title King of Jerusalem, and continued the good work his brother had started. But he too was taken from us just before this last Easter and now we have his distant cousin, Baldwin de Bourcq, as our new King.

"But he does not seem to have the strength and power as his late cousin who always held a strong command over the region. New King Baldwin is still relatively early in his post but his past struggles after assuming control of Edessa are cause for worry. He continues to do battle to maintain control in his part of Outremer as well as providing assistance to others to control theirs. This leaves Jerusalem at risk for attack."

This was the first time I heard anyone refer to the four crusader states by this name, Outremer. I did not know who coined it, but it was appropriate considering it meant beyond the sea.

"There is something else that is worrisome. We have a new Patriarch of Jerusalem, Warmund de Picquigny, who has only been in this position since last autumn. His predecessor, Duke Robert's own chaplain during our crusade, died only a few weeks after anointing Baldwin in April. So, we have a new King and a new Patriarch in Jerusalem, it is no wonder that our adversaries might feel the city is ripe for the taking.

"Saint-Omer can attest to all that I am saying, he has been witness to it as have I," Hugues said gesturing to Saint-Omer who raised his hand and nodded solemnly.

"This brings us to our purpose. Saint-Omer and I believe that a small band such as this could be extremely helpful to the King. With our skills, we would provide extra security for the Christians within the city as well as protection for those wishing to come on pilgrimage, keeping at bay the bandits we are all familiar with," he said, then added when looking at Montbard, "well, most of us are familiar with.

"We brought our proposal to King Baldwin and he gave his permission for me to gather the best men I know who would be willing to come to the Holy City and form this, ah, elite guard, for lack of a better term. And so, we shall set off on this journey the day after the morrow. With the fast ships we have procured, it should take us only a few weeks, possibly less with good winds, to reach the port of Jaffa. Upon our arrival, we will meet with the King and outline what services we shall provide. Does anyone have anything to ask?"

No one did, it all seemed quite straightforward. There was an undeniable excitement in the air, I felt it too, it had been so long since I had left Jerusalem I had to wonder if the city had changed much, undoubtedly it had. I knew the plans that Bouillon had put in place for the repairs and restorations, some work had actually started before the Duke and I departed for Bari. I could not begin to imagine what it would look like after twenty years of Christian occupancy and rule. And of course I had to wonder if Theós was still alive and thriving, I knew he had become a favourite amongst the crusaders who remained after the victory, I could only hope he would still be there.

The rest of the evening was filled with drinking more ale and telling each other stories of our lives over the past years apart and having some fun with Montbard, who had not even been born when we went on crusade which made us feel our age.

The next two days were spent preparing for the journey over sea from Calais to Jaffa, loading our goods, supplies and horses. We would be making a number of ports-of-call along the way to replenish our supplies and to pick up goods and materials for delivery to Jerusalem. With a strong wind at our backs, we reckoned it would take three weeks to arrive at Jaffa and a few more days to make the trek overland to the city.

And on schedule, at dawn on the third day after Hugues and I arrived in Calais, we were on our way, sailing our vessel, an oversized cog with a double mast which would make better use of the strong winter winds. Four other such ships accompanied us, two had Constantinople as their final destinations whilst the other two, along our own, headed for Jaffa. We made a brief stop at La Rochelle to pick up provisions including timber and other building materials that those in Jerusalem were always in need of for the constant repair and rebuilding of the Holy City.

We hugged the coastline of France and then to the west along the north coast of Leon before turning south along Portugal, the winds becoming warmer on our faces the further we travelled. At its tip we turned eastward along the coast of Andalos, being careful to navigate the waters so that the Muslims to the north would not see us and launch an attack. We continued until we landed at Malta where we were greeted warmly by Count Roger of Sicily whose father had taken the island from the Muslims years before we had taken Jerusalem, forcing the rulers to become his slaves. Our sister ships left us once we reached Crete, turning northeast for Anatolia as we continued east towards Cyprus, eventually coming into the port town Lemesos on the south side of the island where we rested for a few days, taking time to exercise the horses and replenish our food and water supplies. We were ready for our final push on to Palestine and, after a brief stop at Acre to off-load some of the building materials for a crusader house that was being built there, we were soon at Jaffa, the very same port Duke Robert, Flanders and myself sailed from two decades years earlier.

Although winter was closing in on the beginning of spring, the dry temperatures had already turned warm compared to the freezing wet squalls we endured at the start of the voyage. I was soon reminded of the arid air and remembered how quickly this would turn to the full heat of the summer. The sun on my face felt good and for the first time in a long while I managed a sort of half-smile which evaporated when I thought of her. I wondered if that would ever cease tearing at my heart.

We had much to do, we had arrived at mid-morning and it would take the better part of a few hours to unload everything and ready it for transport to Jerusalem. We decided to leave immediately, making the most of the afternoon sunlight, aiming to arrive at Nabi Samuil by vespers and avoiding having to travel on horseback at night. If memory served it would only another couple of hours to reach the city and by camping overnight, we could be rested and alert when meeting with King Baldwin the following day.

At Nabi Samuil the firelights of the settlement were burning bright, guiding us to where we needed to go. After having a small meal, I made my way to the crest of the hill, just as I had so many years ago, breathing in the cool night air, exhaling hard upon seeing the lights of the great city in the distance. I could not help remembering more of that night when I met Théos, hearing his story and being filled with anticipation for the coming days of battle that could have cost me my life. A chill went down my spine with the memories that followed, the intense bloody fighting, the deaths of so many and our ultimate victory. I hoped it had not all been in vain.

* * * * * * * * * *

Our entrance into Jerusalem could not have been any more different from the last time we arrived. Instead of being the interlopers attacking and invading, pushing enormous siege engines, climbing over the walls at Herod's Gate and slaughtering those before us, this time we arrived in peace, on horseback, walking up the gentle slope towards and then through Jaffa Gate, the western entrance to the city. I instantly recognized the citadel to our right, passing by the great walls of King David's Tower and remembered the moment we had secured it during the siege. I glanced to my left and down a little alley which I knew held the place of Theós's shop, saw some leather goods sitting outside by the door but could not see anyone milling about. I made a note to visit it as soon as I was able.

We dismounted at the entrance to the marketplace where the open space in front of the citadel turned into narrow alleys, and led the horses slowly on foot, down the wide, well-worn flagstone steps, pressing our way through the crowded market lanes. The image of the bloodied and dead sprang to my mind and I had to shake it free, that had been a long time ago, this was now a different Jerusalem. I could only hope it was.

We had been instructed to come to the Temple of Solomon on the Temple Mount to meet with King Baldwin once we arrived in the city and so we headed there without any delay. Originally the Al-Aqsa mosque, it had since been turned into a palace of sorts, used by the King for his residence and for governing, and a set of stables for his horses. To get to it we had to navigate the marketplace which at this hour was a hive of activity, sellers with all sorts of wares laid out on the floors or hanging above the entrances of their small shops. Noon was approaching and the food vendors were already preparing the mid-day meals, roasting meats and vegetables next to fruit stands with fresh pears, pomegranates, figs and other succulents ready for the taking. Although my belly was full from the morning breakfast, the aromas made my stomach growl for want of them. Hugues had sent word ahead to King Baldwin of our arrival and so there was no time to stop and sample the goods.

We used the stairs on the west side of the Mount next to what was the Jewish prayer wall, crossing a small bridge to reach the Mount's expansive stone platform and soon found ourselves standing at the entrance to Solomon's Temple. The Temple Mount itself did not seem, at first glance, to have changed much in the intervening years, there were still wide-open spaces and gardens and trees for anyone to walk about, we learned later that only the nobles and their families tended to come to the Mount especially as the Dome had been transformed into a church only for their use. But in reality the Temple Mount had become a military complex, its spiritual importance diminished with the Christian crusader triumph and the rebirth of the Sepulchre. I took a moment to look around, wincing a bit when remembering the barbaric scenes of slaughter that were necessary to win it, it was difficult to believe it was the same place.

Bouillon had started to make changes to the Temple before the Duke and I had departed, having wanted to turn it into a residence fit for the ruler of the city and his family but of course I had no idea what to expect. The first King Baldwin had continued the work and now his cousin, our second King Baldwin, was residing there, awaiting the arrival of his family from Edessa.

We by-passed the entrance and turned the corner and saw the stables but stopped short of entering them, instead tying our horses' reigns to some hitching rings embedded in the wall. There were a few empty troughs on the flagstone floor beneath them and Hugues gave a couple of short whistles which caused two stable boys to come running out. Without saying a word he just pointed to the troughs, giving silent instructions for hay and water to be brought, then turned and headed back towards the entrance, everyone else close behind.

The seven exterior arches had not been altered in any way, each still covered in exquisite carvings from floor to ceiling and the doors did not seem to have been replaced as they were still looked to be in good shape even after all these years. Two guards stood on either side and nodded to Hugues as he passed them by, ignoring the rest of us, apparently we were expected.

As Bouillon had intended, the original huge open spaces separated only by enormous square pillars had been somewhat closed in to provide private rooms for various uses, greeting halls for foreign dignitaries, dining halls and of course the private quarters. One section had been turned into a private chapel with an apse and an outdoor cloister, both for the use of King Baldwin, his family and the Patriarch, for private services. But oddly, all of the Islamic decoration had been kept, the beautiful mosaics and frescoes still adorned the walls and ceilings. Paintings of Christian saints and Christ on the Cross hung on top of them but no effort had been made to destroy the vibrantly coloured tiles that had been there long before our arrival more than two decades before.

At the end of a very long hallway we came to a set of closed doors with another set of guards. Hugues told one of them we were here to see the King and the guard disappeared behind the door for only for a few short minutes as he returned and allowed us entrance. This sizable room was sparsely decorated and only had a few pieces of furniture along the opposite wall of the room: two ornate thrones on a slightly raised platform, one larger than the other, and another plainer chair next to them off the platform. Natural sunlight flooded the room from the original arched windows along the high ceilings. This was King Baldwin's private meeting room and here we found him with the Patriarch waiting for us, seated each according to his status. More guards were stationed at four other doors leading off at the corners of the hall, armed and ready should they be needed.

I saw Warmund de Picquigny first and he was just as I had pictured him. Thinning white hair contrasted with the full, long beard that fell straight almost to beneath his chest, the Patriarch of Jerusalem sat in the lower chair, his white alb and a plain brown cloak masking a rather portly build. In contrast was the King, tall and slender, his blue and brown velvet garments hanging off narrow shoulders, and thick black hair which came down the nape of his neck, so thick and curly it almost hid the gold and ruby crown nestled in it. His face was covered by a matching beard and his expression was animated as he and the Patriarch were engrossed in a serious conversation, only looking up once our group came within a few feet of them. We stopped, Hugues and Saint-Omer at the front, and knelt in unison, heads bent. King Baldwin got up from his seat and welcomed Hugues back from his travels.

> "Hugues! It does my soul good to see you returned safe and sound," he said, touching Hugues on his shoulder, indicating he should rise.

We all waited until he had and then did the same.

> "I take it your trip was successful?" he asked, looking at each of us in return.

> "Yes, your Grace, quite," Hugues responded. "I have done what I set out to do, before you are the men I believe are best suited to the task at hand. Their backgrounds and experience will prove to be invaluable in the protection of the Holy City."

> "Whom do we have here then?" King Baldwin asked.

Hugues stepped to his side and answered, pointing as he made introductions. We bowed as we heard our names called.

"Godfrey Saint-Omer, you are aware he has been with me from the time my lord Bouillon became Princeps after the conquest. Payns de Montdidier, cousin to the Count of Flanders, Archambaud Saint-Agnan, Stephen of Blois's senior man in the crusade, Sébastien D'Ivry who served Duke Robert of Normandy, Geoffroi de Bisol, one of my men from Champagne, André de Montbard, uncle of the Abbot at the new Cistercian Abbey in Clairvaux, and two of the Abbey's brothers, Rossal and Gondamer."

King Baldwin looked at each of us and returned his gaze to me.

"You, ah…" he started.

"D'Ivry," Hugues prompted.

"Yes, D'Ivry, you were in the service of Duke Robert of Normandy?"

"I was, your Grace," I said, stepping forward slightly.

"He was one of the great leaders of our crusade, a brilliant strategist. I heard about his battles with King Henry and subsequent imprisonment. Were you with him?"

"Yes, your Grace, I fought with him at Tinchebrai and was also taken prisoner."

"Loyal to the end then? One always needs such devotion in one's life, hmm?" he said and returned to his seat.

The Patriarch, who had gotten to his feet when King Baldwin stood, remained standing and spoke.

"His Grace and I have had many discussions since your request was made prior to your departure," he said to Hugues. "We recognise the need for and importance of protecting the Holy City, a need which is increasing each and every day. Have you conferred amongst your men and are you of one mind?"

"Yes, Patriarch," Hugues replied. "These men here are willing and able to do whatever is necessary."

"Jerusalem is more and more at risk of being attacked. Bandits are harassing Christians travelling here from afar or from neighbouring settlements. They are beaten, robbed, left for dead. We need an organized force not only to deal with these existing problems, but also to put plans in place to prevent them escalating in the future. If they continue, pilgrimages will cease and our support from our Christian allies in the west will diminish. Is this something you are prepared to take on?"

"We are, Patriarch," Hugues responded. "Many of us here took the cross on the first crusade to defend the Holy Land from the infidel, our desires have not changed, nor have they dwindled. We have had the opportunity to discuss this in quite some detail during our journey here. We feel forming a brotherhood is the best way to continue defending Jerusalem, initially with just the nine of us here, later adding more with candidates who are worthy, vetted of course. But a brotherhood with two purposes. A fraternity living by Christian tenets, in particular the austere rule of Saint Augustine, as an example to those who may have strayed from the ways of our Lord. But also a fraternity which is not afraid to use its might to protect our fellow Christians with force if necessary."

Both the Patriarch and King Baldwin were listening intently, nodding and apparently liking what they were hearing.

"And who would lead it?" King Baldwin asked.

Saint-Omer stepped forward to respond.

"Your Grace, we felt it would be best if our leader was elected from within the group rather than, ah," he hesitated a moment, "chosen from outside of it."

The King thought on this. And then acquiesced without challenging it.

"Very well. I assume you already have such a person ready to take his place?" he asked rhetorically.

"Yes, your Grace. It was unanimously agreed that Hugues de Payns lead the brotherhood," Saint-Omer answered, giving a slight nod to Hugues.

That seemed to sit well with both the King and the Patriarch.

"It is settled then. What do you need of me?" King Baldwin asked.

"Your support of this order is critical for its success," Hugues replied. "We need to be seen as a united force, equals with the same authority and power to act. As we are now, we are men from various walks of life, being knighted by your Grace would accomplish creating uniformity in its initial stages. As the order grows, we would define roles and authorities as required."

King Baldwin looked across the group.

"That is easily enough done," he replied. "What of your base? Have you established one in the city?"

"None as of yet," Hugues said.

"Then you shall take rooms here in the Temple. I am expecting the arrival of my Queen and daughters for the coronations later in the year, and so we will be renovating and extending the Patriarch's palace to house the royal quarters and making it my permanent residence hopefully early next year, I see no reason not to allow you the use of the Temple now."

"That is most gracious of you, your Grace," Hugues said, bowing his head slightly. "May I be so bold to make another request?"

The King waited.

"If we are to use meeting halls in the Temple for conducting the Order's business, would it be possible to take rooms above the stables for our own? Although it will need to be clear that our duties have the backing of your royal authority, if the brotherhood is to follow the rule of Augustine, we must shun materialism and live a life that is proof of that. Using the stable rooms will keep us far enough apart from the royal apartments so as not to give any hint of hypocrisy?"

I was not aware that this had been discussed during the voyage but really had no objection to it. Being that close to the stables would also give us immediate access to our horses in case they were needed urgently and I did not really care where I slept. What I did not realize then was that Hugues had other reasons for requesting the stable rooms for our own.

"Very well," King Baldwin agreed with a bit of a shrug, "they are yours. We shall perform the knighting ceremony this evening after vespers," he said, looking at Patriarch Warmund for confirmation.

The Patriarch stepped forward and stopped a few feet in front of me.

"I remember the Duke very well. My predecessor was his personal chaplain, Arnulf was a worthy man and well respected. I have missed his guidance. And, of course, I too was dismayed to hear of the Duke's fall," he said, sounding sincere.

"That was many years ago, Patriarch," I said, "but I must admit I have felt the Duke's absence sorely over the past years. No doubt returning to Jerusalem will raise many memories of our time here."

"You will find the Holy City a much-changed place since then," the Patriarch said, "each of the Kings since have taken great pains to rebuild what had been destroyed and build anew what has been needed. We cannot let this all go to waste and back into the hands of our enemy," he said emphatically.

I remained silent which he took as my agreement. Hugues gave his thanks to the King and the Patriarch for their graciousness and generosity and then we left them to their business.

I was eager to walk about the city to see what had changed and what had not. But with our meeting with the King now at an end and having to return later that evening, we had many things to do to settle into our new quarters. The pack horses with our personal goods had arrived and Hugues very quickly had organized a few servant boys to assist us in moving them into the stables and up to the floor directly above where the horses were kept in their stalls. Whilst Hugues took one room on his own, the rest of us shared rooms, and I found myself in quarters again with Bisol.

It did not take long to bring the chests to the rooms and the Patriarch had small wooden cots with simple but fresh linen brought to us to sleep on. By sharing rooms, we were able to keep others free for work and dining. And having decided that we needed an area just for our prayers, one room was turned into our private chapel, a small, windowless enclosure, just large enough for all of us to fit in. I stood and watched as large, tall tapers were brought to the room and set atop a small table acting as an altar. When he heard that we had created this room, the Patriarch sent a standing wooden crucifix and a piece of white silk edged in lace for it to sit on. It was simple, but would suffice.

Once our rooms had been set, Bisol and I decided to walk about the city to become familiar again with the twisting alleys and lanes that snaked about in an almost maze-like fashion, and to take in the repairs that had been done and new buildings that had been erected since we were last here. We knew construction was still on-going in many places, the building materials we brought with us would be put to good use when they arrived in the next day or two. But still we were excited to become reacquainted with the city that was destined to become our home again for some time.

Exiting the stables and coming out onto the open platform, we crossed in front of the entrance to the Temple and retraced our steps off the Temple Mount and back down into the markets. But rather than going all the way back to King David's Tower, we turned up a wider lane known as Muristan Street towards the Holy Sepulchre for it was the great church we wished to see first.

We passed the refurbished hospital run by the Order of St John of Jerusalem better known as the Hospitallers, who had been providing medical care and protection to the population, Christians, Arabs and Jews alike. Bouillon had endowed their organisation when he was Princeps and Pope Paschal had formalised it in a papal bull years later, they had earned their reputation as hard-working pious men committed to nursing the sick. We could see their emblem, an eight-pointed white cross on a black background, attached to the gates leading to the hospital and just beyond to the Church of St John the Baptist, named for their patron saint. Bisol and I stopped, peering through the iron bars and saw the ribbed vaults and massive pillars inside, the ceiling a few stories high, it could easily house a couple of thousand patients at a time. We watched the brothers dressed in black robes quietly going about their duties, we were impressed with what we saw. We would need to work with the Hospitallers, hopefully our new order could relieve some of their burden of having to provide both protection as well as their medical services.

We continued up Muristan passing the Church of St Mary of the Latins and when we reached the end of the lane we turned left into a smaller alley which we were told would take us to the Sepulchre's new entrance. We had been told that it was no longer on the east side but had been moved to the south, and was accessed down the little lane we now found ourselves in. Within a few steps we emerged into a large stone courtyard and suddenly realized we were not really prepared for what we saw. The three sections we had stood in years earlier had all been enclosed in a single building and covered under a tiled roof. From where we were standing, we could no longer distinctly see the rotunda, nor could we see into the triportico, all were now hidden behind huge stone walls that included the basilica.

From the courtyard there was a stone staircase, to the right of two massive stone arched doorways, that led up and then turned left into the structure itself. We climbed these stairs and entered at the higher level and came upon a platform that surrounded and protected the place of the crucifixion. From this platform we could see how the original courtyard had been enclosed and covered with a new roof and that the basilica's apse, which had previously curved out to the open courtyard now curved into the basilica from the vaulted courtyard. The interior was lit with what seemed to be hundreds of lanterns and candle lamps, and cloths embroidered with gold and silver depicting various saints, hung from the walls which were covered in colourful frescoes. The place simply shimmered, reflecting the candlelight which flickered each time a breeze flowed through from the entrance. It was awe-inspiring to see the Church in such glory. But more was awaiting us.

We knew there had been some additions to the Church and that included the resting places of Bouillon and his brother, the first King Baldwin. They had been entombed in the entrance to the small Chapel of Adam which was next to and behind the rock of Calvary where we now stood. Both had wanted to be laid to rest at the foot of the crucifixion and so they were. Returning the way we came, back out and down the stairs, we re-entered by way of one of the two arched doors and reached the doors of the Chapel of Adam within a few seconds. We stopped upon seeing the two tombs, one on either side of the Chapel's entrance. On the walls above them were engravings dedicated to each man.

> *Here lies the famous Duke Godfrey of Bouillon, who won this whole country for the Christian faith. May his soul rest in Christ. Amen.*

> *Here lies King Baldwin, a second Judas Maccabeus, the hope of his country, the pride of the Church and its strength. Arabia and Egypt, Dan and overweening Damascus feared his power and humbly brought him gifts and tribute. Alas! This poor sarcophagus covers him.*

We knelt and gave prayer to them, remembering them in glorious times. Bouillon had been the most spiritual man I had ever met, even more so than Bishop Odo or any other cleric that had been in my life. His final resting place was a just one.

After a few reverent moments, we left the Chapel, turning west towards the rotunda. Much had been changed here too, the structure that had rested above Christ's tomb had been completely replaced by a limestone and marble aedicule with Latin phrases etched along the top edge and a small capped tower rising up at the west end. But even more stunning was the new dome which soared to the sky, many stories tall with an opening through which the sun and the moon could shine, lighting up the aedicule. Row upon row upon row of arches decorated the circular walls, building up the rotunda to a great height, drawing a visitor's eyes towards the heavens. The scale and magnitude of the work that had been done here in these last years was almost incomprehensible, astonishing really. What the crusaders had done was simply miraculous.

Bisol and I parted ways as we left the Holy Sepulchre. He had some tasks given to him by Hugues to complete before our evening meal and knighting and I had someone I needed to become reacquainted with if I could be so fortunate to find my old friend still alive after all these years. Coming out of the Church I turned west and meandered more of the small alleys and lanes in the direction of King David's Tower and soon found myself on a familiar street, nearing what I assumed was Theós's shop. I slowed my pace as I approached, not wanting to startle anyone. I stood by the open doorway, looking down at the leather goods being sold, perched on small wooden risers and hanging from hooks overhead. But still no one came out to inquire after me, so I ducked my head down and stepped into the shop, standing half-in and half-out of it. And there he was, my good friend Theós, bent over at his bench, intent as usual on his work, so intent he did not hear me until I knocked gently on the open door.

He turned, seemingly annoyed to be interrupted but then froze, his eyes growing large and his mouth dropping open in complete surprise. There was no doubt he recognized me, even though I had grown from a lad to a man in the intervening years, my unusual height even in my youth would distinguish me from others. He too had changed, his lanky frame had filled out somewhat probably due to good food and wine over the years. And his hairline had receded leaving a ring of white circling a bald patch from ear to ear. He got up from his bench and rushed to me, opened his arms for a wide embrace and kissed me, almost violently, on both of my cheeks as was his custom.

"My dear Sébastien, is it truly you?!" he asked excitedly, his face wrinkling in a smile. "I dare not believe my eyes."

"It is me, Theós, I cannot tell you how pleased I am to find you here! I was worried you may not be," I responded.

"You might have just missed me," he said, misunderstanding my meaning, but I did not correct him, I just smiled. "I might have been at the shop in the marketplace, but I prefer to spend my time working on my leather here, away from the crowds."

"You have another shop in the markets?"

"Yes, my friend, thanks to you. With the support from the Duke and his recommendations to those who remained behind, I have been quite successful in my endeavours. But enough of me, what of you? Why have you returned?"

I paused and picked up the harness he had been working on. His workmanship was still of the finest quality. I was pleased for his success.

"It has been a very long time, Theós," I said. "I have many things to tell you. I would like to see your shop, have you time to show me now? And perhaps we can find a place to sit, share some wine and speak a bit?"

Theós could not have been more eager. He called out to a young lad who appeared through a door at the side wall, a door I was sure had not been there when we had returned the shop to him before we left Jerusalem. He saw my puzzled look and chuckled.

"Your eyes do not deceive you. I have been able to acquire the shop next to this one and have turned it into a workshop, come, see," he beckoned me.

I stood at the new doorway and peered in. Sure enough, there were multiple tables and tools and pieces of leather-working machinery and tools and a couple of young lads hard at work. Beautiful, freshly sewn satchels, harnesses and other leather goods hung from hooks along the walls, the aroma of the oils used to strength and protect them filling the room. He said a few words to the boy who had come when he called out and soon we found ourselves heading into the marketplace.

Although the city was made up of what seemed to be one large open-air market containing all the various alleys and lanes, the core actually held a series of three covered markets running parallel to each other on alleys east of Muristan Street. This was the busiest part of the city during the day, with a range of goods being sold from cloths of silver, gold and deep rich colours to fruit, meats and cheeses and many other types of produce. Traders from afar brought their wares to sell here as well as the locals with their own trinkets and specialties that were a favourite of foreign visitors. Bisol and I had made our way past this section of the city as we hurried to the Holy Sepulchre, so I was glad to have the opportunity to visit it with Theós now. His shop was next to an outdoor canopied café, with small tables and chairs that I, with my size, could barely sit on and caused Théos to chortle a bit at the sight of my efforts to get comfortable.

I ordered some wine and bread and olives for us and we spent the next couple of hours talking about the years since the siege, families – he had not remarried and was pained to hear of my heartbreak – and what had been going on in our respective countries. He confirmed the concerns about the city not being secure and that attacks on pilgrims had been increasingly worrying. I told him that I was here with others to help with that, but said no more. Soon the late winter's afternoon sun was beginning to set and I needed to return to the Temple and so we said our good-byes with an invitation to come to supper from Theós as soon as I was able to find some free time from my work. I certainly intended to spend time with him, I had enjoyed our conversations when I was much younger, I felt I had learned much from him and would have much more to learn from him in the future.

* * * * * * * * * *

The evening's knighting ceremony was done quickly and quietly, only a few other than ourselves were in attendance, the King and the Patriarch wishing to keep the formation of our order secret until everything was in place. Each of us knelt, one at a time, to be first knighted by King Baldwin and then blessed by Patriarch Warmund. Although normally our titles would have been "Sir" after being knighted, we requested to be known as "Brother" to emphasize the monastic aspect to our group. When all was done the Patriarch blessed our new brotherhood and endorsed our mission of protecting Jerusalem and its surrounding territories. Whilst doing so, he gave us the name for which we were to become known, the Poor Fellow-Soldiers of Christ and of the Temple of Solomon or the Knights Templar for short. Our nine were all now equal men in the eyes of both the King and God, courtly cousin and monk alike.

After most had retired for the night, I decided to wander about the Temple Mount, the stars and the moon in the cloudless sky providing enough light to illuminate the path across the platform and up the stairs to the Dome of the Rock, or the Templum Domini as it was called now that it had been turned into a Christian church. I did not enter it, I felt there would be plenty of time for that. Instead, I sat on a low stone bench and took it in, the bright mosaics reflecting the moonlight, lifting my gaze upwards to the golden dome glistening in the dark.

It was very quiet, eery and yet comforting at the same time. There was something, was it the air? The gentle breeze that rustled my hair? The stillness of the night? I could not put my finger on it, I shuddered slightly, lost in my thoughts. It was only then that I noticed Hugues had sat down on the stone floor beside me, knees up, laying his arms across them, hands clasped.

"Beautiful, is it not?" he asked.

"It is. I was thinking about Bishop Odo. I wish he had had the chance to gaze upon it. On all of this actually," I said. "It is fitting that we have become a sort of group of military monks, it was what he once was, Bishop of Bayeux wielding a sword beside the Conqueror at Hastings. I think he would have approved."

"No doubt. He would be proud of what we have accomplished, of what you have accomplished. We have much to do still, but forming this order is taking the first step. I hope you are feeling you made the right choice to join us?"

"I believe I have," I responded. "I want my life to have meaning, I am not sure so far that it has had much."

A pang of the loss of her shot across my heart.

"Time will tell," Hugues said and with that he got up and headed back to the stable rooms, leaving me to my thoughts under the cloudless sky.

# VI

# Part Two

# 1119–1128 – Jerusalem

The next weeks turned into months filled with tasks and chores alternating with daily and nightly security checks on the outer perimeter of the city walls. When supplies were on their way from ships docking in Jaffa, some of us would ride out to escort them back to the city so they would not be pillaged by thieves on the roads. Two of our brotherhood, Rossal and Gondamer, had no military skills, so we took turns training them on various fighting techniques, on foot and on horseback until they were almost as good as those of us who had spent our lives wielding swords.

Because of my experience designing and constructing the hunting lodges and farm buildings on D'Ivry land in Oxfordshire, I was selected to work with the architects on the new churches and finding ways of shoring up those structures that needed repair and had been ignored whilst the workers focussed on the Holy Sepulchre, the Temple of Solomon and Templum Domini. The Church of the Probatike by Herod's Gate, which held the healing pool of Bethesda, was in desperate need of restoration and while we surveyed it, we realized that a large plot of land immediately next to it would be ideal for the first church to be built in its entirety by crusaders who had made Jerusalem their home. It was decided that the new church would be named after Saint Anne, Mary's mother because it was believed she had lived in a grotto there. So when I could find the time, I set my mind to it and on occasion found myself sketching late into the evenings, often going through several candles before turning in.

King Baldwin busied himself in the spring with new incursions, attacks by Turks on Antioch and Edessa needed to be quelled and he departed for the northern crusader states confident in the fact that we would remain in Jerusalem and keep it safe for his return. Antioch's Prince was still just a young boy, the namesake of his father Bohemond, and living in Bari and so Baldwin had named his own sister's husband, Roger of Salerno, as his regent and it was Roger who had made the call for Baldwin to come to his aid. But acting precipitously, Roger marched out to meet the Turks before Baldwin could arrive and he and his army were slaughtered. Baldwin was forced to become regent of Antioch which kept him from Jerusalem for the entire summer and most of the autumn.

The summer months passed without incident and without too many days of searing heat which made it easier to acclimatise to the weather which was quite different from our own in France and England. As we moved towards Christmas, an excitement could be felt in the air with the anticipation of being able to spend the holiday in the Holy Land. King Baldwin, finally returned from the northern states, had chosen Christmas Day for his coronation and that of his queen who had not yet moved to the city from Edessa where she still resided with their young daughters Melisende, Alice and Hodierna. They would be crowned in Bethlehem in the Church of the Nativity with all the pomp and ceremony due to the King of Jerusalem. Once it was over we were told by elders in the community the ceremony had been even more spectacular than that of the previous King Baldwin who had been crowned there.

Soon after the new year, our order was officially sanctioned by the council held by King Baldwin and Patriarch Warmund in Nablus, a town half-way between Jerusalem and Nazareth. This was important as it meant we could now be recognized formally beyond Jerusalem and our authority would extend throughout the Kingdom of Jerusalem which stretched from lands south of Ascalon to those north of Acre. But for the most part, our business kept us close to the city as we continued to help the bricklayers and masons who were busy with many more renovations and new buildings sanctioned by King Baldwin, including his new rooms at the Patriarch's palace. He was soon able to vacate the Temple, leaving it completely to our use. The Armenians desired a new church dedicated to St James be built in their section by the Sion Gate in the southwest corner of the city and King Baldwin's permission and our advice was sought. Even smaller structures like the Church of St Julian located down a narrow lane just steps off the Temple Mount required our attention and assistance.

And throughout those months of hard work I was fortunate to grow my friendship with Theós. I had always known he was a wise and intelligent man, having learned much from him during the time we spent together those many years ago. I was amazed to find that he had taught himself Arabic during the time in between, having felt it would make negotiating with merchants easier and keep him safe. And so I asked him if he would take me on as a pupil and teach me the ancient language and he agreed on the condition that I was taught his Coptic language as well. I found the Arabic easier, which no doubt he found frustrating.

And so our second year in Jerusalem had started peacefully and continued to be so for quite some time. We occasionally received news from the West, births, deaths, marriages, conflicts. We were now on our third Holy Father since Pope Urban had died, first Paschal, then Gelsius who had died around the time Hugues was visiting me in Sandford on Thames, and now Calixtus, each having their own anti-pope to challenge them. And the French King, Louis the Fat, who had been crowned after his father King Phillippe's death, was still in power after more than a decade on the French throne.

As the year moved into late summer we were able to celebrate the birth that August of King Baldwin's fourth daughter Ioveta and then in September share in the grief and mourning of our Hospitaller brothers for the death of their founder the Blessed Gerard. We had formed a strong relationship with their order, offering our assistance where and when we were able which was gratefully accepted, taking on some of the non-medical tasks freed their brothers to concentrate on helping their patients. So we shared their pain with the loss of their leader.

Our order began to grow with new members, mostly squires and farriers, both doing what was necessary to take care of the horses and manage the goods and supplies we needed. And a few cooks were brought in to share in the duties of feeding our increasing numbers. But we decided not to admit any further knights with the exception of one: Hugues's old overlord, Hugh de Champagne, the Count who had provided men, horses and funds for Hugues to join the crusade those many years ago. Having visited the Holy Land many times on pilgrimage, the Count had wearied of the responsibilities in Champagne, especially after repudiating his wife who had presented him with a bastard son, knowing he was incapable of creating one. Upon hearing of the order and its purpose, the Count abdicated his position in Champagne, handed the title to his nephew and heir Théobald, and came to Jerusalem begging to be allowed to join the order as a simple knight. His request was granted although he was not considered part of the inner group of nine and spent most of his time travelling to various Christian settlements and reporting any security issues he encountered.

As Christmas approached, we received some truly shocking news. William Ætheling, the son of the English King Henry, had tragically died. After successfully defeating King Louis and Duke Robert's son William Clito in battle, King Henry and his son William decided to return to England by way of the port at Barfleur. On a particularly cold early winter November night, King Henry set out before his son whilst William opted to follow on a newer vessel, the White Ship, which the owner had declared was the fastest ship on earth. But those who sailed with him had been celebrating for most of the day and were very drunk, including the oarsmen. As they headed out to sea under the darkness of the night, the port side of the ship struck rock, smashing some of the hull planks, filling the ship with water. William Ætheling and a couple of companions managed to escape on a dinghy but returned upon hearing the cries of one of his half-sisters, Matilda. But with so many drowning about them, the little boat was soon overwhelmed and sank, killing all on who were on it.

William had been only seventeen years old. And the only legitimate son of King Henry. This, of course, meant that the succession in England was now in disarray. A widower aged fifty-two, his wife having died a couple of years earlier, it was doubtful that the King would be able to sire any more sons even if he remarried. And his only other legitimate heir was a daughter, Matilda, who was living in Italy having become Empress with her marriage to the Holy Roman Emperor. So there was a great question as to who would be heir should King Henry die without having any more sons. And the first male heir in line after Matilda was, astonishingly, William Clito, Duke Robert's son, being the first male descendent of any of King Henry's brothers. We would have to wait to see how it would all be resolved, but I could not help a private wry smile knowing that there was a chance the Duke's son may become King after all that had taken place between the two brothers. I wondered how Duke Robert had received the news of William Ætheling's death knowing that his son was next in the line of succession.

Dispatches received told us that Stephen of Blois was supposed to have been on the ship that night, the same son of Blois who had been with us on crusade and the same who had been my nemesis at the tourneys many years ago. I am sure his mother Adela was forever grateful that her son was spared. Rumour had it that he said he had been concerned about the state of the crew but others have said he suffered from an ill belly. No matter which was true, he must have felt God had protected him from the fate of so many others that night.

Early in the new year of 1121 I received heart-breaking news: my beloved mother had died, the doctors reckoned from consumption. My brother Roger sent a letter detailing her illness which at first had not seemed serious, but then the cold of the January winter took hold and within a few days she was gone. They buried her next to our father in the Abbey of Our Lady of Bec with the ceremony she was due. I was truly sorry not be able to be there and spent many days sitting in the Holy Sepulchre, not really in prayer but deep in thought, wondering about those that had gone from my life. Séraphine, little Isabel, Bishop Odo, my father and now my mother, one by one they were leaving my life, each before their time. My mind meandered, moving from one memory to another, provoking in me a mixture of emotions of extremes which I found exhausting. After two years in Jerusalem I was no further along in finding my way and I was becoming disheartened. I needed to discover my path, the reason why I was here. Until then, I would continue as I was, living each day as it came, doing whatever tasks each day brought whilst at the same time trying, and failing, to understand the purpose of my existence.

\* \* \* \* \* \* \* \* \*

The years passed, a lot of time spent building in the city, providing protection for those on pilgrimage from the west and assisting King Baldwin in his campaigns to wrest more lands from the Turks and the Saracens. But then in our eighth year came the day the future Queen of Jerusalem came into my life.

I saw the hem of her flowing robes before I saw anything else, they came into view as I was bent over, half-kneeling, one of my horse's front legs resting across my knee as he tolerantly waited for me to finish securing a new shoe in the stables next to the Temple. The old one was being stubborn and I worked the hook in and out, trying to loosen the nails as quickly as I could without causing damage to the hoof. My peripheral vision caught the sight first but then I realized the flurry of silks had come to rest in front of me. Grasping hold of the horse's lower leg so as not to lose control of him, I looked up and saw the exquisite face of Melisende, King Baldwin's daughter, looking down at me, a soft smile and an expression of patience mixed with hopeful anticipation.

The eldest of the four princesses, she was now twenty-two years old, the heir apparent who would take control of the kingdom of Jerusalem from her father as he had not sired any sons. And ever since she and her sisters had come from Edessa almost eight years ago, her father had ensured she was educated to the same level as the sons of the local nobles. It was perhaps because of these studies and preparation for the role she would take on with the death of King Baldwin that she had not yet married. She was, without a doubt, the most eligible and worthy match in the Christian world east of Constantinople. Whoever married her would naturally, it was assumed, rule in her name. How wrong they would be.

Few had seen Melisende or spent time in her presence but rumours abounded of her inner strength, intellect and wisdom at such a young age, Baldwin having taken great care with her education knowing she was to succeed him. And now, this mysterious creature was standing in front of me.

I looked up and met her gaze, intense and yet calming at the same time. I immediately lowered my head and greeted her.

"My lady," I said.

"You are the one called D'Ivry, yes?" she asked, her low-toned voice soft and yet commanding.

"Yes, my lady," I responded, surprised that she knew my name. "I am Sébastien D'Ivry."

"My father has spoken to me of the band of men who have taken vows to protect the city and its inhabitants, you in particular seem to have made an impact on him."

This took me aback, not really knowing what to say to her not being able to think what I could have done to receive such recognition. I released the horse's leg and slowly stood to my full height. It was then that I saw the two female servants standing behind her, hands clasped in front of themselves, eyes downcast and two guards on either side of them, equipped with small swords at the ready to protect their mistress.

"Ah, I see now why you might stand out in a crowd," she said with a smile.

I smiled back at her, impressed with her cheeky humour.

"Yes, I have always had great height, even as a boy. It has its advantages," I responded adding, "and its curses."

"No doubt," she agreed with a twinkle in her eye.

"Is there something I may help you with, my lady?"

"Yes, well, actually, it is Master Payns that I seek. It is common knowledge that preparations are underway for ambassadors to travel to Acre to discuss my hand in marriage to Count Fulk, I wish to speak with him regarding this but I cannot gain access to the Temple without an escort."

It was common knowledge that King Baldwin wanted a strategic marriage for his heir and that Count Fulk of Anjou was the desired match. Fulk had been travelling in Outremer on various crusades the past few years and, like Hugh de Champagne, had joined our group as an extended and distanced member, providing funds and goods to us for a few years. But it was the wealth and power he brought to the battles Baldwin was having in Damascus that was his real value. But Melisende would not be able to enter the Temple to meet with Hugues without someone accompanying her.

"Is the Master aware of your desire to speak with him?"

"I am sure he is aware that I would wish to discuss this matter with him, but no, there is nothing formally arranged. I thought it would be opportune since I find myself here on the Temple Mount today," she said carefully.

I was impressed with the way she spoke. Whilst the words were gentle and unassuming, there was no doubt of the meaning and intent behind them. She knew I would know that to come here would have required a significant effort as she and her sisters were mostly confined to the Patriarch's palace and grounds. She was telling me to take her to Hugues without actually telling me to take her. She would indeed make a formidable ruler.

"It shall be my pleasure to bring you to him, my lady," I said and motioned to a stable boy to come finish shoeing the horse.

I escorted her and her entourage to the entrance of the Temple but stopped short of the massive doors.

"Your men..." I started and pointed but she was already ahead of me, gesturing to her two guards to stay put.

We crossed over the threshold and stepped into the large open entry hall and made our way through the relatively new corridors to the rear of the building where Hugues had his private meeting rooms. I asked her to wait a moment so I could announce her and confirm Hugues was available which I knew he would be. After all, this would be the ruler of Jerusalem upon Baldwin's death, it would be insulting to refuse her. Within a few moments, she was ushered in and I left them to their discussions. And even though our encounter had lasted but a few minutes, the lady had left an impression on me.

That evening I was called to a meeting with Hugues. I was hoping he was going to tell me about the discussions earlier in the day with Melisende, I had to admit I was curious. I had not really given any thought to the proposed arranged marriage that was primarily strategic but now that I had met the princess I found myself oddly uncomfortable with this arrangement. Perhaps it was because I was fortunate to have married for love despite the fierce objections of some of my beloved's family, and I was troubled that this special lady may not have such luxury and freedom in choosing her own mate. Hopefully she would follow in her father's footsteps in this regard too.

Hugues was studying some paperwork when I arrived for our meeting. He got right to the point as usual.

"Sébastien, the King has requested that I and five of the brothers travel with the nobles who are negotiating the marriage treaty between the Count of Anjou and Princess Melisende. The talks will be held at the Hospitaller house in Acre, we leave in a few days. I will be taking Saint-Omer, Montdidier, Saint-Agnan, Montbard and Rossal, so I will need to delegate an interim Grand Master, I would like that to be you."

I was at first a bit disheartened not to be accompanying Hugues and the brothers on this mission as I had not been to Acre since we first arrived in the Holy Land so many years ago, but then was honoured to be chosen to step in for Hugues. It was a huge responsibility to be Grand Master and Hugues was demonstrating his trust in me to take this on. I told him I would be honoured to do so.

"There is something else. With the treaty being as important as it and with many who oppose it, the Princess's safety may be at risk. We need extra protection for her."

"I will see to that personally," I said.

"See that you do. Nothing can stop this marriage from going through. Fulk is quite powerful in France and rumours are circulating that negotiations may be underway for his son Geoffrey to be wed to King Henry's daughter Matilda now that she has been widowed. It would do us good to have the backing of the English King for our cause."

I understood his meaning. King Henry's support would naturally come through the alliance between Fulk and King Baldwin if the three families became entwined in marriage. Of course I was witness to many instances where family connections only ended badly even after starting out with great hope and good will. I remained silent on the matter. But something stirred within me.

* * * * * * * * * *

I saw off Hugues and the five brothers before dawn a few days later and wished them well on their travels and mission. I also bid Hugues to speak with King Baldwin when he arrived in Acre from Damascus to give him ease about the protection of his eldest daughter. I had spoken to the lady herself after receiving my orders from Hugues and she seemed pleased to know I would not be going with the others and instead would be remaining in Jerusalem. We had agreed to meet once a week in the reception hall at the Patriarch's palace so I could give her any updates on the negotiations and anything else that she should be aware of. In her father's absence, she was the de facto royal authority in Jerusalem and thus she was entitled to being kept informed.

I quite quickly found myself looking forward to our meetings, she was a breath of fresh air from the brothers' company I had become accustomed to and I found myself relaxing more and more in her presence as did she in mine. She insisted on calling me by my Christian name and allowed me to call her by hers whenever we found ourselves alone which was rare, her ladies or guards were almost always near. But I was delighted nonetheless. Her warmth soon reminded me of what I missed in being near a beautiful woman and her vivaciousness and sharp wit started to bring me out of the shell I had retreated to since Séraphine's death, although this was not without its effect of injecting some guilt into my thoughts. I found myself staying awake thinking of her dark, bright eyes and how she gestured with her hands whenever she was telling a story, but then immediately shut the thoughts down, feeling that I was betraying my long-gone lady. But I also could not escape the feeling that I was being released from my self-imposed prison by this woman who made me laugh.

Our weekly meetings soon turned to a few times a week and eventually began to take place outside of the Patriarch's palace. She felt, and quite rightly so, that if she were to become Queen of the Kingdom of Jerusalem, she needed to become acquainted with more than just her cloistered rooms. So we began our walks, with guards both visible and hidden for her protection everywhere we went. She asked me to show her all the building works that were happening in the city and asked many questions about their structure, design and composition. Her curiosity seemed insatiable and there were times, especially in the beginning, when I suspected she was simply making conversation. But she proved me wrong time and time again, not only remembering everything that I told her, but asking more and more detailed questions. She simply drank in everything she saw, heard, witnessed and always wanted to know more.

She seemed particularly taken with the ruins of the Byzantine basilica with what had been the healing pool in the northwest corner of the city and was impressed that I had many years ago created some sketches for a church to be built next to it. For a variety of reasons the work on the church had yet to start, but she asked to see the drawings any way. And so one evening after supper we found ourselves pouring over them, she again asking her questions with sincere interest. She was eager to see this church built and told me she would see to it if her father did not.

Early one evening we found ourselves exiting the stables after returning from a long hack with two of our best horses. The day had turned cool in the autumn afternoon and the sun in the west cast long shadows across the Temple Mount. Instead of returning to the Patriarch's palace, Melisende and I walked amongst the cypress trees aligning the walkway from the Temple on the south side of the Mount to the stone staircase leading to the Dome of the Rock, or the Templum Domini as it was now called, on the north side. Each time I saw this structure I was captivated by its colourful design, the blues and golds of the mosaics always sparkling in the sunlight, its golden dome a beacon that could be seen for miles.

Oddly enough I had only ever stepped foot inside once, after the city had been given over to the crusaders and before I left the Holy Land with Duke Robert. But even then something made me feel almost unworthy of doing so and since my return I had been satisfied simply to sit and marvel at it from a distance. There was still something awe-inspiring about this having been a sacred holy place for both the Muslims and Jews for centuries. But Melisende headed for its entrance and I suddenly felt my apprehension of entering it dissipate.

Once inside I immediately saw the changes that had been made to turn it into a Christian place of worship. Still remaining were the exquisite immense square marble columns and rounded columns which held the dome aloft, its convex ceiling painted in a myriad of gold and silver. A series of arched openings at the base of the dome allowed the daylight or moonlight to cast their beams throughout the interior and the golden hues of the late afternoon lit up all the gold on the walls. The columns created two ambulatories, one nearer the outside walls and one inside, closer to the Foundation Stone, the rock from which Mohammed ascended and where Abraham was charged to slay his son Isaac. But this is where the most substantial change had taken place: a large marble floor now covered the Foundation Stone to form a choir and altar. And the Islamic scripts from the Qur'an that decorated the walls had been covered over with Latin texts and icons, obviously trying to erase any Muslim presence. I found myself shocked somewhat to see this but did not know why I was having this response, after all what was this Stone to me?

We walked around the inner octagonal walls in silence, looking up at the dome which, whilst a bit smaller than that of the Sepulchre, surpassed it in beauty. Each of the walls had torches which lit up the interior. Upon almost completing the walk around, we came upon a set of steps at the south-eastern corner that led down to a small wooden door. We looked inquisitively at each other and, as if reading each other's minds, we both tried to descend the steps at the same time which only succeeded in us colliding and then stepping back, laughing, both indicating to the other to go first. I took the lead only for protection sake, not sure what or who might be beyond the door.

Surprisingly it was unlocked and, gently opening inward, it creaked slightly and revealed more steps down into a darkened space. I turned to suggested we needed a torch but Melisende was ahead of me – as always – and had quickly retrieved one from the nearest wall and handed it to me. In the flicker of the torchlight, I could see the excitement dance in her eyes, eager for an adventure. This lady never ceased to surprise me.

Stepping down and bending my head carefully so as not to smack it on the stone entry, I held the torch before me to light the way ahead. I felt Melisende place her hand on my back to steady herself as she followed me and I instinctively reached behind and took hold of it, an act that was utterly forbidden for me to do. But she did not let go until we had cleared the last stair.

Reaching the bottom we could see we had stepped down into a cave-like room, walls hewn out of the rock. What looked like a small stone altar, carved out of the bedrock as well, sat facing the base of the Stone. But upon a closer look, it did not seem to be an altar, it was much older than the work that had been done above.

Once I got my bearings I knew it was actually a mihrab, a niche created in the wall that pointed in the direction of Mecca so the Muslims would know which way to pray. I said as much to Melisende but something told me she already knew what it was.

There was an ever so slight breeze that seemed to come from nowhere and we both felt it. We stood still and suddenly it dawned on us where we were. This was the Well of Souls, where the dead go to await Judgement Day. I felt unnerved, as though I was trespassing and was somewhere I really should not be. And then it all came upon me, years of turning inward, of refusing to honestly admit how the loss of her had ripped my very soul, my total inability to grieve. I sank to my knees, my mind's eye mobbed with memories and soon my face was soaked by the tears that now came with gut-wrenching sobs.

Melisende knelt at my side and wrapped her arms around me, practically cradling me. I am sure she must have been shocked to see a man such as myself in this state and bewildered as to why. But she never asked, and I never explained. We stayed like this for some time, her words soothing and calming me. And when she knew I was ready, with a nod of her head she silently suggested we leave this place. She went ahead of me, I followed with the torch firmly in my grip. I turned and shut the door, giving it an extra tug, just to ensure it was closed.

As we returned to the entrance Melisende stopped, turned to me and took both of my hands in hers. She looked up into my eyes and smiled sweetly, her touch gentle and warm. It was then that I knew I was in love with her. And I grimaced inside, knowing she could never be mine. It was as if she read my mind and felt the same for her expression changed to one of slight melancholy. She then placed the palm of my left hand on her face against her right cheek, smooth and softer than anything I had felt since that of my lady. She then kissed it, lingering just long enough for me to know for certainty the meaning of it. And then, without a word, she slipped out into the cool air of the early autumn evening on the Temple Mount.

* * * * * * * * * *

It was in 1128 early in our ninth year of being in the Holy City that the repercussions of a decision made by Hugues upon his return from Acre were going to change our lives forever. When we had first arrived in the city, we had concentrated our efforts on the restoration work above ground across the city but Hugues determined we needed to focus on what lay under the city. We had heard rumours about the original Temple's walled foundations continuing deep beneath the Mount and that the stables, which we now called home, were only the top couple of floors with many more bricked-in layers existing underneath. So Hugues ordered excavations to start on the ground floor of the stables in the far corner, out of sight of anyone visiting the Mount or coming into the Temple. Even those using the stables for their horses could not see our activities as we closed off the area from use. And so, after obtaining the tools necessary for the job, we began to dig, working in pairs, starting first by removing the large flagstone floor slabs.

It was arduous work that was done only when there was time in between our other responsibilities, but it only took a couple of days before we had our first success with Montdidier and Saint-Agnan breaking through what would have been the ceiling of a massive, vaulted room beneath our rooms, causing clouds of dust to swirl up from down below. We all took turns peering into the darkness, we could barely make out the floor so torches were brought and held low so we could see better.

Montdidier, Saint-Agnan, Bisol and I descended one after the other, lowering ourselves with the rope ladder Montdidier had unfurled earlier, bringing the torches with us to get a better look. We found what looked like an almost exact replica of the structure at our ground level, with many square stone pillars and arches, most a man's height in thickness and each embedded with heavy iron rings for tying horses' reins, all surrounded by masses of dust, dirt and other debris covering the floor, knee-deep in some areas and over our heads in others. We could see the structure extend just as far north as did the above-ground stables, and bricked up stone arches along the north edge providing more support for the floors above. And making our way through the rubble with our torches we could see the structure went just as far west as well.

We knew we would have a large task ahead of us clearing it all out. It took a couple of weeks to clean out this floor, finding nothing of any consequence and dumping the dirt in ditches outside the city walls. The Patriarch had told us that Solomon's original temple had been destroyed by the Babylonia King Nebuchadnezzar, and that centuries later King Herod had expanded the second Temple to the east and to the south. The expansion was particularly difficult to the south as the Mount sloped down to the valleys, so he had the ground raised to be level with the north side, building huge stone arches to support the platform and filling in all the gaps with earth and rubble. This meant encasing the lower levels of the stables with an immense amount of earth that had obviously settled over the centuries.

Hugues came down to inspect the work we had done, he seemed pleased with what we had achieved and encouraged us to press on opening up more areas to the west which did not take long once the main hall leading from one section to the next had been discovered and cleared. As soon as the first level down was sufficiently cleared, we were able to move to the next using a set of stairs we had uncovered that had once been used to move from one level to another.

The digging continued for some weeks from the early spring to early summer, the progress slow but steady. It was when we had reached what seemed to be the lowest level that an arch was discovered in the wall facing east and excavating this we discovered a hidden entrance that led out of the city itself, and from the state of it, probably blocked for many hundreds of years. Because of natural rock formations on the exterior of the wall, the entrance had been hidden from sight unless one was practically standing directly in front of it, so we knew we would have a secret entrance if we wanted to open it. But Hugues's concentration was not on the back wall of the stables, but looking for other blocked passageways leading out from the lowest level. And it did not take too long to find what he was hoping we would.

The opening had been cleverly disguised, the original supporting arch that would have kept the stone from crashing down upon heads had been removed when the stones were added to block up the passage. It was Saint-Omer with his sharp eyesight who caught the inconsistencies of the newer stones which had been used versus those of the original wall. Once seen, it was easy to spot the added stones which had settled over the years, breaking the straighter lines of the others in the walls. So with Hugues's permission, we began removing them, being careful to provide support, we did have, after all, several tons of stone pressing down upon us.

After removing the first layer we were greeted by a pile of stones and rocks that rose up as far as we could see. This posed a difficult problem. We did not know how high it actually was, we did not know how deep it went and even if we removed the stones starting from the top we risked more falling into place and potentially into the area we had just cleared. And if that happened, what would else could come toppling down? All of us gathered that night with many torches lighting the area around us to discuss the matter. Eventually it was decided to remove some of the stones at the top of would have been the original passage and this proved to be all that was needed.

After chiselling our way through we revealed that the original arch had carried through which meant the pile of stones we were seeing was simply for hiding the fact the arch existed and preventing anyone from using the passageway. So with increased energy and enthusiasm, we all started pulling out the stones, creating a new heap, and eventually clearing them completely. And what we saw amazed us. The larger passageway led to a smaller arched passageway, a tunnel of sorts, just tall enough for a normal-sized man to stand up straight in. And it was not blocked at all. I, of course, had to bend my head but this did not bother me. I grabbed the nearest torch and headed inside with the others following close behind, excited to see where this would lead.

The tunnel's path meandered, the ceiling occasionally rising, giving my neck and back much needed relief from the aches that had started to set in. Its width fluctuated from very narrow in places to wide enough for two men to stand abreast. The air was dank and the surfaces we walked on well-worn and uneven which was startling when we realized just how long anyone had walked them. We had gone only a short length when we reached a point where the tunnel forked, Bisol, Saint-Omer and I continued on a relatively straight path to the north, the others on a curve to the west. Both ends of the tunnels were blocked with more stone piles which we assumed had other entrances behind just as the one on our end had. It was then that we decided to retreat to the stables, grateful for the refreshing air that hit us as we emerged, the staleness of it in the tunnels was strong.

Hugues decided we should excavate the far ends of the tunnels to see where they came out, it could be advantageous to us depending on where the exits lay within the city. We lined the tunnels with small torches high in the walls, giving just enough light to illuminate the paths. After a couple of weeks of trudging back and forth I began to wonder if there may not be any other tunnels leading off of these. I mentioned this to Bisol one night after we had retired to our rooms and he agreed it was odd that we had found none and that undoubtedly there were more to be found. So, unable to sleep, Bisol and I returned to the tunnel, picked up our torches and began a close inspection of the walls leading from the entrance, he worked the east wall, I worked the west.

We had been at it for what must have been a couple of hours and had covered most of the main tunnel and the extension to the north after the fork, becoming rather disheartened with not having detected a single crack or significant indentation in the walls, when we decided to take a break and give our eyes a rest. We slumped onto the ground on my side of the tunnel and reached for our calf-skin flasks which we had filled with some good wine before descending into the lower levels. Frustrated, Bisol took a swig from his and pressed his head against the wall behind him.

But something was off and he began to feel bits and pieces of the wall crumbling and falling onto his neck. He reached up and felt dirt on the back of his head and turned to see what was causing it. He asked me to bring my torch closer which I did, and both of us knelt on the floor leaning in to scrutinise this section of the wall. To our amazement, we realized it was not stone but hardened mud which was dry and cracked and barely hanging together. The pressure of Bisol's head had ruptured the frail bond and with some ease we were able to use just our fingers to dig away a significant portion of the wall. When we could go no further, we used our handpicks to pull down more, eventually revealing a small, squarish indentation, just large enough for a man to crawl through if more rocks and stones had not blocked the way.

We decided to press on and not wake the others, thinking that uncovering where this led would be better than showing just another blocked tunnel. And the area we were working on was so small, being about a man's shoulder-width wide, that only one man could work inside it at a time. So we painstakingly removed as much as we could both reaching in from our side of the entrance and then taking turns laying on our stomachs and handing rocks to the other who sat outside.

I had been inside on my second turn inside when I inadvertently pushed on the rock pile in front of me and it moved, telling me we were near its end and that there was an opening on the other side. I edged my way back out to tell Bisol what I had found and to reached for some wine to soothe my dry throat. We agreed that the next step would be for me to go back in, on my back and feet first so I could then use the force of my legs pushing against the rocks with my boots, forcing the rocks back and, hopefully, into whatever space there appeared to be. This would also allow Bisol to pull me to safety should there be any sort of collapse.

It only took a few kicks before the rocks fell back revealing a black hole leading to a space the size and depth of which we could not yet judge. I crawled back out and told Bisol what I had done and suggested he be the one who should go back in and see what was inside as it had been his head that started us on this path. He grinned and, taking one of the torches from the wall of the main tunnel, crawled in head first, keeping the flame well ahead of him.

"Sweet Jesu!!" I heard him exclaim and I stuck my head in as far as I could get, trying to see whatever I could but his body was in the way.

He looked back at me with a look of surprise on his face. We both scrambled back out so he could explain.

"I extended the torch ahead of me and into the space and then crawled up to the edge," he said, rather out of breath from excitement and looking up and down the passageway to see if anyone was there. "And when I peered over I saw a cavernous space, large and very deep and wider than I could see with just the one torch. There does not appear to be any steps or way down, I think it would be best if we used another rope ladder to descend. Here," he said offering me the torch, "you take a look."

I took it from him and crawled quickly to the edge of the small tunnel. Bisol had been quite accurate. It took a moment for my eyes to adjust to the dimly lit darkness, but I could see the same cave-like formation Bisol had described. We needed to get down and see what was there.

While I was in the tunnel Bisol had fetched another rope ladder which we affixed with iron pegs at the top of the cave's entrance and rolled it out. Bisol went first, slowly stepping his way down the wooden slats as I steadied the rope ladder at the top. The torch illuminated more and more as he descended and I tried to see what else was down there. Suddenly he lost his footing on the penultimate slat and losing his grip on both the torch and the ladder he tumbled, crying out. For a split second I was quite anxious for my friend as I could not tell how deep the cave was but it was all for nought as its floor was only a few more feet and Bisol landed only with a stumble which did not seem to cause any injury. He picked up the torch which had fallen a few feet beside him, told me he was unhurt and slowly turned, holding the torch up so we both could see.

The cave was quite large, probably twice the size of one of our rooms above the stables. The walls were all stone and undecorated and there seemed to be some sort of shelving carved into them on the north side, leading us to believe that this may have been used for storage. There did not appear to be any entrances or exits to the space except for the one we just descended from and there was nothing else except dirt and dust to be seen. I joined Bisol, being careful on the ladder and bringing with me another torch which we lit using his. We found slots carved into the walls and with some effort made the torches fit so we could look about unencumbered. It was all very perplexing, there was no obvious reason for why such precautions had been taken to protect this room to the extent that it had been.

After a few more minutes we knew we had done enough for the night and that Hugues must be told at first light, hopefully he would be pleased with what we had discovered. When we returned to the surface level we were stunned to find that dawn was already on the horizon and that we had been missed at morning prayers. We found Saint-Omer in his room and asked him where we could find Hugues and were told he was at work in the main meeting hall. We suggested he accompany us as we had news and found Hugues engrossed in discussing the day's tasks with the others and looked up in surprise when we arrived dust-covered and looking a bit rattled. We quickly updated them on our night-time activities and without a moment's hesitation we were leading everyone back down to the tunnels.

The nine of us stood in this cave-like room now well-lit with multiple torches providing an abundance of light. And still nothing leapt out to us as special or unusual and yet Hugues had agreed with our earlier thoughts and musings about the extraordinary fortifications. Somebody did not want anyone in here. We needed to find out why. Hugues was not satisfied to just let it be and so Bisol and I were ordered to spend some time here and to give our daily tasks to others for the next couple of days. But he also ordered us to get some rest once we had told him we had been in the tunnels throughout the night, he could obviously tell fatigue was setting in. Despite our protestations we knew Hugues was right and repaired to our room with Montbard agreeing to wake us at sext. Our mystery room would have to wait.

\* \* \* \* \* \* \* \* \* \*

True to his word Montbard woke us just before the mid-day meal so we were able to join the others in the dining hall in the main building. But our eagerness to return to the tunnels would not be contained and as soon as it was permissible Bisol and I were on our way.

Dropping several lit torches gently down unto the cave floor below us, we descended the rope ladder and quickly secured the torches in more cracks in the walls or using some of the rocks scattered about the room to support them along the edges of floor so that we could get a good view of our surroundings. We also had our small pickaxes ready for whatever we would find that might need their use. And so we began, each of us on either side of the rope ladder that hung down from the tunnel entrance above us, slowly and methodically examining the walls and the floors for something, anything that would give us a clue as to why this cave had been so well sealed. We had been down there for a few hours when Gondamer appeared and lowered a wooden bucket that contained two lambskins of warm ale for us to drink and a few pieces of bread and a jar of olives for when we were ready to rest. He told us that he would be staying in the passageway up top to be of assistance should we need him and to go for help should anything go awry for us down below.

Frustrated, we decided to stop for a moment and take advantage of the refreshments. Sitting down on opposite sides of the cave, we rested, arms on knees, holding onto a lambskin each and taking greedy gulps for though the air was cool our throats were parched.

"I do not think there is anything here, Sébastien," Bisol said dejectedly. "The walls are smooth like the day they were made, I cannot see anything, this must have been used for storage, the only access in and out seems to be at the top," he added pointing up. "Of course why the entrance to a storage room is up there is a bit of a mystery."

I sat quietly, contemplating his words. I looked up at the entrance and let my eyes follow the flow of the rope ladder downward, then my eyes wandered over the walls and towards where what looked to be shelves had been carved out of the stone.

"Indeed. But whatever it was used for…" I stopped, my attention grabbed by what looked like a deformity in the underside of one of the stone shelves my eyes had come to rest on.

Not noticeable when looking at it straight on or from above when standing, it became obvious from the angle I was at sitting on the floor. I was suddenly struck by the memory of the latches that miraculously opened walls to hidden tunnels in the church in Bari when I first met the Holy Father Pope Urban and wondered if something similar might not be here. I got up and walked over to the stone shelves, bending over almost in half to examine the underside of them. Then standing up straight, I ran my hands underneath the shelf at my waist height, my fingertips feeling along, examining every aspect of the shelves which were about a half a palm in height and my lower arms' length wide. I continued feeling where the shelf met the stone wall at the back.

And then I felt it. A gap, just wide enough for the fingers of one hand to reach up into, extending back into the wall. I looked at Bisol who must have read my mind for he was at my side in an instant, kneeling with a torch in his hand to get a good look at what I had found.

I pushed the palm of my right hand against the wall part of the gap and nothing happened. Then curling my fingers into the gap I pushed down and nothing happened. I looked at Bisol who shook his head silently telling me he was seeing no movement. So I reached up with my left hand and felt along the underside of the shelf again until I found the second gap. This time I combined the movements, pushing down with my fingers and against the wall with the palms of my hands and that is when it happened – the wall moved backwards and a section fell away, opening a gap from my waist to my feet, but leaving the shelf in front of it intact and in place. An ingenious device, it took me some time to figure out how exactly it worked.

Unlike the cave we broke into, this space was much smaller, a cubby-hole of sorts, just large enough for me to crawl into and then, once inside, barely kneel upright in. Bisol handed me one of the torches so I could see and, with an involuntary jolt, I suddenly knew the reason for the excessive security measures.

Before me sat three large clay jars, two of them almost three-quarters as tall as the space itself, the third short and squat, all with caps covering rather wide mouths, all looking as though they had not been touched in many, many years. The undisturbed layer of dust at their base reinforced this, it was clear nothing alive had been near them in quite some time.

"We need to fetch Hugues," I said quietly.

Bisol shouted up to Gondamer to bring our leader but quick and then returned to help me get the jars out of their tomb. Still on my knees I examined them, looking first for any cracks or any breaks and found none. But looking at them closely, I could see etchings, shapes and designs I did not think I had seen before. Did they hold any meaning? Was this some sort of language new to me? But there was something familiar about them, but my mind could not pull it from my memory.

I gently moved one of them ever so slightly, not sure of their strength or delicateness, testing them, not wanting to damage them in any way. They needed to be tipped on their sides to get them out of the opening in the wall and into the outer cave avoiding the shelf which was still in place, so together Bisol and I slowly tilted them horizontally and carried them out into the open, carefully setting them upright again, making sure the caps did not come off. By the time the three jars were in the cave, Hugues, Saint-Omer and Gondamer had arrived. We stood in a group looking at our find, walking around them, studying the markings which we could now see more clearly.

We first noticed the crosses that appeared on the sides of each of the jars, all the same design, but not the kind of crosses we used in our daily prayers. Instead of the fourth arm being longer than the other three, all four arms were of the same length, and each end flared out to points. I knew what it was a split second before Hugues spoke it aloud.

"Coptic crosses," he said.

He was right. These and others like them were displayed in the market stalls of Coptic vendors, including Theós's shop which is also where I now knew I recognized the other markings from. They were Coptic writings but none of us knew what they said. The two taller jars had

$$Aλήθεια$$

engraved on two opposite sides whilst the shorter had

$$το ένα$$

on two opposite sides.

"Something is inside of each of them," I said. "I could feel movement when we tipped them over to bring them out here."

"Have you tried removing the caps?" Hugues asked.

Bisol and I both shook our heads.

"We wanted to wait for you before doing anything to do them," I answered.

Hugues stepped up to the jar closest to him, leaned down and studied the lid. There did not seem to be any locking mechanism on it and so with a deep breath he placed his hands on either side and gently twisted, first one way then another. Small granules of sand came out from underneath and fell to the floor which told us the lid was slowly coming free. Hugues waited a moment, then tried again, this time only in one direction and eventually we heard a grinding noise as the lid gave way and turned, scraping against the lip of the jar, eventually coming off. Hugues set the lid slowly onto the floor, reached for a torch and peered in, then straightened with a bit of a start. Handing his torch to Saint-Omer, he put his right arm into the jar as far as it could go, up to his armpit, clasped something and withdrew it. In his hand was a small set of parchment papers bound in leather covers with golden stitching, encircled with twine cord knotted on one side.

We all gathered close around Hugues trying to get a look at our discovery. He turned it over slowly in his hands, handling it with care, looking intently at what seemed to be more writings on the outside of it. Whilst the others were examining it, Bisol opened the second of the three jars and pulled out another packet much like the others, but slightly larger and with plain leather covers.

I went to the third, stouter jar, carefully twisted open its lid, peered in and noticed something sitting at the bottom. Just as Hugues and Saint-Omer had done, I placed my arm inside where my fingers soon hit a hard object covered in what felt like cloth. Taking hold of it I could tell it was quite heavy and I adjusted my grasp to get a better grip so as not to drop it. I pulled the object out and determined it was a slab of some sort, only a finger's width thick, squared in shape at one end but coming to a point at the other, covered in an off-white linen cloth and secured with the same type of cord used on the leather-bound pages from the other jars.

The others were now staring at me and what I held in my hands. I looked at Hugues who nodded his assent. I loosened the knots of the cord, handed it to Saint-Omer, and gently unwrapped the folds of the cloth revealing a most exquisite piece of green gemstone, mostly clear but with cloudy veins winding their way throughout. It seemed almost too much to believe that a piece this size could be emerald, but that is what I assumed it was. More intriguing was what was written on one side, the reverse being smooth and bare. It looked as if more of the same characters that were on the outside of the jars had been written here, finely etched into the almost glass-like surface. Hugues stepped over and leaned down close to examine it but seemingly not daring to touch it.

"The Emerald Tablet," he said, his voice barely perceptible.

He seemed more in awe than surprised and I had to wonder why. But I did not have a chance to ask as he straightened and turned to the rest of the group.

"Do any of you know this language?" Hugues asked.

Everyone shook their heads. Even though I had been getting lessons in the language from Théos, I was not capable of giving the meaning of these words.

"I do not believe any of the other brothers do," Saint-Omer said.

"We need to find someone who we can trust to decipher this," Hugues said.

"I believe I know just the person who can help," I offered up. "He has been here ever since the crusade, he was a Coptic refugee, a leatherworker, who came to work in the Duke's army when we were at Nabi Samuil. After the capture of the city he decided to stay, re-opened his shop after we departed for home. His name is Théos…"

"Of course!" Saint-Omer exclaimed looking at me. "I know him well, Bouillon used him often, King Baldwin still has him in service. He is a good man, I believe him to be trustworthy. Shall he be fetched?" he asked Hugues.

"Yes, but if it is decided he can be useful, let him start with the booklets only for now. If he does well, we can have him look upon the tablet then. Return it to its container and put it back into there," he said pointing to the opening, "making sure it cannot be seen from here. And needless to say, nothing is mentioned outside the highest level of the order about these discoveries," he said sternly, looking at each of us in turn.

Gondamer was sent to bring Théos but only to the meeting hall in the Temple, not to the newly discovered tunnels. Hugues wanted to make sure my old friend was as trustworthy as we believed him to be. We returned the bundled pages and the Emerald Tablet to their respective jars, secured the lids and moved the jar with the Emerald Tablet back into the smaller space, out of sight. Rossal was instructed to keep guard whilst we discussed the matter, not wanting to bring them up into the warmer air in case it damaged them.

Théos came immediately when Gondamer told him he was needed and that Hugues had requested he attend upon him. Even though Bisol and I were covered in dirt and dry mud from our work, we met Théos as we were, hoping he would not take notice. But as he entered into the hall his keen eyes quickly scanned those in the room, stopping only slightly to notice my dust-covered leggings which he must have found odd knowing Hugues's demands that we maintain proper appearances to respect the honour of our Order. But he said nothing, bowing slightly to Hugues who was sitting at the head of the table. The rest of us remained standing.

"Théos," Hugues began, "thank you for coming so quickly."

"Of course my lord," Théos responded, "Anything I can do to assist you and the Order."

"D'Ivry and Saint-Omer tell us that you have been in service to the crusader Kings since Jerusalem was conquered, is this correct?" Hugues asked.

"Yes it is, my lord. I was blessed to have happened upon Sébastien after all the non-Muslims were expelled from the city and was put to work in Duke Robert's army. I was very fortunate. Many were not. I have been filled with gratitude ever since, I debt I may never completely repay."

We all stood silent, waiting for Hugues's next words.

"I remember the Duke well, during the crusade, a great tactician and an excellent judge of men. One of the qualities he passed unto our Brother Sébastien, would you not say?" he asked.

I was honoured to be called out by Hugues in this way.

"Without a doubt," Théos replied with a knowing smile.

Hugues beckoned to Théos to come join him at the table.

"We have a matter of utmost importance that we need your assistance with," Hugues started. "And your utmost discretion."

Théos leaned in resting his clasped hands on the table before him, his interest immediately peaked.

"We are taking you into our confidence. Are we right to do so?" Hugues asked seriously.

"I am here to serve in any manner that I am able, my lord. I attend his Grace, King Baldwin, and am privy to his confidential matters so you may rest assured," Théos responded sincerely.

Hugues pursed his lips and thought for a moment, then took a deep breath.

"We have come across some objects with writing that we have seen before but are not able to decipher. We believe it is Coptic which you, I believe, are fluent in, yes?" he said.

"Yes am I, and in Arabic and Latin," Théos answered.

"Good. We need these examined and translated, would you be willing to take on this task?"

"Of course my lord," Théos said enthusiastically.

Hugues gestured to me.

"Brother Sébastien will take you to these objects. You will see what some of our Brothers have been busy with over the past few months, you must keep what you see to yourself. Do I have your word?" Hugues demanded.

"I swear to God, my lord," Théos said.

Hugues then turned to me.

"Set to it then," he said simply.

I motioned to Théos to follow me and the two of us along with Bisol and Saint-Omer headed to the stables, navigating the ancient stairs to the lowest level and to the entrance to the tunnel. If Théos was surprised or shocked by what he was seeing, he did not show it. Rossal had been busy whilst we were meeting above having cleared more of the entrance to the cave so that a man could crawl through on his knees rather than on his stomach to reach the rope ladder. I went first, reaching the cave, descending the rungs easily and helping Théos navigate them which was not easy for him, not being as agile as he once had been. He immediately spied the two jars and went to them, squatting by them, looking closely at the engravings.

"Ἀλήθεια," he said, saying out loud what was written on each as he ever so gently touched one of the crosses.

"You know what language this is? What it says?" I asked almost rhetorically and immediately felt foolish for asking.

"It is Coptic, which as you know from your learning, is very close to ancient Greek. It is old Coptic, but yes, I can read this. This word," he said pointing to it, "means 'Truth'".

He looked around the cave and spotted the opening in the wall.

"Is this where you found them," he asked, getting up and moving as if to peer into the space.

"Yes, just a few hours ago. But there is more, Théos," I said, beckoning him back to the first jar.

I removed the lid, and reached inside, removing the packet of parchment. This was the first time that Théos's expression turned to surprise and his eyes widened at the sight of it. I placed it in his hands, face up, the knotted cord still in place.

"What of this?" I asked.

He held it carefully and bent over a bit to examine the exterior covering. After a few moments he spoke.

"The leather is very old, I can only just make out more Coptic crosses. The ties will have to come off for me to examine it further, if I am permitted?"

I nodded and watched him struggle somewhat with the ancient cord so I worked the knots slowly for him until they came loose, not wanting to break it. But eventually I was able to unravel it and stepped to the side to let more light in to help him see. Théos cautiously opened the leather cover to reveal pages of light brown papyrus, edges stained dark from age and more Coptic writing.

"'Το μυστικό βιβλίο του Ιωάννη'" Théos whispered, his voice barely audible.

We waited anxiously for him to translate for us. He looked at me with quite a serious, almost stricken expression on his face. I raised my eyebrows slightly, silently asking him to tell us what it said.

"Oh my dear Sébastien," he started, shaking his head. "This cannot be. There have been rumours, stories, throughout the years, but nothing, there has been no…" he stumbled across his words.

I placed my hand gently on his shoulder to help calm him, and told him to take a deep breath which he did.

"This is a codex, a…a collection of writings," he explained. "I have seen others like it, most have to do with medicine or records of doctoring, that sort of thing. But this," he looked serenely down at what he held in his hands, "is something quite different. Ever since I was a boy, I have heard the stories but always thought they were just that, myths that these writings had existed but none had ever been found. But maybe there was some truth to them after all."

Bisol, Saint-Omer and I were rapt with attention. None of us spoke, not wishing to interrupt what Théos had to tell us.

"This first page translates to…" he thought a moment to get the words right, "The Secret Book of John. I will need to read more of it to be sure, but if the remaining pages reflect the first, then these are some of the writings that were discounted at the Council of Nicaea and deemed heretical, along with many others. They were all to have been destroyed, someone has taken great care to ensure this was not."

We all stood still, staring at Théos not really sure if we had heard him correctly. I then moved to the second jar and removed the second codex. Théos's eyes widened when he saw how more elaborate this one was from the first. I handed it to him, taking The Secret Book of John from his hands. He handled it so gently I thought for a moment he was afraid it would disintegrate in his hands. A small gasp escaped from him.

"το ιερό βιβλίο του μεγάλου αόρατου πνεύματος," he murmured, and I noticed tears had just sprung to his eyes.

"Théos?" I asked.

He patted the leather covering and looked at me.

"I am truly honoured," he said looking down at the floor, his chin beginning to quiver. Then adding after gaining some control, "This, this is the Holy Book of the Great Invisible Spirit, writings from my forebearers, holy men of the Egyptian Coptic religion. A sort of Coptic Egyptian gospel if that makes sense?"

"What do you mean a gospel?" I asked. "There are only the four gospels, how can there be others?"

Théos looked at me rather pityingly.

"My dear Sébastien, there have always been others. The Council of Nicaea was held for the specific reason to determine which of the gospels to keep and which to discard when Christianity was becoming the official religion in the Latin world. We have been taught ever since that all writings that were not accepted were heretical and all copies were destroyed. Obviously," he said lifting the book slightly, "this is not the case."

We were dumbfounded. And desperately curious to know what the writings said.

\* \* \* \* \* \* \* \* \* \*

It took Théos a few weeks to translate the Secret Book and the Coptic gospel and make several copies of them. In order to keep this from prying eyes, Hugues had set tables and a supply of candles, parchment, quills and inks, enough to keep him working through the days and long into the evenings, in the cave where the codices and tablet were found. I visited my friend frequently, making sure he had enough food and drink and anything else he needed to complete the task he was given. It was after vespers on such an evening when I came to check on him and his progress. He seemed to be in a bit of a state when I arrived. I pulled up a chair and poured some fresh wine for the two of us.

"You seem agitated this evening my friend," I said, trying to jest with him.

Théos looked at me sternly, I suddenly realized something really was amiss.

"What is it?"

"The work I have been tasked with is almost complete. And I am…" he hesitated.

I waited for him to continue not wishing to press him.

"I am somewhat troubled," he said finally.

"Why is that?"

"The Secret Book speaks to the creation of our world both the physical and the spiritual. But what is written is not totally in keeping with Christian tradition. In fact, it tells quite a different story."

I failed to grasp his meaning. What other story could possibly have been told? The look on my face clearly told him I did not understand and so he patiently explained it to me.

"Do you remember we spoke of the Council of Nicaea that took place during the rule of Emperor Constantine? When he ordered the bishops of the various Christian sects to decide once and for all the divine nature of the Son of God?"

I nodded. I could not help but have the image of those decapitated heads being launched against the city walls all those years ago flash through my mind. That was my memory of Nicaea. I quickly shook it from my mind.

"And that several texts and writings about the Christ were examined by the council and that many were cast aside, destroyed so as not to give any credence to them?"

I nodded again.

"Are you saying you are now certain that these are some of those writings?"

"Yes, that is precisely what I am saying. These words were not intended to have been seen again and someone, or some people, decided they should be preserved and hidden away.

"These are the secret teachings, purported to be the truth of how we came to be. Or another version of it. But one that is certainly in conflict with the church, and have been since they were written."

This was surprising news indeed, but I was not unnerved by what Théos was telling me. More intrigued than anything else. I needed to know more before making judgement, just as I always had about everything I had been told in my life. And I think my calm reaction gave Théos what he needed to share more.

"I want you to read something and when you are done, tell me what you think it means."

With that, Théos selected a few pieces of parchment from the pile next to him and slid them across the table to me. I leaned in and moved one of the candles closer to better illuminate the pages. I began to read his translation:

### The Inexpressible One

The One rules all. Nothing has authority over it.
　　It is the God.
　　It is Father of everything,
　　　　Holy One
　　　　The invisible one over everything.
　　It is uncontaminated
　　　　Pure light no eye can bear to look within.
　　The One is the Invisible Spirit.
　　　　It is not right to think of it as a God or as like God.
　　　　It is more than just God.
　　Nothing is above it.
　　Nothing rules it.
　　　　Since everything exists within it
　　　　　　It does not exist within anything.
　　　　Since it is not dependent on anything
　　　　　　It is eternal.
It is absolutely complete and so needs nothing.
It is utterly perfect Light.


The One is without boundaries
　　Nothing exists outside of it to border it
The One cannot be investigated
　　Nothing exists apart from it to investigate it
The One cannot be measured
　　Nothing exists external to it to measure it
The One cannot be seen
　　For no one can envision it
The One is eternal
　　For it exists forever
The One is inconceivable
　　For no one can comprehend it
The One is indescribable
　　For no one can put any words to it.

The One is infinite light
    Purity
    Holiness
    Stainless,
The One is incomprehensible
    Perfectly free from corruption.
Not "perfect"
Not "blessed"
Not "divine"
But superior to such concepts.
    Neither physical nor unphysical
    Neither immense nor infinitesimal
It is impossible to specify in quantity or quality
    For it is beyond knowledge.
The One is not a being among other beings
    It is vastly superior
    But it is not "superior."
It is outside of realms of being and time
    For whatever is within realms of being was created
    And whatever is within time had time allotted to it
The One receives nothing from anything.
It simply apprehends itself in its own perfect light
The One is majestic.
    The One is measureless majesty
Chief of all Realms
    Producing all realms
Light
    Producing light
Life
    Producing life
Blessedness
    Producing blessedness
Knowledge
    Producing knowledge

Good
 Producing goodness
Mercy
 Producing mercy
Generous
 Producing generosity
It gives forth light beyond measure, beyond comprehension.
His realm is eternal, peaceful, silent, resting, before everything.
He is the head of every realm sustaining each of them through
goodness.


## The Origin of Reality

The Father is surrounded by light.
He apprehends himself in that light
He is conscious of his image everywhere around him,
 Perceiving his image in this spring of Spirit
 Pouring forth from himself.
He is enamoured of the image he sees in the light-water,
 The spring of pure light-water enveloping him.
His self-aware thought (ennoia) came into being.
Appearing to him in the effulgence of his light.
She stood before him.
This, then, is the first of the powers, prior to everything.
Arising out of the mind of the Father
The Providence (pronoia) of everything.

Her light reflects His light.
She is from His image in His light
Perfect in power
Image of the invisible perfect Virgin Spirit.
She is the initial power
glory of Barbelo
glorious among the realms
glory of revelation
She gave glory to the Virgin Spirit
She praised Him
 For she arose from Him.
 This, the first Thought, is the Spirit's image
She is the universal womb
She is before everything
She is:
 Mother-Father
 First Man
 Holy Spirit
 Thrice Male
 Thrice Powerful
 Thrice Named
Androgynous eternal realm
First to arise among the invisible realms.
She, Barbelo, asked the virgin Spirit for foreknowledge
(prognosis).

The Spirit agreed.
Foreknowledge came forth and stood by Providence
Foreknowledge gave glory to the Spirit

And to Barbelo, the Spirit's perfect power,
For She was the reason that it had come into being.

I read the pages three times before I spoke.

"I am not sure I understand. The writer, John, speaks of God the Father
but also about another creator, a female?" I said.

He waited to see if I was grasping the importance of this.

"That is part of it, yes. There is much more of course, in the rest of it. But for you to truly understand, I need you to let go of what you have been taught, what you have believed since your early days with Bishop Odo. Please do not think I am being patronizing, what I am about to share with you is complex and unlike anything you have been led to believe. Do you think you can do this?" he asked, taking a drink from his goblet.

"I will try," I responded as honestly as I could.

Théos nodded.

"The secret writings are to be read in the abstract, in the symbolic rather than the tangible. They are stories with lessons to be learned and are not literal. They recount much of what we have been taught, God the Father, the Christ, even Adam's story, but in terms that are different to our understanding. And with those nuanced differences, some of what is written conflicts with what the church has preached for many centuries.

"In these pages that I have given to you, John refers to God the Father as an Invisible Spirit and calls him 'the One,' a being of a size and magnitude incomprehensible to our poor meagre minds. And this is in keeping with our understanding of God the Father we have understood Him to be since the Council of Nicaea chose the writings to be used to teach us.

But then John goes on to speak of a Mother figure, Barbélo, who was created from the outpourings of thought from the Invisible Spirit. And She becomes the first 'Thought.'

"According to these writings, It is She who first lived in the realm known to us as heaven and it is She who created all that is known to us as both the physical and spiritual worlds and it was She who brought forth all that makes us who we are. She is the Holy Spirit we talk about when we pray to the Holy Trinity. But in what we have been taught, She disappears from the stories completely."

He waited again to see if I was comprehending his meaning. Strangely enough, this all made sense to me, after all, why should not the Holy Spirit be feminine? I could tell he was searching my face for some sort of recognition that I was grasping what he was saying.

"But why would the Holy Spirit being feminine be an issue for the church?" I asked, adding, "They have always venerated Mary, the Mother of Jesus."

"Indeed they have. But think for a moment about what this difference actually means. Mary is revered as the mother of Christ, yes, but that is where her role ends. She is not part of the Holy Trinity nor is she seen as a significant contributor to the doctrines of Christianity. She is set to the side and the focus is always on the trinity and it being wholly male. For centuries the role of woman has been relegated to second class status, man being her complete superior. But here these writings show that, as a female Holy Spirit, She was on equal footing with both God the Father and the Christ who came from her, a concept which is not only very pagan in nature but is quite different from the trinity story the church has taught. The idea that a female was actually the creator of our existence would be an anathema to them. And so they simply removed her. Imagine the revelation that there were, are, beliefs that our Creators were both male and female, and, more importantly, the reaction of the people if they discovered they had been not told the entire truth."

I pondered on that for a moment and thought I was beginning to understand. There had been many occasions that I had witnessed over the years when an untruth or even just withholding the full truth had been outed, resulting in distrust being bred amongst men whether that be between allied kings or parleying adversaries and destroying any good will between them. All it would need would be for these writings to plant the seeds of doubt and men would do the rest. The Christian church would risk collapse and with it the world as we now knew it.

"In the rest of the writings you have not yet read, John speaks to the creation of the Christ, and man and woman, and the good aspects of humanity and of course the evil. But as I said, you must read this as symbolic, it would be very easy to not do this and instead ascribe these attributes to actual beings. Which is of course what the church has done, probably to help the less capable grasp the meaning. What is important are the lessons to be learned."

We sat in silence a moment, and I struggled somewhat with what Théos meant by the symbolism.

"The Coptic Gospel says much of the same. So I have to ask some questions," Théos continued. "First, if the writings on their own were considered having no merit at the time of the Council, why was a decision made to save these in such a way that it would be years, centuries as it has turned out, for them to be found but clearly with the intention that they eventually would be found? Knowing that there were many writings that were rejected at the Council, why were these saved? Who saved them?"

It was then that I decided to share with Théos our final discovery, Hugues had given his permission for me to do so if I felt it should be done. I crept into the smaller cave and removed the covered tablet from its jar and brought it back to the table. Théos watched me with eyes growing wider by the second. I placed the block onto the table and gestured for him to unravel the cord that bound it and to remove the tablet from its wrappings. His jaw dropped upon seeing what it was.

He gently caressed the etchings in the emerald slab before reaching for his quill and paper, slowly going back and forth from the tablet to the parchment in an effort to meticulously translate what was written there. Finally, he sat up and sighed heavily.

"I have finished the translation as best I believe I can," he said, staring at the single piece of parchment before him. "There were not many lines, it will not take you long to read them through."

He handed the page to me. I read:

> Truth! Certainty! That in which there is no doubt!
> That which is above is from that which is below, and that which is below is from that which is above, working the miracles of one thing.
> As all things were from One.
> Its father is the Sun and its mother the Moon.
> The Earth carried it in her belly, and the Wind nourished it in her belly,
> as Earth which shall become Fire.
> Feed the Earth from that which is subtle, with the greatest power.
> It ascends from the earth to the heaven and becomes ruler over that which is above and that which is below.
> This is my honour and that is why I am called Hermes Trismegistus.

Like the pages from the first codex, I read this several times but even though it was brief and only contained a handful of sentences, its meaning escaped me. I was confused, frustrated by the words and feeling inadequate, as if I should understand but clearly I was unworthy. Not wanting to give any hint that the words had perplexed me, I focused on the name that appeared at the end.

"Who is this Hermes Trismegistus?"

Théos squinted a bit, as if trying to decide how to explain this to me.

"He is a bit of a mysterious figure, his name translates to 'Thrice Greatest' – it is interesting that the concept of 'thrice' is here in the philosopher's name as well as in the writings of John, yes? Some say he was a Greek who lived in times far before Christ, who foresaw the coming of Christianity. Some say he did not exist until much later, closer to the time of Constantine. But regardless, he is known as the father of Hermeticism, a nature-based philosophy, ancient beliefs from Egypt, at the heart of which is the art of alchemy."

"Alchemy? Trying to change metals into gold and silver?" I asked incredulously.

"Yes," Théos murmured and I sensed a slight annoyance with me being flippant. "But not only that. Alchemy is not just the study of the construction and changeability of matter, it is also about life, death, and the possibility of rebirth. Many have attempted to create elixirs hoping to achieve immortality, and others hoping to cure the sick and dying. But it is not this part of the philosophy which concerns me, whilst admirable, no one has been able to accomplish such things and nothing on the tablet refers to that. What is important here is the basis of the philosophy, the concept of the 'One'".

"Just as the Secret Book of John writings speak to the 'One'."

"Indeed they do. And it is this that fascinates me."

"So what is this 'One' on the tablet? Is it not also God the Father that John writes about?"

Théos thought a moment.

"Yes, the 'One' is God the Father. But these writings speak of 'The One' being much more than that," Théos mused pointing at the parchment papers, and speaking as if he was thinking and deciphering aloud. "I have deep and distant memories of other stories, told to me when I was a child and beginning my spiritual studies. Stories that have been passed down generations, about a student of Hermes Trismegistus, his name was Asclepius if I recall correctly, supposedly a descendant of the Greek God of medicine by the same name. Asclepius the God was rumoured to be able to bring the dead back to life!

"But the stories of the student Asclepius tell of his discourse with Hermes Trismegistus who was teaching him and a few other students the secret knowledge. And they spoke of the 'One,' in the same way as it is spoken of here. But they also spoke of the 'All'."

"So what is this 'All'?" I asked, adding, "and what does it have to do with the 'One'?"

We were both silent for quite some time thinking on this. And then his face brightened, a flow of energy suddenly emanating from him.

"It is connected," he said simply, beginning to smile. "The 'One' and the 'All' are connected. Or rather, more specifically they are the same. Do you get my meaning Sébastien?"

I had to admit I was still in the dark.

"No, I am afraid I do not, what is connected?"

"We are. With everyone, each of us. God the Father. Barbélo. And the Christ. You. Me. Everyone. And this collective becomes the 'All.' The 'All' is the 'One'."

He picked up the parchment that held the words from the Emerald Tablet.

"'That which is above is from that which is below, and that which is below is from that which is above, working the miracles of one thing. As all things were from One.' It is saying the heavens and our earthly world are one and the same. And it might be even more philosophical, our external existence and how it relates to who we are in ourselves, in our minds and in our hearts, what makes us men. Did not the Gospel of John in the book say, 'Jesus answered them, "Is it not written in your Law, 'I said, ye are gods'?"'"

And now I understood. It was as if waves of illumination washed over me, fleeting moments of doubt as I gradually grasped Théos's meaning replaced quickly with a clarity of understanding and purpose I had not experienced since I woke that first morning with Séraphine next to me and everything had been right in my world.

"But if this is truth, we have no need of priests and bishops who tell us of the retribution of a vengeful God? And we control our own destiny?" I asked, my voice shaking slightly at realizing the enormity of what I was saying.

"And what if this was the true teachings of the one we know as Jesus Christ?" Théos offered up.

That rendered us silent.

"Of course, we cannot know that with any certainty," Théos finally broke the silence. "But it is possible. And we know men keep hidden that which threatens to harm them."

"We need to take this to Hugues," I said.

"Indeed," Théos said. "But not quite yet."

Théos and I spent a long night engrossed in his translations. I knew it was just the beginning of my journey into this new spiritual world and that I had much to learn but it had already explained so much of what I had been questioning ever since I was a child. I had always felt innately ill-at-ease with the blind faith demanded of me by most of the men of the cloth I had encountered throughout my life. Only Bishop Odo and Abbot Faritius seemed to encourage my questioning ways, both probably hoping that after I veered from their intended path I would return to it. But I never did. And now, I never would.

It was early morning when I finally started to make my way back to my room but instead decided to go out onto the Temple Mount and take in the crisp cool breeze of the middle of the night. I quickly crossed over the open expanse and up the steps to the Templum Domini and found myself drawn inside.

Standing next to the marble floor that covered the Foundation Stone I looked around, gradually lifting my gaze to the rotunda and dome above. How many men had stood here before me, praying to their god or gods? How many would die because of those prayers and beliefs? How could we not have known that we are the 'One' and the 'All' and always have been? When will we finally truly believe and understand that the divine is in each of us?

After a few minutes of contemplation, I returned to my room and slept soundly for the first time in many, many years.

\* \* \* \* \* \* \* \* \*

When copies of the codices and tablet had been carefully crafted and bound, we presented the translations, first to Hugues and then to the others once Hugues had given his permission, Théos being careful not to colour his explanations with his own views on their meaning but speaking simply and sincerely. Hugues's reaction was not what I expected, his calm, emotionless manner gave me pause – he was not surprised by what he was hearing or reading. Or at least he did not show it. But I felt I knew him well enough by now to be able to tell if he was concealing anything. I had to wonder if he knew more than he was letting on. When he finally spoke, it was with choosing his words carefully.

"I believe we have something here that could prove to be very dangerous indeed, especially in the wrong hands. I do not need to remind each of you of the oath you took to protect our order from harm. What we have heard this evening is to remain with us until such time that it is agreed to share it. Is this understood?"

We all nodded solemnly as he looked at each of us individually for our agreement. Including Théos. As with everything, the ties of brotherhood would keep these writings secret amongst just the original nine of us who were the only ones privy to these discoveries. No one else was brought into our confidence. Hugues then turned to Saint-Omer.

"Prepare to travel. It is time for us to go to Rome."

# VII

## Part One

## 1128-1129 – The West

Leaving Brothers Saint-Agnan, Bisol, Rossal and Gondamer in Jerusalem and Saint-Agnan as the de facto Grand Master of the Order in our absence, Hugues, Saint-Omer, Montdidier, Montbard and myself departed for France at the end of August, sailing from Jaffa to Montpellier, sending word ahead to have horses and supplies awaiting our arrival. We would have left earlier but Patriarch Warmund died suddenly in July and we needed to stay until his successor had been invested. Stephen de la Ferté was a distant relative of King Baldwin and we had hopes that he would be able to seamlessly step into the role, but only time would tell. We had other pressing matters to attend to.

Our precious cargo, the original codices and a few copies of the Secret Book of John and the Coptic Gospel translated by Théos and his translation of the Emerald Tablet, were all carefully and cleverly hidden amongst our belongings. The late summer weather was fine and encountering no storms that would set us back, we arrived on the shores of southern France a week later. Eager to be on our way, we stayed but a night in the port town before heading out before dawn the next day. We reckoned the trip to Clairvaux would take four days and stopped at inns along the way, including in Lyon which brought back memories of meeting Toulouse and, of course, of the lovely Lady Elvira. The core of the city had not changed much in the intervening years and I took advantage of the stay to walk about, remembering the streets and buildings and especially the hall where we had gathered to make plans for our crusade. They were good memories.

After Lyon we travelled to Montbard, the home of our youngest Brother whose family, especially his nephew the current Count, Bernard de Montbard, was more than happy to welcome us into their Château. We had sworn ourselves to secrecy of course, so excuses were made for our visit. We feasted and slept well allowing ourselves this bit of comfort in beds of relative luxury compared to the cots we were used to in our lodgings at the Temple of Solomon. In the morning the Count saw us off, telling us to wish his cousin the Abbot of Clairvaux well upon our arrival, for despite being in reasonable proximity of the Abbey, the two Bernards had not met for some time.

The last leg of our journey was through the fertile lands of eastern France, recently harvested of their crop, the ground becoming more lush the closer we got to the Abbey due to the nearby river Aube, a tributary of the Seine flowing east from Paris. Seeing its walls from afar, we approached Clairvaux Abbey from the west, entering through the large gate located there, coming upon the Abbot's house almost directly past the gate. We dismounted and tied the horses to some posts at the back of the house and walked on foot around to its entrance. Doing so let us see the rest of the precinct that Abbot Bernard and his followers had started to build when they relocated here from a Cistercian abbey in nearby Cîteaux a little more than thirteen years earlier. In that time, they had constructed their church, the Abbot's house, the monks' quarters and many of the agricultural buildings needed to be self-sustaining. It was impressive considering the small number of men who had done all the work.

The five of us stood by the entrance to the Abbot's House admiring what we saw. A great deal had been accomplished and it was remarkable that it was only done by the monks themselves. Our gaze was interrupted by the sound of the door opening and we turned to see a small man, clothed in the white robes of the Cistercian Order tied at the waist with a black rope belt, arms clasped together and tucked into the robe's wide sleeves. His face was thin, on the verge of gaunt, no doubt a result of his adherence to the very strict rules of his Order. His tonsure was rimmed with a small ring of hair. All of this made him look older than his years. He looked at each of us with a questioning look.

"May I be of assistance?" he asked in a quiet voice.

Hugues stepped forward.

"We seek the Abbot of Clairvaux," he answered.

"I am he," the little monk responded. "Whom am I addressing?"

"Grand Master Hugues de Payns, at your service," Hugues responded, nodding his respect.

Abbot Bernard broke into a huge smile.

"Yes, yes of course, your arrival has been expected. Which of you is my uncle André?" he asked looking at each of us.

Montbard stepped forward and embraced the Abbot.

"My have you grown!" Abbot Bernard exclaimed with delight. "You were but a child the last time I laid eyes upon you. You remind me of my dear mother, your sister Aleth, you have the same eyes," he said, touching Montbard's face gently.

"It is good to see you Abbot Bernard," Montbard replied, "much has happened since you saw me last."

"Indeed, I have heard many things," Abbot Bernard responded cryptically, but with a smile.

"I have brought letters for you from King Baldwin," Montbard continued, patting his side pouch where they had been kept safe and secure.

"Excellent, I shall look forward to reading them." Turning to Hugues, the Abbot continued, "My dear Master Payns, I am pleased to finally see you in the flesh after receiving so many of your letters imploring me to assist you and your fledgling Order. The Poor Fellow-Soldiers of Christ and of the Temple of Solomon, yes? That is what you call yourselves, is it not?"

He was clearly well-informed.

"Yes Abbot," Hugues responded, "that is the name we have taken in honour of our home on the Temple Mount. Templars for short. We are all brothers of the Order, there are more whom we have left in Jerusalem. As I mentioned in my letters, we bring together prayer with hard work, having spent much time restoring the Holy City and repairing much of the damage done over the years."

"How very Cistercian," Abbot Bernard said with a smile. "Come, you must be hungry from your ride. Let us repair to the refectory, it is almost sext, our mid-day meal must be ready for us."

We spent the next hour enjoying the fruits of the Abbey's farm, loaves of bread fresh from the ovens and wines from the Abbey's own vineyards, kept cool stored in the buttery. After the meal, the Abbot took us on a tour of the Abbey's precinct, showing us the progress that had been made in developing farming tools and erecting agricultural buildings, the beginnings of a cloister next to the chapel and the chapel itself where we said prayers and took a blessing from the Abbot. But then it was back to the business at hand and we were soon in the Abbot's House gathered around a table in his small meeting hall. It was fortuitous that only five of us came on this mission, all nine of us would not have fit in the room.

As agreed ahead of time, Hugues discussed our Order with the Abbot and ask him for his advice and support with Pope Honorius. If the Holy Father were to officially sanction our brotherhood, we would be able to reach out much further than we had in the past to ask for support, in particular funding, from the Christian states and add more members to continue doing the good works we had been engaged in since arriving in Jerusalem. We decided not to show him the codices and instead save those for our audience with the Holy Father. We felt it would be best that Abbot Bernard is not involved in those discussions.

We talked for several hours, food and wine were brought and we forgot to attend vespers, so engrossed was the Abbot in hearing our stories. He was impressed with the additions we had done on the Holy Sepulchre and in giving assistance to the Armenians for the building of their church. He had received excellent reports from Patriarch Warmund about our work and how the roads between the crusader states had been made safer with our presence protecting pilgrims as they moved from one place to another. Hugues finally broached the question about asking the Holy Father for his support. Abbot Bernard explained the lay of the land as it currently was with the church and the French crown.

> "Pope Honorius has been these past months mired in troubles concerning the French Bishops and King Louis. The King firmly believes that the crown has the right to choose who shall sit in which see, who shall be Bishop, Archbishop and so on. Some of the French Bishops have been protesting this view and actions the King has taken filling a few positions that have become open recently.

> "I have become involved at the request of the Bishop of Paris and have asked the Pope to intervene and to stop the King from retaliating against the protesters. So there is an unusual level of tension in Rome at the moment, although I personally believe Honorius shares our views of separating the powers of the crown from the church," he said.

"Would this then be an inopportune moment to raise our request then?" Hugues asked.

"Quite the opposite!" Abbot Bernard said emphatically. "Quite the opposite. I think this is just what his Holiness needs at the moment, something to refocus on what is important and that is doing God's work. But your request needs to be different, the Pope has many who seek his support and favour and we cannot afford to be lost in the crowd, this must stand apart. I think you will catch his ear by the name you have chosen for the Order – Poor Fellow-Soldiers of Christ – very good. We need to present the Templars as a new knighthood, a brotherhood of knights, godly men who are not afraid to wield a sword when circumstances demand it."

"Much like Bishop Odo once was," I interjected quietly.

The Abbot turned and stared at me, at first I thought his look was of anger but his eyes widened as he understood my meaning.

"Yes, of course! A Bishop who fought at the side of the Conqueror, the perfect image! His Holiness has called for Council at Troyes just after the new year, this will give us just the opportunity to make our case. We will need a paper praising the order as it is, glorifying its deeds, laying out its potential. And giving some indication of the rules by which this new brotherhood shall live. I shall set my mind to it, a treatise, yes, a treatise which I will present to his Holiness at the Council. What do you think of this?"

Hugues expressed his gratitude as did we all for the enthusiastic support the Abbot was giving us.

"We will need ways of identifying members of the Order from the general population," Abbot Bernard continued. "May I suggest the white hooded robes of the Cistercian monks, they would emphasize the purity of the intention of the Order? I shall think more on that," he trailed off, deep in thought, as if speaking aloud to himself.

We all sat in silence, waiting for him to speak again. Gradually he came out of his contemplation and asked if there was anything else that needed discussing this night as the tapers were growing low and that since we missed vespers, we should attend matins which, much to all our surprise, was to start shortly. For a moment I thought Hugues hesitated in answering, possibly considering telling the Abbot about our discoveries. But perhaps I had imagined that as he said no and thanked the Abbot once again for all he had he had done for us and what he was proposing to do for us. And with that, we were off in the darkness to the chapel for midnight prayers.

* * * * * * * * * *

We spent a mild Christmas that year at the Château Montbard, our host's generosity in providing us with room and board only surpassed by the gifts of the destriers he made to us, including four for the senior Brothers we had left behind in Jerusalem. They were all handsome, magnificent animals and would make a fine contribution to our stables. I had spied a white steed with patches of black on its hind quarters and I was reminded of both Pax and Lux who had been my trusted companions throughout the years. Pax sadly had died a few years earlier but Lux was still with me, awaiting my return to Jerusalem, he was not suited for this long trek. I was leaning on the fence of the Château's paddock. watching the horses graze when Hugues approached. He and Montdidier had just returned after having spent the intervening weeks touring northern France and England even going as far as Scotland, gathering support for our cause, and upon his arrival had seen me from inside the château and made his way over. He suggested I take the piebald as my own and I agreed, very happy to do so.

We discussed his travels and my own to the family holdings in Ivry-la-Bataille. My brother Guillaume had made the Channel crossing from England to come see me and spending time with him and our brother Roger did me good. We did not speak of her, my brothers were careful not to rip open old wounds or cause any new ones with careless talk. Guillaume passed along Osmond's best wishes and letters giving updates on the success of my properties – it appeared they had all been quite fruitful and lucrative, I was even more wealthy than when I had departed England. I sent instructions back with Guillaume asking Osmond to find a way to get some of the excess profit to us in Jerusalem, the Order was in dire need of funding and I was duty-bound to donate it.

It was Roger who told me of the death of Duke Robert's only son, William Clito, and with it any hope the Duke might have had of ever being released from captivity. The boy had grown into a powerful young man and had had the backing of King Louis in making claims of lands that were once ruled by his father and of course was the disputed heir to the English throne. But during a siege in Flanders, his arm had been slashed by a low-ranked enemy soldier, the wound turned gangrenous and he died at the end of July. He was only of twenty-five years. I could not begin to imagine the anguish Duke Robert must have felt at the news of the death of his precious lad. I was filled with sorrow to hear of it.

The Council at Troyes was set for the middle of January and we made the ride in less than a day. We discovered when we arrived in the city that his Holiness Pope Honorius was not going to be attending in person but had sent a legate, the Cardinal-Bishop of Albano, to act on his behalf. Abbot Bernard had taken the weeks between our first meeting and this trip to prepare his treatise on our order, sometimes working feverishly into the night. He had entitled it *"Liber ad milites templi de laude novae militia,"* or in our language, *"In Praise of the New Knighthood"* and it sang admiration of our order and of Hugues in particular. The Abbot had sent it to the enclave ahead of our arrival so they would be well-advised on the reason for our appearance.

The council was mostly clerics but we were heartened to see that seated amongst them hearing our plea was Hugh de Champagne's nephew and heir Théobald who, we could only hope, would have received good views about the Order from his uncle who had been a distant member of our group for several years now. We were fairly certain we could count on his support. Abbot Bernard did not present our cause to the council, he felt it best coming from Hugues as the founder of the Order. Hugues spoke rather eloquently, describing for the council his background and that of the nine founding members, speaking to the experiences many of us had in the crusade those many years ago and how now, after all this time, we were still fighting to maintain possession of the Holy Land and Jerusalem in particular. He spoke to all the good work we had done in the restoration of the Christian sites and recovery of the relics and icons that had been removed or broken during the Muslim occupation, and of the protection we had been providing to the city and to the Christian pilgrims making their way from afar. He concluded by making his request that our Order be supported and championed by the church.

The council was very receptive, believing we were exactly what was needed in these days of discord within the church, and that it would be a shining example for others to follow. They agreed with Abbot Bernard when he suggested that the brother-knights be allowed to wear the Cistercian white mantle to set ourselves apart from lower members of the Order who would wear brown or black, as well as from non-members who worked among us. They also believed a set of tenets by which the brothers would swear to live by was needed. But they did not feel capable of writing such commands, for ours was an Order unlike any other with a dual purpose of both prayer and battle. And so, having been impressed with his treatise, they set Abbot Bernard a task to write our Rule and then instructed us to take it to Pope Honorius to receive his blessing and sanctioning of our Order.

It took him less than a week to compile the list of rules by which we were to live our lives going forward. This was what he wrote:

### The Primitive Rule

*Here begins the prologue to the Rule of Temple*

*1. We speak firstly to all those who secretly despise their own will and desire with a pure heart to serve the sovereign king as a knight and with studious care desire to wear, and wear permanently, the very noble armour of obedience. And therefore we admonish you, you who until now have led the lives of secular knights, in which Jesus Christ was not the cause, but which you embraced for human favour only, to follow those whom God has chosen from the mass of perdition and whom he has ordered through his gracious mercy to defend the Holy Church, and that you hasten to join them forever.*

*2. Above all things, whosoever would be a knight of Christ, choosing such holy orders, you in your profession of faith must unite pure diligence and firm perseverance, which is so worthy and so holy, and is known to be so noble, that if it is preserved untainted for ever, you will deserve to keep company with the martyrs who gave their souls for Jesus Christ. In this religious order has flourished and is revitalised the order of knighthood. This knighthood despised the love of justice that constitutes its duties and did not do what it should, that is defend the poor, widows, orphans and churches, but strove to plunder, despoil and kill. God works well with us and our saviour Jesus Christ; He has sent his friends from the Holy City of Jerusalem to the marches of France and Burgundy, who for our salvation and the spread of the true faith do not cease to offer their souls to God, a welcome sacrifice.*

*3. Then we, in all joy and all brotherhood, at the request of Master Hugues de Payns, by whom the aforementioned knighthood was founded by the grace of the Holy Spirit, assembled at Troyes from divers provinces beyond the mountains on the feast of my lord St Hilary, in the year of the incarnation of Jesus Christ 1129, in the tenth year after the founding of the aforesaid knighthood. And the conduct and beginnings of the Order of Knighthood we heard in common chapter from the lips of the aforementioned Master, Brother Hugues de Payns; and according to the limitations of our understanding what seemed to us good and beneficial we praised, and what seemed wrong we eschewed.*

*4. And all that took place at that council cannot be told nor recounted; and so that it should not be taken lightly by us, but considered in wise prudence, we left it to the discretion of both our honourable father lord Honorius and of the noble patriarch of Jerusalem, Stephen, who knew the affairs of the East and of the Poor Knights of Christ, by the advice of the common council we praised it unanimously. Although a great number of religious fathers who assembled at that council praised the authority of our words, nevertheless we should not pass over in silence the true sentences and judgements which they pronounced.*

*5. Therefore I, Jean Michel, to whom was entrusted and confided that divine office, by the grace of God served as the humble scribe of the present document by order of the council and of the venerable father Bernard, abbot of Clairvaux.*

*The Names of the Fathers who Attended the Council*
*6. First was Matthew, bishop of Albano, by the grace of God legate of the Holy Church of Rome; Renaud, archbishop of Reims; H(enri), archbishop of Sens; and then their suffragans: Gocelin, bishop of Soissons; the bishop of Paris; the bishop of Troyes; the bishop of Orléans; the bishop of Auxerre; the bishop of Meaux; the bishop of Chalons; the bishop of Laon; the bishop of Beauvais; the abbot of Vézelay, who was later made archbishop of Lyon and legate of the Church of Rome; the abbot of Cîteaux; the abbot of Pontigny; the abbot of Trois-Fontaines; the abbot of St Denis de Reims; the abbot of St-Etienne de Dijon; the abbot of Molesmes; the above-named Bernard], abbot of Clairvaux: whose words the aforementioned praised liberally. Also present were master Aubri de Reims; master Fulcher and several others whom it would be tedious to record. And of the others who have not been listed it seems profitable to furnish guarantees in this matter, that they are lovers of truth: they are count Theobald; the count of Nevers; Andrè de Baudemant. These were at the council and acted in such a manner that by perfect, studious care they sought out that which was fine and disapproved that which did not seem right.*

*7. And also present was Brother Hugues de Payns, Master of the Knighthood, with some of his brothers whom he had brought with him. The same Master Hugues with his followers related to the above-named fathers the customs and observances of their humble beginnings and of the one who said: 'I who speak to you am the beginning,' according to one's memory.*

*8. It pleased the common council that the deliberations which were made there and the consideration of the Holy Scriptures which were diligently examined with the wisdom of my lord Honorius, pope of the Holy Church of Rome, and of the patriarch of Jerusalem and with the assent of the chapter, together with the agreement of the Poor Knights of Christ of the Temple which is in Jerusalem, should be put in writing and not forgotten, steadfastly kept so that by an upright life one may come to his creator; the compassion of which Lord is sweeter than honey when compared with God; whose mercy resembles oine, and permits us to come to Him whom they desire to serve. Through infinite ages of ages. Amen*

*Here Begins the Rule of the Poor Knighthood of the Temple*
*9. You who renounce your own wills, and you others serving the sovereign king with horses and arms, for the salvation of your souls, for a fixed term, strive everywhere with pure desire to hear matins and the entire service according to canonical law and the customs of the regular masters of the Holy City of Jerusalem. 0 you venerable brothers, similarly God is with you, if you promise to despise the deceitful world in perpetual love of God, and scorn the temptations of your body: sustained by the food of God and watered and instructed in the commandments of Our Lord, at the end of the divine office, none should fear to go into battle if he henceforth wears the tonsure.*

*10. But if any brother is sent through the work of the house and of Christianity in the East--something we believe will happen often--and cannot hear the divine office, he should say instead of matins thirteen paternosters; seven for each hour and nine for vespers. And together we all order him to do so. But those who are sent for such a reason and cannot come at the hours set to hear the divine office, if possible the set hours should not be omitted, in order to render to God his due.*

*The Manner in which Brothers should be Received*

11. *If any secular knight, or any other man, wishes to leave the mass of perdition and abandon that secular life and choose your communal life, do not consent to receive him immediately, for thus said my lord St Paul: 'Test the soul to see if it comes from God.' Rather, if the company of the brothers is to be granted to him, let the Rule be read to him, and if he wishes to studiously obey the commandments of the Rule, and if it pleases the Master and the brothers to receive him, let him reveal his wish and desire before all the brothers assembled in chapter and let him make his request with a pure heart.*

*On Excommunicated Knights*
12. *Where you know excommunicated knights to be gathered, there we command you to go; and if anyone there wishes to join the order of knighthood from regions overseas, you should not consider worldly gain so much as the eternal salvation of his soul. We order him to be received on condition that he come before the bishop of that province and make his intention known to him. And when the bishop has heard and absolved him, he should send him to the Master and brothers of the Temple, and if his life is honest and worthy of their company, if he seems good to the Master and brothers, let him be mercifully received; and if he should die in the meanwhile, through the anguish and torment he has suffered, let him be given all the benefits of the brotherhood due to one of the Poor Knights of the Temple.*

13. *Under no other circumstances should the brothers of the Temple share the company of an obviously excommunicated man, nor take his own things; and this we prohibit strongly because it would be a fearful thing if they were excommunicated like him. But if he is only forbidden to hear the divine office, it is certainly possible to keep company with him and take his property for charity with the permission of their commander.*

*On Not Receiving Children*
14. *Although the rule of the holy fathers allows the receiving of children into a religious life, we do not advise you to do this. For he who wishes to give his child eternally to the order of knighthood should bring him up until such time as he is able to bear arms with vigour and rid the land of the enemies of Jesus Christ. Then let the mother and father lead him to the house and make his request known to the brothers; and it is much better if he does not take the vow when he is a child, but when*

he is older, and it is better if he does not regret it than if he regrets it. And henceforth let him be put to the test according to the wisdom of the Master and brothers and according to the honesty of the life of the one who asks to be admitted to the brotherhood.

## On Brothers who Stand Too Long in Chapel

15. It has been made known to us and we heard it from true witnesses that immoderately and without restraint you hear the divine service whilst standing. We do not ordain that you behave in this manner, on the contrary we disapprove of it. But we command that the strong as well as the weak, to avoid a fuss, should sing the psalm which is called Venite, with the invitatory and the hymn sitting down, and say their prayers in silence, softly and not loudly, so that the proclaimer does not disturb the prayers of the other brothers.

16. But at the end of the psalms, when the Gloria patri is sung, through reverence for the Holy Trinity, you will rise and bow towards the altar, while the weak and ill will incline their heads. So we command; and when the explanation of the Gospels is read, and the Te deum laudamus is sung, and while all the lauds are sung, and the matins are finished, you will be on your feet. In such a manner we command you likewise to be on your feet at matins and at all the hours of Our Lady.

## On the Brothers' Dress

17. We command that all the brothers' habits should always be of one colour, that is white or black or brown. And we grant to all knight brothers in winter and in summer if possible, white cloaks; and no-one who does not belong to the aforementioned Knights of Christ is allowed to have a white cloak, so that those who have abandoned the life of darkness will recognise each other as being reconciled to their creator by the sign of the white habits: which signifies purity and complete chastity. Chastity is certitude of heart and healthiness of body. For if any brother does not take the vow of chastity he cannot come to eternal rest nor see God, by the promise of the apostle who said: 'Strive to bring peace to all, keep chaste, without which no-one can see God.

18. But these robes should be without any finery and without any show of pride. And so we ordain that no brother will have a piece of fur on his clothes, nor anything else which belongs to

the usages of the body, not even a blanket unless it is of lamb's wool or sheep's wool. We command all to have the same, so that each can dress and undress, and put on and take off his boots easily. And the Draper or the one who is in his place should studiously reflect and take care to have the reward of God in all the above-mentioned things, so that the eyes of the envious and evil-tongued cannot observe that the robes are too long or too short; but he should distribute them so that they fit those who must wear them, according to the size of each one.

19. And if any brother out of a feeling of pride or arrogance wishes to have as his due a better and finer habit, let him be given the worst. And those who receive new robes must immediately return the old ones, to be given to the squires and sergeants and often to the poor, according to what seems good to the one who holds that office.

## On Shirts
20. Among the other things, we mercifully rule that, because of the great intensity of the heat which exists in the East, from Easter to All Saints, through compassion and in no way as a right, a linen shirt shalt be given to any brother who wishes to wear it.

## On Bed Linen
21. We command by common consent that each man shall have clothes and bed linen according to the discretion of the Master. It is our intention that apart from a mattress, one bolster and one blanket should be sufficient for each; and he who lacks one of these may have a rug, and he may use a linen blanket at all times, that is to say with a soft pile. And they will at all times sleep dressed in shirt and breeches and shoes and belts, and where they sleep shall be lit until morning. And the Draper should ensure that the brothers are so well tonsured that they may be examined from the front and from behind; and we command you to firmly adhere to this same conduct with respect to beards and moustaches, so that no excess may be noted on their bodies.

## On Pointed Shoes' and Shoelaces
22. We prohibit pointed shoes and shoelaces and forbid any brother to wear them; nor do we permit them to those who serve the house for a fixed term; rather we forbid them to have shoes with points or laces under any circumstances. For it is

manifest and well known that these abominable things belong to
pagans. Nor should they wear their hair or their habits too long.
For those who serve the sovereign creator must of necessity be
born within and without through the promise of God himself
who said: 'Be born as I am born.'

## How They Should Eat
23. In the palace, or what should rather be called the refectory,
they should eat together. But if you are in need of anything
because you are not accustomed to the signs used by other men
of religion, quietly and privately you should ask for what you
need at table, with all humility and submission. For the apostle
said: 'Eat your bread in silence.' And the psalmist: 'I held my
tongue.' That is, 'I thought my tongue would fail me.' That is, 'I
held my tongue so that I should speak no ill.

## On the Reading of the Lesson
24. Always, at the convent's dinner and supper, let the Holy
Scripture be read, if possible. If we love God and all His holy
words and His holy commandments, we should desire to listen
attentively; the reader of the lesson will tell you to keep silent
before he begins to read.

## On Bowls and Drinking Vessels
25. Because of the shortage of bowls, the brothers will eat in
pairs, so that one may study the other more closely, and so that
neither austerity nor secret abstinence is introduced into the
communal meal. And it seems just to us that each brother
should have the same ration of wine in his cup.

## On the Eating of Meat
26. It should be sufficient for you to eat meat three times a
week, except at Christmas, All Saints, the Assumption and the
feast of the twelve apostles. For it is understood that the custom
of eating flesh corrupts the body. But if a fast when meat must
be forgone falls on a Tuesday, the next day let it be given to the
brothers in plenty. And on Sundays all the brothers of the
Temple, the chaplains and the clerks shall be given two meat
meals in honour of the holy resurrection of Jesus Christ. And
the rest of the household, that is to say the squires and
sergeants, shall be content with one meal and shall be thankful
to God for it.

## On Weekday Meals

27. On the other days of the week, that is Mondays, Wednesdays and even Saturdays, the brothers shall have two or three meals of vegetables or other dishes eaten with bread; and we intend that this should be sufficient and command that it should be adhered to. For he who does not eat one meal shall eat the other.

## On Friday Meals
28. On Fridays, let lenten meat be given communally to the whole congregation, out of reverence for the passion of Jesus Christ; and you will fast from All Saints until Easter, except for Christmas Day, the Assumption and the feast of the twelve apostles. But weak and sick brothers shall not be kept to this. From Easter to All Saints they may eat twice, as long as there is no general fast.

## On Saying Grace
29. Always after every dinner and supper all the brothers should give thanks to God in silence, if the church is near to the palace where they eat, and if it is not nearby, in the place itself. With a humble heart they should give thanks to Jesus Christ who is the Lord Provider. Let the remains of the broken bread be given to the poor and whole loaves be kept. Although the reward of the poor, which is the kingdom of heaven, should be given to the poor without hesitation, and the Christian faith doubtless recognises you among them, we ordain that a tenth part of the bread be given to your Almoner.

## On Taking Collation
30. When daylight fades and night falls listen to the signal of the bell or the call to prayers, according to the customs of the country, and all go to compline. But we command you first to take collation; although we place this light meal under the arbitration and discretion of the Master. When he wants water and when he orders, out of mercy, diluted wine, let it be given sensibly. Truly, it should not be taken to excess, but in moderation. For Solomon said that wine corrupts the wise.

## On Keeping Silence
31. When the brothers come out of compline they have no permission to speak openly except in an emergency. But let each go to his bed quietly and in silence, and if he needs to speak to his squire, he should say what he has to say softly and quietly. But if by chance, as they come out of compline, the

knighthood or the house has a serious problem which must be solved before morning, we intend that the Master or a party of elder brothers who govern the Order under the Master, may speak appropriately. And for this reason we command that it should be done in such a manner.

32. To talk too much is not without sin. And elsewhere: 'Life and death are in the power of the tongue.' And during that conversation we altogether prohibit idle words and wicked bursts of laughter. And if anything is said during that conversation that should not be said, when you go to bed we command you to say the paternoster prayer in all humility and pure devotion.

## On Ailing Brothers

33. Brothers who suffer illness through the work of the house may be allowed to rise at matins with the agreement and permission of the Master or of those who are charged with that office. But they should say instead of matins thirteen paternosters, as is established above, in such a manner that the words reflect the heart. Thus said David: 'Sing wisely.' And elsewhere the same David said: That is to say: 'I will sing to you before the angels.' And let this thing be at all times at the discretion of the Master or of those who are charged with that office.

## On the Communal Life

34. One reads in the Holy Scriptures: to each was given according to his need. For this reason we say that no-one should be elevated among you, but all should take care of the sick; and he who is less ill should thank God and not be troubled; and let whoever is worse humble himself through his infirmity and not become proud through pity. In this way all members will live in peace. And we forbid anyone to embrace excessive abstinence; but firmly keep the communal life.

## On the Master

35. The Master may give to whomsoever he pleases the horse and armour and whatever he likes of another brother, and the brother to whom the given thing belongs should not become vexed or angry: for be certain that if he becomes angry he will go against God.

## On Giving Counsel

36. Let only those brothers whom the Master knows will give wise and beneficial advice be called to the council; for this we command, and by no means everyone should be chosen. For when it happens that they wish to treat serious matters like the giving of communal land, or to speak of the affairs of the house, or receive a brother, then if the Master wishes, it is appropriate to assemble the entire congregation to hear the advice of the whole chapter; and what seems to the Master best and most beneficial, let him do it.

## On Brothers Sent Overseas
37. Brothers who are sent throughout divers countries of the world should endeavour to keep the commandments of the Rule according to their ability and live without reproach with regard to meat and wine, etc. so that they may receive a good report from outsiders and not sully by deed or word the precepts of the Order, and so that they may set an example of good works and wisdom; above all so that those with whom they associate and those in whose inns they lodge may be bestowed with honour. And if possible, the house where they sleep and take lodging should not be without light at night, so that shadowy enemies may not lead them to wickedness, which God forbids them.

## On Keeping the Peace
38. Each brother should ensure that he does not incite another brother to wrath or anger, for the sovereign mercy of God holds the strong and weak brother equal, in the name of charity.

## How the Brothers Should Go About
39. In order to carry out their holy duties and gain the glory of the Lord's joy and to escape the fear of hellfire, it is fitting that all brothers who are professed strictly obey their Master. For nothing is dearer to Jesus Christ than obedience. For as soon as something is commanded by the Master or by him to whom the Master has given the authority, it should be done without delay as though Christ himself had commanded it. For thus said Jesus Christ through the mouth of David, and it is true: 'He obeyed me as soon as he heard me.'

40. For this reason we pray and firmly command the knight brothers who have abandoned their own wills and all the others who serve for a fixed term not to presume to go out into the town or city without the permission of the Master or of the one

who is given that office; except at night to the Sepulchre and the places of prayer which lie within the walls of the city of Jerusalem.

41. There, brothers may go in pairs, but otherwise may not go out by day or night; and when they have stopped at an inn, neither brother nor squire nor sergeant may go to another's lodging to see or speak to him without permission, as is said above. We command by common consent that in this Order which is ruled by God, no brother should fight or rest according to his own will, but according to the orders of the Master, to whom all should submit, that they may follow this pronouncement of Jesus Christ who said: 'I did not come to do my own will, but the will of my father who sent me.'

How they should Affect an Exchange
42. Without permission from the Master or from the one who holds that office, let no brother exchange one thing for another, nor ask to, unless it is a small or petty thing.

On Locks
43. Without permission from the Master or from the one who holds that office, let no brother have a lockable purse or bag; but commanders of houses or provinces and Masters shall not be held to this. Without the consent of the Master or of his commander, let no brother have letters from his relatives or any other person; but if he has permission, and if it please the Master or the commander, the letters may be read to him.

On Secular Gifts
44. If anything which cannot be conserved, like meat, is given to any brother by a secular person in thanks, he should present it to the Master or the Commander of Victuals. But if it happens that any of his friends or relatives has something that they wish to give only to him, let him not take it without the permission of the Master or of the one who holds that office. Moreover, if the brother is sent any other thing by his relatives, let him not take it without the permission of the Master or of the one who holds that office. We do not wish the commanders or baillis, who are especially charged to carry out this office, to be held to this aforementioned rule.

On Faults

45. If any brother, in speaking or soldiering, or in any other way commits a slight sin, he himself should willingly make known the fault to the Master, to make amends with a pure heart. And if he does not usually fail in this way let him be given a light penance, but if the fault is very serious let him go apart from the company of the brothers so that he does not eat or drink at any table with them, but all alone; and he should submit to the mercy and judgement of the Master and brothers, that he may be saved on the Day of Judgement.

## On Serious Faults
46. Above all things, we should ensure that no brother, powerful or not powerful, strong or weak, who wishes to promote himself gradually and become proud and defend his crime, remain unpunished. But if he does not wish to atone for it let him be given a harsher punishment. And if by pious counsel prayers are said to God for him, and he does not wish to make amends, but wishes to boast more and more of it, let him be uprooted from the pious flock; according to the apostle who says: 'Remove the wicked from among you.' It is necessary for you to remove the wicked sheep from the company of faithful brothers.

47. Moreover the Master, who should hold in his hand the staff and rod- the staff with which to sustain the weaknesses and strengths of others; the rod with which to beat the vices of those who sin–for love of justice by counsel of the patriarch, should take care to do this. But also, as my lord St Maxime said: 'May the leniency be no greater than the fault; nor excessive punishment cause the sinner to return to evil deeds.

## On Rumour
48. We command you by divine counsel to avoid a plague: envy, rumour, spite, slander. So each one should zealously guard against what the apostle said: 'Do not accuse or malign the people of God.' But when a brother knows for certain that his fellow brother has sinned, quietly and with fraternal mercy let him be chastised privately between the two of them, and if he does not wish to listen, another brother should be called, and if he scorns them both he should recant openly before the whole chapter. Those who disparage others suffer from a terrible blindness and many are full of great sorrow that they do not guard against harbouring envy towards others; by which they shall be plunged into the ancient wickedness of the devil.

*Let None Take Pride in his Faults*
*49. Although all idle words are generally known to be sinful,
they will be spoken by those who take pride in their own sin
before the strict judge Jesus Christ; which is demonstrated by
what David said: that one should refrain from speaking even
good and observe silence. Likewise one should guard against
speaking evil, in order to escape the penalty of sin. We prohibit
and firmly forbid any brother to recount to another brother nor
to anyone else the brave deeds he has done in secular life,
which should rather be called follies committed in the
performance of knightly duties, and the pleasures of the flesh
that he has had with immoral women; and if it happens that he
hears them being told by another brother, he should
immediately silence him; and if he cannot do this, he should
straightaway leave that place and not give his heart's ear to the
pedlar of filth.*

*Let None Ask*
*50. This custom among the others we command you to adhere
to strictly and firmly: that no brother should explicitly ask for
the horse or armour of another. It will therefore be done in this
manner: if the infirmity of the brother or the frailty of his
animals or his armour is known to be such that the brother
cannot go out to do the work of the house without harm, let him
go to the Master, or to the one who is in his place in that office
after the Master, and make the situation known to him in pure
faith and true fraternity, and henceforth remain at the disposal
of the Master or of the one who holds that office.*

*On Animals and Squires*
*51. Each knight brother may have three horses and no more
without the permission of the Master, because of the great
poverty which exists at the present time in the house of God
and of the Temple of Solomon. To each knight brother we
grant three horses and one squire, and if that squire willingly
serves charity, the brother should not beat him for any sin he
commits.*

*That No Brother May Have an Ornate Bridle*
*52. We utterly forbid any brother to have gold or silver on his
bridle, nor on his stirrups, nor on his spurs. That is, if he buys
them; but if it happens that a harness is given to him in charity
which is so old that the gold or silver is tarnished, that the*

*resplendent beauty is not seen by others nor pride taken in them: then he may have them. But if he is given new equipment let the Master deal with it as he sees fit.*

## On Lance Covers

*53. Let no brother have a cover on his shield or his lance, for it is no advantage, on the contrary we understand that it would be very harmful.*

## On Food Bags

*54. This command which is established by us it is beneficial for all to keep and for this reason we ordain that it be kept henceforth, and that no brother may make a food bag of linen or wool, principally, or anything else except a profinel.*

## On Hunting

*55. We collectively forbid any brother to hunt a bird with another bird. It is not fitting for a man of religion to succumb to pleasures, but to hear willingly the commandments of God, to be often at prayer and each day to confess tearfully to God in his prayers the sins he has committed. No brother may presume to go particularly with a man who hunts one bird with another. Rather it is fitting for every religious man to go simply and humbly without laughing or talking too much, but reasonably and without raising his voice and for this reason we command especially all brothers not to go in the woods with longbow or crossbow to hunt animals or to accompany anyone who would do so, except out of love to save him from faithless pagans. Nor should you go after dogs, nor shout or chatter, nor spur on a horse out of a desire to capture a wild beast.*

## On the Lion

*56. It is the truth that you especially are charged with the duty of giving your souls for your brothers, as did Jesus Christ, and of defending the land from the unbelieving pagans who are the enemies of the son of the Virgin Mary. This above-mentioned prohibition of hunting is by no means intended to include the lion, for he comes encircling and searching for what he can devour, his hands against every man and every man's hand against him.*

## How They May Have Lands and Men

*57. This kind of new order we believe was born out of the Holy Scriptures and divine providence in the Holy Land of the East.*

That is to say that this armed company of knights may kill the enemies of the cross without sinning. For this reason we judge you to be rightly called knights of the Temple, with the double merit and beauty of probity, and that you may have lands and keep men, villeins and fields and govern them justly, and take your right to them as it is specifically established.

## On Tithes

58. You who have abandoned the pleasant riches of this world, we believe you to have willingly subjected yourselves to poverty; therefore we are resolved that you who live the communal life may receive tithes. If the bishop of the place, to whom the tithe should be rendered by right, wishes to give it to you out of charity, with the consent of his chapter he may give those tithes which the Church possesses. Moreover, if any layman keeps the tithes of his patrimony, to his detriment and against the Church, and wishes to leave them to you, he may do so with the permission of the prelate and his chapter.

## On Giving Judgement

59. We know, because we have seen it, that persecutors and people who like quarrels and endeavour to cruelly torment those faithful to the Holy Church and their friends, are without number. By the clear judgement of our council, we command that if there is anyone in the parties of the East or anywhere else who asks anything of you, for faithful men and love of truth you should judge the thing, if the other party wishes to allow it. This same commandment should be kept at all times when something is stolen from you.

## On Elderly Brothers

60. We command by pious counsel that ageing and weak brothers be honoured with diligence and given consideration according to their frailty; and, kept well by the authority of the Rule in those things which are necessary to their physical welfare, should in no way be in distress.

## On Sick Brothers

61. Let sick brothers be given consideration and care and be served according to the saying of the evangelist and Jesus Christ: 'I was sick and you visited me'; and let this not be forgotten. For those brothers who are wretched should be treated quietly and with care, for which service, carried out without hesitation, you will gain the kingdom of heaven. Therefore we command the

Infirmarer to studiously and faithfully provide those things which are necessary to the various sick brothers, such as meat, flesh, birds and all other foods which bring good health, according to the means and the ability of the house.

## On Deceased Brothers

62. When any brother passes from life to death, a thing from which no one is exempt, we command you to sing mass for his soul with a pure heart, and have the divine office performed by the priests who serve the sovereign king and you who serve charity for a fixed term and all the brothers who are present where the body lies and serve for a fixed term should say one hundred paternosters during the next seven days. And all the brothers who are under the command of that house where the brother has passed away should say the hundred paternosters, as is said above, after the death of the brother is known, by God's mercy. Also we pray and command by pastoral authority that a pauper be fed with meat and wine for forty days in memory of the dead brother, just as if he were alive. We expressly forbid all other offerings which used to be made at will and without discretion by the Poor Knights of the Temple on the death of brothers, at the feast of Easter and at other feasts.

63. Moreover, you should profess your faith with a pure heart night and day that you may be compared in this respect to the wisest of all the prophets, who said: 'I will take the cup of salvation.' Which means: 'I will avenge the death of Jesus Christ by my death. For just as Jesus Christ gave his body for me, I am prepared in the same way to give my soul for my brothers.' This is a suitable offering; a living sacrifice and very pleasing to God.

## On the Priests and Clerks who Serve Charity

64. The whole of the common council commands you to render all offerings and all kinds of alms in whatever manner they may be given, to the chaplains and clerks and to others who remain in charity for a fixed term. According to the authority of the Lord God, the servants of the Church may have only food and clothing, and may not presume to have anything else unless the Master wishes to give them anything willingly out of charity.

## On Secular Knights

65. Those who serve out of pity and remain with you for a fixed term are knights of the house of God and of the Temple of

Solomon; therefore out of pity we pray and finally command that if during his stay the power of God takes any one of them, for love of God and out of brotherly mercy, one pauper be fed for seven days for the sake of his soul, and each brother in that house should say thirty paternosters.

*On Secular Knights who Serve for a Fixed Term*
66. We command all secular knights who desire with a pure heart to serve Jesus Christ and the house of the Temple of Solomon for a fixed term to faithfully buy a suitable horse and arms, and everything that will be necessary for such work. Furthermore, we command both parties to put a price on the horse and to put the price in writing so that it is not forgotten; and let everything that the knight, his squire and horse need, even horseshoes, be given out of fraternal charity according to the means of the house. If, during the fixed term, it happens by chance that the horse dies in the service of the house, if the house can afford to, the Master should replace it. If, at the end of his tenure, the knight wishes to return to his own country, he should leave to the house, out of charity, half the price of the horse, and the other half he may, if he wishes, receive from the alms of the house.

*On the Commitment of Sergeants*
67. As the squires and sergeants who wish to serve charity in the house of the Temple for the salvation of their souls and for a fixed term come from divers regions, it seems to us beneficial that their promises be received, so that the envious enemy does not put it in their hearts to repent of or renounce their good intentions.

*On White Mantles*
68. By common counsel of all the chapter we forbid and order expulsion, for common vice, of anyone who without discretion was in the house of God and of the Knights of the Temple; also that the sergeants and squires should not have white habits, from which custom great harm used to come to the house; for in the regions beyond the mountains false brothers, married men and others who said they were brothers of the Temple used to be sworn in; while they were of the world. They brought so much shame to us and harm to the Order of Knighthood that even their squires boasted of it; for this reason numerous scandals arose. Therefore let them assiduously be given black robes; but if these cannot be found, they should be given what is

*available in that province; or what is the least expensive, that is burell.*

## On Married Brothers
*69. If married men ask to be admitted to the fraternity, benefice and devotions of the house, we permit you to receive them on the following conditions: that after their death they leave you a part of their estate and all that they have obtained henceforth. Meanwhile, they should lead honest lives and endeavour to act well towards the brothers. But they should not wear white habits or cloaks; moreover, if the lord should die before his lady, the brothers should take part of his estate and let the lady have the rest to support her during her lifetime; for it does not seem right to us that such confréres should live in a house with brothers who have promised chastity to God.*

## On Sisters
*70. The company of women is a dangerous thing, for by it the old devil has led many from the straight path to Paradise. Henceforth, let not ladies be admitted as sisters into the house of the Temple; that is why, very dear brothers, henceforth it is not fitting to follow this custom, that the flower of chastity is always maintained among you.*

## Let Them Not Have Familiarity with Women
*71. We believe it to be a dangerous thing for any religious to look too much upon the face of woman. For this reason none of you may presume to kiss a woman, be it widow, young girl, mother, sister, aunt or any other; and henceforth the Knighthood of Jesus Christ should avoid at all costs the embraces of women, by which men have perished many times, so that they may remain eternally before the face of God with a pure conscience and sure life.*

## Not Being Godfathers
*72. We forbid all brothers henceforth to dare to raise children over the font and none should be ashamed to refuse to be godfathers; this shame brings more glory than sin.*

## On the Commandments
*73. All the commandments which are mentioned and written above in this present Rule are at the discretion and judgement of the Master.*

With the success of gaining the backing of the council and the order's Rule now completed, we only had to get the Holy Father to give his blessing. So, with our Rule, the written support of the council and our hidden treasure in hand, we departed Troyes for the ten-day trek to Rome.

* * * * * * * * * *

St Peter's basilica was magnificent to behold. The five of us on horseback, dressed in our new white mantles, must have been quite a sight to behold as well. Leaving the horses in the care of Montbard, Hugues, Saint-Omer and I climbed the large staircase in front of the arches and crossed the colonnaded atrium to the basilica itself where we knew the Holy Father was awaiting our arrival.

We were met at the entrance to the basilica by a young priest who had been sent to greet us and bring us to the Holy Father's meeting hall. We entered through an enormous open wooden door and, turning to the right before we entered the core of the church, quickly found ourselves in a medium-sized ornately decorated but rather sparsely furnished room with about fifteen or so men hovering at the base of a few low-level stairs leading to the large dark throne chair, canopied in red velvet and gold trim. And on it sat the Holy Father in his papal white robes and a cloak of gold, a rounded silver head covering with a small cross at its apex atop his head.

An elderly man nearing seventy, Pope Honorius's dour expression barely visible through a thick dark grey beard that fell to the middle of his chest left all those before him in no doubt of his complete lack of interest in whatever they were discussing. He saw his priest servant approach with us trailing behind and raised his right hand in a motion that demanded silence. The chatter stopped immediately and all eyes turned upon us.

Hugues approached the steps and knelt, bowing his head in reverence, we followed suit and waited for the Holy Father to speak. Instead we heard the priest announce us.

"Holy Father, Hugues de Payns and his men," he gestured towards us, "request a private audience."

Honorius grunted and after a moment, shooed away everyone else in the room. With suspicious glances, the others reluctantly departed, unhappy that they were not allowed to stay to hear our story and resenting their time with the Pope being usurped. The doors clicked shut with a heavy thud and the priest motioned for us to rise.

Honorius waved Hugues to approach and offered his ringed hand to kiss. Hugues knelt again, kissed the ring and stepped back to his original place.

"I have received word from the Council of your work and your request to have this, ah, new brotherhood sanctioned and given my blessing," Honorius said getting right to the point.

That was Hugues's cue to speak.

"Yes, Holy Father, the Council has given their approval and Abbot Bernard has written the Rule…."

"Yes, I have read it," Honorius interrupted.

His eyes narrowed and his mouth made a sucking noise through his teeth.

"I have many requests such as this made of me, what makes your Order more worthy of my endorsement than the others?"

We were not expecting this. We had been assured that the Pope was agreeable and supported our efforts, why was he now questioning us? Hugues took a deep breath before responding.

"Our work, Holy Father, is primarily for the Holy Land, creating an Order that is determined to support and maintain our presence there and give assistance to those on pilgrimage whilst protecting…"

But Honorius interrupted again.

"The Hospitallers are already there doing just that. Why not simply join them?" he demanded.

"We believe our Hospitaller Brothers wish to focus their work on providing care to the ill and wounded from the skirmishes with the local bandits…"

"Nonsense!" the Pope growled in exasperation. "They have been in Jerusalem for years and are perfectly capable of continuing to do the work you claim only you are capable of doing. I see no reason to create another Order," he stated flatly, his mind seemingly made up.

Again, this was concerning. What had happened between the time Abbot Bernard had sent the Rule and his treatise to Honorius? Had something happened to cause a falling out with the Holy Father? I could tell Hugues seemed just as bemused as the rest of us and looking at the priest gave us no answers as he stood to the side, hands clasped in front of himself, eyes downcast focused on the floor.

Sizing up the situation, Hugues realized the tide had changed and the Pope was no longer with us. We needed leverage to persuade the Holy Father to move his support back to us. Hugues must have known he now had no choice but to reveal the writings which had lain undiscovered in clay urns in dark, sealed rooms, hidden from human eyes and keeping their secrets for hundreds of years. He motioned to Saint-Omer who handed him a leather pouch which contained a copy of the Secret Book of John codex that Théos had meticulously replicated, in its original language, with the leather coverings etched just as the original had been. The original, of course, remaining hidden far away.

Hugues carefully removed it from the pouch and passed it to the priest who examined it, looking for any sort of hidden danger and, finding none, approached the Holy Father, extending his arms and bowing slightly as he handed it to him.

"What is this?" Honorius said suspiciously, running his hands over the leather cover, tracing the engraved words on it with his fingers before gently opening the cover, his eyes focusing on the strange writings.

His head jerked slightly as he gave a start, he obviously could read Coptic and knew what it said.

"'Το μυστικό βιβλίο του Ιωάννη'" he whispered its title and looked at Hugues incredulously. "How...? Where...?" he stuttered.

Hugues remained calm, giving nothing away.

"There is more," he said adding, "this is but one of our discoveries. We have had it translated..." he continued but the Pope waved his words away.

"I know what it is, I know what it says," Honorius snapped. Seeming to rethink his tone, he asked more softly, staring down at what he was holding, almost not wanting to hear the answer, "What else have you found?"

Hugues did not gesture to anyone else but instead reached into his own leather bag and removed a rolled parchment from it. This time he did not hand it to the priest but rather placed it in the Pope's hands himself. This caused the priest to start but he was quieted with a glance from his master. Honorius placed the codex onto his lap, unknotted the ribbon the roll was tied with, unfurled the parchment and read Théos's translation of the writings on the Emerald Tablet.

The Holy Father was clearly affected, his gnarled hands began to tremble to the point of almost not being able to hold the page. He lowered the parchment so it rested on the codex, the fingers on his left hand rubbing his forehead in small circles as if trying to rid his mind of what he had just read, then moving down his face as if wiping it, finally clasping his bearded jaw as he leaned his elbow on the arm of his chair.

"You…" he began, then took a breath, "you have the originals?"

Hugues simply nodded. The two men stared at each other. We knew at that moment we had won the argument and the Pope would now be forced to make concessions.

"What is it you want?" he eventually asked, dropping his hand onto his lap, knowing he had been outmanoeuvred.

"What we came here for, your Holiness," Hugues responded, keeping the tone of his voice respectful and non-confrontational.

We knew it would be best to keep this Pope as our friend and ally rather than as a foe. Honorius nod was barely perceptible, the muscles in his jaw moving as he clenched and unclenched his teeth. But that soon stopped as his arrogance and haughty demeanour slipped away. Resignation had set in.

"So be it," he stated finally, a weariness having entered his voice.

"And," Hugues added, causing the Pope's lips to purse in worried anticipation, "the Order shall be accountable to no crowned head. The Order shall only be accountable to the papacy."

This had not been discussed prior to our arrival but none of us reacted as though this was a surprise. It was genius of Hugues to think of such a thing, the freedoms this would give us would be almost immeasurable. And it would mean we would have the unfettered support of this and every successive Pope. That gave us power.

Honorius thought upon this for a moment, running through its meaning, the ramifications and the outrage he would face throughout the Christian world should he agree to this demand. And yet, he must have recognized that the damage to the papacy would have been considerable and a far greater concern than the anger of any simpering king, whose very power depended on the existence of the papacy, each feeding the other. One did not challenge the church for very long, the failure of the anti-popes over the years had proved that. He must have realized that saving his position and that of the church was vital and his sole objective now. He knew he had no choice but to agree. Perhaps he thought he could undo this at some point, but whatever his reasoning, he acquiesced.

"Agreed," he said quietly, nodding gently. "But I will insist on regular communication from you, or whomever is Grand Master, we must know what it is the Order is busying itself with. We will not allow the reputation of the church to be abused."

"Agreed," Hugues said with no hesitation.

He stepped forward and for a moment I thought he was going to kneel in front of the Holy Father to receive his blessing but he did not. Instead he leaned down towards Honorius and gently took both the codex copy and the parchment from his lap. If Hugues had wanted to demonstrate the new equality between them, he could not have picked a better way. He then returned to our group, handing everything to Saint-Omer who promptly packed it all away, safe and secure.

We had won the day. And now, with the blessing of the Holy Father for the Order in place, we would soon find ourselves on our way back to Jerusalem.

# VII

# Part Two

# 1129-1135 - Jerusalem

The Holy Father's endorsement drew the attention of the Christian world to our new Order and support began to flow in from various sources. So much interest came from across the Channel in England that Hugues decided to send Montdidier there to set up a monastic house, a sort of headquarters from which our business in the south of England could be conducted. I declined his request that I do so, he did not question me why. Montdidier settled on the village of Guiting, in the county of Gloucestershire, not very far away from some D'Ivry lands in Minstre. My brother Guillaume had been building on the lands there and had established quite a holding, he welcomed Montdidier and insisted he stay with him until the preceptory in Guiting was ready.

Hugues, Montbard, Saint-Omer and I made our way back to Jerusalem, this time over land, following the path we took on our crusade almost twenty years prior, educating Montbard on our adventures and battles that we had encountered along the way. And each time we stopped for the night, we were well welcomed, the news of our new Order having preceded us and reached the ears of the rulers and many of the important men of the city or town we were in. Everyone pledged support and promised funds and supplies would be sent regularly, many asked if they would be able to join us. We instructed them to make their way to Jerusalem where we would be able to vet them properly and test their sincerity, after all they would be sacrificing much to join the Order.

We were treated like royalty, despite our vows of poverty, by Emperor John of Constantinople, the son of Emperor Alexios who had died ten years earlier. And meeting Bohemond's son, named for his father, in Antioch as he had reached his majority a few years ago and was now Prince of that realm, was wonderful. He reminded those of us who knew his father of the great man he had been and we were able to regale the son with stories of how he had won the city. We stopped in Acre as we crossed through Outremer and were treated well by the Hospitaller Brothers, the building works they had been engaged in over the past years was quite impressive. Their large meeting house was close to the harbour, easily accessible to receive the supplies they needed to maintain the properties. I could not help wondering if the rooms we stayed in were the same as those used by the Brothers who had come here late the previous year for the negotiations for Melisende's marriage to Count Fulk. A twinge went through me when I thought of their impending wedding set for early summer. I was hoping my commitment to our new Rule would soon stop those.

We were welcomed warmly by our brothers who had stayed behind and kept the city safe and secure. They were pleased to receive their new horses that were given to us by Montbard's nephew Count Bernard. Théos was very glad to see our return, eager to hear of our travels and how we were received by the council and then by Pope Honorius. He had already heard the outcome, news having reached Jerusalem not only through our own correspondence with the Brothers but just in the various ways that information made its way across the lands. And of course now that Hugues was back in control as Grand Master, he would meet with King Baldwin and Melisende just as he had when he had returned from the marriage negotiations. This should not have bothered me, but it did.

We quickly got settled back in our routine and it was not long before the impact of the announcement of our Order took effect. Requests to join the Order started to roll in and we needed to determine how we would manage them. The Rule had already established the preference for the unmarried and the conditions to be imposed for the married. But that was not the only criteria and we soon realized that we needed someone to help administrate it all.

In our absence, a new member whose name was Robert de Craon had joined us, a man who had travelled from Aquitaine in France to Jerusalem when he had heard our Order had been formed. He had been engaged to be married but abandoned the arrangement upon hearing of the Templars and made his way to Jerusalem expressly to join us. But as most of us had been away these past months, the remaining Brothers had admitted him only as a lay Brother not as a knight. The Brothers told us reports of his valour and military expertise in seeing off a number of bandit attacks on travellers arriving from Arsuf, they seemed to be quite impressed by him. He had attended all masses and made no complaints of the manual labour asked of him and so after a thorough investigation we accepted him and Hugues knighted him just as we had been. He immediately set to work making his way through all the correspondence and papers that had arrived and continued to arrive, there did not seem to be an end in sight.

We quickly realized that our rather simplistic way of organizing the members was not going to be enough and so we set about creating levels of offices to which Brothers would be assigned or could aspire to once they joined at the novice level. We settled on six new major officers to start with in our location in addition to the Grand Master who would, of course, be responsible for the Order across the known world. These high offices included:

The Seneschal - Grand Master Deputy, responsible for advising the Grand Master and performing administrative duties.

The Marshal - responsible for all military activities, battle-planning and responsible for the stable and the horses

The Chancellor - responsible for the mints, all monies, coin, gold, silver, jewels, and any other valuables to be used for trade and barter for supplies for the Order.

The Constable & Standard Bearer - responsible for all prisoners of battle and maintaining all banners and flags.

The Chamberlain - responsible for all housing and sleeping quarters for those in the high offices.

The Butler - responsible for all food, drink, and meals for those in the high offices

We knew there would be other offices required once preceptories began to appear across the Christian world but these could wait for now. Saint-Omer was chosen as Seneschal, Saint-Agnan continued managing what had been meagre funds in his new office as Chancellor, Bisol took on the responsibilities of the Constable and Standard Bearer, Montbard became our first official Chamberlain and Rossal took on the role of Butler whilst I became Marshal. Later on we agreed to an Under Marshal which Bisol took on relinquishing the role of Constable and Standard Bearer to Gondamer. The rest of the Order would continue in the roles they were currently in, squires, cooks, stable hands and suchlike.

Once these roles were decided, we discussed the need for a standard for our Order, a banner that would represent both the monastic and military in us. Lots of designs were brought forward, crosses and shields, different colours and emblems but all of them seemed to be too busy, nothing seemed to be right. I thought it needed to be simplistic and straightforward, its meaning understood upon sight and the others agreed. It was when I was out on patrol late one afternoon in early spring when it came to me.

I had taken one of the two horses given to me by Montbard's nephew for a walk around the outer walls of the city and then through the Garden of Gethsemane to the top of the Mount of Olives and had dismounted so the horse could rest a moment and take a drink from a small stream nearby. I wandered back down the hill taking in the glorious view, pausing many times to revel in its beauty. The sun was setting in the west behind the city, giving an unearthly glow to it and basking me in a soft warmth contrasting against the chill of the approaching evening. Once sated, I turned and began my ascent and glanced up, seeing my piebald horse standing majestically atop of the hill, awaiting my return, the stark contrast in its colouring lit up by the western sun. And I knew instantly what our standard would be.

"Black and white," I said simply to the others the next time we met to discuss these things. "Made of two halves, the top black, the bottom white, signifying the dual-purpose of our Order, the monasticism and the militarism, the evil that we fight underpinned by the good that we do. The duality…of human nature," I said the last almost in a whisper.

They all sat still when I brought this to them at our next gathering, contemplating the meaning of this for a moment. Hugues looked from Brother to Brother and then nodded.

"Yes, it is perfect, let it be done," he said solemnly, and soon Bisol found himself busied with the task of having the banners created for us.

With the rumours that the Muslim world was starting to organise again and the threat of attack in the Holy Land ever-increasing, the need to enhance our military forces became urgent. And that fell to me, which was good because as the spring neared its end, the wedding between Melisende and Count Fulk grew nearer and I was not wishing to be reminded of it. So I kept busy, organizing new recruits into squads and running them through attack and defence tactics, using different weapons but teaching them to trust their sword the most. Eventually we would have to move them to various Christian strongholds throughout the Holy Land, Acre, Jaffa, Ascalon and others would become home to many of them.

Along with the physical skills, we taught the men about the reason for the Order, and how, as a band of Brothers, it had become our life's purpose as it would theirs and the support and caretaking of each other was paramount. Hugues emphasized this by the emblem he designed of two Brothers astride a single mount. The Rule was taught daily, each new member was told to live their life by it, and they were tested regularly. We ran mock battles and it was during one of these that Bisol, as he raised our flag, called out a battle cry which was to become known across the world: "Beauséant!," "Be Glorious!," the same I had used during the tournaments. We decided later to name the standard this.

We instilled an honour code that was second to none, and our Templar Beauséant was hoisted for all to see. Battle protocols even surrounded it, each unit would have its own flag, carried by a standard-bearer whose sole responsibility was to ensure it was always held aloft with other Brothers charged with guarding it. No Templar Brother was allowed to leave a battlefield as long as one such Templar flag was still flying and even if one was not, they were instructed to make their way to any Christian flag they could see was still in the air. Only if none could be found were they then allowed to abandon the fight. And of course, if any unit was set upon unexpectedly, at least one Templar was to make his escape to go for reinforcements – I learned that from my experiences in the woods outside Antioch, which were burned into my memory.

As was meeting the strange lad Zengi who over the years had become Atabeg of Mosul and Aleppo, two of Syria's most important strongholds. I knew he was destined to be a great and powerful leader and I thought of him every once in a while, wondering if he remembered the tall, gangly boy from the west whose life he saved the night Antioch fell to us.

But even though I tried to keep the impending marriage out of my mind, it was the talk of just about everyone in the Order, whether they were involved in preparations for security for the event or attending as guests. Having been one of three Brothers invited – Hugues and Saint-Omer being the others – I tried to beg off saying I was needed more for organizing the policing but both Hugues and King Baldwin were having none of it. And so I had no choice but to attend and maintain a stoic, unemotional façade, but I had become good at that over the years until I met this lady. She had penetrated the armour.

The wedding ceremony was held in the Holy Sepulchre and officiated at by Patriarch de la Ferté much to King Baldwin's chagrin as he did not care for the holy man. But it was the Patriarch's right and Count Fulk was determined to be wed in the most important church in Christendom, intended to certainly outdo his own son's wedding the previous year back in France. Geoffrey Plantagenet, called thus because of a yellow sprig of broom brush he wore in his headgear, had married Matilda, the daughter of King Henry of England after her husband the Emperor had died, and was made Count of Anjou once Fulk had departed for Jerusalem for his own wedding, Fulk expecting to become King of Jerusalem upon Baldwin's death, ruling instead of his wife. Melisende, no doubt, would have other plans.

So on that warm day in early June, I stood at the far side of the nave, hoping to go unnoticed. But of course my great height put me head and shoulders above most of the guests and I could not help but be mesmerised by the sight of her, clad in shimmering gold, practically floating down the centre aisle. Even through her gossamer veil I could see her eyes, fervently searching the crowds of people, seeming to relax upon meeting my gaze. In my arrogance, for a moment I thought she might turn and run to me but of course she did not. She could not.

The wedding celebrations lasted a few days, I made my excuses saying I was needed in Jaffa to oversee the arrival of some supplies, of course that could have been done by any junior knight. But it allowed others to join in the revelry, which I wanted no part of. Aside from how I felt about the Princess, I simply did not like Count Fulk. I needed to keep my distance lest I risk letting my feelings show which would embarrass Melisende and the Order as control of one's emotions was an essential skill taught to all new members and for me to lose mine would not bode well.

And so that was how it was to be for the two of us, each doing our duty, me focussing on training the new recruits and she doing what she needed to do to prepare for her role as Queen of Jerusalem. Providing an heir of course was critical to continuing the royal line of succession and there were celebrations when she presented Fulk with a son named after her father, the third Baldwin who was destined to eventually take the crown of King of Jerusalem. I tried my best to not be in her presence but occasions such as this drew us together and even though we did not speak much and certainly never alone, I sensed the connection between us as the world melted away each time our eyes met. But try as I might, the longing I was feeling for her did not dissipate by not being near her but intensified. I needed to remember my oath as a Templar, easier said than done.

Adding to this difficult time was the unexpected death of two of our founding Brothers early in the new year. Just after the birth of the prince, both Saint-Omer and Bisol took to their beds, ill with sweating sickness. Eventually they were moved to private quarters in the Hospitaller hospital near the Holy Sepulchre and I visited them daily, reporting on their progress to Hugues who was concerned of contagion at first. Eventually he came to understand the fate both were destined for and he relented and began to accompany me. It was maddening to sit and watch them waste away, two strong, resilient men losing the battle to some unknown and unfightable disease, all bringing to the fore memories of the night I lost my lady and finding it infuriating to be unable to help them. It was gut-wrenching to hear from the Hospitallers there was nothing more they could do for them, we felt as though pieces of us were dying with them. And so, despite the constant and dedicated hard work of the Hospitaller Brothers, we lost both of them, within a few days of each other, just before Annunciation Day. Needless to say, we held no feasts on the day and only attended the masses because it was expected of us. But the loss of my good friend Bisol weighed heavily upon me, guilt and shame that I had, in some way, failed them both.

This was followed by the death of King Baldwin later in the same year. Rumours abounded that the marriage between Melisende and Fulk was fraught with tension and discord and the King had been concerned that Fulk would repudiate Melisende and try to rule on his own in his infant son's name. The King had been concerned about this even before the wedding and had made provisions in the marriage treaty to prevent this, but there was no telling what Fulk might try to do. But the nobles made it clear that Melisende was Queen and that she and Fulk should reign together as co-rulers until the boy had reached his majority and the two of them did their best to show a united front. But I knew better. I saw through the façade and felt the unhappiness deep inside her. And there was nothing I could do to alleviate it her pain. Or she mine.

\* \* \* \* \* \* \* \* \* \*

In early spring of the year 1134 I received the news I had been expecting for quite some time and had been rather surprised not to hear it before then: Duke Robert was dead. He had been moved from Devizes Castle after spending almost twenty years as its prisoner, and ended his days locked away in Cardiff Castle. I felt sick to my stomach when I was told. I knew after our last battle against his brother, he was destined to spend the rest of his life under lock and key, such was the fear King Henry had of Robert's ability to raise an army to his cause. But when his pride and heir William Clito had died, I had no doubt Robert had been left utterly bereft. I am surprised he lasted as long as he did. I spent some time in the rotunda of the Holy Sepulchre, sitting on one of the stone benches in the niches along the curved walls, just thinking about him and the adventures we had together. I felt true sorrow at the loss of him. History would probably be cruel to his memory, but I remembered the man who had great love and generosity in his heart for those close to him, the man whose skills at military strategy were surpassed only really by those of Prince Bohemond, and the man whose willingness to take a young boy on crusade helped that boy grow into a man. I would be forever grateful to him for it.

Occasionally I would descend into the lower levels of the Temple Mount and walk the tunnels, quite a few now as we had found more once we returned from Rome. I would go alone now that I no longer had my friend Bisol to wander with and I had not really found anyone to replace him. But although we had excavated extensively and opened other tunnels, nothing else of interest had been found and they all eventually seemed to lead to dead ends.

Our Order had grown extensively with preceptories being built in England and France, but the secret teachings were only shared to a few, those who we determined were of an openness of mind to understand and accept the meaning of the words hidden away for so long. But those who were taught the secret knowledge and prayers knew instantly their power and the vital need for secrecy.

It was late in the afternoon a few months later on an early summer day when Hugues and I received some surprising news. We were in the midst of discussing the succession crisis in England and even though King Henry had remarried after the death of his only male heir in the White Ship disaster, he had produced no more legitimate sons and only had his daughter Empress Matilda to take the crown after his death. She had given Geoffrey of Anjou two sons but although those in the east had accepted the rule of a with woman with Melisende, those in the West had yet to become so enlightened. We expected civil war if this was not resolved quickly. In the midst of this, an excited knock came at the doors and Saint-Agnan entered, a look on his face matching the intensity of his knock.

"We have found it!" he exclaimed breathlessly.

Hugues raised both his hands in an effort to calm him.

"Compose yourself Brother," Hugues said quietly. "What has been found?"

Saint-Agnan took a breath.

"Zedekiah's Cave," he said almost imperceptibly.

Hugues and I were stunned. We had heard rumours of the cave, supposedly where the King of Judea had hidden whilst trying to escape from

Nebuchadnezzar's men after the Babylonian King set siege to the city. But after all these years we had come to believe it was just a myth.

"Explain," Hugues quietly urged him.

"We had been repairing part of the wall between the Damascus and Herod Gates and had some local boys helping bringing some of the tools and supplies the men needed when we noticed one of them had slipped near some rather large boulders at the base of the wall. We rushed over to see if he had been injured but he had simply disappeared, as if the earth had swallowed him whole. It was not until we were right next to the boulders looking for the lad that we noticed a space, only wide enough for a child to slip into, between one of the boulders and the wall. We heard his cries and with the effort of several of us we were able to move one of the largest rocks enough to allow us to get through. And what we saw!"

Hugues raised his hands slightly again as we could tell Saint-Agnan was getting animated again. After taking another breath he continued.

"There is what looks to be a natural cistern or well of some sort, we found the lad crumpled at the bottom, but so far down we could not reach him with just our arms and he had nothing to cling onto to be able to climb out the walls being very smooth. We lowered a rope ladder but when he tried to stand we realized he had injured his leg – it is possibly broken - so I went down to help him. Once we had secured him, the others lifted him safely out."

"And how is the boy now?" Hugues asked.

"He is with the Hospitallers, they expect him to recover fully but it will be a while before he is running about again."

"I am glad to hear it, we must take him something to help his recovery, make sure he has fresh fruit and something to occupy his mind," Hugues said.

"I shall see to it," Saint-Agnan said.

"So, go on, what did you find there?" I pressed him, eager to hear what he had to say once we were assured of the boy's health.

"I examined the space where the boy had fallen and I noticed an opening in the wall at the base of the cistern, it actually extends beneath the wall itself. I called for a torch and knelt to get a better view. The opening is quite small, barely wide enough to get my head and shoulders through and only then by contorting myself. I lit the torch and reached in and I saw that the hole continued right through the wall but what was beyond it I was not able to see. So I ordered a couple of the men to come down with picks and axes to widen the opening enough to be able to get a man through. I think you need to come see for yourself what we found."

Hugues and I looked at each other and were on our feet instantly, and without another word followed Saint-Agnan through the marketplace out of the city to a spot a few hundred steps to the east of the Damascus Gate where we were greeted by the sight of several men standing beside a few massive rocks, looking down at what seemed to be nothing. It was not until we were almost on top of them that we noticed the small dry well at the bottom. With the boulders in their original places, we could see why no one would have known it was there.

The men had removed quite a bit of the rocks around the cistern, we could see the remnants having been dumped on the other side from where we were standing. But even from where we were, we could not see the opening to the cave at the bottom which was set back into the wall, we needed to descend into the pit to actually see it. And so we did.

The depth of the drop was deceptive, much deeper than I initially thought. We saw the work Saint-Agnan and the men had done to widen the entrance and both Hugues and myself were able to crawl through to the other side. And the sight that met us was simply mesmerizing.

We stood to our full height and for a long moment did not move. We just stared. A few of our men had gone before and had laid small candle pots along the rocky floor of the cave creating an eery path of flickering orange lights making the far walls dance with shadows. The cave looked to descend down a steady slope into darkness almost immediately, a few steps from the opening. It seemed to go on forever, we could not see the end, and soon enough those who had gone ahead of us returned to fetch more candles.

Hugues and I then continued on our own, holding lit torches which provided light when the candle pots along the path came to an end. We meandered, veering to the left or right wherever the ground was smoother and easier to pass over. And once the torches became our only source of light, we had to choose our steps carefully, finding our way through sharp-edged rocks that could slice our legs and pebbles we could lose our footing on. The air was muggy and damp, unlike that aboveground, having the hot and dry air of early autumn. The further down we went, the cooler the temperature turned and the sweat on our bodies turned cold.

The walls were bare, no writings or etchings were to be seen anywhere, nothing to give any hint of who had created the cave or who had been the last to be in it. Each time we thought we had reached the end we spied a passageway that led down even further, so much so that a darkness fell in behind us as the light from our torches reached their limits.

"Incredible," Hugues finally murmured, breaking an awe-inspired silence.

I quickly calculated some measurements and orientation in my head.

"This is the bedrock of the city," I said pointing above us. "We are directly under the north-eastern marketplace. It is remarkable that this has not been discovered before now, that no one has dug down far enough to break through from above," I said examining the ceiling of the cave.

As we continued along, our path began to level out and we came to an arched opening in the stone wall. Our torches lit the way ahead and suddenly we saw something glimmering in the darkness and we realized we had come across a pool of water, black as the night and stretching farther than our torch light would reveal. It was impossible to tell what the source of the pool was without actually getting in and following it along but somehow it was being fed. I reached down and dipped my fingertips into the water, it was cool to my touch. I looked up at Hugues who simply nodded as he continued to look about him. We both knew there was much work to be done exploring this cave.

* * * * * * * * *

The summer crept along, each day hotter than the last, and the cave and its black pool and cool waters provided a relief to the searing temperatures outside. We decided that only members of the Order should have access until the cave could be fully investigated and that would take some time considering the size of it and its many meandering passageways. To think this had existed all this time with us walking above it all was almost unbelievable. I had taken to visiting the cave fairly often to cool off and soon found myself enjoying the occasions when I could swim in the pool, especially doing lengths underwater when I could block out the daily noise and have my thoughts to myself. Each time I pushed myself a little further to see how long I could last before needing to surface for air. It was on one such occasion that I made the discovery that would eventually make me a wanted man for years to come.

It was very late on a particularly hot night when the heat of the day had not abated much when I decided to take a quick swim in the pool to cool down. No one else was in the cave and so I felt comfortable enough to strip off my sweat-stained clothing down to my braies. I dove in, my hot body instantly cooled by the water enveloping me completely with its gentle caress. Strong strokes propelled me easily through, I met no resistance until I reached the other side where I turned and swam back to where I started. I did this countless times and eventually stopped to catch my breath, deciding to rest a bit on a recessed ledge along the far side of the pool. But when hoisting myself up and twisting to take a seat, I felt something slip down my chest. Realizing what it was, I quickly reached to stop its descent but I was too late; I saw the St Michael medal and chain my mother had given me as a boy drop silently into the water.

I froze, staring at the spot where it had disappeared, small ripples caused by the medal ebbing quickly until it was gone. I knew I must retrieve it but also knew I would have to do so blindly, the single torch I had brought with me still sitting where I dropped it, providing little light to where I sat, not that bringing it closer would have helped, the water's darkness was almost impenetrable. I would need to use touch and feel my way around the bottom of the pool.

Slipping back into the water, I took three deep breaths and on the third dove downward, feeling the wall of the pool beside me, hoping that I would be close enough to find the medal quickly. Reaching the bottom, I felt the floor, carefully trying not to miss any spot where the medal might be. Frustrated that I was failing, I surfaced to get another breath and then when I was ready, dove again. I traced the wall with my hand again, feeling my way until I reached where it turned into the pool's floor and started my search again. I reckoned the medal could not have been carried too far from the wall and dragged my hand back and forth along, feeling for either the chain or the medal itself.

I was quickly running out of air again when my fingertips came upon the chain and then eventually the medal. Grasping them, I twisted my body around and pushed off the floor with my right foot, pushing hard to get back to the surface as quickly as I could but as I did so, I could feel the floor give way, as if pressing on it had made a part of the floor drop. I did not give it any thought and continued my ascent, gasping for air as soon as I was able and, gripping the chain tightly, I pulled myself out of the pool and sat myself on the ledge. I took a few deep breaths before inspecting the chain and the medal, wiping away the excess water dripping down my face. As I suspected, the clasp had simply worn through, I must have knocked the medal getting out of the pool causing the clasp to finally give way. I made a mental note to take it to the jewellers in the marketplace to have it repaired.

Relieved to have retrieved it, I leaned back into a recessed part of the wall to rest a moment and regain my composure. This medal was the only memento I had from my mother other than her letters, but it had seen me through battles on the field and off, and of course I had memories of my lady tracing it with her soft fingers as it lay on my chest when we were in our marriage bed. The memory was bittersweet and made me realize how important such a little thing was to me.

Taking another deep breath, I prepared myself to get back into the water and return to the other side where my clothes were awaiting me. I stretched and looked up and was stunned to see that the top right of the recessed niche I was sitting in had moved, revealing a narrow open gap in the wall. Suddenly I was filled with the feeling that this was all eerily familiar. I reached up my right hand and felt along the gap and sure enough, my fingers came upon the same formation in the rock that I had felt under the shelf in the hidden room under the Temple Mount.

I turned and knelt, barely fitting in the small space, I could feel the top of my head grazing the ceiling, and reached up again, this time with both hands and within moments I had found the two indentations I was expecting to find. Knowing what had worked the last time, I pressed down with my fingers and in with my palms and felt the rock move backwards, revealing an opening almost the size of my kneeling height and seemingly wide enough for me to squeeze through. Amazed and yet not surprised, Jerusalem kept revealing her secrets to me, I took a moment to marvel at the ingenuity of the opening. It was astonishing to find a second mechanism like the one that revealed hidden secrets. I felt my heart race wondering what might be hidden here.

I could not see into the space as it was pitch black, no light came from within its depths. I had a decision to make: investigate this now or wait until the morning when I could alert others who would come along and explore this with me. It was an easy choice and I quickly made it back to the other side of the pool, secured my chain in a pocket of my vest, retrieved a second torch, lit it using the first and carried it being careful not to get it wet as I swam my way back to the recessed ledge.

I placed the torch near the new opening and hoisted myself out of the water, then held it leaning into the dark space to try to get sight of what was there.

What I saw was a tunnel, a passageway, large enough for a man to walk through, strangely enough even for me which I was grateful for. I crawled through the opening and then stood, my eyes adjusting to the dimness. The torch flame barely flickered, there was no breeze of any kind to move it. The air was stale and thick with a musty scent and it almost hurt to breathe. It was obvious fresh air had not been in here for a very long time.

I stepped slowly down the passage, carefully examining the walls as I went, gingerly testing the floor with each movement before placing my full weight on it. I could see only a few steps in front of me using the light that was cast from the torch and so I was startled to see an object suddenly appear before me, a wooden chest that was so old it was rotting through. It was not large, its width about half that of my arms span and only my calf high. I dropped to my knees to examine it, studying it closely, looking for any kind of trick or trap that might have been set; I could see none. But through the brittle and cracked wooden slats, I could see something shining inside, reflecting the flame as I brought it near. I placed the torch against the wall nearest the box and gently touched the chest's lid, feeling along the top until I reached the sides. I hesitated a moment, thinking again if I should stop and fetch others but reckoned I had gone this far and decided to continue.

I applied enough pressure on the sides of the lid to try to lift it but realized it was stuck. Not because of some locking mechanism, but simply because years of not being opened had caused the lid to latch onto the body of the chest. I tried again, shaking the lid a bit trying to release its grip and suddenly with a splintering noise, it came loose and popped up in my hands, the rusted hinges snapping apart. I leaned forward and laid the lid against the wall behind the chest. Looking inside, I could see some sort of silken cloth, folded and placed tucked as if protecting the contents beneath. I moved the torch closer so I could see better and, although faded due to its years, I could tell the cloth once had been a vibrant mass of colours in swirling patterns now barely perceptible, the skill and artistry exquisite. I marvelled at its beauty.

Ever so gently lifting the cloth, slowly to make sure nothing was wrapped in it, I set it on the floor nearby, keeping it away from the water still dripping from my body. That is when the light from the torch lit up the contents of the chest which glittered as the flickering flame was reflected, dancing across what was there. What I could only assume were precious stones filled the chest, rubies, sapphires, diamonds, gold nuggets. No objects, no rings, jewellery or diadems of any sort, just honed and polished stones in varying shapes and sizes. I tried to estimate what the value might be as I picked up a few one at a time and examined each using the flame of the torch to judge the purity of the stone. And of course I had to wonder where this treasure came from; was it left here by King Zedekiah himself as he desperately fled the city from Nebuchadnezzar as legend had it, thinking he would be able to retrieve it when he returned? That would have been fascinating but I suspected this hoard was much younger than that.

I reached into the chest, digging my hand down into the stones feeling to see how far they went and to see if there was anything else being kept from view. Just as I had when I was searching blindly for my St Michael's medal, I could only use my sense of touch when suddenly I felt my fingertips hit an obstacle buried deep within the stones. I was able to get a grip on it and pulled it through. I held a wooden box, just over my hand's length long with a lid that was held in place by twine that had frayed and stuck to both the lid and box. It did not take much effort at all to undo it - which fell apart in my hands - and remove the lid.

Inside was a parchment of thick vellum, rolled and tied with a single strand of twine. I removed the string by gently working it free from being stuck to the parchment and then sliding it down the length of the scroll, took a deep breath and slowly and gently unrolled the skin, revealing writing in a language I instantly recognized. It was the same as what had been used to etch the words on the Emerald Tablet. I felt my body tense with excitement because I knew that from my studies with Théos that I now could decipher this without his help. And so I began to read.

It was confusing at first, rambling words without any connection, references to different kinds of animals, plants, herbs, some I had never heard of. It seemed to be nonsense but as I read it through again, I began to make sense of it. I suddenly realized that what I was looking at was a list of sorts, a set of instructions bringing together these odd things, but for what purpose I had no idea. I chuckled slightly nervously to myself thinking this is probably just a fool's ruse, surely it meant nothing and the stones were the real treasure? But that extra sense that Bishop Odo always claimed I had gnawed at me; there must have been a reason why this was included in this chest which was so well hidden from sight for so many years. I decided to take it with me and have a better look in daylight before I shared it with anyone. But for now, I needed to get back to the others and let them know about the treasure I had found so they could retrieve it and put it to good use.

I put the scroll back into the box and as I was doing so, I caught sight of what looked to be Arabic writing etched inside on the bottom:

الحياة إكسير

Startled, I read it again.

# Elixir of Life

Surely I had mis-read this. I knew the one person I could trust to ask.

I wrapped the box in the cloth and then replaced the lid on the chest. Making my way back to the pool, I extinguished the torch and left it on the ledge for whoever would return for the chest. I twisted my body and eased myself back into the water and swam on my side using one arm, the other holding the bundle over my head, being careful not to drop it. Once reaching the other side, I climbed out, quickly dressed and retraced my steps back out of the cave, emerging into night air so thick with humidity that I could feel it even before I reached the entrance, my small treasure secreted from sight.

*  *  *  *  *  *  *  *  *

It took Théos but a moment to confirm what I thought it said was correct. I also showed him the parchment which he read wide-eyed and curious after I told him how I had come by it.

"It is the same language as the codices and the tablet," he confirmed, reading it again.

"What does it mean?" I asked.

Théos thought and rubbed his now silvery bearded chin.

"There have always been rumours of magical texts written long ago by those who believed they had mastered ways of healing the sick or dying. That is what this is. Clearly someone has thought enough of this particular text to have hidden it away from dangerous eyes," he answered and then stopped for a moment.

He reached for the box the parchment came in, opened it and picked up the twine the parchment had been tied with. He began to nod almost imperceptibly, pursing his lips. And then he looked at me.

"This," he began, holding up the twine, "this is what the scroll was tied with?" he asked.

I nodded. He made a slight grunting noise. I waited.

"It is interesting, is it not, that this was tied with the same type of twine that was used to bind the codices, the handwriting looks identical and the parchment seems to be made of the same vellum?" he asked.

I had made the connection at the same time he was speaking the words.

"Same time, same writer?" I asked.

"It would seem so. Perhaps he, or she, wanted to tell whoever found these things that they are connected, to be used together. But this is just conjecture, we cannot be sure of that."

He thought carefully before speaking again.

"Sébastien, many have been convinced that they have found the elixir of life only to discover, to their own misery, that they were mistaken. Or others discovered them to be frauds with their claims to have knowledge of how to obtain some unearthly power. Many have suffered painful deaths due to their foolhardiness. I would suggest you rid yourself of this or, at the very least, keep it from prying eyes. For your own safety, I beg of you," he insisted rather earnestly.

"Have no fear my good friend," I said, "I have no god-like delusions."

"We shall see," Théos said.

# VII

## Part Three

## 1135 - 1136 – Jerusalem

The gems were retrieved and nothing further was said about the scroll although I did not destroy it as Théos had advised. As I suspected, the stones were quite valuable and brought a great deal of much needed monies to help fund a number of building works happening within the city walls. Melisende's vision for St Anne's church had come to fruition and we were able to put the finishing touches on the aisle columns and adding a new altar in the crypt below where it was said the Virgin Mary had been born in a grotto there.

Melisende was quite pleased with the result and I of course was happy to see her smile again. For a while now I had watched from afar and seen the light that had shone from her dim, stifled by the enormous presence of her over-reaching husband who desperately wanted to rule by himself, unhappy with the terms that had been set for him by Baldwin as the basis for the marriage. She had already given him one son and during their public appearances he had always deferred to her but it was a false freedom and she knew it – he demanded control of her and her activities were relegated to that of queenly duties rather than that of a ruler.

But Fulk knew that as long as she lived, he would always exist in her shadow. He must have known it would not be long before her thoughts would turn to how she could govern without him and ruling instead as regent through their young heir. But for now, the pretence would be kept up as the two of them seemed to be living increasingly separate lives. And there was nothing I could do to help her.

During this time of relative peace, we had many visitors to the city on pilgrimage or some business that we would assist with. Many members of royal families from across the West arrived to visit the sacred sites along with others, mostly either seeking salvation for some transgression or wishing to satisfy their curiosities about the Holy Land now that it was firmly in Christian hands. What they were not aware of was an undercurrent of dissatisfaction with the state of being in the Muslim world and a desire to reclaim this land for Islam had started to build. What had kept us relatively safe – the disparate, warring factions who would rather fight each other to press their rights to rule Palestine – was now turning to a threat as they began to unite. We had noticed the poetry and stories of jihad being spread across the Levant and reaching us in Jerusalem and it was cause for concern. But for now, the Fatimids to the south and the Seljuk Turks to the east were being kept at bay.

But it was not just the elite who came, people from all walks of life visited, some staying a short while, others longer and some who had heard the call and decided to make the City their home. If it were important enough, one would find the ways and means to make such a voyage that would be both costly and take months possibly years from their lives. Artists and craftsmen from around the world came to Jerusalem, some to sell their wares, others to learn or share their skill and artistry. Young men destined for the priesthood were sent by their families to be indoctrinated by the religious leaders at the holiest place in Christendom. Scientists and mathematicians and other scholars came to study and bring new inventions and ways of thinking.

One of these scholarly visitors to our compound was a very learned man we knew had been travelling throughout the west and east, studying with the Greeks and Arabs their ancient works and translating them into Latin. Adelard of Bath arrived one cool late autumn morning, eagerly anticipated by the senior Templar Brothers who were all very curious about this man who had served several English Kings and wanted to discuss with him his translations of various scientific texts on astronomy, alchemy, philosophy and mathematics. He was shown into the main hall in the Templar Palace on the Temple Mount after ensuring his horses had been taken care of and given one of our rooms to stay during his visit.

Many things were spoken of long into the nights he was with us. But the most fascinating was an object he had brought with him: he unveiled an Islamic astrolabe and placed it on the table before us. A Greek invention to study the celestial bodies and their positions in the night's sky, it was used to aid in determining physical locations, the time of day or night and even calculating the tides. But this astrolabe had been enhanced by the Arabs so it could be used to determine the qibla, the direction of Mecca for Muslim prayers and when the prayers needed to take place each day. It was an ingenious device and I spent much time with Adelard as I could asking him about it and riding with him out of the city and trying it from different places. I was disappointed when he departed but was glad to know he was willing to write and let me know how he was getting on with his various works.

During this time I also had been receiving letters from England on a fairly regular basis, having asked Osmond to keep me apprised of the yield of the many properties there. And of course enquiring what was happening with my daughter Margaux, making sure that she was well-cared for and was receiving the highest education at the Abbey and wanted for nothing. I was aware of her betrothal and subsequent marriage to Godwin de Clare, half-brother to the 2nd Earl of Pembroke. I had sent gifts and supplied her dowry of course, but even after all these years I found it too difficult to write to her myself. Too ashamed I had not written before. One of my many failings.

\* \* \* \* \* \* \* \* \*

In the months that followed, tensions between Melisende and Fulk worsened and we worried that their disintegrating marriage could fracture the tenuous peace that had existed over these years and cause civil war between their supporters. Patriarch la Ferté tried to intervene and provide counselling but his incompetence proved him unworthy of the task and when he failed he turned to Hugues to request assistance in bringing the two sides to an amicable agreement.

The negotiations lasted for weeks and we thought we were reaching a point where all were satisfied with the agreements when Melisende suddenly took ill of a mysterious ailment that seemed to have no discernible cause. The discussions were halted as we waited word on her condition but a day went by and then a few more without word of any improvement. I was desperate to see her but we were all kept away until the physicians determined whatever was ailing her would not be passed to us. But finally, I no longer needed to wait; she called for me.

Entering her private rooms at the Patriarch's Palace, I could not help but see how poorly she was. Laying in the oversized bed she once shared with Fulk, her maids moving quickly but silently around her, trying to cool her fevered body as best they could with cold cloths. And although it had been years, this was all too familiar. I caught the eye of one of chief physicians from the Hospitallers and with a nod of my head beckoned him to come to me.

"What is the cause of this?" I asked tentatively, not really wanting to hear the answer but knowing I must.

But he hesitated.

"I'm afraid we do not know for certain Brother Sébastien," he replied. "There are no open wounds, no rashes, no lesions. The fever and chills come and go, each bout worse than the last."

He hesitated again and made as if he wanted to continue but was nervous.

"Speak honestly Brother," I urged him quietly. "What you tell me goes no further."

He took a deep breath.

"I would not say this to anyone but you, but…" he glanced around the room and lowered his voice, "I suspect this is poison. And not from bad food or wine, but something more potent, something…more insidious."

I understood his meaning, nodded and walked slowly over to the bed. I was struck with fear as I approached, Melisende's body was covered by a thin sheet which could not hide the thinness that had taken hold from lack of appetite. I knelt and pushed aside the beautiful psalter with its ornately ivory carved covers dotted with blue stones which rested by her thigh, a gift given to her by her treacherous husband in better days of their marriage.

I reached for her hand which felt cold and sweaty to the touch. Images of Séraphine's last moments flooded my mind and my stomach lurched. She moaned slightly when I caressed her hand and turned to look at me. A feeble smile came to her face as she recognized me.

"Sébastien," she whispered hoarsely. "You came."

"How could I not?" I said leaning close to her so no one could hear.

"You must take care of my son," she said, seeming to have accepted her fate.

"There's no need to ask of me such a thing," I said trying to be reassuring.

But she became agitated and even tried to lift her head from her pillows.

"No, you must promise me. The Order must take him, protect him from his father…" her pleading trailed off as her head fell back.

Her maids were at her side in an instant, one gently pushing me aside. I stood back and watched them hover over her, just as Séraphine's had hovered over her to no avail. One of her ladies turned to me.

"You must go now sir," she said, softly but firmly.

I looked at her and then at Melisende. And I knew what I needed to do.

Without another word I left the Palace and retrieved the Elixir scroll from where it had stayed hidden since the day I had shown it to Théos. Racing against time, I hurried to collect what I needed to prepare the concoction, searching the marketplace for the herbs and oils I was not familiar with, returning to my room and following the text on the scroll, mixing it all in a small wooden bowl. When I thought I was done, I poured the mixture into a small amulet I had found in our medical supplies. But I knew I could not give this to her without testing it first, I had no wish to be the cause of her death even if doing nothing meant she would pass on her own. And so, after saying a silent prayer to the One and reciting the words from the Emerald Tablet which I had memorized, I drank what was left in the bowl. And waited.

I felt nothing at first. But I soon began to feel strange, slightly dizzy, everything around me starting to rush at me, exaggerating my senses. The sunlight from the window seemed brighter, the sounds and voices from the courtyard louder and more distinct, aromas from our kitchens stronger. I reached for the table to steady myself and it seemed as though I could feel the grain of the wood pressing gently up into my fingertips. I sat and closed my eyes in an attempt to return to normal but my mind then lit up with vivid images, my thoughts danced from my past to the present, seeing people and events in rapid, crystal-clear flashes followed by some scenes I did not recognize and could not place.

But I did not have time to waste trying to make sense of it. I tried instead to concentrate on my physical body, to see what ill effect, if any, this potion was having. I felt none. In fact, I felt rather invigorated but that could have just been my own heightened and anxious state. It took a short while before the assault on my senses calmed enough for me to walk a few steps without the dizziness impeding me. I decided then that I would give this to Melisende to try to save her.

I fastened the amulet with a chain and hung it about my neck, touching the St Michael medal as I did, tied my undershirt at my neck so that it could not be seen then rushed back to the Patriarch's Palace, bounding up the steps three at a time. The guards recognizing me opened the doors without a word. I could see her body twisting on the bed, her condition had worsened.

"Get out!" I barked to everyone in the room.

The ladies and Hospitaller Brothers attending her stopped what they were doing and stared at me, unsure for a moment what to do.

"GET OUT!" I shouted this time, pointing to the doors and making my meaning clear and watched as they dropped whatever they were holding and scattered.

I closed the doors behind them and slid the heavy wooden bar across so we would not be disturbed and then went to Melisende's bedside, untying and reaching inside my shirt for the vial secreted there.

Gathering her up in my arms I held her tightly, pressing her close to my chest, rocking her back and forth as I murmured the sacred words and prayers that Théos had shared with us during our studies of the Hermetic texts and those from the Tablet. I felt her body start to calm, her laboured breathing become slower and steadier, her eyelids twitching ever so slightly until they opened and her beautiful eyes gazed into mine.

"Do you trust me?" I whispered.

She nodded.

Whilst still holding her, I opened the amulet with my right hand and brought it to her lips, repeating the prayers as I did so. She took the liquid without questioning, drinking all of it. I recapped the amulet and replaced it under my shirt and laid her back onto the pillows, watching for any adverse reaction. Her body shivered suddenly and then relaxed, her head sinking into the pillow. For a moment I thought I had lost her but she suddenly took a sharp breath and settled, her breathing becoming steadier with each passing moment.

I stood up and brought a chair over from by the window and placed it next to the bed, sat and watched her for so long I fell asleep, I was only woken by the sound of someone pounding on the wooden doors. Once I got my bearings, I leapt up and leaned over her to see what effect the potion had taken, pressing my ear to her lips to see if she was breathing. Much to my surprise and great relief she was and colour had returned to her cheeks. I stroked her hair and kissed her forehead before moving to the door, removing the wooden bar and letting in those demanding entry. Three of her ladies rushed past me followed by two Hospitaller Brothers and the Hospitaller physician who stopped only to give me a strange look then made his way to his patient.

I stood by the door watching as they surrounded her, waiting word on her condition.

"Her fever has broken," he said finally and looked at me. "If she continues like this, she will live."

I leaned against the door frame, crossed my arms before me and took in a deep breath. In doing so, I unknowingly dislodged the amulet which now could be seen resting on top of my shirt. One of the Hospitaller Brothers made his way to me.

"It is the likes of which I have never seen," he said, cautiously choosing his words.

His eyes met mine and then travelled to my chest where he spied the vial and stared just long enough for me to realize what had happened. I tucked it back under my shirt.

"But," he continued with a barely perceptible smirk, "miracles do happen I suppose."

"Indeed," I replied giving nothing away.

Melisende made noticeable improvements every day. I was determined nothing would harm her again during her recovery and insisted that I sleep in the room with her which may have seemed improper but which no one questioned. When she was feeling well enough to eat unaided, she asked me to join her for her meals and at night I cradled her to sleep, removing myself from the bed before the sun rose so as not to cause any suspicions. I knew I was breaking my vows, but to be so close with her filled me with a joy that had long escaped me and to see her smile and the light in her eyes return I felt a love that had disappeared from my life the night my lady passed from the world. This time together would not last, of course, and eventually I returned to the Temple Mount and to my own room but feeling somewhat whole once again.

Fulk did everything he could to deflect any responsibility for Melisende's poisoning but word of it had spread far and wide and he was blamed for it. He even made show of being seen leaving Melisende's quarters early one morning giving the impression that the marriage was once again in good stead and that marital relations had resumed. I knew better. The negotiations that had started prior to her illness ended quickly once Melisende had fully recovered and Fulk removed himself from Jerusalem ostensibly on a mission to protect the borders, leaving Melisende in full control of the city and surrounding areas that made up the Kingdom of Jerusalem. He eyed me suspiciously whenever we crossed paths for he knew I knew the truth but we never spoke of what had occurred. His plans spoilt, he now had to leave the city in disgrace and yet with enough powers to have his orders followed but not enough to cause any damage to Melisende's rule. I was glad to see the back of him.

Within a few months it was clear that Melisende was with child again and the realm rejoiced with the news that she would be providing another heir to secure the dynasty should anything befall the elder child. The gender did not matter, Melisende had been a strong and competent ruler and no one doubted that a female child would follow in her footsteps if the elder brother did not thrive. And although our contact had been minimal and always formal in the weeks after she returned to her duties, we knew the love between us was strong and that the babe likely was mine. But nothing was ever said. As far as the world was concerned, Fulk and Melisende had done what was required of them, the infighting could stop and peace could return to the area.

Just before Christmas I received word in one of Osmond's dispatches that King Henry of England had died and that he had named his daughter Empress Matilda his successor which he had planned over the years once he knew he would not be able to beget another son. This was of particular interest to those in the East – Empress Matilda was married to Fulk's son Geoffrey and having England as an ally and supporter was essential to the continued supply of provisions and money to Jerusalem and the Order. But as was suspected, the barons were not willing to support a female ruler in England – thankfully for us in the Levant no such prejudices had kept Melisende from her rightful crown – and soon there were rumours of a revolt. We watched from afar as sides were soon drawn.

It was not long before I received another dispatch from Osmond informing me of the coup in England with Henry's nephew Stephen of Blois, son of his sister Adele and my very nemesis of the tournaments. Upon his uncle's death, he had raced to Winchester and had himself crowned whilst Matilda was still in Normandy unable to travel as she had recently discovered she was expecting her third child. It would not take long though for this to spiral into full-scale civil war. I also was sent this news by Stephen's brother Henry, the friend I had made at those same tournaments. He was now the Bishop of Winchester and had been for several years. We had corresponded occasionally, he clearly felt the need to make me aware of the brewing hostilities back home.

I wrote to Osmond instructing him to take all measures to secure the properties and of course Margaux who was now living in Normandy with her husband Godwin FitzGilbert de Clare having followed old King Henry there and remained after his death. I suspected he supported Empress Matilda's cause – if it had been the wish of Henry to have her succeed him, then so it must be. I could only hope they were out of harm's way and I knew I could trust my old retainer to keep her safe. But I did ask him to increase the frequency of his letters so I could keep abreast of the situation.

* * * * * * * * * *

The following February Melisende gave birth to a second son and the realm rejoiced at having another heir. Fulk returned from his exile at the edges of the realm to attend the christening in the Holy Sepulchre. Once again I was merely a quiet observer of an event that I should have had a central part in. All I could do is watch as the man I loathed held up the child who was more than likely my own and receive the cheers and congratulations on his achievement. The boy thankfully looked much like his mother with her dark eyes rather than my grey ones. He was christened Amalric, an old tribal name meaning hard-working prince. It would only take time to see if he lived up to it.

If only Fulk had returned to the borders once the babe was born, life could have settled into some semblance of normalcy. But it was not to be. Instead, he suddenly became the attentive father and husband, lavishing gifts on his wife and new-born son and treating Melisende with the deference due to her as the reigning monarch in the kingdom. This made things increasingly difficult for me, I had no real reason to visit the Queen and especially none to spend time with the boy. I could not share my growing despair with anyone lest I reveal the truth that I had broken my vows. And to do so would mean having Amalric declared a bastard, Melisende removed from power and possibly from the city itself, sent to a distant nunnery to spend the rest of her days away from her sons. Keeping the peace was of the upmost importance.

So I suffered in silence and a sadness overcame me which did not go unnoticed. After several weeks of this I decided I needed to get out of Jerusalem for a while and was given permission from Hugues to visit the Templar House in Acre. I left under the cover of night taking one of the piebald destriers to make the week-long journey, arriving just before mid-day. I was greeted warmly by the Brothers and was impressed with the work that had been done to improve and build on the small house that had been there when we had purchased it. I threw myself into some hard labour helping to lay the stones for what was planned to become a massive fort that would rival that of the Hospitallers in the north of the city. But for now, it was enough to distract me and give me purpose again. But my efforts to regain my sense of self were soon to be dashed.

Montbard arrived by ship in mid-May with dreadful news. Hugues had taken a fall from his horse when on his way back from Jaffa. It happened just outside of Nabi Samuil, the small settlement where the crusade leaders and our armies first laid eyes upon Jerusalem. He had been carried to its monastery and was being tended to by the monks there. Montbard was sent to fetch me and we returned the way he came, taking a ship back along the coastline. It took only a day to sail to Jaffa and another to reach what had grown into a town, having expanded over the years with Christian pilgrims who turned settlers. We rode directly to the monastery, leapt off our horses and raced up the hill and through the large arched entry, took the stairs to the right and headed for the corner room where he had been brought after the accident.

The room was small but brightly lit from sunlight streaming in from the window and balcony door on one corner and two more windows on the other. I did not see Hugues at first, instead I was greeted by the sombre expressions of some of the Templar Brothers: Saint-Agnan, Gondamer and Craon were gathered about the bed. They all turned and looked at us, I met their gazes one by one and each slowly shook his head. My stomach churned but I pushed forward anyway, determined to see for myself. I stood at the foot of the bed and saw the ashen face of our Grand Master, of my dear friend, Hugues de Payns, still and lifeless. Saint-Agnan came up beside me.

"He's gone Sébastien," he said sadly. "He passed just before you arrived."

I suddenly found myself at the mercy of my emotions as tears sprang to my eyes and I sank to the floor on my knees. I reached out and touched his foot through the blankets that had covered him to keep him warm. Thoughts of blame started to race through my mind. Why had I gone to Acre? Why had I not been here when he needed me the most? If I had been here, I might have been able to save him. But there was nothing I could do now and waves of guilt washed over me, unceasing and getting stronger with each pass. 'I'm sorry my friend,' I kept thinking, saying to Hugues in my head or perhaps even out loud, I was not sure. It took two of the brothers to lift me up and carry me out of the room, such was my collapse. I was not sure I was going to survive this sudden loss of a man who had meant so very much to me.

* * * * * * * * * *

Hugues's funeral was understated, in keeping with our Rule and even though it was held in the Holy Sepulchre, only members of the Order were allowed to attend along with a few outsiders including Théos. Melisende, despite being Queen, was not allowed to join us but she had managed to come to me before the service to give me some comfort with her soothing words. But nothing she or anyone else could say could erase the misery I was now in. Knowing what I knew about the potion and its effects on Melisende, I was certain I would have been able to save Hugues had I been there. But I had failed him. And this to me was unforgiveable.

After the funeral, he was buried in a secret location under the Temple Mount, in a place known only to us. I felt his absence sorely; he had been a friend, mentor, father-figure, he had given me my first true sword and believed in me, valued me highly enough to ask me to join him on his mission here, changing my life forever. I would be forever grateful having had him in my life. But I knew my time in the Holy Land was coming to an end. I no longer felt as though I was living the life of a true Templar, I was no longer hearing the calling of the Order. I had failed Hugues, I had no place here in terms of my son, my best friends were gone.

I also knew I had to protect we had uncovered here, the texts of the secret knowledge and the elixir needed to be kept in hands that would do good with them or at the very least protect them from those who would do harm; in the wrong hands, they could be devastating. The Hermetic writings of the Emerald Tablet were shared with members of the Order only once they were deemed worthy enough of receiving them and this was done verbally and committed to memory and only at the highest level. As for the elixir, other than myself, only Théos suspected the power of the potion.

So I went to him and told him of my plans. Although he was very sad to see me go, he understood why I needed to. I then told Craon, our new Grand Master, of my intention to leave and return to the West. I did not say I would not return for I could not see that far into the future. But I knew I would be gone for some time. I did not tell Melisende of my departure. I knew that once she had heard, she would try to make me stay, eventually she would understand why it had to be so.

I packed my few belongings and wrapped the Emerald Tablet and a copy of its translated scroll, copies of the translated books and the box containing the elixir scroll tightly, burying them within my travelling chest, locking it with special locks. I left the originals of the books with the Brothers as they needed them to continue the initiation rites. I knew that my reputation would proceed me and that I would not be harassed on my travels, I was known in the East and would be left alone and treated with deference which is not something I enjoyed but needed until I could secure my treasure.

And so, less than a week after we buried Hugues, I stood on the same spot the crest of the hill in Nabi Samuil that I had when I first arrived as a mere boy on crusade to save Jerusalem. So much had changed and yet so much had not. This would be a land, I feared, of constant conflict and the bloodshed would continue. With one last glimpse across the horizon, I turned, mounted my steed and headed west to Jaffa and the ship that awaited me.

My time here was over. I knew in my heart I would not return.

# VIII

## Part One

## 1136-1145 - France

I was not sure where my travels would take me, free and fairly unencumbered, I had so much to choose from, lands I had visited over the years, and new cities, towns, villages I had yet to experience. I considered visiting Montdidier in England, we had received word just before I left Jerusalem that King Stephen's Queen had given the Order a manor house in Cowley in the east of Oxford and Montdidier was assisting the Brothers there in setting up the preceptory. Osmond had kept me informed about the estates and the family, and I could not bring myself to cross the Channel just yet. I knew I wanted to go to Palermo once again to visit the tomb at the basilica of my old friend and mentor Bishop Odo, so the ship docked at port there for a few days and loaded fresh supplies whilst I paid my respects. I then followed the same path taken with Hugues when we came to get the papal blessing on our order. Disembarking at Montpellier I felt a new sense of loss; the town and harbour had not changed much since my last time here and the reminders of that quickly pushed me to decide to be on my way as soon as the horses were rested.

So I wandered, crisscrossing the various territories from the Aquitaine in the west where I was entertained by my old friend and tournament adversary Duke William and his beautiful daughters Eleanor and Petronilla – it was rumoured the elder was soon to be married to Louis, the Dauphin of France - to the far reaches of the Holy Roman Empire to the east, journeying through some of the most difficult and yet beautiful mountainous areas, before returning to France. I spent some time with Abbot Bernard at the Abbey in Clairvaux, having sent him letters from his uncle Montbard when I first landed at the French coast, making him aware of my travels and receiving his invitation to visit him when I was in Aquitaine. He could tell I was troubled and suggested I stay at the Abbey in Clairvaux and help with managing the crops and the tithes earned from them. I gladly accepted the chance to throw myself into some mindless chores where the only conversation I would have would be about the weather and the state of the fields. The Abbot having become quite powerful in his quiet way had many visitors but I kept out of sight, keeping my head down, trying not draw attention to myself as best I could.

The following summer the rumours we had heard about the young heiress of Aquitaine came true. The Duke passed away suddenly whilst on pilgrimage to Santiago de Compostela and had, with his dying breath, instructed that she be put in the care of King Louis who immediately put her under his protection and betrothed her to his son and heir, also named Louis. She was not allowed to attend her father's funeral at the Cathedral there, such was the concern the King had for her safety and I thought of how much that must have weighed heavily on her knowing the pure love she had for her father. Instead, she was moved away from her childhood home and relatively carefree life in the open expanse of Bordeaux to the suffocating enclosures of Paris, being installed in quarters in the Palais de la Cité. I remembered being awed by it on my visit as a child at the start of the crusade, I wondered how much of it and the city had changed in the years since. But that was many lifetimes ago and I tried to not give it much more thought.

So I was surprised when Abbot Bernard asked me to accompany him to Bordeaux for the wedding of Eleanor to the Dauphin Louis. Although we were roughly the same age, the Abbot's severe austere lifestyle had aged him badly; he was terribly thin and frail and suffering from various joint aches and body pains. At least that was the excuse he gave when he asked me to help him make the journey and to assist him during the trip. I was hesitant, wanting to continue my unassuming life in absentia, and only reluctantly agreed when he pressed his need of me due to his delicate physical state. I could hardly refuse him, he had, after all, recently taken me in without demanding any explanations about my departure from the Holy Land and had never asked a single question about my intentions.

It was a hot July when we made our way to the coast city, the capital of the duchy of Aquitaine. The Archbishop of Bordeaux, who was to marry the couple, kindly gave us rooms in the Bishop's house at the Cathedral of Saint-André where the wedding was to take place. King Louis and Queen Adelaide arrived a few days after we did and then several days of feasts and entertainments were enjoyed by a large number of guests who had travelled from far and wide to attend. Dignitaries or representatives from every corner of the Christian world came to celebrate the marriage of the King's son to quite possibly the most eligible heiress in the world. I was surprised, although I should not have been, to see Grand Master Craon and Brother Montbard amongst the throngs of invitees. We greeted each warmly, I think they were genuinely glad to see me as I was them. Although we spent some time speaking about various matters with the Order in and around Jerusalem, the only mention of Melisende was regarding the success of her reign now that Fulk was kept out of sight patrolling the borders which meant he was no longer interfering with her, which was probably for the best.

The wedding was magnificent, Eleanor made a stunning bride. The youth of the pair – she but fifteen and he merely two years older - was evident in her downcast eyes and blushes on her flawless cheeks and his shyness, one could barely hear the vows he spoke to her. His timid demeanour was understandable as the Dauphin had been destined for the church until his older brother Philip died from after a horrific fall from his horse a few years earlier. No doubt he was unprepared for the direction his life was now going to take. Only time would tell if their marriage would last the test of time.

And tested soon it would be for only seven days after the wedding, King Louis died. No one was aware of how ill he had become during the festivities, quite possibly from indulging too much in food and drink. He was known for this – he was called Louis the Fat after all – but it was still shocking to everyone to hear that the King had collapsed during a tour through the forests north of Paris. He had been brought to the town of Béthisy-Saint-Pierre where after a bout of the bloody flux he passed away.

And so, after such an uplifting celebration of the marriage, all the counties and duchies in France found themselves in a period of mourning for the dead king. And apprehensively looking at a future with his young, inexperienced successor. A sombre funeral was held at the basilica at Saint-Denis – the very place where Duke Robert and the armies had gathered before leaving for the Holy Land. Many memories flooded over me as I stood overlooking the fields where the camps had been. The same guests at the wedding attended the funeral as many had not yet returned home and all eyes fell to the new king who, to his credit, was brave and stoic with his beautiful young bride at his side. I had to wonder what was in store for them.

* * * * * * * * * *

Abbot Bernard was asked by the new King's ministers to remain in Paris to assist with the preparations for the coronation which would take place in

Bourges in December and so I stayed with him to do whatever I could to help make the transition as smooth as possible. We were given rooms in the Palais so King Louis could call on us whenever he needed. Master Craon and Montbard stayed their departure for a while too, wanting to ensure the support for the Templars continued unabated despite the old king's death.

It did not take long for their presence and aid in sorting government issues was rewarded. The new King Louis, being of a very religious mind, not only continued the support of the Order but donated a large parcel of land at the Place de Grève, just to the northeast of the city, dedicating it for the building of a preceptory which was to become the main headquarters for the Templars in Paris. It was a generous gift, a substantial tract of land that we could use as we saw fit, making whatever additions we needed to a small house that already existed there.

The fields that surrounded the house were mostly marshland and needed to be drained for us to be able to build there. Grand Master Craon and Montbard found it very easy to arrange for the help we needed, increasing the number of recruits in the Order, and construction soon began on a massive square tower and round chapel nearby. Eventually Grand Master Craon and Montbard had to return to Jerusalem and they requested that I stay in Paris and oversee the work. I agreed, but on two conditions; first, that I was not asked to be Master of Paris as the new preceptory would require one and, second, that I would be allowed to bring Osmond over from England to assist me. My conditions were agreed to and it was decided to have Montdidier join us as the Paris Master, having been so successful in setting up the preceptory in Oxford. And so the two of them were sent for and Osmond arrived before Montdidier shortly before Christmas.

It did my soul good to see my old retainer and although we had been in regular contact throughout the years with Osmond providing updates on events happening in England, seeing him made the almost two decades seem to fade away. He had aged only slightly, his hair and closely cropped beard speckled with grey and his body slightly more filled out than I remembered. We laughed as we embraced for no other reason than realizing it was a miracle we were both still alive.

We took rooms in the small house that already existed on the site so we could keep constant watch over the labour and provide immediate instructions to the masons and other craftsmen who had been provided with tents nearby to stay in whilst the work was on-going. It was agreed that they would work for five days of the week and the sixth would be spent training them to become Templars, teaching them the Rule and taking them through military drills and strategy. So by the time the preceptory would be complete, we would be able to garrison it with a full complement of Brothers who could serve Master Montdidier however he saw fit.

Osmond and I spent many nights telling stories from the past years. He told me of the conflicts in England between King Stephen and the Empress Matilda who were warring over their claims to the throne. And of how the D'Ivry properties were flourishing, Guillaume had made a success of the holdings in and around Oxfordshire and Gloucestershire and was now expanding into Buckinghamshire. I asked after Margaux and her husband de Clare and was told they had returned to England at the behest of King Stephen who was in need of assistance in quelling a few Welsh rebels. It suited Godwin FitzGilbert to return to England for protecting the Welsh borders meant also protecting his family's holdings and he could do this without raising the suspicions of the King whom he did not truly support. It was all very complicated and I was glad not to be part of it, I had had enough of intrigue. But I was glad to hear of Margaux's safety in Wales, quite the distance from the English court.

The square tower was completed rather quickly - it was a simple design - and the round chapel was not far behind. We were quite pleased with the results and a surge in requests to join the Order meant we now had to turn our attention to building quarters to house all the new recruits and training yards for their military schooling. Pope Innocent issued a papal bull extending the protection of the Order across Christendom and declaring the Order was exempt from taxes and were allowed to keep the tithes and gifts given which meant there was no debt incurred to the overlords of the lands on which Templar preceptories sat. It also meant the preceptories had the potential to become quite rich which worried me.

And so, with much hard work and graft, the main house for the Order was now ready for the senior members of the Paris preceptory to take rooms and start growing the Order, hopefully making it the largest assembly of Templars outside of Jerusalem.

* * * * * * * * *

War in England had taken another turn, this time with Empress Matilda pressing her claims by arriving in England in the autumn with troops, landing at Arundel and eventually making her way to Gloucester. With her half-brother Robert of Gloucester having his base in Bristol, the two of them essentially controlled the entire southwest of the country. Her husband, who happened to be King Fulk's son Geoffrey, stayed behind to rule Normandy in her absence and to oversee the care of their three young sons, Henry, Geoffrey and William. We knew neither side would withdraw from the conflict which no doubt meant civil war would ensue. Although I knew that Margaux was secure in the de Clare castle at Pembrokeshire, I nevertheless was concerned especially upon hearing of the birth of her daughter Alix which happened at the same time as the hostilities worsened. Osmond sensed and shared my worry and increased the number of despatches as well as ordering more men at arms to protect them and the castle.

We watched from afar as reports of the battles reached us with increasing number, showing the winds of fortune turning at an astonishing rate. Many of the Barons who had sworn to the dying King Henry that they would support his daughter Mathilda's rule switched sides whilst many kept their oath believing her right to be more just than Stephen's. The territory controlled by Matilda eventually stretched as far as Oxford and the magnificent castle of Wallingford both of which were unsettlingly close to the D'Ivry holdings and I became concerned they would come to harm should the warring sides wage battled there. But Osmond never received any grievous news, we were relieved to hear Stephen's army kept to the Thames for travel which meant they were far enough away from Shirburn to keep it and everyone there out of harm's way. And despite many attempts, his army never made it past Wallingford, having found the castle too well defended, so those at Sandford on Thames were also safe.

And so the war continued. Lands captured in one campaign were won back in another. Gains for one side became losses soon after. By the time the war had entered its second year, it seemed that neither side had achieved a clear advantage. That is until we received the news of King Stephen's catastrophic loss at Lincoln which ended with his capture and imprisonment in the castle at Bristol. This, we believed, would finally settle the matter of the succession with Matilda preparing for her coronation, but fate would intervene yet again.

She found herself under siege at Winchester, facing fierce fighting from Stephen's men during which her half-brother Robert of Gloucester was taken captive. And thus the winds of fortune changed again. It was also the very same battle, I was told, where my lady's eldest brother and my nemesis John Marshal had lost his eye from a drip of molten lead from the roof of the abbey he had been trapped in at Wherwell. Mention of his name brought back unpleasant memories, his anger at my marriage to his sister and, of course, holding me to blame for her death. I retreated into seclusion every now and then, and Osmond, now familiar with the reason behind my solitude would carry on the business of the Paris preceptory on my behalf.

It was around this time that we lost our dear Brother Montdidier. He had started to feel a weakness in his body and I watched as he lost weight and the strength in his arms and legs. He struggled to ride and spent more and more of his time in the rooms at the Black Tower rather than joining me overseeing the building works or training new recruits. He decided it was time for him to make a visit to his family's lands to the north of Paris which would have been a few days' ride by horse but slightly longer by cart which is how he needed to travel. I was deputised as Preceptor in his absence and was aggrieved to learn he had passed within a few days of arriving at his childhood home. I had no opportunity to help him as I had Melisende, but I may not have been successful even if I had, still being mystified by the power of the elixir and the incantations and when it would work and when it would not. There were only a few of us now left from the original nine that travelled to the Holy Land, we had to look to the future of the Order with its growing numbers.

I wrote to Grand Master Craon in Jerusalem to inform him of Montdidier's death and to ask direction on finding a successor. He offered it to me, I declined without hesitation. So he left it with me to find suitable candidates. I considered Saint-Agnan, but he had taken over the preceptory at Temple Guiting in Gloucester when Montdidier came to Paris and, being several years my senior, probably was not in strong enough health to take the position of what was becoming the headquarters for the Order in the West. I would have to find someone else. In the meantime, I would do my best to continue the diplomatic work we had started and keep the relationship with the French King cordial and agreeable, having Louis as an ally would be advantageous in many ways.

The issue of the English royal succession needed to be resolved. The people were tired of the fighting and wanted peace in the realm. Once an exchange of prisoners had taken place – King Stephen for Robert of Gloucester - the two sides had retreated to their protected territories. Stephen in London and Matilda in Oxford where she was taking up residence in the very town where I had laid eyes on my lady and fixed her horse's broken shoe. I wondered if the castle had changed much in the years I had been absent; I reckoned it must have if Matilda felt safe enough to conduct her war plans and lead her troops from a place so close to London where Stephen's armies were awaiting their orders. But then came the most shocking event of the war.

Stephen had started to wage small, targeted attacks against Matilda's armies along her eastern flank, then circled around to the north and west, taking castles at Cirencester and Bampton, encroaching ever more on Oxford, surrounding Matilda and forcing her to take refuge in the castle itself. But instead of launching a direct attack, Stephen decided to lay siege and set up camps on all sides of the great fortress except to the east where the Thames flowed and there was not enough room for any of his men.

The siege lasted several months until mid-winter, one of the coldest many said had ever been experienced. Matilda knew she was trapped but devised an ingenious plot to escape. Knowing she would soon forfeit her position, lose the castle and possibly be imprisoned, she and a few knights, draped in white cloaks to camouflage themselves in the snow-covered fields, climbed down the walls of George's Tower and escaped through the postern gate. And then fled on foot, crossing the frozen Thames and striding in knee-deep snow to Abingdon where horses were provided for them to reach Wallingford and safety. It was unbelievably daring, very brave and caught Stephen's entire royal army by surprise. I admired her courage and ingenuity. Stephen certainly learned never to underestimate her again.

\* \* \* \* \* \* \* \* \* \*

The Order expanded over the next few years with many new recruits joining the various preceptories across the West or taking pilgrimage to the Holy Land and joining there. The building works in Paris were flourishing under the new Master in Paris, Everard des Barres. He had been selected and installed as the new Preceptor and had easily taken on the responsibilities of the Order from me. I was relieved; Everard was more than capable and had already established a strong friendship with King Louis, so I was satisfied with his assuming the helm and allowing me to slip back into obscurity. Or so I thought.

In November of 1143 King Fulk died after a rather nasty accident with his horse when he and Melisende were holding court in Acre. Master Everard shared with me a letter written to him by the Queen, giving the details of the death. His horse had tripped whilst he and others were hunting outside the city, Fulk was unseated and the horse fell on top of him, the saddle crushing his head but not killing him outright. He had been taken to the Hospitaller Citadel in the city where he lay in agony for three days before succumbing to his injuries. I wondered at first why Melisende did not write me directly but I knew why she could not. She did not really have to write to Master Everard, he would have received the news through King Louis. But she would have known Everard would share this news with me, so I hoped this was her way of reaching out to me without directly reaching out to me. Shortly after Fulk's death, Melisende and the young Baldwin were crowned as co-rulers on Christmas Day in the Holy Sepulchre in Jerusalem. And whilst I was certain of her strength and power to rule, I nonetheless could not help but be apprehensive about the next few years ahead of them both. And of course I thought about Amalric.

Fears which had existed for quite some time of war being waged by the various Arab factions to retake the Holy Land were starting to be realized and it was not long into the new year before I was called to attend upon King Louis to discuss the matter. He understood my extensive familiarity with the area, its cultures and political intricacies and demanded that I come to him. The meeting hall in the Palais had become grander in the intervening years since my first visit, it had been enlarged, more gold and silver had been added throughout, as well as richer tapestries and a larger fireplace which was roaring with flames warming the room when I arrived. I was surprised to see Abbot Bernard from Clairvaux at his side, I had not seen my old friend for quite some time, clearly something was worrying them if he felt he needed to come to Paris. I knelt before the King and waited for the tap on the shoulder just as Duke Robert had done when we met with Louis's grandfather King Philippe when we departed for crusade. King Louis got right to the point.

"D'Ivry, we have been informed that you are familiar with the Turkman Imad al-Din Zengi, is this correct?" he asked directly.

The question took me by surprise, I hesitated, unsure on how to respond.

"I had some interaction with Zengi when I was young, during the crusade, but have not had any contact with him since we departed Antioch," I responded truthfully.

I was well aware of the path Zengi's life had taken, few were not. Around the time we were excavating the tunnels beneath the Temple Mount, Zengi had started making a name for himself by becoming Atabeg of Mosul and then Aleppo, forming a stronghold in the territories east of Palestine and controlling them on behalf of the Seljuk Turks. He had grown tremendously powerful and habitually harassed the towns and cities along the western border with the Crusader states. One such battle at Homs, north of Damascus, resulted in his defeat. And because of the fear that he might come after Damascus, Governor Unur there formed an alliance with Jerusalem for protection against him. He tried again at another settlement near Tripoli and this time won the battle, his enemy being none other than King Fulk himself. Fulk's army had been crushed and only through his surrender were he and what was left of his troops allowed to leave. These attacks simply strengthened the bond between the leaders of the Crusader States and Governor Unur, all now more determined than ever to keep Zengi and the Turks at bay, foiling further attempts at taking Damascus.

This should have been the end of any ambitions Zengi may have had for taking the city and would have been had it not been for the woman he had taken for his second wife shortly after the battle with Fulk. Zumurrud Khatun's reputation was as notorious for brutality as Zengi's was. Her eldest son from her first marriage had become King of Damascus and being unhappy with his rule, she had him assassinated then had his body thrown from a window at the top of a tower in the citadel. She then ruled along with her second son until she agreed to marry Zengi and moved with him to Aleppo. But not long after, her second son was murdered and she pressured Zengi to attack Damascus to avenge the death of her son. Unfortunately for Zengi, those who had murdered her son had also joined the alliance with Jerusalem and were provided protection against any enemy assault. So his desire to take Damascus had been thwarted and he had abandoned his plans and turned his focus elsewhere. I was curious to hear what he was up to that would cause King Louis and others to discuss my acquaintance with him.

"Interaction?" King Louis said inquisitively, squinting at me. "What was the nature of this interaction?"

I quickly recounted the instances when Zengi and I had crossed paths. And how we seemed to have gained a mutual respect for each other in those dangerous times. Despite the reputation he had gained over the years of being a cutthroat enemy of the West, I had to quietly respect him, he had become a brilliant strategist and commanding leader, if not a very merciful one. As I was relaying my experiences, my curiosity increased as I watched King Louis and Abbot Bernard react, raised eyebrows and exchanged knowing glances between them. I finished speaking and waited, knowing they would soon let me know why I had been brought before them.

King Louis sighed heavily and gave a side glance to the Abbot who gave an almost imperceptible nod.

"We have received despatches from Jerusalem. Queen Melisende has written about a troubling development in Outremer," he said with a serious and darkened expression.

The mention of her name startled me though I tried not to show it. After Fulk's demise, Melisende and her young son Baldwin had been crowned co-rulers of Jerusalem on Christmas Day that same year, with Melisende acting as regent on her son's behalf due to his youthful age. So I should not have been surprised to hear she had reached out to the King of France. I set my jaw and hoped I remained expressionless.

"Your old acquaintance Zengi having been successful in his taking of Edessa is now turning his sights to other Crusader States," the King said straightforwardly as he raised the parchment letter with Melisende's seal attached at the bottom and handed it to Abbot Bernard who passed it to me. "Queen Melisende's despatch says he has been turning his attention to Damascus which, as you are aware, has had a treaty with Jerusalem for many years now, having fought alongside King Fulk and Raymond of Antioch in many battles."

The King sighed heavily again. I unrolled the pages and quickly scanned the distinctive writing I knew instantly was hers.

"Those who responded to her call for help last summer were not strong enough to hold him off and now he poses a serious threat to the unity of the remaining Crusader states. This does not bode well..." the King's voice trailed off.

I looked at the Abbot who returned my glance with a slight cock of his head. We waited for King Louis to continue.

"The Queen is now calling upon us to stop this before it escalates and Zengi tries again to capture Damascus."

"How can I be of assistance, sire?" I asked plainly.

King Louis sat back in his chair and tapped the table a few times. Even though he had been King for several years, at twenty-give he still appeared young in both looks and behaviour, having not quite settled into the role yet, at least not when it came to conflict. Politics were his strength, he always shied away from waging battle. Rumour had it that his ministers were concerned about his ability to lead an army if necessary but of course no one had dared raise this with him.

"We want, ah," he started haltingly, "we believe that the best way forward is through diplomatic means, to see if Zengi would be amenable to a treaty through his possession of Edessa. He would have to agree, of course, to cease his attempts to take Damascus and other Crusader territories."

I could see now where this was leading but said nothing as I placed the despatch on the table. Abbot Bernard spoke next.

"We believe, Sébastien, that you would be an excellent emissary, that you should go to Zengi and see if he would agree to meet with you to discuss terms."

Both King Louis and the Abbot looked at me, waiting for me to respond. I did not quite know what to say. Of course I would do as I was bid but surely there were others better suited to this task.

"It is a difficult situation, and your mission must be kept secret," King Louis said, filling in the gap of silence. "You would not be able to take an army. You would only be allowed a few hand-picked men, of your choice of course."

I let the meaning of that sink in. The King was expecting me to go virtually alone and use my past association as the way to gain an audience with the new leader of Edessa, all without the power of the crown behind me. I asked the obvious.

"Why do you think Zengi would grant me an audience if I go on my own, sire?"

The King looked to the Abbot to provide the answer.

"If what you have told us is true, we believe he would remember you. And possibly be indebted to you. And because you would wear the mantle and go as a representative of the Order. And his guards, wanting to curry favour, would be eager to bring him a Templar," Abbot Bernard answered quietly.

This I did not expect and for a moment I let my guard down and expressed my surprise. The Order had been granted the right to wear new garb which still consisted of the white robes and hoods but now with bright red crosses on the chest of the surcoats and on the shoulders of the mantles, making them easily identifiable from a great distance.

"I...I have not worn the new mantle and have not truly been an active member of the Order since I left the Holy Land..." I started to say but the Abbot interrupted.

"Your reputation in the Holy Land was well known, Zengi undoubtedly would have heard of you, been kept informed of your whereabouts. And your work here building the preceptory at Paris and growing the Order proves you have been an integral part of the Order, despite your protestations to the contrary," Abbot Bernard countered. "You are the perfect man to send on this mission."

"And," King Louis added as he pointed a bony finger at the despatch, "you have been requested specifically by Queen Melisende. Surely her judgement in this matter must be taken as sound?"

I was trapped and knew I had no option but to agree. I lowered my gaze and tilted my head down towards the floor. Almost as if with perfect timing, there was a knock at the door and, at the King's bidding, in walked the exquisite Queen Eleanor, heavy with child, their first after many years since the wedding. Following her were her ladies in waiting, one carrying a folded cloth of white.

I bowed upon seeing her as the Abbot stood and the King went to greet her. The ladies curtsied to the King and the lady carrying the cloth waited until the pleasantries between King and Queen were done. Then, at Queen Eleanor's bidding, she placed the cloth at the end of the table, curtsied again and returned to her place standing behind the Queen.

"My dear Sébastien," she said and approached me and I bowed again. "Come, give an old friend an embrace," she insisted and I raised my eyes to meet hers, deep dark grey eyes set afire by her flowing auburn hair.

She truly was the most beautiful woman in the kingdom, possibly all of Christendom. But I remembered the clever girl being schooled at her father's ducal court in Aquitaine in preparation for her future role of Duchess there. I took her hand and raised it to my lips to kiss it, as was the custom. Her smiling face was glowing as she met my gaze, her approaching motherhood wore well upon her.

"Thank you my dear," King Louis said now standing next to where the cloth lay on the table.

"Of course dear husband," she answered him. "I have ensured the sewing and patchwork is of the highest quality," she said nodding to the lady who had carried it in.

"Excellent," King Louis replied.

"I shall take my leave of you," she said and then added turning to me, "please do come and sup with us before your travels."

Clearly she was aware of what her husband had planned for me, I suspected she had more stomach for the fight than her husband. I bowed again and watched as she curtsied before the King and then left the room as if floating on air. Louis beckoned me to stand next to him. As I came closer I suddenly realized it was not one piece of cloth but two that lay before me. The King picked up the top cloth and unfolded it, revealing a white surcoat with a deep red cross in the centre of the chest. He laid it out on the table, then unfolded the other cloth, a long white mantle with a hood and a cross of the same colour red on the right shoulder. I watched the King as he laid it on the table next to the surcoat, rather astonished that he would do this himself.

"These have been made specifically for you Sébastien," he said with a gentle sense of urgency to his voice and I knew then I could not refuse him.

"I shall do as you ask, sire. I have but one request. That I be allowed to take my retainer Osmond as one of the men who will accompany me. He has been with me a long time and I trust him implicitly."

I said it as a statement, not as a question. King Louis squinted at me again, giving the impression of suspicion.

"He is not a Brother is he?"

I shook my head no. He turned to look at Abbot Bernard who shook his head as well.

"Then yes of course," he quickly agreed, trying to erase any sense of doubt. "And I will send a few guards, but you shall be the only Templar, the only one wearing the cross. Zengi must not believe he is under a threat of any kind."

He looked at me for my tacit agreement. I nodded solemnly.

"And whilst you are on your mission, we shall busy ourselves with gathering our armies for another journey to the Holy Land. A show of force from the West should only reinforce our determination not to lose any more of our territories and that we shall defend our allies," King Louis stated with a surety I was not sure was warranted.

And with that, because of a request from the King of France which I could not refuse, I was returning to the lands I had left so very long ago. And to the memories I had hoped to have left there.

# VIII

## Part Two

## 1146 – Baalbek

Osmond did not hesitate to accept my request to accompany me on this journey. He had known of my encounters with Zengi and had been amazed to hear me tell the stories. He agreed the plan for me to speak with Zengi on my own was probably the only way to achieve his army's retreat from Damascus without engaging in full-scale battle, as long as he would accept me. And so he busied himself with packing for our voyage. The white mantle and surcoat with their bright red crosses were tucked away in one of the locked travel chests along with my secrets. As I had done for years, I brought them with me, my only certainty of their security was having them with me. This time I prepared a few vials of the elixir, sealed them with wax, tightly so they would not leak, and hid them in one of the lambskins of wine we would take with us.

A supply ship would take us after Christmas first to the Isle of Cyprus where we would rest at the fort at Paphos so we could exchange our clothes to some more suitable to the warmer air and gather what we needed for the trip across the sea to Tripoli. The Byzantine Emperor Manuel, grandson of the great Alexios whom I had come to know during the crusade, had promised safe conduct and ordered the garrison at Paphos to welcome us.

We departed La Rochelle where the fleet of Templar ships were moored. The port town had grown substantially over the years with the support of Queen Eleanor who had gifted many mills and other textile merchant buildings, all of which of course were exempt from the normal duties and taxes owed to the crown. But the choice to use a supply ship instead of one of the Templar cogs was done intentionally, the purpose of our travel was to be kept secret with as few knowing the details as possible. Even the two knights King Louis had provided from his private guard only had orders to attend myself and Osmond and ensure our safety, it had been left to me whether to take them when meeting with Zengi, assuming he would grant me permission and safe conduct into his camp outside of Damascus.

It was fairly smooth sailing and we reached the Cypriot port within two weeks of departing La Rochelle. As we entered the warmer waters and approached the island, I could feel the heat of the sun get stronger on my face and memories of past began creeping into my mind. The Emperor's bright banners and flags hanging from the walls of the imposing square-shaped fortress, which had been built on a small peninsula that jutted out into the sea, could be easily seen at a distance. They reminded me of the sight of the great Palace of Blachernae at Constantinople, colours of black and gold flapping in the breeze.

We were met by a contingent of the Emperor's men and, as promised, we were greeted as friends and treated well during our brief stay. Emperor Manuel had sent a message to welcome me to the island. It was early in his reign, having become Emperor on his father's death only a couple of years earlier, and he was eager to establish strong relations with the West. Having been alerted by King Louis of my arrival gave him an opportunity to show his favour. But we did not wish for fanfare or anything that would call attention to ourselves and so for the few days of our stay, we mostly kept to ourselves, sorting out provisions for the rest of our trip.

Sailing to Tripoli took less than a day and the grand city that had become the centrepiece of one of the four Crusader States appeared quickly in our sights. King Louis had written to its current leader, Raymond, the Count of Tripoli and great grandson of Raymond of Toulouse, the same Toulouse who had been one of our leaders of the first crusade and who had been determined to have Tripoli for himself. But sadly, it was not to be. Toulouse died whilst besieging the city and was not alive to see it captured. The County of Tripoli was then created and eventually his son and grandson held the post of Count.

We were met in the port and escorted to the citadel where we were told Count Raymond was awaiting our arrival. The citadel was one of the few reminders of Toulouse who had constructed it on the southeast corner of what would have been the borders of the city at that time. But growth and spread of the settlement over the years meant the citadel was now encircled and sat in the middle of the urban sprawl. It bore his family name – Citadel Saint Gilles – and was positioned atop of a hill, its massive walls and the red flags with the gold crosses perched atop them easily seen from the port.

We were led into the heart of the building, each room more and more ornately decorated, a beautiful blend of hanging Byzantine silks swaying with a breeze that carried through the halls and rooms, complimenting the heavy Frankish tapestries that adorned the walls. And the mosaic tiles we walked upon, the original laid by Toulouse's knights, still shone with their bright colours as if they had been set down only the day before. Eventually we came upon two large wooden doors which swung outward towards us as if anticipating us and we were met by savoury aromas of the many dishes that no doubt awaited us within.

Count Raymond was not unlike his great-grandfather. He was slightly smaller in stature but had the same piercing blue eyes and dark reddish-brown beard that seemed to be characteristic of Toulouse and his descendants. Toulouse had not been known as a particularly humourful man, indeed many of his trials and tribulations probably had been caused by his prickly and obstinate nature. It would not take long to see if his great grandson were the same. I hoped not for I had another reason for discovering more about the man: he had been married for the past ten years to Hodierna, one of Melisende's younger sisters.

Rumours abounded that their marriage had not been a happy one. Despite this, they had managed two children, first a daughter named after Queen Melisende, the other a son named for his father and who, if he survived his childhood, would be destined to assume the title Count upon his father's death. But both children were still young, the boy barely but five years and so his future had not yet been determined. I was curious and slightly anxious to see Hodierna, wondered if she would remember me and whether she had been taken into her elder sister's confidence about us.

But my fears were unwarranted. The rumours about the unhappiness in the marriage were true and Hodierna and the children were not even in Tripoli when I arrived, having made their annual visit to another one of the sisters, Alice, in Jableh to the north of the city. In the end, Osmond and I spent the evening listening to Raymond relating the latest exploits of Zengi's armies and his attempts to take Damascus. He was unwittingly telling me exactly what I needed to know.

I had some decisions to make. From the information that Raymond provided we knew that Zengi was camped at Jabal Qasiun, one of the mountains within the ranges southeast of Tripoli and nearest to Damascus. He would need the protection the mountains provided at his back and a continuous source of water from the nearby Barada River would be essential for the survival of his army especially as we were approaching the spring months which would soon lead to a scorching summer. I needed to decide the best route to take to reach him and who to take with me. And finally, I needed a plan on how I be invited into his inner circle.

The first decision about which route to take was made once some reconnaissance was done on the mountain paths. The winter had been harsh with an extreme cold settling in for weeks. But surprisingly, it had also been a dry winter which meant the ground would be frozen but not clogged with snow and thus more easily passable. It would take a few days to traverse the path through two mountain ranges and so Osmond and I began to prepare the horses Count Raymond had provided, a destrier each for riding, and a palfrey each as a packhorse for supplies. I also knew that I would have to take my treasure with me as leaving it in Tripoli would risk its discovery. I would have to find a place along the route to deposit them for safekeeping and return to retrieve them when I could.

The second decision turned out to be the easiest when I decided that only myself and Osmond would make the journey. I did not want Zengi to be alarmed by seeing armed knights advancing even if it would only be four men on horseback. But as Tripoli and the lands between it and Damascus were still under the control of the West, there should be no threat to our safety. The only real danger was what would happen once we reached his camp – and the plans for diplomatic discussions would either work or it would not.

The last decision was more difficult but started to come together once Osmond and I were on our way against the pleas of both Count Raymond and the two knights sent along to be our guards against our going alone. But I was determined not to place anyone else in danger for there was a very good chance we would not make it out of this alive, I had even offered to go on my own but Osmond would not hear of it. We decided to start out in the early hours of the morning before sunrise, Osmond and I both wrapped in winter fur cloaks to protect against the biting cold. I had decided to wait until we were out of Tripoli before dressing in the Templar surcoat and mantle, I wanted to postpone wearing the garb until it was absolutely necessary. The guards accompanied us to the foothills of the mountain range we needed to cross and then turned back. Osmond and I were now completely on our own.

* * * * * * * * * *

As suspected, the path through the mountains was rough but frozen which made the journey easier than it could have been had we encountered warmer weather turning the ground into thick mud making it difficult for the horses to move through. We made good time and as the sun began to fade to the west we found ourselves at the edge of the Orontes, the same river that flowed past the city of Antioch, the same river we had crossed to fight Kerbogha's army. Osmond set about setting up camp, feeding and watering the horses whilst I gathered branches and twigs for the fire. Placing stones in a small circle, I used my flint and soon had flames large enough for us to warm ourselves.

As Osmond prepared our supper, I walked to the river's edge and watched the as the water coursed northward towards its destination, eventually emptying out into the sea just west of Antioch. Returning to the horses, I reached into the saddlebag of the destrier I had been riding and withdrew the leather-wrapped bundle containing the books, the small tin box and scroll within it and the Emerald Tablet. Sitting on a large boulder, I undid the ties and quickly checked their condition; considering all the travels they had been taken on, they were all in a remarkable state, much like the day they were discovered.

Closing my eyes and breathing deeply, I gently ran my fingers over the engravings on the tablet, feeling the indentations of the letters and running the meaning of the words through my mind. Suddenly the sound of the rushing river became louder and the breeze on my face felt stronger and my body felt an energy surge run through it as though every sinew was alight. All my senses were suddenly alive as never before, becoming more intense with each passing moment. I had no idea how long I sat in this manner, I just gradually became aware of Osmond calling out to me to come eat the supper he had prepared. I re-wrapped and re-tied the bundle, placing it securely back in the saddlebag, made my way over to our campfire and ravenously devoured Osmond's simple food.

We were on our way again before sunrise, one of my saddlebags somewhat lighter that it had been, its load having been lightened somewhat by the removal of the bundle I had checked on the night before. I could only hope Osmond would not notice we had one less wine lambskin since I buried the one with the vials in it too. Whilst he slept, I had found an ideal location to secure it and the bundle, buried beneath the brush until I could return and retrieve them. At the last moment I removed my St Michael medal and chain and placed them gently on top of the small pile. I then stepped twenty paces towards the shore, found some rocks and created a small pile, not one large enough for anyone to take notice of, but large enough to jar my memory. In the morning I memorized the landscape around the river where we had set camp before removing all remnants of it and, when we set off, dragged brush behind the pack horses to destroy the hoofprints we would have otherwise left behind.

We travelled south alongside the river which seemed relatively shallow in sections but we dared not try to cross. But that was not our plan anyway, we needed to reach Baalbek, a settlement which we knew had been under Zengi's control for a number of years now, in the past he had even failed in his attempt to exchange it for control of Damascus. We also knew that he had granted Baalbek to one of his chief lieutenants, Najm al-din Ayyub, who had established his base there. My plan was not to approach Zengi directly, which would probably result in our certain deaths, but to try to gain access through Ayyub. If I could convince Ayyub that I was no threat, he might bring me to Zengi himself. I could only hope that the language taught to me by Théos during our time together would not fail me. The trick was not to be captured by any hot-headed Seljuk Turk who thought he might gain a fortune by holding a Templar Knight for ransom.

We reached the outskirts of the settlement by sundown and found a small grotto in which to set up camp. As we had done the night before we created a campfire, one which we knew would easily be seen by the guards on patrol. We ate and attended to the horses. And then I knew it was time to don the Templar garb. They needed to see who I was when they came.

I took the white cloths out of the leather pouch they had resided in since we left Tripoli and unfolded them, careful not to let them touch the ground as it had turned muddy when we were busy building the camp. I laid each across the back of the pack horse and then removed my travel cloak, throwing it over the horse. I undid the belt around my waist which held my scabbard and sword and then removed my plain surcoat, then folded it and the cloak and placed them into the now empty pouch. With a deep sigh, I reached for the Templar surcoat first and pulled it over my head, adjusting it so that the bright red cross sat perfectly positioned on my chest. I re-attached my belt around the surcoat at my waist and adjusted the scabbard so that it hung in place on my left side, easy access for my right hand to withdraw and ready it in an instant. I then reached for the mantle, the hooded cloak with the red cross on the left shoulder, threw it around my shoulders and secured the ties of the hood at the base of my neck. I walked around a bit, practising the movements I would need to do if attacked, making sure the mantle and surcoat did not impede me in any way. They did not. I was ready.

I returned to the fire pit where Osmond was adding more firewood and stoking the flames. He glanced up at me and gave a start.

> "Sweet Jesu!" he exclaimed and then quickly apologised for his outburst. "My apologies, my lord, I have not ever seen you in the Order's garb. Quite the impressive."

I patted the belt holding in the surcoat around my midriff, uncomfortable in my new attire but I knew that if this was to work, I needed to treat it as if it were a second skin to me. I nodded and sat on one of the logs that Osmond had moved closer to the fire to warm ourselves. It did not take long before the fruits of our labour were rewarded.

I sensed them before I saw them as I always did. The flames from our fire had been seen and guards sent to investigate. They had circled the camp and must have spied us, seeing the white cloak with its red cross, which is the reason why I assumed they had not yet attacked. Seeing a lone Knight Templar sitting by the fire must have been quite shocking to them. I waited until I knew they were almost upon us when I stood to my full height, called out to them to show and identify themselves but in my language, not wishing to give away that I would understand them when they spoke in theirs. No doubt this startled and confused them as they instantly froze. It took them a few moments before they tentatively stepped out of the shadows and into the dancing light of the firepit. I kept my hands at my sides and made no movement towards my sword as I spoke with them, Osmond following suit behind me at the edge of the firelight.

Their nervousness was obvious by the shaking of their voices as they talked to each other. As I suspected, they were just simple guards thinking they had been sent to chase off rogue bandits. This was altogether something else, a situation they had not been prepared for. They revealed that Ayyub was in the citadel at Baalbek rather than with Zengi who was camped closer to Damascus. Somehow I managed to get them to understand that I had need of an audience with Ayyub and the smarter of the two seemed to figure out it would be to his master's benefit if I were provided safe conduct into Baalbek. By the looks on the faces of the two, it was clear they were confused by my presence.

They exchanged glances throughout the short discussion, each probably wishing another would take charge of the situation. In the end, they just nodded and retreated. I guessed we would not have to wait long to see what they decided to do.

* * * * * * * * *

My assumption was correct. I half-expected them to re-appear with more men to take us prisoner, take us to the city and then decide what to do with us. Before long we saw a small trail of lit torches being carried by men on horseback as they made their way up the incline to where Osmond and I sat awaiting their arrival. All but three circled our camp and dismounted, the light from their flames brightening the dark space. I ignored them and concentrated on those who remained seated on their horses in front of us. One moved closer, it was clear he was the leader of the group, the others deferred to him. I stood and took a step towards him; instantly all his men reacted and tightly gripped the hilts of their sabres. I raised both of my hands to show the leader I was not reaching for my weapon but the tension did not ease.

Their leader was of medium build and had the dark features of his countrymen, an angular face enhanced by a perfectly trimmed moustache and beard cropped close to the skin. But what caught my attention was the intense expression of his face, an intelligence emanated from his eyes, narrowing as he studied me. He took his time and I waited, giving him the respect he was due, after all, I was trespassing in his land. Eventually he spoke. And to my surprise, he spoke in my language.

"Templar, who are you?" he asked bluntly.

"Sébastien D'Ivry," I responded simply yet firmly and I thought I caught an ever-so-slight reaction upon hearing my name.

But if I had, it was gone in an instant. He pursed his lips and jutted his jaw, contemplating the situation.

"Why are you here?" he demanded.

"I seek an audience with Atabeg Zengi," I said flatly, not wanting to provoke with what could be seen as a confrontational tone.

He raised his eyebrows in surprise. He cocked his head to his left, speaking now in his own language to the one on the horse next to him.

"He wishes to speak with Atabeg Zengi," he said with a tone of incredulity.

"What do you want to do with him General Ayuub?" the other asked.

I was astounded but tried not to show my reaction; the warrior sat on his horse before me was Zengi's second in command, whose fame in battles and warfare was almost as impression as his master's. I decided to take a chance that he had some recognition of my identity and spoke to him but only loud enough for him to hear.

"I have no doubt Zengi would approve my request for an audience," I said plainly.

Although I could not see him, I could almost feel Osmond trying to hide a smirk. The Turkman General stared at me with wide eyes, he had not expected this. He looked me up and down and for a moment glared as if my words had angered him. But slowly his gaze softened somewhat, he nodded and spoke to me in my language.

"You may be correct, D'Ivry," he said. "It takes a very brave or a very arrogant man to come here virtually unprotected," nodding towards Osmond, "and make such a demand. I shall give you and your man quarters in the citadel but you will understand why my guards shall be provided to, ah, assist you?"

"I understand," I answered.

I realized that he had not made any mention of my request. I understood, his was to save face with his own men; he was not going to take any instructions from an infidel, least of which a Templar, whose brotherhood was intensely hated and yet respected by the Muslim armies. I suspected he was extremely curious as to what this was all about and did not want to displease his leader who had, after all, given him Baalbek to govern and relied on him as his best commander. Ayyub wanted to see how this was going to play out. And he knew he had the option to kill us if anything went awry.

And so, we packed up our camp, loaded the horses and were escorted down from the grotto to the city. Even at the distance we were at in our grotto we could see the lights aglow inside the surrounding walls but as we got closer we began to see the true size of the settlement. We had been told it had been built upon Roman ruins and that the temples had been converted to mosques, and we could see the huge white granite columns typical of Roman architecture soaring above the walls surrounding the city. A massive arch opening the city to the north emerged in the early morning light that had appeared on the horizon to the east of us. No one had spoken the entire journey, each of us knew the other understood our languages, not wanting to give anything away.

As we passed through the arch we got our first real look at the temple complex surrounding the citadel as we made our way around to its main entrance facing to the east. It sat atop an immense raised platform, much like that of the Templar Palace on the Temple Mount in Jerusalem, with a massive staircase leading up to it. Getting closer, we could now see that there were twelve columns, each reinforced by iron bands, similar to those I had seen in the Hospitaler citadel in Acre. There were two towers, one of which I guessed was going to be our home for the foreseeable future.

Ayyub was true to his word and had Osmond and myself taken into one of the larger rooms in the citadel's left tower. It was not luxurious nor was it spare, Islamic paintings adorned the walls and the mosaic floor boasted strong colours of blue and yellow and specks of gold. It was obvious that Ayyub wanted to treat his unexpected guests with respect but we also knew it would only take a slight change in the winds of fortune for us to be taken to the dungeon as his prisoners, possibly tortured or executed. We were playing a delicate game and trusting on a man's memory as a young boy hiding in a cave on the outskirts of Antioch.

* * * * * * * * * *

We spent two weeks in isolation with the exception of the guards who brought us food and drink and saw to any of our needs which were few. We had been brought a chess game with exquisite pieces carved out of ivory as well as Qirkat, an Islamic game played on a smoothed animal skin with round, darkly coloured red and blue honed pieces of glass. We were allowed out of the tower only at night to stretch our legs and get fresh air but under strict guard and of course I was not allowed to wear the surcoat or mantle. But they did not take them from me either. Our weapons, of course, had been confiscated.

On the first day of the third week, we had a visitor. Or two rather. At the break of dawn we were awakened as usual by the adhan, the Muslim call to morning prayer being sung from the minaret of a nearby mosque. The sound was strangely soothing and Osmond and I had become accustomed to the almost mesmerizing vibration of the singer's voice over the previous weeks, feeling almost as if we were intruding even though we were still locked in our comfortable rooms, kept away from prying eyes and the general population. I wondered if those making their way to the mosque each morning and four more times throughout the day were even aware that a Knight Templar was in their midst.

Osmond had just finished re-lighting the fire with wood from a small pile beside the hearth. Although the weather was warmer this far south, a chill settled in each night in the tower and our host had extended the comfort of a fire to us as well. We were settling in ready to continue the chess match we had started the night before when we heard the door being unlocked and then pushed open. As we stood, in strode one of the guards followed by Ayyub. Glancing quickly around and having deemed it safe, he waved the guard out of the room but before the door closed behind him, in stepped a young boy, probably no more than nine or ten years of age, dressed in a dark tunic, a leather belt with sabre, and a cloak, much like Ayyub. Ayyub looked from him to me and back again.

"D'Ivry," he said, pointing to the child, "My son, Salah al-Din Yusuf ibn Ayyub."

A remarkable-looking child, he had the intense look in his eyes from his father but there was a serenity that was his own. We stared at each other for a moment and I suddenly got a sense of something other-worldly about the boy, that I was in the presence of future greatness. But I shook the thoughts from my head as quickly as they appeared. He nodded respectively to me as his father continued.

"Shall we sit?" Ayyub asked, pointing to the chairs at the small table with the chess game on it.

Osmond remained standing on the far side of the room and the boy did not move. I waited for Ayyub to take a seat as respect dictated and then took the chair opposite. Ayyub took a long look over the positions of the black and ivory chessmen.

"Interesting strategy here, hmm?" he asked.

I remained silent. He stroked his beard and then pointed at the pieces.

"Ivory has a position of strength here, no? But do you think it will remain?"

He raised his head slowly and met my eyes. The dance had begun.

"Yes, ivory's position is strong. But a man must always be wary of one's opponent, for one small mistake could be the ruin of him," I responded knowing we were not speaking of the chess match.

He leaned back in his chair and nodded. He beckoned the boy to come to us.

"My son has only heard of the great Templar warriors, I wanted him to see one in person. What do you think of him, son?" he asked the boy.

His son studied me for a moment. He surprised me responding in my language, his voice was soft and measured, with a wisdom beyond his years.

"There is a sadness deep in his spirit, perhaps his purpose here will help heal his wounds?"

His words struck me to my very core though I tried not to react. I could not help but be amazed at the insight of one so young.

Ayyub nodded at the boy, then turned and studied me for a moment. He sighed.

"You have been granted one audience with my master Zengi, I am to take you to him. We leave after mid-day prayers."

And with that, he stood and walked out the door which his son had opened for him. The boy turned and looked at me, smiled a gentle smile, nodded, and followed his father out.

# VIII

## Part Three

## 1146 – Jabal Qasiun

I dressed in my full Templar attire, the cloak resting on my shoulders and tied at the base of my neck, the red crosses on both it and my surcoat easily identifiable. Ayyub made no comment on it when I appeared but one of his men handed me an overcoat to wear until we were out of sight of the city's garrison. We travelled south for two days by horse through the mountains before turning east heading towards Jabal Qasiun where Zengi was camping with his army. It was from here that he was launching his battles harassing Damascus and it was here that I was going to see my old adversary and liberator for the first time in many, many years. I reckoned that he must have remembered me else why would he have allowed an audience? I was curious to see him, to take the measure of the man the boy had grown into.

Zengi had chosen to use the myriad of caves that dotted the sides of the mountain so those he was fighting would not be able to easily discover his whereabouts. The Barada River was a short distance from the mountain and provided much needed water to his troops which was critical as all other supplies had to be brought to the army, the mountainside providing little in any kind of sustenance. He must have been very determined to take Damascus, knowing that his supply routes would always be in danger of attack and he would need men to protect the routes and then replenish the supplied if they were intercepted. Considering our history, it was fitting that our reunion would be in such a place.

In the early evening, we halted our journey on horseback near the top on the northwest side of the mountain and made camp for the night, intending to start out again the next morning which we did right after morning prayers. The rocky terrain and lack of any real paths made navigating difficult, so we left the horses at the camp and were guided the rest of the way on foot, carefully picking our way down the mountain side, passing many alcoves and caves along the way. I could see how one could easily get lost amongst them if one did not know the mountain well. Clearly Ayyub did. About halfway down, he stopped at large outcrop with a few tents with some men milling about and motioned to Osmond he needed to stay, he would not be allowed to continue with us. Osmond looked at me or confirmation, I nodded and he settled down to await my return. Ayyub and I continued on our own, without any guards or men accompanying us. We walked in silence. My message was for Zengi and Zengi alone, Ayyub respected that.

We eventually reached a ridge that at first glance seemed bare but the closer we came, a small opening in the mountain face started to appear, invisible to anyone scanning the mountain for signs of activity. But it was here that Ayyub led me, pointing to the mouth of the cave and motioning for me to walk ahead of him. I had to duck at the opening and walked in darkness for several steps, feeling along the walls as they turned to the left before I saw torches flickering, lighting the path ahead. Suddenly the tunnel ended and opened to a cavernous space where a battle base had been constructed and I could see soldiers wandering about, busy with various tasks.

The space was shockingly large with a ceiling well high enough for me to stand up in easily. The look and feel of the cave – spacious and surprisingly damp – reminded me of Zedekiah's cave back in Jerusalem and my mind jumped for a moment to the treasures I found there now safely tucked away in their hiding place. I stood silently observing those in the cave and watched as Ayyub walked over to a group of men gathered around a small table, disappearing amongst them. As the men started to become aware of my presence, the room gradually went silent as each turned and started at me.

And then, like the parting of the sea, the men stood aside, revealing a dark-eyed, black-bearded man facing me, sitting in an ornate chair, his expression serious and dour. Our eyes locked and we knew instantly that there was no doubt of recognition between us. I was looking at Zengi, the great and feared leader of the Seljuk Turks, Atabeg and ruler of many of the largest Muslim cities and harasser of those considered to be the infidel. The boy whose life I saved and who had spared mine. And he was looking at one of the founders of the Knights Templar, the most powerful military orders in Christendom. We were equals.

He waved away everyone in the room except Ayyub. He waited until the men had left the cave before standing and meeting my gaze once again. For a moment, it felt as though the world stood still. He broke our stare and glanced at Ayyub then returned to me. Finally, after what seemed like an eternity, he came out from behind the desk and extended his right arm in the traditional greeting of friends.

"De-verr-eee," he said, his serious expression breaking out into a wide grin.

I took a step forward and grasped his arm. He had grown into an impressive looking man, taller than I remembered, a well-trimmed beard and moustache greying as was the long black hair I had seen so many years ago, now peeking out slightly from the secured bejewelled headdress tightly wound atop his head. We embraced and Zengi stood back to give me a good look, nodding his head as if giving his approval of the Templar attire.

"You have aged, De-ver-ee," he said almost perfectly in my language.

And then he laughed.

"But no less the formidable man I expected you to become," he added.

I returned the smile.

"The same can be said of you," I said sincerely.

"Come, we shall eat," he said, beckoning me to follow him.

We returned out of the cave where I found more of his men standing about waiting for their orders. They all stiffened and bowed their heads as he approached whilst managing at the same time to stare at his unusual-looking companion. Ayyub followed as we made our way down the mountain but to where I did not know.

"My man…" I began but Zengi cut me off.

"He is being well cared for. I have ordered that he be fed and that a place for the two of you to stay be readied for you. Ahhhh," he exclaimed as we reached a wide crevice where I could see a large portion of his army with tents and camps stretching as far as the eye could see.


It was a perfectly defended position, protected on many sides by the mountain's rock-face, the enemy's only avenue of attack was straight on, it was no wonder his armies had been able to continually harass Damascus for so long. We walked in silence until we reached his tent which was not opulently decorated but was rather plain and blended in easily with the many other tents surrounding it. Entering it I could smell the aromas of the exotic dishes I knew would be awaiting us and Zengi pointed to the chair opposite his at the small table I saw before us. I stood by it and bowed my head in respect as prayers were given for the meal and waited for Zengi to sit before taking my own seat. Our goblets were soon filled with delicious wine and I let Zengi begin where he wanted to. We spoke in my language, it was clear he had become fluent in over the years.

"So," he started slowly, "you wear the cross of the Templars. Do I need to be concerned that more are on their way?"

I shook my head.

"No, I come on my own, just with my man Osmond to assist me," I responded matter-of-factly, adding, "he is not of the brotherhood."

Zengi nodded.

"I have heard stories of your, ah, how does one say? Exploits? Throughout the years. A founder of an Order that has become so powerful in such a short amount of time? Remarkable. As are your own skills and expertise with the sword, so I am told," he said as he drank.

"Just as I have heard of your adventures," I responded without a hint of judgement.

He nodded.

"Yes, one needs to do what one must. I have encountered your brethren, sometimes winning the day, sometimes not. I consider the battle at Montferrand a particularly glorious victory," he said tilting his head back slightly, almost as if daring me to make comment.

I knew of course what he was referring to. Ten or so years earlier, he had been attempting to take the city of Homs and in doing so, invoked the anger of Count Raymond of Tripoli. Raymond rushed to the aid of the Christian settlement, calling upon King Fulk to provide assistance which he did, bringing about twenty Templar soldiers with him from Jerusalem. But Raymond had been captured and Fulk's army were hopelessly outmanned and forced to take refuge at the castle at nearby Montferrand but not before sending out the call for reinforcements. Zengi knew they were out of supplies having left most of them on the battlefield and smartly negotiated at once, forcing a surrender, asking for nothing more than the castle itself. Fulk capitulated. Had he only waited a few more days, the outcome may have been quite different and he rued his decision to give in so quickly. His surrender meant Zengi had gained a foothold in the area and probably the permanent loss of a castle within striking distance of both Homs and Tripoli. Fulk had been truly humiliated. I grimaced at the sound of his name, a rare lapse in my usually unbreachable façade. It did not escape Zengi's notice but he said nothing.

"So, tell me De-ver-ee, why are you here? Why have you been sent to speak with me?"

I could not help but smile as he got right to the point as I suspected he would.

"The leaders in the West wish you to stop harassing Damascus. There is a treaty with Jerusalem and as such the city is owed the protection provided by the Crusader States…"

"One of which I have now taken as my own," he interrupted, reaching for some fruit.

This was true. The loss of Edessa had been a tragedy for the Crusader States but now the focus was ensuring no further advancement could be made by the Muslim armies.

"Indeed. That was lamentable. I have been sent to do whatever is necessary to prevent another all-out war."

"Do they know of our past, ah, association?"

"I informed them of our paths having crossed during the battle at Antioch but only after I had been summoned…" my voice trailed off.

"Then it is curious, no? Why your rulers would have selected you to make this diplomatic journey?" he said as he carefully sliced a pear from end to end with a small, curved knife.

I said nothing.

"You lived for many years in Jerusalem, did you not? And as a senior member of your Order, you must have had much to do with its rulers, Fulk and his Queen Melisende?" he continued to probe.

"Yes, I assisted the King and Queen wherever possible," I answered plainly.

"And with Fulk now dead, do you still serve the Queen?"

I hesitated but only slightly.

"I serve the Order's Grand Master and do as he bids."

I answered cryptically knowing full well that Everard had very little to do with my mission. Zengi stared at me, it was as if he could see right through me.

"It is no matter," he said with a slight wave of his hand. "You are here and I must say it does me good to be reacquainted with the one who gave me my life when it could have been so easily taken. I have thought of you often."

"And I you," I said sincerely.

At that moment Ayyub entered the tent and whispered something to Zengi who thought a moment, drank from his goblet and then turned to me.

"A matter I must attend to. I shall have you shown to your quarters where your man awaits you. But we shall continue our discussion, yes? I believe there is much to say."

I watched him leave, drank what was left of my wine and followed the guards who led me to my quarters. The tent that had been given to Osmond and myself was in another camp farthest away from that where Zengi was based. As Zengi had promised, I found Osmond well taken care of, fed and resting on one of two piles of thick blankets that had been provided as makeshift beds. Two lamps provided the only light within in the tent and I could see a small table and two chairs in the far corner of the tent.

I carefully removed the cloak, my belt and surcoat, folding the clothing neatly and placing them on the table, pulled out a chair and sat down, suddenly feeling very fatigued. Osmond stood when I entered the tent and joined me at the table, pouring some wine into two goblets. He told me how the guards had brought him here, brought him food and wine and bade him await my return. He had been treated very respectfully but it was clear we were going to be guarded and watched every minute we were here. I told him everything about meeting with Zengi and that we were just starting to get to the point of why I had come when we had been interrupted by Ayyub giving Zengi some news calling him away. But his parting words were he wished to continue our discussions, which I took as a good sign. At least for now.

* * * * * * * * *

It took another two days before Zengi extended another invite to meet with him. This time he asked me to walk with him about the mountain as we talked, one of Ayyub's guards keeping a discreet distance following behind.

Our discussion that day focused on our military accomplishments, his battles to secure lands and territories that he firmly believed were rightly his. We spent a lot of time discussing Palestine and the history of the region, the claim of so many disparate groups to ownership of the land and the religious importance to those who continued to fight for it. I began to better understand why we were seen as invaders even as I tried pointing out the beliefs of the Christians and the Jews about their Holy Land.

I asked him why he had chosen this mount as the place from which he launched his battle to take Damascus. He carefully took his time in explaining to me the Islamic holiness of this mountain, such a virtuous place that it emanated a glow which constantly shined whether during the day or at night. He taught me that day of the legend of the seventy prophets who had taken refuge in one cave and, only having a single loaf of bread, passed it around from one to another, no one wanting to take a piece if his brother had not. Eventually, all died of hunger in the cave and their spirits now come to the cave at dusk and leave at dawn, and are the source of the light coming from the mountain. When we arrived at the cave, he took a moment to pray, having brought a small prayer rug with him. When he rose, he said the cave was called Maghārat al-Jūʿ or the Cave of Hunger and asked if I wanted to venture inside. Suddenly feeling unworthy, I thanked him but declined.

On other days he spoke about other legends of the caves of the mountain as we continued our walks on Jabal Qasiun. Another not far from the Cave of Hunger was believed to have been the home of Adam, the same spot where Abraham and Jesus had prayed. It was visited by many who prayed to have afflictions and miseries healed, prayers for rain during droughts and sunshine during seemingly never-ending rainfall. But in the Quran, it had been told as the place of the death of Abel by his brother Cain, and so it had been given the name Maghārat al-Dam, the Cave of Blood. This time I stepped inside and was greeted by a strange formation in the rock, shaped like a gaping mouth. I was struck by this, Zengi saw my reaction and said legend had it this was created on the night of the murder, when the cave cried out in pain of the heinous deed.

Zengi brought me to yet another cave on the far side of the mountain, known in the Qur'an as the Aṣhāb al-Kahf, Companions of the Cave. The story he told me was again familiar, where several young men hid in a cave to avoid capture by their enemies and fell asleep for more than three hundred years, emerging to a completely different world to the one they had lived in. They even had a guard in the form of a dog which stayed with them protecting them from attack and which emerged with them. I told Zengi there was a similar story from Christian traditions, but that those who were in the cave were hiding from Roman prosecution of their Christian faiths. The Roman

Emperor at the time had ordered the cave sealed and when emerging these many years later, they were astounded to find Christian symbols and icons in places where once they had been forbidden. We wondered at what the stories the caves told us and how they held meaning for many on the warring sides.

And so this was how it went for weeks as spring moved into summer, Zengi attending to his armies besieging Damascus during the day, spending some of the evenings deep in conversation with me, sharing many stories from Islamic tradition whilst I shared my stories of the conquest of Jerusalem, returning to the West with the Duke and our capture at Tinchebrai, my successes at the tournaments.

Eventually the topic turned to our wives. One evening as we sat together on an outcrop facing away from Damascus, gazing up to the cloudless sky, a myriad of stars blinking like crystals above us, Zengi spoke of Zumurrud Khatun whom he had married as a political match. I knew most of the story he was about to tell me but let him tell it anyway, about her sons' ruling Damascus, their assassinations, one at her own hands. And when her second son was murdered and Zumurrud had begged Zengi to avenge his death, this being one of many reasons for his desire to take Damascus. By right of marriage, Damascus was his.

I listened to Zengi's story, he seemed unaffected by her seemingly cold-bloodedness but as he continued, I got the sense of not pride but honour in his feelings towards her. It would take a remarkable man to have done what she had done and being a woman made it even more impressive. But I was not surprised by him. I had learned from my studies with Théos and spending many years living amongst Muslims that honour was paramount to them and what may appear brutal to those from the West would seem not only expected but celebrated in their culture.

In contrast, my stories about my lady showed her for the beautiful woman she was, gentle and yet with a will of steel.

"I envy you, you married for love," he said to me with a slight wistfulness to his voice, adding "I have not had the luxury."

"You may have been the lucky one in matters of marriage," I said sadly. "I have suffered much from her loss. I still do."

"But there has been another, yes?" he asked quietly.

I knew of course of whom he spoke. I thought of the Melisende and for a brief moment my chest constricted. I knew my silence shouted the truth to Zengi and I wondered just how much I could tell him about her. But he seemed to know a great deal already. Zengi felt my unease and quickly filled the vacuum between us.

> "We have many that affect us, yes?" he asked, not really expecting an answer. "I have heard rumours," he continued, "of a Queen who had been on her deathbed only to be saved by the love of a Templar?"

I should have been shocked by this but I was not. I had often wondered how Melisende's miraculous recovery had been interpreted and spoken of although no one had ever approached me about it. They had not dared.

> "It was not just by love was it?" he asked. "You know, do not you? The ancient rites?"

This I was shocked by. But of course, how could I be so arrogant to have thought I was the only one who possessed such knowledge.

I studied him for a moment and then went with my gut instinct. I told him everything, all of it, from the accidental discovery of the ruins beneath the Temple Mount to the hidden rooms and the treasures discovered there. And the pool in Zedekiah's cave and the chest and its contents. I knew I was taking a huge risk, that I was trusting Zengi with information that I had kept hidden for years now, determined not to let this power fall into the wrong hands. Although many would argue that Zengi's hands were the wrong hands. But he allayed my fears right away.

> "There have been stories throughout the years of this secret knowledge, my father and his father before him and so on have passed down the traditions of the Emerald Tablet and the prayer words that go with it. But it was also known that they would work only in the hands of those with a noble soul and one who truly believes. The powers do not come to those who do not. And they cannot be forced. You clearly have been chosen. It is a blessing but also a burden."

He was right. We sat in silence for a moment and he looked at me through the light cast by the moon and from the small torches resting nearby.

> "You are a man of honour, Sébastien, I have known that from the moment we first met when you spared my life," he said with great sincerity.

"You gave a starving boy food," I reminded him.

Zengi chuckled.

"Yes. At the time it was no doubt self-serving to do so, but we were obviously meant for great things. *Masha'Allah*. God willed it."

"*Masha'Allah*," I repeated after him.

"I have decided to give you an Arabic name, my friend," he said suddenly. "Jadir. I shall call you Jadir. One who is worthy. Those who hear me speak it shall know the respect you are owed."

I was surprised by this and flattered. I was at a loss for words and he knew it.

"I am aware of the trust you have placed in me with this confidence," he said seriously. "Do not fear, I shall not abuse it. It does confirm for me the depth of your character and I am honoured to call you friend."

I slept well that night, for the first time in a very long time. I felt a huge burden had been lifted somewhat from my shoulders by confiding in Zengi although his words did confirm something I had wondered about: if I had been chosen for this, were there others?

A few nights later we took another walk to the outcrop which had become our favourite for sitting, sharing some fruit and talking.

"I have a gift for you, Jadir," he began as soon as we sat, reaching into a pouch which he had placed on the ground by his feet.

He brought out something solid, wrapped in a cloth of dark blue silk with what looked to be stars in silver embroidered on it. I watched, intrigued as he carefully unwrapped it. I knew instantly what it was. An astrolabe, not unlike that which Adelard of Bath had shown me in Jerusalem. Zengi saw the recognition in my face as he handed it to me.

"You know what this is?" he asked and I nodded as I took it from him.

Circular in shape and made of bronze as was Adelard's, I ran my fingers over the markings along the inner and outer rings. I saw the same Arabic notations etched and Zengi took time explaining them to me and reminding me how it worked. The evening sky was perfect for this as it was crystal clear that night. I was touched by the gift.

"Keep this with you always," he said, tapping it gently, "and you will be able to find your way."

"*Shkran lak* my friend," I said quietly, "thank you."

We sat in silence for a long time that night, no doubt thinking similar thoughts, of how our lives had led us to this moment in time and what our futures may hold before us. I also needed to find a way to do what King Louis and Abbot Bernard had instructed of me: to convince Zengi to leave Damascus. I was not sure I was going to be able to accomplish my task.

# VIII

## Part Four

## 1146-1147 – Baalbek

A few days after receiving the gift of the astrolabe, General Ayyub appeared at our tent, waking both myself and Osmond in the early hours of the morning. He had unsettling news: Zengi's armies were moving out, leaving Damascus and were on their way back to Aleppo where Zengi was needed but did not explain why. He did, however, have a message from Zengi which was for Osmond and myself to return to Baalbek with Ayyub and after his business was done at Aleppo, he would come meet us there where we could continue our discussions. I began to dress quickly to try to see him before he left, but Ayyub informed us he had set out just after midnight, much to our surprise. I was disappointed to hear this but heartened by Zengi's message that he would return. To those watching from afar, it would appear as though I had accomplished my task as reports would undoubtedly surface of Zengi's massive army making their way north again, away from Damascus. But I would not know for sure if this departure was permanent or just temporary.

Osmond and I packed up what little we had including the astrolabe now re-wrapped in the silks in which it came and were escorted back to Baalbek and to the tower we had occupied before. But this time we were not imprisoned guests, we were given larger, more comfortable quarters and allowed to roam the city at will which we did but rarely, keeping mostly to the grounds of the citadel. And without me wearing the Templar clothing, I thought it would be wise not to draw any more attention to us than we already had, Zengi's blessing on our presence or not.

Zengi had graciously given us access to a small library, stocked with various texts of Islamic tradition and philosophy, writings on the Qur'an which I painstakingly made my way through, trying my best to understand the complex and passionate beliefs of Zengi's people. I needed to be able to bring whatever knowledge I had gained back to those in the West; the battles for this land had to come to an end and a peaceful co-existence established and I wanted to be part of that. I felt this was now my calling and Osmond regularly found me late in the night, reading by candlelight, reminding me to take my rest.

We had been in Baalbek for a month or so when we received the dreadful news: Zengi was dead. Ayyub had hastened back to Baalbek and came to our quarters immediately upon his arrival in the middle of the night, concerned for not only his own position without his master but ours as well. There were not many details. Zengi and his armies had been diverted to Qal'at Ja'Bar, a fortress overlooking the Euphrates River which had been taken by a group of French mercenaries. Strategically placed between Aleppo and Baghdad, it was important for him regain possession of the fort as quickly as possible and so had set about besieging the besiegers. But he had not died an honourable death in battle. Instead, he had been attacked and murdered by one of his own servants who had come to his tent in the middle of the night in a drunken rage seeking revenge after Zengi had berated him earlier, having caught the man drinking from one of his goblets after the evening meal. Zengi had been stabbed to death in his sleep.

I stood shocked to my core. It was too surreal to believe. I was numb. But I also knew that we were now probably in danger. Knowing the turmoil that deaths of rulers plunged the Islamic world into when they were expected, I could only surmise that this unexpected death would result in chaos. Or, at the very least, we could not rely on the same respect and courtesy shown to us by Zengi to be extended by a new ruler hellbent on establishing his authority. And a Templar in captivity would be a great prize indeed. I asked Ayyub who would succeed Zengi.

"His eldest son, Nur ad-Din Zengi, will be Atabeg of the cities his father had been governing," Ayyub told us. "You must know, the son does not share the respect for your Order as did the father. He sees the crusaders and the Templars in particular as the great enemy in Palestine. You would be well-advised to depart as soon as possible. I have had your destriers readied for you."

Osmond had already started re-packing our belongings in our travel pouches, carefully folding the Templar cloak and surcoat and tucking them out of sight. I reached for the astrolabe which was sitting on the window ledge where I had left it after the previous night's studying of the sky and tightly wrapped it with the silks it came with and packed it into one of my leather bags. Suddenly there was a motion at the door and I turned to see Ayyub's young son standing in the doorway, holding our swords in the palms of his hands. I reached for Osmond's and handed it to him then took mine from the boy nodding my thanks. We grabbed our things and followed Ayyub quickly out onto the landing, down the circular staircase and out the door into the stone landing in front of the citadel's main entrance where we found our two destriers waiting for us as Ayyub had promised. We mounted the horses after securing the leather pouches and made our way to the massive arch entrance lit by torches and waited for the guards there to open the wooden gates.

But the guards only glanced at each other and made no move to unlatch the gates. I looked up to the platform where more guards were positioned; they did not look at us but seemed transfixed by something outside the gates. Suddenly we could hear shouting from afar, fast-paced Arabic that I could not really understand but I knew what was advancing towards us. Osmond and I turned our horses and directed them away from the main gate, riding as quickly as we could throughout the city, shocking many gawking bystanders as we flew past them on our way to exits we knew from our walks existed at the south end of the city, hoping to make our escape there before whoever was arriving from the north reached the city. Luck was with us as the gated entrance there was open and we crossed through, ducking our heads as we made our way. But that is when our luck ran out.

A line of Saracen soldiers greeted us, several deep, preventing us from passing. Our horses reared up with the sudden stop and it took a few moments to get them under control. Torches were lit amongst them, lighting up the area. And then we saw him. Zengi's eldest son, Nur ad-Din Zengi, rode slowly through the men who stepped aside as he approached. As we got closer to us I could see the resemblance to his father, same dark features, beard longer than Zengi's, he sat taller in the saddle. But lacking the spark I had always seen in his father's eyes; his were dull and menacing. He approached us and did not stop until his horse's head was next to mine.

"Ah, my father's Templar friend, yes?" he sneered.

I remained silent for he already knew the answer. He glanced at Osmond who met his eyes without flinching.

"You of course know my father is dead," he started, crossing his hands on the hilt of his saddle and leaning forward ever so slightly, his knowledge of my language almost as good as Zengi's.

I nodded.

"I now govern these lands. And will continue to govern these lands as I see fit," his voice menacingly constrained. "I do not know why you are here Templar, what possessed you to believe you, an infidel, had the right to walk freely amongst the blessed of Mohammed's people."

"Your father and I shared a mutual respect, and we were welcomed here," I responded.

He smirked.

"I am not my father," he snarled.

'More the pity,' I thought but kept silent.

"But what to do with you? I have never shared my father's respect for members of your Order, nor for the invading crusaders who have taken our lands from us, slaughtering our women and children."

I decided not to point out the hypocrisy of his statement. His was not as open a mind as his father's was. I knew we were in peril.

"Well, I cannot let you pass, you must realize that. I think I shall keep you here until I decide what to do with you," he said nodding to himself.

And raising his right hand and making a slight circular motion, guards surrounded us and we had no choice but to dismount. Our swords were taken as were our leather pouches. It was then that I realized Ayyub had arrived at the south gate and was watching the proceedings. Nur ad-Din caught sight of him too and waved him over. He instructed the guards to hand Ayyub our swords and effects; Ayyub took them and handed them to one of his own men. He turned his expressionless face towards me and stared at me, his eyes telling me nothing.

"General Ayyub is one of my commanders now, he does my bidding. You shall stay as his guests but I am afraid the accommodations will not be of the same quality as those you have been enjoying," he said with a nasty smile.

And then, turning to his men, he spoke in his own language, clearly unaware that I was able to understand him. Nur ad-Din gave instructions to his men about our captivity and that he would be sending interrogators to Baalbek from Aleppo. He would know why I was really here. And what I really knew. Ayyub said nothing.

Osmond and I were not taken back to our rooms but rather down into the lower levels of the citadel, where prisoners of war were held in dungeon-like cells, behind thick, heavy wooden doors, locked and guarded all day and all night. We were ushered into separate cells at opposite ends of the stone corridor, far apart enough to prevent us from speaking with one another. I ducked through the doorway and found myself in an almost empty cell, the only sense of the outdoors coming through a grate in the ceiling. I guessed this was a viewing point through which those standing above could watch whoever was in the cell below. No doubt I was to be put on show.

The only other opening in the cell was a slot at the foot of the door which I surmised was what was used to provide food. There was no furniture to speak of, only a bucket of water in one corner and an empty bucket in another for waste. In many ways it reminded me of the cell I was kept in at Devizes Castle after Duke Robert and I were captured after the battle at Tinchebrai. But I did not have any annoyed uncles nearby to help me get out of this situation. I needed to concoct a way to save myself and Osmond on my own.

* * * * * * * * *

Nur ad-Din did not waste any time establishing his position as his father's successor and for the first couple of months Osmond and I were left alone as he busied himself with visiting his cities. I was made aware that he had sent word to King Louis of my capture but was making no demands for my release. His hatred for the West was palpable and he was enjoying playing games with those whom he was certain had sent me on some spurious mission of espionage that his father had been deceived into believing was something innocent. We had had a few conversations before he departed for Aleppo during which I admitted I had been sent to seek out Zengi and to try to convince him to forgo his attacks on Damascus, preventing an all-out war with the West. Nur ad-Din did not believe this was all and even demanded to know why I had been given the Islamic astrolabe. I simply said it had been a gift from his father. This did not satisfy him.

The interrogator arrived from Aleppo shortly into the new year and began first with conversation in the cell with a chair for him and a small stool for me, an obvious attempt to make me feel inferior. But with my natural height I still sat taller than him and so the attempt failed. I think my size, towering over most of the Saracen army, intimidated him although he tried not to show it. But the questions were the same again and again: why was I really there? What was discussed with Zengi? Why did Zengi not simply take me captive and hold me for ransom? I responded truthfully as the answers to these questions did not hold any secrets and it was well known that the rulers in the West wanted to avoid a war.

When that did not give them what they wanted to hear, the threats of violence started. Guards arrived with weapons drawn, ready to do whatever was asked of them. Other attempts were made to frighten me into revealing secrets through threats of torture but this failed as well. But despite the menacing, I was never touched. Finally, after many weeks of this, they allowed me to walk within the well-guarded courtyard of the citadel. This is when I saw what they had done to Osmond.

I was let out first, took a deep breath and looked up at the sun-filled sky, blue and cloudless. Otherwise a perfect early spring's day. Then I heard the sound of the door I had come out of opening again and I saw Osmond limp out, hunched over and cradling his left arm. He lifted his head and I could see he had been beaten about the face, cuts and bruises covering his cheeks and jaw, a nasty gash badly wrapped along the hairline on the right side of his head. My gut lurched with the realization of what had been done to him. I rushed to him and helped him over to a stone bench. I kept my arm around his shoulders, careful not to inflict pain on areas I could see through his ratty clothing. He was severely injured but I had no idea how badly.

"Oh my dear Osmond," I started but he cut me off.

"Do not, m'lord," he pleaded with me.

And so I stopped talking and gently squeezed his shoulder which caused him to place his head on my chest. We sat that way, still, breathing deeply, feeling the warmth of the springtime sun on our faces, imagining other peaceful places. I tried to be brave for my friend whilst at the same time trying to control the racing emotions coursing through me, an overwhelming wave of rage, sadness, guilt that I had brought him to this land on this mission. I felt the strength in him slipping away and I knew if I did nothing, I would lose him.

Once back in my cell I called to the guard to get the interrogator. When he arrived he was dismissive of my anger at the torture Osmond had suffered, callously shrugging and saying the only reason I had not suffered the same was because of my high status and importance to the King and Pope which made my value much much higher than that of Osmond. It was then that I made my position clear: I would tell Nur ad-Din what he wanted to know but only to him and only if they left Osmond alone and let him heal from his wounds. They would not ever get what they were searching for from Osmond, it was me and me alone who had what Nur ad-Din was seeking. And if I needed to go to Aleppo, so be it, but Osmond would be accompanying me, we would go together to wherever Nur ad-Din was.

The interrogator must have acted with haste as within a short while I received word that Nur ad-Din had ordered the two of us to be taken to Aleppo immediately. A locked caged cart was prepared for our journey, its floor thankfully padded with straw and blankets to make the journey comfortable for Osmond. He was carried out and laid down carefully. I was then loaded into the cage, my hands and ankles in chains to prevent me from trying to escape. Once inside, a large piece of canvas was thrown on top of it and secured at the sides, preventing us from seeing where we were going but with enough of an opening at the bottom to let a breeze in.

And so, out of the large arched gate into which we had been brought by Ayyub almost a year earlier, a small convoy of Nur ad-Din's men and an iron-caged cart with precious cargo made their way out of Baalbek.

* * * * * * * * * *

The journey was painstakingly slow and difficult. Osmond had suffered a great deal, his wounds were not healing properly because of the constant jostling of the cart over the uneven roads. The food and water given to us was sparse, I gave most of mine to Osmond although he did not eat much. I worried that his condition was not improving and the guards refused to do anything despite my admonitions that Nur ad-Din would not be pleased if either of us died on route to him. I did my best to keep the wounds clean and watched him closely for any signs of fever setting in.

Eventually we stopped by a lake which I knew was just outside of Homs, having overheard a couple of the guards talking about our progress, unaware that I could understand them. We were to camp for the night and await supplies. I managed to convince them by using gestures to allow me out to stretch my cramped legs and to wash out the rags I had been using for dressing Osmond's injuries. I took the opportunity to bathe as best I could still being shackled, ruing the beard that had been the result of these months in captivity.

I had just been returned to the cage with the canvas sheet pulled down around us and was checking on Osmond when the shouting began, the great cries of men being assaulted, and the sounds of the chaos that ensues when an attack is unexpected. We could hear the clashes of sword upon sword, men in their death throes calling out to Allah. And yet, the only voices I could hear were in Arabic, I could discern no other language.

And then suddenly, it was over as quickly as it began. Silence replaced the cacophony of the raid. I steeled myself for my inevitable death once the attackers untied the canvas cover to the cage and discovered our existence. But that did not happen. I could hear movements around the cart and then some murmuring in the distance and then the sound of horses' hooves as their riders spurred them into gallops leading them away from where we were. And then again silence. Osmond had awakened during the melee and looked at me with raised eyebrows. I shrugged, whispering to him that I did not know what was happening. And then the ropes tying the canvas sheet about the cage started jerking and within a few moments they and the canvas were yanked from the cage revealing to us who it was that had been responsible for the attack.

Much to my astonishment, I was greeted by the sight of two guards on foot, one holding the canvas, the other holding the ropes and behind them, on horseback sat Ayyub and next to him his son. With a few instructions, Ayyub had his men unlock the cage and get me out. One look at him and my rage rose again and I charged him as he was getting off his horse, it was only his men that kept me from striking him down. They held onto me but did not harm me as I shouted my accusations of betrayal at him. His son sat passively by on his horse, watching the scene unfold.

Ayyub waited for my fury to abate before telling his men to let go of me.

"I understand your anger D'Ivry," he said as he handed the reins of his horse to a guard. "I can explain but we must speak quickly and get you on your way as soon as possible."

I waited to hear his explanation as to why he had allowed my friend to be tortured so. He motioned to his men to help Osmond out of the cage.

"The night you were taken prisoner at Baalbek, I had no way of saving you and your man. Nur ad-Din had assumed control of the cities and territories after Zengi's death and I could not take the risk of raising any suspicions of my allegiances. He was the true successor and I needed to bide my time until I could find a way to get you out. And then I was instructed to assist him in Aleppo and so have not been in Baalbek these past months."

He stopped and looked at Osmond.

"I am sorry for the pain caused to your man," he said sincerely.

I believed him. I felt my anger start to abate.

"And the opportunity came when I was told Nur ad-Din had given orders to have you brought to him in Aleppo. I engaged a mercenary tribe with whom I have had dealings before and, on the promise of payment, had them attack this, ah, how do you say..." and muttered his meaning in Arabic.

"Convoy," I said, translating it for him.

He stood still for a moment, with the sudden realization that I understood him dawning upon him.

"Yes, convoy, with the understanding that upon pain of death should they touch the cart. They were paid, they have departed and we now have but a short time to get you to safety."

His son now dismounted and moved behind his horse, fetching our two destriers that we had used to try to escape from the city. Handing me the reins, he spoke.

"Your horses have been fed and watered and are ready for your journey. Your saddlebags have food and wine as well as the contents you had with you when you were captured, including your swords," he said, his dark eyes looking up at me. "I do wish your friend a good recovery. *Alikum asalam*. Peace be with you."

I looked at the boy and suddenly realized he must have been about the same age I was when I accompanied Duke Robert on crusade. And I felt that memory rush through me.

"*Nafs alshay' maeak*," I said, my younger self feeling a strong connection to this boy. "The same with you."

Ayyub's men had attended to Osmond, re-dressing his wounds and giving him fresh clothes, wrapping him tightly in a cloak with ties that would allow him to sit upright on a horse. I was also given fresh clothing to replace the threadbare ones I had worn for months. I knew we must depart quickly as the supplies coming from Homs might reach us soon and Ayyub and his son and men needed to be as far away so as not to be suspected of what would be seen as treason.

Ayyub gave me instructions on how to get to and then cross the Orontes River to reach safe land and eventually Tripoli. I embraced him as a friend and once Osmond was secured on his horse and with a nod to the boy we were off to the south, heading back to safety. As we moved I could hear a slight cry out from Ayyub, turned to look and saw they were gone. Once again I had been saved from certain death by a man whose sense of honour matched that of my friend Zengi. It was a lesson I would never forget.

Osmond and I travelled as quickly as he could bear and we soon came to the edge of the Orontes River and the crossing just as Ayyub had described. We now were only two days ride from Tripoli but I knew that Osmond may not last; I needed to help him. So instead of turning west towards the city, we continued to follow the river south, back towards the place where we had set up camp before crossing the Orontes on our way to Baalbek. In a strange twist of luck, it was almost the exact same time of year, the weather and ground coverings the same, as was the flow of the river. It did not take long before I started seeing familiar landmarks, trees, bushes, the curves of the river, the shoreline indentations and suchlike. I kept my eye trained on the shore knowing I would soon recognize where our camp had been.

Once I was certain we had reached the area, I dismounted and helped Osmond down from his horse and attended to his wounds. The ride had worsened them, the rags wrapped around them were soaked with more blood than they had been outside of Homs. I needed to get the bleeding to stop. I gave him some water to drink and then, making him comfortable, I told him to rest and that I would return shortly. I made my way in from the shore and easily found the little pile of rocks I had created and stepped twenty paces back into the trees and bushes in the direction I thought was correct from my memory. But when I had, I found nothing that spurred my memory of where I had buried my treasures and tried to contain the panic starting to rise in me.

I took several steps in each direction from the twenty-pace mark and it was on the second time I tried that I found it. The shrub had grown and spread over top of the small trench that I had used as my marker which is why I missed it the first time. Dropping to my knees, I quickly dug at the soil, knowing that time of was of essence. Within a few moments, I hit upon the lambskin first and then the St Michael medal and chain. I quickly tied its clasp around my neck and then reached down to find the wrapped bundle containing the Emerald Tablet and the books. Thankfully the leather wrapping had kept everything dry.

Picking up everything, I rushed back to the shore and saw that Osmond was no longer awake and his breathing had become short and shallow, his skin having turned deathly pale. I lifted the bandages from the most serious wound across his stomach and saw that it had turned in colour with an oily black substance oozing out. I had seen this before when tending the soldiers during the crusade and knew that few lived after reaching this state. I ripped open the lambskin and shook out the vials of elixir I had put there for safekeeping and was devastated to see that the first two of the three had broken their wax seals and the little glass bottles were empty and dry. I picked up the third and was hit by a wave of relief – it had not broken and I could see liquid inside.

I gathered Osmond up about the shoulders and began rocking to and for, saying the sacred words and prayers from memory. Opening his mouth for him, I tipped the liquid from the vial into his mouth, tilting his head back slightly to help him swallow it. I continued the recitation of the words until suddenly I felt the winds increase in force, the gentle breeze that had been when I left Osmond now turning into a gale, whipping the sand from the shore at us, stinging my face and hands. Rain started to come down upon us, light droplets that tickled at first then strengthening to a torrent, but I did not stop reciting the prayers. I covered Osmond's body with my own the best I could to shield him from the rain but it was no use, we were drenched within moments. Bolts of lightning lit up the sky, crooked spikes of light stabbing at the ground in the distance. But still I did not stop reciting the prayers. And then I felt as though I was being lifted, as if becoming one with the wind and the rain and the sky and the shore, Osmond being removed from my arms and gently laid onto the sands. I felt tears pouring from my eyes, the grief, the burden, the pain that I had caused this man rushing out of me and I cried out in a burst of emotion, fists clenched, releasing all the anger and agony from my body, as if the world around me was liberating me from all the sorrow and guilt I had carried with me throughout my life. With a tremendous clap of thunder it was suddenly all over and I collapsed next to Osmond, exhausted and unable to move. I fell into a stupor and sleep soon followed, a deep, restful sleep I had not had since my marriage days with my lady.

* * * * * * * * * *

I awoke the next morning feeling the warmth of the morning sun on my face. I sat up and looked about me, nothing seemed out of the ordinary. Had I imagined the storm in my dreams? I crawled over to Osmond not knowing what to expect. He had turned onto his side during the night and I rolled him onto his back and saw right away his breathing was slow and measured and the colour had come back to his face. I lifted his shirt to take a look at the main wound and saw it was still raw but the colour had changed to a light pink and the black ooze had disappeared. A quick look at his other wounds showed improvement too, he was healing. I took a deep breath and sighed heavily, sinking back into the sand. I felt the tears come again, but this time it was relief mixed with joy and I was happy to feel them.

I set about setting up camp and preparing the food that Ayyub had provided. Osmond's recovery was remarkable and we were able to continue our journey back to Tripoli within a few days. He knew he owed me his life but never asked about how he had come to be healed of wounds he knew would have taken a stronger man than he. We never spoke about it.

# VIII

# Part Five

# 1148 – Acre

Upon our return to Tripoli, we were hailed as heroes. I met with Count Raymond who told me that from what the leaders of the West knew, it appeared I had succeeded in my mission to convince Zengi to abandon Damascus; his death simply meant they had a new enemy to contend with and now we needed to wait and watch to see what Nur ad-Din had planned. I told him of my encounter with this new adversary and of our imprisonment and Osmond's torture, both at his hands.

I spent much time in contemplation of what had happened during the past months. I found it difficult to reconcile the brutal Zengi, known in the West to have committed some of the worst atrocities in battles waged against our allies, with the deep-thinking, merciful man I had spent much time with discussing philosophies and our traditions and the similarities between them. Although my head told me we were adversaries, my heart told me otherwise. I had unwittingly made a friend for life in that cave in Antioch, but the world in which we lived kept telling us that our friendship could not be.

News came from Aleppo about Ayyub who thankfully had not been suspected in our escape. But he did have to surrender Baalbek to Nur ad-Din who wanted to use it as his own base for his next moves on Damascus which became clear when we received word that Governor Unur of Damascus, despite an alliance with the West still being in place, had agreed to a treaty with Nur ad-Din. Even more worrying was that part of the agreement included Nur ad-Din's marriage to Governor Unur's daughter, seemingly strengthening the relationship through family ties. But Governor Unur had always fought Zengi's attempts to take over Damascus, and so this new alliance was viewed with scepticism. We just had to wait and see.

The war in England had finally come to an end with the death of Matilda's key military leader, her half-brother Robert of Gloucester. The strength and power of her purpose diminished, she had returned to Normandy having not gained the crown which was rightfully hers, but at least having made her presence felt and leaving many in awe of her energy and determination. She would need to leave it to her son, Henry, to take up the cause when he was old enough. And that would come sooner rather than later, much to King Stephen's chagrin. I hoped I would not have any contact with the English King, I had no desire to be in his service.

Whilst Osmond continued his convalescence in the comfort of Raymond's palace and under the care of Raymond's best physicians, I spent my days writing as much as I could remember and as much as I wished to impart in letters to King Louis and Abbot Bernard. Despite knowing I was on a mission to do whatever I could to prevent war in Palestine, I was disappointed to hear that Abbot Bernard had indeed preached a sermon soon after I had departed, much like Pope Urban's call to the masses in Clermont, but this time in Vezelay to an audience which included King Louis and Queen Eleanor, calling again for the taking of the cross and for another crusade to save the Holy Land.

Massive armies had been formed and had already departed in three waves, the first made up of English, Scottish and Flemish fighters, the second of German fighters led by their King Conrad, and the last of French fighters led by King Louis. He was to be accompanied by the new Grand Master Everard who had been elected to replace Grand Master Craon who had died early in the new year. His selection was not surprising knowing the close relationship he had fashioned with King Louis and he had supported the call for another crusade, and so was travelling with the King and Queen Eleanor to Palestine when I arrived back in Tripoli.

The first wave of crusaders set sail from England and had to make port at Porto in Portugal due to bad weather. But this was not a complete misfortune as the bishop there convinced them to march on Lisbon and back King Alphonso in his attempts to recapture the city from the Muslim invaders. They would spend a few months there eventually winning the city and setting sail again for the Holy Land albeit with a smaller army as many decided to stay.

The second wave of the Germans set out over land, following the same path we had done in the first crusade. And just as our leaders had sworn an oath to Emperor Alexios in Constantinople, so did King Conrad to Emperor Alexios's grandson Emperor Manuel. The third wave of the French followed a few weeks behind the Germans and upon reaching Constantinople, King Louis was greeted royally by the Emperor but was pressed to swear an oath to return Byzantine lands to him should any be won. It was all eerily familiar and having witnessed the brutality of battle and the bloodshed of so many on our journeys, I was uneasy with this new war, wishing those who insisted on bringing the armies had done more with diplomacy before launching this campaign. I knew what the cost would be, and it unsettled me greatly.

And as if more evidence of history repeating itself was needed, the first real battle took place again at Dorylaeum, but this time the West were not the victors. The German troops moved to meet the Seljuk Turks, led by another Arslan, son of the ruler we had defeated at Nicaea. For some inexplicable reason, King Conrad had ordered half of his army to head to Nicaea, leaving only the other half his army to take on Turks. They were hopelessly unprepared and outmanned, their defeat was inevitable. The loss was enormous, and only about one tenth of the fighters made it to Nicaea to join the other armies.

King Conrad himself survived but had become desperately ill and had to return to Constantinople. When he arrived, he requested that a fleet be sent by the Emperor for the remainder of the armies and one was dispatched immediately. Unfortunately there were not enough to take all the crusaders and so King Louis took them for himself and for the nobles to sail to Antioch, leaving the rest to fend for themselves. Most perished over the next few months from disease or attacks by bandits. And when the rest reached Antioch, they were exhausted and starving. The second crusade was off to an ignominious start.

At Antioch, King Louis took time to consider what to do next. Many implored him to turn to Edessa and recapture the Crusader State. Raymond of Antioch, Queen Eleanor's uncle, demanded the armies turn to Aleppo and take it from Nur ad-Din, but King Louis was focused on the vows he made when taking the cross and wanted to press on to the Holy Land. There were reports of King Louis and Queen Eleanor arguing and accusations of incestuous adultery between uncle and niece although there was no evidence of it. I certainly did not believe the rumours, I knew the Queen to be a strong-willed woman and I admired her greatly, but many of the noblemen disapproved of her ways, many had not wanted her to accompany her husband on crusade. And rumours of this sort was just the thing to ruin her reputation and lessen her power, but I knew she would not let this affect her, in fact I think she revelled in it. It did not matter in the end, King Louis simply forced her to go with him to Acre where they would take advantage of a previously arranged meeting of the Haut Cour of Jerusalem, the annual coming together of all the members of the High Court.

But her uncle had been outraged by King Louis ignoring his advice and so he declared he would not attend the Council of Acre. It would be a great loss not to have the Count of Tripoli in attendance as it would be there that the decisions would be made on what should be done with the armies they had amassed, and where they should strike first. I knew I would be called upon to attend on the French King and Queen and waited their instructions.

And so, with the decision made to head to the Holy Land, what was left of the armies set off from Antioch eventually setting up camp outside of Tripoli. Its Count Raymond made preparations for King Louis's and Queen Eleanor's arrival and received them and the nobles with sumptuous fanfare, feasts and celebrations, although I knew not what they had to celebrate. I expressed my concern only to Osmond, one evening as we stood on the battlements of the city's walls, overlooking the camps.

"Is this all there is?" Osmond said as we stood side-by-side looking out at the scores of tents and campfires set up by the crusading army.

"I fear so," I answered, my voice filled with trepidation.

Osmond spoke my unspoken fears.

"There is not enough of them, they will be slaughtered in any battle with the Seljuks," he said plainly and without exaggeration.

I did not know what to say, I just nodded.

"When you have your audience with King Louis and the others, what will you advise?" he asked staring out at the field before us.

"They will not want my advice," I answered. "The King wants his triumph in the Holy Land as others have had before him. If he had the strength and size of an army needed to complete the task, I would have advised him to go to Aleppo as Queen Eleanor's Uncle Raymond wanted, and remove Nur ad-Din from power. But I am no longer certain I can understand what it is they wish to accomplish here."

It was a very troubling thought and the audiences I had with the King did nothing to eradicate my sense of impending doom.

* * * * * * * * *

I met with the King and Grand Master Everard in a private audience the day after they arrived in Tripoli. I told them more details of my meetings with Zengi and the progress I had been making before his untimely murder on his way to Aleppo. I told them I thought we had had a better chance of establishing a peaceful co-existence with Zengi and that Nur ad-Din's hatred for the crusaders and anyone he considered the infidel would be a far more difficult problem to resolve. He had made it clear that he was determined to return Palestine and all its lands back to his people and remove any trace of us at any cost. Zengi had been known to be a brutal leader but the son, I felt, would far eclipse the father given the opportunity. And with the treaty with Damascus still in place, the best option was to take Nur ad-Din at Aleppo, Damascus was not really a threat to us.

But I felt my words were falling on deaf ears. I was providing information taken from the enemy leaders themselves but King Louis was determined to not to heed my advice. I was thanked and handsomely rewarded for my efforts, as was Osmond, but no more was said about the perilous mission they had sent me on. War was what they wanted, and it was war that they would have. I was ordered to head to Acre ahead of the armies and prepare for the arrival of the various heads of state who would be coming to attend the Council King Louis wished to hold to discuss what to do next. I was handed a few lists of the attendees which I looked at after I was given my leave. My heart skipped a beat when I read the names under the Haut Cour of Jerusalem:

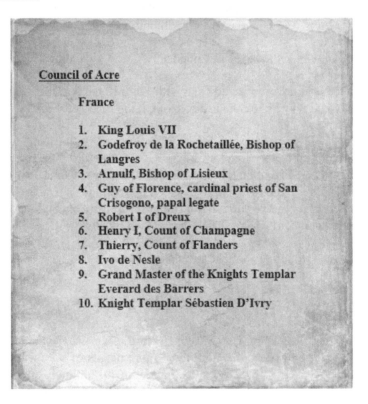

Council of Acre

France

1. King Louis VII
2. Godefroy de la Rochetaillée, Bishop of Langres
3. Arnulf, Bishop of Lisieux
4. Guy of Florence, cardinal priest of San Crisogono, papal legate
5. Robert I of Dreux
6. Henry I, Count of Champagne
7. Thierry, Count of Flanders
8. Ivo de Nesle
9. Grand Master of the Knights Templar Everard des Barrers
10. Knight Templar Sébastien D'Ivry

**Haut Cour of Jerusalem**

1. Baldwin III of Jerusalem
2. Melisende of Jerusalem
3. Patriarch Fulk of Jerusalem
4. Raymond du Puy de Provence,
   Grand Master of the Knights Hospitaller

**Germany**

1. Conrad III of Germany
2. Otto, Bishop of Freising
3. Stephan of Bar, Bishop of Metz
4. Heinrich I von Lothringen, Bishop of Toul
5. Theodwin, Bishop of Porto, papal legate
6. Henry II Jasomirgott, Duke of Bavaria and
   Margrave of Austria
7. Duke Welf VI
8. Frederick III, Duke of Swabia
9. Herman III, Margrave of Baden
10. Berthold III of Andechs
11. William V, Marquess of Montferrat
12. Guido, Count of Biandrate

**The Levant**

1. Baldwin, Archbishop of Caesarea
2. Robert, Archbishop of Nazareth
3. Rorgo, Bishop of Acre
4. Bernard, Bishop of Sidon
5. William, Bishop of Beirut
6. Adam, Bishop of Banyas
7. Gerald, Bishop of Bethlehem
8. Manasses of Hierges
9. Philip of Nablus
10. Elinand of Tiberias
11. Gerard Grenier
12. Walter of Caesarea
13. Pagan the Butler
14. Barisan of Ibelin
15. Humphrey II of Toron
16. Guy I Brisebarre of Beirut

Although I should not have been surprised, both Queen Melisende and her son King Baldwin would be attending. Even though he had reached his majority two years earlier, he was considered a young and inexperienced ruler, having left it mostly to his mother to attend to matters of governing. And although he would officially be the host of the Council of Acre, there was no misunderstanding as to who the true ruler of Jerusalem was. I wondered if she had changed much.

Osmond and I set off with a small contingent of armed guards, horses and carts of provisions to help prepare Acre for the onslaught of visitors on their way. Those at the highest levels and their immediate staff would of course stay in the citadel itself, rooms in the city would have to be obtained for everyone else. It took us three days to reach the city and I was amazed at how it had grown in the years since I had left. King Baldwin had besieged the town a few years after our crusade and had established it as a port settlement used mostly for trade and as a staging place for shipping supplies to and from the West. And over the years it had grown both in size and in population; when I left the Levant it was second in numbers only to those of Jerusalem.

The Templar House I had visited many years ago had increased in size and was quite impressive but nothing rivalled the Hospitaller citadel which had practically taken over the north of the city stretching to the coast. Immense in height and sprawl, with soaring towers that could be seen at quite a distance both on land and at sea, the citadel was the focal point of Acre, built over many years by our brother order, the Hospitallers of St John. Used primarily as a commandery for the brothers, the equivalent to the Templar preceptories which were being built throughout Christendom such as the one I had built in Paris.

When we arrived, the citadel was a busy hive of activity, the Hospitaller Brothers having been given ample warning that they were about to be deluged by a large number of eminent members of royalty, clergy and military, and they knew they also had to prepare for the armies they were bringing with them.

Osmond and I crossed the open courtyard and made our way through the various workmen and servants hurrying about, making way for us upon seeing the new Templar cloak and surcoat I was wearing having obtained them at the Templar House. We stood for a moment at the entrance to the great hall, watching them. Knowing we also had a great deal of work to do, we turned and entered the great hall, greeted by several towering pillars, all wrapped in iron bands, providing the support for the enormous heavy stone roof above. It was a remarkable chambre and was also where the Council would take place. I needed to ensure that tables and platforms were constructed and appropriate seating provided for the attendees by their place in order, Kings before Counts, Bishops before Priests, and so on. I spent much time ensuring this was correct, the last thing we needed was for some Count to be offended by his place at the table.

Whilst Osmond and I took quarters at the Templar House closer to the south end of the city, the senior members of the crusaders stayed in the rooms provided by the Hospitallers in the citadel. They started arriving within a few days after we had and I assisted one of the clerics who attended upon the Hospitaller Grand Master, Raymond du Puy de Provence. This man, Brother Alvisius, was a smarmy little man who had an irritating sense of self-importance, shocking and not in keeping with the Hospitaller ways, busied himself with making sure all the dignitaries were settled comfortably in their quarters. I was assigned to attend on those from France and Germany and as such had no opportunity to see Queen Melisende or King Baldwin before the Council began.

Many of our Templar Brothers had been enlisted to help wherever they could during the proceedings and our white surcoats and red crosses stood out amongst the Hospitaller Brothers in their black surcoats with white crosses. We and they were everywhere. The security of this Council was paramount and Acre, for the time being, had become impenetrable.

On a warm day near the end of June, on the day of the Council, I was standing by in the background, keeping a quiet and watchful eye as the attendees arrived, greeted one another and took their seats. I was dressed in my full Templar regalia including a ceremonial sword and scabbard as was Grand Master Everard who arrived with King Louis but not Queen Eleanor. Rumours abounded that there was friction between the two and the Queen had elected to go to Jerusalem and await the outcome there. This disappointed me, I would have liked to have seen her again.

I escorted the King to his seat on the raised dais facing out to the rest of the tables formed in arcs on the floor in front of them. Grand Master Everard spoke with them for a moment, then took his seat at one of those tables on the floor in front of the dais. I bowed and took my leave and was making my way through the throng of people when the set of doors at the far end opened and all eyes turned to watch as Melisende and Baldwin entered with a large entourage.

She took my breath away, it was as if she had not aged a day. She certainly rivalled Queen Eleanor in pure beauty and grace. She and her son took a few steps into the hall and then stopped, surveying the room and receiving bows from those near to them. She scanned the faces as if searching for someone and then came to rest upon me. Our eyes locked for a moment and I saw what I thought was the tiniest of smiles, just the edges of her mouth turned up as she looked at me before having her attention taken by one of her minions escorting her to the dais. Brother Alvisius startled me out of my thoughts.

"We have planned well, have we not?" he asked surveying the results of all the hard work done by the Hospitallers and Templars.

I had to agree. Although there had been a few issues with the quarters given to a couple of French Counts, they were easily rectified and all seemed to be satisfied. Whilst I tried to appear as though I was looking across the hall from one side to the other, my eyes always lingered on Melisende for a moment or two before moving on. The Hospitaller Brother noticed.

"She is remarkable, no? Strange for a woman to have reigned for so long during her son's minority without a man taking control," he said, a more than a hint of distain entering his voice. "She had Fulk of course, but it is well known that she did not heed or even ask for his guidance."

It made my skin crawl to hear the monk speak of Melisende in this demeaning way. I was insulted on her behalf and wanted to argue the point but had already ascertained earlier that he was a close-minded bigoted sort, whose criticisms against female rule showed the shallowness of his character and mind. I made my excuses and headed to the other side of the hall where I could have direct eye contact with both King Louis and Grand Master Everard, able to do their bidding at a moment's notice. I felt the Hospitaller's eyes watching me as I stood at guard.

The discussions started immediately after the blessings given by the Patriarch and there was no shortage of people willing to voice their opinions. There were several areas in the Levant that could do with the assistance of this crusading army. Many argued that the armies should head to Edessa to win it back and restore it as a Crusader State but others disagreed feeling that Edessa, with its position so far north and surrounded by the Muslim territories, was a lost cause. Aleppo as a target was discussed again as even though Count Raymond of Antioch was not in attendance, his supporters, including Queen Eleanor supported his argument that Nur ad-Din needed to be captured in his most important city, If Aleppo fell, surely others would too. And had Count Raymond of Tripoli been in attendance, he would have put forth his vote for Aleppo as capturing it would certainly be to his benefit. But this argument was disregarded.

It became clear quite quickly that both King Louis and King Conrad were focused solely on Jerusalem and all suggestions to the contrary were dismissed. They believed that to keep true to the vows they made when they took the cross, they needed to defend Jerusalem from the foes who were the most threatening. And to those in the great hall that day, that meant Ascalon to the south of Jerusalem and Damascus to the north. Damascus was set aside, after all, there was a good treaty in place between Damascus and Jerusalem and had been for several years. Melisende and Baldwin had sent warriors and supplies to Damascus when it needed to fend off attempts to capture it and although it was considered an Arab territory, it was an ally of Jerusalem. So the talk turned to Ascalon.

The discussions had taken all morning and having reached this point, it was decided that time should be taken for the noon-time meal and sext prayers which were held at the chapel of St John which was under construction at the far end of the citadel. I followed the French royals as they made their way but hovered outside the chapel's entrance, wanting to give them their privacy but also so I could keep watch. King Conrad soon followed as did King Baldwin but there was no sign of Melisende. The two Grand Masters of the Templars and the Hospitallers passed by without so much as a glance.

I waited until I could hear the Patriarch start the prayers and then closed the heavy arched doors and took my place in front of them. It was a few moments before Melisende appeared. I made to step out of her way and open one of the doors to the chapel but she waved me not to, and told the ladies who were with her to step out of earshot.

"Sébastien," she said as I bowed to her. "I had hoped you would attend on the Council today."

She extended her hand to me in the formal greeting of a Queen. I took her hand and bowed my head again and let my lips barely brush the back of her fingers, I could smell the scent of jasmine. I stood straight and looked at her. Now, closer to her, I could see that she had aged but beautifully. Her skin was still looked as soft as the day I left her, her eyes still bright and fiery, revealing the intellect that flourished behind them. Her honey-coloured hair bore the signs of age having streaks of grey, giving her an almost otherworldly look. No wonder the narrow-minded kept their distance; this powerful, beautiful woman would intimidate the strongest of men.

"Your Majesty," I responded and waited for her to continue the conversation.

"I wanted to thank you for taking on my request to try diplomatic efforts with Zengi," she said. "I have been told of the details of your undertaking and that it seemed to be making some progress before his death?"

"Indeed my Lady, it did seem as though we were about to reach a meeting of the minds. Unfortunately, the son does not resemble the father, in many ways."

She nodded her understanding of my meaning. I decided to press her on her thoughts of the crusade.

"I have noticed that you have remained silent during the discussions today, do you have a view on where the armies should challenge?"

She looked about her quickly then responded.

"King Baldwin," I noticed she did not say her son, "is now of his majority and wishes to rule in his own right. Alas, he does not have the strength of mind nor the experience he truly needs to be able to make the informed decisions he needs to. He has," she hesitated, "taken on some of Fulk's mannerisms which I am trying to dispel him of. We have spoken in private, of course, but he is being petulant. I was disappointed to see the choice of attacking Nur ad-Din at Aleppo dismissed, it is what I believe we should do."

I nodded in agreement.

"So we are left with Damascus and Ascalon...?" I said, trailing off so she would give her views.

"Baldwin will never agree to Ascalon," she said flatly. "Amalric is already Count of Jaffa and Ascalon being so close to Jaffa would mean it be added to his territories, and Baldwin does not wish his younger brother to gain too great a foothold."

She stopped speaking rather abruptly, realizing of whom she had been speaking. Looking at each other, we knew what we were both thinking but neither of us dared say it. But just mention of his name made me smile though I tried to hide it.

"And Damascus?" I asked, changing the subject.

She continued to look up at me, her eyes searching my face.

"Your grey eyes have not changed," she whispered.

A group of Hospitaller knights walked past probably on their way to be fed.

"I have thought of you often," I said when we were alone again.

"And I you," she said and smiled.

And for a moment we were back on the Temple Mount where we first embraced, where I felt the soft warmth of her hand pressing mine against her cheek. My left hand tingled at the memory.

The loud clang of the iron door handle being twisted interrupted us as someone tried and failed to open one of the doors. We gave each other a knowing look that said our moment had come to an end and I reached down to open the door from my side. I came face-to-face with King Baldwin, a tall gangly man-boy who did not look as if he had even started to shave. I had noticed him from a distance but now I could see him up close and could not help but notice the resemblance to his father. I nodded and took a step back. He looked from me to Melisende.

"Mother," he started with an air of haughtiness, "you have missed midday prayers. Come," he said taking her arm, "let us dine, Council is to begin again shortly."

With that, he whisked his mother down the hallway towards the large rooms that had been laden with food. King Louis then followed with Grand Master Everard at his elbow, talking animatedly. Then the others, the last of which was the Hospitaller Grand Master followed by his cleric Alvisius who stopped at my side as the others continued down the hallway.

"Careful there Templar," he said with his smarmy grin.

I turned and looked at him with a cold stony stare.

"I am sure I do not know to what you are referring," I said and, pulling the door of the chapel closed with a clang, abruptly turned and made my way to the food rooms as I was suddenly famished.

I would pay for this perceived rudeness.

The afternoon session started up where the morning had left off. Ascalon was discussed first and as Melisende had said, Baldwin vehemently opposed sending the armies there. An arc of crusader castles had been built and occupied to the north of it so there was no imminent threat and if one appeared, Amalric could take care of it from his position in Jaffa. So the topic turned to Damascus. This was the only time Melisende spoke during the entire Council. She raised again the treaty that was in place with Governor Unur of Damascus but she was opposed by King Louis reminding everyone that Governor Unur had signed another treaty with Nur ad-Din and that Nur ad-Din had even married his daughter to solidify the relationship. But others stated that they knew Governor Unur was suspicious of Nur ad-Din and that this was only a measure to stave off an inevitable attack and that we should be true to our word and provide them with support as we had done in the past.

The debate continued for hours, each point against being countered with a point in favour. In the end it came down to the three leaders of the crusade that mattered most – King Louis, King Conrad and King Baldwin – to make the final decision. And although good arguments had been made about the treaty, they took the view that Governor Unur of Damascus had breached it when signing a treaty with Nur ad-Din and that Damascus needed returning to Christian hands for good.

I thought this was a grave mistake. Damascus had always been in the hands of a Muslim ruler but the treaty had kept the relationship with the Christian Crusader States strong, they aided each other in times of war and provided supplies whenever needed. And having a Muslim-based ally in that region was critical to keeping the territories west of it Christian. Losing this ally could have potentially disastrous implications for all of the Crusader States. I believed that diplomatic means should be attempted first to try to re-invigorate the relationship and offer armies to fight Nur ad-Din at Aleppo, but the decision had been made. The die had been cast.

\* \* \* \* \* \* \* \* \* \*

I returned to the Templar House where Osmond was awaiting word on the outcome of the Council.

"Fools!" I snapped half under my breath.

"It did not go the way you hoped?" Osmond asked knowing the answer.

I shook my head, sighed, then removed my cloak, belt and Templar surcoat before sitting on my cot, slumping my shoulders in defeat.

"It is Damascus," I said.

Osmond sat on his cot opposite and waited for me to continue.

"They would not listen to reason. Louis and Conrad are determined to earn their place in heaven by this war, against a city that we were not even sure is against us! Many do not believe the treaty Governor Unur signed with Nur ad-Din is sound. Sending the armies will certainly turn the Damascenes against us and with Nur ad-Din's army at their back, the crusading army will fail. You saw them," I said emphatically, pointing towards the camps outside of the city.

"What do you intend to do?" Osmond asked.

I sat silently, thinking on this for a moment.

"I think it is time to go home," I said quietly. "I have had enough of war."

Osmond simply nodded, stood and began to gather our belongings. We had acquired a couple of travel chests in Tripoli and brought them to Acre, he reached for one and opened it. I watched him as he began packing, thankful for his presence there. I owed him a huge debt of gratitude for leaving what was surely a peaceful life in England to come to this hot, foreign land, to experience the horrors he had and to still be at my side, all because I bid him to. I needed to give him peace. And myself peace as well.

I had just changed out of my Templar garb when there was a knock at our door and Osmond moved to open it. Standing there was a Knight Hospitaller, helmeted, with his hand on the hilt of his sheathed sword. A warning but not a threat.

"You are requested to attend on King Louis at haste, Brother D'Ivry," he said drily to me.

I knew this was coming. I turned to Osmond and bid him to continue what he was doing and followed the Knight Hospitaller back through the alleys of Acre to the citadel. We approached the King and Queen's chambre and stopped before the closed door. He knocked and we waited until the door was opened from the inside and I was ushered in. Before me at a table sat King Louis and standing before him was the Hospitaller Brother Alvisius who had a strange look on his face. King Louis waved the Hospitaller Knight who brought me out of the room leaving the three of us alone. King Louis beckoned me to come forward.

"Ah, D'Ivry, I see you have removed the Templar attire…?" he said in a sort of question.

"I believe the tasks assigned to me have come to an end with the decision of the armies attack Damascus," I said plainly, not wanting to give any more information to the King than I had to.

"Huh," the King said as if he was giving this great consideration. Then, "Are you in agreement with the decision?"

"It is not my place, sire, to agree or disagree with decisions made by the leaders of this crusade. To do so would be impertinent and improper," I said trying to remain as non-committal as possible.

"But what is your view, D'Ivry?" he pressed, exasperation creeping into his voice.

I paused. And then spoke.

"I agreed, sire, with the other leaders who had proposed the attack on Aleppo, taking Nur ad-Din at his base. Capturing him and taking Aleppo would surely mean the harassment of other Christian states by the various Saracen armies would cease. And I am not sure this new treaty he has with Governor Unur has substance. But," and I looked down as I said this, "you must have your reasons that I cannot understand to have chosen Damascus as you have."

King Louis snorted and took a drink from a gold goblet. I could not help but start to get annoyed by the Hospitaller Brother practically twitching behind me just within my eyesight.

"Of course, one cannot expect the common men to comprehend the God-given knowledge that I have been blessed with. We shall achieve greatness through this battle, D'Ivry, and we shall be welcomed into the Kingdom of the Lord once we have vanquished all of God's enemies!" and with this he pounded the table before him.

I did not move. I waited to hear what was coming next.

"We have assumed that you shall be joining the armies in this conquest, yes?" he asked, sipping again from his goblet once he had calmed down.

I took a deep breath.

"Sire, I feel that I have accomplished all that I can do in Outremer. I have dedicated many years of my life to the Holy Land and to the

Templar Order. It is my foremost desire to return to my holdings in England and try to live a peaceful life."

"Understandable," the King said, nodding, "but of course unacceptable. The battle at Damascus will require all the able-bodied men we have. And especially men of your, ah, special talents," he said, drawing out the "s" a little longer than necessary.

"Special talents? I was a warrior, sire, but that was many years ago and I fear my strength is not what it used to be…" but he interrupted me.

"No, my dear Sébastien, I am referring to your other talents, those that Brother Alvisius has kindly informed me of."

He pointed with his open hand to the Hospitaller who, for some unknown reason, had become hunched in his stance. I turned and looked at him and then it struck me: I knew this man. But no, it could not be. In an instant I tallied the years and came to the dreadful conclusion: this was one of the Hospitaller Brothers who had been scurrying about in the background assisting the physician taking care of Melisende during her illness. What had he seen? What did he think he knew?

I walked slowly over to where he stood. Already towering over him earlier in the day, his stance made him seem even smaller.

"I know not to what the monk is referring, sire, perhaps he could explain himself?"

I looked at Louis who nodded at the Hospitaller. He started out stuttering.

"I was, was, there, that, that night, when the Queen lay dying," he said pointing at himself. "I saw what you did!"

"And what is it you think you saw?" I asked him.

"She was dying! Nothing and no one could save her, we all knew she had poison coursing through her, everyone knew Fulk wanted the crown to himself," he continued hissing. "And then you, you appeared, shouting at everyone to leave, locking the doors behind us. I saw you, I saw the amulet hanging from your neck. You used it, did not you? You performed some ritual, in league with the devil no doubt! I heard you, saying strange words to her, repeating them over and over! The next morning, when you finally allowed us in, the Queen was healed! Weak still, yes, but not in any danger. What did you do to her?"

I stood completely still and stared at him. My mind raced. Then the King spoke.

"Leave us," he ordered the Hospitaller.

He looked shocked at the command and did not move. The King repeated his words, this time barking them. Brother Alvisius snarled at me and then slowly made his way to the door, probably hoping the King would change his mind. The King did not and waited for the door to be completely closed before he spoke again.

"Is it true?" he asked.

I looked at him blankly. I had a decision to make: deny the Hospitaller's claims and insist that he was mad, or tell the truth, knowing in my gut that this prince had not the expanse of mind to be able to grasp the full meaning of my discoveries. I knew that I needed to take extreme care with whom I decided to share this knowledge as it was indeed powerful and may not be used with the best intentions. I quickly decided on a half-way measure.

"The monk is correct that I came to the Queen in her hour of need, sire," I said, "but I am unsure as to what the monk means by ritual."

I stared at him intently, trying to give the expression of earnest. King Louis stared back at me. I knew him to be a very pious man, indeed that was one of Queen Eleanor's complaints that she had married a monk instead of a man. And from my encounters with him and from rumours I had heard coming from the French court I was not sure he was a highly intelligent man. So in this moment, I counted on his strict Christian beliefs to convince him that there could not be any other forces at play here. I was not let down.

"What was in the amulet?" he inquired.

"A mixture of herbs and other natural elements, sire, nothing more. Having dwelt for so long amongst the Arabs who lived and worked amongst the Christians in Jerusalem, I spent much time learning what I could about their ways, traditions, healings. Trying to know my adversary if you will, sire," I said sincerely.

What I was saying was not inaccurate, it simply omitted a few important details. But what I told King Louis was, in fact, true. He stared at me for a long moment as if trying to decide my veracity in that moment. He stroked his trimmed beard.

"You have served the crown well, Sébastien," he said. "Your mission with Zengi might well have been a success had he not met his demise, and your work building the Templar preceptory in Paris has proven your devotion to the Order. So I have no reason to doubt you now."

He stood and adjusted his royal robes about him as he walked over to the open window looking out over the sea.

"But as I said, we now need everyone to fight for this cause…"

"Even if one does not agree with it, sire?" I interjected, taking a risk at angering him.

He let out a loud sigh and turned to look at me.

"I shall forgive the impertinence," he said more annoyed than cross. "Damascus must be brought to heel, and once it has, the rest will follow. It is God's will."

My mind cast back to the last time I had heard that and realized this King would not listen to reason. His mind was set and he and the others would lead their armies into certain carnage.

"But I shall not command you to fight, you have done enough of that. You shall attend on me and bring with you your little amulets of elixir to save us, just in case the monk was right," he said with a bit of a smirk.

That was it. Once again I had no choice but to follow his orders. To Damascus I would go.

# VIII

# Part Six

# 1148 – Damascus

It took the armies about a month to travel the distance from Acre to Damascus in the searing heat of mid-summer. Melisende had returned to Jerusalem immediately after the Council of Acre had concluded. She needed to govern there as King Baldwin was going to lead his army in his first crusade to fight for the Christian states. With so many people in the citadel, it had been impossible to see her alone and especially with Brother Alvisius spreading rumours, I did not want to give him any more fodder. We would have to be content with our moment knowing as I did the probable outcome of the siege of Damascus, I may not live long enough to see her again.

Osmond was dismayed to hear we were not returning to England but had, once again, declared his loyalty to me and his determination to accompany me despite my insistence that he return home. I admired his courage, he had sacrificed much. but he was firm in his refusal to go home without me. My debt to him was ever-growing.

At the King's request, I brewed more of the elixir and placed it in little vials hidden away on my person. I secretly hoped that no situation would arise where I would be called upon to use the potions as I was determined not to reveal the full powers that the elixir and the secret words gave a believer.

King Baldwin's armies departed first, followed by King Louis's and the King Conrad's pulling up the rear. It was with great annoyance that I saw Brother Alvisius riding with a few other Hospitaller Knights in King Conrad's contingent; King Louis explained that the Hospitaller Grand Master had offered a few knights to be added to Conrad's personal guard. He needed them after the rout at Dorylaeum.

King Louis's army had been added to by a group of Knights Templar. Everard had obtained the funds by mortgaging several Templar properties which allowed him to pay for a large number of the Brothers to join King Louis's army. This would cost Louis half his annual income to repay.

And so the trek to the city began. Knowing that the Saracens would have spies watching our moves, just as we had our own watching theirs, it would not be long for word to reach the city of our approach. And I knew that Governor Unur would immediately send to Nur ad-Din for help, for there would be no confusion over the purpose of these armies marching towards Damascus.

The plan was to march to the west of the city and camp near the orchards found there. They would provide food and shelter the armies needed whilst they regrouped and the leaders continued strategizing the attack. But the orchards were extremely thick, impassable using the phalanx formations that had become a familiar tactic of crusading armies. And we soon discovered that within the orchard were fortified towers from which armed enemy soldiers would shoot their arrows and jab their spears at crusader fighters who dared to make their way through the trees. The leaders had to find a way to get through them.

But they were not to be deterred. True to his word, King Louis did not order me to fight and I made no move to join either the vanguard or the rear guard. My size in a wooded area such as this was a disadvantage and I had no desire to take part in the combat. Instead, I kept watch along with King Louis from a nearby hilltop as King Baldwin led the charge of small units of fighters through the orchards to meet the city's defenders on the banks of the River Barada. From our position we could see the walls of the city in the distance as watched as Seljuk warriors poured out of the city and crossed the river to meet our fighters.

On the first day the fighting was vicious, frenetic and brutal. The crusader armies had been successful in beating the defenders back across the river and into the city taking refuge. Upon his return to King Louis to report on the day's battle, King Conrad recounted how he had fought a Seljuk Turk so fiercely he cut the warrior in two, slicing his head, neck and left shoulder off with one stroke of his sword. Following the fleeing defenders back across the river, our armies immediately laid siege to the walls of the city, using the wood from the orchard to build platforms and huts to protect themselves from objects being hurled at them.

The mood in the camps the night was upbeat and optimistic as warriors shared their stories of success amongst each other, confident that God was with them. I had heard these stories so many times before. I had believed them then. I wondered how many of them would be alive to tell them once all was said and done.

On the second day, Damascus's defenders suffered many losses but somehow managed to keep our fighters from breaching the city walls. This was when the crusading leaders made their first egregious error: they did not encircle the city to prevent aid from reaching the city. This was monumental as they should have known that Nur ad-Din and leaders from other Arab provinces were bound to send more reinforcements and the only real entry to the city was from the north. A last-minute attempt made on the third day to cover the north gates failed and the defenders managed to push our armies back to the west of the city, leaving the north entrances open for the arrival of Nur ad-Din and his men.

On the fourth day, a decision was made to move the armies to the east of the city because the plain there was better for an onslaught as there were no orchards for enemy soldiers to hide in or to break up the army formations. And this was the second egregious error: the east of the city might have given the advantage of level ground but it was barren and provided no food and little water. And now that Nur ad-Din and his army had arrived and made camp in the place we had just abandoned to the west of the city, there was no chance of returning to the orchards.

Arriving on the east of the city, we found a few wells that might have provided the water we so desperately needed but the concern was that they had been poisoned. Upon hearing this, Brother Alvisius raced to King Louis's tent and requested a private audience with the King and myself during which he offered to test the water. After all, he reasoned, did not the King's Templar protector have the power to save those who had been poisoned? King Louis turned to me and asked what I thought.

"I am against this, sire," I said firmly. "Despite Brother Alvisius's adamant assertions, I cannot say the potion will work. I would not want to put anyone's life in danger under a false hope of being saved."

But Brother Alvisius was not having any of it. He begged the King to allow him to do this.

"Sire, I have seen this work. It will work again, I am convinced of it. And think what this might mean for the crusade, what kind of power this could give a King such as yourself, to be able to resurrect dying soldiers…" his voice trailed off as his eyes widened, imploring the King and playing to his vanity.

His ploy worked. King Louis's expression changed as he recognized the implications should the elixir work. I knew to argue any further would be a waste of time and waited for the King's instructions. But for a moment, I thought the King was going to decide not to go through with it.

"You realize, monk, that if this fails, you will die?" he asked sternly.

Brother Alvisius was unwavering.

"I shall not die, sire, if your Templar does what is necessary," he replied.

The King thought a moment. Then decided.

"Take this goblet and get some water from the nearest well and bring it back here, Hospitaller. I shall be witness to this for I need to see with my own eyes the power of this potion. If you survive, we shall decide then what to do with you. Sébastien, do you have an amulet with you?"

I nodded. But I had also decided I could not let this happen. I could not give someone so unworthy the power to save life. What was it Zengi had said? A chosen one cannot be forced? I took my leave and followed the Hospitaller out of the royal tent and to the well closest to our camp. He lowered the bucket found there down into the well, waited until we heard a splash then pulled it up. Careful not to touch any of the water, he filled the goblet and then we made our way back to King Louis's tent. He had a small cot brought to him and was waiting for our return. I took one of the amulets from a pocket under my surcoat and showed it to him. Brother Alvisius sat on the edge of the small cot and raised the goblet to his lips.

"I shall be known across Christendom for this," he boasted, his voice dripping in bravado. "Kings and Emperors shall ever be in my debt for providing them with this power!"

His eyes glowed with the anticipation of his future glory. I warned him again that the potion may not work but he refused to listen. With a swift flick of his wrist, he gulped down the goblet of water in one turn, then lay back on the cot to await the effects of the poison if the well had in fact been poisoned. It did not take long.

His face showed the first effect as it turned from the typical pale white of a Hospitaller Brother to pink to deep red. His breathing became laboured and he clutched at his gut from the pain as the poison started to eat away at it. Within a moment he was convulsing with foam starting to form at his mouth and I moved to the head of the cot and knelt, holding his head down with my left hand. With my right, I held the amulet and uncorked it with my teeth and managed with some struggle to pour its contents into the monk's mouth, then closed his jaws so that he had no choice but to swallow. I said nothing throughout all of this. King Louis stood nearby enthralled with the spectacle.

Brother Alvisius's convulsions started to subside and for a moment I feared that the elixir on its own had worked. I moved to the foot of his cot watching him, wondering how long it would take. Suddenly he bolted upright and clutching at his throat he screamed at me.

"THE PRAYERS, YOU MUST SPEAK THE PRAYERS!!!"

But I stood still and said nothing. He fell back onto the cot and his body began a series of spasms, stiffening and then relaxing, tremors taking over. And then with one final lurch, the monk became still, his legs slowly releasing from being bent at the knees, his fists unclenching as death took him. King Louis and I both stared at the monk, laying lifeless before us. 'Ma-sha' Allah,' I thought to myself. God willed this.

"What did he mean by 'speak the words'?" King Louis asked quietly.

I hesitated. And then spoke my only lie.

"I do not know. I believe the monk was mistaken in his remembrances," I answered looking the King directly in the eye.

"Is that so?" he asked with a raised eyebrow. "So be it."

* * * * * * * * * *

The second crusade fell apart quite quickly after the armies moved to the east of the city. Quarrels broke out amongst the leaders as to who should rule the city reminding me of Tancred and Toulouse fighting over Antioch. Would they never learn? Without good water nearby, and with Nur ad-Din's forces continuing to arrive in vast numbers, the crusading army was outnumbered and dispersed before any further lives could be lost. Four days and it was over.

I only found out about the result weeks later as Osmond and I had left the camp the night of the monk's death. I wanted no more part of any of it. I had seen how men, King and monk alike, changed when they thought they were on the verge of god-like power and I strengthened my resolve not to allow it to fall into the wrong hands. And so we had slipped away in the dead of the night with only the clothes we wore.

It was time to go home.

# IX

## Part One

## 1148 – 1149 - England

Obtaining passage on a ship from Tripoli back to the West did not take long as we expected as ships were arriving almost on a weekly basis. We did not take the horses and only had a few travel pouches and found ourselves on a Byzantine Dromon which would take us as far as Malta. Oaring was difficult as late summer storms battered the seas and fought the ship as it made its way through the sea, passing Cyprus, Crete, and Palermo. We made port and disembarked to switch to another ship as the one we had been on was returning to the East. The second ship was a French cog and we were on our way again within a day of arriving at Malta. This ship would take us to La Rochelle, the harbour used by many pilgrims on their way to the Holy Land and the main port where the Templars were starting to build their fleet. As we approached, we could see the flags of the Order, the black over white bars of the Beauséant, flapping atop the masts of three ships. No doubt with the way the Order was rapidly growing, this number would be increasing soon.

We needed to stay in La Rochelle for two weeks as most of the English ships travelling to and from France sailed from Dover to Calais and I did not wish to return through Dover. I had a few options in England to choose from but had decided on another of the Cinque Ports, the five ports of entry created by King Edmund who ruled England before William the Conqueror. Amongst the five – Sandwich, Dover, Hythe, New Romney and Hastings –

Hastings was the only harbour that didn't have a formal port but rather boats and ships would anchor offshore and use smaller boats for reaching the sandy beaches. As Osmond and I did not have much to bring with us, I decided this would be the best entry to England for one who did not want to draw attention to himself; Dover would have been too conspicuous. And so we had to wait for a ship which would take us to my entry point of choice.

Whilst Osmond secured lodgings for our stay, I wandered through the harbour, wearing my Templar garb figuring it would be the last time I would do so. Some of the Brothers working on the deck of one of the ships saw I was a Brother and welcomed me onboard, happily showing me the latest in design – these boats were meant for speed and yet were sturdy enough to fend off any adversary foolish enough to fight them. I could not help but be impressed.

We spent the rest of our stay writing and receiving despatches to and from various people in England alerting them to our imminent arrival. Osmond wrote to the households in Shirburn and Sandford on Thames and arranged to have horses and supplies brought to us on our arrival in Hastings. It was also through this correspondence that he discovered my daughter Margaux and her husband Godwin FitzGilbert de Clare were actually at Striguil Castle on the Welsh-English borders. This was another stronghold now owned by her brother-in-law Richard FitzGilbert de Clare, inheriting it and the title after the death of their father, Gilbert FitzGilbert de Clare, the 1st Earl of Pembroke. I was determined to go there as soon as was possible.

I also wrote to my brother Guillaume and told him of my plans to return to England. I was not sure when I would be in Oxfordshire but assured him that we would see each other soon and that I was looking forward to meeting his wife whom he had married over a decade earlier.

Our path by horseback would take us first to Pevensey, another castle held by Richard FitzGilbert de Clare, where we would spend a night and then continue traveling along the west of London on our way to Shirburn. I realized the plans would take us close to Ferneham where my old tournament competitor Henry de Blois had built a castle as part of his holdings as Bishop of Winchester. I wrote to him about my return and requested permission to visit him there; I reckoned he would be a good source of information about the lay of the land, the outcome of the war between his brother King Stephen and his cousin Matilda and anything else that might be pertinent for me to know. His reply granting my request came surprisingly quickly.

When the day of departure arrived, we were ready to leave France. It was bittersweet, for I was leaving behind my life both there and in the Holy Land, knowing I was unlikely to return to either. I had packed my Templar surcoat and cloak into one of the leather pouches we had brought with us but I knew I would probably not wear them again. Instead, I dressed in new clothing bought from the merchants within the town of La Rochelle; I made sure to purchase some for Osmond as well.

For the first time, I was apprehensive about my future, not knowing how my arrival back in England would be taken. Out of my own failures as a father came a fear of rejection by my daughter and she would have every right to be unwelcoming. Even though she had been provided for, nurtured, educated, and wed to a man of high-standing - Godwin FitzGilbert de Clare was the bastard son of Gilbert de Clare, the first Earl of Pembroke, and despite his status had been treated almost as though he had been legitimate – none of this made up for the total absence in her life of her father. I struggled with how our reunion would be, considering I left when she was a mere babe, I would be a stranger coming into her life.

As we boarded, I was told by the captain to watch for the tall sandstone cliffs, light brown in colour, unlike the white chalky cliffs at Dover. It would be quite a different experience to that in Dover which was always a busy hub with merchant and trading ships clogging the port. And the docks would be awash with loading and unloading goods heading to markets in England or afar. In comparison, Hastings would be quiet, a small coastal town that thrived with small fishing boats but mostly by-passed by the larger ships.

The Channel was calm for most of the trip, the stillness of the late-August air settling the waves that would sometimes make the crossing impossible during the winter months. And as I was promised, the dark cliffs soon appeared on the horizon and the deckhands busied themselves bringing the galley as close to shore as they could. It was done quickly, the small rowboat brought us the short distance and soon we found ourselves standing on the sands of England basking in the warmth of the early evening sun.

Osmond's correspondence had been successful and we were greeted by a man on the beach holding the reins of three horses, two for riding, one as a packhorse which already had bulging travel sacks hanging on its sides filled with what I assumed would be supplies for our journey. We knew it would take a couple of hours to reach Pevensey and decided not to waste any time spending the night in Hastings and set off right away. Darkness had fallen by the time we reached the castle further along the coast to the west of Hastings. Godwin FitzGilbert had been kind enough to alert those working at the castle of our arrival and we were made comfortable for the night, fed well with delicious food and wine. We had been given the best rooms available, it was the first time in a very long time that I slept in a proper bed.

We were on our way by dawn the next morning having received fresh horses from the stables. It took us two days to reach Ferneham, spending the night in between at an inn along the way. It was both strange and wonderful riding the paths of southern England, seeing the lush landscape, the green forests, the rushing creeks and rivers. It was quite a difference from the harsh, dry rock and sand of Palestine. The warm summer heat in the English countryside felt gentle on my face compared to the scorching, relentless sun of the summers spent in the Holy Land. But I could not help but feel the pull, the tug on my heart of Jerusalem and the life I had been leading there which I thought was extraordinary despite what some might think was a harsh way of life. It might seem that way, but it was where I had found myself, my purpose after losing my one true love. I knew it had been where I needed to be. Now I would have to find the purpose for the remainder of my years.

\* \* \* \* \* \* \* \* \* \*

We arrived in Ferneham in the early evening having passed Waverly Abbey on the road to the town. We walked the horses through an open archway in the low walls which created the bailey that surrounded a small market and various buildings and the castle which sat atop the motte further ahead. Eventually, we stopped at the guard house at the base of the motte where we were told we were expected and to wait for a guard to be sent from the castle's keep where Bishop Henry resided. I looked around and saw some stone structures to the right of us at the base of the motte, I figured those to be some sort of domestic buildings, possibly living quarters for the Bishop's staff. To the left was the large staircase which led from the bailey up to the keep.

Once the guard arrived, we were escorted around the base of the motte to the stables, dismounted and then followed the guard back to staircase and up to the motte's plateau and the keep. It was larger than it looked from the base, I guessed possibly four levels with battlements at the top but I could not see any guards patrolling which I thought was rather lax. But then again we were in the home of a Bishop as well as the brother to a King. Perhaps he did not feel he needed such protection. I would have thought otherwise.

The castle keep sat alone on the motte. The actual entrance was at the second level via another staircase, this one attached to the keep itself, leading up the western side of the structure. We were ushered into the great hall, which was decorated luxuriously, Bishop Henry certainly did not want for anything. I reminded Osmond how we had met on the tournament fields in France, the same fields which had brought himself to me. He remembered the animosity with which Henry's brother Stephen, now the King, had held for me and wondered if it had abated. Our reminisces were interrupted by Bishop

Henry's arrival from one of the four spiral staircases at the corners of the room.

"My dear Sébastien, how it does my eyes good to see you!" he exclaimed, holding both arms open for an embrace.

"Bishop Henry, your Grace," I responded as we hugged then stood back to look each other over.

"Now, now, no need for formality with us, it is just Henry when we are on our own," he insisted with a wide smile.

I introduced Osmond and I was amazed that the Bishop remembered him from the tournament in Valenciennes. He bade us both to take a seat but Osmond declined saying he would rather attend to our quarters if the Bishop would be so kind as to indicate where they would be.

"Ah, yes," he started snapping his fingers at the page who stood near the door we entered from. "I have ordered rooms be prepared for you in one of the domestic buildings, you passed them on the way up to the keep," he said adding directly to the page, "please escort Master Osmond to guest quarters."

Osmond bowed to the Bishop, picked up our bags and followed the page. Henry and I were now on our own. He took a seat at the head of the large table with his back to the fire and bid me to sit, pointing to the chair to his right. I sat.

Our conversation practically took up from where we left off after we both departed from the tournament. He told me how he had completed his studies in Cluny and that King Henry had brought him over to England to be the Abbot of Glastonbury, a title he still held. Then in 1129, he was given the bishopric of Winchester, and ordained as its Bishop in November of that year. And after his brother Stephen had become King, he had worked extremely hard on his relationship with Rome and as a result was made a papal legate, which meant that for the lifetime of Pope Innocent III, he would be the most important churchman in England, even more powerful than the Archbishop of Canterbury. But much to his disappointment, when Innocent died, the title of papal legate was rescinded and he had been spending much of his time over the past few years trying to get it back from a new Pope who had more pressing matters to attend to.

"It has been frustrating Sébastien," he said with a sigh. "The Popes who followed - there have been three! - have not reinstated the title despite my many efforts to convince them to. The latest, Eugenius, has been difficult to get an audience with. He cannot reside in Rome – the people there have revolted against papal power in secular, non-church matters and did not allow him to return once he had left to attend an abbey's consecration outside the city. And so, he has been spending most of his time in France.

"But," he continued, "I have received word that he has returned to Italy, not to Rome but to Viterbo, a town about two- or three-days' ride from Rome. I prepare now to travel there as he has finally granted me an audience. So your timing for your visit is excellent for I leave in two days' time."

I did not know quite how to take that comment, but I assumed he would explain it.

"I am aware that Pope Eugenius did not have Abbot Bernard's support when he was elected, but perhaps if I wrote to the Abbot, I could persuade him to support your cause?" I suggested, and then explained my longstanding relationship with the Abbot of Clairvaux.

Bishop Henry smiled.

"That is kind of you, Sébastien. I may very well take you up on that if the audience with Eugenius does not go well, or does not happen," he chuckled knowing how unpredictable the Pope was. "You are correct, Abbot Bernard did not support Eugenius in his election but over the past couple of years he has seen how he has been able to influence the Pope, Eugenius is not of the strongest mind. Your assistance might be very helpful indeed."

It gladdened my heart to see him in such good form. With the civil war raging in England whilst I was away, and he being King Stephen's brother, he could have found himself in peril in many ways. But now that Empress Matilda had returned to Normandy and set up court in Rouen, it would seem the major battles had dissipated, although small outbreaks always threatened.

I found him exceptionally easy to talk to. I recounted to him my life in England after the tourneys, my holdings in Oxfordshire and of course of my marriage. And how Séraphine's death was the catalyst for my decision to accompany Hugues when he came requesting my assistance with founding the Order. It was exactly what I needed at the time, gave me a new purpose and the years I spent in the Holy Land did much to heal the wounds if not resolving them completely.

He listened in silence, nodding every once in a while, never questioning, never judging. And I confessed my shame at having left my daughter Margaux to be raised by others, how I had not been a proper father to her. And now she had a young daughter that I was bound to meet soon. He said he understood why I left England, how it was unfortunate but probably necessary for me to have done what I did. And by what I had told him about my daughter and her successful marriage to a de Clare, he was certain it had worked out for the best. He offered a blessing to help me assuage my guilt, but I politely declined.

We then turned to discuss his interest in the several building works he had underway at the many properties he had been given over the years. I marvelled at his eye for architecture and his determination; if Ferneham Castle was anything like the others he had built over the years, he must have some very impressive properties. He thanked me for the compliment.

"Well, my dear Sébastien, I must come now to something that I have been considering since I received your letter from La Rochelle telling me of your impending return and even more so now that I have heard of your woes. And the reason I think your timing is excellent! I am sure you will not wish to return to Shirburn or to Sandford on Thames, the memories would be difficult, yes?"

I nodded. Although that had been my plan, just discussing the time I spent there made me realize it would be a very difficult task indeed.

"As I mentioned," he continued, "I shall be departing for Italy shortly. Would you be willing to stay here and take care of the property in my absence? It would be a tenancy to start but I am not sure of when, or if, I will return and so I would need eventually to divest myself of it. It is within my gift and I cannot think of anyone more deserving. But of course that is not something you would need to think about, for now it would be your home until you decide what is best. What say you?"

I was taken aback by this generosity. He must have seen something in me that told him to make this offer. I stuttered my gratitude and accepted.

"Outstanding!" he exclaimed. "This takes a great burden off my mind and I am glad to do it, you are actually doing me the favour. And now I wish to show you something."

He got up from the table and went over to one of the massive chests against the far wall. He reached inside his cloak for a ring of keys and unlocked one of them, reached in and pulled out what looked to be some sort of manuscript bound by two dark wood intricately engraved covers. He brought it to the table and laid it before me. I knew instantly what it was.

"The Qur'an? In Latin?" I said, shocked.

"Yes," he said nodding. "During my studies at Cluny, I met and studied with the man who eventually became the abbot there, Peter of Montboissier. After I came to England, we stayed in touch…"

"Peter of Cluny?" I interrupted. "The same who defended Peter Abelard from accusations of heresy by Abbot Bernard?"

I had heard the stories of the conflict between Abbot Bernard and Peter Abelard, Abbot Bernard had shared his frustrations with me about Abelard's teachings. I had listened but was not convinced that Abelard had actually been heretical but this was overshadowed by the scandal of his relationship with a young lady of low nobility named Heloise that had occurred many years earlier. Abelard and Heloise had fallen in love when Abelard had been hired by her uncle Fulbert – she had been his ward - to teach Heloise, They had kept their relationship hidden, even hiding the fact that they managed to have a child which they named Astrolabe and then married in secret. But when Fulbert discovered the marriage, he and Heloise fell out and Abelard rescued her and placed her in a convent for safekeeping. But the uncle had misconstrued this, had assumed Abelard had deserted his niece and so an attack on Abelard was ordered during which he was castrated. Abelard spent the rest of his life moving from monastery to monastery until Abbot Peter of Cluny gave him refuge during the conflict with Bernard.

"Yes, the one and the same. I understood why Abbot Peter felt the need to protect Abelard. In the end, he was able to reconcile him with Bernard and he convinced Pope Innocent to lift the sentence of excommunication."

But with regards to this," he said tapping the top cover of the manuscript, "Abbot Peter commissioned this. He obtained copies of a number of Islamic texts from Toledo and sent translators to La Rioja where there is a Cluniac monastery, Santa María la Real of Nájera. There they spent a few years translating these texts, about five of them. There only a few copies in existence, Abbot Peter sent me this for safekeeping here in England. I thought you would be interested in seeing it."

He slide the manuscript towards me. I stared at it, scarcely breathing.

"Obviously I cannot take this with me to Italy," he said, "I would need to entrust it to you."

"I am honoured. I shall not let it leave my custody," I vowed as I leaned in to take a closer look.

I could not wait to examine it further and spent a considerable amount of time after Bishop Henry had retired for the night exploring it.

It was in the early hours of the morning when I made my way back down the motte and to the domestic building that housed the quarters we were staying in. After a few hours' sleep, I met Osmond for breakfast and informed him of the developments that had taken place the night before. He took these in as he always did, passive acceptance without asking questions. We spent the day inspecting the castle grounds and he took notes of areas needing improvement or changes that I pointed out along the way.

We then wandered down to the town that was surrounded by the settlement's walls and saw a small but vibrant marketplace with an inn, an alehouse, and blacksmith is along its eastern side. We stopped in at the alehouse and met the owner, a jovial man who was happy to get to know us over a couple of tankards of his best. He pointed out the River Wey just on the south side of the town, we had bypassed it on our route up from Pevensey. It was the source of the trout and other fishes we had seen for sale in the market stalls and decided to take a look at the river to see how passable it would be for barges and small boats and if there was a pier in place. There was not, only a small dock with a couple of oar boats tied to it. But I could see the potential in this place which I had agreed to call my home for now. After settling in, I could then visit my properties and deal with the memories they would bring on my own time.

* * * * * * * * * *

Bishop Henry departed two days later after insisting that I take his quarters in the keep as my own once he had left. He had issued instructions to his servants and staff that did not accompany him that I was the new steward of the castle and that they were to obey my orders as though they were coming from him. I wished him well on his journey and luck on the tasks he had before him. He had written to his brother the King letting him know of my return and that I would be taking on the tenancy of the castle in his absence. He told me later in his first letter that the King's response never mentioned me, so inconsequential he must have found news of my return. Which suited me just fine.

We had only been in the castle for a few days making decisions about storing Henry's goods and furnishings as I did not feel comfortable using them - after all he was a Bishop and I a mere knight - when we received news from Striguil. Margaux was gravely ill and I was advised to travel to the Welsh border as quickly as possible. We were on our way within the hour and even riding at breakneck speed and stopping only for a few hours rest and to switch out the horses it would take us near three days to reach them.

Striguil Castle, built on the cliffs above the River Wye in the Wye Valley, was a massive fortification and the second most important in the holdings of Richard FitzGilbert de Clare, the 2nd Earl of Pembroke, the most important being the castle in Pembrokeshire. From these two strongholds, the de Clare family had managed to secure the south of Wales for the English King, routinely putting down skirmishes and larger battles with various Welsh princes who tried to claim the land back. Richard had allowed his older half-brother Godwin permission to reside in Striguil when he was in the other, thus keeping control by always having a presence in both. I was thankful that Margaux and her family were in the castle closest to me.

We arrived in the evening on the third day, exhausted and yet anxious to know the state of Margaux's heath. The message we had received had not given any details as to the nature of her malady, just to arrive at haste. We approached the castle from the east and saw the two towers and the entrance arch situated on the other side of the drawbridge we would cross to gain entrance to the castle enclosure. The guards had been given notice of our arrival as they did not stop us from galloping through and heading to the rectangular keep. I practically flew off my horse, dropping the reins where they were, ripping off my riding gloves as I raced up the stairs, Osmond hot on my heels.

But once reaching the great hall, we found nothing. No one to meet us. And a silence that unnerved me. I glanced at Osmond who looked as perplexed as me. I had never been in this castle before and really had no idea which way to turn. But the shouts from the guards as we crossed through the entrance must have been heard as just as I was about to call out, we heard the creak of a door at the far opening and out walked Godwin FitzGilbert de Clare looking as though he had the weight of the world on his shoulders. I knew that look.

Godwin walked up to me, extended his arm in greeting and then told me the news.

"I regret," he started, his voice breaking, "I regret, your daughter, Margaux, died this past night."

I stood in shock. Not again. Not another member of my family taken before her time. Séraphine. Isabel. Margaux. Would this ever end? And I fail yet again to protect those that I needed to protect.

I could not respond. Taking in the reality of what Godwin was telling me, I was unaware that another door had opened and someone else had come into the room. My clouded eyes could barely make out the small figure standing beside Godwin and it took a moment before I realized who it was.

"Sébastien, this is Alix, your granddaughter," Godwin said, putting his arm around the young girl at his side.

I blinked to focus and looked at the cherubic face of Margaux's only child and my mouth dropped. She was the very image of my Séraphine at about the same age. The same blond locks, hazel eyes a touch greener than her grandmother's but with that same dark, piercing intelligence. She walked slowly to me, hesitant and yet with a curiosity about this tall, old stranger that was her unknown grandfather. She curtsied. I wondered what they had told her about me. I knelt to get a better look at her and to make her feel less intimidated. But if she had any of her grandmother in her, she would not be.

"Alix," I said, "I am your grandfather," I said slowly.

She stared at me for a moment as if examining my face for some sort of hint of the man that I was, but then let down her guard and wrapped her arms about my neck in a tight hug. This I did not expect, but after a moment, I returned the hug, and enveloped her little body with my big arms.

"Mama is gone," she whispered in my ear.

"Yes, ma chère," I said, "she is. But I am here, a poor substitute, but I shall love you as she did."

I surprised myself with the power of my words. That seemed to give her comfort and me as well. She asked if I wanted to see her horses and I said I most certainly would but Godwin pointed out that it was getting late and that the horses would have to keep until morning. With another hug she bid me good night and then followed her nurse who was waiting for her at the door. With a last glance at me over her shoulder, she stepped through and disappeared from sight.

"She is beautiful," I murmured quietly.

Godwin nodded.

"Yes, she is. She takes after her mother and, from what I have heard, also takes after her grandmother."

"What happened to Margaux?" I asked softly.

Godwin ushered both Osmond and myself into another more comfortable room where a fire had been set in a sizable fireplace and chairs had been placed close enough where we could warm ourselves. A servant arrived with lambskins of wine and goblets as we settled down to talk. Godwin waited until the servant left the room before speaking.

"We had been visiting the Brothers at Tintern Abbey – my Uncle Walter had helped establish them there and I took over the support after his death – and decided to take a barge rather than ride. Shortly after we left in the late afternoon, a storm came upon us, the rains were heavy and we were quickly drenched. I did not think anything of it, the weather here has always been inconstant. And Margaux was accustomed to it. But this time was different and a fever set in. The doctors thought it would be brief and she would recover but alas she did not. We sent word to you as soon as we realized this had turned dangerous, we just did not know…" his voice trailed off as he looked into the fire thinking about the loss of his wife.

I knew how he felt and was saddened by it.

"When will the funeral take place?" I asked.

"In two days' time at the Abbey. I have commissioned a grave next to my father and near to my uncle in our family plot."

I nodded. We sat in silence for a while and then Osmond took his leave with the excuse of tending to our quarters. Eventually Godwin spoke.

"I find myself in a, ah, bit of a predicament, Sébastien," he said tentatively.

"Tell me," I said hoping that I could be of assistance.

"The Welsh princes are rousing trouble again, they have been attacking and robbing travellers on the roads between here and Pembroke and I have received word that they are about to harass Castle Usk to the northwest of here. This castle is at risk especially since it has become known that my cousin, Roger, who was in possession of Usk, has moved permanently to Hertford now that he had inherited the Earldom there. I need to go to the castle as soon as possible to fortify and defend it," he explained.

"What do you need from me? Men? Arms?"

He shook his head.

"No, I have plenty of both. And this is not your battle. What I need from you is much more personal…" he hesitated.

"Speak man," I urged him to continue.

"I am concerned about leaving Alix here alone. Would you take her to your holdings in Oxfordshire until I can quell the uprisings? I do not believe it will be long, I hope to deal with the Welsh quickly, I do not wish to have any protracted fighting. The de Clares need to remind everyone that we hold the power in these lands. I would think she could be back before Christmas."

This I was not expecting. He was right of course, the de Clare family and its land battles in Wales were none of my concern but my granddaughter was. I agreed in an instant. But I told him of my change of plans and intention to remain in Ferneham instead, which he found even more agreeable knowing that it belonged to King Stephen's brother. I could only hope that Alix would find it so as well.

The funeral at Tintern Abbey was a sombre affair attended by many of the de Clare family and supporters, some coming from afar. I tried to be as inconspicuous as possible, difficult enough when being a stranger in these lands and even more so when people began to discover who I was. The morning after my arrival we spent some time as I promised we would at the stables and Alix showed me what a good rider she was becoming. Watching her in the practice yard reminded me of the first time I laid eyes on Séraphine riding about the gardens at Marlborough Castle, they were so much alike. Afterwards, she took me for a walk to her favourite places to play and she surprised me that she had been learning how to read. Godwin and Margaux had not been able to have more children and had wanted to make sure Alix had the best education available. I made a note of this and later instructed Osmond to start a search for the best tutor available. Her studies would not halt because of her stay with me.

And when she was told of this plan, she agreed to it almost gleefully. I think it gave her a sense of some freedom and even though this might have been imagined, I was glad to see her excitement at coming to stay with me. Osmond had tactfully pointed out that the castle we were staying in had been made to suit a clergyman and not a young child. I told him to immediately reach out to carpenters and furnishers in the town and nearby upon our return to start making over the rooms to make them suitable not only for Alix but for ourselves as well. I needed to make her as comfortable as I could.

A few days after the funeral Godwin departed for Usk Castle. There were a few tears from Alix but we did our best to remind her of the journey she was going to be taking going to England and the new places she would be seeing and exploring. And we assured her that her favourite pony would be brought with us. As would her kindly maid Joan who had been with her as a nurse since she was born.

So we busied her with packing her things and we loaded two carts of goods as Godwin thought taking her bed would be the best option to make her feel at home in a strange place. And after waiting for a summer shower to pass, we set out to return to Ferneham, a new adventure for Alix, a new purpose for me.

\* \* \* \* \* \* \* \* \* \*

Life at the castle moved rapidly once we had arrived. The servants had removed Bishop Henry's personal effects from his rooms in the keep and had placed temporary furnishings in what was Henry's bedchamber on the top floor so I would have somewhere to sleep and did the same for one of the two smaller rooms on the same floor for Osmond's bedchamber. The second of the smaller rooms would be changed into Alix's room, I was glad that we had taken on the burden of bringing her bed. We made it a priority to set up and she fell into it, asleep quickly, exhausted from the four-day trip.

Osmond had done what I had instructed and was soon meeting with tutors to decide who should be employed to have Alix continue with her studies. He also alerted Pascal, my old squire and now retainer of both Shirburn and Sandford on Thames, that he would be coming to Oxfordshire to oversee the packing and moving of my personal goods from both properties to be brought to Ferneham.

Whilst I was still in Striguil, I had written to Bishop Henry to inform him of the changes in my circumstances and he was very happy to know I would have my granddaughter stay with me. He felt it would be good for me. And of course, expressed his sorrow at the loss of my daughter. I wrote again, raising again my concerns that the castle required more fortification and he was satisfied with my recommendations of what could be done, almost relieved that I was agreeing to take this on. I needed to move quickly on this for the summer was at an end and we only had a few months of autumn before the frozen earth and snow-covered ground of winter would bring most of my building works to a halt until spring's thaw.

I found men who understood what I intended to do and were enthusiastic as such works had never been attempted before. I needed to erect a curtain wall around the entire motte because the keep already took up most of the top of it and there was no space for walls there. So they were going to be substantial and the foundations would need to be deep and a considerable amount of earth would be needed for infill between the new walls and the motte. I knew this could be done, we had learned how Herod had done something similar at the Temple of Solomon.

The design also called for twenty-three sides to the curtain wall as it made its way around the motte. And I included five towers, each with living quarters fit for nobility and guardrooms and anterooms for servants if necessary. All the towers would have battlements for guards to patrol and privies which would empty into pits outside the walls which would be routinely emptied. It would be my intention to take one of these towers as my personal residence whether the Bishop returned or not. But the keep's rooms sufficed for now. And Alix was having fun racing up and down the four circular staircases at the corners of the keep and helping out in its kitchen, all of which allowed for many hiding places.

The infill work would need to be done after winter had left us but the men could press on with building the walls as the stone required was in abundance nearby and the masons were more than eager to become involved as quickly as possible. Whilst they busied themselves with the walls and towers, I turned to the domestic building which now would sit outside the walls and worked with Osmond to find a way to include it in the overall plans. I had intended on making this a working castle, helping the town grow, making the marketplace thrive. And so, we would need quarters for the workers at the castle if they so wished to stay there and a great hall and sizable kitchens to feed them. More builders were employed, the domestic building that had been the quarters where Osmond and I slept when we first arrived slowly transformed into a massive great hall, sleeping quarters above and kitchens attached.

I then turned my mind to the staircase which led from the bottom of the motte to the top. When the space between the curtain wall and the motte was completely filled, the staircase would need to lead from the new great hall up to the castle but with increased security as this would be the main entrance. A clever young engineer brought me a plan that showed the staircase doing just that but coming to an end at a drawbridge that could be retracted if the castle were under attack. He had included a gatehouse built into the new curtain wall with a wooden balcony protruding out from which sentries could keep watch. And the staircase would now have a landing that would lead not only to the great hall and kitchens but also down to the courtyard. It was ingenious.

Once the building works were underway and Alix's tutor hired, I sent Osmond to Shirburn and Sandford on Thames to organize the transport of my goods and furnishings that I had left there to Ferneham. Although many had connections with my lady, they had been gifted to me by Duke Robert and I wanted them with me. I was glad I did, I had forgotten the exquisite artistry in the carvings of the pieces of furniture, the chests, the great hall table and chairs. Our marriage bed, however, stayed where it was.

I replaced Bishop Henry's chests with those my own but made sure the precious manuscript was kept locked in my bedchamber until I could secure a safer place for it. I took it out occasionally to read it, the translation was fascinating. I was not sure of the accuracy, the translators had no doubt brought in a bias against the Muslims. But it was a start to those in the West trying to understand them, I had to hope.

Shortly after the arrival of the furnishings, I had a visit from my brother Guillaume and his wife, Matilda de Beaumont. They brought with them their son, Richard, who was slightly older than Alix and the two cousins became fast friends, each trying to outdo the other in their games and horsing skills. It brought us much joy and laughter watching their antics. It was wonderful to see my brother and to hear everything about his family's lives since I departed from England. The properties had flourished under his guidance and expanded to the northwest of Oxford, adding more of the lush Oxfordshire farmland to our holdings.

But he also brought some ominous news about my old adversary, Séraphine's brother John Marshal, who was aware I had returned to England and had no concern about voicing his displeasure about this to whomever would listen. Guillaume recounted a few stories about the man who had become universally feared and hated, switching sides many times during the civil war had left him with a reputation that he could not be trusted.

Guillaume told me about the battle at Lincoln where he had abandoned King Stephen and of the incident at Wherwell Abbey where he was disfigured and lost an eye. And that John currently found himself in an especially foul mood as Empress Matilda's son Henry had brought a small army through the south of England continuing to press both his and her claims for the crown, and had taken over Marlborough Castle, ousting John and his family. They had to return to their castle at Hamstead Marshall just outside of Newbury. And despite the fact that John was purportedly supporting Matilda at the time, Henry clearly did not trust him. I knew the man would hold his hatred of me until his death.

It was a sad day when Guillaume had to return to Oxfordshire for even though we were now physically closer to each other than we had been in decades, I also knew our busy lives would make it difficult to make time for more visits. But I was determined we would find that time.

Autumn soon turned into early winter and I was amazed at the speed at which the walls and towers were being constructed. I had been receiving despatches from Godwin on a fairly regular basis giving updates on the fighting with the Welsh rebels and asking about Alix. I wrote him frequently, assuring him of his daughter's safety and her health and well-being. But when we passed All Saints Day in November and I had not heard from him for a few weeks, I knew something was wrong.

Alix had already retired to bed when the messenger came with dire news. He had been sent by Godwin's younger half-brother Richard. Godwin had been killed, not in battle in defence of Castle Usk, but in broad daylight as he travelled to Pembroke to meet with Richard to discuss his successes against the Welsh. Bandits had attacked his small group and all were murdered for the few gold coins they carried. Richard made clear that he would avenge his half-brother's death and that the murderers would pay dearly for his death. But I now had to tell Alix that her father was gone. I also knew this meant she had suddenly become a wealthy heiress which added to my concerns of her safety.

After her meal the next morning, I sat her down in the great hall of the keep so we would have some privacy to talk. Osmond offered to stay and help but I told him I needed to do this on my own. She was now my full responsibility – I would not fail her as I had her mother. She was understandably upset to hear the news, she loved her father dearly and had been looking forward to seeing him at Christmas. And her nine-year-old mind immediately went to what would happen to her pony rather than what would happen to herself, I had to smile inwardly when I heard her pleas for me to look after him. I told her she had nothing to worry about, that both her pony and she would be taken care of, that her life would be with me now if she wanted it. And that I would do anything in my power to protect her.

Upon hearing this, she threw her arms about my neck and cried. She then asked me if she could call me "Papa" as she now had none, I told her I would love it if she did. I informed her maid of what had transpired and instructed her to sleep in Alix's room for the next few weeks. And that if the girl awoke with night terrors that she was to bring her to me, no matter what the time.

We did not return to Wales for the funeral, what was happening with the Welsh rebels made it too dangerous to bring Alix and even Richard agreed that the best place for her was with me. We held a small service at Waverly Abbey but as Bishop Henry, who was its Abbot, was in Italy, one of the senior Cistercian monks agreed to take on the official duties for us. Alix lit candles in remembrance of both her father and her mother, it was very touching to see how brave she was being, but I expected nothing more from Séraphine's granddaughter.

# IX

## Part Two

## 1149-1152 – Ferneham, England

I tried to make Christmas as pleasant as I could under the circumstances and although Alix tried, I knew she was missing her parents. I had a portrait made of her which I then sent to the best tapestry artisans in Flanders with specific instructions on what I wanted, two ladies in a garden, and for them to use the portrait to model from. It arrived just in time to gift it to Alix for Christmas. She adored it and insisted we hang it in the great hall of the keep so it could be seen by many. I had to admit, I was taken aback by how much one of the ladies in it resembled both Séraphine and Alix, so similar were they.

As winter turned into spring and the building works started in earnest again, I kept her occupied helping with sorting the decorations for each of the living quarters in the five towers. As soon as the land thawed, I began work on constructing a proper dock on the part of the River Wey closest to the town. This allowed easier access to the traders to come to the markets to sell and trade their wares.

With each passing day I could see the changes I was making coming to life and was pleased with the results. The townsfolk came to know me not only through the business I was doing with them but also for the frequent walks I took with Alix around the town, we became a familiar sight. I took on a number of responsibilities for governing the town, settling disputes fairly, made sure all sides were as satisfied as possible. And tried to make the quality of life for those working at the castle and the townsfolk as pleasant as possible. The town grew as people were attracted to it through a reputation that was spreading nearby. I would soon find out that that would have an unpleasant impact as well.

By the end of the first year living in Ferneham, most of the major the building works had been completed, the castle felt sound and secure and our farms and gardens were thriving, as was Alix. Now ten, she was starting to grow in height and I realized she had at least one of the characteristics I had at that age, she was tall for her age. She was still a child who needed to be taken care of but I also knew that as a wealthy heiress she would be sought after as she reached marriageable age, I knew I had to be extra vigilant as she got older. I worked with her uncle Richard who had hired retainers to assist with the administration of the Welsh properties left to her by her father until she was old enough and married at which point her husband would take control. With our assistance of course.

It was shortly before the next Christmas that I received a message from Bishop Henry. From previous despatches I knew that his discussions with Pope Eugenius had been fruitful and that he was gaining new favours for many of his abbeys. He had also been present for the return of King Louis and Queen Eleanor who, after staying in the Holy Land a while longer debating what to do with the remnants of their armies, had finally returned. Their relationship was clearly strained, the two were barely speaking to each other and he and the Pope were doing their best to resolve their issues and bring them back together but his personal belief was that the situation was hopeless.

But this despatch also had other news. Henry had decided to stay for the foreseeable future and as such he wished to divest himself of some of his houses in England, Ferneham being one. And after hearing of the massive building works I was having done to the castle and the surrounding property, he could not in all good conscience ask me to purchase it. Instead he wished to gift it to me and if I were willing, he would put the deed in my name. I was delighted with this, although I wished my friend would return, I was also heartened to know that I and Alix could make this our permanent home. I accepted and by the time the following Easter had passed, I had become the new official lord of Ferneham Castle.

And so our lives fell into the peaceful routine of running the castle and the lands surrounding it, helping to build the town. Whilst Alix was going to remain in her room in the keep, I had decided it was time to move into the newly completed southwest tower which had terrific views of the valley and a pretty little stream as well as the town in the distance. And beneath it were the new gardens which I had given to Alix, letting her do what she wanted with them. The tower was also closer to the gatehouse and I could be anywhere on the walls within moments, much quicker than if I stayed in my room on the top floor of the keep.

It only took a day to move my bedchamber furnishings to the new rooms, as well as the chest containing the Qur'an manuscript. At the end of that day, late in the evening I was preparing for bed when I opened my of my chests looking for a belt I thought I had misplaced and came upon the silk-wrapped gift from Zengi that had remained packed in this chest since I packed it there when we took the rooms in the keep.

I reached for it and took it to the bed, slowly undoing the ties that held the silk in place and then gently removed them, careful not to disturb any of the settings on the astrolabe as I revealed it. The gilt bronze danced with the fireplace flames that reflected from it. I lightly touched the markings along the discs, remembering the evening when Zengi gave me this gift. I had to admit, I rued the loss of our friendship but was glad to have had the time we did. I had learned so much from him, I could only hope he had felt the same.

I got up and placed the astrolabe on the mantel above the fireplace. Looking at it made me realize it was time for me to share this with Alix. Her curiosity would undoubtedly get the better of her once she saw it and I needed to be ready to share with her the meaning and importance of it. Even though she was still young, she had gravitated to her lessons eagerly and with a passion to learn everything put before her. She received the education usually reserved for boys in a household but the intellect I suspected was in her became more and more obvious every day. I felt she was ready.

As I suspected, Alix practically ran towards the astrolabe when I called her to my chambers one early afternoon. She moved so quickly I had to call out to her to stop her reaching for it, my voice sounding so urgent that she stopped in her tracks turning to me with a look of surprise on her face. I apologized for the harshness that she may have heard and gently reached for the astrolabe and bid her sit next to me at the table by the window when the afternoon sunlight was streaming in.

She was fascinated by it all. I told her of the crusade, focusing on my encounters with Zengi, how we had come together just before his death and how this had been his gift to me. I showed her how it worked, explaining all the markings and the ways in which it could be used. And our discussions did not stop with the astrolabe. As the afternoon hours passed and turned into evening, I told her everything. Almost all of it.

* * * * * * * * * *

It was in the middle of the night not long after when my past in England came back to haunt me. I was actually surprised that it took him this long to come looking for me but I also knew it was inevitable. And I knew he would use Alix as the pretext for starting hostilities with me, especially as she was nearing marriageable age. She would now be useful to him. As was his style, he and his men arrived in the dead of night, thinking he would have the advantage of surprise. He was wrong of course.

I was awakened by Osmond's knocks at my door. He quickly apprised me of the situation. John Marshall and about ten men had reached the courtyard of the castle and were demanding my presence. I told Osmond to make sure Alix was safe and secure and then got dressed, binding my belt with my sword and scabbard attached and resting at my side. As I descended the spiral staircase from my quarters, I could see through the arrow slits in the stairwell the men on horseback surrounded by my men holding torches and weapons and a number of my guard facing them, armed and ready to fight. It looked as though tensions were already high.

I made my way to the gatehouse and ordered the drawbridge down so I could cross it and descend the massive stone staircase. But I remained on the landing rather than continuing to the bottom. This gave me the advantage. I stood staring at the man who had hatred for me going back decades. More of my guards raced past me and, armed themselves, were ready for whatever John and his men would do.

Even though it was in the dead of night with a cloud-filled sky that prevented any natural light from the moon and the stars, the light cast from all the torches lit up the scene almost as though it was broad daylight, and I could see my adversary plainly. I could not help but notice that his face had been hideously scarred down his left cheek, beneath the black patch he wore to cover the fact he was missing an eye. The civil war had taken its toll. I waited for him to speak.

"D'Ivry! DOG!" he shouted out.

I waited.

"I am surprised that you have the gall to show your face in England after all these years!"

I resisted the urge to make comment on the state of his face, I knew it would only inflame him.

"What is it you want Marshal?" I asked, trying to get him to the point.

"Do you have her?" he barked.

At that, one of the men with him rode up beside him and whispered something I could not hear. I narrowed my focus to this man, I was certain it was his younger brother Anselm who had been but a small child the last I had seen him. His countenance was somewhat softer than his wretched older brother.

"Her?" I played dumb.

"You know very well who I mean," he said, waving his brother away like a bothersome gnat. "Séraphine's granddaughter Alix. You have her here."

"If you mean my granddaughter Alix, then yes, she is here. And is here to stay. What do you wish with her?" I demanded knowing full well why he was here.

"You cannot believe that you are fit to raise her D'Ivry!" he growled. "I am here to take her to Hamstead Marshal. She needs to be with the Marshal family, and not poisoned by the likes of you!"

I was silent, carefully scanning the scene before me, counting the men and their positions, knowing there was no chance he could make it anywhere near the keep and Alix. Then I walked down the remaining stairs and towards the man who was still on horseback. Suddenly, more of my men, all armed, piled in behind me and even more still encircled Marshal and his men.

"She is going nowhere," I said quietly but steadfast in my resolve. He needed to hear it in my voice.

John did not dismount as would be the custom if the visit were friendly. I did not expect him to. But his men had all drawn their weapons when I approached his horse, all except his brother Anselm who obviously was the only member of this party with a clear head. This of course meant all of my men had drawn theirs. I raised my hands palms outward indicating everyone should remain calm. Although in my head I was seething – no one was going to take my Alix from me.

John unwisely believed that he had the better of me, now having the higher position, he thought he could conceal the dagger as he flung his far leg over his horse's head and in an instant was on the ground lunging for me. But I was prepare for this, John was clearly unaware of the military skills I had earned through my years as a Knight Templar. Before he knew what was happening I had disarmed him of the weapon, twisted him around and forced him to a half-kneeling position, his arms locked behind his back in my vise-like grip, his dagger now in my right hand, precariously resting against the centre of his throat. Any move and he would be cut instantly. He knew this and he stopped struggling to free himself as soon as he felt the blade's cool edge against his skin. It happened so quickly that his men had no chance to react or come to his aid and were stopped from doing so by the threat I was now making against their master. My men surrounded them and they were forced to sheath their weapons. I leaned in close to his right ear.

"Listen to me and listen good, Marshal," I whispered in his ear so that only he could hear. "You come to my land, uninvited, and threaten me and my family…"

"She is MY family," he hissed back at me and I tightened my grip on his arms.

"Let me make myself perfectly clear. Alix is mine, she stays with me. You *ever* trespass on my land again or make *any* attempt whatsoever to take her, I will kill you. Do you understand me?"

"And you, a Knight Templar! So much for your oaths, I shall take this to your Grand Master!" he threatened.

"I no longer wear the mantle, Marshal. But please do reach out to Brother Everard, I beg you," I said so confidently that he stopped talking, knowing his threat was baseless.

"Have you understood me?" I asked again.

Now it was his turn to be silent which I took as his assent. I pushed him away from me and tossed his dagger to one of my men. I watched him scramble to his feet and in doing so his eyepatch became dislodged and I glimpsed his monstrous face in its entirety. He quickly pulled it back into place before anyone else noticed and remounted his horse. And without so much as a grunt, he turned and spurred his horse into a gallop towards the entrance through which he came. His men did the same and within a few moments the courtyard was quiet, with only the slight flapping of the torches' flames in the light wind making any sound.

I looked around at the men who had come to assist me and nodded my thanks to them all. Then I turned to the staircase to return to my quarters. I saw Osmond standing on the landing, having witnessed all of it.

"That will not be the end of it," he murmured as I passed him.

I stopped.

"No, it will not. Double the guards on the walls and on the battlements. I have no doubt we have made this castle as impenetrable as possible, but that will not mean he will cease trying to breach it. And I want guards to be with Alix wherever she goes for the time being."

Osmond said it would be done. I retired to my bedchamber, cold and weary. I had hoped to be done with all of this. But old grudges rarely ever die.

* * * * * * * * * *

The following months were relatively quiet although the thought of John Marshal and his threats were never far from my mind. His attentions were elsewhere as his fallout with the King was having ramifications, especially as Matilda was providing him support in harassing the King by staging small incursions at a ring of the King's holdings to the west of London. I kept aware of his activities, always keeping abreast of his whereabouts and increased the guards whenever he was found to be in the vicinity of Ferneham.

I continued to correspond with Bishop Henry and with Abbot Bernard, each giving me news of events happening in France and beyond. When Brother Everard decided to retire from the Order and live his life as a monk at Clairvaux Abbey, I was saddened to hear it – I had been appreciative of his work as Master in Paris and I thought he had done well navigating the complex and sometimes hazardous relationship with King Louis and his determination to go on crusade despite the advice many had given him not to.

I did not know his successor, Grand Master Bernard de Tremelay so I wrote to Montbard who had reached the Order's highest echelon and was one I could trust. He had given his support of de Tremelay's election and hoped he would be a strong leader as the harassment of Jerusalem continued, this time from the Egyptian Fatimids to the south. I wished him well; Montbard was the only other original founding Brother still alive and in Jerusalem. Archambaud Saint-Agnan had died the year after Montdidier and the two monks, Gondamer and Rossal had left Jerusalem, Gondamer returning to Portugal and Rossal to Clairvaux. I missed the camaraderie I had shared with the Brothers, but was glad not to be involved in the battles, I had had enough of the bloodshed.

Things came a head between King Stephen and John as soon as Matilda's son Henry had returned to Normandy for his marriage to Eleanor of Aquitaine who had just had her marriage to King Louis annulled. After their return from crusade and despite intervention from many, the strife between King Louis and his wife had been declared irreparable and Pope Eugenius eventually agreed to annul the marriage on the grounds of consanguinity, as the two claimed to be related within the forbidden degrees. Of course, the fact this had been allowed in order to create the marriage in the first place was ignored. The annulment was made easier since the marriage had not produced a male heir even though two daughters had been born and thrived.

The King and Queen were mismatched from the beginning, he needing a mate who was much more pious and subservient, she needing a mate who could equal her spirit. Most importantly, Eleanor received her duchy of Aquitaine in the annulment which made her a prized heiress, but her next match had already been made. It was said Henry fell for Eleanor on first sight and she him. And politically, since Henry had been made Duke of Normandy two years earlier, the match united two of the largest duchies on the continent; they would make a formidable pair.

As soon as word reached the King of Henry's departure, King Stephen was on the move, deciding to lay siege to John's castle in Hamstead Marshal near Newbury. A hastily built but strong fortress, it had been deemed illegal as it had been built without royal assent. And Stephen, wanting to punish John for this insult, moved his army to encircle the castle. The siege lasted longer than either had expected, John having designed the castle to have an interior well and constructed supply stores larger than most castles, knowing he would need them should it be besieged. King Stephen was not able to make much of an advance on it. But John also knew that eventually he would start to lose ground and so he offered a truce to give him time to write to Matilda and ask her permission to surrender the castle. The King allowed it and, as was traditional when temporary truces were agreed to, the King demanded that John provide a hostage from within his own family who would be held by the King until the matter had been settled.

John acquiesced. He sent his six-year-old son William.

This was when Bishop Henry wrote to me and begged me to assist in keeping the peace whilst the terms of surrender were being worked out. I thought I was an odd choice for the task – John's hatred of me was obvious and King Stephen's dislike of me at the tournaments many years ago could still hold. Perhaps I was the best person after all. And I could not turn down my old friend who had been so generous in his gift to me of his castle and so I gathered a few of my guards and made the day and a half ride, reaching King Stephen's encampment on the south side of the castle in the late afternoon. The autumn rains had held off for a couple of weeks and the ground had dried enough for more of the King's siege engines to be moved into place.

As I approached the camps, I understood why John appeared to be capitulating. The King's army's tents were everywhere the eye could see, curving around the base of the motte and out of sight. I was amazed that John had lasted as long as he had, I surmised there must be supply tunnels running underneath the land and exiting somewhere the King's men had been unable to find.

The King had been alerted to my eventual arrival by his brother the Bishop and so I passed the guard points without too much interrogation, especially once I showed the letter from Bishop Henry. Being led through the tents I was reminded of the many times I had witnessed similar sights: at Saint-Denis, at Nicaea, at Antioch, at Damascus. And all the others. The tents were a much better quality, sturdier and larger, being able to accommodate more men, I was sure Duke Robert would have wanted to have had such in his armies.

King Stephen's tent was a bit of a distance from the castle, keeping him out of range of any arrowshot coming from the battlements and situated up on a hill within a small copse. His guards brought me to the entrance where I was told to wait until I was called. I took the opportunity to examine the castle. Although hurriedly constructed, it was remarkable in size and strength, the deep ditch surrounding it made it more difficult to attack as any attackers would have to traverse it and then the motte the castle sat upon and without cover they were easy prey for John's archers.

The wind began to pick up and tree branches swayed slowly in a rhythmic dance that in any other circumstance would be calming and peaceful. I felt a pang of sorrow remembering the reason I was asked to come here. And then suddenly, I heard the squeals of a young lad, happy and carefree, coming from the far side of the tent. This must be John's young son for no one would bring a youth of such tender age to this place.

I told one of the guards where I wished to go and was escorted around the corner of the tent where I was taken aback by the sight that greeted me. John's young boy, playing with a small wooden sword and shield in a fenced-off area, laughing and giggling as he came at his enemy. And his enemy was no other than King Stephen himself, laying on the grass, feigning injuries and letting the little one win before rolling over and grabbing the boy, wrestling him to the ground and tickling him, making the squeals come faster and louder. It would have been a truly heart-warming scene had the reality not been that young William was King Stephen's captive.

I stood still for a moment, not wanting to interrupt but then decided I should wait back at the entrance to the tent and not intrude. I had barely turned to walk away when I heard my name being called out.

"D'Ivry!" King Stephen shouted.

I watched as the King disentangled himself from the young boy's grip on his tunic and got up off the ground.

"Your Majesty," I responded, bowing my head respectfully.

I could not help but think the man had not aged well. He looked much older than I expected, possibly the years of his tumultuous reign had taken their toll. He took hold of the boy's hand and walked him through the gate of the enclosure, bringing him towards me.

"Young William," he said to the boy, "here is a great man indeed. Sir Sébastien D'Ivry. He is a Knight Templar. And part of your family, he is your uncle by marriage to your father's sister Séraphine. Do you understand?"

The boy looked up at the King and nodded. Then he turned to me.

"Hello Uncle," he said to me in the sweetest voice I think I had ever heard come from a boy. "Does my Aunt Séraphine not come with you?"

My heart skipped a beat hearing this little boy mention my lady's name. I could not help but grin at his question, so forthright and innocent.

"No, no, young William," answered the King before I could, "your Aunt Séraphine is no longer with us. But I do not doubt she was much loved when she was?"

He said the last part looking directly at me. I knew why. His own wife the Queen had succumbed to a fever but a few months earlier, his grief no doubt spurred his decision to wage war against John. I suddenly realized I had something in common with this man who had dismissed me all those years ago as an unimportant person born of a family of no consequence. I nodded at him, letting him know I understood his meaning.

"Right, you must run along now boy, your King has matters to discuss with your Uncle."

The boy began to protest as he wanted to continue playing and the King shot him a stern look. But clearly he could not deny the boy much as the look turned quickly into a bit of a chuckle.

"Get on with you, I will send for you soon and we can play at Hannibal and the Romans!"

"Can I be Hannibal?" the boy asked endearingly. "Please?"

"Yes of course. And if you ask nicely, perhaps your uncle here will be willing to be one of your elephants?"

The boy skipped away happily, completely unaware of the danger he was in. The tone of my exchange with the King changed as soon as the boy was out of earshot.

"So, my brother Henry feels you may be of some assistance here?" he asked as we started walking to the rear entrance to the tents.

Once inside, he removed his tunic, dirty from all the child-play and sat in his royal chair, drinking from a gold goblet of wine that one of his servants had handed to him.

"Bishop Henry was gracious enough to believe so, yes, sire," I responded.

King Stephen grunted. Apparently he did not share his brother's views.

"I do not know what you could possibly do to improve this situation?" he snorted.

"I can tell you that John Marshal cannot be trusted, sire," I stated plainly. "Whatever terms you have agreed to in this temporary truce, he will not abide by them."

The King looked at me with scepticism. He knew John Marshal had deserted him at the battle of Lincoln and had switched sides to support Matilda, but truces were based on honour and were not to be broken, such was the rule of war.

"How do you believe John will break the truce?"

"He will continue to bring in food and supplies against the rule, I believe he has contrived some secretive manner in which to continue the supply that your men have not located. Unless of course you have given him leave to do so?"

The King grimaced.

"No, I have not. He knows better than to do this. What else?"

"I do not believe he has any intention of surrendering the castle. I believe he has more than likely requested Empress Matilda to send men rather than asking for her permission to relinquish control here."

That seemed to take the King by surprise.

"That is nonsense, he would be a fool to do so!"

"How long has it been since the truce was put in place?" I asked.

The King thought a moment, calculating the amount of time that had passed since the truce had been agreed and John was to have sent despatches to Matilda. It had been too long. The King ordered one of his guards to gather the captains of his army and advisors to discuss my observations, he had to admit that I might have a point.

I was not privy to those discussions but was aware that the advisors were soon busying themselves with creating the order to be sent to John to cease all supply activities and to surrender the castle immediately. Which of course meant having to use the one pawn that King Stephen had at his disposal – the threat of harming the life of young William. This shook me to the core but I also knew how important family was to John – he certainly made me aware of it every chance he had – so I believed that the threat against his son would result in his capitulation.

Signals were exchanged and a meeting arranged for a representative of the King to deliver the order to a representative of John. This is where my presence became useful to the King. He chose me to be his man and although I did not think this was wise considering my relationship with John, I did his bidding. I found out soon enough why he had chosen me.

I was provided a suit of mailled armour as well as a helm but no weapon as was the custom when meetings between adversaries and their men were held during a truce. I mounted one of the King's great steeds and tucked the scrolled order under my shoulder plate and walked the horse slowly down from the King's location on the faraway hill to the ditch and waited for John's man to arrive.

The massive doors of the castle opened just wide enough for a single rider to get through and begin the descent down towards the ditch. I thought for a moment my eyes deceived me but no – the person John had chosen was wearing a Knight Templar surcoat over top of a maille hauberk. His head was protected by a maille coif and as far as I could see he was carrying no weapon. But this is what King Stephen had wanted: Templar versus Templar.

The rider walked his horse down into the ditch and I matched his moves until we were face to face. I raised my visor to get a better look at the Knight but I could not place him. But he knew me.

"You are Sir Sébastien D'Ivry, Knight Templar?" he asked in a tone that was more of a statement than a question.

"I am," I replied, not wishing to say anything more, if he did know me, he would know I had not been part of the Order for many years.

"I am Father William Heath, Master of the Templar preceptory in Bristol. I see you no longer wear the mantle. I know of you, your reputation is well known throughout the Order," he said with respect. But then added, with a change in tone to disparaging, "And of course, from what Sir John has told me."

I ignored the dig.

"Marshal is in breach of his truce with King Stephen. He is hereby ordered to surrender the castle forthwith," I said calmly as I handed him the scroll containing the order.

He took it from me.

"There are rumours about you Brother D'Ivry. You know what I refer to. A Queen of Jerusalem?"

Again, I ignored the snide remark.

"The King expects a response by sext tomorrow. He will not hesitate to do what he must," I stately flatly, then directed my horse to climb out of the ditch and then cantor back to the King's tent, feeling the Templar's eyes on my back.

In my mind, Heath was not a true Knight Templar. Montbard had told me of some Brothers who were abusing their power and had turned their backs on the Order when the opportunity came to advance themselves either in power, wealth, or prestige. That was not our way. And for a Templar to align themselves with one so despised by his own countrymen was disheartening.

I reported back to the King what I had said to Heath, he had not been surprised to see the Templar appear from within John's castle. He had guessed John would be using the Bristol Master to give the impression he had the Order's backing. I did not speculate on the reasons for the Knight's appearance. But his words told me all I needed to know about any stories about Queen Melisende's mysterious illness and recovery from near death. Those who had heard them were out there. And I needed to be aware that some might come searching for me.

We saw the signal from the battlements near noon the next day that John's response to the King was ready to be delivered. Once again, I donned the armour and met Heath at the same place but this time I did not engage in any talk. He was of no consequence to me. I took the scroll from him and returned immediately to the King who bade me stay whilst he read it. It was not good news.

"He must be mad!" the King snorted, clearly surprised by what he read. "He has been told that I have no choice but to have his boy tied to a trebuchet and kill him by launching him into the castle, and this is his response!" he roared, throwing the scroll to me.

John's answer to the threat to his young child was monstrous.

> *I have no intention of ever surrendering this or any other castle I am in possession of. As for the threat made against my son, I dare you to make good on it! I have both the hammer and the forge to make more, and better, sons!*

The King was enraged and launched into a tirade against his enemy. Once he seemed to have calmed somewhat, one of his advisors pronounced that the King would have to carry out the threat or his position and strength would be diminished. Upon hearing that, King Stephen's anger flared again and he stormed out of the tent demanding the boy be brought to the place where the trebuchet stood.

I could not believe the King was actually going to follow through with retribution against this innocent lad and walked with him hoping to be able to convince him not to do this. We were both standing by the huge siege engine when the boy was brought by one of his guards. At one point, he ran ahead of the guard and over to one of the King's knights, asking him if he could play with his shiny sword. We watched as the knight tussled the boy's head and told him the King was waiting for him.

Young William was completely oblivious to what was truly happening around him. He skipped over to the King and hugged his leg before letting go and moving over to the trebuchet, looking at it with awe. He stood by the bucket and then called out.

"Sire," he said grinning and looking back at the King, "the bucket is just my size! Can I play on the ropes please?"

It was heart-breaking. I leaned towards the King and whispered in his ear.

"Sire, you cannot…"

Everything stood still, as the King stared at the boy and then to the castle battlements where he knew John would be watching. Two of his guards moved towards little William.

"HALT!" the King bellowed and marched over the boy, sweeping him up in his arms and carrying him away. And calling out to his advisors as he passed them by, "One would have a heart of iron to see such a child perish!"

I breathed out my relief in an audible sigh. Thank god the King had seen to do right. I watched as King's minions scurried after the King and the boy, back to the royal tents, leaving me alone by the trebuchet. I turned and stared at the battlements. Such immoral, barbaric behaviour had not been seen before and it I knew that once word spread, it would cement John's brutal and ruthless reputation.

John did not shift his position. Only when word reached him some time later that the Empress had safely reached Wallingford did he capitulate, but by then young William had been taken to Windsor and remained King Stephen's captive for several months. But having seen how the King reacted to the boy, I knew he would have been treated well.

I also knew that John would have been made aware of the stories the Knight Templar had referred to during our short exchange. And that he would always be looking for ways to gain the upper hand against his enemies. And this, combined with his arrogance and overblown sense of self-importance, would mean that he too would more than likely make the same mistake Brother Alvisius did in believing his was worthy of the powers of the knowledge and the elixir. I had to be on my guard now at all times. I was glad to return to my life at Ferneham and embraced Alix a little more tightly when I saw her.

# IX

# Part Three

# 1153-1154 - England

With Empress Matilda's arrival at Wallingford Castle, we knew that the likelihood of one of King Stephen's sons inheriting the crown would become less and less as support for her son Henry as heir being the grandson of the Conqueror was growing. Stephen had legitimate sons but those who survived into adulthood – one, Baldwin, had died when he was nine – were not seen as strong contenders by the barons and nobility in England, especially once being introduced to the raw power that was Henry, Duke of Normandy. Stephen had tried to have his son Eustace crowned while Stephen was still alive in the style of the French, but the barons refused to allow it. And whilst Eustace was alive, the youngest son, Guillaume would have to be content to stay as Earl of Surrey through his wife, Countess Isabelle de Warenne.

My darling Alix was now of marriageable age and despite the attention given to her by many suitors, some worthy, many not, she settled her heart on the worldly Jordan de Lacy. His family was of good standing, nobility in the east of England, having lands and at least one castle, Pontefract, in their holdings. But it was not the riches that came with Jordan or the connection to the de Lacy family – Alix was wealthy herself and there were many suitors who came from prominent families – it was a love match between the two which pleased me as I had wished this for her.

And so a lavish but small wedding was held in Waverley Abbey, presided over by Bishop Henry himself having returned to England specifically for the event. Throughout the months of courting, I was certain John would make some attempt to take Alix and force her into a marriage of his making. But with the eventual return of Matilda's son Henry after his own wedding, he found himself too busy forming an alliance with Henry and continuing to harass King Stephen whenever and wherever he could. But the wedding went ahead without any sign of John or his men, not that he would have been able to accomplish anything. The entire town was aware of the threat he posed and the love they had for Alix meant protecting her at all costs. But the threat of him would always remain.

Although I was so proud of my granddaughter, who made a truly beautiful bride, it broke my heart to see her things being packed for her move to the east of the country, the tradition still being that wife would stay with husband. She was stoic on her leaving day but I felt her tremble as she embraced me farewell. She promised me she would write often and she did.

Shortly after the wedding, I received news that Montbard had become Grand Master of the Knights Templar in Jerusalem after a battle at Ascalon had gone badly. Grand Master Tremelay had led a group of Brothers to the walls of the city with siege engines and had been set to besiege the city for as long as it took. But one of the wooden towers caught fire from flame-lit arrows and in tumbling down it destroyed a section of the walls. Tremelay and the Brothers hastened across to gain entrance quickly before any of King Baldwin's men could join them. It was not really known why but rumours were spread saying Tremelay wished to keep the best spoils for himself and the Order.

But whatever the reason, he paid dearly for the rush forward. He and the Brothers who accompanied him were captured and executed, their heads sent to the Fatimid Sultan and their bodies hung from the battlements to show the Christian armies what would befall them. But as life tends to turn especially in the winds of war, when hostilities resumed there was no desire for further fighting and a truce was agreed. The Christians took the city and the Muslims were given three days to leave. Once firmly in the hands of Baldwin, he gave the fortress to Amalric, which, ironically, was the very thing he had wished not to do at the Council of Acre. I smiled at the mention of Amalric's name, I hoped he had grown into a strong, intelligent young man. As for the Templars, with Montbard now as Grand Master, I knew the Order was in good hands.

King Stephen made one last attempt at reclaiming control of England when he made the futile decision to come at Henry and his mother the Empress Matilda at Wallingford. The stand-off of the armies facing each other from opposite sides of the River Thames lasted a few months before the two sides agreed to parlay and Henry put forth convincing arguments for becoming Stephen's heir apparent. All agreed that the war needed to end, it had lasted Stephen's entire reign and he was tired. Queen Eleanor had just given birth to Henry's first son, named William after her father the last Duke of Aquitaine, and so the dynasty of the Plantagenet family seemed secure. And when word was received in the midst of the discussions of Eustace's death during a skirmish outside Bury St Edmunds, it was all but said and done. Henry, Duke of Normandy, would become Henry II, the King of England upon Stephen's death.

Whilst the battles at Wallingford had raged on, I was saddened to hear of the death of my brothers within two months of each other. First, Roger, who had collapsed one afternoon when inspecting his fields after a particularly violent hailstorm had caused substantial damage to his land. And then Guillaume, who, according to a letter sent to me by his wife, had been in Leicester on business and had been found in his bed by the innkeeper. I was not able to travel to France for Roger's funeral but made sure to pay all the costs for it and his interment next to our father and mother at the Abbey of Our Lady of Bec. But with Guillaume, I owed it to him to return to Shirburn which had been his home. And it was time for me to go visit the past and try to rid myself of the ghosts.

* * * * * * * * *

Osmond accompanied me to Oxfordshire. He had business with Pascal at Sandford on Thames and had wanted to give his respects to my brother at the funeral. Arriving at the property, I was surprised by its size, it had grown considerably over the years. But I really should not have been surprised, Guillaume had always been the consummate businessman, and would have done our uncle Roger D'Ivry proud with his achievements.

Because of his standing in the village and surrounding area, the Abbey at Dorchester had offered a resting place for him but his widow had decided that he would have preferred the small church of All Saints that had been in the village long before he or Roger had even arrived. I thought this was perfect as well and the service given him was modest but still befitting a man of his stature. I was invited to stay for a few days afterwards, but I declined saying I had business elsewhere. But in reality, I only had one place to go.

The day after the funeral, Osmond and I set off at dawn by horseback for the half-day ride to Sandford on Thames. We were silent most of the way, I was glad for it, I was certain Osmond knew why I was not feeling the need to speak. As we neared the village, certain pieces of the landscape jogged my memory, a small bridge here, or a dovecote there. And as we rounded the bend in the road on the final leg of the journey, I could see the tops of some of the farm buildings appear on the horizon. My chest began to swell.

We entered a new gate, at least one that had appeared since I was last there, and as we did so saw various workers and servants hustling about doing chores for the farm. Each stopped to look at us as we passed them by and bowed their heads in greeting, but no one said anything, I suspected they had been made aware of our arrival. We trotted the horses up to the main entrance of the house and by the time we had dismounted my old squire Pascal had come out and was standing on the doorstep with his arms crossed and a massive grin on his face. He had aged but still possessed a body of wiry strength. It was good to see him.

"Master D'Ivry!!" he called out with great joy and came rushing out to greet me.

We embraced as old friends and we could not count the years since we had seen each other last. Stable hands came to take care of our horses and we were led into the house and with each step memories started flooding into me. In front of me was the grand staircase leading up to the private quarters and I saw in my mind Séraphine's mother Margaret, standing at the base of it, receiving the news of her daughter's death and collapsing there. Looking up to the landing where the staircase turned into two, I saw Séraphine standing there, smiling at me before floating down then leaping into my arms as she so often did.

We turned to the left and entered the dining hall where I had sat with the man who would become my mentor, brother, friend. Different chairs now sat in front of the fireplace but that did not matter, I could still see Hugues and myself sitting there as if it had happened the day before, quaffing ale and talking about going back to the Holy Land. I felt a pang go through me, I missed my friend.

I excused myself once Pascal and Osmond starting to speak about the management of the property and went outside to walk about. Everyone I met seemed to be so cheerful, it made me glad to see such happiness in a place that had caused me such happiness before tragedy struck. I went to the stables and saw all the horses, many piebald which made me think of Pax and Lux and the others. Then I wandered down to the river and discovered that the old mill had been rebuilt and was a much larger, fully functioning version of its former self. Several men were working inside and all nodded to me as I insisted they continue their work and not stop because of me. I watched them as they milled the grain and piled newly filled sacks on carts ready to go to market. Or up to the kitchens. It was good.

The afternoon turned to early evening. Pascal had arranged for a hearty meal which I gobbled down quickly, surprised at how hungry I was. The wine was the best from the cellar and before long fatigue started to set in. Pascal excused himself to check that our quarters were ready. Osmond turned to me.

"I was not sure, m'Lord, where you would feel most comfortable for the night, so Pascal has readied two rooms, one on the west corridor and the one you shared with your lady on the east. Which shall I tell him you will take?"

I was touched by how sympathetic Osmond had been, not many would have considered the impact of sleeping in the room where I had cradled my lady as she died would have on me.

"I shall take the first Osmond, but I shall visit the other before I go to bed. And thank you, my friend, for being so thoughtful," I said warmly.

Osmond simply nodded. Pascal returned to the room and somehow managed to understand I would take the first room he had prepared for the night.

"The quarters I have readied for you, Master, are in the west wing of the house, at the end of the corridor."

I stood and thanked him, patted Osmond on the shoulder and made my way up the staircase I had climbed so many times so many years ago. But instead of turning right on the landing, I turned left, towards the east wing of the house and wandered the hall until I came to the door to the anteroom of our bedchamber. I opened the door and entered, finding it empty of any furnishings – obviously this room was not being used and I suspected the bedchamber was not either. I walked up to the closed door on the far side of the anteroom and stood still, staring at it.

I took a deep breath and suddenly felt weary. I placed my hands on each side of the door frame and leaned my head against the door, chastising myself for this perceived weakness. I had battled adversaries under the most extreme conditions, I had endured imprisonment, twice, and escaped dangerous situations simply by my wit or by the strength and skill of my sword. Surely I could survive this.

With another deep breath I opened the door and found that Osmond had been correct, the room had been readied. I stood in the doorway, slowly looking around the room, from the large lead windows to the left to the fireplace on the right. The bed was the same one my lady and I had for our marriage bed, large, ebony with intricate carvings along the base and the four posters, gifted to me by Duke Robert. It was the only piece I did not, could not, bring to Ferneham.

Flashes of the night of her death started running through my mind and then I found myself reliving it. The news of the birth of the twins, followed by the midwives telling me she had asked for me, laying next to her as we slept and the horror I saw when her convulsions woke me. The shouts of the midwives and the panicked movements of the physicians trying to do everything, anything, to save her.

My body felt the assault of the memories and the tears came, rushing forth in a torrent of emotion I had not felt in a very long time. I became unnerved, shaking and feeling weak in my legs, I sank to my knees at the side of the bed and leaned in on it, clutching my head with my hands, trying to make the memories stop. I started to rock, begging her for forgiveness for not being able to save her. And then the words came to me. The secret prayers and the words etched on the Emerald Tablet came to me in a clarity of mind I had not experienced before. And so I spoke them. Again and again and again. As I did, the pain began to ebb, the sobs became fewer until slowly they went away completely. And eventually, I felt a peace settling in, a true calm came upon me and I could lift my head again.

And I knew at that moment, she had been my One and my All. And I was saved.

# X
## November 1154 - Ferneham England

Anselm sighed heavily and leaned back in his chair, massaging his hand trying to ease the cramping in his fingers. He looked at the stacks of papers covering the table – here was written a man's life. He watched as Sébastien threw another log on the dwindling fire knowing it would probably be the last as the candles giving the hour had burned to almost to four. They had been talking almost the entire night. The castle would soon be waking.

"So, there you have it," Sébastien said. "The story has been told. Now, what are you going to do with it?"

Anselm thought for a moment.

"I think if everything you have spoken about tonight is true, and I believe it is, then there will be others who have been chosen like you. And I think allowing this to be told may bring harm to many by those who falsely believe they have been chosen when they have not. What will be done in the name of this secret knowledge and power…" his voice trailed off.

"Indeed," Sébastien agreed, nodding. "Now you understand why I have refused to tell it before now."

"What *shall* we do with it?" Anselm asked. "We cannot destroy it, we need to protect it."

"I have known since you were a young lad that you have a good heart Anselm, you and Séraphine were the best of the Marshals. But you also know that this cannot reach those with malice in their hearts. I am probably not long for this world, I am not sure how I have lasted until now. Alix and Avice are now under the protection of the de Lacy family and with the young Duke of Normandy being crowned King next month, I am certain the power of that family will only increase as Henry favours them."

Anselm listened intently.

"Then I think," he said, looking into the dying embers in the fireplace, "that I should secure this, away from Alix and Avice, and let it come to light only when it must?"

Sébastien nodded.

"You will have to tell those who ask that I revealed nothing and let them come for me, you must not risk your life in order to protect me. I have had enough of others being punished for what I am responsible for. Agreed?"

"Agreed."

"Good. Well," Sébastien said standing up and stretching, "I can see dawn is nearly upon us. You should rest before you return to Ludgershall, I suggest you return to your quarters, I can have Osmond wake you mid-morn?"

Anselm gathered the papers he had created recording Sébastien's words, there were many.

"Yes, I think I shall take some rest. I want you to know," he said stopping the rustling of the papers and looking Sébastien in the eye, "that you can trust me. We are brothers, you and I, through Séraphine, my love for her knew no bounds. And I knew of her deep love for you. And despite the unfounded and unreasonable hatred John has for you, you must know I do not share any of it. I will protect this for you. And for Alix. I shall not let any harm come to her because of this. But please be wary, if I keep our plan and say nothing, they will still come for you."

Sébastien knew Anselm was speaking the truth. But John and his underlings were his problem, not Anselm's. They shook arms in friendship and then embraced as brothers. Sébastien suddenly felt a sense of relief, as if a huge burden had been lifted from him.

\* \* \* \* \* \* \* \* \*

Anselm hurried back to his quarters in the southwest tower, his bundle of papers tucked under his cloak to keep from prying eyes. But he need not have worried, he only saw a couple of early rising servants scurrying about and they were too busy getting to their chores to give him much notice.

The first glow of dawn's light began to rise to the east just as he reached his chambre. He knew he needed sleep but was too excited by the revelations over the past several hours to go to bed just yet. He lit a few candles, two on the mantlepiece and caught sight of the astrolabe. He stared at it in wonder but dared not touch it.

Looking for somewhere to secure his bundle for the few hours whilst he slept, Anselm opened one of the chests against the wall. It contained what he thought were just extra furs for the bed but when he removed them to make space for the papers, he noticed that he had gathered up something else along with them. Dropping the furs onto the floor beside him, he saw what it was: a small, almost ebony-coloured leather ladies glove. Anselm picked it up, examined it and then looked into the chest for its mate but found none. And then he realized what it was: it was Séraphine's riding glove. Sébastien must have kept this remembrance of her and had it brought to Ferneham when he had his furnishings moved. And then a second thought dawned on Anselm: this was Sébastien's bedchamber for such personal items would not be left in guest quarters. He must thank Sébastien for this kindness before he left for Ludgershall.

Anselm placed the papers in the chest, disrobed and climbed into the bed. Exhaustion set in and sleep took him.

\* \* \* \* \* \* \* \* \*

Sébastien knew he had one last thing to do. He rose and climbed the stairs to the chapel on the floor above, an area of the keep he rarely entered, no longer having any need for religion in the traditional sense. The staircase he used to get there opened up at one of the corners behind the altar, near where the piscina used for washing the communion cups was set into the wall. He stood before the piscina and reaching up into the recess, he grabbed hold of the lever he had put there, the same type of mechanism that was used in the hidden room under the Temple Mount but a much smaller version.

Once the lever did its work, a small hidden space opened up revealing the Bishop's translated Qur'an. Sébastien had reckoned he needed to secure this book and had devised its hiding place whilst all the building works were taking place. Only Alix knew of it, and had been fascinated by how it worked. She had asked his permission to examine the book and try to read it wanting to practice her Arabic, he had given it gladly but reminded her always to return it to its place in the chapel.

Returning to the dining hall, Sébastien took an empty piece of parchment that had been left by Anselm and drew:

And on the back, wrote:

عكّ

He waited until the ink was dry, folded it and placed it as close to the middle of the Qur'an as he could figure, closing the book afterwards. And then he took it with him up to his old bedchamber in the keep where he was staying the night.

\* \* \* \* \* \* \* \* \*

After only a couple hours of sleep, both Anselm and Sébastien were up and ready to get on with a new day. Sébastien was eager to get back to the meadow to complete the wood cutting he had been working on before Anselm's arrival as the nights were now only going to get colder and the castle was always in need of wood for the many fires in the various kitchens and private quarters.

Sébastien dressed and made his way down one of the keep's spiral staircase to the kitchens. He was early for breakfast but luckily there was warm fresh bread and some breakfast meats already available and he quaffed a tankard of ale to wash it all down. He then returned to his bedchamber, retrieved the Qur'an and took a seat in one of the large chairs he had spent most of the night in whilst talking with Anselm. Servants arrived shortly to set the table for breakfast for the others and it wasn't long before he started to hear the noises of his guests as they made their way to the dining hall.

"Good morning Papa!!" Alix cried out with a huge smile as she floated into the room.

The nurse followed carrying little Avice who was still rubbing her eyes having recently been awakened from a deep sleep. The journey and late night had worn her out and being roused had made her grumpy. Sébastien greeted Alix who kissed him quickly on the cheek and then he reached out to take Avice from the nurse in an attempt to soothe her. He felt a slight spasm across his chest as he did so. 'Perhaps the wood cutting had affected me more than I realized,' he thought.

"Where are you off to this morning?" she asked as she took her seat at the table.

"I have wood cutting awaiting me in the meadow down by Waverley Abbey, my visitor interrupted my work yesterday and I did not get as much done as I had hoped," he replied, bouncing Avice slightly which made her giggle.

"Yes, your visitor," she said, reaching for her goblet of breakfast wine. "How long did he keep you?"

"Many hours, we had much to discuss. He is leaving today, he might have already left."

"Oh Papa, I know he is my great uncle but you must not let any of the Marshals keep you for so long," she said, knowing full well the history of his relationship with her relatives on her grandmother's side.

"Anselm is a good man," Sébastien said, dismissing her concerns.

Wanting to change the subject he asked the whereabouts of her husband.

"He is still asleep," Alix answered. "He does not have the same penchant for early morning breakfasts as we do. And he did not sleep much on the journey down from Pontefract."

He realized it was time to get on with his chores and so handed Avice back to her nurse who busied herself with helping Avice eat.

"Shall I bring her to the Abbey and have food brought so we can lunch there?" Alix suggested. "It looks to be another glorious day, we need to take advantage, they will become more infrequent as the winter approaches."

Sébastien told her he thought that was a lovely idea and that he had better set off. He gave her a kiss on the cheek and turned to leave. But as he did, he placed the Qur'an on the table next to her.

"There are some passages that I read this morning that I think you will find interesting," he said, tapping the cover lightly.

"Really?" she asked.

"Yes, I have marked the place," he said, pointing to where a corner of the parchment was protruding from the book.

"Ok, Papa, I'll take a look and let you know what I think," Alix said, reaching for a piece of fruit.

Sébastien leaned down and kissed her on the top of her head. It was time to work. He would look forward to chatting with her by the fire later in the evening as they had always done.

* * * * * * * * *

Anselm was packed and ready to leave by the middle of the morning. Osmond had brought a hearty breakfast to his room which he had downed greedily, the long night and short sleep had caused him to be very hungry this morning.

Osmond had his horse ready and saddled by the time Anselm reached the stables. He took his time attaching the burgeoning saddle bags to the sides of the horse, cargo he would need to protect with his life. When he asked, Osmond informed him that Sébastien had already departed the castle but did not say to where. No other words were exchanged between the two men, there seemed to be a shared understanding of what had transpired during the night and there was nothing left to say.

As he directed his horse down the path towards the guardhouse, he stopped and turned to take a last look at the castle. It was another beautiful day and the D'Ivry red and gold flags fluttered in a gentle breeze atop the towers. 'This night's revelations have changed my life,' Anselm thought. But then a thought occurred to him: what had happened to Sébastien's treasure? Where was the Emerald Tablet, the books and the scroll containing the formula for the elixir? 'Save that for another time,' he thought. 'I can ask him at King Henry's coronation at Westminster Abbey next month.' And with that, he turned his horse and spurred him on to the east.

\* \* \* \* \* \* \* \* \* \*

Sébastien arrived at the clearing where he had worked the day before chopping wood for the castle. It was going to be another warm autumn day and small beads of sweat had already appeared from the brisk walk he took to get there. He filled the wooden bucket he had brought with him with water from the River Wey tributary and placed it on the ground next to the axe he had also carried from the castle. Taking off his tunic, he untangled the St Michael medal which had become caught in the shirt as he lifted it over his head. He felt the medal for a moment, then pressed it against his chest, tapping it slightly reassuring himself it was there.

The air was still which, although meant rain was unlikely, would mean he would not be cooled whilst cutting the wood. He picked up the axe and a large piece of tree trunk, placed it on the cutting block and swung the axe, cleaving the wood easily in two. Picking up one of the chopped pieces to halve it, he swung again when he was ready. And did the same to the other piece. But just before the fourth swing of the axe, he froze. He heard it again. The laugh. He shrugged it off knowing the wind had caused the same noise the day before. Then he realized: there was no wind today.

Sébastien looked about himself, trying to find the source of the laugh. Putting down the axe, he walked slowly toward the Abbey and paused at the magnificent yew tree which had fooled him into thinking he could hear his lady's sweet laugh. The yew tree's wide expanse of branches provided a large amount of shade and suddenly he was grateful for it. He took a seat on the ground on the side of the tree facing out to the meadow and leaned back against the trunk. And there it was again. Spent, Sébastien closed his eyes thinking he would nap a while.

In the dream that came upon him, Séraphine appeared, beckoning him. He smiled.

And then, he was gone.

# Coda

## 1148 - Acre

The heat was searing as it always was in the middle of the summer in Acre. Sébastien knew that the Council was not going to make the decisions he wanted it to and had to figure a way of secreting away his treasure to keep it out of the hands of the unworthy. He had memorized the ingredients of the elixir and the prayers and the words from the Emerald Tablet. The books of the secret knowledge would not really be understood except by those who had been initiated in ancient ways. And he knew the chances of being searched once word spread of what had happened in Jerusalem with Melisende increased every day.

He reached under his cot for his leather pouches and pulled the astrolabe out of one of them and tucked it under his tunic. The sky that evening was cloudless and clear, the moon and the stars shining brightly, making it easy to see his way as he grabbed the other pouch and slipped out of the Templar House walking at a pace to the beaches south of the city. Just as he had done on the shore of the River Orontes, he counted so many steps back from the waterline but added more for the sea was a much stronger force than the river had been. And there he found the perfect spot and, setting down the astrolabe, began moving a few large boulders and digging down a considerable way. He took the other items out of the pouch one by one, unwrapping them to give each a last look, running his fingertips along the Emerald Tablet engravings as he had done so many times, even now feeling an intensity surrounding and within him. He re-wrapped and placed each item gently back inside the pouch and secured it deep into the ground, protecting the pieces from nature's forces so they would be undamaged in case he needed to retrieve them.

After replacing the boulders he took the astrolabe and held it up to the night's sky and set the markings on the dials so they aligned with the stars overhead, locking them into place. He then tucked the astrolabe back under his tunic and quickly and quietly returned to his room in the Templar House.

# Acknowledgments

The author would like to thank the following for their support in writing this labour of love:

- ❖ Elizabeth Sandor for her constant support and willingness to give up her time to read the chapters as I wrote them.

- ❖ Julian Humphreys for welcoming me into the world of English history and introducing me to sooo many castles, forts, and garderobes.

- ❖ Linda Sabathy-Judd for her proofreading and for her patience in listening to me drone on about this book.

- ❖ And to Samantha Piper for being there at the very beginning in a beautiful little holiday let in Akko, patiently pouring over family trees and encouraging me every step of the way.

# Picture References

**Waverley Abbey Tree:** https://www.shutterstock.com/image-photo/tree-frame-by-spectacular-ruins-cistercian-1855361521

**Bayeux Cathedral:** https://www.freepik.com/premium-photo/cathedral-our-lady-bayeux-calvados-department-normandy-france-people-background_23708106.htm

**Normandy Coat of Arms:** https://commons.wikimedia.org/wiki/File:Arms_of_William_the_Conqueror_(1066-1087).svg

**Vermandois Coat of Arms:** https://commons.wikimedia.org/wiki/File:Arms_of_Raoul_de_Vermandois.svg#mw-jump-to-license

**Taranto Coat of Arms:** https://en.m.wikipedia.org/wiki/File:Coat_of_Arms_of_the_House_of_Hauteville_%28according_to_Agostino_Inveges%29.svg

**Komnenos Coat of Arms:** https://wappenwiki.org/index.php/File:Komnene.svg

**Flanders Coat of Arms:** https://en.wikipedia.org/wiki/Coat_of_arms_of_Flanders

**Blois Coat of Arms:** https://commons.wikimedia.org/wiki/File:Old_Arms_of_Blois.svg

**Champagne Coat of Arms:** https://en.wikipedia.org/wiki/Count_of_Champagne#/media/File:Blason_Champagne_primitif.svg

**Toulouse Coat of Arms:** https://en.wikipedia.org/wiki/House_of_Toulouse#/media/File:Arms_of_Languedoc.svg

**D'Ivry Coat of Arms:** https://wappenwiki.org/index.php/File:Ivry.svg

**Coat of Arms of Jerusalem:** https://commons.wikimedia.org/wiki/File:Arms_of_the_Kingdom_of_Jerusalem.svg#/media/File:Arms_of_the_Kingdom_of_Jerusalem.svg

**Rod of Asclepius:**
https://www.shutterstock.com/image-vector/rod-asclepius-staff-asklepian-vintage-woodcut-438696679

**Two Templars on Horseback:**
https://en.wikipedia.org/wiki/File:Templari_Paris.jpg#/media/File:Templari_Paris.jpg

**Templar Preceptory in Paris:**
https://www.parismuseescollections.paris.fr/fr/musee-carnavalet/oeuvres/le-donjon-du-temple-vers-1795#infos-principales

**First Page of the Corpus Cluniacense:**
https://en.wikipedia.org/wiki/File:First_page,_Summa_totius_haeresis_ac_diabolice_secte_Sarracenorum.png

**Astrolabe:**
Istanbul Turkey 051818 Medieval Astrolabe Museum Stock Photo 1404973931 | Shutterstock

Made in United States
Orlando, FL
25 May 2025

61570679R00350